THE SOOKIE STACKHOUSE COMPANION

THE SOOKIE STACKHOUSE COMPANION

EDITED BY
CHARLAINE HARRIS

GOLLANCZ

LONDON

First published in Great Britain in 2011 by Gollancz
An imprint of the Orion Publishing Group
Orion House, 5 Upper St Martin's Lane,
London WC2H 9EA
An Hachette UK Company

A CIP catalogue record for this book
is available from the British Library

ISBN 978 0 575 09714 8 (Cased)
ISBN 978 0 575 09753 7 (Export Trade Paperback)

1 3 5 7 9 10 8 6 4 2

Printed in Great Britain by Clays Ltd, St Ives plc

The Orion Publishing Group's policy is to use papers
that are natural, renewable and recyclable products and
made from wood grown in sustainable forests. The logging
and manufacturing processes are expected to conform to
the environmental regulations of the country of origin.

www.charlaineharris.com
www.orionbooks.co.uk

ACKNOWLEDGMENTS

Paula Woldan, Danna Woldan, Lauren Dodson, Victoria Koski, Debi Murray, Beverly Battillo, Denise Little, and Rachel Klika volunteered their skills and talents in assembling various parts of this book. My gratitude to them for their vision and hard work. I also appreciate the enthusiasm of the many readers who submitted questions for me and Alan Ball, and recipes for the cooking section. I wish we could have included every single one.

CONTENTS

The World of Sookie Stackhouse

Sookie and I go back a long way. We're practically sisters. Many years ago, when my mystery career was languishing, I thought it might be a good idea to shake up my writing style by trying something new. It might be fun to write a book that contained all the elements I loved: mystery, the supernatural, bloody adventure, and a dash of romance. And since people had told me for years that I had a great sense of humor, I thought it would be interesting to try to include that in the book, too.

Without a contract, without a soul being at all interested, I began to establish the character of my protagonist. My grandmother's best friend's name was Sookie, and since it was a fine old Southern nickname, I thought it would do well for my heroine. And "Stackhouse" just flowed right after it. I wanted to write from the point of view of a human, not a vampire or other "supe," and since I have to live with Sookie, I wanted to make her as interesting as I possibly could. I decided she would date a vampire, as the entrée into a completely different world, and I had to establish a reason for sensible Sookie to do such a crazy thing. After a long thinking session, I came up with telepathy, which I wouldn't wish on my worst enemy.

Up until then, most vampires in fiction had exotic, sexy names. My vampire, I decided, would be named Bill. Instead of setting my books in the picturesque, touristy part of Louisiana, I'd make do with the distinctly unromantic northern part. Instead of being angsty brooders, my vampires would be trying their hardest to be in the forefront of business; they'd be hard workers, and they'd have their own internal system of checks and balances.

I finished *Dead Until Dark* and turned it in to my agent, the great Joshua Bilmes. It took Joshua a long time to warm up to the Sookieverse, but he dutifully did his best to sell my favorite book. After two years of rejections, *Dead Until Dark* seemed likely to live up to its acronym. Then a young editor at Ace, John Morgan (now at DC Comics), decided to take a chance, and his boss, Ginjer Buchanan (my present editor), okayed the deal.

We've never looked back.

Readers seemed to want more details of the Sookieverse, and the website (www.charlaineharris.com) has always bubbled and seethed with questions. How *do* you make Caroline Bellefleur's chocolate cake? What about that pesky fairy genealogy? What book contains the famous shower scene? (I'm just kidding on that last one; everyone knows the shower scene.) How do the short stories fit into the chronology of the books?

We've assembled *The Sookie Stackhouse Companion* to answer all of these questions and hopefully a few more, to give readers a thorough look at the world of Bon Temps, and to provide extra snippets of interesting information about Sookie's world and the people who live and die in it. Though this book is about the books, we also give a nod to our favorite television show, *True Blood*, by including an interview with one of my favorite people, Alan Ball.

Lots of people helped me assemble this companion, and I tried to thank all of them in the acknowledgments. But let me just say here that without the help of my assistant and best buddy, Paula Woldan, I would have torn out my hair and cast myself upon the floor in despair at a few points. So thanks, Paula, and I think I had some of the most fun ever drawing the map with you.

I'm sure the second *The Sookie Stackhouse Companion* is on the shelves, I'll think of something I should have included, but it's time to let this project go. I hope you all find something in the book to entertain, enlighten, and engross you.

See you in Bon Temps.

—Charlaine Harris

THE SOOKIE STACKHOUSE COMPANION

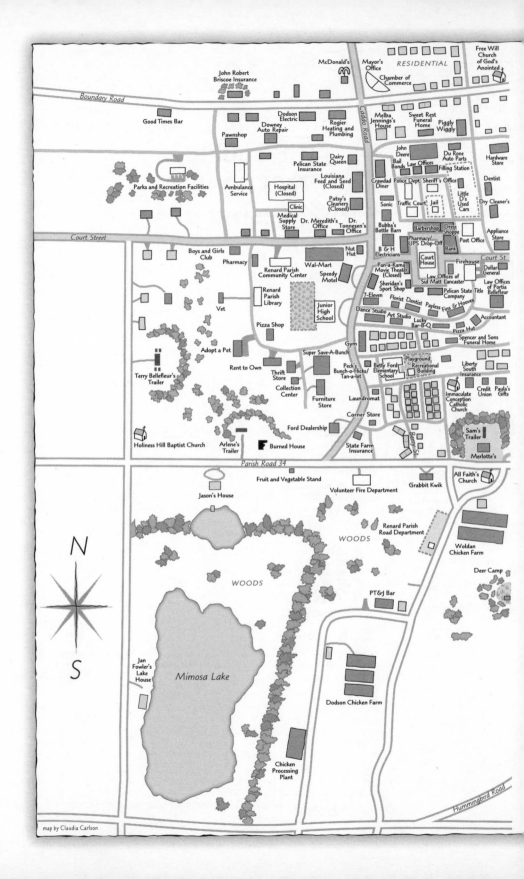

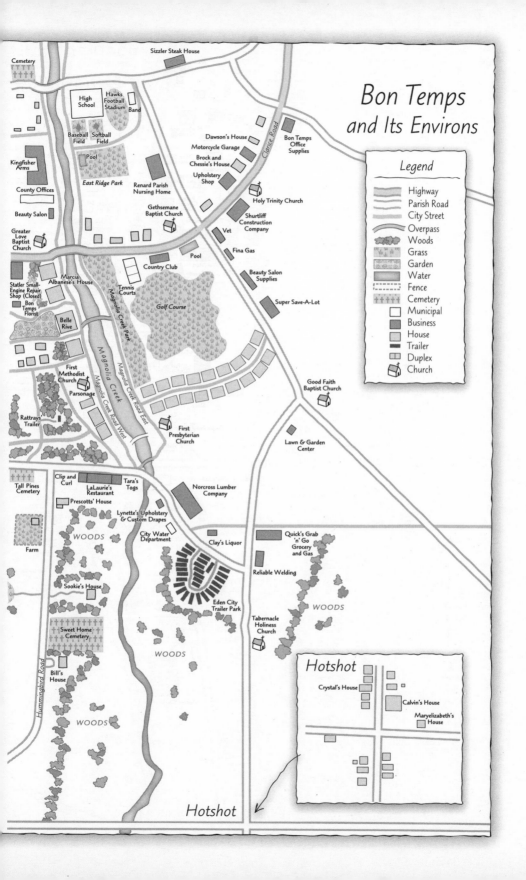

Bon Temps
and Its Environs

Legend

	Highway
	Parish Road
	City Street
	Overpass
	Woods
	Grass
	Garden
	Water
	Fence
	Cemetery
	Municipal
	Business
	House
	Trailer
	Duplex
	Church

Cemetery

Sizzler Steak House

High School

Hawks Football Stadium

Band

Baseball Field

Softball Field

Pool

Kingfisher Arms

County Offices

East Ridge Park

Renard Parish Nursing Home

Beauty Salon

Gethsemane Baptist Church

Greater Love Baptist Church

Dawson's House

Motorcycle Garage

Brock and Chessie's House

Upholstery Shop

Bon Temps Office Supplies

Clarice Road

Holy Trinity Church

Shurtliff Construction Company

Vet

Fina Gas

Pool

Country Club

Statler Small-Engine Repair Shop (Closed)

Marcia Albanese's House

Bon Temps Florist

Belle Rive

Tennis Courts

Golf Course

Beauty Salon Supplies

Super Save-A-Lot

Magnolia Creek Park

Magnolia Creek

First Methodist Church

Parsonage

Rattrays' Trailer

Magnolia Creek Road West

Magnolia Creek Road East

First Presbyterian Church

Good Faith Baptist Church

Lawn & Garden Center

Tall Pines Cemetery

Clip and Curl

LaLaurie's Restaurant

Tara's Togs

Prescotts' House

Lynette's Upholstery & Custom Drapes

City Water Department

Norcross Lumber Company

WOODS

Farm

Clay's Liquor

Quick's Grab 'n' Go Grocery and Gas

Reliable Welding

Sookie's House

Eden City Trailer Park

WOODS

Sweet Home Cemetery

Tabernacle Holiness Church

WOODS

Hummingbird Road

Bill's House

WOODS

WOODS

Hotshot

Crystal's House

Calvin's House

Maryelizabeth's House

Hotshot

Small-Town Wedding

BY CHARLAINE HARRIS

There are a lot of people to thank, for a relatively short work! I forgot to mention my CSI niece Danielle, who helped me on a previous piece; so here's to you, Dani! And Ivan Van Laningham offered me help on that same piece. My college buddy, Dr. Ed Uthman. Victoria Koski, my continuity queen, who struggles against my tide of fuzzy thinking. And the many people who were kind enough to help me attempt to pronounce Dutch: Geja Topper, Dave Bennett, Hans Bekkers, Jochem Steen, Leighton Gage, Sarah Bewley, and Simon Wood. And Duane Swierczynski, who is standing by to help me dispose of a body.

CHAPTER ONE

I t was May, I had a great tan, and I was going on a road trip, leaving vampire politics behind. I felt better than I had in a long time. Wearing only
my underwear, I stood in my sunny bedroom and went down my checklist.

1. Give Eric and Jason address and dates

I'd done that. My boyfriend, Eric Northman, vampire sheriff of Area
Five of Louisiana, had all the information he needed. So did my brother,
Jason.

2. Ask Bill to watch house

Okay. I'd left a letter pushed under my neighbor Bill Compton's door.
He'd find it when he rose for the night. His "sister" Judith (sired by the
same vampire) was still staying at his place. If Bill could tear himself away
from her company, he would walk across the cemetery separating our
properties to have a look at my house, and he'd get my mail and my newspaper and put them on my front porch.

3. Call Tara

I'd done that; my pregnant friend Tara reported all was well with the
twins she was carrying, and she'd call or get her husband to call if there
was any news. She wasn't due for three more months. But twins, right? You
never knew.

4. Bank

I'd deposited my last paycheck and gotten more cash than I usually
carried.

5. Claude and Dermot

My cousin and my great-uncle had decided to stay at Claude's house in
Monroe while I was gone. Claude had been living with me for about a
month, and Dermot had joined him only two weeks ago, so Dermot said he
still felt funny being in my house without me there. Claude, of course, had

no such qualms, since he's about as sensitive as a sheet of sandpaper, but Dermot had carried the day.

All my clothes were clean, and I thought I was packed. Though it would be a good idea to review my packing list, which was completely separate from my "things to do" list. Since my friend and boss, Sam Merlotte, had invited me to go with him to his brother's wedding, I'd been in a nervous tizzy about forgetting something essential and somehow making Sam look bad in front of his family.

I had borrowed a pretty dress, sleeveless and blue, like my eyes, to wear to the wedding, and I had some black pumps with three-inch heels that were in great condition. For everything else, I packed the best and newest of my casual clothes: two pairs of good shorts, an extra pair of jeans. I threw in a yellow and gray skirt outfit, just in case.

I counted my underwear, made sure I had the right bras, and checked the little jewelry pouch to be sure my gran's pearls were there. I shut the bag, triumphant. I'd done my best to cover every contingency, *and* I'd fit everything into a hanging bag and a weekender bag.

Just as I reopened the bag to make sure I'd included my blow-dryer, I heard Sam's truck coming up the driveway that wound through the woods. In thirty seconds I pulled on my khaki shorts and a very thin white tank top with a teal tank layered over it. I had a little gold chain on, and I slid my feet into my new sandals. My toenails were a happy pink ("Run Run Rosy"). I felt great. I hurried to the front door and opened it just as Sam was about to knock.

He was wearing his usual jeans and Merlotte's Bar and Grill T-shirt, but he was sporting ancient cowboy boots. Yep, we were going to Texas, all right. His red gold hair was shorter these days, and I could tell he'd taken special care shaving.

"Sorry I'm a little late," he said. "I had to give Kennedy and Terry some extra instructions." The two substitute bartenders were going to be in charge while Sam was gone, and Sam was pretty nervous about it.

"No problem. I'm ready." He picked up my overnighter while I got my hanging bag and locked the door behind me. Luckily, Sam's pickup had an extended cab, and we were able to put our clothes on the backseat.

"You looking forward to this?" I asked him, when we were on the interstate. We were going across the state line from Louisiana into Texas to a small town called Wright, south of the interstate past Dallas, where Sam's folks had settled after his dad got out of the service.

"This is the first nice thing that's happened in my family in months, and for a while I didn't think this wedding would ever come off," he said. "I really appreciate your going with me."

"Are they putting pressure on you to get married?" I should have realized before that there might be another reason Sam wanted me to accompany him, something beyond the pleasure of my company. Some women have long careers as bridesmaids; I had a long career of being a pretend girlfriend. I hoped that wasn't going to be a perpetual pattern.

"That might be overstating it," Sam said. He grinned at me. "But my mom and my sister sure are ready for me to show them I'm thinking about the subject. Of course, the shifters going public and my mom's troubles kind of put my own marital status on the back burner."

The Weres had revealed their existence on television a few months before, following the vampire model. Many of the other two-natured (or "twoeys," as the pop-culture magazines had immediately started calling them) had shown themselves at the same time. Oddly, the American public seemed to be more upset about the werewolves and werepanthers living among them than they'd been when they found out vampires were real.

"Does your mom try to set you up with nice shifter girls all the time?"

"So far she hasn't been able to find another pure shifter like me, though my sister, Mindy, told me Mom had gone online trying to track one down." Sam could turn into anything: lion, dog, raccoon. His kind was pretty rare.

"Gosh. Are you sure you shouldn't have brought Jannalynn? She may not be exactly who your family wants you to bring home—at least, that's what you said—but she's a werewolf, and that's better than a human like me, right? At least to your mom. If your mom's looking for a woman for you online, that's kind of . . . desperate, huh?"

Sam laughed. "Definitely. But Mom means well. She was really happy with my dad, and their first date was a setup. If she can find an unattached female shifter the right age, she's hoping lightning will strike twice in the Merlotte family."

"You told me that you'd almost gotten married once."

"Yeah, when I was in the army. She was a good ol' girl, regular human. My dad would have liked her. But it just didn't work out."

I wanted to ask why, but I knew it was none of my business.

He asked, "You think you and Eric might get married now that it's legal?"

I started to tell him we were married already, according to my big blond vampire boyfriend, but decided it would be better to skip that discussion entirely.

"He hasn't asked me," I said, which was the truth. He hadn't asked me about the vampire marriage rite, either. I'd handed him a ceremonial knife in front of a witness without asking a single question, which proves how little sense I could have when I was around Eric.

As the miles carried me away from Eric, the bond between us stretched but did not break. Eric was a silent presence. Miles of Texas interstate rolled by, and though I knew Eric was in his bed, dead to the world, I couldn't help thinking about him. It wasn't nearly as bad as it would have been if he'd been awake, though.

"A penny for your thoughts," Sam said.

I jumped because my thoughts weren't family-rated at that moment.

"I was hoping Bill recovers from the silver poisoning. I found a vampire sibling of his, and I got her to come visit. He'd told me if he got some blood from a sib, it would really help him heal."

Sam looked a little nonplussed. "How'd you do that?" he asked.

When I told him how I'd tracked Judith down, he shook his head. "How'd you know he wouldn't get mad at you?"

"I was doing it for *him*," I said, not understanding Sam's point. "Why would he get mad?"

Sam said gently, "Sook, Bill obviously knew where this Judith was, and he didn't call her on his own. He must have had a reason."

I knew that. But I'd gone ahead and contacted her anyway. I'd only thought about how worried I was about Bill. I could feel myself tearing up. I didn't want to admit to Sam that he was right.

I looked out the window so Sam wouldn't have to watch my eyes brim over.

"Sook?" he said, and from his voice I could tell he had leaned forward to try to see my face. "Sook? Hey, I'm sorry. Listen, I was just blowing hot air. You were watching out for him, and I'm probably just jealous."

I could read his mind enough to know he wasn't being entirely truthful—but he did sincerely want me to feel better, and he was truly sorry I was upset. "You're right," I said, though my voice wobbled in a pathetic way. "Sam, you're absolutely right. I've made so many mistakes."

"Don't we all? I've made more than a few, and I don't seem to stop making them," Sam said, and there was bitterness in his voice.

"Okay. We're both human; we got that settled," I said, making myself smile. "Or, at least, we're mostly human."

He laughed, and I felt better. I rummaged around in my purse for a Kleenex and patted my eyes carefully to keep my makeup intact. I got a Coca-Cola out of the ice chest behind Sam's seat and popped it open for him, and got myself one, too. We talked about the sorry season the Bon Temps Hawks baseball team was having, and I told Sam about watching the softball team practice the week before. I felt good when I was confident everything was back to normal between us.

When we stopped to get gas outside Dallas, I watched a black Ford Focus shoot by. "That's funny," I said to Sam, who was punching his PIN into the pump. "That's the same car I saw when we pulled over to find out what that noise was." A branch had caught under the truck and had been making an alarming *whap-whap-whap.*

Sam glanced up. "Huh," he said. "Well, the interstate is always busy, and the Focus is a popular model."

"This is the same one," I said. "There's a place on the driver's side of the windshield where a rock hit."

Then I went inside the station to visit the ladies' room, because I could tell Sam didn't want to be worrying about a Ford Focus. I didn't, either, but there it was.

I kept a sharp eye out for the car after that, but I didn't bring up the subject again. As a result, we made pleasant conversation past Dallas and Fort Worth, all the way to the turn off the interstate that would lead us south to Wright.

I'd offered to drive, but Sam said he was so familiar with the route that he didn't mind being at the wheel. "I'm just glad to have company making the drive, for once," he said. "I've had to go over to Wright so often since the announcement." Sam's mom had had a huge crisis the evening of the big two-natured reveal, broadcast worldwide; her second husband had been so startled by the fact that his wife could turn into an animal that he'd shot her.

"But you've got the one sister and the one brother," I said.

"Yeah, Mindy and Craig. Mindy's twenty-six. She's married to Doke Ballinger. She went to high school with him. They have two kids, Mason and Bonnie. They live about thirty miles away in Mooney."

"What's the name of the woman Craig's marrying? Daisy? Denise?"

"Deidra. She's from Wright, too. She and Craig have both been going to UT Dallas. She's a real pretty girl, only nineteen, and Craig's twenty-four. He went into the army before he started college."

"Lots of military service in your family." Sam and Craig's dad had been retired army.

Sam shrugged. "Because of Dad, we're all used to the service as an option. It's not a huge leap like it is for some families. Craig always liked Deidra, but when he was in high school, she was way too young for him to think about as a date. He did call her when he found out another kid from Wright was going to UT Dallas, and he says they were gone on each other after the first date."

"Aw. That's so sweet. I guess all this trouble has been really hard on them."

"Yeah. Craig was pretty mad at me and Mom for a while, and then he accepted it, but Deidra's folks freaked out. The wedding got postponed a couple of times."

I nodded. Sam had told me how his brother's fiancée's family had reacted to the news that her about-to-be mother-in-law sometimes ran on four feet.

"So instead of sending out new invitations, the Lisles just put a notice in the Wright paper."

"How big is Wright?"

Sam laughed. "About as big as Bon Temps. Except in the tourist season. There's a river that runs a little west of Wright, and there's a lot of rafting and camping. At night, those rafters and campers are looking for something to do, so there're a couple of big bars that have live bands. And there's a western-wear store and a riding stable for beginners on up, for when people want to take a break from the water. Stuff like that. Wright's a pretty conservative place, though. Everyone's glad when the tourists leave in the fall."

"Has your mom had any trouble with the rest of the town since the shooting?" Sam had been the target of one protest in the Merlotte's parking lot, but since then things had died down—for good, I hoped.

"I'm reading between the lines, but yes, I think people haven't been as friendly as they used to be. Don's a local guy. He's got cousins and stuff all around Wright."

"He's in jail now, right?"

"Yeah, he couldn't make bail. He never denied he shot Mom. I don't understand why there's any sympathy for him."

I didn't say anything, but I could sort of understand feeling sympathy for someone who'd suddenly discovered his wife changed into a different creature. Of course, shooting that wife was a gross overreaction, but watching your wife transform into a dog . . . That would shake any man. However, that was not my problem to solve, and I was certainly sorry the whole incident had happened.

I was not walking into a normal, happy family wedding. I already knew some of what Sam was saying, but maybe I should have asked more questions before I got in the truck. I thought of the shotgun my brother had given me, sitting uselessly in the closet in my house.

"You look kinda worried, Sookie," Sam said, and I could read the dismay in his brain. "I wouldn't have brought you if I thought there was a way in the world something bad would happen to you."

"Sam, I hope you have the whole picture of what's going on in Wright," I said. "I know you asked me to go with you before you started dating Jannalynn, but I really wouldn't have minded if you'd wanted to take her." He understood the subtext. Though he'd told me Jannalynn's habits and manners weren't family-pleasing, she had excellent natural defenses. In fact, she was the enforcer for the Shreveport pack. What was I going to do if we were attacked? Mind-read someone to death?

"This isn't any mob situation," Sam said, and he laughed. "I finished high school there when my dad retired from the military, and Mindy and Craig did even more of their growing up in Wright than I did. People will get used to the new things in their world, even the people in a conservative little place like Wright. These are just regular folks. They've known us for years."

Pardon me if I felt a tad skeptical.

I saw the black Focus one more time, and then I didn't spot it again. I told myself that there were hundreds of cars on this section of interstate, and a hell of a lot of them were going west like we were.

The landscape got less and less green, more and more arid. Trees were smaller, rocks were more plentiful, and there were cacti in the scrubby brush. After the turnoff south, towns were fewer and farther between. They were small, and the stretches of road were lined by fences of all kinds. This was ranching country.

Wright looked very normal when we rolled in. The highway ran through Wright going north–south, and it was the main drag. In its stretch through Wright, it was called Main Street, which made me smile. It was a one-story town. Everything was low and long and dusty. I looked at the people we passed, the gas stations, the Sonic, the Dairy Queen, the McDonald's. There were three motels, which seemed excessive until I remembered that Sam had told me about the river west of the town. The trailer park was full, and I saw a few people walking west, flip-flops on their feet and towels over their shoulders. Early vacationers. We passed a rental place for canoes, tubes, rafts, grills, and tents.

"People can grill on the sandbars in the river," Sam said. "It's fun. You take your ice chest out there, a tube of sunblock, drink your beer, and grill your meat. Get in the water whenever you want."

"I wish we had time to do that," I said. Then, thinking that might sound like a complaint or a hint, I said brightly, "But I know we're here to get this wedding done! Maybe you can bring Jannalynn over here sometime later in the summer."

Sam didn't respond. I'd seen Jannalynn be aggressive, physical, even savage. But surely she had a softer side? I mean, it couldn't be all skull-cracking, bustiers, spike heels, and kill-my-enemies. Right?

It was a warm feeling, seeing the town where Sam had done a lot of his growing up. "Where's your school?" I asked, trying to picture the young Sam. He turned east to take me by the little high school where he'd played sports and been named Mr. Yellowjacket. Yellowjacket Stadium was about the same size as Bon Temps's Hawks Stadium and in much better repair, though the old high school had seen better days. The town library was brand-new, and the post office was proudly flying the flag. It whipped in the warm wind.

"Why'd your dad decide to retire here after he left the service?" I asked. "What do people do here besides cater to tourists?"

"They ranch, mostly," he said. "A few of them farm, but mostly the land's too rocky, and we don't get much rain. A lot of people make the bulk of their income during the tourist season, and they just coast along on odd jobs the rest of the year. We get a big influx of hunters when the tourists run out, so that's a major source of income, too. My dad commuted to Mooney, where Doke and Mindy live now. He had a job doing security for a big plant over there. It manufactures wind turbines for wind energy. Doke works there now."

"And you-all moved here instead of Mooney because . . . ?"

"My dad wanted us to have the whole small-town experience. He thought it would be the best way to finish out my teen years and to bring up Mindy and Craig. Some of my mom's family was still living in Wright then, too. And he loved the river."

I looked at the people coming in and out of the businesses we passed. There were lots more brown faces than I was used to seeing, though even Bon Temps had experienced an upsurge in its Spanish-speaking population in the past decade. Some were identifiably Native American. There were very few black faces. I'd really traveled somewhere different. In addition to the differences in skin color, there were more people in western-style clothes, which made sense. We'd passed a rodeo ground on our way into town.

We took a left when we were within sight of the south boundary of the city limits, turning onto a narrow street that could be anywhere in the United States. The houses were small ranch styles, one or two had a trailer in the backyard where maybe a mother-in-law or a newlywed child lived, and most had a prefab toolshed tucked into a corner of the yard. There were lots of open windows. People in Wright didn't turn on their air conditioners as early as we did in Bon Temps. Instead of garages, there were carports attached to almost every house, some to the side, some added on in front.

At Sam's mom's home, the awning extended over half of the front of the house, covering enough area to park two vehicles. Unattractive, but efficient. "This is the house you lived in after you-all moved to Wright?" I asked.

"Yeah, this is the house Mom and Dad bought after Dad got out of the army. Don moved in here when he and Mom got married. By the way, she's still Bernadette Merlotte. She never took Don's name."

Bernadette Merlotte's home was a modest house, maybe twelve hundred square feet, with white siding and ornamental dark green shutters. The little yard space had barely any grass because it was almost entirely given over to beds containing flowers, smooth river rocks, and concrete statues, which were various in the extreme. One was a little girl with a dog, one was a large frog, and one was a creature that was supposed to be a fairy. (Any fairy I knew would want to kill Sam's mom after a good look at that statue.) From the dry state of the patches of grass and dirt, it was evident that Sam's mom cared for her flowers lovingly.

There was a little sidewalk winding to the front porch from the covered driveway, and the "porch" was flush with the ground. This was a slab house.

After an almost imperceptible sigh and a moment of bracing himself, Sam jumped out. I didn't stand on ceremony. I slid out, too. I wanted to stretch my legs and back after sitting in the truck for so long, and I was almost as nervous about meeting Sam's family as if I were his real girlfriend.

A screen door slammed, and Sam's mother hurried down the sidewalk to hug her son. She was about my height, five-six, and very slim. She'd had his hair color, but the red gold had faded now. She'd obviously spent a lot of time out in the sun, so at least we'd have that in common. Then she was in Sam's arms and laughing.

"It's so good to see you!" she cried. After giving Sam a final, hard hug, she pulled away and turned to me. "You must be Sookie. Sam's told me a lot about you!" The words were warm and welcoming, but I could tell how she really felt . . . which was more like cautious.

Shaking hands seemed a little too distant somehow, so I half hugged her. "It's good to meet you, Mrs. Merlotte. I'm glad you're doing so well."

"Now, you just call me Bernie. Everybody does." She hesitated. "I thank you for taking care of the bar while Sam came down when I was shot." It was an effort for her to so casually mention what had happened.

"Are you going to let them come in, Mama?" said a young woman standing in the doorway.

"You just hold your horses," Bernie said. "We're coming!"

There were a few moments of confusion as we got out our hanging and overnight bags. Finally we went into the house. Bernie Merlotte's right-hand neighbor, a man in his sixties, came out into his yard—ostensibly to check his mailbox—while all this was going on. I happened to catch his eye, and I gave him a friendly nod. To my amazement, he looked right through me, though I knew from his thoughts that he could see me plainly.

That had never happened to me in my life. If I'd been reading a Regency romance, I would have termed it "the cut direct." No one else had noticed, and he wasn't my neighbor, so I didn't say anything.

Then we were inside, and I had to stuff my bafflement into a corner of my mind because there were more people to meet. The small house was crowded. First there was Sam's sister, Mindy, a young mother of two. Her husband, Doke Ballinger, was as thin and laconic as Mindy was plump and chatty. Their children, five-year-old Mason and three-year-old Bonnie, eyed me from behind their mother. And finally I met the groom, Craig, who was like a more carefree clone of Sam. The brothers were the same in coloring, height, and build. His fiancée, Deidra Lisle, was so pretty it hurt to look at her. She was lightly tanned, with big hazel eyes and reddish brown hair that fell to her waist. She couldn't have stood five foot two, and she was all compact curves and femininity.

She shook my hand shyly, and her smile showed that her teeth were as perfect as her complexion. Wow.

She was pregnant. She was hoping she wasn't showing, that no one could tell. Now that I knew, I could sort of sense that other mind floating around inside her, but it was a weird read—no language, no thoughts.

Well, another thing that was none of my business. More power to them. I was the only one who could sense that other presence in her womb.

By that time Bernie was showing me to a very small room that contained a pullout couch, a sewing machine, a computer desk, and a card table that was cluttered with scrapbooking materials. "We're not fancy here," Bernie said. "I hope you don't mind sleeping in what the magazines call the all-purpose room. Course, I just call it the room-Mindy-finally-left-out-of-so-I-could-have-it-back." There was a hint of challenge in her voice.

"No, ma'am, I don't mind at all." I set my bag down by the end of the couch. "I'll just hang these up in the closet, if that's okay," I said, taking my hanging bag over to the closet door in the corner and waiting for her permission.

"Go right ahead," Bernie said, and she relaxed a bit.

The closet had *just* enough spare room right in the middle.

"Oh, I'm sorry," Bernie said. "I meant to get in there and make you some more space. It's taken me longer to get over this injury than I'd figured."

"No problem," I said. There was a hook on the outside of the closet door, so I hung my bag there rather than cram it in and wrinkle my dress.

"What's the matter with your neighbor?" I said, my mind suddenly leaping back to my previous source of misgiving.

"Jim Collins? Oh, he's such a grouch," she said with a half smile. "Why do you ask? Was he giving you a mean look when you came in?"

"Yes."

"Don't pay any attention," she said. "He's just a lonely man since his wife died, and he was a big friend of Don's. Don helped him out in the yard all the time, and they went fishing together. He's blaming me for all Don's problems."

That seemed a strange way to refer to Don's being in jail for shooting her. "Jim Collins hates you," I said.

She gave me a very strange look. "That's a lot to read into a look across the yard," Bernie said. "Don't worry about Jim, Sookie. Let's go get you some ice tea."

So Sam hadn't told his mom that I could read minds. Interesting.

I followed Bernie down the short hall and into the kitchen. The kitchen was quite a bit larger than I'd expected, since it also encompassed an eating area set in a bay window. Deidra was sitting at the big round table with Mindy's little girl, Bonnie, in her lap. The child was holding a soggy cookie and looked quite happy. Through the bay window, I saw Mason and his dad in the backyard playing catch with Craig and Sam. I went to the door and looked out at the family scene. When he saw me, Sam darted an inquiring look my way, to ask if I was okay. He was willing to come in if I needed support.

I smiled at him, genuinely pleased. I nodded reassuringly before I turned to the table. There was a pitcher of tea and a glass filled with ice ready for me. I poured my tea and sat down beside Deidra. Mindy had put a laundry basket full of clean clothes on the kitchen counter, and she was busy folding them. Bernie was drying dishes. I'd thought I might feel like an intruder, but I didn't.

"Sookie, you're the first girl Sam's brought home in years," Mindy said. "We're dying to know all about you."

Nothing like cutting to the chase; I appreciated the direct approach. I didn't want to lie to them about our relationship, but Sam had brought me here to deflect the wedding fever. I would have felt worse if Sam and I hadn't been genuinely fond of each other. After all, I told myself, I was literally Sam's "girl friend," if not his "girlfriend," so we were more bending the truth than breaking it.

"I've worked for Sam for several years," I said, picking my words carefully. "My mom and dad passed away when I was seven, and after that my grandmother brought me and my brother up. Gran died a couple of years ago, and I inherited her house. My brother lives in my parents' house," I added, so they'd know that was fair. "I graduated from high school in Bon Temps, but I never got to carry my education any further than that."

This Sookie-in-a-capsule got a mixed reception.

"Is your brother married?" Mindy asked. She was thinking of her own brother who was getting married, and the possibility of another grandchild to make her mother happy. Bernie was going to get one sooner than Mindy imagined.

"He's a widower," I said.

"Gosh," Deidra blurted, "people in your family don't have a long life expectancy, huh?"

Ouch. "My parents died in a flash flood," I said, because that was the public story. "My grandmother was murdered. My sister-in-law was murdered. So we never got to find out how long they would live." Actually, they'd *all* been murdered. I'd never put it to myself like that before. People in my family really, truly had a short life expectancy. If I followed the family trend, I could expect to meet my end through violence in the not-too-distant future.

I glanced at the appalled faces of Sam's womenfolk, who'd gotten more than they'd expected. Guess they wouldn't be asking me any more personal questions, huh? "But my brother's still alive," I said brightly. "His name is Jason."

They all looked relieved. Deidra grabbed a napkin and began dabbing at Bonnie's smeared face. "Bonnie, you have a chocolate mouth," Deidra said, and Mindy and Bernie laughed while Bonnie stretched her mouth into a wide grin, enjoying the attention.

"How big is your family, Deidra?" I said, to get off the topic of my life.

"I got two sisters," Deidra said. "I'm the oldest. They're seventeen and fifteen, still in high school. And I've got two brothers, both older. One brother works here in Wright, and one brother's in the army."

"How about you, Bernie? Do you have any younger brothers or sisters?" I asked Sam's mother, to keep the conversational ball rolling.

"Oh, they have to be younger? I must be showing my age." Bernie turned a wry face to me. She was stirring something on the stove.

"You have to be the oldest, if you're the shifter."

Then they were all looking at me, this time in surprise. "Sam did tell you a lot," Mindy said. "Humph. He doesn't usually talk much about his heritage."

"I'm not sure if I heard it from Sam or from a werewolf," I said.

"Unusual," Bernie said. "Have you dated other shifters?"

"Yes," I said simply. "And my brother's a bitten panther."

There was another round-robin of exchanged glances among the women, broken by Bonnie demanding to go potty. Mindy stopped matching socks to sweep her up and carry her off to the hall bathroom.

"So you have no problem with wereanimals at all," Bernie said.

"No," I replied, and I'm sure I sounded as surprised as I felt.

"We just figured . . ."

"What?"

"We just figured," Deidra said, "that your family wouldn't like the idea of you marrying into a shifter family, like my family didn't. I mean, they've come around *now*, but when they saw the woman change on television, they freaked out." The two-natured, following the vampire pattern, had sent their most personable representatives to local television stations to change on the air.

Don hadn't been the only one who'd reacted with panic.

"If I had a big family, there might be more of a problem. But my brother wouldn't mind me marrying into a family with the shifter gene," I said. "He's all I've got to worry about." And I wasn't any too worried about his opinion. "Not that I have any plans to get married," I added hastily. I hadn't even planned on getting married in the vampire way, for that matter. "Are you going to wear the traditional white dress, Deidra?" I had a doomed feeling that no matter how I tried to keep the conversation on the actual wedding about to take place, the women of the family were going to continue to steer it toward a possible future match between Sam and me.

The bride nodded, smiling. Gosh, Deidra was a dentist's dream. "Yeah, it's pure white and strapless," she said. "I got it on sale at a bridal shop in Waco. It was worth the drive."

"How many bridesmaids?"

A cloud crossed her face. "Well," she began. After a perceptible pause, she tried again. "Two," she said, smiling for all she was worth. "My sisters."

"Two of her friends backed out after the shooting," Bernie said, her back to us. Her voice was flat.

Mindy had come back into the kitchen with a scrubbed daughter, and she let Bonnie out into the backyard with the men. "Incoming," she yelled, and shut the door. "Bitches," Mindy said abruptly, and I knew she was referring to the bridesmaids who'd reneged on their obligations.

Deidra flinched.

"I'm sorry, sweetie, but that behavior was low," Mindy said. "Any true friend would be thinking more about you and your feelings than about their disapproval of our family."

Mindy had good sense.

"Well, you still got the two best ones," Bernie said, and Deidra smiled at her mother-in-law-to-be. "Sookie, I hope you like baked chicken."

"I sure do," I said. "Is there anything I can be doing to help?"

Bernie said no, and I could see that the cooking area would be easier for one person to manage without a newcomer getting in her way. To keep the conversation going, I told them about having to step in at the Bellefleur double wedding when one of the bridesmaids had had a sudden attack of appendicitis. They all laughed when I described trying not to breathe in the too-tight dress or move too quickly in the too-small high heels, and I began to feel a little more at ease. Mindy finished folding clothes, Bonnie came in crying with a skinned knee, and Craig accidentally threw the ball over Doke's shoulder and into Mr. Collins's backyard.

In the background, I'd heard the men's voices as they called to one another and to Mason, and I was alerted when they all fell silent. I listened.

Then I was out the door and looking to my right. Jim Collins was standing there at a gap in the overgrown hedge, his balding head shining under the sun, the baseball in his age-spotted hands. I knew what he was going to do before he did it; I knew it as his intent formed. Collins was in his sixties, but hale and fit, and the ball went right toward Sam with impressive force. My hand shot out to intercept it. It stung like hell, but I would not have winced for all the cotton in the Delta. I caught Collins's gaze and held it. I didn't let myself speak. I was afraid of what I'd say.

There was a long moment of silence. Mindy's husband, Doke, took two steps forward. He told Collins, "Don't think about acting out in front of my son." Doke was so angry he had to exercise all his restraint.

At that moment, I wished I were a witch so I could throw Bernie's neighbor's malevolence back at him. But I didn't have any superpowers or any supernatural powers, or any kind of power at all. All that I had that was mine was my unpredictable ability to read minds and my unexpected strength and quickness, which came from taking the occasional sip of Eric. My arm dropped to my side, the ball clenched in my fist, and Sam came over to put his hand on my shoulder. We watched Jim Collins, still expressionless, turn to go back into his house.

"Was he trying to hit me?" Sam asked quietly.

I was too angry to speak. I turned my head to look into Sam's eyes. I nodded.

"Thanks, Sookie," he said. "That would have been bad. Maybe I could have caught it in time. Maybe not." Sam was very, very quick, like all twoeys—but he'd been caught off guard.

"I only moved quicker because I knew about it ahead of time," I said, leaving Eric and his blood out of the conversation. "That creep wants to provoke you. I hope none of the rest of your neighbors are like him."

"They never used to be," he said, his voice bleak. "Now it's hard to tell."

"To hell with them," I said. "You-all are good people, Sam. There's nothing wrong with you and your mother, except maybe your mom didn't pick her second husband too well."

I could hear the other men going into the house, Mason's piping voice exclaiming over my good catch.

"Mom understands that now," Sam said. "I think it never occurred to her that Don would be so angry about her other nature, because she was so sure he loved her."

Time to change the subject. "Your mom's fixing chicken," I said. "Oven baked, with Parmesan cheese and bread crumbs."

"Yeah? She's a pretty good cook." Sam's eyes brightened.

"I don't know how we're all going to squeeze in around that table."

"I'll get the other card table out of the closet. We'll all make it."

And we did. No one mentioned Jim Collins again, and no one asked me any questions about what I'd done. The Merlottes (extended version) seemed to be a clan that accepted the odd without a blink . . . at least, they did now.

It was a long evening after a long day, and I was ready to retire when the dishes were done and Deidra had departed to her parents' house. Mindy and Doke had left for home soon after supper was eaten so they could bathe the kids and get them to bed. The next day, Saturday, would hold both the wedding rehearsal (in the morning) and the wedding itself at four in the afternoon, followed by a reception. All three events would be at Deidra's church.

Craig made a point of having a conversation with me while I was washing dishes and he was drying them. He told me that the reception would be only a punch and cake affair, which is often the case in the South. "We made up our minds too quick to do anything else," he said with a smile. "After Deidra's folks—the Lisles—kicked up a fuss and postponed the first date and made us go to counseling, we didn't want anything to get in the way of this one. We don't care about having a sit-down dinner. Punch and cake is fine with us, and a lot cheaper."

"Where will you live?" I asked. "In Dallas? Sam said you-all went to college there."

"I took an apartment in Houston after I graduated," Craig said. "I got a job doing tech support for a big firm of CPAs. Deidra's got to finish training as an EMT."

I assumed she'd have to put that off because of the pregnancy, but it was none of my business to say anything.

"She'd really like to become a physician's assistant, after we get on our feet," he said.

"I hope she can do that," I said. Deidra would have a hard row to hoe, with a new husband and a new baby.

"What about you?" Craig asked.

"And my future?" I actually had to think about it. Craig and I were alone in the kitchen. Sam had gone outside to move his truck because it had been blocking Deidra's car. Bernie was in the bathroom.

"I've got a good job working for this really nice guy," I said, and Craig laughed. I hesitated. "Maybe I'll take some online courses. I don't do well in classroom situations."

Craig was silent for a few moments. He was thinking he could tell I wasn't dumb, so what could my problem be? Maybe I had ADD, or just a total lack of ambition? Why hadn't I advanced further in life?

Though I felt a flash of resentment, I realized that Craig naturally wanted his brother to be dating a girl who had some goals and aspirations. It was hard to resist showing off, trying to impress Craig with my one unique ability.

For example, I could have told him that I knew he'd recently quit smoking at Deidra's request and that right now he was craving a cigarette. Or I could have told him that I knew he and Deidra were going to be parents. Or I could have told him that my boobs were real, which would have answered another unspoken question.

When you opened yourself up and stayed in a person's head for more than a second, you could really pick up on a lot of stuff.

Analyze what you've thought of in the last few minutes. Would you want anyone else to know about it? No. Sam had asked me once if I thought I could do a good job for Homeland Security. I tried to imagine how. Standing in an airport by the search line? Would any bomber or terrorist be going over his plan mentally, in detail, in an airport chosen at random? No, I thought not. I'd have to have a little more direction than that.

I wanted to discuss this with Craig, as I'd wanted to say it to so many people in the past. I'd often wished that other people understood my daily path, understood what I lived with. Not that I wanted to act all whiny and put-upon—"Poor Pitiful Pearl," as my grandmother used to call me when she thought I was in danger of being sorry for myself.

I sighed. It wasn't Be Kind to Telepaths week, and I had better tighten up my suspenders and get on with my life. I told Craig good night and took my turn in the bathroom when it was empty. It felt good to shower away the long day, and I belted my robe around my waist and emerged with the bundle of clothes I'd removed.

Sam was waiting by the door to my assigned bedroom. He looked tired but relaxed, and I could tell he was happy to be at home. He stood aside to let me enter first, and I put my clothes down on top of my tote bag and straightened up to find him looking at me with affection. Not lust, not frustration . . . affection. My heart went all gooey. We hugged, and it felt wonderful to breathe him in. He didn't mind the damp hair, the bare face, the worn bathrobe. He was happy I was here. He stood off a little, though he didn't entirely let go. "Thanks for coming with me, Sookie," he whispered. "And thanks for defusing that situation with Mr. Collins." Sam thought Jannalynn would have sprung over into the old man's yard and given him a shellacking. He seemed to believe that the problem with his mom's neighbor was over. I didn't know what to say to him. I decided, *I should let him sleep well and be happy. Tomorrow is the wedding.*

"No problem," I said. "I'm glad my softball training came in handy."

Sam went to the doorway. "I'm down there, in my old room," he said, jerking his head toward a door on the other side of the hall and down a bit. "Craig's in there with me. Mom's at the end of the hall."

I started to ask him why he'd told me, but then I realized I did indeed feel better knowing where he'd be in the night.

"You going to call Eric?" he said, almost inaudibly.

"I may try," I said. "He'd probably appreciate it."

"Tell him . . . Nah, don't tell him anything." Sam was not a big fan of the Northman. "I was going to say, 'Tell him thanks for letting you come,' but you can go where you damn well want to."

I smiled at Sam. "Yes, I can, and I'm glad you know that." Over his shoulder, I saw the door at the end of the hall open just a crack, and I could see Bernie's eyes peering at us. Sam gave me a little grin, and I knew he could tell we were being observed. I winked at Sam with the eye away from Bernie, and I kissed him. It wasn't long, but it was warm. There was a look in Sam's eyes when we let go of each other, a look that let me know he might've enjoyed putting on a much longer show for his mom, but I laughed and stepped back.

"Night," I said, and shut the door. I heard Sam's steps move away, and I fished my cell phone out of my purse. "Hey, you," I said quietly when Eric answered. Bernie would surely have the sharp shifter hearing.

"Are you well?" he asked. I could hear some noise in the background. It didn't sound like the familiar bar noises.

"I'm fine," I said. "There seems to be a lot of hostility here in this town against Sam and his mom, and I'm a little bit worried about that. Maybe the hater is just their cranky old neighbor, but I got a feeling there's more to worry about." This was what I hadn't discussed with Sam, so I was glad to pour it out to Eric.

"That's worrisome," he said, but he didn't sound too worried. "Can you handle it, or do you need help? What's the name of the town?"

"I'm in Wright, Texas," I said, and I may have said it a little sharply. After all, you expect your boyfriend to listen when you tell him stuff, and I knew I'd told him about the wedding. "It's west and a little south of Dallas."

"How far?"

I described the route we'd taken to Wright, and Eric said, "That would still be in Joseph Velasquez's territory. When Stan became king, he gave Joseph the sheriffdom."

"Your point?"

"I'd have to ask Joseph for permission to send someone to help you."

"Well, I appreciate the thought." Though I noticed that Eric hadn't actually said he'd *do* it. "But the wedding will be tomorrow afternoon in the daytime, so I don't think a vampire would be a big help."

"If you're really worried, you could call Alcide," Eric said reluctantly. "Maybe he knows the leader of the nearest pack down there, and it's possible the packleader would be willing to come to make sure things go well. Though surely Sam and his mother know the other two-natured in the area."

I didn't know how seriously to take one man's malice, but I did know from the shadow of his thoughts that there were more people in the town who believed the way he did. Maybe sending out a request for help would be a good idea. On the other hand, that was hardly my call to make.

"What's going on with you?" I asked, trying to sound completely focused. Eric had his own political problems, and the representative of the Bureau of Vampire Affairs was breathing down his neck about a violation of one of the rules for operating a vampire-owned business. A barmaid had promised a female customer that she (the barmaid, Cyndee) could bribe one of Eric's vamps to bite the woman. Cyndee'd been blowing smoke, but the BVA had to investigate the allegation. Plus, there was a tense situation with Eric's boss, Victor Madden.

"I think the BVA investigation is going to exonerate us," he said, "but Victor was here today with his own accountant, going through my books. This is well-nigh intolerable. I can fire Cyndee, and I have. I understand that's all I can do to her."

"Don't worry about things down here, then," I said. "You've got your hands full."

We talked a little longer, but Eric was preoccupied, and so was I. It wasn't a very satisfactory conversation.

I'd unfolded the couch to find it was already made up, and I discovered a folded bedspread and a pillow lying on the sewing machine. The evening was warm and the windows open, so I didn't exactly need the bedspread, but the pillow was nice and fluffy. I turned off the overhead light and stretched out on the lumpy mattress. As I adjusted my spine, I wondered if there was any foldout couch in the world that was as comfortable as a bed. I reminded myself to be glad I wasn't sleeping on the floor.

I could hear a muffled conversation coming from the room Sam was sharing with Craig. The brothers laughed. Their voices died away gradually. Through the open window, I heard a small animal outside, and the hoot of an owl. The breeze coming in didn't even smell like the wind at home.

I considered the possibility of calling Alcide Herveaux, the Were pack-leader in Shreveport. He was the werewolf I knew the best, and he might have some insight for me about the situation in neighboring Texas. But not only was I harboring a great resentment toward Alcide since he'd pressured me into taking hallucinogenic drugs so I could solve a pack dispute; I knew he was feeling resultant guilt himself. People who felt guilty lashed out, in my experience. It would be just my luck if he sent Jannalynn to provide backup.

Awkward.

Geez Louise, I'd be on the chopping block in no time flat. I wondered what kind of conversation Sam had had with her before we'd left. ("Yes, I'm going to my brother's wedding, but I'm taking Sookie because she's more presentable." I thought *not*.) And truly, it was another thing that was none of my business.

Then I fell to wondering if there were any other two-natured in Wright or its environs. If there were, maybe Sam could ask them to help when—if— trouble arose. The two-natured didn't always stick together. Of course, neither did any other minority group I'd ever heard of. . . . The owl hooted again.

I woke the next morning to the welcome smell of coffee and pancakes with a side of bacon. Oh, *yeah*. I could hear a couple of voices in the kitchen, and the water was running in the bathroom. The household was up early. This was the day of the rehearsal and the wedding. I smiled up at the ceiling in anticipation. My room looked over the front yard, and I got up and padded over to the window to see what kind of day it was.

It was a bad day.

Chapter Two

I pulled on shorts and a T-shirt, and hurried out into the kitchen. Sam and his mother looked up as I appeared in the doorway. They'd been smiling, and Sam was raising his coffee cup to his lips while Bernie was flipping the bacon in the frying pan. Sam put down his cup hastily and jumped to his feet.

"What?" he said.

"Go look in the front yard," I said, and stood aside while they hurried from the kitchen.

Someone had stuck a big sign in the yard, facing the house. The message was definitely for Bernie. DOGS BELONG IN THE POUND, it said. I'd already jumped to a conclusion about its meaning.

"Where is it?" I asked Sam. "The pound? I hope I'm wrong, but I have to check."

"If you go back to the highway, head south," he said. There was a ring of white around his mouth. "It's on Hall Road, to the right. I'm coming."

"No. Give me your keys. This is your brother's wedding day. You have to take care of your mother."

"It's not safe."

"Whatever's happened there, if anything has . . . it's already done."

He handed me his keys without another word. I hurried out to the truck, noticing along the way that not a soul was outside in any of the yards, though Saturday mornings are good for washing cars, yard work, garage sales, shooting hoops. Maybe Bernie's neighbors had already seen that trouble was brewing and wanted no part of it.

In fact, not that many people were out and about in the entire town of Wright. I saw a stout man about Sam's age putting gas in his car at the filling station. I caught his eye as I drove by, and he turned away pointedly.

Perhaps he'd recognized the truck. I saw an elderly woman walking her dog, an equally elderly dachshund. She nodded civilly. I nodded back.

I found Hall Road without any trouble and took a right. It was a dusty stretch of asphalt with a few straggling businesses, places in little faux-adobe structures spaced far apart. I began looking at signs, and it didn't take long to spot the one that read LOS COLMILLOS COUNTY ANIMAL SHELTER. It stood in front of a very small cement block building. Roofed pens extended in a long line on either side of a concrete run behind the building.

I turned off the motor and jumped out of the truck. I was struck by how quiet it was. Outside any animal shelter, I would expect to hear yapping and barking.

The pens out back were silent.

The front door was unlocked. I took a deep breath, let it out. I steeled myself and pushed it open, left it that way.

I stepped into a little room containing a desk topped with a battered and grimy old computer. There was a phone with an answering machine, half-buried under a pile of folders. A dilapidated file cabinet stood in a corner. In the opposite corner were two huge bags of dog food and some plastic containers of chemicals that I supposed were used to clean the pens. And that was all.

A door in the center of the rear wall stood open. I could see that it allowed access to the runway between the pens where the ownerless dogs were kept.

Had been kept.

They were all dead. I'd stepped through the door with dread in my heart, and that dread was justified. Bundles of bloody fur were in every cage.

I squatted simply because my knees gave way. My face was wet without my even realizing I'd started crying.

I'd seen dead human beings plenty of times, and the sight hadn't made me feel this awful. I guess, in the back of my mind, I believed most people could defend themselves to some extent, if only by running away. And I also believed people sometimes—sometimes—shared responsibility in the situation that brought about their deaths, if only by making unwise choices. But animals . . . not animals.

I heard another car pull into the parking area. I looked out through the open doors to see the black Ford Focus with the cracked windshield. If

I could have felt more frightened, I would have. Its doors opened, and three ill-assorted people got out and approached the animal shelter slowly, their heads swinging from side to side as they sniffed the air. They came through the little room very carefully, the tallest man in the lead.

"What's happened here, babe?" he said. He was tall and muscular, with a shaved head and purple eyes. I knew him fairly well. His name was Quinn, and he was a weretiger.

"Someone shot all the dogs," I said, stating the obvious because I was trying desperately to pull myself together. I hadn't seen Quinn in weeks, not since he'd tried to visit me at my home. That hadn't worked out too well.

Quinn knew they were dead already. His sense of smell had told him that. He squatted down by me. "I came to Wright to make a chance to talk to you," he said. "I didn't want it to be here, with all this death around us."

One of Quinn's companions came to stand by him. The two of them were like a pair of amazing bookends. Quinn's friend was a huge man, a coal black man, with his hair in short dreads. He looked like some exotic animal, and, of course, he was. He stared down at me with an incurious assessment, and then his eyes moved to the sad corpses in the pens, the streaks of blood running everywhere. The blood was beginning to dry at the edges.

Quinn extended his hand to me, and together we stood up.

"I don't understand why anyone would do this to our brothers," the black man said, his English clear and crisp but heavily accented.

"It's because of the wedding today," I said. "Bernie Merlotte's younger son is getting married."

"But a younger son will never change into anything. Only the oldest son." His accent was sort of French, which made the whole conversation more surrealistic.

"People here don't seem to know that," I said. "Or maybe they just don't care."

The third wereanimal was pacing outside the pens, circling the area. She would pick up the scents of the shooter. Or shooters. Tears were streaming down her face, and that wouldn't help her sense of smell. She was also furious. The set of her shoulders was eloquent.

"Babe, I don't know that this wedding is going to go off without more trouble," Quinn said. His big hand took mine. "I have a lot to say to you, but it's going to have to wait until later."

I nodded. The wedding day of Craig Merlotte and Deidra Lisle had definitely gotten off to a sad start. "Anything that upsets the Merlotte family upsets me. How did you come to be here?" I tried to keep my gaze away from the pitiful, limp forms.

"I was checking the twoey message board for information about the Shreveport area," Quinn said. "Sam posts on there from time to time, or sometimes I talk to the members of the Long Tooth pack." The Long Tooth pack was Alcide Herveaux's. "Someone posted that you were coming to Wright with Sam, and I already knew Trish and Togo here. Texas is part of my territory, you know." Quinn worked for Special Events, a branch of the national event-planning company E(E)E. Special Events staged important rites of passage for the supernatural community, like vampire weddings and first changes for the two-natured. "I knew Trish has a ranch outside Wright. I decided to take the chance to see you without the deader around." That would be Eric. "I flew into Dallas, and they picked me up. We were able to track you. I didn't want anything to happen to you on the way. I should have worried about what would happen when you got to Wright."

"This town is full of hate," the man called Togo said.

"I'm afraid so." I looked up at the broad nose, the high cheekbones, the gleaming skin. He was quite extraordinary. He stood out in these surroundings like a bird of paradise in a wren flock . . . not that there was anything avian about him.

The third wereanimal had finished her prowling, and now she appeared beside us. "I'm Trish Pulaski," she said. "You must be Sookie. Oh my God and his angels! Who would ever conceive of hurting poor dumb dogs to make a point?" She was lovely, and she was also clearly in her fifties. Her hair was solid gray, thick and curly. She didn't wear glasses, and her eyes were bright chips of blue in a tan face. Her jeans left no doubt she was in excellent shape. She wasn't thinking about herself or her companions. She was beside herself with rage and pain. I understood at that moment that the pound was her special project, that she'd raised the money to build it, she came every day to feed the animals, and she'd loved them all.

I said, "They left a sign in Bernie's yard."

"Bernie? They're targeting *Bernie*? Those fools!" she said, and her anger blazed like a flame within her. She turned to Quinn. "When we agreed to come out like the vampires did, this is the last thing I imagined would happen." She looked around at the dead dogs and the pools of blood, her gray curls dancing gaily and incongruously in the morning wind. She sighed, and her shoulders straightened. She said to me, "I'm sorry we had to meet here. This big guy is Togo Olympio. Quinn tells me you two are old friends. What was on the sign?"

I wanted to ask a lot of questions, but now was clearly not the time. I explained the little I knew. I also told them about Jim Collins.

"On Craig's wedding day," Trish said. She was angry and tearful and hurt. "Assholes!" Togo put a huge hand on Trish's thin shoulder. She laid her cheek on it for just a moment. "I'm not surprised to hear Jim Collins is involved," she continued. "Ever since we came out, he's been posting hate messages on his website."

"He has a website?" I said stupidly.

"Yeah, he's Mr. Right Wing. One of my jobs is monitoring websites like his. They've sprung up everywhere since the vamps came out, and they sprouted like mushrooms when we did. I watch Jim's especially closely since we're in the same area. He's even had postings from the Newlins." Steve and Sarah Newlin were the leaders of the radical religious underground in America. "Jim's website backs every extreme conservative position you can think of. Some of his principles I actually agree with, though it chokes me to say so. But most of his beliefs are so radical they scare me, and he doesn't seem to care how people will be hurt as a consequence of acting on those beliefs. Obviously, he doesn't care about animals," she added quietly.

Togo Olympio had entered one of the pens and bent over to touch the side of one of the fallen dogs. Flies were swarming now, and though I hadn't noticed their buzzing before, it droned in my ears. His dark eyes met mine, and I shivered. I was glad we were on the same side.

"I have to go back to the house and tell them," I said. "What will happen at the wedding if people are this determined to do them harm?"

"That's the big question, isn't it?" Trish said. She was pulling herself together. "Quinn says you're a friend of the shifters and the vampires though you're human."

I saw Quinn twitch out of the corner of my eye.

"But you're not completely human, right?" Trish persisted.

"No, ma'am." My bloodline wasn't exactly her concern, I figured, so I stopped at that.

"If you're Sam's friend, you're special already," she said, nodding to indicate she'd made a quick decision. I felt absurdly pleased. "Well, Sookie, Togo roams through every few weeks, and he and I are the scandal of the county. I've known Quinn, here, for years. Together, maybe we can hold back this hatred long enough for the young people to get married. After the wedding's over, I'm hoping like hell that feeling dies down and things go back to normal."

"Did you come out?" I asked. "With the other wereanimals?"

"This town's always thought I was a wild card, and no one was that surprised." Trish smiled broadly. "Bernie—she shocked everyone because she always seemed like Hannah Housewife; she and her first husband had such a great marriage, such good kids. Then, after she married Don . . . That was the trouble, Don's going nuts like that. His reaction was so violent and public, though I don't think he was in his right mind. Look, let's get out of here. All of this is making me sick."

I glanced at Quinn, and he nodded. "Togo and I'll come back later and dig a pit," he said, answering a question I hadn't wanted to ask.

To my surprise, Togo brought out a digital camera and began taking pictures. "My brothers and sisters need to know," he told me when he saw me watching. "This is to post on our own websites."

This just got more and more interesting.

"I've got to get back. I'm sorry I can't help you clean up," I said, which was a total lie. I was hugely relieved to have good reason to avoid burying the poor dogs. "Where are the cats?" I asked, struck by the fact that all the corpses were canine.

"I keep the cats at my place, thank God," Trish said, and I could only say *Amen* to that.

I walked back through the little building. When I got to the parking lot, I leaned against Sam's truck. The awfulness of the morning rolled over me again like a heavy wave. It was abominable that someone had slaughtered innocent dogs in a vicious attempt to ruin a day that should be happy. I felt the swell of a huge anger. I'd always had a slow temper. I didn't get *really* angry very often. But when I did, I did it right and proper. Since my time in the hands of the fae, my control over that anger seemed to have slipped. The second wave, the weight of my rage, threatened to pull me under. *I'm not myself,* I thought distantly.

It took a moment for the feeling to pass. When I was sure I was in control, I opened the door of the truck, dreading my return to the Merlotte house with the burden of my bad news.

What a lousy, rotten way to start the day.

"Sookie," Quinn said, and I turned to show him my face. I paused with one foot on the running board.

"All right," he said carefully. "I get it that you're way upset now, and so am I. But I've got to talk to you sometime."

"I understand," I said with equal care. "And we'll try to make the chance. Putting all personal issues aside, I'm glad you're here. Sam's family is up against more than we know. You're willing to help?" My eyes were telling him I'd think less of him if he wasn't.

"Yes," he said, surprised. "Of course I'll help. Trish will put out a bulletin on the Web. It's probably too late for much of anyone to come, since Wright's out in the middle of nowhere, but we'll all help. And I'm putting personal problems aside. For now." I looked up into his eyes, and I read in his head that he was serious, determined, and unswerving.

"I'd better go," I said. "You know where Bernie lives?"

"Yeah, we followed you at a distance. You spotted us, right? I hope you didn't call Eric."

I was a little shocked. "I wouldn't do that, Quinn."

"You didn't protest too much when Bill showed up at your house and beat the hell out of me the last time I tried to talk to you."

Eric had ordered Bill to intervene, since he'd banned Quinn from his area. "Excuse me," I said sharply. "You'll remember I was knocked unconscious! What happened to putting personal issues aside? You got Sam's number? You got the same cell as you did?"

We swapped phone numbers before Quinn returned to the building. I had to face the fact that there was nothing to keep me from driving back to Bernie's house. As I negotiated the streets of Wright, I found myself looking at each person I passed. Who was our friend? Who was our enemy?

A lightning bolt of a thought hit me. I was almost all human. I could legitimately claim this wasn't my fight.

No, I couldn't. I'd be as bad as Deidra's bridesmaids.

I'd been Sam's friend for years, and his family was human, too. I'd already taken a side, and there was no point in reviewing it.

I pondered Quinn's appearance. His story had amazed me. He'd gone to a huge amount of trouble and inconvenience to rendezvous with me here in Texas, and he'd only been acting on a tip.

I'd had a brief but ardent relationship with Quinn before I'd broken up with him—awkwardly and painfully—over family issues . . . his family issues. I'd been feeling guilty ever since, though I still thought I'd made the wise decision. Quinn seemed to think we had more to discuss, and possibly he was right, but I wanted to get through one crisis at a time.

I looked at the dashboard clock when I parked in front of the house. I'd been gone only forty-five minutes. I sure felt a lot more than forty-five minutes older. I got out and crossed the yard to the front door.

As I came close to the damn sign, I ripped it out of the ground. Moving with a lot more velocity, I strode over to the neighbor's house. Jim Collins was looking out of his open front window when I jabbed the stake into his dirt. Well, yee-haw. "You damn *murderer*," I said, and then I made myself walk away before I climbed through the window to choke Collins.

His creased face had been shocked and almost frightened, and for a blinding second I'd felt sorry that he didn't have a weak heart. After seeing the pathetic heaps of blood and fur, I would have enjoyed the sensation of scaring him to death.

I didn't knock on Bernie's door since I was staying there, and once I was inside, I went right to the kitchen at the back of the house. Sam, Bernie, and Craig were all there. They looked eerily alike as I appeared in the kitchen: apprehensive, upset, unhappy.

"All the dogs at the shelter are dead," I said. "They were shot."

Sam rose to take a tentative step toward me, and I could tell he wanted to offer me comfort. But I was too angry to accept it, and I held the palm of my hand toward him to let him know that.

"I moved the sign into Jim Collins's yard," I said. "That man's a murderer." My rage deflated just a little.

"Oh, Sookie," Bernie began, sounding both alarmed and a little reproachful, and I held up the same palm to her.

"It was him," I said. "He was not the only one, but it was him."

She sat back and looked at me with more objective attention than she'd given me since I'd met her. "And you know this how?" she said.

"He's condemned by his own words, from his own brain."

"Sookie can read minds, Mom," Sam said, and after a second's thought, Bernie flushed a dull red. She had thought a few unflattering things about me. I'm a big girl; I can live with that. It wasn't like I hadn't heard plenty of similar things before.

"Shapeshifters are hard to read, if that makes you feel any better," I offered, and I sat down at the table with a thud. As the rage oozed out of me, it left an empty space, an aching hole. I looked down at my leg as if I could see it through my clothes, see the thickened, whiter flesh of the scarring. I made myself sit straighter. This family had enough on their plate without having to bolster me up.

"My friend Quinn showed up," I said, and from the corner of my eye I saw Sam start. "He came with a couple you know, Bernie," I said, looking at Sam's mother. "A woman named Trish Pulaski and a man named Togo Olympio."

"Trish and I have been friends since we moved to Wright," Bernie said. "You probably remember her as Trish Graham, Sam. She divorced a while ago, took back her maiden name, and started up with Togo. I'll never understand that relationship, but I tell myself it's none of my business." Bernie's face suddenly reflected much more of the woman behind it and less of the mom, as if she'd switched hats internally.

"The point is, they're very concerned about Craig and Deidra's wedding going off without a hitch." I watched Bernie's face pass from incomprehension to reluctant horror.

"You think there may be *more*?" she said.

I found myself understanding why Bernie had been stunned when her husband had reacted so drastically to her revelation. As well as being unimaginative, Bernie was a wee bit on the unrealistic side.

"Mom," Sam said, "if they're starting off by killing all the dogs in the pound, I think you can assume there's going to be something else happening. Maybe we should think about postponing the wedding? Move it somewhere else?" He looked at his brother.

Craig said, "No." His face hardened as I watched. "We put it off once because Deidra's family wanted to understand more about what she'd be getting into, being married to me. We got the couples counseling. We got the totally unnecessary genetics counseling. Deidra's ready to marry me.

Her family is used to the idea, if not exactly thrilled. We set another date, and then we had to move it up." He cast a quick glance at me. He was wondering if I knew exactly why. "Because of Deidra's brother going overseas."

"Next month," I said helpfully.

"Right. Well, we didn't want to wait till the last minute. In fact, we don't want to wait another day."

Sam was looking from me to Craig.

"But everyone has been pitching in to help," Bernie said, still stuck on the hate. She'd lived here for years, and I could tell she was having a very hard time believing that people she'd known for more than a decade could turn on her. "I mean, the ladies in the church, the pastor . . . they've all been so happy that Craig and Deidra were going to get married. They threw Deidra a wedding shower in the fellowship hall."

"See, most people aren't bad," I said, as if I were reassuring a child. "I'm sure it's a minority here in Wright, a handful of people, but we don't want anything bad to happen that would ruin the wedding. Craig and Deidra need happy memories of this day, not . . ." My voice trailed off as I thought of what I'd seen at the shelter.

"Yes, I understand," Bernie said. She sat up a little straighter. "Craig, honey, I think you need to call Deidra right now. I hope nothing has happened over at her place."

Nothing could have gotten Craig moving as fast as that idea, and he had speed-dialed his fiancée almost before his mother had finished speaking. He stepped into the living room while he spoke to her, and he snapped his phone shut and came back into the kitchen with an air of relief.

"They're fine," he said. "I didn't tell them about the animal shelter. I hope they won't find out until after the wedding. Deidra's at the Clip N Curl, getting her hair done."

It was all of eight thirty in the morning. Despite the important issues we were facing, I shuddered at the idea of how long a day it was going to be for Deidra.

"When are Mindy and Doke and their kids coming?" I asked.

"They're supposed to be here in an hour," Bernie said. "Should I call their cell, tell them to turn back?"

"No," Sam said. "No, this wedding is going to take place. We are not going to let a few crackpots make us back down. That is," he said more qui-etly, "if that's what Craig and Deidra want to do."

Craig smiled at Sam briefly. "I'm getting married today," he said. "I don't want to put anyone in danger, but we're having this wedding." He shook his head from side to side. I could see the unhappiness, the bewil-derment, the determination. "They all know us. Why do we seem like we're any different from the way we've always been? And it's not like Deidra or I turn into anything."

Sam stared at his brother, and Bernie winced.

To his credit, Craig noticed. He said, "Sam, we talked this all out a couple of months ago. You're my brother, and you and Mom are like God made you. If they've got a problem with that, they can take it up with him."

Sam laughed, though unwillingly, and I nodded at Craig. That was a good little speech. I hoped the next time Sam felt down about being differ-ent, he would remember his brother's words. I wouldn't forget them myself.

I went to the guest room to put on my makeup. I'd dashed out of the house in such a hurry that morning, I'd left out several important steps in my daily routine. I wasn't an essential part of the rehearsal (or the wed-ding), but the family clearly expected me to go with them.

I tried to think of some tangible help I could provide—besides looking at dead animals and/or threatening a neighbor who already hated the fam-ily. (In retrospect, that hadn't been a smart thing.) When Sam knocked on the door thirty minutes later, I let him in. I'd pulled on the yellow and gray skirt outfit with matching yellow sandals. The top zipped up the back, and I turned around so Sam could finish zipping for me. I didn't have the flex-ibility in my arms that I'd had before . . . Oh, the hell with it. Not today.

Sam zipped me up as though this were our routine. He was wearing a dress shirt and khakis, and his loafers were shined. He'd brushed his hair neatly back. I admired the new look, but I found myself missing the long tangle of hair he'd had before.

"Listen, I did something I shouldn't have done," I said when I was zipped. I picked up my brush and began untangling my hair, which was very long now.

"If you're about to tell me what you said to Collins, I heard. So did Mom. Shifters have real sharp hearing, you know . . . and the windows were open."

I could feel my cheeks turn red. "Sorry," I said.

"I would have gone in and hit him," Sam said, and that was so close to what I'd been thinking that I jumped.

"I almost did," I confessed.

"Sook," he said seriously, "I appreciate your caring about my family so much."

"But it's not my family or my business, and I should back off and let you handle it? I know," I said, turning away and brushing my hair forcefully.

"I was going to say I'm glad I brought you." Pause. "Jannalynn's got her good points, or I wouldn't be going out with her—but she has no restraint, and she'd have gone batshit crazy this morning. The good thing about Jannalynn is that she's fully into her animal nature, and the bad thing is, it seems like she likes it *more*."

Without revealing how close I had come to going batshit crazy myself, I turned to face him, brush in hand. "I get what you're saying. Eric loves being a vampire. He loves it more than anything." *Maybe more than he loves me,* I thought, surprising myself. "You remember that black Focus we thought might be following us? Well, it was Quinn. Trish and Togo are his local contacts. He came here to talk to me."

Sam said, "Didn't you tell me that Eric had banned Quinn from Area Five?"

"Yeah, but he found out I was coming here from some kind of website. Isn't that crazy? Quinn flew from wherever he was working, and he got Togo and Trish to pick him up at the airport and bring him here."

"You and he . . ."

"Yeah, we had a thing, but I kind of told him to take a hike—I didn't put it that mean—because his family is . . . well, complicated. His mom's not really sane, and his little sister is a real piece of work, though I guess I never really had a chance to get to know her. I didn't break up with him well," I admitted. "He wants to have some kind of conversation about it. I sure don't need that, though I guess I owe him. I just don't understand how my being here got on the Internet."

Sam looked embarrassed. "That might be my fault," he said. "We keep track of each other now, all of us who change. Since the announcement, we never know what people are going to do. Humans don't always react in predictable ways. You know that better than anyone."

"So you put it *on the Web* that you and I were coming here to this wedding?"

"No! No! But I did mention it when I was talking to Travis." Travis, a trucker who was a Were not affiliated with a pack, stopped in at Merlotte's about once every two weeks.

"But why would you have mentioned me?"

Sam closed his eyes briefly. "You're kind of famous in the supe community, Sookie."

"What?" This made no sense at all.

"You're unique. Weres like something different as much as anyone else. You're a friend of the Shreveport pack. You've done a lot for twoeys."

"Okay, several thoughts. I haven't seen a computer around here, or I'd ask you to check Jim Collins's website. I want to know what he's saying about what's happening in Wright. And here's my second thought—I've been assuming that Jannalynn knows I came with you . . . right?"

"Sookie, of course Jannalynn knows I brought you to this wedding. I explained that I'd asked you before we'd started dating." Sam looked even more embarrassed, which I didn't think was possible. He'd already more or less admitted that that wasn't the only reason he'd left Jannalynn at home.

Plus, Jannalynn would realize that anyone who saw on the Web that I was going with Sam to his family home would know that she was not the only woman in Sam's life. Even though Sam and I had a platonic relationship, I knew I would have been pretty jealous if I'd been in her shoes. Or on her paws.

"Jannalynn's going to want to kill you," I said flatly. "Or me. And I guess I wouldn't really blame her."

Sam flushed, but his gaze was unwavering. "She's a big girl. She knows better than anyone else that . . ."

"That you've lost your frickin' mind? Well, it's done now." I sighed and regrouped, realizing that worrying about Sam's indiscretion would have to wait until later. We needed to focus on getting Craig and Deidra married without any violence disrupting the ceremony.

"Have you thought about how Quinn and Togo and Trish can be useful? I've got Quinn's cell phone number. They're probably at the pound . . . cleaning up. Of course, I'll help however I can." I handed Sam the scrap of paper with Quinn's number.

"What I'm going to ask them to do," Sam said, "is stand guard. When we get to the church for the rehearsal, I hope you four will set up a perimeter outside. That way we'll have plenty of warning if Collins and his buddies try something. The time of the rehearsal isn't public knowledge, not like the wedding time. That was in the paper because the whole community was invited."

That was a common practice in Bon Temps, too, so I wasn't surprised. Many engagement announcements included the particulars of the marriage ceremony with the invitation, "All friends of the couple are welcome."

"Sure," I said. "I'll be a lookout." I'd feel better standing watch with a shotgun in my hands, but I figured that if I had the Benelli, (a) I might actually shoot someone, and (b) I might get arrested. I didn't know Texas gun laws, and there was no telling how stringently they'd be enforced on a local level.

"You look too pretty to be standing out in the churchyard. I'm sorry," Sam said, shaking his head. "This isn't how I thought we'd be spending this time."

"Sam, it's not your fault. I'm glad I can help out. I only regret it's necessary." There was a chance that planting the sign and killing the dogs was the end of the protest against the marriage. But that was a remote possibility.

"I'm sorry you had to see the dogs; I guess . . . Well, that's just sad. No one should have to see something like that." Sam stared down at his feet.

"I agree," I said, my voice as steady as I could manage.

From the flurry of voices in the living room, I could tell that Doke and Mindy and the kids had arrived. Sam and I went out to join them. We told them all the news. After some quiet discussion, they decided they'd stay at the house with the kids until it was time for the wedding. Mindy said, "All we'd do at the rehearsal is find out when to come down the aisle and sit in a pew, and I think Doke and I can manage that, right?" They were worried about Mason and Bonnie, and I didn't blame them.

When it was time to leave the house, I walked out with the others to find that a car was parked in front that didn't belong to anyone in the family.

"Hey," called a short brunette who was leaning on the hood of the Saturn. She straightened and came forward to hug Sam.

"Hey, yourself," he said, and hugged her back.

"That's Sister Mendoza," Craig explained. "They've been friends a long time." Craig was afraid I'd get mad at Sam touching another woman.

"She's a nun?"

"What?" Craig stared for a second. "Oh. Oh, no! Sister is her name." He laughed. "She and Sam have been friends ever since we moved here. She's a deputy at the sheriff's department."

"Why is she here?"

"I have no idea. Hey, Sister! Did you come because of that parking ticket I forgot to pay?"

"Hell, no," Sister Mendoza said, letting go of Sam. "I come here to be a watchman. Me and Rafe." A short, thick-bodied man got out of the car. He was as pale-haired as Sister was brunette.

"Rafe played football with Sam," Craig told me, but I think I would have figured it out by the way they were thumping each other.

Sam beckoned me over. "Sookie, these are some old friends of mine, Sister and Rafe," he said. "You two, you be nice to this woman." Sam was in no doubt that they would be. His brain was practically rolling with pleasure at seeing his old buddies.

The two friends gave me a quick once-over, seemed okay with what they saw. Rafe gave Sam a fist to the shoulder. "She's way too pretty for you, you old dog," Rafe said, and they laughed together.

"I'm taking the backyard," Sister said, and she left.

Rafe gave Sam a sharp nod. "You-all go to the church and don't worry about things here," he said. "We got your back. You got someone coming to the church?"

Sam said, "We got the church covered." He paused. "You two aren't in uniform," he said carefully.

"Well, we're off duty," Rafe said. He shrugged. "You know how it is, Sam."

Sam looked pretty grim. "I'm getting the picture," he said.

I felt much better about the safety of both the kids and the house itself as Sam and I got into his truck to drive behind Craig and his mom to the church.

It wasn't a long drive. Wright was no bigger than Bon Temps. Drier, dustier, browner—but I didn't imagine it was essentially different. We'd had trouble with demonstrators in front of the bar, but they'd gotten tired of getting hustled out of the parking lot, and they'd gone back to writing letters. Could my fellow townspeople do what someone had done here at the dog pound?

But there wasn't time to worry about that because we were two blocks west of Main Street at the corner of Mesquite (the north–south street) and St. Francis (the east–west). Gethsemane Baptist Church was a faux-adobe structure with a red-tiled roof and a squat bell tower. I could hear the organist practicing inside. The sound was strangely peaceful.

There was parking at the front and at the left side, between the church and the parsonage. The fellowship hall was directly behind the church, connected by the umbilical cord of a covered walkway. The yard was full of thin grass, though what grew there was neatly mown.

A man who could only be the pastor was walking over from the parsonage, which looked like a smaller version of the church. He was middle-aged with a big belly and graying black hair. From my first dip into his head, I concluded that Bart Arrowsmith was a genial man who was not equipped to handle a situation this volatile. I knew that by now word must have spread all over Wright about what had happened, and I knew this situation had spooked Brother Arrowsmith.

This was a day when I had to know the capabilities and weaknesses of the people around me, no matter how invasive it felt to enter their thoughts. What I saw in Brother Arrowsmith's head gave me the sad suspicion that he was not going to be the tower of strength we needed today. He was a conflicted man who couldn't decide what God wanted him to do when he was faced with a situation he couldn't interpret scripturally.

He was troubled on this day that should be so happy. And that made him feel even worse. He liked Craig and Deidra. He had always liked Bernie. For that matter, he liked Sam, but when he looked at Sam, he now saw something subhuman.

I took a deep breath and got out of Bart Arrowsmith's head. It wasn't a healthy, happy place to be.

A light breeze had been stirring the leaves on the short trees. Now it gained power. It hadn't rained in Wright for a while, and my cheeks felt the sting of the sandy particles picked up by the wind. I didn't know who'd appointed me Grim Nemesis, but I was in a weird state of apprehension.

I intercepted the minister as he reached the steps. I introduced myself.

After Bart Arrowsmith shook my hand and asked me if Craig was already inside, I told him, "You need to take a stand on this."

"What?" he said. He peered through his wire rims at me.

"You know what's happening here is wrong. You know this is hate, and you know God doesn't want hatred to happen here."

See? Like I was the voice of God. But I felt *compelled*.

Something shifted around behind Bart Arrowsmith's eyes. "Yes, I hear you," he said. He sighed. "Yes." He turned to go into the church.

Next I'd be nailing a list of demands to the door.

Trish, Quinn, and Togo drifted across the dry yard. Their feet hardly made a sound on the crisp grass. I hadn't seen them approach, but they all looked the worse for the wear. Quinn and Togo had been digging.

"Quinn will take the front," Trish said, sounding calm and authoritative though her eyes were red from weeping. "Togo, honey, you take the rear. Sookie and I will take the right side." I hoped we could take it for granted that no one was going to attack from the parsonage on the left.

I nodded, then exchanged a glance with Quinn as I started moving east into position.

Deidra and her parents arrived in one car, her sisters and her brothers in another. Mrs. Lisle was almost as pretty as Deidra, but with shorter hair and a few more pounds. Mr. Lisle looked exactly like a man who worked in a hardware store: capable, skilled, and unimaginative. The whole family was obviously very anxious.

Mr. Lisle wanted to ask us what we were doing standing around the churchyard, but his nerve failed him. So he and Mrs. Lisle, Deidra and her sisters, and Deidra's oldest brother scurried across the yard to the open doors of the church. Deidra's other brother, the one in the service, took up a stand beside me. Since I was sure he was armed, I was glad to see him. He nodded at my companion. "Miss Trish," he said politely. She patted him on the shoulder. "Jared Lisle," he said to me.

"Sookie Stackhouse. I came with Sam."

And then we watched.

A pair of girls arrived and scooted up the sidewalk and into the church, casting a glance at Jared as they hurried. He smiled and raised his hand in greeting.

"They're singing," he explained. "I'm kind of surprised they showed up." Sam and Deidra's oldest brother were Craig's groomsmen, so the wedding party was complete.

Through the open church windows, I listened to "Jesu, Joy of Man's Desiring" as the organist ran through some opening music. I could faintly hear Brother Arrowsmith giving instructions to the wedding party.

A car or two drove by, with nothing more than a curious glance from the drivers. I fidgeted, unable to find a casual way to be just hanging around the side of the church. I felt both conspicuous and awkward.

Jared didn't have that problem. Since he was in the army, he was used to spending time being on alert. He didn't talk to me or Trish for a long time, but I figured that was okay because he had something more important to think about.

As for me, I was wondering what on earth I would do if there was some kind of attack. Read their thoughts really, really quickly? *That* wouldn't be much help. I missed my shotgun more than ever. Could I shoot another human being if he attacked the church or tried to disrupt Sam's brother's wedding?

Yes, I thought I could. Hell, yes. My back stiffened.

It's both interesting and unpleasant to get a big revelation about your own character, especially at a moment when you can't do a damn thing about it. I couldn't abandon my post, run to the nearest gun store to make a purchase, don some black leather and high-heeled boots, and reinvent myself as a kick-ass heroine. A gun would make me *feel* tough, but it wouldn't make me *be* tough. The desire to shoot someone wouldn't make me an accurate shot with a handgun. Though if I had my shotgun, it would be hard to miss.

I had a hundred scattered ideas in the space of a few seconds. And those few seconds multiplied as the assorted band I'd joined kept watch over nothing. Only Jared and Trish showed no signs of impatience or restlessness, but they did relax enough to exchange a few comments. I gathered that Trish had taught Jared in high school—English and composition. She was enjoying her early retirement. She'd been doing a lot of volunteer work and selling her handmade jewelry. Jared told her about his posting in Afghanistan. He was ready to go.

Then we heard the sounds of several engines approaching the turnoff to the church from the main drag. We all stiffened, and our eyes went to the stop sign at the end of the street.

Three motorcycles turned onto the street, motors rumbling. And there was a Suburban right behind them, full of people.

We formed a line across the sidewalk without saying a word.

The engines were turned off, and there was silence. The only sound in the neighborhood was the wind through the branches of the live oak in the front yard and the organ music wafting from the church windows.

I tried to develop a plan, and finally I decided the only way I could stop someone from entering the church was by tackling him. The three people astride cycles swung off and removed their helmets. They were all women. Ha! That was unexpected. And I realized after just a moment that they were all shifters, something Togo and Trish had picked up on in a fraction of a second.

"What are you doing here, sisters?" Togo said, his wonderful accent and deep voice fascinating.

The people in the Suburban began to climb out. Two of them were male; two were women. They were also two-natured.

"Hey, buddy," called the man who'd been driving. "We heard about the problem here, from the Web. We've come to be of service."

There was a long moment of thoughtful silence. Then Trish stepped forward. She was holding back her wind-tossed gray curls with both hands. She introduced herself. "I'm a friend of the groom's family. We're here to keep strangers out of the church. You know there've already been a couple of incidents today. All the dogs in the pound were killed to protest this wedding."

I was a little unnerved to hear the newcomers growl. Most two-natured didn't let themselves express their animal sides when they were in public. Then I realized that Deidra's brother and I were the only humans around. We were in the minority.

The newly arrived Weres, both the Suburban wolves and the Biker Babes—I didn't make that up; that's what their jackets said—reinforced our picket around the church. A couple of trucks drove by, but if the men in them had pictured themselves stopping, they changed their minds when they saw the assortment of people waiting.

I introduced myself to a Biker Babe named Brenda Sue, who told me she was a trauma nurse at a hospital about fifty miles away. This was her afternoon off. I told her about the four o'clock wedding, and she looked as if she was working something out in her head. "We'll be here," she said.

At the moment, I thought that Trish, when she'd posted that call to arms on the twoey website, had done us a good deed. And maybe Jim Collins had actually given us a present by killing those poor animals. He might as well have shot a flaming arrow into the sky.

I heard the traditional music a couple more times, and I could hear the voice of an older woman giving some quick instructions. The rehearsal was over much more quickly than I'd anticipated. I didn't know if that was because Brother Arrowsmith was hurrying it up or if forty-five minutes was normal for the rehearsal for a small family ceremony.

The wedding party came out of the church. They were obviously shocked to see the increased number of watchmen in the yard. Sam and Bernie grinned, and though the regular humans held back a little, all the two-natured had a great meet-and-greet. After some conversation all the way around, Jared Lisle shook my hand and got in a car with his brother and his sisters. No one wanted to linger in this exposed space. Trish and Togo had volunteered to feed the out-of-town visitors an impromptu lunch out at Trish's ranch, and they led the little procession south out of town. Sam's mom and Craig got into their car to go home, leaving Sam and me in front of the church.

"You and I are going to the police department," he said briefly, and I scrambled up into the truck. Sam was silent on the short drive—everything in Wright was a short drive—and by the time we parked in front of the small brick structure labeled LOS COLMILLOS POLICE DEPT, I understood that Sam was angry, stressed, and feeling responsible for a certain amount of this persecution.

"I'm sorry," he said to me abruptly.

"What?"

"I'm sorry I bring you here and this all happens. You have enough on your plate without having this added to it. I know you wish you'd stayed home in Bon Temps."

"What I was wishing was that I were more use," I said, trying to smile. "Maybe you should have brought Jannalynn, was what I was thinking."

"She would have broken each of Jim Collins's fingers and laughed while she did it."

Oh. Well, in that case. "But at least she would have accomplished something," I said ruefully. What had I done that morning? Did *not killing the neighbor* count as a positive?

We were out of the truck and walking into the police department as we had this exchange. After we passed through the scarred door, it seemed like a good time to stop talking about finger breaking.

"Sam," said the middle-aged man behind the desk. "When did you get back?"

He had thin lips and a square jaw that came to a point, and a pair of eyebrows that were straight and bushy. He was smiling, but he was not happy. I wasn't sure what the cause of his unhappiness was. I suspected it was us.

"Hey, Porter. We got in yesterday. This is my girl friend, Sookie."

"If you're going out with Sam, you've got a high bullshit tolerance," Porter said. He was trying to smile, but it wasn't reaching his eyes.

"I put up with him somehow," I said.

"I guess you aren't here just to say hi?" The name on his tag read "Carpenter." Was his name Porter Carpenter? Almost as challenging as Sister Mendoza.

"I wish," Sam said, and I realized that his speech had slowed down a bit and his body had relaxed. He even looked a little younger. He was *home*. Funny I hadn't noticed that until now. "I'm afraid we had some trouble this morning."

"I been out to the animal shelter," Porter said. "Your problem related to that?"

I let Sam tell Officer Carpenter all about it, and he did a quick job of it.

"So you think this was at least partly Jim Collins's doing?" Carpenter asked. "Jim wasn't too bad until the vampires came out, but that tipped him over the line because that was about when Della died."

Della had been Jim's wife. I filled that in from Sam's brain.

"Then the weres . . . Well, it just made him nuts. Especially when Don shot your mom. He and Don were big buddies."

"So it was okay for his big buddy to shoot his own wife?" Sam asked bitterly.

"Sam, I'm just saying." Porter shrugged.

"I didn't see any evidence Jim Collins put the sign on Sam's mom's lawn or that he killed the dogs at the animal shelter," I said, trying to get the conversation back on track. "At least, none that you could take to court. Maybe you found something?"

Carpenter shook his head. I knew he hadn't looked. I was getting a whole lot from his head that scared me.

Sam said, "The dogs are dead, and nothing's gonna change that. I'd like whoever did that to go to jail. But right now, I'm more worried that someone's going to disrupt the wedding."

"Do you think they'd do that?" Porter Carpenter asked, genuinely taken aback. "Ruin your brother's wedding day?" He answered his own question. "Yes, I reckon there are a few people who would." He thought for a moment. "Don't worry about it, Sam. I'll be there in my uniform, right outside the church. I'll have another deputy with me, too. We'd have traffic duty anyway. Where's the reception going to be? Church hall?"

Sam nodded.

Good. Close and quick to get to, not much exposure, I thought.

Though Sam and Porter talked a little more, there wasn't much else the cop was willing to do until the anti-two-natured took a more drastic step. He was only being as helpful as he was because he'd known Sam and his mom and dad a long time. If it hadn't been for that bond, he would have given us a much cooler reception. A deputy came in while Sam and Carpenter were talking, and he regarded us with the same reserve.

When we left the police station, I thought Sam was more worried than when he'd gone in. The cops who were on our side were already at the Merlotte home, and they weren't in uniform.

We arrived at Bernie's house to see at least ten cars parked up and down the street and in the driveway. I was filled with dismay, thinking these were people who were showing up to give the family some more grief; but then I saw that the new arrivals were positioning themselves all around the little lot. They were facing outward. They were there to protect the Merlotte family.

Unexpectedly, tears welled up in my eyes. I groped for Sam's hand, felt it grip mine. "Hey, Leonard," Sam said to the nearest man, a gray-haired guy wearing a khaki shirt and khaki pants.

"Sam," Leonard said, bobbing his head.

Sister nodded at us. "We'll get this done," she assured Sam. "Day's half over. Bring Sookie to the next class reunion, you hear?"

Though I knew Sam had a real girlfriend and I was only standing in for the weekend, I had a giddy little tingle of warmth at the welcome I'd received from his family and friends. I had to stop in amazement when we went in the front door. The little house was a beehive of activity inside as well as out.

There were some bouquets of carnations on the occasional tables in the living room. One had balloons attached, which made the atmosphere weirdly cheerful. While we'd been gone, not only had the florist van stopped by, but someone had delivered a platter of cold cuts and cheese, and bread. Sliced tomatoes and everything else that might conceivably go on a sandwich were set out beside the platter, along with some "wedding" paper plates. Sam and I helped ourselves, as everyone else had done. Mindy's children were running around in high excitement.

The house felt very small, very full of life, and all the brains were buzzing with excitement and happiness.

While Sam and I ate in the living room, sitting side by side on the couch, Mason brought me a glass of sweet tea, carrying it very carefully. "Here, Aunt Sookie," he said proudly, and though I opened my mouth to correct the title, I just said, "Thank you, darlin'." Mason grinned, looked instantly bashful, and dashed away.

Sam put his arm around me and kissed me on the cheek.

I took a sip of the tea because I didn't know what else to do. I thought Sam was getting a little *too* into his role-playing.

"After all, you are my girlfriend this weekend," he said close to my ear, and I stifled a laugh because it tickled.

"Uh-huh," I said, infusing the words with a little hint of warning.

He didn't remove his arm until he needed it to pick up his sandwich, and I shook my head at him . . . but I was smiling. I couldn't help it. I was so uplifted at the community rallying around the Merlottes and the Lisles. I hadn't felt this hopeful in . . . forever.

That lasted about five more minutes. The brains outside grew jangled with agitation. It began about the same time that I noticed an increased number of vehicles passing in front of the house. Given the general turmoil, I didn't think much of it. However, I glimpsed movement out the front window, and I half stood to look through Bernie's sheers. There were four cars parked across the street and at least twenty newcomers standing around, blocking the cars of the volunteers, and the family cars, too.

Sister was yelling, poking her finger at the chest of a man three times as big around as she was. He was yelling back. And finally, he shoved her and she went sprawling.

Sam had jumped to his feet to look out the window. When he saw his friend fall, he yelled and shot out of the house, Doke and Craig following him. Bernie zipped through the living room soon after, pelting out the front door like the strong woman she was.

There was lots of shouting, lots of commotion, and I wondered if I should join them, if I could be of any help. Then I thought twice. There was something contrived about the whole incident. Why would a confrontation be staged in front of the house?

So something could happen at the back.

Mindy and her children were standing in the hall, and I understood that Mindy didn't want the kids to see any violence through the front or back windows. I nodded at her, held my finger over my lips, and eased into the kitchen. The small wooden bat the men had been using to lob balls to Mason the day before was by the back door, and I picked it up and hefted it. I was glad it was wood and not plastic. I looked out the window cautiously. Yes, someone was creeping through the backyard. A teenage boy, lean and lanky and angry. He had something in his hand.

My heart was pounding a mile a minute, and I had to make myself calm down so I could read his thoughts. He had some kind of a bomb, and he was planning on opening the back door and tossing it in and running like hell. I had no idea what kind of device it was. It might be a stink bomb or a smoke bomb . . . or a firebomb.

I felt a movement behind me, and I glanced over my shoulder to see Mindy creeping into the room. She'd made the kids lie down on the hall floor, and had come in to provide backup. I felt an unexpected surge of emotion. My resolve got a shot of adrenaline.

So here's where I may have overreacted.

When the teenager opened the back door, so very cautiously, and stuck his hand in, I shoved the door all the way open, took a half step, and swung the bat as hard as I could.

CHAPTER THREE

I broke his arm. And here's the thing: Though what he was holding turned out to be a stink bomb, not something that would actually physically harm Sam's family, I never did feel bad about it afterward. In fact, in a savage kind of way I was glad I'd broken a bone.

This was the new me. Though I could regret I'd changed, it was a done deal. I couldn't regenerate the tenderhearted me. I didn't know how much of this alteration in my character was due to the blood bond I shared with a big, unscrupulous Viking and how much of it was due to the torture I'd undergone ... but I wasn't exactly the same nice person, as this boy had just found out.

He screamed in pain, and people came running from all over, both his buddies and the Merlotte family and their friends, and then the police, both in and out of uniform, and it was all chaos for a good forty minutes.

Since Mindy had been standing there while the boy came in the back door—and when he was blubbering in pain, he himself admitted it—I was in the clear.

In fact, his hastily summoned parents were absolutely horrified, didn't try to dodge the facts or excuse his actions. They were stand-up people, which was a huge relief, because the boy was Nathan Arrowsmith, the only child of the Reverend and Mrs. Bart Arrowsmith. Talk about your touchy situation.

What did Sam's family do? Sam's family had a prayer meeting.

My gran had been a religious woman, and I liked to think of myself as a striving Christian. (Lately, I'd been more striving than Christian.) But we'd never had a family prayer circle. So I felt a little self-conscious about standing in the living room holding hands with Doke and Sam while all of us bowed our heads and prayed out loud, one by one.

Bernie identified herself to God, which I thought was kind of unnecessary, and then asked God to make her enemies see the light of tolerance. Mindy asked that God grant his blessing to the wedding and keep it peaceful. Craig very manfully asked God to forgive Nathan Arrowsmith and those who had conspired with him. Mason asked God to give him back his baseball bat. (I winced at that one.) Doke asked God to cure the hatred growing in the people of Wright. I asked God to restore peace in our hearts, which was something we all needed. Sam put in a request for the safety of everyone involved in the wedding. Bonnie got too self-conscious to say anything and started crying—pretty understandable in a three-year-old.

I felt a little better afterward, and I think the family did, too. It was definitely time to get ready to go over to the church again, and for the second time that day I retreated to the guest/sewing room to get dressed. I put on the sleeveless blue dress I'd borrowed from Tara. I wore Gran's pearl necklace and earrings and the black heels. I pulled my hair off my face with a pearl comb—also Gran's—and left it loose. All I'd had to buy was a lipstick.

Sam wore a suit, lightweight blue seersucker. When I emerged, we looked at each other speechlessly.

"We clean up pretty good," I said, smiling at him.

He nodded. And I could tell he was thinking that Jannalynn would have worn something really extreme, and his family wouldn't have liked it. I felt a twinge of irritation with Sam. Why was he dating her, again? I was beginning to feel sorry for the girl. All weekend, Sam had been glad he hadn't brought her to meet his family. What kind of relationship was that? Not one founded on mutual respect.

When we came out to go to the church, Jim Collins was standing in his yard holding a sign that read NO ANIMAL MARRIAGES IN HUMAN CHURCHES. Offensive, yes. Illegal, no.

I hadn't forgotten from which direction Nathan Arrowsmith had come with his stink bomb.

I stopped on my way to Sam's truck. I took a step off the driveway. I caught Jim Collins's eyes. He wanted to look away, but he didn't. He thought his pride required that he meet my gaze. He was full of hate and anger. He missed Don, thought Don was right to shoot Bernie since in Jim's view she'd been a faithless liar. He knew Bernie hadn't cheated on her husband, but concealing what she really was counted in his book. The constant pain that nagged at Jim Collins's joints made his mind restless and angry. Advanced arthritis.

I said, "You're alone, and lonely, and miserable, and you'll stay that way until you get rid of all that hate." And I turned, walked away, and met Sam at the truck.

Sam said, "Feel better, Sookie?"

I said, "That wasn't a good thing to do. I know. I'm sorry." A little.

"Too bad you couldn't break his arm," Sam said, and he was smiling. A little.

As we opened the truck doors, we both glanced down the street toward Main, alerted by the buzz of voices. The street that had been so oddly empty that morning was now lined with people.

"What the hell?" Sam said. The whole Merlotte party, including the children, froze in place by their vehicles. While we'd been dressing for the most important day in Craig's and Deidra's lives, people with other plans had been gathering.

There were signs, signs bearing hateful messages. HUMAN BEINGS WALK ON TWO FEET, read the mildest one I saw. The others ranged from biblical quotations to obscenities about Craig and Deidra's wedding night. My hand flew up to cover my mouth as I read some of them, as if I could suppress my horror. Mindy covered her children's eyes. Even though I didn't think they could read the signs—and "abomination" is a pretty long word, even for older kids—I understood exactly how she felt.

"Oh my God," Bernie said. "Has the world gone mad? My husband shoots me, and everyone hates *me*?"

"Maybe we should go back in the house," Doke said. He'd picked up Mason, and Mindy had lifted Bonnie into her arms.

"I'll never go back in the house," Bernie growled. "You got the kids, you do what you think you have to. I'll *never* let them win."

Sam stood by his mother, his arm around her shoulders. "We go forward, then," he said quietly.

"All right," I said, bracing myself. "All right, here we go. Craig?"

"Yeah," said Craig. "I'm going to the church. I hope the Lisles can get there. I'm not making Deidra wait for me on our wedding day."

The excitement in all those brains, the churning emotions and thoughts, battered at me, and I staggered. Sam jumped over to grasp my arm. "Sookie?" he said. "This doesn't have to be your fight."

I thought of the dead animals at the shelter. "This is my fight." I took a deep breath. "How did all these people get here?"

"The Internet," said Sister. She and Rafe were looking around them, alert to approaching danger. "Everyone just showed up, said they'd heard about it on the Internet. That Twitter thing maybe."

A television news van pulled up at the end of the street.

"That's probably good, I think," Sam said. "Witnesses."

But I thought people would act out worse, so their protest would make the evening news. "We better get going," I said. "Before the assholes build up their courage."

"Do you figure the majority of the crowd is pro or anti?" There were signs for both camps. More for the anti, but haters are always the most vocal.

I scanned the signs. "The signs are mostly anti," I said. "The anti folks are better organized, which isn't a big surprise. People of goodwill don't have to carry signs."

We got welcome reinforcements from an unexpected direction. Togo, Trish, and the Biker Babes, along with the Suburban people, came through the backyards to arrive at our sides.

"Road was blocked farther on," Trish explained. "Pile on in your cars. We have a plan."

Bernie said, "Trish, maybe . . ."

"You-all get in, but drive slow," Trish said. "We're going to walk alongside the cars. Don't want any of them getting close to the kids."

"Doke?" Mindy said. "Are we doing the right thing?"

"I don't know." Doke sounded almost desperate. "But let's go. If we all stay together, it's better than being divided." The two parents crowded into the backseat of Bernie's car, their kids between them, buckled into the parents' seat belts. Craig got into the driver's seat, and Bernie ducked in the passenger side. Sam and I hugged, and then we got into his truck. We pulled away from the curb slowly and carefully, and Togo got on my side of the truck. He smiled in at me. Trish was on Sam's side. The bikers and the other shifters who'd come from out of town surrounded Bernie's car, which would be behind us.

We started down the street, and the yelling began. The people who were trying to keep the peace pushed to get in front of the protesters, linking arms to provide us clear passage to the corner. The news crew had scrambled out and gotten their equipment set up, and the reporter, a handsome young man in a beautiful suit, was talking earnestly into the camera. Then he stepped out of camera view so the lens could pick up the scene of our approaching vehicles.

Sam was punching in a number on his cell. He held it to his ear. "Porter," he said, "if you're in front of the church, we're headed your way, and in case you have your head up your ass, we're in a lot of trouble."

He listened for a moment. "Okay, we'll be there. If we get through."

He tossed the phone onto the seat. "He says it's worse the closer you get to the church. He's not sure he could get through to help us. He's having trouble just keeping the crowd out of the church. The Lisles have made it, because they came early so Deidra could dress in the bride's room."

"That's something," I said, trying to keep my voice steady. I was scared to death. I was looking out the front windshield, and I saw people's mouths moving, their faces distorted; I heard human beings hating, hating. They didn't know Sam or Bernie. They didn't care that the engaged couple couldn't turn into anything at all. They were waving signs. They were screaming at us. Again Togo smiled through the window at me, but I couldn't smile back.

"Courage," Sam said to me.

"I'm trying," I told him, and then the rock hit the windshield. I shrieked, which was stupid, but I was so startled and it was so sudden. "Sorry, sorry!" I gasped. There was a crack in the glass.

"Shit," Sam said, and I knew he was as tense as I was.

The next rock hit Togo in the shoulder. Though he didn't bleed, he did react, and I knew it must have hurt. Togo, so big and aggressive, probably seemed a better target than Trish, who was gray-haired and a woman.

"I wish I had my shotgun," I said out loud, though I'd thought it twenty times.

"If you had it, you'd shoot someone, so maybe it's better you don't," Sam said, which amazed me.

"You don't feel like shooting some of these yahoos?"

"I don't feel like going to jail," Sam said grimly. He was staring ahead, concentrating on keeping the truck moving at a slow and steady pace. "I'm only hoping none of them throw themselves in front of the truck." Suddenly, a tall figure appeared directly in our way. He turned his back to us and began walking ahead at the right pace to be point man for our little procession. Quinn. Bald head gleaming, he led us forward, looking from side to side, evaluating the crowd.

Sam's phone rang, and I picked it up. "Sookie here," I said.

"There are more of your people here," Brother Arrowsmith said. "I'm sending them to meet you."

"Thanks," I said, and flipped the phone shut. I relayed the message to Sam.

"So he finally grew a pair," Sam said. "And just in time."

We'd gotten to the corner by then, and we had to turn right on Main and go north a couple of blocks to turn onto St. Francis. While we waited for traffic to pass—amazingly, some people were actually trying to go about their everyday routine—I saw someone running toward us out of the corner of my eye. I twisted to see Togo looking out at the traffic, and he met my eyes briefly before he was broadsided by a short, heavy man swinging his sign at Togo's head. Togo bled and staggered and went down on one knee.

"Quinn!" I yelled, and Quinn turned to see what was happening. He bounded over the hood of the truck with a leap that was truly astounding, and he plucked Togo's attacker off the ground and held him there.

The crowd was shocked, and some of them stared, stunned by Quinn's speed and strength. Then they became enraged because this difference was exactly what they feared. I glimpsed more swift movement, Sam yelled, and I saw a tall woman, brown hair flying behind her like a banner, loping across Main at an inhuman rate. She looked normal in her jeans and sneakers, but she was definitely more than human. She went right to the knot of Togo, Quinn, and the protester. She seized the man from Quinn's grip and carried him over to the side of the street. With elaborate care, she placed him on his feet, and then she did an amazing thing. She patted him on the head with one long brown hand.

There was a scattering of laughter from the crowd. The man literally had his mouth hanging open.

She turned to Quinn and Togo, who'd lurched to his feet, and she grinned.

Togo's shoulders relaxed as he realized the crisis had passed—for the moment. But Quinn seemed frozen, and then . . . so did she.

He bowed his head slightly to her. I couldn't hear what he said, but she bobbed her head at him in return, and she said one word. And though I couldn't really hear her, somehow I knew what it was: "tigress."

Whoa. I wished like hell I had time to think about that, but the road cleared in both directions and it was time to turn. I rolled down the window to let the people on foot know what we were planning, and then we moved out, the shifters running easily beside our little motorcade. We drove only a short distance before the left turn. Just two more blocks west to the church.

If Bernie's street had been crowded and frightening, St. Francis was even more crowded, and emotions were jacked up accordingly.

Sam was concentrating so hard on driving while watching the crowd for any sudden moves that I didn't dare talk to him. I crouched in my seat, every muscle twanging with tension.

The tigress and Quinn were loping ahead of the truck in tandem, their paces matched as if they were in harness. It was beautiful to watch. A woman darted in front of them with a bucket of paint in her hand, and before she could aim it at them, the tigress bent to hit the bottom of the bucket. The paint splashed upward all over the woman, who had the neat, casual look of a soccer mom . . . one who'd strayed way out of her league. Covered in red paint, the woman staggered back the way she'd come, and half the crowd laughed while the other half shrieked. But tiger and tigress kept on running at their easy pace.

I looked in the rearview mirror to see how Bernie's car was faring, and watched, horrified, as a group surged forward with pieces of wood and bats in their hands to pound on the roof. The children! Togo, drawn by the noise behind him, turned and then cast a quick, doubtful glance at me.

"Go!" I yelled. "Go!"

Togo didn't hesitate but sprinted back to the crowd and began pulling people away from the car and tossing them to the side of the road as if they were cockleburs he was removing from his pants hem. Sam had stopped, and I glanced over at his agonized face. I realized that he didn't know whether to leap out of the car and go to help, or if that would leave the truck—and me—open to attack. Trish was back at Mindy's car helping Togo.

Then I saw a blur move by the truck and recognized Quinn. I swiveled in my seat and looked through the rear window. Quinn vaulted into the pickup bed, making the truck rock on its shocks.

I thought we were all done for, that this violence would spread and spread, and we'd be attacked and overwhelmed. Instead, the people of the town and the shifters who'd come in to support us began to shout for calm.

For the first time in its existence, most likely, the town of Wright heard a tiger roar. Though the sound came from an apparently human throat, it was unmistakable.

The crowd fell nearly silent. Togo and Trish, both bleeding, covered the windows of Mindy's car with their bodies. I could see Trish heaving for breath, while Togo's shirt was soaked on one side with blood. I peered through the windshield to see if help was coming from the church direction. I saw a thick crowd, and way at the rear I could glimpse the brown of the Wright police uniform. Two uniformed officers were trying to make their way through to come to us, but they'd never be here in time if the crowd decided to rush us. I looked back through the window to see Quinn drawing himself up tall.

"There are children in this car!" Quinn called. "Human children! What example have you set them?"

Some protesters looked ashamed. One woman began crying. But most seemed sullen and resentful, or simply blank, as if they were waking up from a trance.

"This woman has lived here for decades," Quinn said, pointing at Trish, whose hair was soaked with blood. "But you harm her enough to make her bleed while she's protecting children. *Let us pass.*"

He looked around, waiting to see if he'd be challenged, but no one spoke. He leaped down from the truck and jogged back up to resume point position with his new friend. She touched him, her brown hand resting on his arm. He looked directly at her. It lasted a long moment.

I had the feeling that Quinn might not need to have a talk with me anymore.

Then the two weretigers began their run again, and we moved behind them.

Porter Carpenter and another uniform had kept an area in front of the church blocked off for our arrival, and they moved the sawhorses aside so we could park. They looked relieved.

"They didn't come help us," I said, and I found that my lips and mouth had been so tense that I could hardly talk now.

Sam turned the truck off and shuddered, having his own reaction. "They were trying," he said, his voice ragged. "I don't know how hard they were trying, but they were on their way."

"I guess this was a little more than they could handle," I said, making a determined attempt to be less than furious.

"Let's not beat them up," Sam suggested. "What do you say?"

"Right. Contraindicated," I said.

Sam managed to laugh, though it was a sad little snort of amusement.

"Are you okay?" he asked. "Before we get out and the madness starts all over again . . . forgive me for dragging you into this."

"Sam, not necessary!" I said, genuinely surprised. "We're friends. Of course I'm here, and glad to do it. Don't bring it up again, you hear? I'm just glad Mindy's already married!"

My weak joke lightened his mood. He grinned at me and leaned over to give me a kiss on the cheek. "Let's get this over with," he said, and we both opened our doors.

The noise had begun rising again. The car's passengers had emerged, too. Mindy and Doke, carrying their children, hurried up the steps of the church. Bernie, her fists clenched, faced the crowd, her eyes fixing on face after face. Some people had the grace to look ashamed, and some people were cheering for her, but some faces were twisted with loathing for this small, ordinary woman. Sam stood by his mother, his back straight.

I was so proud of him.

Craig moved to flank them, and I seized his hand. "Craig, you need to go on in the church now. We'll be in there in a second," I said, and I felt the anger come through him for a second before he understood that I was right. After giving his mother and brother one more look, he hurried into the church to reassure his bride that he'd arrived intact.

"Sam, you and your mom need to go in," I said. "See, Togo's brought Trish."

All the two-natured who'd flooded into Wright were pressed into service by Quinn and his new friend. Togo carried the stunned and bleeding Trish into the church and laid her on a back pew before he took his place in the shifter barrier that formed around the church. The three Biker Babes and the Suburban Weres were joined by the Wright law enforcement officers, though some were more willing than others to man the barricade. They were joined by a score of others.

I saw a tiny woman I knew. "Luna!" I exclaimed, and gave the twoey a hug. I hadn't seen her since I'd stayed in Dallas; it seemed like years ago, but it wasn't.

"You always in trouble?" she asked, flashing me a grin. "Hey, look down the line."

A few bodies away in the living chain, two Weres grinned and waved. One called out, "Hey, Milkbone," and I realized that they were the ones who had picked us up in Dallas. Amazing.

"It's like playing Whac-A-Mole," Luna yelled, to be heard over the noise of the crowd. "We may have busted up that phony church in Dallas, but I bet some of the same people are still here yelling that we ought to die. In fact, I already saw one of 'em. Sarah's here!"

I gaped at her. "Sarah Newlin?" She was the wife of the founder of the Fellowship of the Sun, and she'd gone underground with her husband after the raid.

Luna nodded. "Ain't that something?"

"I got to get into the church," I said. "I came all this way to go to a wedding, and I better go watch it. I hope I get to talk to you later."

She nodded back and turned to scream in the face of a man twice her size who said he wanted to get into the church to shoot the minister who'd perform such a travesty of a ceremony. That's exactly what he said, though he stumbled over "travesty." (Prompted? I think so.) Luna didn't even use words to respond. She just screeched. She scared the hell out of the man, who stumbled backward.

I ran quickly up the steps to the double doors of the church, amazed at Luna's revelation and cursing my high heels. (Today had turned out to be about so much more than looking good.) The FBI had been looking for the Newlins since the night Luna and I had escaped from the Fellowship building. They'd found all kinds of interesting things—guns, a body— concealed in the huge building, a former church. Steve and Sarah Newlin had continued their ministry of hate while on the run. The pair had a huge following. I would love to catch Sarah Newlin and turn her over to the law. It was no thanks to her that I hadn't been raped or murdered at the Fellowship building.

Nothing could drown out all the noise from the street, but the vestibule of the church was calm and relatively quiet. I could see through the open doors into the sanctuary that the candles were burning and the flowers were in place. Deidra's army brother, Jared, had brought a rifle with him, and he was standing by the church door ready to use it. Sam was with him.

I could see that the Lisles were waiting in the aisle, though Deidra's mother was struggling not to cry, and Deidra's father looked very grim. He had come armed, too. I didn't blame him. Craig and Bernie were right by them, along with Brother Arrowsmith's wife. She'd brought their son with her, cast and all. He looked angry and horrified and humiliated, and most of all he looked ashamed, because Bernie stood in front of him and looked him right in the face, not letting the boy dodge her gaze.

A door in the east wall of the vestibule opened, the door to the bride's room, and Deidra's sisters peeked out in their bridesmaid dresses, both pretty and very young. And very frightened. Their older brother nodded at them, trying to look reassuring.

"Where are Denissa and Mary?" the younger sister asked.

"The girls who were supposed to sing? They didn't make it," Jared said. The door closed. I knew Deidra was waiting in the little room in her wedding dress. "Their parents were too scared to let them come," Jared told Sam and me. "Sookie, you want to sing instead?"

Sam snorted.

"That's one thing I can't help with. You hear me singing, you'd run the other way." I wouldn't have thought anything could make me laugh, but I did. I took a deep breath. "I'll stay right here and watch the door. You two are members of the wedding."

Jared hesitated. "You know how to use this?" he asked, handing me the rifle. It was a .30-.30. I looked it over. "I prefer a shotgun," I said. "But I can make this work."

He gave me a straight look and then vanished through the double doors. Sam patted my shoulder and followed Jared.

I heard the music starting up in the sanctuary. The older of Deidra's sisters came out of the side room, her lavender dress rustling around her feet, and her eyes widened at the sight of me standing there with the rifle.

"I'm just insurance," I said, trying to look reassuring.

"I'm going to ring the bell," she told me, as if she had to get my permission. She pointed at the door in the west side of the vestibule, the bell tower door.

"Good idea." I had no idea whether it was or not, but if tradition demanded the bell be rung at the time of the wedding, then the bell would be rung. "You need me to help?"

"If you wouldn't mind. My little sister needs to stay with Deidra. She's real nervous. You'll have to put down the rifle for a second." She sounded almost apologetic. "My name's Angie, by the way."

I introduced myself and followed her through the little door into the bell tower. A long red velvet rope hung down like a big thick snake. I looked up at the bell hanging overhead, wondered how many pounds it weighed. I hoped the builders had known what they were doing. I laid down the rifle, and Angie and I seized the rope, braced ourselves on our heels, and pulled. "Four times," she said jerkily, "For a four o'clock wedding."

This was actually kind of fun. We almost came off our feet when the bell swung up, but we managed the four rings. And I heard the crowd go quiet.

"I wonder if there's a speaker outside," I said.

"They put in one for Mr. Williston's funeral," Angie said. "He was in the state legislature." She opened the door to an electrical panel and flipped a switch.

I could hear a crackle outside, and then "Jesu, Joy of Man's Desiring" poured over the heads of the crowd. I heard a yell or two, but I could tell that people were turning to listen.

Angie went over to open the door to the bride's waiting room, and

Deidra and her youngest sister came out. Mr. Lisle joined them, and I could tell he was trying to focus on his daughter instead of on the mob in the street. Deidra was a vision in white, and her hands were holding a happy bouquet of sunflowers and daisies.

"You look beautiful," I said. Who could not smile at a bride?

"That's our cue," Angie told her sister, and she opened the door to the sanctuary. The bridal march began, and I could hear it from in the church and from outside. Deidra turned to me, startled.

"All rise," said Brother Arrowsmith's sonorous church voice, and though there were precious few to rise, I could hear a rustle of movement.

Angie went down the aisle first, then her sister. Finally Deidra, her face glowing, took her father's arm and went slowly down to join her fiancé.

I had retrieved the rifle, and I stood in the vestibule halfway between the outer and the inner doors, glancing from one to the other. I saw Deidra's father step forward to whisper something to Brother Arrowsmith, who said, "Please join me on this holy occasion, as all of us, inside these walls and outside, stand together in God's sight to say the Lord's Prayer."

He really came through in a pinch. I stepped closer to the outer doors, put my ear to one of them. After a moment, I could hear voices outside saying the prayer right along with the wedding party. Not all the people outside were joining in, but some were.

I risked going into the bell tower to look out one of the small windows there, and what I saw amazed me.

Some people had fallen to their knees to pray. The few protesters who felt like keeping up with the yelling were being decisively silenced by means both fair and foul by the devout. I dashed to the inside double doors and gestured to the minister to keep it up. Then I went back to look some more.

And I saw her. Sarah Newlin. She was wearing a hat and dark glasses, but I recognized her. She had a sign, of course: IF YOU BARK AND GROWL, IN HELL YOU WILL HOWL. Nice. She was looking around with baffled resentment, as if she couldn't believe we'd played the God card and it had trumped hatred.

Next we had the Apostles' Creed. "I believe in God, the Father Almighty . . . " chorused voices inside the church and out. Brother Arrowsmith's voice rang with sincerity. There was a long moment of silence when the creed was over.

"Today we gather together to join in holy matrimony. . . ." Brother Arrowsmith was off and running with what was probably the most ceremonious, solemn wedding ever held in this church; I was willing to put money on that. The people outside listened as Deidra, her voice shaking, agreed to be the wife of Craig, who sounded both strained and reverent.

It was beautiful.

It was just what we needed to turn the corner.

Gradually, the hostiles began dispersing, until only a few die-hard haters were left. All the two-natured stayed. When Craig and Deidra were pronounced man and wife and the organ music swelled triumphantly, there was actually applause out in the street.

I leaned against the wall by the church doors. I felt like I'd just run a marathon. The little wedding party milled around, hugging and congratulating, and Sam detached himself and hurried down the aisle to join me in the vestibule.

"That was some good thinking," he said.

"Figured it couldn't hurt to remind everyone where they were, and who was watching," I said.

"I'm calling the closest liquor store to get a keg delivered at the house and a lot of snacks from the grocery," Sam said. "We've got to thank everyone that came from so far away."

"Time to go to the reception?" The bride and groom, who looked as happy as two young people can be, were leading the way out of a rear door of the church to go back to the fellowship hall.

"Yeah." Sam was busy on his iPhone for a few minutes, making the arrangements for an impromptu party following the church reception.

I didn't want to distract Sam from this happy family occasion, but there were a few things we had to talk about. "How'd they all know to get here on time?" I asked.

"I don't know," Sam said, startled. "I thought Twitter or the Internet. . . ."

"Yeah, I get that. But some of those people had to travel for hours. And the trouble started just this morning."

Sam was intensely thoughtful. "I hadn't even thought about that," he said.

"Well, you've had other fish to fry."

He gave me a wry grin. "You could say that. Well, do you have a theory?"

"You're not going to like it."

"Of course not. I don't like anything about this. But spill it anyway." We were standing on the covered walkway between the church and the fellowship hall, and I realized the entire property was ringed by the two-natured, and they were all looking out. They hadn't relaxed their vigilance, though perhaps seventy percent of the protesters had left. I was glad of that because I didn't really think this was over. I thought the worst had been staved off, at best.

"I thought about this some when I saw how many people were here. I think that this was all planned. I think the word about the wedding spread, and someone decided this was the chance to see how an organized protest went . . . kind of a testing of the waters. If this went well for the assholes who were out there screaming—if the wedding had been put off, or if the weres had attacked and killed a human—then this would have become a model for other events."

"But the weres showed up, too."

I nodded.

"You mean the twoeys were also alerted early? By the same . . . ?"

"By the same people who alerted the anti-furries."

"To make this a confrontation."

"To make this a confrontation," I agreed.

"My brother's wedding was a *test-drive*?"

I shrugged. "That's what I think."

Sam held open the door for me. "I wish I could say I was sure you're wrong," he said quietly. "What kind of maniac would actually make things worse than they are?"

"The kind of person who is going to make his point no matter how many people have to die in the process," I said. "Luna told me she saw someone in the crowd. And then I saw her, too."

Sam looked at me intently. "Who?"

"Sarah Newlin."

Every supe in America knew that name. He turned that over in his mind for a few seconds. Bernie, resplendent in beige lace, glanced back at us, clearly wanting Sam to rejoin her. The bride was ready to cut the cake, a traditional moment that demanded our attendance. Sam and I drifted over to join the knot of people around the white-draped table. Craig put his hand over Deidra's, and together they sliced the bridal cake, which turned out to be spice cake with white icing, homemade by the bride's mother. This was the most personal wedding I'd attended in some time, and I enjoyed the hominess of it. The little plates for the cake were paper, and so were the napkins, and the forks were plastic, and no one cared. The cake was very good.

Brother Arrowsmith came over to me, and though burdened with a plate and punch, he found a way to free a hand to shake mine. I got a huge gust of his relief, his pride that he had done the right thing, his worry about his son, and his love for his wife who had been by his side all day, both in her prayers and physically.

The minister's chest was burning, and he was having heartburn, which he seemed to have pretty frequently these days, and he thought maybe he'd better not drink the punch, though of course it wasn't alcoholic.

"You need to go to a heart specialist in Dallas or Fort Worth," I said.

Brother Arrowsmith looked as though I'd hit him in the head with an ax handle. His eyes widened, his mouth fell open, and he wondered what I really was, all over again.

Dammit, I knew the signs of possible heart problems. His arm hurt, he had heartburn, and he was way too tired. Let him think I was supernaturally guided if he chose. That might up the chances he'd make an appointment.

"You were really smart to turn on the speaker," Brother Arrowsmith said. "The word of God entered those people's hearts and changed them for the good."

I started to shake my head, but then I had second thoughts.

"You're absolutely right," I said, and I realized I meant it. I felt I was such a bad Christian that I hardly deserved to call myself that anymore, but I understood at that moment that I still believed, no matter how far my actions had strayed from those of the woman my grandmother had raised me to be.

I gave Deidra and Craig a hug apiece, and I automatically told Bernie how beautiful it had been, which was simply weird. I met the Lisles, and it was easy to sense their profound relief that this wedding was done, that Deidra and Craig would not be living here, and that they could maybe regain some semblance of their former life. They liked Craig, it was easy to tell, but the whole trauma of the controversial wedding after the revelation of Craig's mom's heritage had smothered their initial pleasure at his joining their family. Mrs. Lisle was hoping fervently that the other two girls would never, ever give a were or shifter a second look, and Mr. Lisle was thinking he'd greet the next two-natured boy who came to call for one of his daughters with a shotgun.

This was all sad, understandable, and inevitable, I guess.

When it was time to leave the church, the tension ratcheted up again.

Sam stepped outside and explained to the waiting shifters what was about to happen. When Deidra and Craig stepped out of the fellowship hall, they went through the church so they'd be protected by a building for as long as possible. By the time we'd gotten back to the church vestibule, I cracked the doors open to look outside. The two-natured had formed a solid phalanx of bodies between the doors of the church and the parked cars. Trish and Togo had recovered enough to join them, though the dried blood on their clothes looked awful.

Craig and Deidra came out first, and the people still there began clapping. Startled, the couple straightened from their hunched-over postures, and Deidra smiled tentatively. They were able to leave their wedding reception almost normally.

The plan was that we would all go to Bernie's house. Deidra's parents had suggested that maybe Deidra should change into her going-away clothes there, and I didn't want to think too hard about why they'd thought it was such a good idea. They'd also told their two younger girls to get in the car and go home with them, and they hadn't made it an option. I managed to hug Angie, who'd pulled the bell rope with me. I had high hopes for her future. I don't think I ever spoke two words to the younger girl or Deidra's other brother.

I was looking around in the remaining crowd. There were still a few protesters, though they were notably quieter about their opinions. Some signs waved in a hostile way, some glares . . . nothing that didn't seem small after the ordeal of getting to the church. I was looking for a particular face, and I spotted it again. Though she looked older than she should have, and though she was wearing dark glasses and a hat, the woman standing with a camera in her hands—she'd discarded the sign—was Sarah Newlin. I'd seen her husband in a bar in Jackson when he was supporting a follower who'd come prepared to assassinate a vampire. That hadn't worked out for Steve Newlin, and this wasn't working out for Sarah. I was sure she'd taken my picture. If the Newlins tracked me down . . . I glanced around me. Luna caught my eye.

I jerked my head, and she came over. We had a quiet conversation. Luna drifted over to Brenda Sue, one of the Biker Babes, a woman nearly six feet tall who sported a blond crew cut. The two started a lively conversation, all the time moving closer and closer to Sarah, who began to show alarm when they were five feet away. Brenda Sue's hand reached out, twitched the camera from Sarah's grasp, juggled it for a moment, then tossed it to Luna.

Luna, grinning, passed it from her right hand to her left hand behind her back. The blonde made several playful passes with it. All the while, Luna's hands were busy. Finally, the blonde was able to retrieve the camera, and she tossed it back to Sarah.

Minus the memory chip.

By that time, those of us who had ridden to the wedding were back in the vehicles. Luna and Togo and Trish got into the truck's flatbed, and the bikers each gained a passenger. Somehow we all got back to Bernie's house without any bad incidents. There were still a lot more people in the streets of Wright than normal, but the protest had lost its heart, its violence.

We pulled up in front of the house to find that the beer was being unloaded and carried into the backyard, and that even more people were bringing food. The manager of the grocery store was personally unloading more sandwich platters and tubs of slaw and baked beans, plus paper plates and forks. All the people who had been too frightened to come to the wedding were trying to find some way to make themselves feel better about that, was the way I took it. And I'm usually pretty accurate about human nature.

All of a sudden, we were in the party business.

The two-natured who'd flooded into Wright now surged through the house and into the backyard to have a drink and a sandwich or two before they had to take the road home. With a pleasing sense of normality, I realized I had work to do. Sam and I changed from our wedding finery into shorts and T-shirts, and with the ease of people who work together all the time, we set up folding tables and chairs, found cups for the beer, sent the rapidly healing Trish to the store with Togo, and arranged the napkins and forks and plates by the food. I spotted a big garbage can under the carport, found the big garbage bags to line it, and rolled it to the backyard. Sam got the gas grill going. Though Mindy and Doke offered to help, both Sam and I were glad when they went home with the kids. After such a day, they didn't need to hang around. Those kids needed to go back to Mooney.

Few humans remained to party with the twoeys. Most of the regular people had seemed to get a whiff of the otherness of the guests, and they'd drifted away pretty quickly.

Though we were short on folding chairs, everyone made do. They sat on the grass or stood and circulated. When Togo and Trish returned with soft drinks and hamburger patties and buns, the grill was ready to go and Sam took charge. I began putting out the bags of chips. Everything was going very well for an impromptu celebration. I went to pump beers.

"Sookie," said a deep voice, and I looked up from the keg to see Quinn. He had a plate with a sandwich and some chips and some pickles on it, and I handed him a cup of beer.

"There you go," I said, smiling brightly.

"This is Tijgerin," Quinn said. He pronounced it very carefully. It sounded like "Tie" plus a choking noise, and then "ine" as in "tangerine." I practiced it in my head a couple of times (and I looked up the spelling later). "That's 'Tigress' in Dutch. She's of Sumatran and Dutch descent. She calls herself Tij." Pronounced "Tie."

Her eyes were as dark a purple as Quinn's, though perhaps a browner tone, and her face was a lovely high-cheekboned circle. Her hair was a shiny milk-chocolate brown, darker than the deep tan tone of her skin. She smiled at me, all gleaming white teeth and health. I figured she was younger than me, maybe twenty-three.

"Hallo," she said. "I am pleased to meet with you."

"Pleased to meet you, too," I said. "Have you been in America long?"

"No, no," she said, shaking her head. "I am here just now. I am European employee of Special Events, the same company Quinn works for. They send me here to get the American experience."

"You've certainly gotten to see the bad part of the American experience today. Sorry about that."

"No, no," she said again. "The demonstrations in the Netherlands were just as bad." Polite. "I am glad to be here. Glad to meet Quinn. There are not so many tigers left, you know?"

"That's what I've heard," I said. I looked from her to Quinn. "I know you'll learn a lot while you're here, Tij. I hope the rest of your stay in America is better than today."

"Oh, sure, it will be!" she said blithely. "Here we are at a party, and I am meeting many interesting people. And the praying at the church, that was very interesting, too."

I smiled in agreement—"interesting" was one word for it. "So, Quinn," I asked, since we were being very polite in front of Tij, "How's your mom?"

"She's doing all right," he said. "And my sister's gone back to school. I don't know how long it'll last, but she seems a little more serious about it this time."

"That's good to hear," I said.

"How's Eric?" Quinn was really making an effort. Tij looked mildly inquiring.

"Eric is my boyfriend," I explained to her. "He's a vampire." I automatically looked out at the backyard to gauge how much sunlight was left. Eric wouldn't be up for another hour. "He's fine, Quinn."

Tij seemed intrigued, but Quinn took her arm and steered her away. "We'll talk later," he said.

"Sure." They fell into conversation with Togo. The three looked like trees among regular people.

Deidra and Craig had already made a round of handshaking, thanking the people who'd come to save their lives and their wedding. Then the newlyweds changed and slipped away on their honeymoon, which was the most sensible thing in the world for them to do. Quinn and Tijgerin walked them out to Craig's car, and when they came back inside, Quinn tracked me down in the kitchen, where I was mining Bernie's pantry for some more garbage bags.

Quinn looked very serious. We were alone in the kitchen, which was pretty amazing.

"Hey," he said, and leaned against the counter. I pulled a bag from the cardboard box and shook it out. Then I pulled the crammed bag from the kitchen garbage can and cinched it shut.

"It's been a long day, huh? What did you want to talk about?" Might as well get right to it. I stuck the full bag by the back door and inserted the new one.

"The last time I saw you, Bill and I got stupid and you got hurt," Quinn said. "Eric ordered me out of Area Five, and I had to go. I don't know if you realized that E(E)E and Special Events are mostly vampire owned?"

"No." I wasn't surprised, though. The two catering and event companies employed both humans and shifters, but I was sure they'd required lots of capital to start up, and they'd begun their operations in a very luxe way. That's kind of a vampire signature.

"So I can't afford to offend a lot of deaders," Quinn said, looking away as if he were sure this admission would make him look weak. "They're silent partners in the rest home my mother stays in, too." Quinn had already paid off one family debt he owed the vampires.

"They've got you every which way," I said. We looked at each other directly.

"I want you to know," he said. "I want you to know that if you don't want to be with Eric, if he's using any kind of coercion on you, if he's got any leverage on you the way they do on me . . . I'll do anything in my power to get you free."

He'd do it, too. I suddenly saw a whole different life opening up before me, and my imagination painted it rosy, for a moment. I tried to picture living with Quinn, who was warm and generous and a magnificent lover. He really would do everything he could to pry me away from Eric if he thought I had the slightest misgivings about my relationship with the vampire, no matter what the consequences were for him.

I'm not a saint. I thought of how wonderful it would be to be with a man who could go shopping with me in the daytime, a man I could have a baby with, a man who knew how to treat a woman well. But even if I decided I wanted to leave Eric, Eric would always be sure, through his vampire contacts, that Quinn paid and paid and paid.

I looked past his shoulder out the bay window to see Tijgerin, who was happily devouring her third hamburger. I didn't know much about her, but I did know there were very few weretigers left in the world. If Quinn and Tijgerin mated, they could have a tiger baby. And from the way she'd looked at Quinn, I thought I could assume she was unencumbered by a boyfriend at present. She and Quinn had been smacked in the face with their mutual attraction, and I admired him all the more for sticking to his declared program in making this offer.

I took a deep breath before I spoke, aware that this was a huge honor he'd paid me.

"Quinn, you're a great man, and you're *so* attractive, and I am so fond of you," I said. I looked him right in the eyes because I wanted him to see how much I meant every word. "But . . . and some days I think, unfortunately for me . . . I love Eric. He comes with a thousand years of baggage . . . but he's it for me now." I took another deep breath. "With regret, I'm going to turn you down, but I am your true friend, and I always will be."

He pulled me close. We hugged each other hard, and I stepped back. "You go have a good time," I said, blinking furiously, and then he was gone.

After a few moments of recovery—and feeling definitely on the noble side—I drifted into the backyard to see if Sam needed anything. The gas grill had been turned off, so he'd cooked everything there was to cook. The outside lights were on, but there was a sharp contrast of light and shadow in Bernie's backyard. Someone had brought out a CD player and turned the volume up. I wondered why Jim Collins hadn't appeared to protest.

I saw a small figure emerge from the shadows at the corner of the house. It was a woman wearing a vest with a bra under it, and a tiny skirt, and gladiator sandals. The evening was cooling off rapidly, and I figured the newcomer would be covered in goose pimples soon. Her short dark brown hair was slicked back smoothly.

And then I recognized her.

Jannalynn was dressed to kill. I'd imagined her being here in a moment of craziness, and here she was.

Awkward.

Sam saw her at the same moment I did, and I could read him like a book in that moment. He was happy to see her, but he was also flabbergasted—and that's the best way I can put it.

"Hello, young woman," said Bernie, stepping in the Were's path. "I don't believe I've met you yet. I'm Bernie Merlotte."

Jannalynn took in the cheerful gathering, saw all the twoeys having a good time, and I guess she had her own black moment when she wondered why Sam hadn't invited her when there were so many other two-natured guests. I was glad I wasn't in her line of sight. I stepped back into the kitchen ... because frankly, I was scared to death of Jannalynn. I'd seen her in action, and it was no fluke that the packleader of Shreveport had named her his enforcer.

"Hey, honey," she called, spotting Sam over his mother's shoulder.

CHAPTER FOUR

Bernie turned to check that this young woman was addressing her son. It was hard to read Sam's face, especially from the kitchen. I was looking out the window, thinking it would be better not to make an appearance until this situation had been smoothed out a little. Though this was a minor problem compared to the terrors we'd faced today, I still wasn't rushing into some kind of touchy greeting with Sam's girlfriend.

I didn't know if I was being a coward or simply being prudent. Either way, I was staying put until I got a cue.

"Jannalynn!" he said, and he embraced her quickly. It wasn't exactly a boyfriend hug, more a "Hi, buddy, good to see you!" thing. "I didn't expect you could come." When he took a step back, I could see that his brows were sort of knit with doubt.

"I know, I know, you brought Sookie to meet your family. And I know why. But I couldn't stay away when I heard the news on the Fur and Feathers website."

None of this was scanning naturally. Jannalynn was smiling too brightly and doing a weird imitation of a brittle socialite. She looked exactly like someone who knew she was making a huge mistake.

Maybe I should just stay in the kitchen? For a long time? Maybe the rest of the night? I was pretty tired, but I also didn't want to feel I was being held hostage by my own social sense.

I heard the toilet flush, and Luna came into the kitchen, making a beeline for the back door. When she saw me, she stopped by my side and took in the scene.

"Okay, who's the fashion-challenged skinny chick?"

"Sam's real girlfriend." Luna raised her eyebrows at me, and I hurried to explain. "He'd already asked me to come to the wedding with him, and he hasn't been dating Jannalynn that long. Plus, she has some social issues that he kind of wanted to prepare his family for, and not while they were trying to deal with a pressure situation like a wedding."

"Hmmm. So he brings home the more presentable date, leaving the skinny . . . and *very* weirdly dressed . . . one at home. And then she shows up. And you think she's his real girlfriend? You *are* having a hell of a day, Sookie."

"Unfortunately, it's not only me who's having it. It's Sam and his mom, too." I scanned the crowd. "Well, at least I only see one or two more humans." Sam's friend Sister was still partying, and I glimpsed Jared Lisle talking to one of the Biker Babes. They were flirting in a major way.

"So, you know, I just thought I'd tell you," Luna said offhand, "I went through the hedge into the yard next door to make out with that cute guy in the camo pants, the Chinese guy? He's a Were cop from Fort Worth, on the tactical response team." She paused for my reaction.

"A hunk," I said. "Way to go, Luna." Lots of pairing off going on at this after-the-reception reception.

She looked pleased. "Anyway, while we were locking lips right on the other side of the hedge there, I smelled something funky in the house next to this."

I closed my eyes for a long moment. Then I told Luna the history of the past two days with Jim. "Can you get more specific than 'funky'?" I asked.

"Funky, as in dead meat. So someone's killed that guy, maybe." Luna's chirpy voice didn't sound especially dismayed. "He doesn't sound like a great loss, but you know the twoeys are going to get the blame."

"I guess I better go check it out," I said, and I can't tell you how reluctant I was. If Jannalynn hadn't shown up, I would've asked Sam to go with me. But that was out of the question at the moment.

I didn't want to try entering the Collins house through the front door. Who knew who might still be watching Bernie's house, maybe taking pictures? I didn't know if the TV stations had gone home or not. Probably yes, but there might be a few die-hards out there with their own cameras. But if I went out the back door, I'd run into Jannalynn—and although that was going to happen sooner or later, the longer I could postpone it, the better. I was trying not to watch her. She was working the party—shaking hands, laughing, with a beer she took long swallows from every few seconds.

"Fuck," I said.

"She's looking good," Luna admitted. "I bet Sam comes inside to get her a jacket within the next three minutes."

I admitted to myself that I didn't like Jannalynn because I thought Sam deserved someone much better, someone with some impulse control. Here I was, peering out the window like a criminal trying to make my escape, just so this girl wouldn't get her panties in a twist.

"She's hungry," Luna said. "She'll go for the food in a minute."

Sure enough, Jannalynn completely turned her back to the house so she could bend over the table, putting condiments on her hamburger bun. I slid out of the house and across the lawn going west at a smooth, fast clip . . . and Luna was right on my heels as I went through the gap in the overgrown hedge.

"You didn't have to come," I muttered. With a yard full of shifters, I had to take care to keep my voice down.

"I was getting bored anyway," she said. "I mean, I get to make out with gorgeous Chinese guys all the time."

I smiled in the darkness. There weren't any lights on in the Collins backyard or in the Collins house, which was odd because it was getting dark now.

There was a living brain in the house. I told Luna that, and she rolled her eyes at me. "Big whoop," she said. "So what?"

"That's my specialty," I said.

"But *I* can smell something dead," she told me. "Hasn't been dead long, but it's dead. That's *my* specialty. I know a dog or a Were would be better at this, but any twoey nose is better than a oney nose."

I shrugged. I'd have to concede that one. To knock or not to knock? As I stood flattened against the wall by the back door, debating furiously with myself, I heard a little whimper from inside. Luna stiffened beside me. I crouched and pulled open the screen door. It made the wheezy noise so common to screen doors, and I sighed.

"Who's here?" I said, keeping my voice hushed.

A sob answered me. I felt Luna come in, and she crouched beside me. Neither of us wanted to present a target against the faint light from the Merlotte backyard.

"I'm turning on the light," I told Luna in a tiny whisper. I patted the wall where the switch should be, and sure enough it was there. There were two. One would control the outside lights, and one the kitchen light. Was there a rule? If so, I didn't know it. I flicked the one on the left.

I couldn't have been more shocked by what I saw.

Jim Collins was absolutely, messily dead. He lay sprawled across the low kitchen counter, gun resting loosely in his right hand. Closer to the doorway into the interior of the house, Sarah Newlin sat on the floor. She was hurt somehow, because there was blood on her arm and more on her stomach. Her legs were extended in front of her. She was crying almost silently. There was a gun lying by her side, though I couldn't see what make.

"Call the police from his phone," I said instantly.

"No," Sarah said. "Don't!"

Luna punched in numbers so fast that I thought the phone was going to break.

With convincing hysteria, Luna said, "Oh my God! Bring an ambulance to Jim Collins's house! Some woman has shot him; he's dead and she's bleeding out!" She hung up and snickered.

Sarah Newlin made a halfhearted attempt to climb to her feet. I went over to her and put my foot on her gun. I didn't think she had enough sand in her to grab it, but better to be sure.

"You're not going to get away," I said dispassionately. "They'll be here in two shakes of a lamb's tail. You're hurt too bad to escape. If you don't go to the hospital, you'll die."

"I might as well," she said drearily. "I've killed a man now."

"You're counting this as the first?" I was shocked. "You've been responsible for so many deaths, but *this* is the one that matters?" Of course, this one counted to Sarah because Collins had been human and on her side, and the others who'd died had been vampires and weres and humans who didn't believe what the Fellowship of the Sun advocated.

"Why'd you shoot your disciple here?" I asked, since Sarah seemed to be in confession mode.

"Steve and I knew Collins from his website," she said weakly. "He had all the right ideas, and he was full of the fire of God. But the plans we had for today failed. God must have changed his mind, turned his face from us. Collins never came to the church. I came here to ask him why, but he was angry, angry with me, with himself. I think he may have been drinking. He challenged me to go with him, to shoot you-all next door. He said we could kill most of you, just like he killed the dogs."

"You weren't up for that?" Luna asked bitterly. "You sure missed an opportunity to get a bunch of us at once."

"Couldn't risk myself," Sarah whispered. "I'm too important to the cause. He even thrust a gun in my hand. But God didn't want me to sacrifice myself. When I told Collins that, he went nuts."

"He was already nuts," I said, but she wasn't listening.

"Then he said I was a hypocrite, and he shot me."

"Looks like you shot him back."

"Yes," Sarah whispered. "Yes, I shot him back."

A police car pulled up in front of the Collins house, the flickering light visible from the kitchen. Someone called from the front door, "Police! We're coming in!"

"Hurry with the ambulance," I called back. "There are two of us who came and discovered the situation. We're unarmed."

"Stand with your hands against the wall!" the officer's voice called back, and it sure as hell sounded like Porter Carpenter.

"Porter," I said. "It's me, Sookie Stackhouse, Sam's friend. And my buddy Luna Garza is with me."

"Hands!" Porter said. "Anyway."

"Okay." I appreciated his caution. Luna walked over to me, and we turned our backs on the doorway and put our hands on the wall. "We're ready," I yelled.

You'd think I'd be distraught and upset. You'd think I'd be overwhelmed, having seen this horrible scene.

But you know what? I was tickled pink. I'd never been a squeamish person, and I'd seen other and worse scenes of carnage, featuring people I cared about to some extent or other.

As it was, it was hard for me to suppress a smile when I saw Sarah Newlin hauled off to the hospital under arrest. And since the dead man was Jim

Collins, I didn't feel a moment's grief for him, either. He would have loved it if the tables had been turned, if he'd walked in on someone who'd just killed Bernie and Sam. He'd have patted them on the back. And I'm being honest when I say that after the hate I'd seen that day, I couldn't be sorry that if someone had to die, that person was Jim Collins, and if someone had to be a murderer, I was fine with that murderer being Sarah Newlin.

"Sookie," said Luna into my ear, "it doesn't hardly *get* any better than this."

"I think you're right," I said.

Porter Carpenter himself took our statements. I could tell that Luna—and the fact that she'd smelled the dead body—made him uneasy. But he wrote everything down, made note of our phone numbers, and then sent us on our way. Finally, we got to go back to the Merlotte house, where everyone was waiting anxiously to find out what had happened. I'd heard Sam's voice raised outside several times while I'd been answering questions—or simply waiting to be asked questions—and each time I'd smiled involuntarily. Sam was on the offensive.

Luna and I were glad to enter Bernie's kitchen, still crowded with weres, though the bulk of the party had drifted away—including Tijgerin and Quinn.

Sam grabbed me by the shoulders, looked intently into my face, and said, "You okay?" He was vibrating like a tuning fork with anxiety.

"Yeah, I'm okay," I said. I smiled at him. "Thanks. I could hear you yell."

"I wanted you to hear me."

"We had quite an evening over there," Luna said. "Man, getting questioned by the cops is thirsty work!" Her cute Chinese cop took the hint and got Luna a beer from the refrigerator.

"We still have some food, if you're hungry," Bernie said. I could tell she was exhausted, but she was upright.

"Not me," I told her. Luna shook her head, too. "First, let me be sure you-all know Luna Garza from Dallas. Luna did me a good turn at the Fellowship of the Sun church some time ago, and seeing her here tonight turned out to be lucky for me again. . . ."

When we'd related the whole story, Brenda Sue began laughing. And she was joined by some of the other twoeys. "That's just too good," she said. "It's perfect. I know this is probably wrong of me, but I can't help feeling okay about this." There was a lot of silent agreement in the room.

Gradually, the remaining guests of the unofficial party began to leave. I couldn't avoid talking to Jannalynn anymore. She'd been sitting behind the table within reach of Sam since I'd returned, and she hadn't said a word. I knew this situation was hard for her, and I felt sorry it was, but there was nothing I could do about it. She'd known when she'd come to Wright that it was the wrong thing to do.

What could I see in her brain? I saw grief, resentment, and envy. Jannalynn was wondering why Sam couldn't see that she was just like me. She was brave and pretty and loyal, too.

"I have a boyfriend," I said. "You know I go with Eric Northman."

"Doesn't make any difference," she said stoically, not meeting my eyes.

"Sure it does. I love Eric. You love Sam." Already I could tell that saying anything at all had been the mistake I'd thought it would be, that we were compounding the unhappiness. But I couldn't simply sit there in silence staring at her.

Jannalynn could do that, though, and she did. She stared a hole through me and didn't say a word. I didn't know where she proposed to sleep that night, but it wasn't going to be in the sewing room with me, and I was going to bed.

Luna was ready to depart (by a huge coincidence, so was the cute cop), and I gave her a hug and told her I hoped to see her in Bon Temps someday.

"Girlfriend, just say the word," she murmured, and returned the hug.

I didn't see Sam anywhere, but I told Bernie good night and took my turn in the bathroom.

I don't know what anyone else did after that, but I took the quickest shower on record and slipped into my nightgown and unfolded the couch. I had time to pull the sheet up over me about halfway before I was out like a light. My phone buzzed a couple of times in the night, but all I did was moan and turn over.

The next morning, it was raining like hell when I woke. The clock told me it was after eight o'clock, and I knew I had to get up. I could smell coffee and a trace of a sweet scent that made me suspect someone had gone to a bakery.

In fact, Bernie had gone to the store and gotten some Pillsbury cinnamon rolls. Sam and Bernie were sitting at the table. Sam got up to get me a cup of coffee, and I hunched over it gratefully.

Bernie shoved the paper over to me. It was the Waco paper. There was a short article about the upset at the wedding.

"Was it on the TV?" I asked.

"Yeah, apparently," Sam said. "But Jim's murder is upstaging the wedding."

I nodded. All my glee had faded, leaving me feeling sort of dirty.

"Bernie, you did great yesterday," I said. Bernie looked ten years older than she had the day before, but there was vigor in her step and purpose in her voice.

"I'm glad it's over. I hope I never have to go through anything like that again. I hope Craig and Deidra are happy." Three true things.

I nodded emphatically. I agreed all the way around. "You going to church today?" I asked.

"Oh, yes," she said. "I wouldn't miss it for the world."

Sam said, "Sook, you think you can be ready to leave in an hour or so?"

"Sure. All I have to do is grab up my stuff and put on some makeup." I'd pulled on my shorts and a shirt and packed my nightgown already.

"No hurry," Sam assured me, but I could tell from the way he was sitting that he wanted to get on the road again. I wondered where Jannalynn was. I sort of felt around the house for her mentally, got no other brain signal. Hmmm.

We were actually out the door in forty-five minutes, after I said all the correct things to Bernie. I didn't want her to think I hadn't been brought up right. She smiled at me, and she seemed sincere when she told me she'd enjoyed having me in the house.

Sam and I were silent for a long time after we left Wright. I checked my cell phone for messages, and sure enough, I had two from Eric. He didn't like to text, though he would if he had to. He'd left voice messages. First message—"I've seen you on the evening news. Call me." BEEP. Second message—"Every time you leave town you get into trouble. Do you need me to come?" BEEP.

"Eric all bent out of shape?" Sam asked.

"Yeah. About like Jannalynn, I expect." I had to say something. Better to get it over with.

"Not exactly. You and Eric have been together longer, and you seem to know each other a little better."

"As well as a human and a thousand-year-old vamp can, I guess. You don't think you and Jannalynn know each other?"

"She's a lot younger than me," he said. "And she has some impulse control issues. But she's really brave, really loyal."

Okay, that was just weird. It was like listening to an echo of Jannalynn's thoughts the night before.

"Yes," I said. "She is."

Sam shrugged. "When she left last night, we agreed we'd talk when I got back to Bon Temps and recovered from the wedding. We have a date for next weekend."

I had a limited menu of responses to choose from. "Good," I said, and left it at that.

We continued our near-silence most of the way across Texas. I thought of the hateful crowd the day before, their distorted faces. I thought about the flash of sheer pleasure I'd felt when I'd realized who'd killed Jim Collins. I thought of how much fun the party had been before Jannalynn had shown up and Luna had told me about the smell in the house next door.

"I was surprised that the police didn't come over to ask any questions last night," I said.

"Sister called this morning and told me that they were going to, but—well, it seemed so obvious what had happened—"

"That's great. You're free and clear."

This was good. Now we were talking like we had before. A knot in my stomach eased up.

"She said that even before they knew Jim was dead, the Arrowsmiths prodded their son to come forward and tell Porter that he'd seen the e-mails between Sarah Newlin and Jim about marshaling both sides to clash at the wedding. She'd urged Jim to make trouble, to enlist his like-minded neighbors and friends to take action, and encourage them to disrupt the wedding in any way they could. In turn, Jim had insisted she come to town herself to witness the work he was doing. The theory is that the shooting started when the two of them were arguing because the plan didn't work out."

That was pretty much the truth and should sure clinch the case against Sarah. "Why do you think we didn't hear the shots?" I asked Sam.

"According to Sister, all the windows were shut. Probably because the noise of a yard full of folks he hated enjoying themselves was bothering Jim," Sam said. "And with our CD player turned up loud . . . Sarah Newlin told them that she'd been at Jim's house almost an hour before he got worked up enough to suggest they go over and shoot us all. But then her lawyer arrived, and she clammed up."

"You think there's any way she'll get off?" I asked incredulously.

"She won't go to prison for murder. Maybe manslaughter. Of course, she'll claim self-defense." He shook his head and accelerated to pass a beat-up minivan that was poking along in front of us.

"Just think on it, Sook—if Luna hadn't gone on the Collins side of the hedge to make out in private, maybe Sarah Newlin would have called someone to come get her, or managed somehow to crawl out of the house. She might even have made it into her car. Then I think Mom and I would have had a visit from the police for sure."

But that hadn't happened, and now Sarah Newlin would be in jail for a while anyway. That was something, a big something. "I'm not drawing any big life lesson from yesterday," I said.

"Were you sure you were going to?"

"Well, yes."

"We survived," Sam said. "And my brother got married to the woman he loves. And that's all that's important."

"Sam, do you really think that?" I didn't want to pick at him, but I was genuinely curious.

My boss smiled at me. "Nah. But what would you say the moral of the day was? There was a lot of hate, there was some love. The love won out for Craig, the hate did Jim Collins in. End of story."

Sam was right, as far as his "moral" went.

But I didn't think it was truly the end of the story.

Life in Bon Temps

BY VICTORIA KOSKI

Dead Until Dark

Timeline

SATURDAY, JUNE 12, 2004. Sookie Stackhouse, telepath, is working the evening shift at Merlotte's bar when a vampire comes in to order a drink. Although vampires have been "out of the coffin" for two years, Bill Compton is the first one to come to her little town of Bon Temps, and she is delighted by the new experience. Local lowlifes Mack and Denise Rattray soon move to Bill's table, where Denise flirts with the vampire. Worried by their avid interest in Bill, Sookie "listens" and finds, to her horror, that the Rattrays have been in jail for draining vampires, a practice that involves forcibly restraining a vampire (a feat unto itself), draining its blood to sell on the black market, and leaving the vampire to die in the rising sun. When Bill leaves with the Rattrays, Sookie dithers but finally follows them to the parking lot, only to find Bill wrapped in silver chains with Denise crouched over him holding a Vacutainer and with several vials of blood already beside her. Grabbing a heavy chain from her brother Jason's truck, Sookie manages to drive off the Drainers. She unwraps Bill, pulling him out of the way when the Rattrays attempt to run them down on the way out of the parking lot. Sookie is stunned to realize that she cannot "hear" Bill. The vampire, who is being less than gracious after being rescued by a human woman, asks if she wants the blood already taken by the Drainers, suggesting that she sell it when she assures him she does not need its medicinal properties. She is insulted but begins to laugh upon finding out that his name is the very mundane Bill, and she cheerfully leaves him. She shares the encounter with her grandmother, Adele, when she gets home from work.

SUNDAY, JUNE 13. Jason arrives at the Stackhouse home, upset after hearing that Sookie beat up the Rattrays the previous night. Sookie explains what really happened. Jason then tells Sookie and Adele that Maudette Pickens, a former classmate of Sookie's, was found dead in her apartment that morning and that she had several vampire bites on her thighs, although that wasn't the cause of her death. On the subject of vampires, Adele wonders how old Bill is and if he remembers the Civil War, hoping that he will speak to the Descendants of the Glorious Dead. Sookie promises to ask him.

When Sookie arrives at Merlotte's for her shift that afternoon, Sam pulls her into the storeroom and berates her for taking on the Rattrays in the parking lot. She is close to tears but finally realizes that Sam was frightened for her. After touching him, she also perceives that her boss has feelings for her that she did not expect.

MONDAY, JUNE 14. Sookie is relieved that she and Sam are able to return to their comfortable relationship.

TUESDAY, JUNE 15. Bill returns to Merlotte's. Sookie is once again aware that she cannot read his thoughts and feels more relaxed in his silence. While taking his order, she arranges to meet him in the parking lot after closing so she can ask the favor for her grandmother. She looks around for him after work, but when he doesn't appear, she heads to her car to drive home. The Rattrays attack her, beating and kicking her. Although she tries to fight back, a kick to her spine does great damage. As she's lying on the ground, she hears a dog's growl from one direction, a snarl from another, and the screams of the Rattrays. When silence falls, the dog licks her ear, but she is unable to respond. A bloody Bill appears in front of her, picking her up to take her back into the woods. Although she is certain that she is dying, after checking her over Bill assures her that she will live. He offers his blood to speed the healing process, and as she drinks from his wrist, she begins to feel better and finally slips into sleep. She wakes in the woods sometime later to find Bill lying beside her, licking the blood from her head wounds. Feeling much better, she admits to Bill that she is a telepath and reveals that it causes her to avoid dating and relationships. She makes her request, and he agrees to meet her grandmother and to speak to the Descendants of the Glorious Dead. He also asks if he can visit Sookie at her home.

WEDNESDAY, JUNE 16. Adele gets a phone call about a tornado touching down in the vicinity of the Rattrays' trailer, killing them both. While Gran finds the local gossip interesting, she is more excited about the idea of Bill coming to the house, and she vows to make sure it's spotless. Sookie stops by the Rattrays' place on her way to work and is stunned by the amount of damage Bill did to the area.

Rene Lenier—Jason's co-worker, and ex-husband of Sookie's fellow waitress Arlene—is in the bar and comes to Sookie's defense when someone makes an inappropriate pass at her. Rene tells Sookie that she reminds him of his sister, Cindy.

THURSDAY, JUNE 17. Adele and Sookie spend the day cleaning in preparation for Bill's visit. After inviting him in, they discover that the vampire is actually a local—just not a recent one. A Confederate soldier, he returned safely from the Civil War only to fall prey to a vampire. As was customary for vampires at the time, he then left the area so that he would not be recognized. Now that the vampires have revealed themselves, he's finally come back to reclaim his ancestral home, which lies across the cemetery from Sookie's house. Adele happily questions him about the past and about her late husband's family, and they set a date for him to speak with the Descendants. Sookie and Bill go for a walk, and he meets her cat, Tina. Sookie is able to completely relax in Bill's presence, and he admits that he is enjoying her company as well. She carefully asks questions about vampires, and they discover that she cannot be glamoured. She also gets Bill to levitate for her. They speak a bit about Sookie's telepathy and how hard it has been on her, about Bill's family before his turning, and about his difficulties in getting workers to come to his house for renovations. Sookie offers to help. She gives in to her impulses and kisses him good night when he walks her back to her door.

FRIDAY, JUNE 18. Sookie finds various contractors willing to be called at night by a vampire. Sam calls to tell her that Dawn, one of the Merlotte's waitresses, did not show up for work, and Sookie arranges to take part of Dawn's shift that evening. While at work, she inadvertently reads Arlene's mind, and Arlene snaps at Sookie, bringing her almost to tears. Sam comforts her, reminding her that it's not her fault that she can read minds, and she reveals the torment of trying to function with the thoughts of others in her head. After she confirms that she cannot read Bill's mind, Sam invites her to read his sometime, something she has always tried to avoid doing.

She takes the list of contractors over to Bill's after work but finds that he has company. She meets vampires Malcolm, Liam, and Diane, along with their human companions, Jerry and Janella. Bill fears for Sookie and claims her as his to protect her from the other vampires. Diane disbelieves Bill's claim, telling him he obviously needs real blood and offering him the two fangbangers. Janella is busy performing sexual acts with Liam, so Jerry willingly steps up. Bill is tempted, but before he can indulge, Sookie reads the human's mind and discovers that he has Sino-AIDS, a virus that weakens and can even kill vampires, and that he wants to infect as many vampires as possible in revenge for his lover leaving him for a vampire. Jerry attacks Sookie, choking her, and Bill breaks Jerry's wrist to free her. Malcolm slings the unconscious human over his shoulder, and the group leaves. Sookie is certain that Jerry will be made to suffer before his death. She is appalled at the behavior of the trio. Bill reassures her that not all vampires are the same.

SATURDAY, JUNE 19. Sookie is dragged out of bed early by a phone call from Sam. He informs her that Dawn hasn't shown up for work again and asks if Sookie will stop by Dawn's house and check on her because she is not answering her phone. After Sookie dresses for work, she reluctantly heads to Dawn's duplex. There Sookie looks in the bedroom window and sees Dawn's murdered body. Rene is across the street at his home and calls the police and Sam. JB du Rone, a friend of Sookie's who lives next door, sees her standing outside the duplex and comes out to help. Police officers Kenya Jones and Kevin Pryor soon arrive, with Sam not far behind. Sookie is surprised that Sam has keys to the duplex until JB informs her that her boss owns the building. She also realizes that Sam is able to shut her out of his mind and picks up that he is not quite human. He apologizes for involving Sookie in this situation. Detective Andy Bellefleur comes to the scene and, after questioning Sookie and Sam, allows them to return to Merlotte's.

Bill is waiting for Sookie in her yard when she gets off work. She informs him of Dawn's death, and he casually lets her know that Dawn stopped by his house the previous night after the vampires and Sookie left. He also tells her that he doesn't think he would have bothered to protect Dawn from Malcolm, Diane, and Liam had she arrived while they were still there. Sookie asks him why he protected her, and he responds that she is different—although she is not like vampires, she is also not like regular humans, a statement that sends Sookie into a violent rage. She strikes out at him, but he effortlessly controls her until her rage subsides. He continues their discussion as if nothing has happened. He tells her that while he physically could have killed the murdered women, he would not and did not. Sookie knows that Bill will be a suspect in the deaths, so she decides to have him take her to the vampire bar in Shreveport to investigate other possibilities.

MONDAY, JUNE 21. Merlotte's is full of talk of the killings, and half the patrons suspect Bill was involved. Jason also falls under suspicion, as he had relationships with both women.

Sookie dresses carefully for the visit to the vampire bar Fangtasia. She finally chooses a bright dress that flatters her figure and her tan, but when Bill sees her, he worries that her attire will draw unwanted attention. Once at Fangtasia, Sookie is able to briefly question the bartender about Dawn, Maudette, and even Jason, asking if they've been in the bar. She and Bill find a booth, and she watches with distaste as human fangbangers offer themselves to Bill. He points out that she has caught the eye of the powerful vampire owner of the bar, Eric Northman, and takes her over so she can speak to him. When she shows Eric and his vampire associate Pam the pictures of Dawn and Maudette, Eric acknowledges that he has been with Dawn, and Pam admits to seeing them both at the bar. Sookie thanks them and turns to leave, but Bill remains in front of Eric and Pam, holding her beside him. When Eric asks about Sookie, Bill once again states that Sookie is his.

They return to their booth, and Sookie idly scans the bar, "hearing" that the place is about to be raided by the police. She and Bill quickly exit, and Bill gives Eric a sign to leave while Sookie looks at the bartender who answered her questions and gestures for him to get out as well. Once in the parking lot, Eric questions their obvious certainty of the impending raid, and Sookie admits that she read someone's mind. After they flee the lot, a sexually excited Bill pulls the car over, and they have a romantic moment, which is interrupted by the police.

TUESDAY, JUNE 22–WEDNESDAY, JUNE 23. The police continue to question men from Bon Temps and the surrounding areas about Dawn. Detective Bellefleur visits Merlotte's several times, sitting in Sookie's section and trying to get her to react to his thoughts.

THURSDAY, JUNE 24. While eating lunch at Merlotte's, Andy thinks an especially disturbing image at Sookie, so she pours a drink down his shirt and goes out the back door in tears. Sam is furious at Andy's actions. When the detective attempts to apologize, Sam tells Andy to sit in another section if he ever returns. Sam later asks Sookie to accompany him to Bill's speech to the Descendants of the Glorious Dead that evening and then go out for coffee. Sookie agrees, and they arrange for Sam to pick her up.

Bill's speech goes well. When he is asked about a member's great-grandfather, Bill remembers him as a friend and shares the story of his death. Afterward, Sookie and Sam go to the Crawdad Diner for coffee, and Sam suggests that he would like to be more than a friend. Sookie asks why he waited until someone else showed an interest, and they drive back to Sookie's house in silence. Sookie enters the house and immediately senses that something is wrong. She finds her grandmother's bloody body in the kitchen. Her screams bring Bill, who comforts her until Andy Bellefleur arrives. Sookie calls several places to find her brother, including Merlotte's. When Sam hears that she is in trouble, he returns to her house. A distraught Jason arrives, and in his despair and anger, he first verbally assaults Sookie and then slaps her. Bill is about to attack Jason to keep him from hitting her again when Sam tackles Jason, taking him to the ground. Andy manages to calm Bill and tries to defuse the situation.

TUESDAY, JUNE 29. Sookie and Jason maintain a truce during Adele's funeral, the largest ever held in the parish.

FRIDAY, JULY 2. While packing up her grandmother's things, Sookie decides it would be better to move into Adele's bedroom than lie across the hall knowing why it is empty. After that job is done, an exhausted Sookie showers and is combing out the tangles in her hair when Bill knocks on the door. Sookie allows him to comb her hair. As they talk and he soothes her with his touch, the mood between them changes, and Bill begins to make love to her. He is surprised to discover her virginity. The two begin a passionate affair.

SATURDAY, JULY 3. Jason comes into Merlotte's for lunch and tells Sookie that the police have questioned him again about the murders. When her co-workers learn of her intensifying relationship with Bill, they all warn her away. But Sookie is happy to see Bill come into the bar. Malcolm and Diane arrive, and their behavior shocks and angers all the human patrons. The other vampires mock Bill for his devotion to Sookie as they leave for their home in Monroe. Bill waits outside for Sookie to make certain his former friends have left. Sookie follows him to his home, where they enjoy his hot tub together.

SUNDAY, JULY 4. Bill takes Sookie to the movies and out to eat—he abstains. As they lie in bed later, Bill makes a casual remark about his childhood that causes Sookie to tell him that her great-uncle sexually molested her as a child.

MONDAY, JULY 5. As she leaves Bill's house in the morning, she is surprised to find Jason waiting for her with the news of her great-uncle Bartlett's death during a robbery the night before. Jason's shocked Sookie doesn't mourn. Sookie tells her initially disbelieving brother what her uncle did to her and their aunt Linda, and how Adele protected her after she found out, kicking her brother out of their lives. It isn't until Sookie arrives at work that day that she realizes Bill had him killed. She confronts Bill, who doesn't deny it. Although they exchange "I love you"s for the first time, she tells him she can't see him until she decides whether their love is worth the misery she might face by caring for him.

Sookie works hard to create a life without her grandmother and Bill. Adele's lawyer works to wrap up her estate, and Sookie is surprised to receive twenty thousand dollars from Uncle Bartlett's estate. She donates it to a local mental health center.

THURSDAY, JULY 8. During her separation from Bill, Sookie begins to realize the amount of resentment that the human bar patrons are feeling for the Monroe vampires, who have apparently been traveling around the surrounding area and behaving very badly. She catches thoughts of a plan to burn down their house with them in it.

TUESDAY, JULY 13. Bill comes into Merlotte's with visiting vampire Harlen Ives, who was turned when he was a teenager. When Bill and

Harlen announce that they are going to Monroe to visit Malcolm, Sookie gives Bill a vague warning, uncertain of what to do and how much to say. The level of anger and frenzy grows in the bar after they leave, and she calls Bill when she gets home to let him know.

WEDNESDAY, JULY 14. Jason wakes Sookie with the news that the Monroe vampires' house has been burned. She rushes to Monroe and sees four damaged coffins and one body bag with human remains. Unable to ascertain whether Bill was at the house, she realizes that Sam has arrived and allows him to take her home. Sam gets her to clean house the whole day to help her pass the time until the sun sets and she can find out if Bill was home and not in Monroe.

Sookie waits until dark and then heads out to the cemetery between their houses in the rain, calling Bill's name. When Bill rises from the earth, she is overcome and falls to her knees. Sookie tells him of the death of the Monroe vampires, and he is lost for a moment in his anger and rage. Sookie deliberately changes his focus to sex, and they make love in the mud. When he comes to himself, Bill carries her to his home to bathe in his hot tub.

THURSDAY, JULY 15–SATURDAY, JULY 24. Sookie and Bill resume their relationship. They spend nighttime hours together, watching TV, going to movies, playing Scrabble, and making love. Sookie works while Bill sleeps; Bill reads, roams the woods, and does yard work at night while Sookie sleeps. They are uneasy because of the Monroe fire and the still-unsolved deaths of Maudette, Dawn, and Sookie's grandmother.

Jason begins to come into the bar nearly every day to talk to Sookie. He tells his sister that the police have questioned him two more times and that he has spoken to a lawyer. Sookie asks why the police keep questioning him, and Jason confesses that he makes videos of his sexual encounters with women, including the two deceased, and that the police found copies. Jason asks Sookie to "listen" to see if she can find out if anyone who comes into the bar is the murderer.

Arlene asks Sookie if she can babysit for her the next night but angers Sookie when she decides that she cannot leave her children in the company of a vampire. To release her frustration, Sookie digs a hole in her backyard, telling a watchful Bill that she will plant a tree. After she calms down and they make love, he informs her that Eric has ordered him to bring her to Fangtasia. Sookie doesn't want to go but realizes that she must obey for both her sake and Bill's. Bill has her take his blood to strengthen her for the encounter.

SUNDAY, JULY 25. When Bill and Sookie arrive at Fangtasia, Eric reveals that someone has embezzled from the bar. He wants Sookie to use her gift to identify the thief. She promises to willingly help him now and in the future if he promises to go to the proper authorities rather than taking justice into his own hands. He agrees, and she interviews the human employees, discovering through one of them that the embezzler is the bartender, Long Shadow. Before she can inform Eric, Long Shadow attacks to keep her from speaking and is staked by Eric. As Long Shadow dies, his blood gushes out all over Sookie. Bloodlust begins to infect the vampires, so Sookie grabs Bill and flees for home. She has Bill drop her off at her house to spend the rest of the night alone.

MONDAY, JULY 26. Deciding to stay away from vampires for a while to remind herself that she is human, Sookie cannot help but notice that having Bill's blood again has changed her, enhanced her. Her hair, eyes, and complexion are brighter; she is stronger and faster. When she gets to work, her fellow employees notice the difference in her as well. As the lunch crowd rolls in, she does as Jason asked and listens to the thoughts floating in the bar. She doesn't pick up anything about the murders of Dawn and Maudette but does hear a group of men thinking about their involvement in the Monroe fire. Thinking that she might pick up more from the night crowd, she heads back to Merlotte's in her casual clothes and sits at the bar next to an unusually alone Jason.

Bill enters Merlotte's with a young woman in tow and informs Sookie that Eric sent her over as a reward and that Bill needs to send her back. Jason volunteers to drive her back to Monroe so that Sookie and Bill can talk, and Sookie takes Bill to the pond on Jason's property, not wanting to go to either of their houses. She confesses her fear of Eric and the other vampires who could use her love for him and her family to control them. Bill ponders their situation and tells her that he may have a way to get around Eric's dominion.

Bill goes to his own home to make phone calls, and a nervous Sookie cautiously scans her yard before hurrying into her house. Suddenly something hits her front door, and she immediately calls Bill, who rushes over to find Sookie's cat Tina dead, strangled, on the front porch. Sookie bursts into tears but finally calms enough to bury her pet in the hole she previously dug in the backyard. Bill spends the night with a mourning Sookie.

TUESDAY, JULY 27. Sookie notifies Bud Dearborn about the death of her cat, and he tells her they may have to dig the pet up to check if the method of strangulation matches Dawn and Maudette. Arlene once again asks Sookie to babysit, this time not mentioning Bill, and Rene brings Arlene's children, Lisa and Coby, over after work before getting ready for his date with Arlene. The children meet Bill, accepting him without many questions, although Lisa does suggest that he bring Sookie flowers occasionally, and the unusual foursome enjoy their evening. Another vampire arrives just as Arlene and Rene are packing up the kids, and Sookie is stunned to meet the Man from Memphis. Bill introduces him as Bubba and tells Sookie that Bubba will be watching over her while he goes to New Orleans for a few days. He warns her to never call Bubba by his real name, explaining that something went wrong with the turning and that Bubba is a few bricks shy of a load. He also likes pets, especially cats, and not in a healthy way. He is, however, loyal and obedient. Bubba strolls off into the woods as Bill says good-bye to Sookie.

WEDNESDAY, JULY 28. Arlene and fellow waitress Charlsie Tooten are impressed that Bill got Sookie a bodyguard while he is out of town, and Arlene comments on Bubba's resemblance to a certain musical icon. Sookie assures them that Bubba isn't like him at all once you get to know him, an honest truth as Bubba is no longer of the same mind.

Sam tells them that he needs to hire a new waitress. He asks Sookie to go through the applications he has on file. She reads Maudette's application and reluctantly becomes suspicious as she realizes that her brother isn't the only man with a connection to the murdered women. Sam knew them both as well. Sookie remains uncomfortable with her boss for the rest of the day and finds herself nervous and restless once she gets home. Terry Bellefleur calls from the bar to let her know that Jason is there and wants to buy her a drink, so she drives back over to Merlotte's, parking in the employee lot and taking a moment to pat a stray dog on the head. Terry denies having called her. Since the dog is still out back, Sookie decides to take him home for company for the night. She names him Dean, and he watches attentively as she gets ready for bed. She initially makes him sleep on the floor but doesn't push him back off the bed when he climbs on as she is falling asleep.

THURSDAY, JULY 29. Awaking the next morning, Sookie is stunned to find a naked Sam in bed with her. He confesses that he is a shapeshifter and can turn into any animal he wants. He admits that he wanted to guard her overnight. He planned on being out of the house before she woke, but he overslept. Sookie realizes that shapeshifting is definitely supernatural and accepts that vampires are not suffering from a virus. She understands that Bill is really dead, but she loves him anyway.

Sam has to return to being a dog when Andy arrives to let her know that another woman has been murdered. She persuades the exhausted detective to rest in her old bedroom, and Sam shifts back to human form so that Sookie can sneak him back to the bar. They are stunned when they arrive to find Jason unconscious in his truck and covered in blood. Panicked that he is seriously hurt, Sookie has Sam call an ambulance for her brother. The police, believing that Jason killed the latest victim and then got drunk, arrest him at the hospital. Sookie leaves a message for Bill at his New Orleans hotel and then contacts lawyer Sid Matt Lancaster about representing her brother.

Later that night, Sookie hears Bubba shouting. When she calls out to him, he tells her that someone was in her yard.

FRIDAY, JULY 30. Jason makes bail. He is too ashamed to even speak to Sookie. She sits in the bar, doggedly listening into the thoughts of the patrons until Sam sends her home. She is washing her face when she hears something outside and goes to the door to yell for Bubba. He doesn't answer. She calls 911, but her phone is dead. She decides to run to Bill's house, figuring his phone will be working. She looks in the hall closet for an old gun Adele kept there but finds it missing. Sookie is horrified to realize that the killer has been in her house. She creeps out her back door and is stunned when she finally gets a peek into the killer's mind. It is Rene Lenier, and she reads in his tangled thoughts that his first victim was his own sister, who was dating a vampire despite her brother's protests. Rene catches Sookie and begins to beat her, but he is surprised by her strength when she fights back. She falls to the ground, and he straddles her, trying to hold her while he feels around for his rope to strangle her. Sookie's left hand is free. She is able to get his work knife off his belt and stab him. When he falls to the ground, she stumbles to Bill's house and calls 911 before losing consciousness.

SATURDAY, JULY 31. When Sookie wakes up in the hospital, she finds that Rene has confessed to everything. She has visitors and flowers from the Merlotte's employees, from Sid Matt and his wife, and from Eric. She dozes and awakens to find Bill at her side. He considers killing Rene, but Sookie tells him to let the law deal with the killer. Bill promises to take care of her at night when she is released. She turns down his offer of blood and asks him what he accomplished in New Orleans. He announces that he is the new investigator for Area Five, Eric's area. This puts Bill and, thereby, Sookie under Eric's protection. As Bill looks forward to getting back to normal, a collie looks into the room before continuing down the hall, and a smiling Eric floats past the hospital window.

The Secret Dialogues of Bill and Eric

> To: Eric Northman,
> Sheriff of Area Five, LA

Dear Eric,

With the permission of Sophie-Anne Leclerq, Queen of Louisiana, I will be returning to claim my ancestral home in Bon Temps.

Sincerely,
William Compton

~ ~ ~

> To: WILLIAM COMPTON

DEAR BILL,

LONG TIME NO SEE. AS YOU KNOW, THE VAMPIRES IN MY AREA PAY THEIR FEALTY BY WORKING AT FANGTASIA. PLEASE CONTACT PAM TO SET UP YOUR SCHEDULE.

ERIC NORTHMAN

~ ~ ~

> To: Eric Northman,
> Sheriff of Area Five, LA

Dear Eric,

I understand that your vampires may offer a tithe as an alternative to working at Fangtasia. I have other obligations and fear I will not have the time to dedicate to your club.

Sincerely,
William Compton

~ ~ ~

To: William Compton

Dear Bill,

A tithe is acceptable, but I would much prefer your time at Fangtasia. As a former Confederate soldier you would be quite a draw. I
understand that you have work to do for the Queen, but surely you
can spare me, your sheriff, some of your valuable time as well.

Eric Northman

~ ~ ~

To: Eric Northman,
Sheriff of Area Five, LA

Dear Eric,

Please find enclosed my certified check for six months' tithe.

Sincerely,
William Compton

Phone: Eric calling Bill.

ERIC: "Bill."

BILL: "Eric."

ERIC: "I need you to bring your human to Fangtasia tomorrow night."

BILL: "Why?"

ERIC: "I need her services."

BILL: "Eric, you know she is mine."

ERIC: "Of course, Bill. There will be none of that."

BILL: "Then why?"

ERIC: "It is enough that I am sheriff and I order you to bring her."

BILL: "Eric . . ."

ERIC: "Bill, you know it will be much better if you bring her willingly. You
wouldn't want me to have to send someone to get her, would you?"
(Silence.)

BILL: "We will be there."

Phone: Bill calling Eric.

BILL: "Eric."

ERIC: "Bill."

BILL: "I received your gift."

ERIC: "And you're calling to thank me. It was my pleasure, Bill."

BILL: "I've sent her back unopened."

ERIC: "You didn't like her?"

BILL: "I have no need for her."

ERIC: "I see. I'll have to find some other way to show my appreciation to you and your human."

BILL: "That's not necessary. I'll consider your absence in our lives reward enough."

Phone: Eric calling Bill.

ERIC: "Congratulations on your new position as Area Five Investigator, Bill. I had not realized you had such aspirations."

BILL: "I thought it wise to secure a position."

ERIC: "Technically, you now work for me."

BILL: "Technically, I work for Sophie-Anne, as do you."

ERIC: "Yes, I suppose you are right." *Pause.* "I understand your human has captured a killer. She's quite resilient."

BILL: "Indeed she is. Don't float around her windows anymore, Eric. It makes her uncomfortable."

Living Dead in Dallas

Timeline

TUESDAY, SEPTEMBER 21, 2004. Sookie calls Portia Bellefleur to come to Merlotte's and get her brother, Andy, who has gotten drunk after a particularly bad day at work. Leaving his car in the parking lot, Portia drives Andy home.

WEDNESDAY, SEPTEMBER 22. When she gets to work in the morning, Sookie notices that Andy's car door is open. She discovers the body of the bar's short-order cook, Lafayette Reynold, in the backseat. She blows her own car horn to get Sam's attention, and he calls 911. The police arrive and question Sookie, who tells them that Lafayette bragged about attending a sex party a few days earlier. She and Sam privately discuss whether someone from the orgy could be responsible for Lafayette's death. Terry Bellefleur, Andy's cousin, comes in as a fill-in cook and informs them that Lafayette's neck was broken and that there is evidence of sexual assault.

Summoned to Fangtasia by Eric, Bill and Sookie begin to argue in the car on the way to Shreveport. When the car suddenly dies, an angry Sookie gets out. Bill tells her he is going to get a mechanic and leaves the car unlocked for her, but she resolutely begins to trek back to Bon Temps. She hears movement in the woods beside her and calls out, figuring she might as well know what she is dealing with. Much to her surprise, a woman steps from the woods, a feral razorback hog by her side. She identifies herself as a maenad and tells Sookie that she needs a message taken to Eric Northman. Sookie is able to turn away just as the maenad slashes at her, catching her on her back instead of her face and chest. Sookie is in agony as she falls to the ground.

Bill returns and rushes a mortally wounded Sookie to Eric for help. Dr. Ludwig, a supe herself, is called in, and after cleaning Sookie's wounds with her tongue, the doctor instructs the vampires to drain Sookie's poisoned blood and replace it with transfusions of real and synthetic blood. Sookie passes out and wakes to find Pam watching over her. After cleaning up, Sookie waits in Eric's office with Bill until Eric, Pam, and the new bartender, Chow, finish closing the bar. Eric informs them that he is sending Bill and Sookie to Dallas so that she can use her "gift" to help the vampire leader of Area Six solve a problem. Sookie has no choice but to consent, per her agreement with Eric. She brings the conversation to a stop when she asks why a maenad is in the woods, and the vampires explain that maenads feed off the violence associated with alcohol and, therefore, are very interested in bars. They expect tribute from those who profit from drink.

THURSDAY, SEPTEMBER 23. Sam agrees, albeit reluctantly, to give Sookie the time off to go to Dallas. He initially reacts with laughter when she solemnly warns that there is a maenad roaming the woods, but he quickly sobers when Sookie shows him her scars. He gently kisses her back, and then he kisses her more deeply on the lips. She briefly responds to his warmth but then pulls away, and they try to resume their conversation. Portia comes into the bar with a request from Andy for Sookie to "listen" for information because he is a suspect in the death. Sookie agrees, but for the sake of her friend Lafayette, not for the Bellefleurs.

FRIDAY, SEPTEMBER 24. Arriving at the airport in Dallas, Sookie heads to the cargo plane Bill traveled on, waiting for his casket to be unloaded. She is accosted by a man dressed as a Catholic priest who attempts to pull her away with him; however, just then Bill's coffin appears, and the lid opens as Bill wakes. The "priest" runs as Bill rushes to Sookie's side, and they consider the meaning of the incident as they make their way to the Silent Shore Hotel, where Sookie is startled and delighted to realize that the hotel bellboy, Barry, is also a telepath, although very unschooled. They are met at the hotel by Dallas vampire Isabel Beaumont, who waits while they check in and freshen up before taking them to the home of the sheriff of Area Six, Stan Davis. Stan tells them that one of his nest mates, Farrell, is missing, and Stan wants him found. He brings in humans known to have been in the vampire bar where Farrell was last seen. By reading their memories, Sookie is able to tell that Farrell entered a bathroom with another vampire. She also realizes that the "priest" from the airport was in the bar as well. Bill steps away to use a computer and returns with the identity of the second vampire based on the description Sookie elicited. Stan is appalled to realize that Farrell was probably kidnapped by Godric, aka Godfrey, an ancient vampire who has become a renouncer and plans to meet the sun in a ceremony arranged by the anti-vampire Fellowship of the Sun.

Sookie asks how the "priest" could have known that she would be at the airport and suggests, in writing, that Stan's house is bugged. She locates the bug under the table, and the vampires drop it into a bowl of water after acting out a little scenario for the listener's benefit. Isabel's human companion, Hugo Ayres, offers to escort Sookie to the Fellowship to gather information.

Stan, angry about the bug, asks if there are any strangers visiting the house, and Isabel brings in Leif, actually Eric, who came to Dallas to watch over Bill and Sookie. Leif/Eric denies planting the bug, and Sookie points out that the bug had to have been there for a few days in order for the listener to know when she and Bill would be flying in. Isabel takes Sookie and Bill back to their hotel, where they attempt a little romance but are interrupted by Eric.

SATURDAY, SEPTEMBER 25. Sookie is watching the news while waiting for the front desk to procure her clothing that will serve as an appropriate disguise during her visit to the Fellowship. She is dismayed to see a segment on the execution-style death of Bethany Rogers, whose mind Sookie read the evening before and whose body was later found in a Dumpster behind the Silent Shore. Pushing aside her tears, she gets ready for her assignment by donning a wig and frumpy clothes and meets Hugo in the lobby. They come up with a cover story as they drive to the Fellowship, where they meet the director, Steve Newlin; his wife, Sarah; and Polly Blythe, the ceremonies officer. The Newlins and Polly take Sookie and Hugo on a tour, leading them down to the basement. Sookie hesitantly follows Hugo, trying to be reassured by his casual acceptance of what is going on, but finally she tries to escape and is pulled back down the stairs by Gabe, another Fellowship member who is guarding the area. The couple is then locked into a small room. Injured and in pain, Sookie concentrates on reading Hugo's thoughts and discovers that he is the traitor. She confronts him. He tells her that he betrayed the human race when he became enthralled with Isabel. Sookie pushes him to tell Gabe that the gig is up, that she knows of his betrayal of the vampires, to test whether they will let him go. As she already suspected, the Fellowship has no intention of allowing Hugo to live, and Gabe takes Hugo to the room where Farrell is chained. Gabe returns to torment Sookie, trying to rape her, but is stopped by Godfrey. Sookie begs Godfrey to let her out, challenging him when he tells her that Steve Newlin's plan is to tie Sookie to Farrell and put them out for the dawn. Godfrey is reluctant to force others to do what he has willingly chosen, and he helps Sookie escape. Unable to use the phone, Sookie reaches out with her mind to the telepath Barry the Bellboy, frightening him with the contact. She pleads with him to let Bill know that she is in danger. A shapeshifter working undercover in the church, Luna Garza, manages to get Sookie out of the church and informs her that the shifters of Dallas have been monitoring the Fellowship. Sookie lets her know that the vampires will probably attack as soon as the sun sets to retrieve Farrell. Luna debates whether or not to leave but hops in her car when they hear an alarm raised in the building. Sookie jumps in, and they take off. Sarah and Polly follow by car, ramming them and causing Luna's car to overturn. Sarah and Polly attempt to get to Sookie and Luna, but there are too many witnesses to the accident. The police and an ambulance are called. Once at the hospital, Luna has a shifter doctor examine Sookie, delete her records, and then spirit them both out to a waiting ride. Sookie is blindfolded, driven to the hotel by two Weres, and delivered to the front door. Eric, standing outside, is startled by her sudden appearance and calls Bill, then takes her up to their room to start cleaning her up.

Bill returns quickly and confirms that the vampires attacked the Fellowship and freed Farrell, but tells them that Godfrey managed to escape. Bill gently bathes Sookie and puts her to bed.

SUNDAY, SEPTEMBER 26. Sookie wakes just before dawn with the feeling that there is something that she needs to do. She dresses and takes a taxi to the now-deserted Fellowship grounds, where she waits for Godfrey. The vampire emerges from the shadow, and her tears begin to fall as she looks at his young face. He is touched that someone is there to cry for him as he meets the sun, hoping to see the face of God. Sookie returns to the hotel and falls deeply asleep until Bill rises.

She and Bill go to Stan's mansion to tell him about Godfrey and discover what punishment Isabel and Hugo have earned. Sookie is relieved to find Hugo alive and forces herself to accept the punishment the vampires have devised for him. Invited to stay and celebrate Farrell's return, Leif/Eric and Sookie are talking when she "hears" the Fellowship followers preparing to attack the house. Sookie yells a warning and is protected from a bullet by Eric. Bill leaves to hunt the attackers without even checking to see if she survived the attack. Hurt, she walks out and takes the next plane back to Bon Temps.

MONDAY, SEPTEMBER 27–WEDNESDAY, OCTOBER 20. Sookie keeps her distance from Bill.

THURSDAY, OCTOBER 21. Jason stops by the house for lunch and tells Sookie that Bill has been seen over in Monroe with Portia Bellefleur, and Sookie later sees them drive by in Bill's car.

FRIDAY, OCTOBER 22. Sookie decides to attend a high school football game and meets up with her friend Tara Thornton, Tara's date Benedict "Eggs" Tallie, and JB du Rone. Sookie encourages JB to pursue a woman he had been seeing, believing that the woman will be good for him. He kisses her cheek in thanks, and just as she gives him a quick peck on the lips in return, she spots Bill staring back at her from where he is sitting with Portia. When she gets home, Bill is waiting, and they engage in passionate make-up sex. Afterward, she questions him about Portia, and he tells Sookie that he thinks Portia is seeing him in hopes of being invited to the sex club to get information that will help Andy.

SATURDAY, OCTOBER 23. Bill and Sookie decide to keep their reunion quiet, and Sookie receives an invitation from parish coroner and funeral director Mike Spencer to Jan Fowler's lake house to "get a little wild," since he thinks she is a single woman now. Hoping to discover who killed Lafayette, Sookie accepts. She leaves a guarded message for Bill, who has been called back to Dallas, and she's forced to ask Eric to go along to provide protection.

SUNDAY, OCTOBER 24. Eric arrives to take Sookie to the orgy up at Mimosa Lake, and she asks him to make certain nothing happens to her. Eric is surprised that she trusts him but tells her that she will be safe. They enter the cabin to find several Bon Temps residents in various states of undress. Jan Fowler, Mike Spencer, Tom and Cleo Hardaway, and Tara and Eggs are all in attendance, apparently regulars. Eggs is attempting to undo Sookie's shorts, all the while thinking lewdly about Eric, when Eric comes up behind her, and Sookie turns into his kiss, letting her mind roam while he keeps her safe. She finds the memory of Lafayette's murder in Mike's mind and sees that Tom was also directly involved. Sickened, she whispers to Eric to get her out, and he slings her over his shoulder, telling the others that he is taking her outside to get her warmed up. He lays her on the hood of his Corvette, intent on his own desires, and tries to seduce her, but she reminds him that Bill is her boyfriend. Bill emerges from the woods, followed by a drunken Andy, who holds them all at gunpoint, demanding to know who was responsible for Lafayette's murder. Sam, in collie form, joins the group, with the maenad not far behind. She introduces herself as Callisto, telling them she was called to the cabin by the lust and drunkenness of the orgy participants. She reminds them of her first visit. She claims that Lafayette was a fitting offering to her and thanks them for leaving his body at Merlotte's. She names Mike and Tom as the killers, indicating Cleo as well. Tara hides under a table on the deck, and Eggs stands entranced in the yard. Sookie feels the madness of the maenad overwhelm the group on the deck, and she is almost caught up in it herself, but Bill and Eric hold her between them. When Sookie is able to look at Callisto again, the maenad is smiling and covered in blood. She bids a fond farewell to Sam and drifts off into the woods.

Sam shifts back to his human form as Eric and Bill examine the carnage on the deck. They find Tara alive, and after Eric erases her memory of the evening, Sam drives her and a still almost-catatonic Eggs home. The vampires then set fire to the cabin to burn the evidence of the slaughter. Portia Bellefleur pulls up, frantic about her brother, and Bill wakes him from his trance. Sookie tells him that Mike and the Hardaways killed Lafayette, but Andy bemoans the lack of proof. Eric searches the cars and finds blood, Lafayette's wallet, and his clothing in the trunk of Mike Spencer's Lincoln. Andy tells them to leave everything as it is so that the police can find it and clear his name.

MONDAY, OCTOBER 25. Sookie sleeps through the day, and Bill wakes her when he rises. He finds a foil-wrapped chocolate cake on her front porch, a gift from Andy and Portia's grandmother, who has left a message thanking Sookie for helping Andy. When Bill hears that she is named Caroline Holliday Bellefleur, he asks Sookie to get his family Bible from his house, and they look over his family tree together, realizing that Caroline is Bill's great-granddaughter. After more than a century of hating the Bellefleurs for their ancestor's responsibility for the death of one of his friends during the Civil War, Bill decides to secretly assist his struggling descendants financially and shares a warm moment with Sookie.

The Secret Dialogues of Bill and Eric

To: William Compton,
Area Five Investigator

Investigator Compton,

You are summoned to a meeting with me at Fangtasia tomorrow night.

Eric Northman
Sheriff of Area Five

In person at the meeting:

BILL: "Why am I here, Eric?"

ERIC: "Area Six in Texas has need of your services."

BILL: "For what purpose?"

ERIC: "A vampire is missing, a nest mate of the Area Six sheriff. You and Sookie will help locate him."

BILL: "Sookie?"

ERIC: "Yes, per our agreement, Sookie will assist us."

BILL: "I believe her agreement was that she would assist *you*."

ERIC: "And so she shall. It will be of assistance to me to have the sheriff of Area Six in my debt. You will bring Sookie here tomorrow night, and I will inform her of the assignment."

Phone: Bill calling Eric after Sookie's escape from the Fellowship of the Sun.

BILL: "Eric, we have raided the Fellowship. Sookie has gone but there is a dead man with her scent. I believe she had help escaping. We came upon a car accident. Sookie and a shifter were in the car and they were taken to the hospital, but Sookie's name disappeared from their computers even as I asked about her."

ERIC: "I'll go outside and check for her. Perhaps she is unwilling to enter by herself."

BILL: "Or unable."

ERIC: "She is strong, Bill. She will be found."

Phone: Eric calling Bill later that same evening.

ERIC: "Bill, she is here. Some shapeshifters brought her in."

BILL: "How is she? Is she badly injured?"

ERIC: "Battered but walking."

BILL: "Can she get into our room? I will be right there."

ERIC: "Bill, I'll take her up and start doctoring."

BILL: "Don't try anything, Eric. She is mine."

ERIC: *"Bill."*

BILL: "I mean it, Eric. This is not the time for your games. I will be there shortly."

ERIC: "All right then. Good-bye."

Phone: Eric calling Bill.

ERIC: "Bill, the shifters in Dallas have contacted Stan about compensation for their aid. He feels their demands are too much, and I agree. I need you to go back to Dallas and parley with them."

BILL: "You made the original deal with them, Eric. Surely this is your responsibility."

ERIC: "I have another, more important matter to attend to."

BILL: "And that would be?"

ERIC: "The maenad was not satisfied with our tribute. While you are in Dallas negotiating with the shifters, I will be in the woods of Bon Temps negotiating with her."

BILL: "Your tribute was substandard?"

ERIC: "*Our* tribute was a perfectly acceptable bull, a magnificent specimen, and I didn't hear you making any better suggestions. She is just being difficult, as usual. I can only be grateful that she has remained in

Bon Temps for whatever reason. There's been no sign of her in Shreveport, and I'd like to keep it that way."

BILL: "I'll fly to Dallas this evening."

ERIC: "I may ask Sookie to join me as a sign of good faith that I understood the importance of Callisto's message to me."

BILL: "I would prefer you didn't."

ERIC: "Ah, but nonetheless, I still may."

BILL: "Eric, once again, I remind you that she is mine."

ERIC: "For now."

BILL: "And you will do nothing to change that."

ERIC: "For now."

BILL: "Eric, even you cannot so flout the rules."

ERIC: "Of course not, Bill. I accept that Sookie is yours, by her own choice. But should she ever indicate that she is no longer interested in that status . . ."

BILL: "That won't happen."

ERIC: "But if it should?"

BILL: "Then you would be within the rules to pursue her yourself."

ERIC: "Exactly."

BILL: "But you agree that you will not make overtures?"

ERIC: "I agree."

Club Dead

Timeline

As this book was written prior to Definitely Dead *and the inclusion of Hurricane Katrina into the series story line, which established a definite time frame for the events of the series, the events in* Club Dead *do not correspond with the actual full moon.*

WEDNESDAY, DECEMBER 1, 2004. Sookie goes to Bill's house after work and is devastated that Bill has become so consumed with work that he rebuffs her attempts at intimacy. He tells her he is leaving for Seattle soon and that he has been working on a secret project for Sophie-Anne Leclerq, the vampire Queen of Louisiana. He also tells her that he is planning to hide his computer equipment in the hidey-hole in her closet while he is gone. If anything happens to him before he brings the computer, Bill asks Sookie to go to his house during the day and get it. Sookie is even more disturbed when she realizes he is lying to her about where he is going.

THURSDAY, DECEMBER 2. Sookie deliberately drives by Belle Rive, the Bellefleur home, and sees the work being done courtesy of the mysterious legacy left them by a relative who had "died mysteriously over in Europe somewhere." She knows that the legacy actually came from Bill, whom the Bellefleurs despise, and Sookie tries not to be bitter though she herself struggles with money problems.

FRIDAY, DECEMBER 3. Bill calls to let Sookie know he has arrived safely in "Seattle."

MONDAY, DECEMBER 6. Much to Sookie's surprise, Bubba shows up at her door and tells her that Eric has sent him to guard her. When Sookie arrives at work with Bubba in tow, she is attacked by a Were wearing a gang vest, but Bubba saves the day. Pam soon arrives and explains that Bill is missing and that he has been in Jackson, Mississippi, not Seattle. Pam calls Eric and puts Sookie on the phone. Eric tells Sookie to be careful until he can get over to her house to explain. She goes home and cries herself to sleep.

TUESDAY, DECEMBER 7. A depressed Sookie spends the day in bed, rousing only long enough to confirm that Bill has left his computer equipment in the closet hidey-hole. When she awakens again, she finds Eric with her, and he forces her to get up and dressed. Eric tells her that humans who live in the kingdom of Mississippi have informed him that Bill has been kidnapped. He speaks of the work Bill was doing for the Queen of Louisiana and eventually reveals that Bill had actually gone to Mississippi to see a vampire that he had been involved with long ago. He had become enamored with her again but had planned to return to Bon Temps to make "financial arrangements" for Sookie's care. Eric admits that he has not informed the queen of the kidnapping or Bill's missing project because of fears she will punish him and Pam for Bill's misadventure. He asks Sookie to go to Jackson with a Were who owes him a debt, and use her "gift" to try to discover where Bill is being held. Sookie agrees to try to find and rescue Bill.

WEDNESDAY, DECEMBER 8–THURSDAY, DECEMBER 9. Sookie prepares to leave for Jackson.

FRIDAY, DECEMBER 10. Alcide Herveaux arrives to take Sookie to Jackson. They are immediately at ease and realize they are attracted to each other.

Once in Jackson, Alcide suggests that Sookie visit his sister's beauty salon while he takes care of some business, and she learns that his ex-girlfriend, Debbie Pelt, will be celebrating her engagement that evening. Later, Sookie and Alcide eat at the Mayflower Café before heading for Josephine's, a supe club. Debbie is indeed at the club, and since Sookie is posing as Alcide's new love, she immediately earns Debbie's hatred. Alcide realizes Sookie's talent, and they use it to put Debbie in her place.

Sookie casts about in Josephine's to see if she can "hear" anything about Bill. Sookie zeros in on a human with a vampire at the bar and finds that Bill is being tortured for information about the work he has been doing. When Sookie is assaulted by Jerry Falcon, a Were gang member, she is rescued by the King of Mississippi, Russell Edgington, who insists that she and Alcide return to Josephine's the next night as his guests. Sookie and Alcide return to Alcide's apartment and are surprised by a visit from Eric, who has come to Mississippi himself to keep an eye on things.

SATURDAY, DECEMBER 11. Alcide runs errands in the morning, so

Sookie finds herself back at Janice's salon. Later that afternoon, she and Alcide sit down for a friendly game of Scrabble, and afterward, while putting the game away, Sookie discovers the source of an odor both had been noticing: the body of Jerry Falcon, his neck broken, has been stuffed in Alcide's hall closet. They work together to dispose of the body, fearing they will be blamed for the murder. The moon is full as they return that evening to Club Dead, the locals' name for Josephine's. As they are chatting with the guests at Edgington's table, Sookie "hears" the thoughts of a human assassin who plans to stake Edgington's second-in-command, Betty Joe Pickard. While attempting to foil the attack, Sookie is staked and seriously injured. Compelled to shift by the full moon and the excitement of the blood, Alcide runs after the would-be killer's accomplice. It is left to a thinly disguised Eric to assist Sookie. Edgington insists that they return to his compound, where one of his people can use his healing gift to save Sookie.

After the healing of her wound, Eric and Sookie are surprised when Bubba appears. Eric gives Sookie his blood to heal her quickly and orders Bubba to look for Bill. Bubba returns with the news that he has found Bill on the property, and Eric and Sookie make plans for his rescue.

SUNDAY, DECEMBER 12. Sookie sneaks out of Russell's house at dawn and finds a tortured and starved Bill in the garage, but as she is trying to remove his bonds, Lorena Ball appears. Lorena is Bill's maker, and she taunts Sookie and then attacks. Unfortunately for Lorena, Sookie is carrying with her the stake taken from her side at Club Dead. She kills Lorena. Sookie then gets Bill into the trunk of a car and cautiously drives out of the compound.

Arriving at the garage of Alcide's apartment building, Sookie opens the trunk to check on Bill but is pushed inside. The lid slams shut. The worst comes to pass as the starved and uncontrolled Bill wakens and rapes and almost drains her. Coming to his senses just in time, Bill is horrified by his actions. Eric arrives, and he and Bill take an unconscious Sookie to Alcide's apartment, where the three men work to revive her. To Alcide's dismay, Sookie reveals that it was Debbie Pelt who pushed her into the trunk. While going over the day's events, they realize from a comment made by one of Russell's guards while Sookie was leaving that Bubba has been captured. The Mississippi vamps, not knowing he is the real deal, are planning to execute him. Sookie calls Russell's mansion and is able to convince them of Bubba's true identity, and Russell's vamps are excited by the possibility that Bubba might sing for them. Debbie soon arrives at the building, and Alcide hides Sookie, Eric, and Bill next door, where they overhear Alcide tell Debbie that he and Sookie had engaged in an affair. Questioned by Bill, an angry and hurt Sookie denies the accusation but confronts him with the fact of his own betrayal. Disgusted with his perfidy, Sookie asks Eric to take her home.

Thugs hired by Jerry Falcon's gang attack Eric and Sookie as they stop for gas. They escape but fall into an argument about the financial hardship that Sookie is experiencing because of Eric's demands on her time. As they arrive at her home, an angry Sookie storms away from Eric and straight into the waiting fists of more of Falcon's gang. Sookie is severely beaten before Eric and Bill arrive and kill her attackers.

MONDAY, DECEMBER 13. When Sookie wakes the next afternoon, she finds she has a newly graveled driveway, a gift from Eric. Alcide stops by with her suitcase, and they consider the possibility that they might explore their relationship after both recover from their present heartbreak. Pam arrives soon after dark, instructed by Eric to assist Sookie. Bubba follows, still well-groomed and flashily dressed after his performance for the Mississippi vamps, and it dawns on Sookie that he is the one who killed Jerry and stuffed him in the closet. He leaves shortly after Bill and Eric arrive, and Pam slips out as they begin to argue. An exasperated Sookie rescinds their invitations to her home, and they are forced to leave. Alone, she is amused to realize that she still has Bill's computer and the work that started all the trouble.

The Secret Dialogues of Bill, Eric, and Pam

Phone: Bill calling Eric.

BILL: "Eric."

ERIC: "Bill."

BILL: "Lorena has summoned me. I will be leaving the area for a short time to see what she wants."

ERIC: "It's been quite some time since you've seen her, hasn't it?"

BILL: "Yes."

ERIC: "Hmmm. Have you told Sookie?"

BILL: "I have told her that I am leaving on business."

ERIC: "Tsk, tsk. Lying to her already?"

BILL: "What I tell Sookie is none of your concern, Eric. I am merely informing you that I am leaving your area. You would have known about Lorena soon enough."

ERIC: "What of your work for Sophie-Anne?"

BILL: "I'll take care of it."

Phone: Bill calling Fangtasia.

PAM: "Fangtasia."

BILL: "Pam, it's Bill."

PAM: "Hi, Bill. Do you want to speak to Eric? He's in his office."

BILL: "No. I don't need to speak to Eric. Pam, I am in Mississippi. Lorena has called me, and I . . . I am with her again. I need to make arrangements for Sookie."

PAM: "Arrangements?"

BILL: "For her future."

PAM: "One that does not include you?"

BILL: "Yes. I will be returning to set things up for her. It will have to be a short trip. I don't want Lorena to know about Sookie. She's not . . . She wouldn't approve."

PAM: "I see. Well, I don't approve of this, Bill. I don't usually care about keeping secrets from humans, but Sookie is valuable and keeping things from her will discourage her from working for us in the future. It would be much better to keep her cooperation."

BILL: "This is how it must be, Pam. Please let Eric know that I will be staying with Lorena and that I will contact Sophie-Anne myself. I'll speak to you again when I get back."

Phone: Bill calling Eric after their return to Louisiana.

BILL: "Eric, I've spoken with Sophie-Anne. You have nothing to worry about."

ERIC: "Good. I believe I'll visit Sookie this evening, see how she is."

BILL: "I'll probably see you at her house, then."

Dead to the World

Timeline

SHORTLY AFTER CHRISTMAS, 2004. Bill leaves a note on Sookie's door asking to see her. When she agrees, he tries to explain about Lorena. He tells her he is going to Peru to collect more information for his vampire database.

SATURDAY, JANUARY 1, 2005. Sookie finishes working the Merlotte's New Year's Eve party at three a.m. and heads home. Stunned to see a nearly naked Eric running down the road to her house, she stops to ask what he is doing and realizes he doesn't know her or his own identity. She gets Eric to come with her, calls Fangtasia when they get to her house, and finds that the vampires are under some kind of attack. Sookie reluctantly agrees to keep Eric until Pam can come for him. Jason comes to visit that evening and meets Eric. Afraid to leave Eric alone, Sookie asks Jason to buy clothes and synthetic blood for the vampire. Pam and Chow arrive and explain that the leader of a group of witches wants to take over Eric and his businesses. The witches had sent a representative to Fangtasia the night before with an offer: If Eric would spend seven nights with the coven leader, they would only demand one-fifth of his business. Eric refused, and Chow attacked the representative, causing a spell to activate that left Eric on Sookie's road several hours later with amnesia. Jason returns from shopping with the news that the witches have posters all over town offering a fifty-thousand-dollar reward for information on Eric's whereabouts. The vampires reason that the witches don't know about Sookie, so Eric should be safe with her. Jason negotiates a deal, and a surprised Sookie finds herself responsible for Eric.

SUNDAY, JANUARY 2. Sookie is disturbed the next day when Jason's boss, Catfish Hennessy, calls and tells her Jason didn't show up for work. Sookie reports his disappearance to the police, but they discount it based on his reputation. Going to Jason's home, she discovers Alcee Beck, a police detective, searching the area. A blood smear, later determined to be a panther print, is found on Jason's deck. After leaving Jason's house,

Sookie pulls over on the side of the road to try to gather her thoughts. While she is sitting there, Tara Thornton pulls up behind her. Claudine Crane, who is helping Tara at her store, Tara's Togs, is also in the car. Sookie tells Tara that Jason is missing and asks if there are any witches in the area. Sookie is surprised when Tara tells her that her fellow waitress at Merlotte's, Holly Cleary, is Wiccan.

Sookie visits Holly at the Kingfisher Arms Apartments and learns that a group of Were witches, who use vampire blood, are trying to gain control of the witches in the area and that they have threatened Holly and her son.

Still seeking some clue about Jason, Sookie goes to Shreveport to speak to one of his old girlfriends, but the young woman hasn't seen Jason. Hoping to get help from Pam, Sookie goes to Fangtasia to question the daytime employees and leave a message, but she is horrified to find that they have been attacked by the witches in a brutal attempt to find Eric. One woman is injured and another dead. Sookie decides to contact Alcide to learn if the Shreveport pack knows anything about the group. As soon as Alcide hears the story, he contacts his packmaster, Colonel Flood. The packmaster immediately suspects that a missing member of his pack, Adabelle, may have been contacted, and Alcide and Sookie go to Adabelle's business to question her. They find her dismembered body, and the Weres realize they have a serious problem.

Upset by all the terrible events of the day, Sookie returns home that evening to a kind and compassionate Eric. They begin an affair, and she realizes that she cares for this gentle stranger.

MONDAY, JANUARY 3. Still determined to find Jason, Sookie travels to Hotshot, the secretive community where Jason's date from New Year's Eve, shifter Crystal Norris, lives. Sookie meets Calvin Norris, Crystal's uncle and the packmaster of the Hotshot shifters, who helps her question the girl. Sookie discovers that something happened to Jason in the yard at his home while Crystal was waiting for him in the house. As Sookie is leaving Hotshot, Calvin makes her an unusual offer.

Sookie is appalled when the witch leader, Hallow, and her brother come into Merlotte's seeking information about Eric. As the witches question Sookie and Sam, they learn that Bill Compton's home is temporarily empty. Sookie realizes that they plan to search Bill's home, so she rushes home to tell Eric to stay out of sight. To her horror, he wants to see what is going on, and they go over to the Compton home, finding the yard full of Weres: Alcide's pack has arrived and is hoping a surprise attack will result in the witches' defeat. The witches escape and seriously injure a Were woman, Maria-Star Cooper, whom Sookie rushes to the hospital. As an exhausted Sookie drives back toward Bon Temps, she falls asleep at the wheel but is startled awake when Claudine suddenly appears in her car. Sookie returns to Merlotte's to find that the Weres and vampires have joined forces to fight Hallow and her followers. She is disturbed when Debbie Pelt arrives, obviously involved with Alcide again. Sookie and Eric return to her home after the meeting. He declares his feelings for her and tells her that when he is restored, she will share all he has. Sookie is touched but knows it is a fantasy.

TUESDAY, JANUARY 4. Jason's friends organize a search around his house for clues to his disappearance. The fruitless search ends in disaster when a feral hog gores Crystal Norris. Sookie returns to her home to find a message from Pam, letting her know that the vampires and Weres will be attacking the coven that night and telling her to bring Eric for the battle. She falls asleep, exhausted by the events of the day, and awakens to find Eric in her bed. They share another intimate moment before leaving for Pam's house.

When they arrive at the gathering at Pam's, they are surprised when Bill appears, having returned from Peru. He questions why Debbie Pelt is present and reveals that she participated in his torture in Jackson. Finally confronted by irrefutable proof of Debbie's true nature, Alcide shocks the gathering when he abjures her.

The coalition is able to defeat the witches, and Hallow is taken prisoner so that she can free Eric from the curse. Debbie attempts to kill Sookie during the confusion of the battle but is stopped by Eric and flees. Sookie is disappointed when Jason is not found with the witches.

Returning to her home, Sookie and Eric enter the kitchen and are surprised to find Debbie with a gun in her hand and murder in her eyes. Debbie fires to kill Sookie, but Eric steps between them and takes the bullet. Before a shocked Debbie can fire again, Sookie grabs her shotgun and kills the werefox. Sookie revives Eric with synthetic blood, and as she cleans the kitchen, Eric takes the body and Debbie's car and hides them.

WEDNESDAY, JANUARY 5–THE EARLY HOURS OF THURSDAY, JAN-UARY 6. When Eric rises the next evening, his memory is restored, and he has no recollection of the time he has spent with Sookie. She is relieved that he will not remember the killing of Debbie but is saddened that he doesn't remember caring for her. Pam arrives to accompany him back to Fangtasia, and Sookie gets ready for work.

As Sookie tells Sam about the previous day's unusual events, she learns for the first time that the shifters at Hotshot are not werewolves as she believed but werepanthers, and that Felton Norris is in love with Crystal. Sam and Sookie rush to Hotshot to confront Calvin with the evidence of the panther print, and he leads them to Felton's home. Jason is found imprisoned and weak after being repeatedly bitten by his rival. As they leave with Sookie's injured brother, Calvin assures them that Felton will be punished and that Calvin will help Jason during the next full moon, when Jason will find out if he's been turned into a werepanther by Felton's bites.

Sookie and Sam get Jason to her house, where she puts him in the shower, feeds him, and then sends him to bed. Sitting at the kitchen table to talk with Sam, she spots a check from Eric for fifty thousand dollars.

THURSDAY, JANUARY 6. After Sookie calls the police to let them know Jason has returned, Andy Bellefleur and Alcee Beck arrive to question him. She and Jason stick to the story that he was knocked out and taken from outside his home and then just dumped in Sookie's yard with no memory of what had happened or where he had been. Sookie takes Jason to his own home to recuperate. Eric visits later that night and questions Sookie about their time together and why he found brain tissue on his sleeve. While he is still at her home, one of Alcide's pack members, Amanda, arrives to question Sookie about the apparent disappearance of Debbie. While they talk, Eric explores the house. When Amanda leaves, he tells Sookie she should destroy her old coat and get another.

FRIDAY, JANUARY 7. Sookie is not surprised to receive a cranberry red coat from Eric.

The Secret Dialogues of Bill and Eric

To: WILLIAM COMPTON,
AREA FIVE INVESTIGATOR

BILL,

PER SOPHIE-ANNE'S ORDERS I HAVE CONTACTED SEVERAL VAMPIRES I KNOW IN PERU AND ARRANGED YOUR SAFE PASSAGE. YOU WILL BE MET AT THE AIRPORT IN LIMA. AFTER THAT, I BELIEVE YOU HAVE MADE YOUR OWN ARRANGEMENTS.

MERRY CHRISTMAS AND HAPPY NEW YEAR. I MUST SAY THAT I AM SURPRISED THAT YOU ARE NOT SPENDING THE HOLIDAYS WITH SOOKIE. HUMANS HOLD THIS TIME IN SUCH REGARD.

ERIC NORTHMAN,
SHERIFF OF AREA FIVE

~ ~ ~

To: Eric Northman,
Sheriff of Area Five

Thank you for your prompt attention. I'm certain our queen appreciates it. You've often said you enjoy having people in your debt, so perhaps you can use this to your advantage.

Since I imagine you've never celebrated Christian holidays, I'm surprised by your well wishes.

William Compton

~ ~ ~

To: WILLIAM COMPTON

ONLY A FOOL WOULD USE AN ASSIGNMENT FROM THE QUEEN AS LEVERAGE, AND AS YOU KNOW, I AM NO FOOL. SHE SEEMS CONVINCED THAT YOUR DATABASE WILL BE NOT ONLY A VALUABLE TOOL IN HER BUSINESS DEALINGS BUT ALSO A PROFITABLE ENTERPRISE IN GENERAL. CONGRATULATIONS, BILL, YOU'RE NOW A BONA FIDE COMPUTER WHATEVER-YOU-ARE. GOOD TO SEE THOSE NIGHT CLASSES PAID OFF.

As for my holiday wishes, never let it be said that I cannot adapt to my environment. Christian holidays are important to humans—such as Sookie. I wonder how she'll be celebrating? Rumor has it you two are no longer involved, so perhaps I'll drop by to make certain she's not alone for the holidays.

All my best,
Eric

~ ~ ~

To: Eric Northman,
Sheriff of Area Five

Dear Eric,

Fuck off.

Bill

Dead as a Doornail

Timeline

TUESDAY, JANUARY 25, 2005. Sookie drives her brother, Jason, who may be a werepanther as a result of being attacked by Felton Norris, out to Hotshot, leaving him with Calvin Norris, who will guide him through his first change. Sookie can tell his eyes are different before she leaves.

WEDNESDAY, JANUARY 26. Jason returns to Sookie's house the next morning, almost exhilarated by his new experience. Although at first he becomes ill at the sight of food, she is ultimately relieved that he seems able to handle the changes in his life. Working the late shift at Merlotte's, Sookie is surprised to see her friend Tara sitting with an unfamiliar vampire named Mickey. Since Sam is out enjoying the moon, Terry is left in charge of the bar, and he and Sookie work together to relieve a Drainer of her cache of vampire blood and send her from the bar.

THURSDAY, JANUARY 27. Claudine arrives at Merlotte's with the upsetting news that Calvin Norris has been shot and seriously wounded, and that apparently a shooter is targeting shifters. As Sookie and Sam leave the bar after closing up, Sam is shot in the leg.

FRIDAY, JANUARY 28. Laid low by his broken leg and fearing to expose any other shifters, Sam asks Sookie to visit Fangtasia to bargain with Eric for the loan of a bartender. Eric sends vampire Charles Twining back to Bon Temps with Sookie. Hearing that Mickey came into Merlotte's, Eric warns her that Mickey is a rogue and to stay away from him.

SATURDAY, JANUARY 29. The next day at Merlotte's, Sookie is visited by private investigators Jack Leeds and Lily Bard Leeds, who want to question her about the disappearance of Debbie Pelt. Sookie agrees to talk with them at her home the next day.

Jason and Sookie go to the hospital in Grainger to visit the wounded Calvin. The werepanthers keeping guard over their packmaster keep Jason out but allow Sookie in the room. She is upset at the seriousness of his injuries but is horrified when Calvin tells her the Hotshot shifters suspect that Jason is the sniper. He reassures her that he has ordered that nothing be done to Jason, but Sookie realizes that to save her brother, she must find the shooter before the next full moon.

Alcide comes by Sookie's house with the news of the death of Colonel Flood and invites her to attend his funeral the next day. She tells Alcide of the visit of the detectives, warning him that the Pelt family is looking into Debbie's disappearance.

SUNDAY, JANUARY 30. When the detectives arrive, Sookie is surprised at how much they know about her relationship with Debbie, but she is straightforward about her dislike of the shifter. They leave with no apparent reason to suspect her, and Alcide arrives to pick her up for the funeral.

Once at the church for the service, Sookie realizes that her attending with Alcide has a larger import within the pack. She learns from Christine Larrabee, wife of the former packmaster and escorted by Alcide's father, Jackson Herveaux, that her appearance with Alcide signifies her support of his father in his bid for packmaster. An angry Sookie confronts Alcide with the deception but remains at the service to honor Colonel Flood. Sookie also comes to the notice of Patrick Furnan, the other candidate for packmaster. A tall, handsome bald man at the service catches Sookie's eye.

That evening at work, Sam asks Sookie if Charles Twining can stay at her house, since the bar does not have an adequate light-tight space. Tara and Mickey arrive at the bar, and Sookie has an angry confrontation with Mickey.

Sookie is asleep when Charles awakens her with the news of a prowler and slips outside. She turns on the porch light to see that Charles has captured a furious Bill Compton. Returning to bed, she is awakened again by Claudine with the news that her house is on fire. Charles kills the man who apparently started the fire, and the fire department is able to save her house. It appears that the man is a member of the Fellowship of the Sun. With Sookie's home seriously damaged, Sookie and Charles go home with Bill for the rest of the night.

MONDAY, JANUARY 31. Sookie's insurance agent, Greg Aubert, arrives to assess the damage, the first of a steady stream of visitors, including Tray Dawson, who's been sent by Calvin Norris with a message of support and an offer of his home while he is in the hospital. Sookie does not want to be obligated but worries where she will stay until her home is repaired.

Sookie is dismayed when the family of the dead arsonist comes to see her at work. They struggle with his guilt but leave when the evidence seems overwhelming. Sam comforts Sookie, and they have a passionate moment, which is interrupted by Bill, who fights with the injured Sam. When Sookie is harmed trying to stop the fight, an angry Bill leaves, and she decides to spend the night at Jason's.

TUESDAY, FEBRUARY 1. Terry Bellefleur has offered to help Sookie by demolishing the fire-damaged areas of her house and disposing of the refuse for a nominal fee. They are working at her house in the morning when Alcide arrives, anxious after hearing about the fire. Contractors Randall and Delia Shurtliff come by to arrange the repairs, and after they leave, Alcide asks Sookie to move in with him for the duration of the renovation. She refuses, admitting that she shot Debbie in self-defense, and although he claims it doesn't matter, she tells him that now is not the time to consider starting a relationship.

Sookie is upset when Bill brings a date, Selah Pumphrey, to the bar that evening. She is further disturbed when Eric arrives, angry that Charles had not rescued Sookie from the burning house. Eric tries again to get Sookie to tell him what happened between them when he had amnesia, but she is able to distract him. Sookie agrees when Sam offers her one of his rental houses until her own is repaired. She is pleased to have to spend only one more night at her brother's place. She is surprised to find Crystal at Jason's but relieved that the female werepanther doesn't believe Jason is involved in the shootings.

WEDNESDAY, FEBRUARY 2. Sookie salvages enough linens and kitchenware to move into the duplex on Berry Street and makes her first meal in her temporary home. She visits Calvin at the Grainger hospital and decides to stop at the library on the way back. Out in the parking lot, Sookie feels another presence and ducks just as a shot rings out, creasing her shoulder. She wakes up in the hospital to her brother's voice and later gets a visit from Detective Andy Bellefleur. Bill arrives to watch over her and spends the night.

THURSDAY, FEBRUARY 3. Sookie is released from the hospital the next morning and is mystified to find that her bill has been paid. She is just realizing that she has no way to get home when Claudine's brother, Claude, arrives to take her back to the duplex. Tara comes to visit, and Sookie is horrified when she learns how Mickey is controlling her terrified friend. Tara begs Sookie not to interfere. When Tara leaves, Sookie realizes that she has only one alternative, and she calls Eric, who comes over immediately. Sookie tells Eric the full story of Tara's problem with Mickey. She is not surprised that the price for the favor is the truth of the time they spent together. Sookie tells him all they did and what he promised her while he had amnesia. After a few minutes of stunned silence while he processes the information, Eric calls Mickey's maker, Salome, and asks her to deal with Mickey, since he is acting against their laws and without permission in Eric's territory. Eric is beginning to get amorous when a furious Mickey arrives with a beaten Tara and attacks, striking Eric with a rock. Sookie is able to revive Eric but is forced to let Mickey into the house when he threatens to kill Tara. Mickey attacks Sookie, but she is able to rescind the invitation. He is forced to leave and answer his maker's call. Eric calls Salome back to inform her of Mickey's disobedience and then calls Bill to help repair the apartment.

FRIDAY, FEBRUARY 4. Sookie and Sam realize that the shooter has to be a supernatural being of some kind. They decide to investigate the sites of the earlier shootings after work with Sam in bloodhound form. They are searching the alley across from the Sonic, where the first shooting took place, when they are interrupted by Andy Bellefleur. As Sookie is arguing with Andy, Sam barks to let them know someone else has arrived. Sweetie Des Arts, the new cook at Merlotte's, is in the alley with a rifle pointed at them. She confesses to being the shooter, admitting that she has murdered many other shifters in retaliation for being attacked by a bitten Were, which causes her to partially shift each full moon. She plans to kill Sookie and the dog, but when Sweetie hears a noise and turns to fire, Andy is able to pull his gun and kill her. Sookie rushes over to see whom Sweetie shot and finds a seriously injured Dawson, whom Calvin had told to follow and protect her. Sookie is able to keep him alive until the ambulance arrives.

SATURDAY, FEBRUARY 5. Alcide comes by the duplex in the morning to invite Sookie to the Shreveport packmaster contest, but she is too weary to appreciate his presence and sends him away, telling him to leave the invitation. After finding a note on her door from Sam telling her not to come in for her evening shift, she decides to visit Calvin, who has been released from the hospital.

Sookie prepares a chicken dish and biscuits to take to Calvin, and she is surprised to find a crowd already at his house to welcome him home. After being introduced around, she is led to his bedroom, where he is eating the food she prepared for him. As she is leaving, she finds Patrick Furnan—the other contestant for Shreveport packmaster, who has also been visiting Calvin—waiting for her with a strange warning about her being unprotected. Once in her temporary home and able to relax, Sookie considers the shifter shootings and calls Andy to question him as to whether all the bullets matched.

SUNDAY, FEBRUARY 6. Alcide calls to tell Sookie that the packmaster contest is being held that afternoon in Shreveport. When she arrives at the deserted industrial park, she is relieved to see Claudine and Claude in attendance and stands with them. Before the contest begins, Sookie is surprised to see the handsome bald man she had noticed at the funeral and realizes he is the referee, finally "hearing" that his name is Quinn. As the contestants perform the second of three tests, Sookie realizes that Furnan is cheating. She calls out her accusation, and the contest is halted. When investigation proves her to be correct, the pack sends out the non-pack members, so they can vote on whether the contest will continue to the final test. As they wait, Quinn questions Sookie and learns from Claude that she is a telepath. The pack decides that the final test, one of battle, will continue but must be a decisive victory. Quinn asks Sookie to enter the cage where the final fight will occur to try to determine whether Furnan plans to somehow cheat again. He guarantees her safety, but Furnan lunges at her, and her leg is slightly injured as Quinn pulls her out of the cage. As he administers first aid, a definite attraction springs up between them, and he promises he will see her again at a better time. Furnan defeats and kills Herveaux in the final contest and is declared packmaster. A devastated Alcide rejects Sookie, and she leaves, realizing he somehow blames her for the outcome.

At work that evening, Sookie is surprised by a visit from Bubba with a cryptic message from Eric. As she is talking with Charles, she suddenly realizes that he has been lying about his past. He apologizes as he tries to kill her, but she is able to stuff her silver chain in his mouth, and the male patrons at the bar come to her aid, restraining him and staking him at his request. Charles's body has already flaked away when Eric dashes into the bar to save Sookie. Eric explains that Charles was sent by a vampire named Hot Rain to kill Sookie in an effort to punish Eric for the death of Long Shadow, who was staked the previous summer for embezzling from Fangtasia. As Sookie recounts the events of the day, they both agree she is a lucky woman.

The Secret Dialogues of Bill and Eric

Phone: Bill calling Eric.

BILL: "Eric, I understand one of your vampires is staying at Sookie's house."

ERIC: "I loaned my new bartender to Sam Merlotte. So he's staying at Sookie's? Good. I want him to keep an eye on her."

BILL: "Why?"

ERIC: "I have my reasons."

BILL: "Well, he has not done a good job 'keeping an eye on her.' Her house was set on fire last night."

ERIC: "Did she get out?"

BILL: "Yes. But she was not rescued by your 'Charles.' She was rescued by a fairy. She was able to wake Sookie and get her out of the house."

ERIC: "She?" *Pause.* "A *female* fairy. Sookie certainly has interesting friends."

BILL: "Charles did manage to kill the culprit. He was carrying a Fellowship membership card."

ERIC: "I see. I'll need to have a talk with Charles."

Phone: Eric calling Bill.

ERIC: "Bill, I understand that Sookie is no longer staying at your house."

BILL: "True. We had a little . . . misunderstanding."

ERIC: "So you brought a date into Merlotte's."

BILL: "I am free to see whomever I please."

ERIC: "And who is it you are pleasing, Bill? She was attractive in her own way."

BILL: "No one you know."

ERIC: "It's no matter. She was not my type. Where is Sookie staying?"

BILL: "Her brother's."

ERIC: "I doubt that will last very long. Please keep me informed as to where she winds up while her house is being repaired. Charles remains at your house?"

BILL: "Yes. I have a place for him to sleep."

ERIC: "Good. Have you seen Mickey?"

BILL: "I've heard he's in town."

ERIC: "He's involved with Sookie's friend Tara."

BILL: "That won't end well."

ERIC: "No, I'm quite certain it won't."

Phone: Bill calling Eric.

BILL: "Eric, Sookie has been shot."

ERIC: "Is she all right?"

BILL: "She will recover. I spent the night with her in the hospital."

ERIC: "Just to keep her safe, I suppose."

BILL: "Sookie is staying at one of Sam Merlotte's rental houses. I believe that a fairy picked her up from the hospital."

ERIC: "The same fairy who rescued her from the fire?"

BILL: "I don't believe so. From all reports, this one was very much a male."

ERIC: "Very much a male?"

BILL: "Apparently a quite attractive male."

ERIC: "So yet another fairy. Interesting."

Phone: Eric calling Bill.

ERIC: "Bill, I'm at Merlotte's rental with Sookie. Mickey broke in. He was angry because I called Salome."

BILL: "Is Sookie all right?"

ERIC: "We ask each other that a lot, don't we? Yes, Sookie is fine. She had to invite him in because he had her friend, but once they were both inside she rescinded his invitation. I've already let Salome know that he is on the run."

BILL: "She'll have him soon."

ERIC: "Undoubtedly. Right now, we need supplies to repair the window for the night."

BILL: "I'll be there shortly."

Phone: Eric calling Bill.

ERIC: "Bill, have you heard anything about Sookie in an alley with a naked man?"

BILL: "Yes."

ERIC: "And?"

BILL: "And what? Sookie was in an alley with a naked man. And the woman who was shooting the shifters. I assume the naked man was a shifter as well. There was also a dog, so Sam was there, too."

Phone: Eric calling Bill.

ERIC: "Bill, are you in Bon Temps?"

BILL: "No, I'm with Selah in Clarice."

ERIC: "I need information from your database."

BILL: "I have my laptop. Give me a few minutes."

ERIC: "Look up Charles Twining."

BILL: "Charles? Didn't you . . . ?"

ERIC: "Now, Bill."

BILL: "Charles Twining. His sire was . . . Eric, his sire is dead, but he is pledged to Hot Rain."

ERIC: "Goddammit!"

BILL: "How could you have sent him to Sookie without checking him out?"

ERIC: "I did. I called Russell. He thought Charles had been at his home. Fucking idiot!"

BILL: "You or Russell?"

ERIC: "I'm sending Bubba to Merlotte's to warn Sookie."

BILL: "I'll return to Merlotte's immediately."

ERIC: "No. She just needs to stay clear of Charles until I deal with Hot Rain. Killing Charles after Long Shadow's death would not go well for either of us. I'm calling his ruler now to advise them that he has gone against the ruling and sought revenge."

"One Word Answer"

Timeline

THURSDAY, MARCH 3, 2005. Sookie is out in her yard at midnight raking up bush clippings with Bubba when a black limousine pulls into her drive. Bubba immediately vanishes into the woods, and Sookie can only hope that he has left to find Bill, her nearest neighbor, as she faces the large man who emerges from the limo. From his brain pattern Sookie can tell that the man is some sort of supernatural creature. The stranger, Mr. Cataliades, informs her that she is the beneficiary of a legacy from her cousin Hadley, who had not only become a vampire—and personal favorite of Sophie-Anne Leclerq, Queen of Louisiana—but met her final death a month prior. Mr. Cataliades summons his driver, a vampire named Waldo, from the car at Sookie's request. Bubba returns with Bill, who joins Sookie in questioning Mr. Cataliades and Waldo as to the circumstances of Hadley's death. Waldo claims that he witnessed Hadley's murder at the hands of members of the Fellowship of the Sun, but Sookie soon suspects him of doing the deed himself, an accusation confirmed by Mr. Cataliades. He reveals that Sophie-Anne has realized Waldo's duplicity and sent him on the trip to Bon Temps so that Sookie can stake him. She refuses, telling him she will send Waldo back to the queen instead. Heartbroken that his queen knows of his betrayal, certain her torture will make him wish for death, Waldo attacks Sookie, knowing that Bill and Bubba will stop him and put an end to his existence. As Waldo flakes away in Sookie's yard, the queen herself steps from the limo. She questions Sookie as to the events of the night, wondering if Sookie set it all up to play out just as it did. Sookie carefully responds with enigmatic one-word answers, and the queen and Mr. Cataliades are soon on their way back to New Orleans.

The Secret Dialogues of Bill and Eric

Phone: Eric calling Bill.

ERIC: "Bill, Bubba has told me that Sophie-Anne was at Sookie's house, and the two of you killed a wrinkled, red-eyed vampire. What the hell is he talking about?"

BILL: "Sophie-Anne was at Sookie's house, and Bubba and I killed a wrinkled, red-eyed vampire."

ERIC: "Bill . . ."

BILL: "Cataliades arrived to inform Sookie of her cousin Hadley's death."

ERIC: "The queen's favorite was Sookie's cousin?"

BILL: "Yes."

ERIC: "Why wasn't this information in your vaunted database?"

BILL: "Including information about the queen's favorite didn't seem like a good idea, Eric."

ERIC: "I see your point. A red-eyed, wrinkly . . . Wait, you and Bubba killed Waldo?"

BILL: "Yes."

ERIC: "May I ask why?"

BILL: "He killed Hadley. The queen brought him here so that Sookie could exact vengeance."

ERIC: "But you did it instead."

BILL: "Sookie could not bring herself to do it and was sending him back to the queen. He attacked her, and I took care of it for her."

ERIC: "I thought Sophie-Anne was there."

BILL: "She was. She remained in the car until after we staked Waldo."

ERIC: "Interesting."

BILL: "Indeed. Sookie knew she was in the car. I cannot help but feel that Sookie was actually in control of the situation more than we realized at the time."

ERIC: "It wouldn't surprise me. She has unexpected depths."

BILL: "Indeed."

Definitely Dead

Timeline

MONDAY, MARCH 14, 2005. Sookie spends the early part of the day at Alfred Cumberland's studio in Shreveport, posing for photographs with Claude, who is building his portfolio for the Mr. Romance contest. She is pleasantly surprised to see Maria-Star Cooper, the Were she took to the hospital after the skirmish with the witches at Bill's house, fully recovered and working as Al's assistant, although Sookie experiences a flicker of pain when she realizes that Maria-Star and Alcide Herveaux are now dating.

After the photo shoot, Sookie hurries home to work the evening shift at Merlotte's, where she speaks briefly with Bill Compton, who asks if he can accompany her to New Orleans when she travels there to wrap up the estate of her late cousin, Hadley. Catholic priest Dan Riordan and Episcopal priest Kempton Littrell are also in the bar for their biweekly dinner, and Sookie is disconcerted when the priests call her away from Bill's table, telling her that they were concerned that she was consorting with an "imp of hell." Before leaving the bar, Father Riordan informs her that he has been contacted by the Pelts, who are searching for information about Debbie and want to meet with Sookie. She denies their request.

TUESDAY, MARCH 15. Quinn walks into Merlotte's shortly before last call and tells Sookie he'd like to speak with her about both business and pleasure, and she agrees to let him follow her home after closing. He tells her that he's wanted to see her again and asks her on a date. She happily agrees. He then tells her that the vampire Queen of Louisiana has asked him to request Sookie's services for her own use at the upcoming vampire regional summit. The queen outranks Eric, who has also requested Sookie's presence. She unhappily acknowledges to herself that she will have to deliver the bad news to Eric. She and Quinn end their meeting by planning their date for the following Friday.

WEDNESDAY, MARCH 16. Pam calls Sookie at Merlotte's and informs her that Eric wants to see her on Friday night. Sookie declines, telling Pam that she already has plans. Pam is gleeful that she gets to let Eric know that not only has Sookie refused his summons but she has a date. Andy Bellefleur stops Sookie on her way back from the phone call to ask a favor: He is proposing to his girlfriend, Halleigh Robinson, and wants Sookie to hide the ring box in Halleigh's food order. Sookie unabashedly eavesdrops as Halleigh finds the box and eagerly accepts Andy's proposal.

As Sookie is washing dishes at home after work, she realizes that there is something out in her woods when all the night cries from the insects and frogs come to an abrupt stop. She locks her doors but holds her ground, refusing to panic. Only when the sounds resume outside does she relax enough to sleep.

THURSDAY, MARCH 17. Sookie leaves the house early to go to the grocery store and to Tara's Togs to get a new outfit for her date. Once at Tara's shop, she waits while Portia Bellefleur makes plans with Tara to outfit a double wedding. Not only are Andy and Halleigh getting married; so are Portia and her fiancé, Glen. After an excited Portia leaves with a catalog, Tara happily helps Sookie pick out an outfit. Sookie then heads to the store and back home in time to fix lunch for Jason. Her brother arrives and tells her that Crystal has suffered a miscarriage. Crystal refuses to go to the hospital because she is afraid of the personnel noticing the advanced healing abilities of the shifters. Sookie calls Dr. Ludwig, the physician who treated her for the maenad poisoning and who attended the packmaster contest, and arranges to have the doctor meet with Jason and head over to his house.

Sookie is dismayed to find Father Riordan waiting for her with the Pelts in Sam's office when she gets to work. She is once again forced to deny being involved with Debbie's disappearance. Sam gets a phone call letting him know Holly's son is missing from his school, and Sookie hurries over to see if she can help with her special ability. She finally locates the injured child in a trash bin, where he was hidden by the custodian after she thought she had accidentally killed him. Returning to the bar, Sookie is suspicious of the new barmaid, Tanya Grissom, whom Sam has called in to cover for Holly.

Sookie gets another visitor that night in the person of Calvin Norris, Crystal's uncle and the leader of the Hotshot panthers. They discuss Calvin's interest in Sookie, and he reluctantly acknowledges that they are not meant to be.

FRIDAY, MARCH 18. Dressed and ready for her date with Quinn, Sookie is surprised when Eric arrives on her doorstep. He is not pleased to see her looking beautiful for another man, and they are arguing when Quinn arrives. He not only establishes his interest in Sookie but calmly informs Eric that the queen intends for Sookie to be in her retinue at the vampire summit. They leave a fuming Eric and head for the theater in Shreveport. Sookie and Quinn enjoy each other's company, and Sookie is pleased that she can read only admiration from Quinn, who apparently has no fear of her gift. As they are leaving the theater after the show, two young half-changed werewolves attack them in the parking lot. Sookie is slightly injured as Quinn fights them off. The police arrive. They are questioned by the police, who are somewhat uneasy about the power that Quinn has displayed. After their questioning, Quinn takes Sookie to a werewolf bar, the Hair of the Dog, where he challenges the local pack over the attack on Sookie, who has been named a friend of the pack. As they return to the car, the attraction between them explodes, and Sookie decides that she needs to go more carefully with Quinn.

SATURDAY, MARCH 19. Sookie doesn't hear from Quinn the next day but does read in the newspaper that two juveniles were found strangled in the Shreveport holding cells—Sookie and Quinn's attackers had been silenced. A lovely female vampire comes into Merlotte's that night and introduces herself as Felicia, the new bartender at Fangtasia. She informs Sookie that Pam has told her to beg for her mercy, as Fangtasia bartenders don't last long around Sookie.

SUNDAY, MARCH 20. Sookie is suspicious and displeased when Tanya Grissom arrives at her house uninvited and makes obvious overtures of friendship. Sookie's inhospitable attitude soon sends the shifter away, but her negative feelings are soothed when Quinn calls and they set up another date for the following night. Much to her surprise, Mr. Cataliades soon arrives, expecting her to be ready to accompany him back to New Orleans to settle her late cousin Hadley's estate. He is equally surprised that his niece Gladiola did not deliver his message and sets out with his other niece, Diantha, to find Glad's body, knowing that only death would have kept her from her task. Diantha locates Gladiola, cloven in two, at the edge of the woods, and Diantha and her uncle burn the body in Sookie's driveway. Sookie goes to Sam's trailer to arrange the time off and leaves the two supes to their solemn pyre. Remembering that Bill has asked if he can join her when she travels to New Orleans, Sookie calls him to let him know they will be leaving soon. As they travel, Sookie tells her companions about the Were attack in Shreveport and about the visit she and Quinn paid to Hair of the Dog. Bill is unhappy because it's clear Quinn is becoming a part of Sookie's life. When Sookie asks Mr. Cataliades's opinion, he suggests that Quinn knows that the Shreveport pack may already be planning a challenge to the new packmaster.

Arriving at Hadley's apartment in New Orleans, Bill again offers to help. Exhausted, Sookie just wants to be left alone to rest.

MONDAY, MARCH 21. The landlady and apartment owner, Amelia Broadway, who is also a practicing witch, startles Sookie awake. She assures Sookie that wards and a stasis spell (which has kept the place just as it was on the day Hadley died) have protected the apartment. After Amelia returns to her own apartment downstairs, Sookie begins to explore and is disturbed when she finds bloodstained towels in the bathroom hamper. She opens the hall closet and discovers a man's body. Realizing the body must have been there since Hadley died, she goes in search of Amelia to tell her they have a problem. They have just decided that the stasis spell has kept the body from decomposing when Sookie notices the man's fingers moving. She realizes they have a rising vampire to deal with. Amelia just has time to call for help before they are attacked and must fight for their lives against the hungry new vampire, Jake Purifoy, a Were. Both are seriously wounded before they are rescued by the vampire police.

While she is awaiting treatment at the hospital, Sookie is surprised by Eric's arrival. She accuses him of following her. He reminds her of the bond that exists between them because he has given her his blood. He also tells her that he has met with the queen to negotiate for Sookie's services at the vampire summit. As they are talking, Bill suddenly appears, much to Eric's displeasure. When Bill accuses Eric of tiring Sookie and asks him to leave, an angry Eric retaliates by forcing Bill to disclose what Eric discovered when he met with Sophie-Anne. Bill confesses that he was sent to Bon Temps by the queen to attract Sookie's notice and even to seduce her in an effort to gain the use of her gift. Her heart broken by Bill's betrayal, a physically and emotionally devastated Sookie stumbles back to the apartment.

TUESDAY, MARCH 22. Claudine and Amelia are at Sookie's bedside when she awakes in deep emotional pain. Claudine reveals that she is Sookie's fairy godmother, sworn to protect her, and tells Amelia the reason for Sookie's unhappiness. They decide they need to determine how Jake was killed and turned, so Amelia suggests an ectoplasmic reconstruction of the events on the day of Hadley's death. Amelia leaves to make preparations, and Claudine explains to Sookie that she must keep her appointment with the queen that evening. They leave to shop for the perfect dress and accessories.

Sookie, correctly clad, arrives at Sophie-Anne's headquarters and is admitted to the queen's presence by her twin bodyguards, Sigebert and Wybert. The queen introduces her new husband, the King of Arkansas, Peter Threadgill. His personal bodyguard, Jade Flower, stands guard behind her king with a long sword strapped to her back. Sophie-Anne's personal bodyguard, Andre Paul, armed with a saber and a gun, stands guard behind his queen as well. As Sookie and the queen discuss the conversion of Jake Purifoy, Sookie tells Sophie-Anne about the planned ectoplasmic reconstruction. The queen agrees to pay the expenses of the ritual and declares that she wishes to witness it. She inquires briefly after Bill, and Sookie rather sharply informs her that they are no longer a couple. As they ready themselves to go, the king insists that Jade Flower accompany Sookie and Sophie-Anne.

Amelia is waiting at the apartment with three other witches, who will help her with the ectoplasmic reconstruction. The spectators watch in amazement as the ghostly events of the day Hadley died appear before them. They see the attack on Jake but are not able to identify the attacker. They do, however, witness Hadley's desperate attempt to save him by making him a vampire. It is apparent that someone wanted Hadley accused of his death, and the atmosphere is getting tense when Quinn suddenly arrives. When alone in Hadley's apartment with Sookie and Andre, Sophie-Anne tells Sookie that a jealous Hadley stole a valuable bracelet, a gift to the queen from her new husband. The queen will face political and personal disaster if the bracelet is not restored to her before the ball scheduled in two days' time. Sophie-Anne tells Sookie that they must pretend that she and Andre had sex as Sophie-Anne watched, to justify this private meeting to Jade Flower. As they exchange an uncomfortable embrace to add evidence to the illusion, Andre reveals to Sookie that she has a trace of fairy blood. Although Sophie-Anne has instructed Sookie not to reveal any details, Sookie carefully tells Quinn that she did not have sex with Andre, and they have a romantic moment together.

WEDNESDAY, MARCH 23. Sookie begins to pack up Hadley's possessions and is delighted when Quinn reappears to help. They make love that afternoon, but while they are relaxing afterward, Sookie suddenly senses danger. They are attacked and kidnapped by a group of werewolves who subdue the powerful Quinn with a stun gun.

The kidnappers force Sookie and Quinn into a van but do not seem to consider her a threat. She is able to locate Quinn's cell phone and call for help. The kidnappers quickly pull over and search them, binding Quinn's legs before starting off again. Because Quinn has undergone a partial change during the fight, Sookie encourages him to bite through the duct tape binding her wrists. She is able to get free and to unbind his hands and feet. As Sookie stabs the Were in the passenger seat with a screwdriver, Quinn opens the door of the van, and they escape into the swamp. They only stop to rest when they are certain they have lost their kidnappers. Sookie suddenly realizes who is behind the abduction and explains to Quinn, who shifts fully into his tiger persona and leads her through the swamp to a house where they find the kidnappers' van. Looking through the window, Sookie realizes that her feelings were correct when she sees the Pelt family. Sookie and Quinn attack the house and are soon joined by Eric and the queen's guard, Rasul. Sookie confronts the furious family and tells them the truth about the death of their daughter Debbie. Reluctantly recognizing that Sookie was acting in self-defense, Gordon and Barbara Pelt, much to their daughter Sandra's dismay, promise not to harass Sookie further. Sookie also learns from them that Tanya Grissom is a relative who was sent to spy on her and find out more about Debbie's death.

THURSDAY, MARCH 24. Mr. Cataliades accompanies Sookie to Hadley's bank to receive the contents of her cousin's safe-deposit box, but the missing bracelet is not there, as he obviously hoped. Sookie returns to the apartment to find a message on the answering machine: The queen expects to see Sookie that night at the spring ball. She debates whether or not she should go. Continuing to pack, she hears a strange noise when she shakes a can of coffee and realizes she has found the queen's bracelet. Sookie knows she must attend the ball after all and goes down to Amelia's to borrow a dress and shoes.

Quinn and Sookie arrive at the queen's party house, a former monastery. Both are immediately uneasy as they observe the extreme security and the unusual outfits of the king's guards. As Sookie and Quinn greet Mr. Cataliades, she tells him she has heard that someone with a long sword was seen on her way to Bon Temps, letting him draw his own conclusions about who killed his niece Gladiola. Sookie is able to secretly pass the missing bracelet to the queen, much to her relief. As Sophie-Anne joins her new husband in a dance, he notices the bracelet and is obviously furious. Sookie learns from Quinn that the bracelet had been a part of the king's marriage gift to the queen. If he'd been able to prove she'd given it to a lover, he could have taken her kingdom and everything in it for his own.

Thwarted, Peter Threadgill and his people resort to violence. Sookie and Quinn are enjoying a dance when a severed head flies by them. Violent chaos erupts, and Sookie and Quinn become separated during the melee. As she struggles to flee the room, Sookie is forced to fight for her life when she is attacked by an enraged Jade Flower, mysteriously missing one leg. Sookie is rescued by Bill, who beheads the Asian vampire. Fleeing through the queen's bedroom, Sookie flips on the lights and sees a seriously injured Sophie-Anne lying on the bed, with Andre and Peter facing each other across it. Andre immediately shoots Peter twice in the face and then receives permission from his queen to finish the job. Sookie continues out the door before seeing how he does the deed. Once she is out on the lawn, Quinn joins her in tiger form, and they escape over the wall of the monastery. Andre follows them, carrying the injured queen, and they all pile into the queen's limo.

The queen expresses her gratitude to Sookie for the return of the bracelet. The limo drops Sookie and Quinn off at Hadley's apartment, where Amelia waits with a large black-and-white cat. She sheepishly admits that she and Bob, one of the witches who helped with the reconstruction, got a little carried away during sex and that he is now the cat. She needs to get away from New Orleans for a time.

An exhausted Sookie has just finished her shower, and Quinn is taking his turn, when there is a soft knock at the door. Bill is there and asks to talk with her. Sookie listens as he explains that although the queen sent him, when he came to know Sookie he began to truly love her. However, she no longer feels she can trust Bill and tells him that just saying the words will not restore her feelings for him. She leaves him to return to Quinn, and as they lie in bed together, she puts her head on his chest as he sleeps and listens to his heart beating.

FRIDAY, MARCH 25. Quinn departs early the next morning for his next job, leaving behind a spicy note. Sookie and Amelia pack up for Bon Temps, and as she heads home, Sookie is optimistic about the future.

The Secret Dialogues of Bill and Eric

Phone: Eric calling Bill.

ERIC: "Bill, is Sookie going to New Orleans to see about her cousin's estate?"

BILL: "Why don't you ask her yourself?"

ERIC: "Since you are such a good neighbor and keep such a close eye on her, I thought you might know."

BILL: "I don't."

Phone: Eric calling Bill.

ERIC: "I thought you'd want to know that Sookie finally arrived back at Hadley's apartment safely."

BILL: "I am aware, although *safely* is a relative term. Why have you done this, Eric?"

ERIC: "She deserved to know."

BILL: "So you told her the moment you found out. If you wanted to destroy whatever chance I had with Sookie, couldn't you have at least waited until she was not bleeding in a hospital?"

ERIC: "I did not do it to—"

BILL: "Bullshit. You did it to make her hate me so that you could proceed with her without my interference. Unfortunately for you, there is already another man interested in Sookie, one who is not constrained by vampire politics as I am."

ERIC: "Quinn."

BILL: "Yes, Quinn. He should give you a run for your money, and at this moment, I can only wish him well."

Phone: Eric calling Bill.

ERIC: "Bill, you may be interested in knowing that an ectoplasmic reconstruction was performed at Hadley's apartment last night to try to discover who turned the Were, Jake Purifoy."

BILL: "I know."

ERIC: "You seem to know a lot, Bill."

BILL: "Does that bother you, Eric?"

ERIC: "It bothers me that you entered my territory on an assignment from the queen that I was not made aware of."

BILL: "You'll have to take that up with Sophie-Anne."

All Together Dead

Timeline

Though it would seem from the text that All Together Dead *begins around the third week in September, accurate continuity would have it start earlier—more like the second week.*

SATURDAY, SEPTEMBER 10, 2005. Sookie arrives at Fangtasia and is met by a happy Pam as they join the planning meeting for those who will attend the vampire summit in Rhodes. The death of the King of Arkansas, Peter Threadgill, and the destruction of New Orleans by Hurricane Katrina have had a profound financial effect on the empire of Sophie-Anne Leclerq, Queen of Louisiana. Eric, now one of the most powerful sheriffs in the state, is hosting the queen's representative, Andre Paul, as they plan the trip. Sookie learns that the queen will be facing a criminal suit filed by the former king's second-in-command, Jennifer Cater, who alleges that Sophie-Anne lured Peter to Louisiana to assassinate him. If she is found guilty, the queen could lose all she has. Bill Compton will be attending to promote the sale of his database in the hopes of replenishing the coffers of the cash-strapped queen. Jake Purifoy, the Were who was turned by Hadley, is also at the meeting and will be attending, much to Sookie's discomfort.

SUNDAY, SEPTEMBER 11. When she returns from attending a wedding shower for Halleigh Robinson, Sookie is delighted to find Quinn on her doorstep. Her understanding roommate, Amelia, leaves them alone, and Sookie and Quinn discuss their relationship and their need to spend more time together. Quinn tells her he has taken a month off after the summit and wants to spend it with Sookie in Bon Temps. That afternoon Sookie receives a call from her brother, Jason, inviting her to his wedding. He is marrying his shifter girlfriend, Crystal Norris. Sookie is apprehensive about the marriage, especially as it is taking place that same night. When Sookie, Quinn, and Amelia arrive at the wedding celebration, Sookie is surprised at the excited reaction of the shifters to the presence of Quinn.

To her dismay, she discovers that as Jason's only relative she must vouch for him in the marriage ceremony, just as Calvin vouches for Crystal. With many reservations, Sookie witnesses the wedding between the selfish Jason and the wayward, determined shifter he is marrying.

MONDAY, SEPTEMBER 12. Quinn leaves in the morning, and Sookie yawns her way through work after their late night at the wedding and later night together. Bill's girlfriend, Selah Pumphrey, comes in for lunch and accosts Sookie, accusing her of planning the trip to the summit with Bill so that she can get him back. Sookie's fairy godmother, Claudine, comes to Sookie's house that evening to express her misgivings about Sookie attending the summit.

TUESDAY, SEPTEMBER 13. In the morning, Sookie shops at Tara's Togs, where Eric has arranged a line of credit for her to buy suitable clothing for the trip. Later, she is surprised when Pam comes into Merlotte's to challenge her about her relationship with Eric. As Sookie readies to leave, Arlene expresses her distaste at Sookie's choice of company, and Sookie snaps at Arlene and stalks out, crying. Pam follows Sookie into the parking lot to continue their conversation, and a relieved Sookie learns that Pam and Eric had not known why the queen sent Bill to Bon Temps. Pam shares her history with Sookie and tells her how she was turned by Eric. Sookie is astonished when Pam pleads with her to have mercy on Eric. Pam believes he has deep feelings for Sookie. Both are startled when he unexpectedly appears. Eric abruptly dismisses Pam and begins to question Sookie about her relationship with Quinn. Sookie replies that since Eric had shown no interest in her over the past few months, she felt free to pursue a relationship with Quinn. Frustrated, Eric leaves.

THURSDAY, SEPTEMBER 22. Sookie boards the Anubis airplane and is greeted by the queen's lawyer, Mr. Cataliades, and his niece, Diantha. He introduces Sookie to the rude lawyer Johan Glassport, who will represent the queen in the murder case brought against her. Realizing that Sookie is a witness to the killing of Peter Threadgill, Glassport begins to question her intensely about the events of that night. Afterward, Sookie explores the plane and examines the coffins of the vampire contingent. Mr. Cataliades joins her and begins to brief her on what to expect at the summit in Rhodes. They arrive at the Pyramid of Gizeh hotel in the afternoon. Sookie is delighted when she telepathically locates Barry the Bellboy, who is attending as a member of the King of Texas's entourage. That evening, Sookie reports to the queen's room for instructions. Sophie-Anne is surprised and pleased when they are interrupted by a visit from Stan Davis, now King of Texas. As the queen and Stan converse, Barry and Sookie begin a wordless conversation that catches the attention of their employers. Sookie apologizes and asks if they can leave, since they are not needed during the visit. Barry and Sookie go to the lobby to practice combining their gifts to read the thoughts of those in the room. Sookie is suddenly confronted by a belligerent and threatening Jennifer Cater, who vows to take down Sophie-Anne and drain Sookie dry.

Quinn arrives and is greeted with delight by Sookie, much to Barry's dismay. Barry, who knows Quinn by reputation, pushes him to tell a mystified Sookie about his past. As they talk, they are joined by one of the most frightening women Sookie has ever seen. The woman identifies herself as Batanya and tells them she is the bodyguard hired to protect the King of Kentucky. She begins to complain to Quinn about the dangerous lack of security at the summit, but Quinn explains that he is not involved in that aspect of the meeting and tells her whom to see. When she leaves to return to her employer, Quinn explains that she is a Britlingen, an elite bodyguard brought at great expense from another dimension. Quinn leaves to set up an impromptu wedding, and Sookie and Barry are called back to serve their respective employers.

Sookie waits for the visitors to leave Sophie-Anne's suite before recounting the confrontation with Jennifer and the encounter with the Britlingen. The queen decides to call Jennifer and offers to negotiate with her. Jennifer agrees to see the queen, and after some dawdling, the party leaves to visit the room of the Arkansas contingent. Upon arriving at Jennifer's door, they realize that something is wrong. A quick reconnoiter shows that Jennifer and her companions have been brutally murdered. Hotel security is called, and as the queen and her entourage answer questions, a distraught man suddenly appears and identifies himself as Henrik Feith, the only survivor of the Arkansas contingent. He escaped the massacre because he went downstairs to make a complaint to the management. Sophie-Anne immediately offers the terrified man a place with the Louisiana party, and he leaves with Sigebert to go to the queen's suite to rest.

As the queen and her party continue downstairs, Mr. Cataliades recommends that Sophie-Anne marry immediately to form an alliance. Sookie suggests that the queen name Andre as King of Arkansas and marry him. Both vampires are pleased with the idea. They locate the booth in the convention hall where Bill is selling the database CDs, and Sookie gets to say a nervous hello to Russell Edgington, the King of Mississippi, who is getting married that evening to the King of Indiana, Bartlett Crowe. After Russell and Bart exchange vows—and blood—in a ceremony that Eric conducts, Sookie persuades Jake Purifoy to fill her in on Quinn's past and learns he became famous as a pit fighter. Forced to go to the vampires for help when his mother was brutally attacked and raped, he was contracted to fight for them for three years and was known as a most ferocious and successful fighter. Jake also tells her that the event employee who passed out potpourri bags for the wedding is Quinn's younger sister, Francine, a result of the rape. Disturbed by the story, Sookie leaves Jake to return to work for the queen. When Isaiah, the King of Kentucky, realizes that Sookie can sense his visually camouflaged Britlingens, he asks Sophie-Anne to dismiss her, so Sookie is sent to retrieve luggage that apparently belongs to the Louisiana party from down in the loading bay.

As Sookie turns to leave, she is approached by Andre and led into an isolated service corridor, where he informs her that she needs to be bound more tightly to either him or Sophie-Anne. He orders her to take his blood. She resists, and he is about to force her when Eric suddenly appears. Eric reminds Andre that he himself is pledged to Sophie-Anne and suggests that since he and Sookie already share a bond, it would be better for her to take his blood. Then he will be able to control her for Andre and the queen. Realizing that Eric is trying to protect her, Sookie is nevertheless furious when she is forced into a significant blood exchange with Eric in front of the watching Andre. Just as it is finished, an infuriated Quinn appears and demands an explanation. Sookie leaves, devastated, wondering what changes she will now face in her relationships with both Eric and Quinn. She locates the errant luggage and is taking it to Sophie-Anne's room when she notices a soda can sitting discarded in a planter and decides to throw it away. The can is heavier than it should be. Sookie looks more closely. She realizes that it is a fake, probably some sort of bomb. The police are notified, and she stands frozen, afraid to put it down, until they arrive. Quinn demands she hand it to him, as he will heal better should it go off. Eric appears as well, called through the new blood bond by Sookie's panic.

The bomb is finally taken by a vampire bomb-disposal expert, and Sookie and Quinn breathe a sigh of relief as they hug, while Eric slips quietly away. After being questioned by hotel security, Sookie returns to her room to find Quinn waiting for her in the hallway. After checking to see that her roommate is out, Sookie invites Quinn in, and they spend a quiet night sleeping in each other's arms.

FRIDAY, SEPTEMBER 23. Sookie is dressed and waiting for Quinn to escort her to the ball when he calls with the news that the lawsuit against the queen is going to be heard immediately. She is escorted into the proceedings by Andre, who sits beside her. Sookie learns that the judge (a vampire) is the Ancient Pythoness, the blind oracle that Alexander the Great consulted. Henrik Feith has continued the case against Sophie-Anne. Sookie reads the mind of Henrik's lawyer—and quite possibly that of Henrik—and learns that Henrik has been told the queen plans to kill him. He is pursuing the case in the hopes of saving his own life. Sookie stands and reassures the terrified man of the queen's sincerity in offering him a place. The Ancient Pythoness eventually finds Sophie-Anne not guilty, and by the terms of her contract with her deceased husband, the queen inherits the entire kingdom he formerly controlled. Henrik is then asked to name the person who lied to him. Just as the terrified man is about to obey, he is struck in the heart by a wooden arrow thrown by a vampire in the audience. Quinn leaps across the stage to protect Sookie and takes a second arrow in his shoulder. Batanya decapitates the assassin with a throwing star as Sookie tries to aid Quinn.

Quinn is taken to the infirmary by Were paramedics for further treatment. Since the trial is over, the ball begins. Sookie enjoys dancing with Eric, but when she begins to dance with Barry, Eric steps in, disapproving of the way that she is shaking her assets on the dance floor. Barry slips away, and she and Eric have a confrontation that is only alleviated when two professional dancers, both vampires, step in to dance with the angry couple.

Sookie decides to find Quinn. She heads to Jake's room to track Quinn's whereabouts. Jake says he doesn't know where Quinn is, and Sookie is disquieted when he tries to conceal that he has guests in his room. After finally locating Quinn in the infirmary, Sookie has an intense conversation with him about their relationship. As she leaves, Sookie finds Batanya's second-in-command, Clovache, waiting for her. Clovache reveals that the King of Kentucky hired the Britlingens after discovering a Fellowship of the Sun spy in his entourage. She also discloses that the spy revealed under torture that a splinter group of the Fellowship is planning a strike of some kind against the vampires during the summit, and that she and Batanya feel that security is lax at the hotel.

Back in the ballroom, Sophie-Anne, now cleared of all charges, is enjoying her success at the ball. She releases Sookie from further duties. Sookie goes to her room to ponder what she has learned.

SATURDAY, SEPTEMBER 24. Sookie joins Barry in the hotel restaurant for a late breakfast, and they look over their itineraries together. Later that evening there will be interstate vampire trials to attend, where they are to surreptitiously read the human witnesses, and they both wonder at the purpose of a four-hour block of time labeled "Commerce." The waiter gives Sookie a packet from Bill with information on the four area archery ranges. Sookie asks Barry to accompany her as she investigates at Eric's behest, looking for information on the vampire who threw the arrows the previous night. They hit pay dirt at the third range, and Barry takes over the questioning as a flirtatious employee offers to let them review the security tapes later. When they return, they find the door ripped off its hinges, two dead employees, and a smoldering pile of security tapes. They hurry back to the hotel, and Sookie reports to Eric, then goes to her room to dress for the vampire trials. She is astonished to find that vampire justice is swift and permanent; a vampire is staked when the judgment goes against him.

The commerce part of the evening consists of business deals between the various vampires. Sophie-Anne negotiates for goods and services to help her rebuild Louisiana, while Sookie assists by reading the minds of the human vendors. After they retire to the queen's suite for drinks, Sookie realizes that Christian Baruch, the vampire hotelier in charge of the Pyramid, has his own agenda and is likely responsible for planting the soda-can bomb in an effort to alarm the queen, so she would blindly accept his protection and courtship. To Sookie's surprise, Jake approaches her and strongly suggests she get Quinn to take her out the next day. He seems pleased when she agrees to consider his suggestion. As she is leaving for the night, Sookie alerts Andre to her suspicions about Baruch.

SUNDAY, SEPTEMBER 25. A panicked Barry speaking in her mind awakens Sookie. Pulling on her clothes, she hurries down the corridor to meet him and finds the unconscious body of Jake, apparently felled by the sun as he tried to reach her room. Barry joins her just as Sookie puts all the pieces together and realizes that Jake has taken part in the plot against the vampires. Calling Mr. Cataliades and Diantha while Barry gets his human roommate, Cecile, Sookie tells them she fears that bombs have been placed all over the hotel and will soon be detonated. Sookie calls Quinn to warn him and his sister, Frannie. Cecile pulls the fire alarm in the hopes that the human occupants will evacuate before the bombs destroy the building. They all run to try to save the vampires in their groups, and Sookie feels the first explosion just as she reaches the room Eric is sharing with Pam. She is barely able to rouse Eric, and together they place an unconscious Pam in her coffin and close the lid. More bombs are rocking the collapsing building as they push the coffin out the ninth-floor window. Wrapped in the ceremonial cloak he wore to officiate at the wedding, Eric is barely able to fly them both safely to the ground, and Pam's coffin lands hard. Both vampires are burned, but they are taken to a nearby basement for treatment and protection. Sookie saves a seriously injured Bill and is greatly relieved when she locates Quinn. As she climbs over the destroyed building to reach Quinn, she discovers an unconscious Andre nearby. Quinn is terribly wounded, both his legs broken by fallen beams, and his sister, Frannie, is lying near him with a head injury, but when Sookie tells him an unconscious Andre is nearby, Quinn encourages her to leave them. Surprised, Sookie reluctantly goes to help others, but as she walks away, she hears Quinn begin to move and knows she will never have to fear that Andre will force her to take his blood again. Sookie locates Barry, and they begin to use their gifts to help rescue workers find those still alive but trapped in the rubble. They work all day to find survivors, but as evening begins to fall, they know they have to leave before they are forced to account for themselves with the authorities. Sookie is able to call Mr. Cataliades, who is in the basement with the vampires, and he calls a cab to take the two telepaths to a hotel for the night.

MONDAY, SEPTEMBER 26. Mr. Cataliades arrives at the hotel with the news that a plane will be leaving in three hours, stopping first in Dallas and then in Shreveport, and that if they want a ride home, they need to be at the terminal. As they part, Sookie discovers that Quinn has been taken to a nearby hospital. She elects to visit him rather than catch the plane. Sookie finds Quinn unconscious with a weary, hungry, filthy Frannie at his bedside. She gives the younger girl money for a change of clothes and a meal, and Frannie offers Sookie the use of her car to drive home, since she will have to take Quinn home in his van.

WEDNESDAY, SEPTEMBER 28. After two days of driving, a relieved Sookie returns home to an ecstatic welcome by Amelia. Tara soon arrives with the news that she and JB du Rone have gotten married. Sookie tries to be happy for her friends and tells herself that if she just stays away from vampires and Weres for a while, she'll be okay.

The Secret Dialogues of Bill and Eric

To: WILLIAM COMPTON

BY THE ORDER OF OUR QUEEN, YOU ARE SUMMONED TO A MEETING WITH
ANDRE PAUL TOMORROW NIGHT AT FANGTASIA.

ERIC NORTHMAN,
SHERIFF OF AREA FIVE

Phone: Eric calling Bill.

ERIC: "Bill."

BILL: "Eric."

ERIC: "Quinn is in town."

BILL: "Yes."

ERIC: "Is he with Sookie?"

BILL: "Is that any of your business, Eric?"

ERIC: "I like to know who my employees are associating with."

BILL: "Your employee? I believe that Sookie is in the employ of the queen,
not you. If Sophie-Anne calls to ask me who Sookie is spending time
with, then I'll see what I can find out. Not until then."

ERIC: "As if you don't already know."

 (Silence.)

ERIC: "Need I remind you that you are still a resident in my territory?"

BILL: "I remember that quite well, Eric. I am also in the employment of the
queen and am too busy performing my duties in preparation for the
summit to spy for you. And as you well know, Sophie-Anne trumps
you every time."

Phone: Eric calling Bill.

ERIC: "Bill, did you go upstairs? What has happened?"

BILL: "There has been trouble on Jennifer Cater's floor. I believe the Arkansas vampires are all dead, except perhaps one."

ERIC: "Well. That's certainly convenient."

BILL: "My thoughts exactly."

Phone: Eric calling Bill.

ERIC: "The trial is going forward. Meet us in the exhibit room where the wedding was held."

BILL: "Has Sookie been contacted?"

ERIC: "Yes, Andre sent her a message. He'll wait for her and escort her in. We will kneel before our queen to show our support."

In person:

ERIC: "Please get a picture of Kyle Perkins to Sookie. Tomorrow she will be looking for the place where Kyle learned to throw the arrows with such accuracy."

BILL: "I'll provide the locations of the local archery ranges as well."

ERIC: "Good thinking. You can leave them for her at the front desk."

In person:

ERIC: "Sookie and Barry found the archery range, but the employees have been killed and the security tapes destroyed."

BILL: "Who else knew you were sending Sookie out to look?"

ERIC: "That's the question, isn't it?"

BILL: "I'm a judge for the first judicial sessions, so I must go. Think this over carefully, Eric: Who is the enemy here?"

From Dead to Worse

Timeline

SATURDAY, OCTOBER 8, 2005. While working at the Bellefleur double wedding with Sam, Sookie is surprised when she is asked by a tearful Halleigh to be a fill-in bridesmaid after one of the original bridesmaids has an appendicitis attack. Sookie participates in the ceremony and requisite pictures, then changes back into her work clothes to tend bar. Portia's new husband, Glen, has invited several of his vampire clients and honors them with a bottle of Royalty Blended, a premium mixture of real and synthetic blood, so that they can toast the happy newlyweds. Jonathan, a Nevada vampire, introduces himself as he gets another drink at the bar, and Sookie is a little concerned at his interest in her. She notices a tall, slim man observing the proceedings from a distance, a man whom the vampires all acknowledge with nods of respect.

Jonathan startles her as she is getting into her car and claims to have spoken to Pam about her, but Sookie knows he is lying. As they speak, she again sees the slender stranger watching them.

Sookie returns home and recounts her extraordinary evening to her roommate, Amelia. Amelia has her own news. Her father, Copley Carmichael, a wealthy building contractor from New Orleans, is visiting the next evening.

SUNDAY, OCTOBER 9. Sookie attends church in the morning, stopping at the grocery store before heading home to help Amelia, who has been on a cleaning spree. Her father arrives. He is a clear broadcaster like Amelia. Since Sookie has no trouble picking thoughts out of his head, she is able to control her reaction when Copley deliberately brings up Sookie's cousin Hadley. He tells Sookie that he knows Hadley's ex-husband and child. Copley also tells Amelia that a woman named Octavia Fant has called his house, looking for her. After he leaves, Amelia reveals to Sookie that Octavia is her mentor and the head of her coven. Octavia is the reason she left New Orleans after her magical mishap with Bob, convinced there would be a terrible punishment for turning her lover into a cat. Resigned, Amelia knows that she will soon have to deal with Octavia. She also confesses that Eric called the previous evening but that she had forgotten to tell Sookie. Anxious to ask him about the strange incident with Jonathan, Sookie calls Eric at Fangtasia. To her surprise, Eric invites her out to dinner and informs her that he will be introducing her to someone who has asked to meet her. Intrigued, she agrees to go to dinner with him in Shreveport the next evening.

MONDAY, OCTOBER 10. When Sookie and Eric arrive at Les Deux Poissons restaurant, she discovers that the man she is to meet is the beautiful stranger she saw at the wedding. He shows her his ears, and she realizes he is a member of the fae. Eric introduces the man as Niall Brigant, then leaves after reassuring Sookie that he will be nearby if she needs him. To her astonishment, Niall tells her he is her great-grandfather. As the evening progresses, Sookie learns the story of her grandmother Adele's involvement with Niall's son Fintan, who is revealed as her true grandfather. She shares part of her own life. By the time they part, she is pleased, albeit disconcerted, to have found a loving new member of her family. Eric and Sookie are speeding back toward Bon Temps when they are pulled over by a police car. As the officer approaches, Sookie realizes something is wrong and that the man is a Were just as he reaches the open window with gun drawn. When he tries to shoot Sookie, Eric takes the bullet but is still able to disarm the Were by breaking his arm. As a bleeding Eric gets caught in bloodlust and begins to pull the assassin in through the window, Sookie gets out of the suddenly crowded Corvette and checks the attacker's car to see if she can discover who sent him and why. Eric's car is empty when she returns, but Eric appears beside her and kisses her, still caught up in the lust of feeding. They quickly get back on the road, and Sookie doesn't question what Eric has done with the body. When she arrives home, Amelia tells her that Alcide called.

TUESDAY, OCTOBER 11. Octavia Fant appears on Sookie's doorstep, informing Sookie that she is there to see Amelia. Sookie leaves them to talk and goes in to make herself some coffee and read the paper. She is shocked and saddened to read of the death of Maria-Star Cooper, Alcide Herveaux's girlfriend, and her grief is compounded when Alcide calls to tell her that Maria-Star was murdered, warning Sookie that she may be in danger herself. She tells him about the attack the night before by the Were, and he immediately offers protection. However, Sookie declines. Alcide asks Sookie to tell Amanda, a member of his pack, the entire story. Amanda inquires if Amelia can do some sort of reading to try to ascertain who was involved in Maria-Star's death. Amelia agrees, but Octavia questions her decision, pointing out the previous failure that led to Bob's transformation. Sookie challenges Octavia to turn Bob back herself, but she fails in her attempt. Amelia, Sookie, and Octavia then go to Maria-Star's home, where they meet up with Tray Dawson, a Bon Temps lone wolf, who is guarding the apartment. The two witches are able to perform an ectoplasmic reconstruction, and they all witness Maria-Star's murder by the Were Cal Myers and a half-wolf, half-man accomplice. Amelia and Octavia leave for home, and Sookie accompanies Tray to Amanda's house, where Alcide is lying low. Sookie and Tray report what they have learned about Maria-Star's death. The Weres involved in her murder as well as in the attack on Sookie all work for the current packmaster, Patrick Furnan. When Alcide reacts angrily to the information that Sookie had dinner with Eric, she loses her temper with him and storms out. Tray drives her home.

Already weary from the events of the day, Sookie goes to work and is disheartened to see members of the Fellowship of the Sun in the bar. To her surprise, Pam comes in, followed shortly by Amelia, and the two have drinks and then leave on a date. The Fellowship members are indignant about a vampire being in the bar, but after they leave, Sam tells Sookie she must suck it up and treat them as she would any other customers. She knows he is right, but the admonishment stings. She leaves quickly after closing and finds Tray waiting for her in the parking lot. The Were tells her that he is following her home to check out her house. Once he makes certain the house is clear, they sit down, and he informs her that Alcide found Christine Larrabee, the widow of a previous packmaster, dead that afternoon. Patrick Furnan is suspected in both Christine's and Maria-Star's deaths.

WEDNESDAY, OCTOBER 12. Sookie visits the local library and greets the librarian, Barbara Beck, wife of Detective Alcee Beck, before checking out the new book arrivals. Sookie hears a sound from Barbara and looks up to see her being held by a huge Were with a knife to her throat. Sookie senses Alcee coming quietly in the back door and warns the attacker in a loud voice what Barbara's husband will do to him if he hurts Barbara.

Alcee is able to silently come up behind them and put his gun to the assailant's neck, but the quick-thinking attacker pushes Barbara toward her husband and rushes, knife raised, at Sookie. She flings a hardback in his face, tripping him, and he falls to his death on his own knife.

A fed-up Sookie finally decides to confront Furnan, and she calls him and demands to know why he has ordered the attacks upon her and the murders of the Were females. An angry and frightened Furnan denies any involvement and claims that his own wife, Libby, has been kidnapped. Sookie convinces him to call Alcide and set up a meeting, but his one condition is that she attend as a friend of the pack to read both sides for honesty.

Later that night Sookie, accompanied by a concerned Sam, travels to the same industrial park where the packmaster contest was held. She grasps Alcide's and Furnan's hands as they question each other. Just as they realize that neither of them is responsible for the attacks and murders, a voice calls from the roof of a nearby building. Priscilla Hebert, the widow of a packmaster from another part of the state and Cal Myers's half sister, announces that she committed the murders of Maria-Star, Christine, and Libby in a plot to set Alcide and Furnan against each other so that she could more easily take over their pack. Both Alcide and Furnan strike with suddenly clawed hands, Furnan eviscerating Cal as Alcide takes off the back of his head. Howling with fury, Priscilla leads her wolves in attack, and Sam and Sookie find themselves in the middle of the warring Weres. Sam tells her he is going to change, and a surprised Sookie turns to find that Sam has shifted into a lion. Taking down the enemy with a swipe of his huge paws, Sam draws the attention of Priscilla, now a wolf. Amanda, also in wolf form, attempts to distract Priscilla as she works her way over to Sam, but Priscilla manages to break Amanda's neck and leaps on the lion, sinking her teeth into his neck. Seeing Sam attacked, Sookie launches herself onto Priscilla's back and begins to strangle her. Priscilla must release Sam, who then turns and kills her. When Sookie falls to the pavement, vulnerable, Claudine suddenly appears standing over her to protect her through the remaining battle. When the action finally ends, Priscilla and most of her wolves, as well as Furnan and Amanda, are dead, and Alcide declares himself the new packmaster.

Claudine helps Sookie to her feet and reveals that Niall is also Claudine's grandfather. She urges Sookie to leave before the wolves celebrate the ascension of Alcide, and Sam marches Sookie out to his truck.

When she gets home, Sookie finds Pam sitting in the kitchen with Amelia, and Sookie knows that the vampire will report the events of the evening back to Eric.

THURSDAY, OCTOBER 13. Sookie works the day shift and is not pleased when Tanya Grissom shows up to speak with Sam. Her fellow waitress Holly tells her that Tanya has been living out at Hotshot with the panthers, and Sookie is surprised to find that Holly believes that the shifters will come out someday. Sookie again finds Pam at her house with Amelia when she returns home from work that evening and questions Pam about whether Eric has heard anything more about Jonathan. Pam suggests Sookie call Eric to find out, so she calls Fangtasia. During the conversation, Sookie learns to her dismay that Eric believes that the queen's weakened state has left Louisiana open to a hostile takeover.

Uneasy and unable to sleep, Sookie is startled when Bill suddenly appears in her bedroom. He reports that Pam called him to come guard Sookie when she herself left for Fangtasia after becoming concerned because she couldn't reach either Eric or Cleo Babbitt, the sheriff of Area Three. A terrified Frannie Quinn appears suddenly at the door with a warning from her brother. The vampires of Las Vegas are on their way to take over Louisiana. As a shocked Sookie, Amelia, and Bill hear Frannie's story and are preparing for the worst, Eric arrives with the news that his people have gathered at Fangtasia, but he was cut off from the club.

The Vegas vampires arrive in Sookie's yard, and the king's representative, Victor Madden, asks to enter the house to negotiate with Eric. Sookie is distressed to learn that Quinn is with the Vegas vampires, who have used his mother and sister to blackmail him into their service. Victor reports that Sophie-Anne and the other sheriffs have been killed, but they feel Eric can be useful to them if he will swear allegiance to the King of Nevada, Felipe de Castro. Sookie attempts to call Niall, but Eric prevents her from making contact. Victor finally asks Eric whether he intends to fight to the death or accept the takeover, informing him that Fangtasia is surrounded and that he is prepared to burn it down with the Area Five vampires inside. Knowing that his people will die for nothing, Eric accepts the sovereignty of the king. Eric wanders off to have some privacy as he calls Fangtasia to tell his people to surrender and swear fealty to the new king. Bill comforts a shaken Sookie and then goes out to speak with the new leadership.

Sookie escapes to her bedroom only to find Eric sitting on her bed, his head in his hands. When she sees his face, Sookie believes that the shock on it is because of the takeover, but he tells her he has suddenly remembered everything that happened between them during the time he spent with her when he had amnesia. Overwhelmed by the events of the evening, Sookie tells him they will talk about it another time. Eric agrees but warns there will one day be a reckoning between them.

FRIDAY, OCTOBER 14. Sookie wakes to find Quinn sitting in her bedroom. Realizing she can never be first in his life because of the needs of his mother and sister, Sookie breaks off their relationship and sends the man she had hoped to love away. She gathers herself and goes to work, buying Crystal lunch when her pregnant sister-in-law comes in with Jason, who is fed up with his wife's spendthrift ways and now refuses to give her any money. Sookie and Sam later read in the newspaper about several people missing in Shreveport who actually perished in the Were war. Sookie then sees the obituary of Sophie-Anne Leclerq, which lists the cause of death as Sino-AIDS, but Sookie knows the weakened queen was assassinated by order of Felipe de Castro. Sookie arrives home after work to face even more unwelcome visitors: Frannie Quinn and her mother. Frannie is furious with Sookie for her treatment of Quinn, and although Mrs. Quinn is generally confused, she identifies Sookie as the woman her son loved.

SATURDAY, OCTOBER 15. Copley Carmichael stops by Sookie's house to ask her to arrange an introduction to members of the new vampire leadership so that he can do business with them. She reluctantly agrees to call Fangtasia to see what she can find out. Sookie leaves the house to run errands—and get away from Copley as he visits with his daughter—and comes across Arlene and Tanya having a conversation in Tanya's car in the Sonic parking lot. Sookie deliberately tries to tune them in, first picking up Arlene's thoughts about her new boyfriend's conviction that the world should be free of vampires. She zeros in on Tanya, discovering that she is still in the pay of Sandra Pelt, who continues to be determined to make Sookie's life miserable. Sookie decides to consult Amelia and confesses the entire story of Debbie Pelt's death. They decide to bring in Octavia to try to find a long-term fix without hurting Tanya.

Sookie remembers her promise to Copley, and right before she goes into work she calls Fangtasia to ask Eric whom Copley should contact. During the conversation Eric tells her more of his memories of their time together. Claudine and Claude come into Merlotte's to bring greetings from Niall, who is concerned about his great-granddaughter. Copley has obviously jumped on the opportunity to ingratiate himself with the new vampires and arrives for a meeting with Sandy Sechrest, Felipe de Castro's area rep.

Sam and Sookie talk a bit after closing, and he tells her about his family, inviting her to his brother's upcoming wedding. As they leave the bar, they come across Niall standing in the moonlight, and Sookie introduces him to Sam. Niall is worried that Sookie has been in danger the previous two nights and is not at all happy that she was prevented from calling him for protection during the takeover. He expresses his love for his great-granddaughter and his desire to do something for her, but Sookie tells him she just wants him in her life. After he leaves, she tells Sam that she wants to love Niall but finds him a little frightening.

SUNDAY, OCTOBER 16. Sookie awakens to find Octavia and Amelia in the kitchen discussing how to deal with Tanya. Much to Sookie's surprise, she realizes that Amelia has already invited Octavia to move in, based on a casual offer of Sookie's. The two witches have Sookie ask Calvin Norris, who is currently seeing Tanya, to stop by at lunchtime. The leader of the Hotshot werepanthers immediately knows to whom Sookie is referring when she tells him that they have a problem. When Sookie tells Calvin the whole story of her involvement with the Pelts, he promises to bring Tanya there that night for the witches to work on if they promise that Tanya won't be harmed. Bob the cat strolls in, and Calvin recognizes straightaway that Amelia's magic doesn't always work.

True to his word, Calvin arrives shortly after seven that evening with Tanya carefully trussed up and slung over his shoulder. After the struggling young woman inhales smoke from a potion lit in a bowl, she is placed on a chair surrounded by chalk drawings, and Octavia begins to chant, pulling Tanya out from under Sandra's sway. When the spell is over, Tanya doesn't remember why she has been causing the mischief she has and is rid of Sandra's influence. A relieved Calvin takes Tanya back to Hotshot.

Sookie takes a break outside while the witches clean up. She sits in a lawn chair out in the chill night air. Bill soon steps from the woods and sits with her. After a few moments of silence, Bill tells Sookie that Selah Pumphrey has moved to Little Rock to work for a firm that specializes in vampire properties and that he always knew that Selah was more interested in him as a vampire than as a man. After telling Sookie that there have been many like Selah, he informs Sookie that there is only one her and leaves.

MONDAY, OCTOBER 17. After the turmoil of the previous week, Sookie enjoys a quiet and peaceful day off.

TUESDAY, OCTOBER 18. Sookie works the day shift, serving lunch to Jason and several of his co-workers. Jason tells her that he needs to ride over to Clarice to pick up some fencing after work and asks her to check on Crystal after her shift. Sookie stops by his house, calling out to Crystal as she opens the front door. She hears a muffled moan and, worried that Crystal is miscarrying again, rushes into the bedroom, only to find her pregnant sister-in-law having sex with one of Jason's co-workers. As Sookie marches out of the house, furious and disgusted, Calvin pulls up, having also been asked by Jason to check in on Crystal. Jason knew that both Calvin and Sookie would catch his wife being unfaithful. Calvin shares Sookie's anger and disgust, informing her that they will need to have the ceremony to punish Crystal. Sookie remembers that at the couple's wedding, she agreed to stand in for Jason just as Calvin agreed to stand in for Crystal under certain circumstances. Calvin calls Sookie later that evening to tell her to come to Hotshot the following night.

WEDNESDAY, OCTOBER 19. Sookie drives out to Hotshot alone after work, determined to face whatever may come. As Calvin stood for Crystal at her wedding, promising to take the punishment for her actions should she violate the covenant and be unable to face the penalty herself, Jason declares that Sookie will administer the punishment to Calvin in his stead as well. The sentence for the breaking of the wedding vows is the breaking of the symbolic panther claw, and Sookie is forced to break Calvin's fingers with a brick.

THURSDAY, OCTOBER 20–FRIDAY, OCTOBER 21. Sookie struggles with her actions as she tries to go about her life. She knows that she was only following the laws of Hotshot, but she feels guilty for hurting a man she respects and considers a friend. Unwilling to even speak to Jason, she turns her back on him when he comes into the bar. She hears through the grapevine that Calvin has passed his injury off as the result of an accident that occurred while he was working on his truck.

SATURDAY, OCTOBER 22. Sam finally calls Eric in to speak to Sookie, hoping to find out what is wrong. She is angered by Eric's lack of compassion and stomps out of Sam's office, but she eventually manages to shake her black mood. When she leaves work, she finds Eric waiting for her in the parking lot. She asks him about the visiting Nevada king, Felipe de Castro, and they are both startled when Castro suddenly appears to talk with Eric. After introducing herself to the dramatic King of Nevada, Louisiana, and Arkansas, Sookie gets in her car to go home, but she has to pull over when she suffers a panic attack caused by her worry over Eric. She heads back to Merlotte's, parking in the front lot and sneaking around to the back, uncertain of what she will find. To her shock, she sees that Sigebert, Sophie-Anne's loyal bodyguard, didn't die with his queen and has come seeking vengeance. Both Eric and Felipe are bound with silver chains, obviously having already suffered at Sigebert's hands. Sam, an innocent bystander, is tied to the bumper of his own truck. Sookie decides that her best weapon is her car, and she creeps back to it, trying to figure out the best way to charge Sigebert without hitting anyone else. Pulling around to the back, she accelerates and is able to hit him from the front and then back over him. She jumps from the car to free Eric but is unable to unwrap the chains. She frees Sam first so he can help. The moment Eric is able he leaps on Sigebert and decapitates him, sending him to join his beloved maker. Felipe proclaims himself in Sookie's debt, but he and Eric both wonder how it is Sigebert survived the takeover. Sam takes Sookie home, questioning her about whether the price she has paid to know more about the supernatural world has been worth it.

SUNDAY, OCTOBER 23. Having been contacted by Felipe, Tray Dawson has repaired Sookie's car and returns it to her in the morning before she is due for her shift at Merlotte's. The big Were asks her to put in a good word for him with Amelia.

MONDAY, OCTOBER 24. Running errands in town, Sookie sees Alcide, who thanks her for her help. When she returns home, Amelia and Octavia are working in the yard, and as they talk, Bob strolls over. Octavia proves her power by turning Bob back into his human form, later admitting that she faked her initial failure so that Amelia and Sookie would need her. Bob's initial anger turns to devastation as he learns about Hurricane Katrina.

TUESDAY, OCTOBER 25. Sookie takes Bob to Wal-Mart to buy clothing and shoes, and she fixes an early supper of his favorite foods for them all before leaving for work. She says good-bye to Bob, knowing he will be gone by the time she comes home. He is heading back to New Orleans to find his family. Sookie contemplates getting a real cat on her way to work.

Alcide stops by Merlotte's to thank both Sam and Sookie for their help in the Were war, and Eric and Pam soon arrive to announce that Felipe has given them leave to offer Sookie their formal protection. Sam, Sookie, and Arlene decorate the bar for Halloween after closing.

Sookie finds Niall waiting for her on her front porch when she gets home, and he again asks if he can do any favor for her. After a bit of thought, she asks if he can find a man named Remy Savoy. He leaves, happy to have some way to please his new great-granddaughter.

WEDNESDAY, OCTOBER 26. Sookie wakes to find a magical message with an address. Sookie drives out to Red Ditch to introduce herself to Hadley's former husband, Remy, and his four-year-old son, Hunter. She finds that the child shares her telepathic gift. When she leaves, she promises his father that she will be there to help the boy when the time comes.

The Secret Dialogues of Bill and Eric

Phone: Eric calling Bill.

ERIC: "Bill, did you see a strange vampire at the Bellefleur wedding?"

BILL: "I saw several who were not familiar to me. They were mainly business associates of Portia's groom. Is there one in particular you are asking about?"

ERIC: "Sookie has told me of an Asian vampire called Jonathan who claimed he had heard a lot about her and is staying in the area. He told her that he had checked in with me, but he has not. I'm concerned that he would bother to lie."

BILL: "I'll see what I can find in the database, but *Asian* and the first name Jonathan are not much to go on. If that even really is his name."

ERIC: "I'm seeing Sookie tomorrow night. I'll see if she can remember anything more about him."

BILL: "You're seeing Sookie? I thought she was still with Quinn."

ERIC: "She hasn't heard from him since Rhodes, but this is not that kind of seeing. I'm introducing her to someone who wishes to meet her."

BILL: "Someone who wants to meet her? Is this someone you trust?"

ERIC: "Yes."

Phone: Eric calling Bill.

ERIC: "Bill, have you discovered anything?

BILL: "I'm still working on it. I've eliminated several possibilities and am pursuing several others."

ERIC: "Something is definitely going on."

BILL: "Did something else happen?"

ERIC: "Yes. We were attacked on the way home."

BILL: "Vampire?"

ERIC: "Were."

BILL: "But you still think there is some connection?"

ERIC: "I don't know."

BILL: "Was the assailant after you or Sookie?"

ERIC: "I took the bullet, but I believe he was after Sookie."

BILL: "Do you still trust this person you took her to meet?"

ERIC: "Yes. He would do nothing to harm her."

BILL: "I'll continue my research and call you as soon as I find anything definite."

Phone: Eric calling Bill.

ERIC: "Bill, the Shreveport pack is divided and going to war. I believe the attack on the way home the other night was part of that, an attempt to kill a friend of the pack, because Sookie is Alcide's friend, not Furnan's, although I'm not certain she considers Alcide a friend."

BILL: "That makes sense, but it doesn't explain the vampire Jonathan at the wedding. Is Sookie being attacked on two fronts? The last time she was stalked by a vampire, it was because of the death of Long Shadow. Has your disagreement with Hot Rain been resolved? Or is he even more determined now that his child and his acquired child have met their final death?"

ERIC: "The judgment was upheld, and I have heard nothing more from Hot Rain since Twining's death. After losing two I don't think he will send any more after us."

BILL: "Then who?"

ERIC: "That's what we need to find out."

BILL: "What of the pack war?"

ERIC: "Despite the bullet I took, it is none of our affair. We will intercede only for vampire interests or to protect Sookie."

BILL: "Understood."

Phone: Bill calling Eric.

BILL: "Eric, the Were situation has been resolved. Alcide Herveaux is now packmaster of the Shreveport pack."

ERIC: "I assume Sookie is fine."

BILL: "Yes. Merlotte was there to protect her, and I understand Claudine stepped in as well."

ERIC: "Claudine. Of course she would."

BILL: "I'm told the vampire Jonathan has been seen in other places."

ERIC: "He has. He had even come to Fangtasia, coincidentally enough on a rare night I was not there. I'm very suspicious. We are not in a strong position with Sophie-Anne disabled and Andre dead."

BILL: "You are the strongest sheriff of the four of you."

ERIC: "Yes."

BILL: "Yet you do not wish to lead."

ERIC: "No."

BILL: "Then we can only do what we can with what we have."

Phone: Bill calling Eric.

ERIC'S VOICE MAIL: "It is Eric. Leave a message."

BILL: "Eric, Pam was unable to contact Cleo. She has gone to Fangtasia. Call us as soon as you get this message."

Phone: Bill calling Eric.

ERIC'S VOICE MAIL: "It is Eric. Leave a message."

BILL: "Eric, the Las Vegas vamps are attempting a takeover. They have already attacked some of the other sheriffs and are surrounding Fangtasia as we speak. I'm here at Sookie's. Call me!"

Phone: Bill calling Eric.

BILL: "Do you have time to speak with me, Eric?"

ERIC: "You phrased that so well, Bill. Yes, I am alone. In my car, in fact. Hosting Felipe and his entourage has been rather stressful, so I decided to take a drive."

BILL: "Who was Sookie trying to call?"

ERIC: "When?"

BILL: "Don't be evasive, Eric. When you knocked her phone from her hand."

ERIC: "Ah, well, perhaps it's better that you know. You are closest to her if she needs help. She was calling her great-grandfather."

BILL: "Sookie has no living great-grandparents."

ERIC: "Actually, she does. His name is Niall Brigant."

BILL: "Niall Brigant, as in Prince of the Fairies?"

ERIC: "I didn't know you knew him."

BILL: "I don't, but I've heard of him. Well, that explains some things, doesn't it?"

ERIC: "Yes. So now there is yet another player in the game."

BILL: "Yes, but is he friend or foe?"

ERIC: "I get the distinct impression that he will be friend to Sookie's friends and enemy to her enemies. But I could not involve him in our battle. That would have been the end for too many of us. On both sides."

BILL: "I agree."

ERIC: "While I have you, I did want to give you a heads-up that Felipe wants to meet with you to discuss your database business."

BILL: "When?"

ERIC: "Within the next week. I'd advise you to drive a hard bargain. He is enterprising, and I'm certain he will want you to branch out into other computer endeavors. And for the time being, at least, I believe he is willing to be more generous than Sophie-Anne to keep you content."

BILL: "I'll await his call. Thank you."

ERIC: "You're welcome."

Dead and Gone

Timeline

TUESDAY, JANUARY 10, 2006. When Sookie arrives for her evening shift, Sam tells her that the shifters are ready to reveal themselves on TV and in various public locations. Her brother, Jason, and some friends are in the bar, as are Bill and fellow vampire Clancy, and Tray and Amelia soon enter. Sam comes out of the office just as the bar television flashes a "Special Report," and everyone at Merlotte's watches as the shifters announce their existence to the world. To the amazement of the bar patrons, Sam and Tray step forward and change. Sam in collie form takes his place beside a smiling Sookie, while werewolf Tray is hugged by his girlfriend, Amelia. Although most of the patrons begin to accept the shifters, Arlene reacts with anger and hate, quitting and storming out of the bar with her Fellowship of the Sun friends. A happy Sam has just changed back to his human form when he receives a call from his stepfather, who did not know about his wife's other nature. He tells Sam that he shot her (though not fatally) when she shifted in front of him. Sookie agrees to watch the bar as a distraught Sam leaves to be with his family.

WEDNESDAY, JANUARY 11. Sookie goes into Merlotte's early to work on finding a replacement for Arlene. When none of her first choices are available, she reluctantly contacts Tanya Grissom, tracking her down at Calvin Norris's house in Hotshot. Tanya agrees to pick up a few shifts in the evenings, and they arrange for her to start the next night. Terry Bellefleur handles bar duty while Sookie works a double shift in Arlene's absence. Sam calls at closing to let Sookie know that his mom is expected to make a full recovery and that his stepfather is in jail.

THURSDAY, JANUARY 12. Duff, Merlotte's beer-delivery driver, calls Sookie at home when no one is at the bar to accept a shipment, so she rushes to the bar, nervously signing the invoice on Sam's behalf. She remains at Merlotte's and is on the phone with Amelia when Bobby Burnham, Eric's daytime guy, arrives. Amelia tells her that Eric called the night before and that Octavia finally told Bobby this morning where Sookie could be found. Bobby tells Sookie that Eric has requested that she come to Fangtasia that evening to meet with Victor Madden, the lieutenant of Felipe de Castro, the new king of Louisiana and Arkansas, as well as Nevada. Sookie agrees, and Bobby hands her a black velvet bundle, telling her to present it to Eric in front of Victor. After Bobby leaves, Sookie goes about her day. The customers and employees at Merlotte's continue to adjust to the news about the existence of shifters. Tanya arrives early for a little brushup training before her shift, and Sookie is able to head to Shreveport in time for the meeting.

Pam greets Sookie as she enters and instructs her to go into Eric's office and respectfully present the velvet package to Eric. Victor watches as Eric receives the velvet bundle from Sookie, dramatically opening it to reveal the shining ceremonial knife that he used to officiate the vampire marriage in Rhodes and later used to cut himself during the blood bond. As Eric kisses the knife, she becomes uncomfortably aware that she does not understand the ramifications of all that is happening. She is stunned when Victor states that Quinn had requested a private meeting with her that will now be denied and that Felipe will acknowledge Eric's prior claim on Sookie. Her discomfort gives way to anger as the vampires explain that shifters who do business with the vampires must get Eric's permission to enter Area Five, a stipulation he specifically negotiated when he allied with the new regime. She becomes even more furious when Victor explains that because she and Eric used the ceremonial knife in a blood ritual, they are now effectively wed under vampire law. Her outrage is not assuaged when Eric tries to appease her by claiming that his actions were taken for her own good, and she leaves, promising him that they will discuss this later.

FRIDAY, JANUARY 13. Sam calls with a quick update about his mom's condition. Sookie is shocked when she is visited by Agent Sara Weiss from the New Orleans office of the FBI and Special Agent Tom Lattesta from the Rhodes branch. After showing Sookie a photograph of herself and Barry the Bellboy in the ruins of the bombed hotel, they begin to question her about Barry and the events of that terrible day. The phone rings, and a shaken Amelia interrupts them to tell Sookie that she is needed at Merlotte's because a woman has been crucified in the parking lot.

Sookie arrives at the bar with the FBI agents in tow. Sookie is devastated to see that the woman is her pregnant sister-in-law, Crystal. She calls

Sam as the police begin to gather evidence. A stunned Jason, notified of the death, arrives first, followed shortly thereafter by a grief-stricken Calvin Norris, who is accompanied by Tanya Grissom. Sookie escorts the Hotshot leader back to the scene, where he hopes to get a scent of his niece's killer. He tries to force his way through to her body but is stopped by the law-enforcement agents present, and Sookie is moved by Sheriff Bud Dearborn's careful treatment of Calvin, realizing that the old sheriff was aware of the panthers long before the Great Reveal. Jason's friend Mel Hart arrives and persuades the dazed Jason to go home while Calvin waits for Crystal's body to be taken down from the cross. Sookie decides to leave when the police tell her that Merlotte's will remain closed for several more hours at least. When she doesn't get word that it is okay to reopen by the time darkness falls, Sookie heads to Fangtasia to see Eric.

Sookie is comforted by Eric's presence and listens quietly when he begins to tell her of his early life and how he was turned by Appius Livius Ocella. She then shares her concern about the FBI's interest in her and Barry, and her fears that they want her to work for them. Eric explains that he wed her in the vampire way to protect her from King Felipe who, even though he owes her a debt, wants to take her to Las Vegas to use her gift to help him in his business dealings. Sookie wants details about their pledge but is too weary from the day's events to pursue the conversation and goes home.

SATURDAY, JANUARY 14. Andy Bellefleur gives the okay to open the bar, and Sookie is relieved when Sam walks in as she is setting up for the day. His mother is healing, but the situation with his stepfather is very tense. When Sookie reveals her marriage to Eric, Sam's reaction causes her to leave Merlotte's in a fury. She turns to her best friend, Tara, for advice, telling her the whole story. Tara says that while Sookie could have been smarter about the situation, only the vampires will know about the pledge and she has time to figure things out. Despite her own bad past with vampires, Tara concedes that there are benefits to Sookie's relationship with Eric. Tara then shares her own news: She is pregnant, and she is fiercely determined to give her baby the childhood she never had.

Returning to her own house for lunch, Sookie takes a phone message for Octavia from Louis Chambers. When she hands Octavia the note with Louis's phone number, it is obvious that the gentleman means a great deal to Octavia, and she promptly returns his call.

Sookie enters Merlotte's to work her shift that evening to find Sam arguing with Bobby Burnham, who hands her an envelope and tells her that Eric has instructed him to always be at her disposal, much to his humiliation. Sookie enters the dining area and sees agents Weiss and Lattesta at one table and her great-grandfather, Niall, at another. Niall informs Sookie that the agents have been discussing her, and she tells him her fears about being forced to work for the FBI. She asks if he knows about Crystal, and although he has shown no interest in Jason, he tells Sookie that he is always concerned when someone connected to him dies and will look into it. He then makes a vague comment about there being trouble and assures her that he will take care of it, but advises her to be wary of fairies she does not know. She and Sam remain on the outs for the evening.

Louis Chambers has arrived to take Octavia back to New Orleans by the time Sookie gets off work. After they leave, Amelia tells Sookie that he is a sorcerer, and the two agree that the older couple has little to fear in the Big Easy.

SUNDAY, JANUARY 15. Andy and Agent Lattesta come by in the morning to discuss Crystal's death, and after they leave, a slightly chilly Sookie is sunbathing in her yard when she is surprised by a visit from Diantha, who brings a message from Mr. Cataliades. The lawyer has sent his niece to warn Sookie that fairies are moving about in this world and that they will try to hurt her if they can. Sookie learns from Diantha that Niall has many enemies, the most important one being the other fairy prince, his nephew Breandan. When Diantha leaves, Sookie calls her fae cousins Claudine and Claude to meet her for a talk, during which she learns about her fae lineage and why her great-grandfather has enemies. She is told that Breandan hates all humans with fairy blood and believes they should be eliminated because they dilute the fae magic. He wants to close off Faery from the contamination of humans. Claude and Claudine also warn her that her great-uncle Dermot is the spitting image of her brother, Jason, and that she should be very careful because he was involved in her parents' deaths.

Disturbed by the warnings, a restless Sookie returns home and decides to work off her disquiet by weeding the flower beds. She is busy with her old trowel when she suddenly hears someone say, "I'll enjoy killing you for my lord," and she instinctively lunges upward, shoving the trowel into the speaker's stomach. As he falls to the ground, she retreats into her house, locks the doors, and calls Niall. Her great-grandfather arrives with his son Dillon, the father of Claudine and Claude, and is pleased that she has killed one of his enemies. As the body disintegrates into a fine glittery dust, Niall warns her again and then leaves.

A troubled Sookie is pondering the events of the day when Quinn unexpectedly pulls up. Feeling Eric's rage at Quinn's presence through the blood bond, Sookie becomes upset as Quinn questions why she is harder on him than on anyone else and voices his fear that Eric is trying to cut her off from the others who care about her. Alerted by Eric, Bill arrives, and the two men begin to fight. When an angry Quinn throws Bill with all his strength, he cannons into the helpless Sookie, knocking her unconscious. She wakes in her darkened bedroom with Eric. The taste of his blood is on her tongue. The passion between them ignites. After lovemaking, Eric and Sookie talk, and she tells him of the events of the day. Eric invites a stunned Sookie to move in with him but is surprised when she gently declines. They discuss their feelings for each other, and Eric regretfully leaves for his home. As Sookie looks out her kitchen window, she sees Bill silently watching over her from the woods.

MONDAY, JANUARY 16. A forlorn Jason visits, waiting for Sookie out in the backyard. While she believes she will be able to forgive him for his past actions, their relationship remains strained. He asks her to attend Crystal's funeral and tells her that if she hears who killed his wife, either she can tell the police or she can simply tell him and Calvin, and they will take care of it.

Sookie is surprised to have a message from Arlene asking her to come over to her house to talk. When she learns from Sam that Arlene has tried to get her job back and that he is planning to refuse, Sookie decides to visit her former friend to try making peace with her. She calls Arlene and tells her she will come over, but Sookie senses something is not right and leaves immediately to scope out the situation before she is expected at Arlene's trailer.

Sookie watches from the burned-out house next to Arlene's as she sends her children away with a friend and then talks with two men from the Fellowship of the Sun. Sookie is able to discern that they are going to do to her what was done to Crystal. She calls Andy Bellefleur, who is with the FBI agents, and they tell her they will come if she would be willing to go in and try to trap the men in the act. As she is waiting for the law, Sookie sees Arlene leaving and comes out of hiding to confront her. Just as the police arrive, Arlene begins to scream, and the men come out of the trailer with their rifles in their hands. Special Agent Lattesta calls a warning for them to lay down their arms, but one fires at Sookie, who flings herself to the ground. The bullet slightly grazes Arlene but hits Agent Weiss in the upper chest. The men all open fire, and one of the attackers is killed, the other wounded. As a stunned Sookie sits on the ground, she realizes the two men did not kill Crystal but were planning a copycat murder. While the wounded are taken away, Sookie looks over to see a fairy watching from the woods. After she is questioned, Bud Dearborn sends her home.

Sookie goes into work and is relieved when nothing else happens and she is able to go about her shift just like any other waitress at Merlotte's.

TUESDAY, JANUARY 17. Amelia tells Sookie of a hot new guy named Drake who has been asking her and Tray about Sookie, but Sookie passes on the opportunity to meet him. Remy Savoy calls with a request for Sookie's help with Hunter, who will be starting kindergarten soon, but she has to put him off. Because of the threat of the fairies, she is unwilling to possibly jeopardize the little boy or his father. She promises to contact him when things have settled down, hoping that she survives whatever it is that is coming. While Amelia gets ready for a date with Tray, she again mentions Drake and his desire to meet Sookie. When Amelia says that the man looks a lot like Jason, a panicked Sookie warns her friend to stay away from him. Sookie calls Eric to ask for the protection of the vampires, and he tells her he will present her request to Victor, who is there at Fangtasia. Once at work, Sookie struggles to function normally while trying to listen for information about Crystal's murder, but Sookie hears little but the usual mundane thoughts of the people surrounding her. She gets one text message from Eric, assuring her that the protection she requested is coming, and another from Alcide, who has learned of her problems from Tray and offers pack protection as well. Before leaving Merlotte's, Sookie fills two water pistols with pure lemon juice as a defense against the fairies.

She finds Bubba waiting beside her car in the parking lot as the protection promised by Eric, and when she arrives home, Tray is at her house as the protection from the Weres.

WEDNESDAY, JANUARY 18. Sookie awakens to hear Tray being desperately ill. He tells her of meeting a woman in the woods who compelled him to drink poisoned vampire blood. A worried Sookie sends him home, promising to contact Jason to guard her. Niall appears in her living room, looking as if he has been in a battle, to let her know that Breandan has retaliated for the death of his follower. Niall warns her to be even more careful. Sookie calls Jason to come protect her and is horrified to hear that he has had a visit from Dermot, who attacked Jason's friend Mel. Mel accompanies Jason but briefly leaves to get an ice bag for his injured shoulder, and Sookie tells Jason of their family fairy connection, warning him of the danger they face from Dermot. Jason tells Sookie that he wants to go home for his rifle and that she should come pick him up there so he can be with her for the day, and he and Mel leave. As she drives to her brother's house, she begins to think of some things she has learned and starts to suspect that she knows who killed Crystal, so she calls Calvin.

When she arrives, she finds Jason and Mel sighting Jason's rifle behind his house. She begins to question Mel, and when her brother realizes what the questions mean, he holds Mel as she examines his thoughts. Sookie tells her horrified brother that his friend killed Crystal, just as Calvin arrives with two of Crystal's other relatives. Mel confesses that he is gay and in love with Jason and that he hated Crystal for her treatment of him. Crystal knew of Mel's love for Jason, taunting him when she saw him alone at Jason's house one day, and he struck her down in anger. Mel tells them that he did not crucify her but left the body in the back of his truck, from where it was stolen. Sookie leaves as the werepanthers administer their justice.

Sookie manages to get through her shift at the bar, but she remembers on the drive home that she promised to meet Amelia at Tray's house to check on him. When she arrives, she is alarmed when no one answers the door and there is no sign of her roommate. Fearing the worst, she calls Bill to come and check the house for her. As she waits outside, she is relieved when Amelia calls to tell her that she was unable to get an answer at Tray's, so she went home. Bill returns from the house with the unwelcome news that there has obviously been a fight and that Tray is gone. Frightened and worried that the fairies have done something to Bubba as well, Sookie heads home in her car with Bill following. As she walks to her door, Sookie is abducted.

Sookie awakens in what appears to be an abandoned house, a captive of two fairies, Lochlan and his sister Neave. She learns that they are the ones who crucified Crystal and that Breandan has given them permission to do what they want with Sookie, short of killing her. As the two gleefully torture her, Sookie soon realizes that they will not be able to control themselves and simply waits for death. Barely conscious, she believes she is hallucinating when she sees Bill and Niall stealing up behind her tormentors. She manages a smile as Niall beheads Lochlan and Bill tears out Neave's throat. Finally, Sookie succumbs to the unbearable pain and slips into darkness.

THURSDAY, JANUARY 19. Coming to, Sookie finds herself clean and bandaged in a strange bed, with Dr. Ludwig and Claudine by her side. Dr. Ludwig tells Sookie that her kidnappers are dead but that Bill was badly injured during the rescue. Claudine informs Sookie that the war has begun between Niall and Breandan and that Claudine's own disheveled appearance is due to being ambushed. She is knitting and shares that she is pregnant by a fae lover. Eric arrives and begins examining Sookie's wounds, giving her his blood to strengthen her for the coming battle with the fae. As Sookie begins to weep, Eric comforts her, praising her for remaining strong and intact under the terrible torture. She pulls her makeshift weapons from her bag before Eric carries her to the room where Bill and Tray lie. Bill is gravely ill from silver poisoning, and Tray's wounds will be mortal. As Clancy gives Bill blood, he explains to Sookie that he saw her taken but knew he could not defeat the twins alone, so he called Eric to notify Niall. Bill and Niall were then able to track Sookie and her captors through the fae and human worlds to where she was held captive.

Eric receives a call that Breandan's forces have arrived and the attack is imminent. Eric, Bill, and Clancy, armed with iron swords and long knives, face the door as it splinters under the force of the attacking fae. Clancy decapitates the first fae as he enters, and Bill steps in front of Sookie, throwing his knife into the throat of the second fairy and then reaching back to take Sookie's trowel. Breandan enters, already bloodied and with a knitting needle protruding from his shoulder, followed by a female swinging a mace. Eric is able to avoid it, but Clancy is hit and then beheaded by Breandan as he moves to confront Bill. Tray, knowing he is dying, makes a superhuman effort to distract Breandan, gripping the enemy fairy's shirt. As Breandan plunges his sword into Tray, Bill stabs the fairy under the arm with Sookie's trowel, and he falls. The female fairy moves in on an unsteady Bill and Sookie, who squirts the fairy with her lemon juice–filled squirt gun. The fairy screams in pain, and Eric has the chance to kill her. Niall arrives to find all his enemies dead. Niall takes his great-granddaughter into his arms, and Sookie weeps for her fallen friends but is able to smile when she realizes that at least Bill survived—though Claudine did not. Eric calls Pam to come pick up the living and the dead.

FRIDAY, JANUARY 20–SATURDAY, JANUARY 21. Amelia mourns Tray, whose death is attributed to a case of mistaken identity. Sookie publicly explains her own injuries as a pedestrian hit-and-run but tells Sam the entire truth when he comes to visit.

SUNDAY, JANUARY 22. Niall comes to tell Sookie that he has decided to close all the portals to the fae world to protect humans, but that they have not located Dermot and that the rest of the fae who have lived in the human world will have to choose whether to stay or return to Faery permanently. Jason arrives, startling Niall, who for a moment believes he is Dermot. Jason expresses hurt and resentment that his great-grandfather didn't deem him worthy of attention or acknowledgment, and tells Niall that he hopes the fairies are gone for good.

When Niall kisses his great-granddaughter on the cheek, Sookie senses his power and immediately feels a bit better. She watches Jason's tension relax as Niall kisses his great-grandson on the forehead before leaving.

The Secret Dialogues of Bill and Eric

To: WCompton@vmail.com
From: Eric@Fangtasia.com
02:15 am

Bill,

I've gotten word that the shifters will reveal live on TV in three nights while local shifters simultaneously change at several public venues. I will be sending as many vampires as I can to keep an eye on the situation and lend aid if needed. I will personally watch as Alcide Herveaux shifts at the Shamrock Casino. I'll send Clancy to you to watch over Merlotte's as Sam and Tray Dawson shift.

Eric

To: Eric@Fangtasia.com
From: WCompton@vmail.com
02:35 am

Eric,

So we are going with the "enemy of my enemy is my friend" philosophy? Allying ourselves not so much as with the shifters as possibly against the humans? I do see the reasoning behind it, and I'll be at Merlotte's with Clancy watching the reveal.

BTW, glad to see you've finally moved communication into the twenty-first century.

Bill

To: WCompton@vmail.com
From: Eric@Fangtasia.com
02:40 am

Pam insisted I start using e-mail.
   What the hell is BTW?

To: Eric@Fangtasia.com
From: WCompton@vmail.com
02:42 am

By The Way.

To: WCompton@vmail.com
From: Eric@Fangtasia.com
02:44 am

So why don't you just type "by the way"?

To: Eric@Fangtasia.com
From: WCompton@vmail.com
02:47 am

It's faster to abbreviate.

To: WCompton@vmail.com
From: Eric@Fangtasia.com
02:48 am

Obviously not, if one has to ask what the meanings are.

To: Eric@Fangtasia.com
From: WCompton@vmail.com
02:50 am

Get a list of them from Pam.

To: WCompton@vmail.com
From: Eric@Fangtasia.com
02:51 am

I hate computers.

~ ~ ~

To: WCompton@vmail.com
From: Eric@Fangtasia.com
06:01 pm

Bill,

I assume by now you've heard that Merlotte's mother was injured by
her husband when she revealed her second self. He has gone to
her, leaving Sookie to mind the bar, and now her brother's wife,
Christy, has been found nailed to a cross in the parking lot. I don't
know what to make of all this, but, needless to say, keep your eyes
and ears open.

Eric

To: Eric@Fangtasia.com
From: WCompton@vmail.com
06:13 pm

Her name was Crystal. I will keep watch over Sookie.

Bill

Phone: Eric calling Bill.

ERIC: "Bill, get to Sookie's immediately. Quinn has entered the area without permission, and you are to make certain he does not harass Sookie in any way. Keep him from her if you can."

BILL: "I'm on my way to her house."

Phone: Bill calling Eric.

BILL: "Eric, Sookie has been taken by fairies. I believe it was the ones called Lochlan and Neave. You must contact Niall, tell him to come to her house so we can track her. Now, Eric, NOW."

ERIC: "I'll call him and then come find you."

Dead in the Family

Timeline

THE FIRST WEEK OF MARCH 2006. Grieving the death of her lover, Tray Dawson, Amelia decides to return to New Orleans and pick up her life there. Sookie, too, is struggling with the emotional and physical aftermath of the torture she endured at the hands of the fairies. Amelia questions Sookie about her feelings for Eric as they pack up the car, and Amelia offers to help Sookie find a way to free herself of the blood bond. Sookie accepts, and she and Amelia say an emotional good-bye. As Sookie thinks over the events and losses of the past few months, she acknowledges that there are people she wants dead for the pain they caused and wonders if her own life is worth the cost.

THE END OF THAT WEEK. Sookie wakes one morning to find her cousin Claude sitting on her front porch. He asks how his sister died, and Sookie tells him that while she didn't witness Claudine's death, she believes Breandan was responsible. Claude sits silently, and Sookie waits for him to strike and kill her. He finally leaves, walking toward the road. Sookie enters her house and falls to her knees, trembling; she realizes that she wants to live, after all.

THE SECOND WEEK OF MARCH. Sookie works out with her friend JB du Rone at the health club in Clarice, where he is a personal trainer, and then she talks with his wife, her best friend Tara, about the upcoming birth of the couple's child. When Tara tells Sookie the baby will call her Aunt Sookie, she begins to plan a future.

THAT SAME WEEK. Spending the night with Eric, Sookie wakes in a panic, an event that has been occurring far too often. Eric weeps with her, but as he explains why he did not come to her aid during her torture, she is at first skeptical. Eric says that Victor Madden chained him to a wall with silver so that he could not rescue her. Victor alleged that Eric's actions would force the vampires into the Fae War. Although Pam was also held, she was not chained, and vampires loyal to King Felipe allowed her to call him to remind him of his personal pledge to protect Sookie. Felipe then demanded that Victor free both Eric and Pam. Hearing the pain and rage in Eric's voice, Sookie accepts his explanation but tells a surprised Eric that Victor must die.

THE THIRD WEEK OF MARCH. Jason invites Sookie over to enjoy a barbecue with him and Michele, and she is happy to see that not only is he recovering from the losses he has suffered but he seems to be maturing as well. Jason admits that he hasn't come out as a werepanther yet and still wants to keep his status private, but he has told Michele, who accepts him as he is, including his fairy heritage.

THE FOURTH WEEK OF MARCH. Watching Sookie at work, Sam lets her know that he is pleased to see her smile again. They talk, and he asks if she has seen Bill. When she admits that she believes Bill has been avoiding her, Sam encourages her to visit her former lover.

THE END OF THAT WEEK. Sookie goes over to see Bill and is alarmed when she sees his condition. Although he has been taking blood from his fellow vampires, he still has not recovered from the silver poisoning he suffered during the Fae War, and he admits that he no longer has any interest in his computer or in anything else. When Sookie asks what will help him, he tells her that he would have completely healed already if he could have taken blood from his maker, Lorena. Sookie asks if Lorena had created other children, and Bill tells her that Lorena turned a woman but he cannot reach out to his only sibling for help. Sookie leaves, determined to find a way to help her friend.

Having seen Bill and decided to help him, Sookie finds a level of peace and is able to sleep through the following nights. She finally relaxes enough to fully enjoy making love with Eric again.

WEDNESDAY, APRIL 12. Alcide calls, asking if the Long Tooth pack can use Sookie's land for their full-moon run the next night. She agrees, telling him to also contact Bill, whose land shares a property line with hers. She is curious about why Alcide can't use his own land as usual. He tells her that fishermen who claim that his late father allowed them to camp on the land are staying there. Both Alcide and Sookie are a bit uneasy at the sudden arrival of strangers on the Herveaux land so close to the full moon. When she gets to work, Sookie tells Sam about Alcide's call and suggests that he join the Weres for the evening. Sam casually mentions that he is dating someone from the pack and that while it might be fun, since he could shift into a wolf if he chose, he ultimately feels that it wouldn't be right. He confirms that Sookie will still attend his brother's wedding with him when it is rescheduled, admitting that he doesn't think that he should take a shifter to the event.

THURSDAY, APRIL 13. The Weres arrive for their run, and Sookie meets Alcide's new girlfriend, Annabelle Bannister, and his new second, Basim al Saud. She recognizes Alcide's friend Hamilton Bond as well as the slender young woman she met at the Hair of the Dog and two women from Priscilla Hebert's pack who surrendered to Alcide after the Were war. Sookie settles into her home for the evening with the doors locked and curtains drawn as the pack leaves for the hunt.

FRIDAY, APRIL 14. Basim comes to the door as the Weres are leaving to report to her that they have discovered signs of a vampire and at least one fairy on her land as well as a buried body. Sookie immediately realizes that the body must be that of Debbie Pelt and thanks him, considering the implications as the last of the Weres drive away.

Hearing a knock at the back door, Sookie is surprised to find Claude standing on her doorstep, a large tote bag in hand. He confesses that he is lonely in the house he once shared with his sisters and asks if he can stay with her for a while. He feels as if he is starving without the company of his own kind, and Sookie has enough fae blood to help him. Claude also delivers a letter from her great-grandfather, Niall Brigant, written on the skin of the water sprites that murdered her parents. The letter informs her that before leaving the human realm, Niall used profits from the sale of his pharmaceutical company to ensure that the FBI would no longer bother her. Niall's letter also states that Claudine had left Sookie all the money in her personal bank accounts and that Mr. Cataliades, who is handling the estate, will be sending Sookie a check. She calls Amelia to see if she plans to return to Bon Temps, and when her friend tells her she must stay in New Orleans, Sookie tells Claude he can have the room upstairs. She asks Claude if he had been in her woods recently, and when he denies visiting, she tells him of the scent of fairy that the Weres reported. After asking him why the news doesn't make him want to rush out to find whomever of his kind has remained on this side, Claude tells her that he fears it is her great-uncle Dermot and that Dermot would not be happy to see him. Sookie comes to the conclusion that Claude is realizing that he needs others, especially family, after the loss of both his sisters.

At work at Merlotte's, Sookie is thrilled when Holly shows off her new ring and announces her engagement to Hoyt Fortenberry. Sookie continues thinking about matrimony, and Tara, her pregnancy showing, comes in to satisfy one of her cravings. Sookie later decides that since Eric is her boyfriend—she is resolutely determined not to use the word "spouse"—she will seek his advice about the events of late.

Eric sends Pam to pick up Sookie after Merlotte's closes, and Pam immediately scents fairy in Sookie's house. Sookie explains that Claude has come to stay with her, but Pam doesn't buy Claude's loneliness and offends Sookie by telling her that she is foolish to be taken in by the fairy. They discuss Victor Madden on the drive to Shreveport, a discussion that continues at Eric's house. Sookie informs them that the Weres used her land and tells Eric that not only is there an unidentified fairy but there is a body buried on her property. Eric asks Pam to leave and then verifies that the body is Debbie's. They enjoy some passionate sex before Sookie leaves. As Pam is driving Sookie home, Pam reminds Sookie that she didn't tell Eric that Claude is living with her. She also expresses her reservations about Sookie and Eric's relationship, telling Sookie that in his position in Felipe's new regime, Eric cannot afford to be distracted by anything or anyone. Pam sees a car on the side of the interstate and identifies Bruno Brazell, Victor's second, standing beside it in the rain, waving them down. Realizing that Bruno has another vampire, Corinna, with him and that the obvious intention is to kill Eric's second and his lover, Pam hands Sookie a silver dagger, telling her that she cannot take them both on, so Sookie will have to help fight for their lives. Pam slips out the driver's side door, and Sookie steps out to approach Bruno. Corinna is standing to Bruno's right, looking around warily for Pam. Bruno admits that Victor has someone watching Eric's house, and the decision was made to attack Pam and Sookie when they were spotted leaving together. Sookie wonders aloud why Victor cannot simply enjoy having Eric on the payroll, but Bruno tells her that Victor fears Eric's power and his access to Sookie's ability. Bruno suddenly grabs Sookie by the neck. She is able to pull the knife out as she and Bruno struggle, falling and rolling down the embankment, and she stabs him up under his ribs, killing him. Pam makes her move at the same time, sending Corinna to her final sleep as well.

Pam immediately calls a panicked Eric to tell him that they are all right and that he is not to come to them in case Victor still has him under surveillance. She and Sookie decide to move Bruno's car to a location far away from the two disintegrating vampire bodies. When Pam and an exhausted Sookie finally reach her home, Sookie is surprised when her vampire friend hugs her and tells her she did well.

SATURDAY, APRIL 15. Sam notices that Sookie looks tired when she gets to work in the morning. When he asks about the Were run, she tells him that it seemed to go okay, leaving out the news of trespassers and the buried body. Sam reveals that he is dating Jannalynn Hopper, the young woman Sookie first met at the Hair of the Dog and who later participated in the Were war, dispatching the wounded enemy Weres with great efficiency. Their discussion is interrupted by Tanya Grissom, who announces that she and Calvin got married, so she needs to change her paperwork at Merlotte's to reflect her new last name. Claude comes in to tell Sookie that her water heater isn't working, and Terry Bellefleur, overhearing Claude's complaint, offers to take a look at it. Claude flirts with Terry, who bluntly states that he isn't gay. Sookie takes Claude aside before they leave and warns him that Terry is fragile because of his wartime experiences. She is relieved when Terry returns an hour later, seemingly none the worse for his time with Claude. She pays him for the part he needed, but he lets her know that Claude took care of the labor.

Kennedy Keyes, Merlotte's new bartender, arrives for her evening shift. Worried that someone will take advantage of Kennedy or see her as a challenge because she served time for manslaughter, Sam has also hired former serviceman Danny Prideaux to watch the bar when Kennedy works if Sam is not there.

After work, Sam and Sookie go to dinner at the Crawdad Diner to catch each other up on their lives. As they leave the restaurant, Pam calls to let Sookie know that Bruno and Corinna have not shown up for work in New Orleans, but no one suspects Pam and Sookie. As she closes her phone, Sookie finds a troubled Sam standing behind her. He tells her to remember that he is always there for her if she needs help and, touched, she promises him the same.

FRIDAY, APRIL 21. Sookie is startled when a nude Claude hands her a towel and the phone as she steps out of the shower. Remy Savoy is calling to ask Sookie if she can babysit his son, Hunter, overnight while Remy attends a family funeral, feeling that the grief-filled situation would be hard for the telepathic five-year-old to manage. Sookie agrees, and they set a time for Remy to drop Hunter off. When the two arrive that evening, she is delighted when Hunter remembers her. Remy is nonplussed that his son, whom he's never left for so long before, seems totally unconcerned as he leaves. As Sookie and Hunter communicate, Hunter reveals his worry that he will never be a regular man like his dad and the other men he admires, and Sookie is able to reassure him that she knows another telepathic man who has been able to make his telepathy work for him. As they are talking, Heidi, a vampire tracker sent by Eric, arrives to check out Sookie's woods. Hunter is fascinated by the vampire, who tells Sookie that she was turned when her son was the same age as Hunter and that her son is now a drug addict. As Heidi leaves to scout through the woods, Sookie reflects on the heartbreaking story.

After dinner, Sookie and Hunter talk about their telepathy a bit, and she tries to explain to the little boy why most people will not understand his gift and how he must learn to be respectful of the privacy of others. She soon realizes that not only is Hunter very adept at picking up thoughts but he can also feel when she is listening to him.

Heidi returns to report that two fae have recently been in her woods and that neither of them is the fairy she smells in Sookie's house. Heidi also identifies the vampire who wanders the woods at night as Bill Compton. She confirms that there is an old grave back in the woods but startles Sookie with news of a brand-new grave in a clearing near the stream.

SATURDAY, APRIL 22. Hunter wakes Sookie early, telling her of his dream of a tall man with yellow hair who came into his room, smiled at him, and then walked into the closet. Her suspicion that Eric is in the house is confirmed when she finds a note from him on the coffeepot, telling her he will see her that evening. Claude joins Sookie and Hunter as they are preparing pancakes and bacon, and Sookie is surprised that he seems to genuinely enjoy being with the child.

Their pleasant morning is disturbed by Agent Tom Lattesta, who is in town for a hearing on the shootings in January. He informs Sookie that the FBI is no longer investigating her. Lattesta is resentful that someone pulled strings for Sookie, and he vows to restart the investigation if he gets any new information on her.

Sookie, Hunter, and Claude decide to go to Magnolia Creek Park. When Tara stops by, Sookie introduces Hunter and Claude and is dismayed when Claude asks Tara if she would like to know the sex of her child. Tara agrees that she would like to know, so Claude informs her that she is carrying twins and will have a boy and a girl. Tara tells him her doctor has reported only one heartbeat, and Claude cheerfully insists she is carrying two healthy babies. As Hunter and Claude wander off to play ball, Sookie tells her stunned friend that Hunter is Hadley's son and that Claude is a cousin from the wrong side of the blanket. They enjoy a visit until Tara has to leave for work, and Sookie goes in search of Claude and her charge. Claude also has to leave to open his club in Monroe, so Sookie and Hunter go to McDonald's for a Happy Meal. When Hunter reads the mind of a playmate's weary mother at the restaurant, Sookie tries to use the unfortunate incident as a teaching moment, then she takes the tired and overexcited child home for a nap.

Remy arrives shortly after Hunter wakes, and father and son greet each other ecstatically. Hunter tells his attentive dad all about his visit, and as the child leaves to gather his possessions, Sookie tells Remy that all has gone well. As they leave, Sookie is pleased when Hunter unexpectedly gives her a hug. Eric rises as the sun sets, and before she can tell him about the second body Heidi scented on her land, he begins to explain the vampire hierarchy to her. Not pleased by her initial lack of interest, he insists that there are things she needs to know to ensure her safety. Afterward, they make love, but Sookie suddenly begins to feel strange and chatters randomly while braiding Eric's hair, finally sinking to the floor, certain that someone with Eric's blood is near.

Eric turns to the window and sees his maker, Appius Livius Ocella. Struggling to maintain cordiality, Eric asks his sire what is wrong with Sookie, and Appius informs him that he has another of his children with him and that the proximity of so many with his blood is confusing Sookie's thoughts and feelings. Sookie regains her senses and invites the two vampires to enter her home, even though she guesses correctly that her invitation is not necessary since Eric has permission and they are of the same blood. She is disturbed that Appius's other child is barely a teenager and then appalled when he is introduced as Alexei Romanov, a member of the Russian royal family.

Jason meets Appius and Alexei when he drops by to pick up an unused end table he wants. After some conversation about the past, Sookie asks if the newcomers are responsible for the fresh body on her land. She explains Heidi's discovery to Eric, who immediately blames the Weres who had been hunting and calls Alcide for a meeting. Fortunately, Alcide is nearby and soon arrives with Annabelle and Jannalynn. When Alcide denies any wrongdoing, the decision is made to identify the body. They all troop through the woods to the spot, and Alcide and Jason start digging. To the horror of the Weres, the body is that of Alcide's second, Basim. As they are trying to determine what could have befallen the werewolf, Annabelle admits to being with him the day after the hunt and reveals that he received a call from someone who was paying him, a call he didn't want her to hear. When Basim made an excuse to get her out of his apartment and then left, she followed him but lost him before she could find out where he was going. Jannalynn strikes Annabelle for her betrayal of Alcide and the pack, knocking her to the ground. Alcide names Jannalynn his new second and states that the pack will call a meeting to deal with the situation. As the Weres turn to leave, Sookie questions why the body was left on her land and demands that it be moved, fearing that the murderer is trying to get her involved. Eric says that he and Sookie should attend the meeting. Alcide tells Eric that vampires are not allowed but that Sookie can bring Jason. Jannalynn assures her that someone will come for the body that night as Alcide, his now former lover, and new second take their leave. Sookie wants the corpse off her land now, so Eric flies the wrapped body of Basim to the woods across the road. She, Jason, and Alexei then fill in the grave, disguising it to blend into the surrounding area.

As soon as the vampires depart for Eric's house in Shreveport, Sookie calls Pam, who is stunned at the arrival of her grand-sire. She then reluctantly notifies Bobby Burnham, warning him to be extra careful when he goes for his nightly briefing with Eric.

SUNDAY, APRIL 23. Sookie wakens to the smell of cooking and stumbles into the kitchen to share breakfast with Claude. He breaks their comfortable silence to tell her that Dermot came to his club the night before, seeking the company of another fae, and states that the Dermot he used to know would never have done that. Claude doesn't know why his uncle went crazy. Claude goes up to his room, and Sookie washes up, then decides to try to relax and read for a while. Her heart sinks when she sees two police cars coming down her drive, and she calls up to let Claude know, prompting him to join her as Sheriff Dearborn, accompanied by Andy Bellefleur and Alcee Beck, tells her that they received an anonymous tip about a body buried on her land in the woods, confirming her suspicions that someone is trying to tie her to the murder. Once again, Claude is introduced as a relative born on the wrong side of the blanket. While the men search her woods, Sookie decides to check her e-mail and reads a message from Andy's pregnant wife, Halleigh, letting Sookie know matriarch Caroline Bellefleur's health is fading fast and that Caroline is determined to locate the family Bible. Knowing that the Bible is on Bill's coffee table, Sookie forwards the e-mail to him so that he can decide what to do. The lawmen return to report that nothing was found.

WEDNESDAY, APRIL 26. Bill knocks on Sookie's door, formally dressed with the Bible in hand. Sookie is pleased to realize that he is finally going to reveal his family connection to the Bellefleurs and agrees to accompany him when he asks.

Halleigh answers the door, and Sookie explains that Bill has brought the family Bible to give to Miss Caroline. They are ushered upstairs to Caroline's bedroom. After she and Bill begin to discuss family history, Caroline is amused and delighted to learn that Bill is her great-grandfather and the one who arranged the financial windfall that allowed her to refurbish her home. As she begins to tire, she thanks Bill, and he tells her to rest easy as he and Sookie leave. Andy and Portia follow them from their grandmother's bedroom, and Bill graciously accepts Portia's extended hand and then gently chides Andy when he is less accepting. Bill asks them to hold Caroline's funeral in the evening so that he can attend, and an understanding Portia readily agrees.

THURSDAY, APRIL 27. Caroline Bellefleur passes away in the early hours of the morning.

FRIDAY, APRIL 28. Portia keeps her promise, and Caroline's funeral is held the next evening. Bill sits with the family. Sookie realizes at the funeral how terrible Bill still looks, and she resolves to take action. When he leaves after the funeral to go with the family to Belle Rive, she sneaks into his home and steals a CD of his vampire database, determined to locate the living child of his sire and save his life.

SATURDAY, APRIL 29. Sookie is able to read the CD and discovers that Lorena's only other child, Judith Vardamon, lives in Little Rock. An e-mail address is included, and after some soul-searching, Sookie decides that Bill's illness is more important than other considerations and that the vampire should be given the opportunity to help him if she can. Sookie sends an e-mail explaining Bill's situation and then leaves to return the CD to Bill's home. As she is crossing the cemetery, she sees Andy by Miss Caroline's new grave. When he comments that he hates that the family received charity from Bill, Sookie tells him that it was not charity, that Bill was simply a man who cared for his family and wanted to help them. A bemused Andy then tells her that Miss Caroline has left her famous chocolate cake recipe to the town and that it was received with great excitement at the newspaper office. He visibly brightens at Sookie's equally thrilled response to the news. Sookie hurries on to Bill's home to return the borrowed CD.

As Sookie works the afternoon shift at Merlotte's, she is stunned when she accidentally reads the thoughts of the cook, Antoine, and discovers that he is a government informant. When he realizes she knows, he begs her to talk to him before she does anything, but Sookie goes directly to Sam. Antoine tells them that he had gotten in trouble with the law over the theft of a car when he was desperate after Katrina and that Agent Weiss came to see him in jail, bringing Agent Lattesta, who offered him a deal. Lattesta already knew that Antoine's uncle was a Were, and the agent was convinced not only that the shifters would come out, just as the vampires did, but that there were other things out there as well. Not quite certain of Sookie's nature, Lattesta sent Antoine to Merlotte's to keep an eye on her. After Lattesta was ordered to leave Sookie alone, he continued to expect Antoine to report the activities of Sam and all the other supes that came into the bar. Antoine tells them he had already decided not to spy anymore and is relieved when Sam believes him and lets him keep his job. When Antoine goes back to the kitchen, Sam and Sookie begin to share their personal troubles, and both agree to go out to dinner again the next night if they don't hear from their significant others.

Sookie is surprised to see her brother waiting for her on her front porch after work. She calls out a greeting before realizing that the man is actually Dermot. A terrified Sookie wonders if he has finally come to kill her. Dermot tells her not to be afraid and that he only wants to get to know her and Jason better. He claims he had nothing to do with the death of her parents and that Breandan had lied to him and told him that Niall had killed his brother. As they converse, Sookie realizes that her uncle is desperately trying to warn her of something but has somehow been bespelled, so he is confused and crazed. He is able to tell her of another fairy who wishes her ill and that he will be looking over her, and then he vanishes. She calls Jason, letting him know to be especially vigilant.

Going through the past few daily newspapers while her dinner is cooking, Sookie realizes that there is still a great deal of tension about the shifters. She also reads about two especially brutal gang killings in Shreveport. She receives a message from Alcide with the time and date of the pack meeting and calls Jason again to give him the information. Finally giving in to the desire to contact Eric, from whom she has not heard a word in several days, she telephones him about the upcoming pack meeting, and he asks her to come see him.

Arriving at Fangtasia, Sookie is shocked by how few customers are in the vampire bar. She finds Eric sitting with Alexei and Appius. Alexei begins to speak of his human family, taking Sookie's hand and showing her his memories of all that was done to him and his family in order to justify his current sense of entitlement and desire to be allowed to go his own way. Sickened, Sookie tells him he still has a responsibility to live the right way. Pam interrupts them with the unwelcome news that the new area BVA representative has arrived in the bar, and Eric asks Appius and Alexei to go to his office so that he can greet her. Although it is obvious that Eric's business is down, the rep is pleasant and too polite to comment.

Once they are alone, Eric tells Sookie that Alexei is insane and that Appius has brought him to Eric in the hopes that he could help the boy. Alexei escaped somehow from their supervision and is responsible for the two supposedly gang-related deaths. Sookie is not happy that Eric is only concerned about the interests of vampires, especially his own, and is ignoring the deaths of the two young men. As they part, Eric wearily reiterates his love for her and promises to come to her house the night after her meeting with Alcide. As Sookie walks to her car, she is joined by Pam, who tells her that Alexei will ruin Eric if he stays much longer. Sookie warns Pam to let Appius handle the situation because Eric will have to let him kill her if she takes out Alexei. Pam is touched that Sookie cares and calls her a friend.

Sookie returns home exhausted and is ready to go to bed when the doorbell rings. She doesn't recognize the vampire female on her doorstep but, curious, opens the door, knowing the vampire can't enter the house without an invitation. When Sookie's unexpected visitor identifies herself as Judith Vardamon, Sookie invites her in, much to the vampire's surprise. As they talk, Judith tells Sookie the story of Lorena and her maker, Solomon Brunswick, and about how she changed Bill because she'd fallen in love with him after seeing him through the window of his home with his family. Bill hated her and was miserable with her, but Lorena remained obsessed with him. After thirty years together, Lorena tried to make him happier by turning Judith because she resembled his wife. Lorena believed that if Bill had a companion, he would be content to stay with her. When Judith confesses her fear of Lorena, Sookie tells her of Lorena's final death. An overjoyed Judith demands to know where to find Bill and delightedly exclaims that they are finally free to be together without Lorena's influence. As she hurries away to find Bill, a stunned Sookie tries to come to terms with her mixed feelings and ponders the fact that she will grow old while the vampires will go on living.

SUNDAY, APRIL 30. Sookie finds two envelopes that were shoved under her front door in the night. The first, from Mr. Cataliades, is her inheritance from Claudine. A stunned Sookie finds a check made out to her for $150,000. The second note is from Bill, who tells her that Judith's blood is already healing him and that she will be staying for a week to catch up on old times. Sookie is again pondering her feelings when Claude joins her on the porch. She tells him of Dermot's visit and of her suspicion that he has been bespelled. She confronts Claude about whether he knows anything about the other fairies still on this side, but he tells her he doesn't want to be killed and leaves. Sookie goes to church for comfort, and she is surprised and pleased to see Sam there. She joins her friends Tara and JB for lunch and then spends the afternoon doing laundry. Jason calls, and they decide to ride together to the Shreveport pack meeting the following evening.

MONDAY, MAY 1. Sam is away at a final tax meeting with his accountant when Sookie arrives at work. An anti-shifter protester enters the bar, and Sookie tells Kennedy to call the police and then notify Sam. Sookie and the bartender persuade the protester to leave, but to their dismay, there are about thirty other protesters in the parking lot. Police officers Kevin Pryor and Kenya Jones manage to disperse the crowd without incident, and Sam, having parked elsewhere and come in the back, arrives to thank them for their help. Sookie tries to be helpful by suggesting that Sam arrange to talk to the church the protesters attend, but Sam furiously refuses to have to explain who and what he is.

Sookie stops at the grocery store on her way home from work and is aware of the silence that greets her as she shops, knowing that word of the protest at Merlotte's has already gotten around town. She is disturbed to realize that some of the townspeople support the pending legislation that would restrict the rights of shifters.

Jason picks up Sookie on time for the drive to Shreveport, and they discuss the various suspects in the killing of Basim on their way to Alcide's house. Jannalynn greets them at the door and escorts them into the living room, where Annabelle is on her knees all alone in the center of the floor. Jannalynn instructs Sookie to go upstairs to Alcide. She finds him in the study waiting for her, and he bluntly tells her that a pack shaman would be able to determine what had happened to Basim. They haven't had one in four years; she is the closest they've got. By drinking a shaman's potion, she should be able to discern who was involved and their degree of guilt. When she tells him that a year ago he wouldn't have asked her to do this, he replies that a year ago she wouldn't have hesitated. Sookie drinks the potion.

As Alcide helps an increasingly unstable Sookie downstairs, she realizes with a sense of relief that she is becoming unable to feel the vampires through her bond. Sookie views the pack through the effect of the drug, and as she concentrates, she realizes she can see them as colors and knows immediately what colors to look for. She accuses Hamilton Bond of betraying the pack by inviting government people to camp on Alcide's land, even knowing that they were looking for dirt on the Louisiana packs to use to push through anti-shifter legislation. She gets him to admit that he was jealous of Basim, and he finally confesses that he saw Basim meeting with a fairy and heard their plan to implicate Sookie in a murder by burying a body on her property. Ham decided to kill Basim and bury him instead, and then collect the reward promised by the fairy himself. Ham tells them that he was supposed to meet the fairy on Sookie's property after the meeting that evening. Sookie names Patricia Crimmins, originally from the St. Catherine Parish pack, as Ham's accomplice. Patricia tries to throw herself on the mercy of the pack, as she did after the Were war, claiming that her only crime has been loving the wrong man, but Ham declares that her motive was purely retaliation for not being chosen by Alcide as his lover. Annabelle is guilty only of being unfaithful to Alcide. Jason and Sookie leave as the Weres are deciding on the punishment, and Sookie is confident that enforcer and second Jannalynn will successfully argue for the deaths of Ham and Patricia.

The drug is already wearing off as they exit the house, and Sookie is sick in the yard before she and Jason reach the truck. As her mind clears, Sookie suddenly begins to feel Eric through the bond again and becomes aware of his unhappiness and physical pain. She urges Jason to get her to Eric's house as quickly as possible, and she fears the worst until they enter the home and Eric answers her call. They find him horribly wounded, and Bobby Burnham and his vampire girlfriend, Felicia, have been murdered. Eric tells them that Alexei finally snapped, killing the two when Appius left him alone to speak to Eric and then fleeing. Appius has gone after Alexei. Sookie orders her brother to push Eric's broken ribs back in so that he can heal, and after doing so, Jason goes to the bathroom to wash off the blood. Sookie confronts the defeated Eric and taunts him until he reacts. When Jason staggers back into the room, he reports finding a severely injured Pam and that he has given her blood. Jason's cell phone rings, and his girlfriend tells him that Alexei has been to his house looking for him, that Appius arrived soon after, and that she has sent them both to Sookie's house. Sookie immediately calls Claude and warns him to get out, since the vampires can enter her house. She and a recovering Eric leave Jason with Pam and rush to Sookie's house.

They have almost reached the house when Eric doubles over with pain that is not his own. They arrive in her yard to find the security light on and Claude and a fairy Sookie has never seen before standing back to back, armed with knives and a sword, while Alexei circles them, occasionally darting in to strike. Appius lies nearby, head bloodied, and Eric asks him if he still lives. Appius replies that his spinal cord is severed and that he cannot move until he heals. As Sookie pleads with Alexei not to kill the fairies, she learns that the stranger is Colman, the father of Claudine's baby, and that he blames Sookie for the death of his mate and child. Alexei dashes forward between the fairy blades to punch Colman and is wounded by Claude.

Sookie realizes that Alexei is beginning to tire and runs into the house to retrieve the silver chain that the Drainers had used to restrain Bill so long ago. Returning to the yard, she edges cautiously toward the whirling Alexei, and when he comes near, she throws it over his head and pulls it tightly around his neck. The boy falls screaming to the ground, and Eric sends his sibling to his final death using a broken tree branch. While Eric stands guard over the two fae, Sookie takes advantage of his distraction to take the stake from a disintegrating Alexei and crawl toward the helpless Appius. She tells him she wants to kill him, but he answers that if she was going to do it, she would not have spoken. He predicts that she won't keep Eric. Eric pleads with her not to kill his maker, so she comes up with a better idea. She hears a shout from Eric as Appius's eyes look past her, and she feels Appius tell her to move. She throws herself away from the vampire just as a fairy blade slashes past her and into Appius's body. Colman stands, stunned, looking down at his unintended victim, and then he begins to sway, a dagger protruding between his shoulder blades. Sookie turns to see who threw the blade but sees only Claude, who is looking at both of the knives still in his hands. Eric begins draining the wounded Colman.

Claude and Sookie sit side by side on the grass, and Claude explains that he had tried to persuade Colman to return to Faery and had moved in with Sookie to protect her. Dermot steps out of the woods and tells them he threw the dagger into Colman to protect Sookie. He is able to indicate to Claude and Sookie that the spell that is on him was put there long ago, and Sookie realizes that it must have been placed by Niall. She tells Claude that spells are broken by a kiss in human fairy tales, and they both lean forward to kiss Dermot. He shudders all over and intelligence begins to fill his eyes as he weeps. Claude takes Dermot into the house, and Eric and Sookie are left alone. Eric asks Sookie why she was going to spare Appius and what she was going to say to him, and she replies that she was going to make a deal to let him live if he would kill Victor. A startled Eric admits it was a good idea.

Sookie watches as the fairy blood he took finally begins to energize Eric, and he realizes that he is free forever from his maker. Telling Sookie that she is his dearest, Eric promises to return to her when he has checked on Pam and dealt with the things he must do now that Appius has died. Sookie watches him launch into the air to return to Shreveport. She wearily showers and prepares for bed, grimly satisfied that her enemies have perished and she has again survived. As she opens the door to her bedroom, she is surprised to find Dermot and Claude, who want to share the bed with her. Too exhausted to argue, she climbs into the bed with her fae kin on either side, and to her astonishment, she feels relaxed and comforted. She falls asleep surrounded by family.

The Secret Dialogues of Bill and Eric

Phone: Eric calling Bill.

ERIC: "Bill, how are you feeling?"

BILL: "Not well."

ERIC: "Victor is expecting a sales report for the database."

BILL: "There are orders. They need to be packaged."

ERIC: "Do you need help?"

BILL: "Yes."

ERIC: "I'll send Felicia over to your house several times a week to assist you. She can also give you blood while she is there. Perhaps that will help you heal."

BILL: "Thank you."

ERIC: "Bill?"

BILL: "What?"

ERIC: "If Sookie had died, I would let you suffer."

BILL: "If Sookie had died, I would already be dead."

Phone: Eric calling Bill.

ERIC: "Bill, I need your help dealing with Victor. Come to my house Thursday night."

BILL: "You need *my* help?"

ERIC: "I need your knowledge of computers. Bobby and Pam have been backing up all of Area Five's financial records on the computer. I want several copies and I want them to be safe. And I want to be able to tell if anyone tries to access them. Can you do that?"

BILL: "Bobby can't?"

ERIC: "I would like you to do this."

BILL: "Of course. I'll be there after Fangtasia closes."

ERIC: "Should I send Pam to get you?"

BILL: "Pam? Not Felicia?"

ERIC: "Not Felicia, not for this."

BILL: "I see." *Pause.* "No. I can drive."

ERIC: "It might be a good idea for you to drive around a bit, make certain you're not followed."

BILL: "Do you believe we are all being watched?"

ERIC: "I'm certain Victor knows you've been . . . ill and staying close to home. If you suddenly drive to Shreveport, he may hear of it. I don't feel like coming up with an explanation."

BILL: "You really are concerned, aren't you?"

ERIC: "Yes. For us all. Victor has already sent Sandy back to Vegas and is running the entire state himself from New Orleans. I would not be surprised if he has bigger plans. Area Five's dealings must be aboveboard and strictly accounted. There can be no reason for Felipe to doubt us, no way for Victor to cast aspersions upon us."

BILL: "I'll take steps to ensure I am not followed."

Phone: Eric calling Bill.

ERIC: "Bill, have you seen either Bruno or Corinna lately?"

BILL: "No. Why?"

ERIC: "I've heard rumors that they are missing from New Orleans."

BILL: "And . . . ?"

ERIC: "And I was wondering if by chance you'd seen them, if they'd stopped by."

BILL: "No, they did not. Have you seen them?"

ERIC: "No, I can honestly say that I have not."

BILL: "I see."

ERIC: "In fact, I cannot imagine why Victor's second would be in my area without my knowledge."

BILL: "Of course not. It would be a violation of protocol."

ERIC: "Indeed it would. And any of my people would be well within their rights to defend themselves if they were accosted by Victor's second."

BILL: "Absolutely."

ERIC: "Yes, so it's a good thing that no one has seen them in the area. However, it's probably best that you don't speak of this to anyone."

BILL: "Speak of what?"

ERIC: "Exactly."

Phone: Bill calling Eric.

BILL: "I'm calling to inform you that I have a visitor. She arrived Saturday night and will be staying with me for a week or so."

ERIC: "She?"

BILL: "Yes. Judith Vardamon, my . . . Lorena's other child."

ERIC: "Well. This is a good thing for you, is it not? You already sound stronger."

BILL: "Yes. I'm feeling much better. Please thank Felicia for me. She was here just before Judith arrived and has been a great help, but I will no longer need her."

ERIC: "I'll let her know."

BILL: "Forgive me, Eric, but you don't sound yourself. I know I have been out of sorts these past weeks, but is there something I should know? Have there been more problems with Victor?"

ERIC: "I only wish it were Victor. You are not the only one with family visitors, Bill. My maker has arrived with his child. Things are not going well."

BILL: "I see."

ERIC: "He is my maker. It is not for me to advise him; he must reach his own conclusions. He's trying, but the child is . . . I see this ending badly. But he's . . . He's my maker."

BILL: "I remember the feeling all too well, Eric."

ERIC: "I imagine you do. She would have been of help to you now, though."

BILL: "I would rather die than have asked her. If Sookie had not contacted Judith, I would never have bothered her after what Lorena did to her, did to us both."

ERIC: "Sookie contacted her?"

BILL: "Yes. She got Judith's e-mail from my database and told her I was ill and needed her. She and Judith then spoke when Judith arrived. Judith was much relieved to know that Lorena had met her final death, and surprised it was at Sookie's hands. She was most impressed."

ERIC: "Sookie is most impressive. Bobby has just arrived with some paperwork for me. Felicia is with him, so I will pass along your thanks. Good night, Bill."

BILL: "Good night, Eric."

Phone: Bill calling Eric.

BILL: "Eric, we've just arrived home. What happened at Sookie's tonight? All was quiet when we went out, but now there are strange scents through the woods."

ERIC: "My maker has met his final death, Bill. His child as well."

BILL: "This is not what you wanted?"

ERIC: "I don't know. I feel strangely free." *Pause.* "What is it like to live without your maker, Bill? How did you feel when Lorena died?"

BILL: "She had been torturing me, Eric. When she died, I felt relief. Afterward, I felt somewhat adrift. I imagine it is much like any child when a parent dies, even if the parent was a poor one."

ERIC: "I cannot remember a time when I did not feel Ocella's presence, but I did not hate him."

BILL: "I believe I hated Lorena, as much as a vampire can hate their maker. Twice she took me from a woman I loved."

(Silence.)

BILL: "I take it Sookie is all right?"

ERIC: "Yes. I left her with her fairy cousin and uncle."

BILL: "Her uncle? I thought he was dangerous."

ERIC: "He was bespelled, and he was freed tonight as well. He killed a fairy who meant Sookie harm, a fairy who killed Ocella instead." *Pause.* "Bobby and Felicia are also dead. Bobby died trying to protect me."

BILL: "I'm sorry, Eric."

ERIC: "So am I. Pam was injured but is recovering."

BILL: "Eric, is there anything I can do?"

ERIC: "Perhaps you could look through Bobby's computer, help Pam with what needs to be taken care of until I find another daytime employee."

BILL: "Of course. Shall we come to Fangtasia tonight?"

ERIC: "Please. I need to rely on you and Pam while I am attending to Ocella's final arrangements, Bill. I cannot afford to let anything slide. *We* cannot afford it. Victor remains a threat to us all."

BILL: "I'll see you tonight."

Dead Reckoning

Timeline

WEDNESDAY, MAY 24, 2006. Sookie decides to take advantage of the fact that Dermot and Claude are still staying at her house and enlists the pair to help her clean out the attic. Setting aside the family photos, documents, and other items Sookie thinks might be worth selling in the living room, they eventually pile the most obviously dilapidated and worthless in the driveway to be burned. At work at Merlotte's that evening, Sookie tells Sam of their activity, and much to her surprise, he is able to recommend a shop in Shreveport that appraises and purchases antiques. Sam tells her that he needs to stop in to look for a birthday gift for Jannalynn, so they make plans to visit the shop the next day.

Business is sparse that night. Not only has Sam come out as two-natured, but there is also a new bar nearby that is drawing a crowd. Kennedy Keyes and Danny Prideaux come in for a drink just as it is getting dark, and Sookie is closing the front curtains when she sees suspicious activity in the parking lot. A Molotov cocktail is thrown through the window, setting a table on fire and scattering flaming napkins through the bar. Sam grabs the fire extinguisher to extinguish the flames. As customers race out of the bar through the back door, Sookie grabs pitchers of tea and water to put out the small fires created by the burning napkins. Sam sees Sookie's hair catch on fire and sprays her with the fire extinguisher before she even realizes what has happened. Together, they are able to douse the blaze before the fire department arrives. Eric storms in a few minutes later, having felt Sookie's distress through their bond, and insists on taking Sookie home; however, she convinces him to allow Sheriff Bud Dearborn and the fire chief to question her for their investigation into the arson.

Eric contacts Pam to bring a hairdresser to Sookie's house, and the female vampire is waiting with Immanuel Earnest, a stylist from Shreveport, when Eric and Sookie arrive. Immanuel sets up in the kitchen and gets to work, cutting off several inches of Sookie's hair while Eric glowers.

While showering, Sookie thinks about the firebombing and suspects that the being that did it was not human. She returns to the kitchen, and Immanuel cuts again, evening out her hair. Pam, who is in a bad mood after receiving a text, begins complaining about Victor still being in charge, then she shifts her annoyance to the items from the attic piled in Sookie's living room and driveway. She finally questions Eric on what kind of husband he is, allowing his wife to live with other men, and Eric attacks her. Immanuel pulls Sookie out of the kitchen while the two vampires battle it out. The hairdresser reveals that Pam is frustrated because she wants to turn her lover, Miriam—Immanuel's sister who is suffering from leukemia—but has not been given permission to make her own child. Sookie finally has enough, fills a pitcher from the bathroom with cold water, goes into the kitchen, and throws it on the two vampires rolling around on the floor, then leaves the two to settle down. When Eric and Pam finally emerge, Sookie sends everyone home, shooing the vampires out of the front door as Claude and Dermot arrive home from work and enter from the back. Exhausted, Sookie heads off to bed.

THURSDAY, MAY 25. Sookie is awakened by someone knocking and finds Sam at her door, ready to head to Splendide, the antique shop in Shreveport. Sam is dismayed at the mess left in Sookie's kitchen from Pam and Eric's fight, but Sookie tells him she expects Eric will replace any damaged items. They straighten up, and then Sam shares donuts with Dermot while Sookie showers. As Sookie and Sam get into his truck to head to Shreveport, he comments on how well Dermot treats Sookie. Sam tells her that he has researched fairies in the library of information kept by shifters about supes and that a familial connection would not deter a fairy from pursuing a possible relationship. Sookie assures him that she doesn't think of Dermot that way, and that they regard themselves as family only. The conversation shifts when they both admit that they believe that the arsonist was a twoey. Although Sam doesn't think that it was a hate crime targeted at shifters and their supporters, he does feel that there is hatred involved. The question is whose.

They arrive at Splendide, and Sookie pokes around while Sam picks out a gift for Jannalynn, who loves antiques. He finally selects a pair of earrings, with Sookie's input, and then she makes an appointment for the shop owners to come to her house to appraise the items from her attic. After leaving the shop, Sam suggests that they stop for lunch. He expresses concern about his relationship with Jannalynn, worrying that they are not on the right track, and then Sookie expresses her own concern about the side effects of her proximity to her fae family. She asks Sam if he could do more research for her in the shifter library, but he suggests going right to the source and asking Claude and Dermot in person. They decide to detour to Claude's club, Hooligans, on the way back. Remy Savoy calls while they are at the restaurant and asks Sookie if she can babysit Hunter for the weekend, but she isn't sure of her work schedule and is unable to commit. After asking Sam about her schedule, she calls Remy back to tell him she can't babysit, and he takes the opportunity to ask her to accompany him and Hunter to kindergarten orientation. Sookie is surprised but agrees.

Sookie and Sam are greeted at Hooligans by an elf named Bellenos and taken to Claude's office. Dermot accompanies them. Sam cuts to the chase, bluntly asking why Sookie is feeling more and more fae. He reprimands the two fairies for not educating Sookie about her heritage and suggests that they have ulterior motives for staying with her. Instead of answering, Claude leads them farther into the club, which is filled with beings of varying degrees of fae blood. One of them welcomes her as one of their own, but Sookie declines the invitation and leaves the room, asking Claude and Dermot what is going on. Dermot tells her that he and Claude will speak with her that evening when they get home. She quietly mourns her gullibility on the way back to Bon Temps.

Sookie works the late shift again and stays up for a while after getting home to wait for Dermot and Claude, who do not come home at all.

FRIDAY, MAY 26. Sookie works the early shift but stays an extra two hours when her replacement suffers a flat tire, and Eric is waiting for her by the time she gets to her house. He has a dress for her and tells her they are going to Vampire's Kiss, Victor's new dance club. Immanuel arrives to do her makeup and hair. On the way to the club, Sookie finds out from Eric that it is Victor who has forbidden Pam from turning Miriam.

Sookie and Eric arrive at Vampire's Kiss to find that Pam has been assaulted by Victor's minions for trying to get into the club to make certain it is safe for Eric. He is furious, as is Pam. Once inside, they see that Victor has brought Miriam there to provoke Pam. Sookie finds out that Victor is also the owner of Vic's Redneck Roadhouse, the new bar that is drawing patrons from Merlotte's. Victor serves Eric and Pam bottled blood along with glasses. The server "thinks" to Sookie not to allow her vamps to use the glasses, as they have been rubbed with fairy blood. Sookie sends a wave of negativity to Eric, who drinks from the bottle. Pam follows suit.

After exchanging words with Victor, Eric, Sookie, and Pam leave, taking Miriam with them. They are approached in the parking lot by two of Victor's followers, who claim they wish to ally themselves with Eric, but he sends them away, believing they are trying to trap him. When Sookie comments on the tension between Eric and Pam, Pam blurts out that Eric has received a letter. Before she can continue, Eric grabs her throat and orders her to be silent. As he is driving at the time, Sookie is disturbed on many levels. He tells Sookie to leave it be. When they arrive at her house, Sookie does not invite the vampires in.

SATURDAY, MAY 27. Dermot and Claude are home when Sookie wakes, and they are ready for their talk. They mention troubles at the club, and Sookie guesses that a fairy is missing and tells them about the fairy blood Victor used the night before. The two fairies are angry to have lost a female, Cait, to the vampires.

The fairies tell her that Niall was able to arrange a visit with Jason when he was a baby and realized that he lacked the "essential spark." Niall assumed Sookie would also lack any fairy traits and didn't attempt to contact her, but eventually he thought to ask Eric, with whom he had business dealings, to check up on her. It was Eric who informed Niall that she wasn't a normal human. Niall first sent Claudine and then decided to meet Sookie himself. Unfortunately, it was Niall's interest in his great-granddaughter that precipitated the fairy war and the sealing off of Faery, leaving not just the two of them but others outside. Claude and Dermot acknowledge that Sookie is gaining power from them and that the fae are all gaining power from each other. They are greater than the sum of their parts. Claude and Dermot also reveal that there is still a fairy portal in her woods. Sookie continues to question their motives, but they all finally settle down in an uneasy truce. They discuss the firebombing at Merlotte's, and Sookie asks them to let her know if they hear any talk about it at Hooligans.

Dermot helps Sookie clean the attic and suggests that she could partition off another bedroom while still leaving an area for storage. To her shame, Sookie realizes that she did not give any consideration to Dermot and Claude having to share a bedroom. Dermot has actually been sleeping on a cot in the sitting room. They discuss what to do, and Dermot is excited at the prospect of having his own space.

The owners of Splendide, Brenda Hesterman and Donald Callaway, arrive to appraise the goods from the attic. Donald finds a secret cubby in the big desk and gives Sookie its contents, a faded letter in an old envelope and a velvet bag. She immediately recognizes the handwriting on the letter as her grandmother's and puts it aside to read privately later. The partners buy several pieces, taking a few items with them and arranging for one of their trucks to pick up the rest.

Jack and Lily Leeds, the private investigators who questioned Sookie about Debbie Pelt's death, come into Merlotte's while Sookie is working that night to give her a warning about Sandra Pelt. Sandra is still obsessed with Sookie. The Leedses reveal that the attorney for Sandra's parents' estate, Mr. Cataliades, instructed them exactly when to arrive at Merlotte's to speak with Sookie, and she instantly realizes that Mr. Cataliades somehow knows there is going to be trouble and sent the Leedses in as backup. Sure enough, four toughs come into the bar, high on vampire blood. Sam, who is standing behind the bar talking with Jannalynn, tries to calm the situation even as both he and Jannalynn react instinctively to the danger. Most of the patrons move away, with the exception of the Leedses, Andy Bellefleur, and Danny Prideaux. The thugs indicate that they are after "the blonde," and weapons are drawn on both sides. There is a short struggle, resulting in one bullet wound, a few minor injuries, and several broken bones. The four thugs are subdued, the police are called, and Lily takes Jack, who took the bullet, to the hospital. Because Lily and Sookie were standing together when the comment was made about "the blonde," the police assume Lily was the intended target, and Sookie breathes a sigh of relief.

SUNDAY, MAY 28. Sookie wakes to an empty house. After going over the events of the previous evening, she calls Mr. Cataliades but is only able to leave a message on his machine. She then calls Amelia to ask if she can help locate Sandra Pelt, and Amelia decides to come up, bringing Bob Jessop, who is back in her life, to help out and renew the wards around the house. Sookie decides to read the letter from her grandmother, which explains, to the best of Adele's knowledge and ability, Fintan's involvement in her life. According to the letter, the object in the velvet bag is a cluviel dor, a gift from Fintan delivered to Adele by a stranger whom Sookie recognizes from the description: Mr. Cataliades. A fairy gift, the cluviel dor holds a powerful spell that will work only one time. Sookie feels an attachment to the object and gains pleasure in holding it. Worried about its potential, she hides it in her makeup drawer.

MONDAY, MAY 29. Andy, who is in Merlotte's with Bud for lunch, tells Sookie that he and his wife, Halleigh, are expecting a girl, whom they will name Caroline Compton Bellefleur, and that his sister, Portia, is pregnant as well. He shyly asks if Sookie will tell Bill, who is his great-great-great-grandfather, the good news. After Andy leaves to take Halleigh a milkshake, Sandra Pelt storms into the bar and screams at Sookie. Sandra admits her attempts to harm Sookie and asks what it will take to kill her. Sam passes the wooden bat he keeps behind the bar to Terry Bellefleur, who hits Sandra as she pulls a gun on Sookie. Terry freaks out, and Sookie comforts him as he mumbles about the shining man and the blond man who told him to keep watch over Sookie and keep her safe. The EMTs give Terry a shot to calm him, and she and Sam take him to Sam's trailer to sleep off the effects. Terry whispers that the men promised to protect his dog and make his dreams stop.

Having again felt Sookie's fear through their bond, Eric is waiting for her outside Merlotte's. They go to her house to talk about the blood bond, their marriage, and their future. Eric is amazed when Sookie tells him that she doesn't want to be a vampire. Amelia and Bob arrive, interrupting the discussion, and Eric soon leaves. Tired from their drive, Amelia and Bob turn in. Sookie hears a quiet knock at the back door and opens it to find Bill, who asks her to come outside to talk with him. Thanks to the blood of his "sibling," Judith, he is healed from the silver poisoning he suffered while rescuing Sookie from the fae, but he explains that he had not contacted Judith himself because she had previously been somewhat obsessed with him. Once she arrived, he hoped to love her and that a relationship with her would free him from Sookie, but he still doesn't have feelings for Judith. Having followed him to listen in, Judith overhears his words and, with great dignity, announces that she will leave and will get over her attachment to Bill. When Bud Dearborn calls with the news that Sandra has escaped from the hospital where she was taken for treatment, Bill tells Sookie that he will guard her house that night.

TUESDAY, MAY 30. Sookie works half of the early shift so that she can attend Hunter's kindergarten introduction with Hunter and Remy in Red Ditch. She and Hunter both get a reading from one of the prospective teachers, and Sookie advises Remy to make sure Hunter is not assigned to that classroom. They stop at Dairy Queen afterward for Blizzards and run into Erin, Remy's new girlfriend, who joins them. Sookie ask Erin to sit with Hunter for a moment and takes Remy outside to offer the money from Hadley's estate for Hunter, but Remy turns her down. He prefers to provide for the child Hadley left behind himself.

Sookie arrives home to find Amelia and Bob renewing the wards around her property. Sookie wanders off to find the fairy portal, which she locates in a clearing less than a quarter mile from her house. Over dinner Amelia tells Sookie that she knows how to break the blood bond, and the trio performs the ceremony at sunset. Eric calls almost immediately, concerned that Sookie has suddenly been cut off from him. He is furious that Sookie has intentionally severed the link, and he ultimately hangs up on her.

WEDNESDAY, MAY 31. Sookie goes to work but is so distracted that Sam sends her home early. She asks Bob and Amelia to go to the movies, certain Eric will come by. He arrives after sundown. They reaffirm their love for each other and have passionate monkey sex on the front porch swing. Afterward, they discuss the situation concerning Pam and Miriam, and the vampire politics currently affecting them all. Sookie suggests that they contact the waiter who warned her about the drinks. Sookie and Eric drive over to Vampire's Kiss. While they wait in the lot for the bar's closing, Eric tells Sookie that he has hired a lone-wolf Were to replace Bobby as his daytime guy. When the waiter, Colton, leaves the bar, they follow him to his trailer and identify themselves. They meet his girlfriend, Audrina Loomis, and find out that Victor killed Colton's mother. They make plans to meet again the next night at Sookie's place to plot the death of Victor.

Exhausted, Sookie spends the night at Eric's, alone in an upstairs bedroom.

THURSDAY, JUNE 1. Sookie leaves bright and early to drive back to her house. She finds Alcide half-naked and asleep in her bed; having heard from Amelia that she broke the blood bond, he came to Sookie's house to try to reignite their chemistry. Sookie is offended and sends him away. Mustapha Khan, Eric's new day guy, arrives with a friend to pick up Eric's car. After they leave, Sookie chastises Amelia and Claude, who let Alcide in, for interfering in her life. Sookie tells everyone to get out of her house. When the others have departed, she finds Dermot sitting on the back steps. Knowing Claude was the real instigator of the two fae, she allows Dermot to stay. She gives him some money and lets him take her car to Home Depot to get more supplies to refinish the attic area.

At Merlotte's, Sam confides that the bar is in a real slump, the worst he's ever faced. Sookie doesn't know what to say and can offer only small comfort. She leaves work late, stopping to fill up her gas tank and to get some milk and synthetic blood. Pulling up to her house, she is first irritated by the open back door but then recognizes danger and tries to retreat, only to be blocked by a tree falling across the drive. She escapes from her car, smacking a potential attacker with a quart of milk, and runs toward Bill's house in the pouring rain. She's able to find the spare key on his front porch and get into his house, but first she discards her soaking clothes and shoes into the bushes so she won't leave a trail.

Though Bill never told her, Sookie had figured out the likely location of his daytime resting place while they were dating. Aware of the renovations he has done, she zeros in on a small room off the kitchen and is able to pry up a trapdoor hidden in the floor. Naked and in the dark, she carefully feels around for Bill and finally locates his inanimate naked body in the corner. Sookie can hear her pursuers overhead as Bill struggles to wake, but it takes him several attempts to fully rouse. He finally comes to completely and leaves to search for her assailants while Sookie waits. He returns and dresses, and she wraps herself in an old shawl for the drive back to her house. They find Dermot bleeding and unconscious in the attic, and Bill is intoxicated by the scent of the fairy blood. He manages to leave the house and checks the property. Sookie calls Hooligans to get help for Dermot, and Claude sends Bellenos, who arrives in a matter of minutes. Sookie apologizes to Dermot, explaining that Amelia's protection wards should have kept the intruders out, but Dermot admits that he deconstructed Amelia's wards, planning to put up his own because he felt they would be much stronger. Bellenos treats Dermot's head wound by breathing into him. As soon as Dermot is able, the two leave to hunt for Dermot and Sookie's attackers. A bit later, Pam and Eric arrive just in time for Dermot and Bellenos to return with the severed heads of the attackers.

After the fairies leave, taking the heads with them, Sookie, Pam, and Eric discuss who could be behind the attempted kidnapping. When Eric quickly leaves the room to take a phone call, Sookie realizes that something is going on. Sookie faces Eric down and forces him to admit that his maker, before his death, had arranged a marriage for Eric with a vampire queen. So far, Eric has not succeeded in extricating himself.

Bubba peers in the window, concerned for Sookie because Eric sent Pam outside. Sookie puts her feelings aside as Audrina and Colton arrive, and Pam reenters the house as well to start planning Victor's assassination. Several ideas are put forth, but Sookie finally comes up with a winner involving Bubba.

Alone again, Eric asks Sookie for understanding, but she cannot imagine honoring such a deal brokered by a dead maker. Eric doesn't stay the night. Sookie sees Bill in the yard and goes out to talk to him, briefly telling him about the situation, but Bill actually does understand Eric's responsibility to his maker.

FRIDAY, JUNE 2. After sleeping late, Sookie begins preparations for Tara's baby shower, which is to be held the next day. Dermot returns home and, upon hearing about the shower, asks if he can attend. He begins looking at the old photographs from the attic and points out that some photos of Mitchell, Adele's husband, are actually Fintan in Mitchell's form.

Thinking about her own current fiscal health, Sookie suddenly figures out a simple way to help Sam through his financial hardship and takes him a check to pull the bar through until it can get back on its feet. Sam reluctantly accepts her offer but insists that they draw up legal paperwork for the loan.

Afraid Sookie wouldn't accept her call, Amelia asks Sam to tell Sookie to check her e-mail, which Sookie often forgets to do. Sookie has not only an e-mail from Amelia but also one from Mr. Cataliades. He advises her to think hard before using the cluviel dor and also warns her about Sandra Pelt. Amelia apologizes in her e-mail and tells Sookie that a cluviel dor is a fairy love token that contains a wish for the bearer, a wish so powerful that it can drastically change a life. When Sookie leaves for the Kill Victor party, she takes the cluviel dor with her.

Once at Fangtasia, Sookie waits in Eric's office for the bar to close. Pam is silent, and Sookie realizes that Miriam has passed away, another victim of Victor, who denied Pam permission to turn her sick lover. After closing, a few vampires loyal to Eric casually spread themselves around the bar as they help the human staff clean up and set the stage for the show. Bubba is going to sing. Colton and Audrina remain, ostensibly as potential donors. Immanuel and Mustafa Khan stay as well. Victor and his entourage, including his new second, Akiro, arrive and settle in for the spectacle. Bubba is breathtaking during his ballads, easily holding the visiting audience's attention, but the faster rock numbers aren't as riveting. Eric makes his move, swinging a stake at Victor's heart. Unfortunately, he is thwarted by Akiro, and the battle begins.

Sookie is able to send Bubba to the relative safety of the back hall, and he is led away by Bill. Pam is taken down by Victor. Seeing Sookie with Akiro's sword in her hands, Pam orders Sookie to kill Victor. She wavers, afraid that she will swing too hard and kill Pam as well, but is able to bring the sword down hard enough to incapacitate him, giving Pam the opportunity to get up, grab the sword, and do it herself. A badly wounded Akiro refuses to yield to Eric, who ends the other vampire's suffering. When the blood and ash settle, all of Victor's loyal minions are dead. Audrina has been killed as well, and Colton weeps over her body. Thalia struggles to reattach her severed arm, a procedure only old vampires can accomplish. Although Sookie is unable to respond physically to Eric when he kisses her, she still offers him her neck to help him heal his wounds. He strikes carelessly, angered by her conflicted emotions. She finally pinches his ear to get him to stop and pulls away, flinching when he tries to kiss her good night. Bill drives her home, and he calmly reminds her that she knew there would be death and blood, and that they only did what they needed to do to survive. Sookie knows he is right but is still disheartened by the carnage. She changes the subject, asking Bill about the Queen of Oklahoma and telling him Freyda is the bride Eric's maker arranged for him. Bill is surprised by the prospective bride's identity, and he tells Sookie that Eric will have to put her aside if he marries Freyda. Sookie admits that she broke the blood bond, and Bill gives her advice as a friend to let Eric make up his own mind. Sookie goes into her home, cleans herself up, and gets into bed, both relieved and disquieted that she thinks she'll be able to sleep.

SATURDAY, JUNE 3. Mr. Cataliades knocks on Sookie's back door during Tara's baby shower, which is a rousing success. He waits in the kitchen until the shower winds down and the guests depart. Sookie questions him about his history with her family, both fae and human, and discovers that Fintan had his good friend Desmond Cataliades give a gift to Fintan's progeny, a gift they could only accept if they had the essential spark. As their sponsor, Mr. Cataliades gave the family the gift of telepathy, a gift that he believed would give Fintan's descendants an advantage over most of the rest of humanity. Mr. Cataliades then tells Sookie that he is being pursued by some of his enemies and must leave.

Sam calls to let her know that someone dropped off a package for her at the bar, and Sookie can tell by his tone that there is something amiss. She asks him to bring her the package instead, and after a muffled consultation with another person, he agrees. Sookie grabs her shotgun and hides in the woods to wait for Sam and whoever is with him. They pull up in Jannalynn's car, and Sookie is not surprised to see Sandra Pelt get out of the vehicle with a rifle in her hands. Sookie emerges from the woods and fires, hitting Sandra in the left arm and cheek. Jannalynn takes full advantage of Sandra's shocked reaction and attacks, taking the other shifter on in hand-to-hand combat. Sookie and Sam circle the battling women, trying to help Jannalynn, and Sam gets a broken nose for his efforts. Sookie is finally able to grab Sandra's arm and forestall a punch, giving Jannalynn time to get her own punch in. The fierce Were breaks Sandra's neck with one blow. When she realizes that Sandra isn't yet dead, Jannalynn finishes the job. They debate calling the sheriff but opt instead to dispose of the body, with Sookie suggesting a place it won't be found. She helps Sam carry Sandra's body to the fairy portal, and they squeeze it through, hearing a yapping and snarling from the other side. Convinced that there is nothing left of Sandra Pelt, they make their way back to the house. After Sam washes off Jannalynn's car and the blood spots on the ground, Jannalynn sets his broken nose, and the two leave, taking Sandra's gun to toss into the woods on the way back to Sam's place.

Sookie muses over recent events and decides to settle back to watch *Jeopardy!* on TV with a glass of ice tea.

The Secret Dialogues of Bill and Eric

To: Eric@Fangtasia.com
From: WCompton@vmail.com
05:33 am

This is to inform you that Judith Vardamon is no longer staying in Area Five.

William Compton

To: WCompton@vmail.com
From: Eric@Fangtasia.com
05:46 am

Lost another one, Bill?

Eric

To: Eric@Fangtasia.com
From: WCompton@vmail.com
05:52 am

GFY. Let me know if you need help with that abbreviation, Sheriff.

Bill

Phone: Bill calling Eric.

BILL: "I had an interesting discussion with Sookie after you left."

ERIC: "She talks to you too much."

BILL: "Perhaps you talk to her too little. I assume you're trying to get out of the contract."

ERIC: "Of course I am."

BILL: "Be sure to let me know how that goes. Have a good sleep, Eric."

Phone: Eric calling Bill.

ERIC: "Did my wife get safely home?"

BILL: "Of course. But from what I understand, she may not be your wife for much longer, Consort."

ERIC: "Watch yourself, Bill."

BILL: "A queen. Bad enough any marriage, but I doubt a queen will release you, Eric. I understand that Pam had to push you into telling her." (*Silence.*)

BILL: "Just as you pushed me. As my human neighbors say, 'What goes around comes around.' Now you know how it feels to be forced by a queen to betray Sookie."

ERIC: "I did not betray Sookie. This was Ocella's doing, not mine."

BILL: "I actually do understand your loyalty to your maker, Eric. I even respect that you still wish to honor his word. Nonetheless, Sookie will see it as a betrayal. And your treatment of her tonight didn't help."

ERIC: "Don't think this means you will get her back, Bill."

BILL: "Perhaps not. But I do take pleasure in the possibility that you won't keep her, either."

The Sookie Short Stories and Related Material

BY CHARLAINE HARRIS

Writing short stories is not like writing a very short novel. The pacing is different, the timing is different, and the way you end the story is *really* different.

At this moment, there are seven Sookie short stories and one novella. They weren't published in the order in which they should be read if you're trying to stick to Sookie's chronology. I backtracked and filled in a little as ideas came to me. For clarity, I'm discussing them in the order in which they fit chronologically between the books.

By the way, the first five of these stories can now be found in one volume: *A Touch of Dead*. Before my publisher put the collection together, you had to buy separate anthologies to read about Sookie's adventures. I think that's a good thing, because then you get to sample a lot of outstanding stories by other writers, but there's no denying it's convenient to have the one book.

On to the discussion.

Though not the first short story I'd ever written, "Fairy Dust" was the first piece of Sookie short fiction I'd attempted, and I learned a lot in the process. The story first appeared in a wonderful anthology, *Powers of Detec-*

tion. In "Fairy Dust," Sookie is asked to investigate the death of Claudette, the triplet of Claude and Claudine, Sookie's fairy acquaintances. Since Claude and Claudine are questioning human co-workers from the strip club that employed both Claude and Claudette, they believe Sookie can help them get to the bottom of the mystery. Of course our heroine can help, and we learn a lot about the fairies and their outlook on life in general and on humans in particular. These events take place after *Dead to the World*.

On the heels of "Fairy Dust" follows "Dracula Night." I really enjoyed writing this one because we get to see an almost childlike side of the usually pragmatic Eric. Sookie, along with other members of the supernatural community, is invited to celebrate one of the few big dates on a vampire's calendar—the annual party held in honor of the first modern vampire, Vlad Tepes, popularly known as Dracula. The vampires believe that every year the real Vlad makes an appearance at one of these parties, and Eric hopes it will be at his. Eric gets his wish . . . and he doesn't. The timing of the party in the original version of "Dracula Night," published in *Many Bloody Returns*, was gradually perceived to be improbable, and by the time the story appeared in *A Touch of Dead*, the invitation date had been changed to a more credible January 13. The book that follows this bit of lore is *Dead as a Doornail*.

"One Word Answer" is the most serious of the short stories and contains information important for understanding the action in the next book. (It falls between *Dead as a Doornail* and *Definitely Dead*.) I apologize to readers who for years wondered if they'd missed a book somehow. I won't put vital information in a short story again. I've returned to treating the short stories as little side trips from the main action of the books.

In "One Word Answer" (which first appeared in *Bite*), Sookie and her friend Bubba are raking in Sookie's yard (at night, of course) when a limousine arrives. It contains the lawyer Mr. Cataliades, the vampire Waldo, and a secret passenger. Sookie finds out about the death of her cousin Hadley Delahoussaye, she discovers that Hadley had become a vampire before that second death, and she is told that Hadley had become the lover of the vampire Queen of Louisiana. In the course of their conversation, Sookie realizes that Waldo was so jealous of Hadley he may have had a hand in her death. The secret passenger in the limo is Sophie-Anne, Queen of Louisiana, and she's come with her own agenda.

"Lucky" was first published in *Unusual Suspects*, and it's lighter in tone. Sookie's insurance agent, Greg Aubert, has been casting spells to ensure that he won't have to pay out on policies. His clients simply have better luck than other people in Bon Temps, thanks to Greg's witch training. But Greg is worried because someone is coming into his office at night, and as Sookie and her friend Amelia investigate, they discover that other insurance agents are really suffering because of Greg's track record. And maybe one of them has decided to do something about that. "Lucky" should be read following *All Together Dead*.

My Sookie Christmas story, "Gift Wrap," should be read before *Dead and Gone*. It's the only thing I've ever written about Sookie that contains another point of view. Sookie is lonely at Christmas; everyone seems to have big plans but her. Her great-grandfather Niall knows this, and he collaborates with some supes to give Sookie a wonderful Christmas Eve gift, though it's not one she would have normally accepted. I got several messages of protest after the publication of "Gift Wrap" in *Wolfsbane and Mistletoe*, but I wrote the story to let the reader know something important about Niall.

"Two Blondes," the sixth of the Sookie short stories, is one of my favorites. It's in the anthology *Death's Excellent Vacation*, and it's a Sookie-and-Pam story set after *Dead and Gone*. Victor sends the two to investigate an offer he's gotten from the owner of a sleazy "gentleman's club" north of the casinos in Tunica, Mississippi. Sookie and Pam enjoy a little entertainment at a casino show before they drive up to keep their appointment. It's not a huge surprise that this meeting turns out to be a trap, and Sookie and Pam form close acquaintances with stripper poles before the night is through. "Two Blondes" was published after *A Touch of Dead* was on the shelves, so it's not included.

The novella "Small-Town Wedding," which appears in this book, occurs chronologically between *Dead in the Family* and *Dead Reckoning*.

The seventh story, one I finished not too long ago, is "If I Had a Hammer," included in *Home Improvement: Undead Edition*. This story should be read after *Dead Reckoning* because the du Rone twins have been born. While Sookie and Sam are helping Tara and JB with some much-needed home renovation, they uncover a terrible secret that has lain buried for decades.

RELATED STORIES

Dahlia Lynley-Chivers

I thought I'd enjoy writing about another character in some short fiction, so I've written several pieces about Dahlia Lynley-Chivers, a little, very old, very cold vampire who loves her high heels and her men. The adventurous and judgmental Dahlia lives in Rhodes, the city Sookie visits in *All Together Dead*, and Sookie sees her there, but the two do not talk. Some of the Dahlia stories ("Tacky" from *My Big Fat Supernatural Wedding* and "Bacon" from *Strange Brew*) take place before the summit at Rhodes. "Tacky" is about the wedding of Dahlia's best friend—yes, even Dahlia has a best friend—which is rudely interrupted by terrorists, who don't live to regret it. "Bacon" is a revenge story in which Dahlia hatches an elaborate plot to bring a witch to justice.

In "Dahlia Underground" (from *Crimes by Moonlight*), my favorite vampire is hauled up out of the rubble by rescue workers after the explosion of the hotel housing the vampire summit. After a bit of recuperation, she's directed to pursue the perpetrators by her sheriff, Cedric.

And finally, in *Glamour*'s holiday issue, we have a Dahlia Christmas story: "A Very Vampire Christmas." Dahlia actually embraces the spirit of the season in her own way, and she gets to kill some elves in the process.

Another Dahlia story is scheduled for release in *Down These Strange Streets*, publishing in October 2011.

Sean and Layla

Sean, an Irish vampire with freckles, and Layla, a modern young woman who has a serious problem with a stalker, meet in the novella "Dancers in the Dark," which first appeared in *Night's Edge*. The beautiful Layla, who's trying to remain anonymous in the Northern city of Rhodes, has fled from the South to hide from her stalker, a rich man who attacked and mutilated her after getting her pregnant. Layla is running out of money, so she auditions for a job with Blue Moon, a company that keeps a stable of dancers who appear at parties and gala events. The teams are usually composed of one vampire and one human, and the human gets bitten at the end of the dance. Layla comes to know and sympathize with the other members of the dance troupe, and they in turn respect her talent and help her when her stalker catches up with her. Sean falls in love with her in his quiet way. In the end, he has to bring Layla over when she suffers terrible blood loss during an attack by her stalker.

Sookie meets Sean and Layla in Rhodes at the vampire summit in *All Together Dead*.

The Britlingens

Sookie meets the Britlingens in *All Together Dead*, too. Batanya and Clovache are hired to protect the King of Kentucky at the summit in Rhodes, and against all odds, they succeed in their mission. They're incredibly tough bodyguards from another dimension. Clovache and Batanya were raised and trained by the Britlingen Collective, whose motto is "What is the law? The client's word." We learn more about the two women in "The Britlingens Go to Hell," in *Must Love Hellhounds*. Burdened with a dubious client (a thief) and an impossible task (to retrieve a ball from Hell), the two saddle up and head into trouble. Along the way, they encounter Amelia Earhart, Narcissus, assorted strange beings, and the Lord of Hell himself. They also discover that their client is one of the few surviving members of a race with an unusual physical attribute.

Vampires, Two-Natured, and Fairies, Oh My!

Sookie Discusses the Creatures She's Met

BY CHARLAINE HARRIS

The last couple of years have been one big learning curve. I got nothing against change. Considering I wasn't a happy camper before I met my first vampire, I have to say that change is a good thing. Some days I just feel like I have learned as much new stuff about the world as I can handle. However, so far I'm coping.

There is one real positive thing about my hometown of Bon Temps, Louisiana: Though it isn't all that big, it can sure adapt.

Back in high school we were studying Shakespeare, and there was this quote in *Hamlet* that seems to describe the last few years: "There are more things in heaven and on earth, Horatio, than are dreamt of in your philosophy." Everyone trots that out in bad horror movies, but there's a reason for that. It really does say it all.

I always thought that life, and society, wouldn't change in my little corner of Louisiana. That was before the whole world got shocked one evening when we found out that vampires were real and not just something that you saw in cheesy late-night movies.

Two years later, a real vampire walked into my life one night in Merlotte's and pulled me smack-dab into the middle of his world. There are times that I wish I had not been working that night, but I know it would have happened one way or another.

THE VAMPIRES

I love the sun. I felt so sorry for vampires when I really considered what it would mean to live your life in the darkness—to never see the blue sky, watch butterflies, see a hummingbird at a feeder . . . just enjoy the day. And some vampires haven't seen the light of day for over a thousand years. A thousand years of night! It's hard to wrap my mind around.

And all the time they kept their existence as secret as they could. They'd still be skulking around picking off humans if some Japanese scientists hadn't managed to create a form of synthetic blood that was just like the real stuff; in fact, in English they named one brand TrueBlood. I figure there were probably stories in the newspaper or on television about this product when it was getting approved for the market, though I don't remember seeing any.

But the vamps were all over it. It gave them the impetus they needed to start networking, trying to form a plan to coordinate their entrance into the modern world. After a lot of palaver, they decided to, as they say, "come out of the coffin" to let us know they are here and have been here for a long time. The vamps were very anxious to present themselves as no threat to the normal human population. They wanted everyone to know that they were the person next door—except for the "not going out in the day" thing, the fangs problem, and the blood addiction. They downplayed that part, emphasized the "not Eurotrash in a tuxedo" aspect.

A lot of vampires, like my ex-boyfriend Bill Compton, wanted to "mainstream," to live as much like humans as possible. That presented a few problems; when you can only go out at night, you can't exactly be running a Main Street shop. But they all seem to manage to make a dollar or two; that's the American way, isn't it? Bill invests in real estate and does computer programming; my current love interest, Eric Northman, owns the vampire bar Fangtasia over in Shreveport. I know there are vampire strippers and builders, and it wouldn't surprise me in the least if there's a vampire private detective or electrician. There are a lot of tandem partnerships—someone does the job during the day; someone of the fanged persuasion takes over at night.

A few of the countries around the world went wacky and killed all the vamps they could get their hands on. But the good old U.S. of A. was always a melting pot, so we figured they were just another minority wanting a new home, a dangerous minority if pressed the wrong way, but still one that wanted the same freedoms as the rest of the people in this nation. There's been a lot of arguing about whether vampires should have equal rights with humans; even if they get them, there will always be people opposed to the idea.

Oh, things weren't all just hunky-dory once the vamps had stood up and said, "We're here." It didn't take folks too long to find out that vampires' blood is almost a narcotic for humans plus helps injured people heal faster. (I know that last part from personal experience.) Since America's the land of free enterprise, before much time had passed scumbags were lining up to make money pushing vampire blood. And the vampires weren't willing donors. Teams developed methods to subdue vamps and drain them. And if you drain too much blood from vampires and leave them out in the open, they die, usually from exposure to the sun. That first night that Bill came into Merlotte's, I had to save him from a couple of Drainers who had trapped him outside the bar.

The humans who prey on vampires don't care who they sell the blood to or how diluted or old it is. The addicts or recreational vamp-blood users can go stark raving mad when they drink the stuff dealers sell. And blood dealers have a short shelf life. Both the mainstream vamps and the rogues love to pick off the dealers.

I'm not sure what's worse: knowing that there are Drainers out there or knowing about the rogue vampires. A rogue is a vamp who refuses to live by the rules that the human population has laid down. When the other vamps find out about one, it's up to the sheriff of the area to deal with him. Eric is very thorough and isn't bothered all that much if he has to put an end to a rogue. Rogues are bad for business.

Of course, since there are humans who live off preying on vampires, there are humans who live to be preyed on *by* vampires—fangbangers. They get off sexually from letting vampires feed on them. I've heard that some of them get off erotically from just being in the same room as a vampire. But loving to have your own blood taken is just as dangerous as taking vampire blood yourself. Even if you're in a committed relationship, like I was with Bill and am now with Eric, the vampire has to be very, very careful about how much blood he takes.

The big problem with the fangbangers is that they can get really addicted to the bite and will keep coming back for more and more frequent feedings with any vamp they can attract. If the vampire isn't careful, and some of them aren't, the fangbanger ends up being accidentally drained or even turned.

You can't be born a vampire. There's only one way to become one. A human being has to be "turned" by a vampire, the way Bill was by that bitch Lorena.

Bill told me it isn't easy to make a new vampire. The victim has to be drained of blood at a single sitting or over a period of no more than three days, till he's almost at the point of the true death. Then the sire has to donate most of his or her own blood to the prospective vampire. After that, it can take up to three days in the dark for the whole change to occur, and it doesn't always turn out right. Sometimes the vampire-to-be doesn't make it. Sometimes they have to be destroyed, they're so damaged. If the baby vampire survives, it's the obligation of the sire to teach the child how to be a good vampire.

Just like a newborn child, the newborn vampire is hungry and doesn't have a lot of control over his or her baser instincts. Amelia and I had first-hand experience with this when a shapeshifter named Jake Purifoy turned into a vampire and rose in a closet in my cousin Hadley's apartment. We got lucky. We were able to call the vampire cops, who could control him during his hunger pangs.

That's another reason the accidentally flipped fangbangers usually don't survive. Not many older vampires are willing to take responsibility for controlling and educating the new vamp.

I'm always astonished when I read about someone who wants to become a vampire. There are actually people who are willing to give up the daylight for the night, who have no problem with the idea of watching all their loved ones wither and grow old. I guess they want the enhanced speed and strength and the glamour ability more than they want their human life. Are they just scared of dying? I don't understand it. A wooden stake through the heart will take them out in a jiffy. They're not stake-proof, and a beheading will end anyone's existence, vamp or human.

It's true that a vampire cannot cross the threshold of a private home uninvited—the resident has to say the express words to allow the vamp to enter. Even more interesting, that permission can be revoked, rendering a home safe from vampire intrusion. I've had a little fun with that rule myself in the past, and it's good to know that it works.

All in all, there are times that I regret ever setting eyes on a vampire, or even seeing a six-pack of TrueBlood at the convenience store, but in the end you have to adapt to the world around you. I've become pretty good at adapting.

THE TWO-NATURED

When the vampires let people know that they were real, everyone thought that the world had been turned upside down. Heck, the first time I met an actual vampire, my universe *did* turn upside down. Of course, I fell in love with him. If I hadn't, my life might have stayed on more of a predictable path.

Finding out shortly thereafter that some people can change themselves into other creatures was another serious shock. My favorite boss, Sam Merlotte, was the first person I saw in both forms.

There are apparently two kinds of the two-natured: shifters, who can change into any type of animal, and weres, who change into only one animal. By far the most numerous clan is the werewolves, and they're so proud of that that they just refer to themselves as Weres, with a capital *W*. Of course, in the strictest sense, they're all shapeshifters. They can change their physical form. But you wouldn't ever hear a Were refer to himself as a shapeshifter, and Sam would never call himself a were-anything.

Within those two big divisions, there's a caste. You're either bitten or born. If you're born, you're the child of two pure-blooded two-natured humans. And you're the first child of that particular pair. Your little brother or sister won't be able to change. If you're bitten, you had an unfortunate encounter with a two-natured individual when he or she was in animal form, and you got (of course) bitten. Most often, that won't take, and you'll be fine. But if it does take, you'll start feeling weird at the full moon. You'll assume a half-human, half-animal form when the moon is up. (Think Lon Chaney Jr. in *The Wolf Man*.) You'll maintain your health and vitality longer than your regular human buddies, but sad to say you probably won't live as long.

Sam's a pureblood shifter, so he can change into any kind of animal form, though he prefers that of a dog. Most shifters tend to stick to a form they've become comfortable with, like a favorite shirt or a pair of shoes that fits just right. But Sam makes a great lion, let me tell you.

The wolves are a lot more secretive than the vampires. Let's face it—not having to sleep in a coffin and remain unseen during the day lets them blend in a lot easier. I know a lot of Weres, and I'm still finding out things about them. If someone had told me there is a hidden shapeshifter bar in Shreveport, I would have thought they were nuts, which is probably the pot calling the kettle black, if you stop and think about it. Quinn took me to a drinking establishment called the Hair of the Dog, and it's not a place for the fainthearted.

Most wolves group together in packs, with the strongest taking the role of packleader, a position that must be defended against challengers. I've been around Shreveport's Long Tooth pack mostly, and it certainly isn't a democracy. What the packmaster says goes. And if the packmaster needs backing up, the pack enforcer steps in.

There are some negatives to dating one of the two-natured, though the facts that they can go out in the sun and are physically warm are *huge* plusses as far as I'm concerned. But the icky part is that the necessity to keep breeding true can dominate mating choices. And if you're a rare breed, like a weretiger or a werepanther, you're kind of obliged to seek out a same-breed mate of the opposite sex and try to have a baby. Take Hotshot, for example. It's a tiny enclave way out in the boondocks, and the werepanthers who live there form a nearly closed society.

Breeding true is all the more important because the two-natured have a high mortality rate. So the leader of a pack is required to have children with as many of the pureblood women in his group as possible. I found this out from Calvin Norris when we were semiromantically involved for a while. As much as I thought I might care for him, this secret breeding program was something I couldn't handle. I'm the sort of woman who wants her husband home in bed with her, not out having kids with the nice lady down the street.

The two-natured young start manifesting their abilities when they hit puberty, as if teenagers don't have enough problems already. According to what I've been told, the kids are mentored and taught how to handle both the physical and emotional changes that their condition entails.

Sometimes, though, shapeshifters will find that they have to mentor a nonchild. That's what happened with my brother, Jason, though there are times when (with the way he acts) you'd think he was a prepubescent kid. After he got involved with Calvin's niece Crystal, one of her werepanther ex-boyfriends took it into his head that the only thing that attracted her to Jason was that he was a full human. So he decided to turn Jason into a werepanther and win Crystal back that way—which, by the way, didn't work. This transformation is not an easy thing to go through, but my big brother survived. In fact, after the first time he changed, Jason described it as "the most incredible experience" of his life.

Go figure.

THE FAIRIES

Just when I thought I had things figured out, with the vampires and the shape-shifters and all, I ended up having everything turned upside down again.

I found out that fairies are real; and no, I'm not talking trash about gay guys. I am talking about fairies—you know, those guys with the pointed ears? They're actually a lot like the elves in *The Lord of the Rings*. I'm sorry, but Tolkien got them wrong. You don't want to meet a real elf. They can take off your hand with one bite.

Unlike vampires and shapeshifters, fairies aren't actually from the world we know. They come from a world that is pretty darn close to ours but is separated by some kind of magical barrier; at least, that's the way I understand it. This world is called Faery, and all the ... well, the creatures that live in it are the fae. Fairies are only one branch of the fae, but they're the most populous and the most humanlike in form.

I've met elves, demons, and goblins. You don't want to know them, though Mr. Cataliades, the mostly demon lawyer, is an okay guy.

Why am I interested in the fairies? I found out that my brother and I are part fairy. Out of nowhere my great-grandfather Niall Brigant invited me to dinner in Shreveport. He explained that his half-human son had been my grandfather and that he wanted to get to know me better; after all, we were family. Now I'm pretty sure that explains my being able to read minds.

He wasn't the first fairy I met. That was Claudine Crane, six feet tall and drop-dead gorgeous, who turned out to be my fairy godmother. She definitely was not one of those fairies in a kid's story; you know the kind I'm talking about, small, winged things that giggle and dart around like a demented firefly? No, Claudine wasn't one of those; she knew magic, but she knew sex appeal as well and didn't hesitate to use it. There wasn't an eye, male or female, that didn't look up and notice her when she walked into the room. Though she didn't tell me so, Niall had sent her. Claudine was a full fairy, and she was also my cousin.

Magic is part of the very nature of the fae, and although they might all have the ability, it can manifest differently in each branch. Kind of like the way we humans have the same basic bodies but wildly different talents and capacities. I wonder if I should even be saying "we" anymore. Can I include myself with humans, since I'm part fairy? That's something I've got to give some thought to.

Claudine said that the fae live a very long time, but they're not immortal; they just don't age at the same rate that humans do. I don't think that fact really sank in until I met my great-grandfather. He doesn't look much older than late fifties or early sixties, and he's been alive for centuries, maybe even millennia. The fairies don't keep track of time very well.

Not all that many of the fae actually live in our world for any extended period. Most of them prefer to stay away because of iron. That stuff is to them like Kryptonite is to Superman; oddly enough, so is lemon juice. I'm not a scientist, but that allergy seems a little weird to me. However, I went to school with people who were allergic to things like eggs and peanuts, so why not? Of course, that also means that a squirt gun full of lemon juice is an effective weapon against them.

I wonder if I could go to the world of the fae for a visit? I doubt I would be very well received. Most of those who reside in Faery look at humans as if we were an insult to their own wonderfulness. But a few fae choose to live on earth because humans are full of energy and emotions of a type that they can't enjoy anywhere else. Claudine's twin Claude lives among us, and Claudine did until her death.

Some fairies enjoy finding humans to mate with. Though these unions seldom result in a pregnancy, some do. The resultant kids have a compelling quality and sometimes strange abilities. Though it makes me squeamish to think of Gran and a fairy, I'm glad she was able to have my father and my aunt Linda.

The gateways, or portals, into Faery are hidden away in a number of places around the world, and those locations are guarded jealously. I can take a few guesses on general locations based on things that my great-grandfather and Claudine have said. The fae don't like extremes in temperature, so I doubt that there will be any portals off in Siberia or down in Central America somewhere.

I know there's a portal in the woods in back of my house.

The biggest danger for fairies who choose to reside in the human world—beyond even iron or lemon juice—is vampires. They find the very presence of a fairy intoxicating, and if they have the chance to drink the blood of a fairy, it's an orgy of sensation for the vamp. So it's not always fun to see them in the same room together. Thankfully, I've never been pushed into having to choose between the vampires I know and my cousins who are fae.

God willing, I never will be.

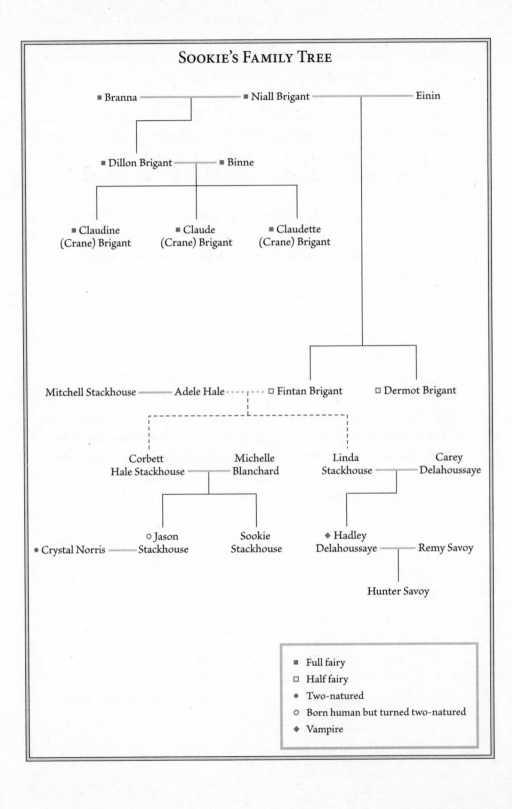

SOOKIE'S FAMILY TREE

■ Branna ——— ■ Niall Brigant ——— Einin

■ Dillon Brigant ——— ■ Binne

■ Claudine
(Crane) Brigant

■ Claude
(Crane) Brigant

■ Claudette
(Crane) Brigant

Mitchell Stackhouse ——— Adele Hale ····· □ Fintan Brigant   □ Dermot Brigant

Corbett
Hale Stackhouse ——— Michelle
Blanchard

Linda
Stackhouse ——— Carey
Delahoussaye

● Crystal Norris ——— ○ Jason
Stackhouse

Sookie
Stackhouse

◆ Hadley
Delahoussaye ——— Remy Savoy

Hunter Savoy

■	Full fairy
□	Half fairy
●	Two-natured
○	Born human but turned two-natured
◆	Vampire

Sookie Stackhouse Trivia

How Much of a Sookie Fan Are You?

BY BEVERLY BATTILLO AND VICTORIA KOSKI

As Sookie herself might say, "The devil's in the details." We've assembled a whole host of trivia questions to test your knowledge about Sookie and the people, places, and things in her world. The first set is pretty easy, and then we've thrown in some stumpers later on. Turn to pages 236–44 for the answers. Have at it, and have fun!

Part One: The Easy Stuff

Dead Until Dark:
1. What are the names of the couple who attempt to drain Bill?
2. What is Gran's full name?
3. What are Gran's two favorite organizations in Bon Temps?
4. What is Rene Lenier's sister's first name?
5. What is the name of Sookie's uncle whom Bill arranges to have killed?

Living Dead in Dallas:

1. What is the name of the Bellefleur mansion in Bon Temps?
2. What is the name of the vampire cook who worked at Merlotte's the night before Lafayette's body is discovered in the parking lot?
3. What kind of creature uses Sookie to send a message to Eric?
4. What airline do Bill and Sookie use on their trip to Dallas?
5. In Dallas, Sookie interviews a girl named Bethany, who later turns up dead. Bethany has a roommate. What is her name?

Club Dead:

1. Name the road where Belle Rive is located.
2. What is the name of the vampire King of Mississippi?
3. What hold do the vampires have over Alcide Herveaux's dad?
4. What is the name of Debbie Pelt's fiancé?
5. Whom do Sookie and Alcide find dead in the closet?

Dead to the World:

1. What is Sookie's New Year's resolution for January 1, 2005?
2. What color is Tara's new Camaro?
3. What amount of money is Sookie to receive for taking care of Eric?
4. Name the manager of the bridal shop who is murdered by the witches.
5. What is the witch Hallow's true name?

Dead as a Doornail:

1. What is the name of the early-night DJ for the all-vampire radio station KDED?
2. What is the name of the sniper's first were-victim in Bon Temps?
3. What was Charles Twining's profession before he was turned?
4. Name the two detectives who come to interview Sookie about Debbie Pelt.
5. How does Sookie's insurance agent, Greg Aubert, protect his clients' property?

Definitely Dead:

1. What is Bill Compton's favorite bar beverage?
2. What is the name of Sookie's cousin who died in New Orleans?

3. What is the name of the little boy whom Sookie uses her gift to find?
4. What theater and what play do Sookie and Quinn enjoy on their first date?
5. What do the names of Sophie-Anne's guards Wybert and Sigebert mean?

All Together Dead:

1. What state was Thalia thrown out of after the Great Revelation?
2. Where was Pam living when Eric summoned her?
3. Where and at what age was Pam turned?
4. Name the three conscious travelers in the airplane with Sookie on the trip to Rhodes.
5. What is the name of the security officer who handcuffs Sookie?

From Dead to Worse:

1. Sookie takes the place of which bridesmaid in Halleigh's wedding?
2. What is the name of Copley Carmichael's chauffeur and bodyguard?
3. What is the name of the restaurant where Sookie first meets Niall Brigant?
4. Name the female Were who instigated the Were war.
5. What position does Sandy Sechrest hold?

Dead and Gone:

1. Name the two cohosts for the show *The Best Dressed Vamp*.
2. Who is the FBI agent from New Orleans who visits Sookie and is shot at Arlene's?
3. What is the full name of Eric's maker?
4. What is the name of the church where Crystal's funeral is held?
5. What are the real names of Thing One and Thing Two?

Dead in the Family:

1. What is Jannalynn's last name?
2. Why was Kennedy in jail?
3. Where is Basim from?
4. Where is Debbie Pelt's car?
   Bonus: What kind of car is it? (This info is from another book.)

5. What does Sam buy as a wedding gift from the Merlotte's employees for Tanya and Calvin?

Dead Reckoning:
1. What is Brenda's last name?
2. What is Claude's secretary's name?
3. Who teaches in the Puppy Room?
4. What color are Colton's eyes?
5. What's the first song Bubba sings for Victor?

Part Two: The Tough Stuff

Think you're a real *Sookie Stackhouse fan? Prove it by answering these harder questions about the world of Sookie Stackhouse.*

Dead Until Dark:
1. What town does Bon Temps "love to hate?"
2. What color is the Rattrays' car?
3. Who calls Gran with the news about the Rattrays?
4. What is the name of the funeral home used by people of color in Bon Temps?
5. What color is Dawn's car?
6. What plants are in the hanging basket by Dawn's front door?
7. Where does JB's cousin live?
8. Where is JB working?
9. What does Sam eat at the Crawdad Diner?
10. What kind of mattress does Bill buy?
11. Where does Diane dance naked?
12. On what street is the house of the Monroe vamps (Malcolm, Liam, and Diane)?
13. How much money does Sookie find in the couch while cleaning with Sam?
14. What is the "Secret Vampire Knock" Bill uses when he takes Sookie to read the humans about the stolen money?
15. What is Bruce's wife's name?

Living Dead in Dallas:

1. What color are Lafayette's toenails?
2. What game do the Merlotte's employees play while waiting to open after the discovery of Lafayette's body?
3. Where did Khan work prior to Merlotte's?
4. What color is Dr. Ludwig's hair?
5. Who did Sookie's best friend Marianne hook up with on the senior trip to Six Flags?
6. What is Stan's former name?
7. What is the name of the bar owned by Stan and the Dallas vampires?
8. When Bethany was a little girl, what was her dog's name?
9. What is Bethany's hairdresser's name?
10. What is the name of the detective investigating Bethany's death?
11. What is the name of the church attended by Hugo Ayres?
12. What is the name of the bartender at the party at Stan's house?
13. Where is Jan Fowler's cabin?
14. What is the name of the physician whom JB du Rone dated for a few months until she had to move to Baton Rouge?
15. What were Bill's children's names?

Club Dead:

1. What is the name of Jane Bodehouse's son?
2. What is the name of Arlene's new beau?
3. Whose Depends failed?
4. Who gives Sookie a manicure and pedicure at Janice's salon?
5. What does Janice's customer attempt to steal?
6. What song do Sookie and Alcide dance to at Josephine's?
7. Who calls with word that Bill's house has been searched?
8. What is the name of the Shreveport packmaster?
9. What is the name of the Were motorcycle gang based in Jackson?
10. What is Alcide's nephew's name?
11. Where do Alcide and Sookie dump the body from the closet?
12. What is the color of the dress Sookie's wearing at Club Dead when she's staked?
13. Who keeps the doctor company at Russell's house?
14. Who is the vampire who heals Sookie after the stake is removed?

15. What is the name of the Were who tells Sookie about the crucifixion?

Dead to the World:

1. Who is sitting beside Chuck Beecham at Merlotte's at the New Year's Eve party?
2. Where does Holly Cleary's ex-husband live?
3. What is Cody Cleary's stepsister's name?
4. What day of the week is Verena Rose's Bridal and Formal Shop closed?
5. What is the name of the officer Sookie and Alcide speak with at the bridal shop?
6. What picture is hanging on the wall over the TV at Crystal's house?
7. According to Sookie, what is Amendment 29 to the Constitution?
8. What is Dawn's child's name?
9. What was the name of the sheriff who disappeared while trying to arrest a Hotshot resident?
10. Who was the sheriff trying to arrest and why?
11. What is the name of the doctor who treats Maria-Star?
12. What are the names of the officers investigating Maria-Star's accident?
13. What is the name of Amanda's companion at Merlotte's?
14. What is Kevin Pryor's mother's name?
15. What is Pam's address?

Dead as a Doornail:

1. Where is the shooter when Sam is shot?
2. What is the name of the serviceman who interrupts Eric and Sookie at Fangtasia?
3. Where was Charles's ship when he was turned?
4. What did Heather Kinman have in her hands when she was shot?
5. What do Jack and Lily drink at Merlotte's?
6. What is Calvin's room number at the Grainger hospital?
7. According to Claudine, what name did Jeff Marriot give her at Merlotte's?
8. Where did Gran buy the material for the curtains she made for the kitchen?

9. What is Randall Shurtliff's ex-wife's name?
10. What does Selah drink the first time Bill brings her to Merlotte's?
11. What is the name of the clerk in the Grainger hospital business office?
12. What is Bud Dearborn's wife's name?
13. What does Calvin send Sookie after she is shot?
14. Where did the second elf war take place?
15. Who hands Catfish the stake?

Definitely Dead:

1. What animal is the young man shifting into in the photo album at Al's?
2. What is Danielle's mother's name?
3. Who is the principal of Betty Ford Elementary School?
4. What is the principal's husband's occupation?
5. What does Sookie buy from Wal-Mart as a shower gift for Halleigh?
6. What else does Sookie buy during that trip?
7. What are Debbie and Sandra's parents' names?
8. Where is the Fellowship of the Sun branch Arlene has gone to?
9. What color are the bloodstained towels in Hadley's apartment?
10. What weapon does Sookie use to fight off Jake Purifoy at Hadley's?
11. What did Hadley wear to the party the night before Sophie-Anne's wedding?
12. What is Melanie wearing at the queen's reception at the monastery?
13. Who decapitates Wybert?
14. Where is Quinn's next event?
15. What is the event?

All Together Dead:

1. What is Halleigh's mother's name?
2. What does Selah give Halleigh as a shower gift?
3. How many seats for humans does the Anubis airplane Sookie takes to Rhodes have?
4. Who are the sheriffs of Louisiana, and which areas do they oversee?
5. What is Barry's room number?
6. What is Barry's real last name?

7. What does Carla wear the first night of the summit?
8. What floor is the Arkansas contingent staying on?
9. What color is Russell's ceremonial robe?
10. Whose lackey is also searching for an "unclaimed suitcase" with Sookie?
11. According to his driver's license, where was Kyle Perkins from?
12. What is the name of the ladies' room attendant?
13. What is the name of the vampire lawyer who argues for the parents against Cindy Lou?
14. Who is the head of the Michigan state terrorist task force?
15. What is the name of the hospital where Quinn is taken after the explosion?

From Dead to Worse:

1. What is Halleigh's sister's name?
2. Where are Portia and Glen going on their honeymoon?
3. What is Hoyt's father's name?
4. What color is the carpet in Maria-Star's apartment?
5. What kind of sandwich does Sookie make Tray while he checks out her house after following her home from work?
6. What business does Cleo run?
7. Who is with Sigebert and Sophie-Anne during the takeover?
8. What is Mrs. Prescott's first name?
9. Who is the author of the hardcover book Sookie throws at the man in the library, causing him to trip and fall on his own knife?
10. What is the name of the owner of the RV park where Priscilla and her Weres were staying?
11. Where does Sam's aunt live?
12. What is the name of the facility where Quinn's mom was held?
13. What is Octavia's niece's name?
14. What landscaping shrub is Sookie allergic to?
15. What is Kristen's last name?

Dead and Gone:

1. What is the name of Devon's friend who called *The Best Dressed Vamp*?
2. How many dogs does Sara Weiss have?

3. What official did Lattesta speak to in Rhodes about Sookie and Barry?
4. Who pays on her daughter's prom dress while Sookie is at Tara's Togs?
5. What does the name Dillon mean?
6. What caused the fire at the Freer house?
7. What color are Sookie's water guns?
8. Besides Jane, who was Merlotte's other "resident alcoholic"?
9. What is Mel's ex-wife's name?
10. What is Octavia's boyfriend's name?
11. What is the name of the fairy Sookie kills with Gran's trowel?
12. What is the name of the fairy Breandan kills in retaliation?
13. Who are Tray's next-door neighbors?
14. What business do Tray's next-door neighbors own?
15. What is the name of the fairy who ambushed Claudine before she went to the hospital to watch over Sookie?

Dead in the Family:

1. How old is Jannalynn Hopper?
2. What is Annabelle's last name?
3. How long has Basim been in Shreveport?
4. Who is the area rep for the BVA?
5. What is the BVA area rep's lover's name?
6. What kind of car are Bruno and Corinna driving when they flag down Sookie and Pam?
7. Whose funeral is Remy Savoy attending?
8. Where is the viewing and funeral being held?
9. Who is Jenny Vasco?
10. What book does Sookie read to Hunter and then give him?
11. What needs replacing on Sookie's water heater?
12. What is the name of Caroline Bellefleur's nurse?
13. Who does the nurse work for after Caroline Bellefleur passes?
14. What is the name of the white-haired male protester at Merlotte's?
15. Why did Basim leave the Houston pack?

Dead Reckoning:

1. What is Brenda's business partner's name?

2. What business was previously in Splendide's location?
3. Who is Kennedy Keyes's aunt?
4. Where does Immanuel Earnest work?
5. From what city is the police badge Sam considered getting Jannalynn?
6. Where is the Ruby Tuesday in Shreveport?
7. What color is the sign at Hooligans?
8. Whose arm does Pam damage at Vampire's Kiss?
9. What is the name of the fairy whose blood is used at Vampire's Kiss?
10. Whom is Lola Rushton dating?
11. What flavor milkshake does Halleigh ask Andy to bring her?
12. Who teaches in the Pony Room?
13. What kind of car does Colton drive?
14. How many children does Kelvin have?
15. Who mows Victor's yard?

PART ONE ANSWERS

Dead Until Dark:

1. *Mack and Denise Rattray*
2. *Adele Hale Stackhouse*
3. *The Descendants of the Glorious Dead and the Bon Temps Gardening Society*
4. *Cindy*
5. *Bartlett Hale*

Living Dead in Dallas:

1. *Belle Rive*
2. *Anthony Bolivar*
3. *A maenad*
4. *Anubis Air*
5. *Desiree Dumas*

Club Dead:

1. *Magnolia Creek*
2. *Russell Edgington*

3. *They hold the markers for his casino gambling debts.*
4. *Charles Clausen*
5. *Jerry Falcon*

Dead to the World:

1. *To stay out of trouble!*
2. *Black*
3. *$35,000*
4. *Adabelle Yancy*
5. *Marnie Stonebrook*

Dead as a Doornail:

1. *Connie the Corpse*
2. *Heather Kinman*
3. *He was a pirate.*
4. *Lily and Jack Leeds*
5. *By casting protective spells*

Definitely Dead:

1. *TrueBlood type O*
2. *Hadley Delahoussaye Savoy*
3. *Holly Cleary's son, Cody Cleary*
4. *The Strand Theatre in Shreveport;* The Producers
5. *Wybert—Bright Battle; Sigebert—Bright Victory*

All Together Dead:

1. *Illinois*
2. *Minnesota*
3. *In London at age nineteen*
4. *Mr. Cataliades, Diantha, and Johan Glassport*
5. *Officer Landry*

From Dead to Worse:

1. *Tiffany*
2. *Tyrese Marley*
3. *Les Deux Poissons*

4. *Priscilla Hebert*
5. *Area representative for Felipe de Castro, the new King of Louisiana*

Dead and Gone:

1. *Bev Leveto and Todd Seabrook*
2. *Agent Sara Weiss*
3. *Appius Livius Ocella*
4. *The Tabernacle Holiness Church*
5. *Lochlan and Neave*

Dead in the Family:

1. *Hopper*
2. *Manslaughter*
3. *Houston*
4. *Sunk in a pond about ten miles south of Sookie's house*
   Bonus: *Mazda Miata (from* Dead to the World)
5. *A wall clock*

Dead Reckoning:

1. *Hesterman*
2. *Nella Jean*
3. *Miss O'Fallon*
4. *Gray*
5. *"Kentucky Rain"*

PART TWO ANSWERS

Dead Until Dark:

1. *Homulka*
2. *Red*
3. *Everlee Mason*
4. *Sweet Rest Funeral Home*
5. *Green*
6. *Begonias*
7. *Springhill*

8. *His father's auto-parts warehouse*
9. *Key lime pie*
10. *Restonic*
11. *Farmerville*
12. *Callista Street*
13. *$1.05*
14. *Three quick knocks, then two spaced apart*
15. *Lillian*

Living Dead in Dallas:
1. *Deep crimson*
2. *Bourré*
3. *The Shrimp Boat*
4. *Golden brown*
5. *Dennis Engelbright*
6. *Stanislaus Davidowitz*
7. *The Bat's Wing*
8. *Woof*
9. *Jerry*
10. *Tawny Kelner*
11. *Glen Craigie Methodist*
12. *Chuck*
13. *Mimosa Lake*
14. *Dr. Sonntag*
15. *Thomas Charles, Sarah Isabelle, and Lee Davis*

Club Dead:
1. *Marvin*
2. *Buck Foley*
3. *Velda Cannon's*
4. *Corinne*
5. *Janice's earrings*
6. *Sarah McLachlan's "Good Enough"*
7. *Harvey*
8. *Terence*
9. *The Hounds of Hell*

10. *Tommy*
11. *The Kiley-Odum Hunt Club property*
12. *Champagne*
13. *Josh*
14. *Ray Don*
15. *Doug*

Dead to the World:
1. *Terrell*
2. *Springhill*
3. *Shelley*
4. *Wednesday*
5. *Coughlin*
6. The Last Supper
7. *Shifters don't have to talk to Sookie Stackhouse.*
8. *Matthew*
9. *John Dowdy*
10. *Carlton Norris, for statutory rape*
11. *Dr. Skinner*
12. *Stans and Curlew*
13. *Parnell*
14. *Jeneen*
15. *714 Parchman Avenue, Shreveport, LA*

Dead as a Doornail:
1. *In the trees north of the parking lot*
2. *Dave*
3. *The Tortugas*
4. *A chocolate milkshake*
5. *Jack has hot tea, and Lily has a Diet Coke.*
6. *214*
7. *Marlon*
8. *Hancock's*
9. *Mary Helen*
10. *A screwdriver*
11. *Ms. Beeson*

12. *Greta*
13. *A gardenia bush*
14. *Iowa*
15. *Dago (Antonio Guglielmi)*

Definitely Dead:
1. *A bear*
2. *Mary Jane Jasper*
3. *Mrs. Garfield*
4. *Methodist-Episcopal minister*
5. *A two-quart CorningWare casserole dish*
6. *Fruit juice, sharp cheddar, bacon, gift paper, and a really pretty blue bra and matching panties*
7. *Barbara and Gordon Pelt*
8. *Minden*
9. *Medium blue terrycloth*
10. *A candlestick*
11. *A skintight, cut-down-to-here red dress decked with darker red sequins (and some gorgeous alligator pumps)*
12. *A pretty yellow dress with low heels*
13. *Ra Shawn*
14. *Huntsville, Alabama*
15. *A Rite of Ascension*

All Together Dead:
1. *Linette Robinson*
2. *Dish towels*
3. *Fifteen*
4. *Sophie-Anne Leclerq presides over Area One, Arla Yvonne over Area Two, Cleo Babbitt over Area Three, Gervaise over Area Four, and Eric Northman over Area Five.*
5. *1576*
6. *Horowitz*
7. *A glittery green cocktail dress, fuck-me shoes, and a see-through thong*
8. *The seventh floor*

9. *A heavy brocade of gleaming gold cloth worked in a pattern of blue and scarlet*
10. *Queen Phoebe Golden's*
11. *Illinois*
12. *Lena*
13. *Kate Book*
14. *Dan Brewer*
15. *St. Cosmas*

From Dead to Worse:

1. *Fay*
2. *San Francisco*
3. *Ed*
4. *Dark blue*
5. *Meatloaf*
6. *An all-night grocery*
7. *Audrey, the child of Gervaise's lieutenant, Booth Crimmons*
8. *Lorinda*
9. *Nora Roberts*
10. *Don Dominica*
11. *Waco, Texas*
12. *Whispering Palms*
13. *Janesha*
14. *Nandinas*
15. *Duchesne*

Dead and Gone:

1. *Tessa*
2. *Three*
3. *Fire Chief Trochek*
4. *Riki Cunningham*
5. *Lightning*
6. *Bad wiring*
7. *One blue, one yellow*
8. *Willie Chenier*
9. *Ginjer*

10. *Louis Chambers*
11. *Murry*
12. *Enda*
13. *Brock and Chessie Johnson*
14. *An upholstery shop*
15. *Lee*

Dead in the Family:

1. *Twenty-one*
2. *Bannister*
3. *Two months*
4. *Katherine Boudreaux*
5. *Sallie*
6. *A white Lexus*
7. *His father's sister's*
8. *Homer*
9. *A child Hunter knows who has a birthmark on her face*
10. The Poky Little Puppy
11. *The element*
12. *Doreen*
13. *Mr. DeWitt*
14. *Mr. Barlowe*
15. *He killed a human who attacked him with a hoe while he was in wolf form.*

Dead Reckoning:

1. *Donald Callaway*
2. *A paint store*
3. *Marcia Albanese*
4. *Death by Fashion in Shreveport*
5. *New Bedford*
6. *Youree Drive*
7. *Shocking pink*
8. *Pearl's*
9. *Cait*
10. *India*

11. *Butterscotch*
12. *Mrs. Gristede*
13. *A Dodge Charger*
14. *Three*
15. *Dusty Kolinchek*

What's Cookin' in Bon Temps

A Selection of Down-Home Southern Recipes

Southern cooking has a style—and a flavor—all its own. When I decided to include recipes that would celebrate the tastes of Louisiana, not to mention the entire South, I decided to throw the doors open to my fans, who had already created a cookbook under the auspices of Charlaine's Charlatans.

I was wonderfully surprised by the response—the recipes came pouring in! After taste-testing all of them, we selected a range that showcased Southern cooking, from breakfast to dessert, including drinks. I hope you have the chance to try and enjoy some of these true down-home Southern recipes—I know I sure did!

BREAKFAST:

Belle Rive Brunch Eggs
Eggs Benedict
French Market Beignets

LUNCH:

Burgers Lafayette Sauce
Cold-Weather Chili
Merlotte's Chicken Strips
Mitchell's Favorite Meatloaf

SUPPER:

Calvin's Catfish
Crawdad's Country-Fried Steak
Crossroads Jambalaya
Sookie's Chicken Casserole
Stackhouse Smothered Pork Chops

SIDES:

Antoine's Fried Pickles
Bon Temps Sweet Potato Harvest
Gran's Easy Baked Apples
Hotshot Hush Puppies
Jannalynn's Golden Biscuits
Mardi Gras Corn Salad
Michele's Homemade Buttermilk Ranch Dressing
Michele's Parmesan Garlic Croutons
Pinkie's Fried Green Tomatoes
Sister's Mashed Potato Casserole

DESSERTS:

Adele Hale Stackhouse's Blue-Ribbon Chocolate Cake
Aunt Patty's Sour Cream Cake with Praline Frosting
Caroline Holliday Bellefleur's Chocolate Cake
Diner Key Lime Pie
Louisiana Pralines
Perdita's Bread Pudding with Bourbon Sauce
Portia's Sweet Potato Pie
Wicked Peach Cake

DRINKS:

Classic Southern Sweet Tea
Country Porch Lemonade

Breakfast

BELLE RIVE BRUNCH EGGS

TIME: PREP TIME 30 MINUTES, MARINATING TIME 8–12 HOURS, BAKING
TIME 90 MINUTES · SERVES 8–10

INGREDIENTS:

8 slices bread, torn into cubes

1 dozen eggs

2¼ cups plus ½ cup milk

¾ tsp. dry mustard

Salt and pepper, to taste

1 lb. ham, cubed, or 2 lb. cooked bacon, crumbled

½ cup green onions, finely chopped

½ cup red bell pepper, finely chopped

1 cup fresh mushrooms, coarsely chopped

1½ cups shredded cheese (cheddar, Monterey Jack, or a blend, your choice)

1 can (10¾ oz.) cream of mushroom soup

Place the bread cubes into a greased 9 × 13" pan. Beat the eggs, 2¼ cups milk, mustard, salt, and pepper. Pour over the bread cubes in the pan. Evenly sprinkle the ham or bacon, onions, bell pepper, and mushrooms over the top of the egg mixture. Top with the cheese. Cover with foil and refrigerate overnight.

In the morning, preheat the oven to 300 degrees F. Mix the can of soup with ½ cup milk and pour over the refrigerated egg mixture. Bake, uncovered, for 90 minutes. The dish will puff when baking but will deflate after it is removed from the oven. Cut into squares and serve hot.

 ∾ *Submitted by Debi Murray*

EGGS BENEDICT

TIME: 15 MINUTES • SERVES 4

INGREDIENTS:

¼ cup mayonnaise (*not* salad dressing)

1 rounded tsp. brown mustard (not honey mustard, but horseradish mustard or champagne mustard works very well)

¼ cup plain yogurt or sour cream

2 English muffins or 4 leftover biscuits

4 slices sandwich ham or Canadian bacon

⅔ cup water

Pinch of salt

A few shakes of Tabasco sauce (or your preferred pepper-vinegar sauce)

4 eggs, room temperature, as fresh as possible

This takes a little practice in terms of timing because the heat goes on the sauce, the eggs, and the meat from different directions at the same time. Once you get the timing down, however, it's the easiest Eggs Benedict you'll ever cook.

Mix the mayonnaise, mustard, and yogurt or sour cream in a small, cold saucepan. Set aside. Split your muffins or biscuits and lay them, torn side up, on a cookie sheet. Preheat the broiler but don't put the bread in yet.

Lay the meat in a cold skillet, preferably with a touch of bacon grease, and place the skillet over low heat to brown the meat. If not using a cast-iron skillet, start with a very low heat. Allow meat to cook, making certain it does not burn. Note: The meat cooks better if it is cut into strips before being laid in the pan, but then it looks less like Eggs Benedict.

As soon as you have the meat pan on the heat, turn to the eggs. Pour ⅔ cup water into a 1-quart bowl. Salt it. Shake in a few good jolts of Tabasco or your favorite vinegar-based pepper sauce. Stir. Crack the eggs and gently slip them (minus the shell) into the water, pricking each yolk once with a toothpick.

Cover the bowl with plastic wrap. Microwave on full power for 2–3 minutes. Let the eggs stand, covered, to give the whites time to completely set and the yolks time to thicken, about 2 minutes.

As soon as you turn on the microwave, put the saucepan with the mayonnaise mixture over low heat and stir pretty constantly for about 5 minutes, until heated through.

When the microwave dings, pull the sauce off the heat long enough to put the bread under the broiler to toast the torn side lightly. While the bread toasts, put the sauce back over low heat and stir. Allow the bread to lightly toast, and then remove it from the oven. The sauce is done when the bread is.

Once the bread is out, quickly drain your eggs and roughly divide them. Shuffle your hot bread onto plates. Top with the meat, then the eggs, and then the sauce. Don't agonize over the nonround eggs or piles that slip over sideways.

ᴄᴠ *Submitted by Amber Green*

French Market Beignets

TIME: PREP TIME 15 MINUTES, REFRIGERATION TIME 8 HOURS, COOKING
TIME 15 MINUTES · SERVES 8

INGREDIENTS:

1 package dry yeast

½ tsp. plus ½ cup granulated sugar

½ cup water, warm to the touch

1 cup evaporated milk

1 tsp. salt

1 egg

3 cups unbleached all-purpose flour

Oil for frying (preferably canola, but whatever oil you've got in the Fry
     Daddy will do)

1 cup powdered sugar in a brown paper lunch bag

The night before you plan to eat these, dissolve your yeast and ½ tsp. granulated sugar in the warm water in a big mixing bowl. Stir gently until the yeast dissolves; let rest for 5 minutes until the yeast is nice and bubbly.

Add the evaporated milk, ½ cup sugar, and the salt to the bubbly yeast. Crack the egg into a small bowl, beat it well, and add the beaten egg to the big bowl. Stir until well blended. Add the flour, ½ cup at a time, blending well. Cover the bowl with a wet towel and refrigerate overnight.

In the morning, fill your Fry Daddy, your electric wok, or a deep and sturdy saucepan or skillet at least 3" deep with oil. Heat the oil to 375 degrees F.

While the oil is warming, roll out the dough on a well-floured surface. The thickness is a personal preference, but anywhere from ¼" to ½" is traditional. Cut the dough into 2" to 3" squares, also a matter of personal preference. Let the dough rest while the oil heats up.

Drop the beignets, three at a time, into the hot oil. Cook until they are nicely brown, and then turn them over to brown the other side, approximately 1 minute per side. Pull the hot beignets out of the oil with a slotted spoon. Let any excess oil drip off. Drop them into the bag of powdered sugar. Close the bag and shake it. Take the sugar-coated beignets out of the bag and serve immediately. Continue with the rest of the beignets.

Tip: Beignets are best served hot.

∾ *Submitted by Denise Little*

Lunch

Burgers Lafayette Sauce

TIME: 30 MINUTES · SERVES 4

INGREDIENTS:

1 medium onion, chopped

¼ stick margarine

¼ cup vinegar

½ cup water

½ tsp. salt

Dash of cayenne pepper

2 Tbsp. Worcestershire sauce

2 Tbsp. brown sugar

1 Tbsp. prepared mustard

½ tsp. pepper

½ cup ketchup

Sauté the onion in the margarine. Add all of the other ingredients. Simmer for about 20 minutes.

Place cooked hamburgers or leftover roast in the skillet and steep for at least 10 minutes.

Place the meat on a bun and put a spoonful of extra sauce on top. Makes enough sauce for about 4 hamburgers.

∾ *Submitted by Charlaine Harris*

COLD-WEATHER CHILI

TIME: PREP TIME 15 MINUTES, COOKING TIME 15 MINUTES, SIMMERING
TIME 1 HOUR 30 MINUTES • SERVES 6–8

INGREDIENTS:

½ lb. ground chuck or ground round

2 medium onions, sliced

1 can (28 oz.) whole tomatoes

1 can (6 oz.) tomato paste

1 cup water

1 beef bouillon cube

2 Tbsp. green peppers, diced

2 cloves garlic, minced

2 tsp. salt

2 tsp. oregano

2 tsp. chili powder or ground cumin

½ tsp. crushed red peppers (or to taste)

1 whole bay leaf

2 cans (16 oz. each) red kidney beans

⅛ tsp. ginger

Combine ground beef and sliced onions in a large saucepan. Brown the meat and drain off the fat. Add remaining ingredients and stir to blend. Cover and simmer about 1 hour 30 minutes, stirring occasionally. Remove bay leaf before serving.

Tip: Top with shredded cheddar or mozzarella and sour cream.

Variation: Omit the kidney beans for a thicker chili to serve over French fries. Top with cheese and bacon bits for cheesy chili-bacon fries.

ᕰ *Submitted by Mary Helen Klein*

Merlotte's Chicken Strips

TIME: PREP TIME 40 MINUTES, MARINATING
TIME 8 HOURS · SERVES 2–4

INGREDIENTS:

¼ cup buttermilk or unsweetened yogurt thinned with a touch of milk

1 tsp. cayenne

1 tsp. adobo or ½ tsp. curry powder

6 boneless, skinless chicken breast halves

2 cups oil or bacon grease

1 cup flour, as needed

Salt to taste

Black pepper to taste

Mix buttermilk or yogurt, cayenne, and adobo or curry powder into a gallon-sized ziplock freezer bag. Slice meat into thumb-thick strips. Put them in the ziplock bag, mash out all the air, and seal. Allow to marinate 8 hours in the refrigerator.

Heat oil or bacon grease in a large skillet. Season flour with plenty of salt and pepper, and pour into a brown paper bag or a gallon-sized ziplock bag. Shake chicken pieces, a few at a time, in the flour, then fry until golden brown. Drain on paper towels. Serve hot.

Tip: Serve with French fries and either honey mustard or ranch dip.

✑ *Submitted by Terri Pine*

MITCHELL'S FAVORITE MEATLOAF

TIME: PREP TIME 15 MINUTES, BAKING TIME 75 MINUTES · SERVES 4–5

INGREDIENTS:

1 lb. ground beef

1 egg

1 cup Italian bread crumbs

1 cup Parmesan cheese

Nonstick cooking spray

Preheat the oven to 325 degrees F.

Mix together ground beef, egg, bread crumbs, and cheese to form a loaf. Place in a pan sprayed with nonstick cooking spray. Bake for 75 minutes (a little longer if necessary).

Tips: Can be glazed with your favorite tomato-based sauce 20 minutes before done. Great cold for sandwiches.

∾ *Submitted by Charlaine Harris*

Supper

CALVIN'S CATFISH

TIME: PREP TIME APPROXIMATELY 15 MINUTES,
COOKING TIME 5–7 MINUTES • SERVES 5

INGREDIENTS:

Peanut oil (enough to fill fryer—the typical home fryer holds 2 quarts but
ours holds 10 gallons)

2½ lb. pond-raised catfish fillets (½ lb. per person)

2 cups yellow cornmeal

1 tsp. salt (or to taste)

½ tsp. black pepper (or to taste)

Heat oil in deep fryer to 355 degrees F.

If catfish is frozen, thaw in cold water.

Add cornmeal to a small bowl and season to taste with salt and pepper.
Roll catfish fillets in cornmeal mix, lightly shake off excess mix, and slip
fillets into hot oil. Cook the fillets for about 5–7 minutes until they float;
they are done when the crust is golden brown. Watch closely so that they
do not overcook. Remove and let drain on folded paper towels.

Tip: Serve with coleslaw and hush puppies or French fries. Use ketchup,
hot sauce, or tartar sauce for additional seasoning.

∾ *Submitted by Joe Jackson*

CRAWDAD'S COUNTRY-FRIED STEAK

TIME: PREP TIME 45 MINUTES–1 HOUR,

BAKING TIME 1 HOUR 10 MINUTES–1 HOUR 25 MINUTES · SERVES 4–5

INGREDIENTS:

1½ cups flour (plus ½ cup if using second gravy-making method)

½ tsp. salt (or to taste)

1 tsp. pepper (or to taste)

2–3 cups plus 1 cup milk (plus 2 cups if using second gravy-making method)

2 lb. tenderized steak, cut into serving pieces

½ cup cooking oil

Nonstick cooking spray

½ cup water

Preheat the oven to 325 degrees F.

Combine 1½ cups flour, salt, and pepper in a bowl; pour 2–3 cups milk into a separate bowl. Dredge the meat in the flour mixture, dip it in the milk, then dredge it in the flour mixture again. Heat oil in a large skillet. When the oil is hot, add the meat and brown it. You may need to add more oil.

When all the meat is browned, place it in a glass pan, whatever size will serve, sprayed with nonstick cooking spray. Leave a little space between the pieces. Pour the water around the meat and cover dish tightly with aluminum foil. Bake for 1 hour to 1 hour 15 minutes, then remove aluminum foil and bake uncovered for 10 more minutes.

While meat is baking, pour the leftover seasoned flour into the leftover milk. You will need to add more milk when it's time to make the gravy, probably another cup. If this process seems unhygienic to you, discard the seasoned flour and leftover milk. Instead, while meat is baking, combine ½ cup flour, salt and pepper to taste, and 2 cups fresh milk.

Drain most of the grease out of the skillet the meat was browned in, leaving enough to make the amount of gravy desired, usually about ¼ cup of grease or less. When the meat is almost done, reheat the grease. Slowly add the flour and milk mixture, stirring constantly until the gravy reaches the desired consistency. Remove meat from oven, remove foil, and pour gravy over meat. Serve immediately.

    ∾ *Submitted by Charlaine Harris*

Crossroads Jambalaya

TIME: 45 MINUTES · SERVES 6

INGREDIENTS:

2 Tbsp. olive oil

1 boneless chicken breast, cubed

2 hot smoked sausages, andouille, or hot links

1 small onion, chopped

1 bell pepper, chopped

1 cup long-grain white rice (not instant, uncooked)

3 garlic cloves, minced

Salt, to taste

Tabasco sauce, to taste

Cajun spice (2 tsp. cayenne, 2 tsp. black pepper, 1 tsp. oregano, ½ tsp. thyme), to taste

2 cups chicken stock

1 cup chunky hot salsa

1 cup canned black beans, rinsed and drained

Heat the olive oil in a sauté pan or frying pan. Brown the chicken, sausage, onion, bell pepper, rice, and garlic until the onion and rice are translucent. Drain if necessary. Add the salt, Tabasco sauce, Cajun spice, and stock. Bring to a boil. Sprinkle the salsa and black beans over the surface. Taste and add any additional seasoning now. Bring to a boil again, and then reduce the heat to a slow simmer. Do not stir. Simmer for 15–20 minutes, or until the rice has absorbed the liquid. Remove from the heat. Leave covered for 5 minutes. Toss and serve.

    ∾ *Submitted by Ali Katz*

SOOKIE'S CHICKEN CASSEROLE

TIME: 45 MINUTES • SERVES 6

INGREDIENTS:

2 cups cooked rice

Nonstick cooking spray

4 large cooked chicken breasts, boned and diced

8 oz. sour cream

1 can (10¾ oz.) cream of chicken soup

1 can (10¾ oz.) cream of celery soup

2 tsp. poppy seeds

1 roll butter crackers, crushed

½ stick margarine, melted

Preheat the oven to 350 degrees F.

Spread the rice on the bottom of a 9 × 13" casserole dish sprayed with nonstick cooking spray. Combine the chicken, sour cream, soups, and poppy seeds, and mix well. Spread over the rice. Sprinkle the crushed crackers over the top and drizzle with the margarine. Bake for 30 minutes, or until hot and bubbly.

∾ *Submitted by Beverly Battillo*

Stackhouse Smothered Pork Chops

TIME: 60–80 MINUTES · SERVES 6

INGREDIENTS:

2 eggs

2 Tbsp. milk

1½ cups seasoned bread crumbs

6 bone-in pork chops, ½" thick

Olive oil for pan-frying

2 packets pork gravy mix

Preheat the oven to 350 degrees F.

Whisk together the eggs and milk in a shallow bowl. Place the bread crumbs in a separate bowl. Dip each pork chop first into the egg-milk mixture, then into the bread crumbs until fully coated, pressing to make sure each chop is covered in the bread crumbs.

Heat a few tablespoons of olive oil in a frying pan and brown each pork chop until golden brown on both sides. Add oil in small intervals throughout the frying process.

Place the browned pork chops in a 9 × 13" baking dish and cover. Bake for 30–40 minutes.

Meanwhile, combine the gravy mix with the correct amount of water, as indicated on the packet, but do not cook the gravy. Just add it to the water and whisk until smooth.

Remove the pork chops from the oven, remove the cover, and pour the gravy mix over the pork chops. Cover again and bake for another 30–40 minutes. Remove from the oven and keep covered until ready to serve.

Tip: Serve with rice or buttered egg noodles.

ॐ *Submitted by Pam Wilbur*

Sides

ANTOINE'S FRIED PICKLES

TIME: 20 MINUTES

INGREDIENTS:

1 cup self-rising flour

1 tsp. baking powder

¼ tsp. paprika

Dash of red pepper

⅓ cup milk

⅓ cup beer (any brand)

Whole dill pickles

Oil

This is a variation on a recipe that became famous after its use at a restaurant close to Tunica, Mississippi.

Sift together all of the dry ingredients. Add the milk and the beer in equal amounts until the mixture is the desired consistency. Slice the dill pickles into round ¼" to ⅜" thick chips. Dip the slices in the batter until the batter is gone, and fry in deep oil. Turn once or twice to brown evenly.

Tip: Enjoy them with cold beer.

∾ *Submitted by Charlaine Harris*

Bon Temps Sweet Potato Harvest

TIME: PREP TIME 1 HOUR 30 MINUTES (IF SWEET POTATOES ARE
PRECOOKED), BAKING TIME 1 HOUR 15 MINUTES · SERVES 6

INGREDIENTS:

10 Tbsp. margarine

2¼ cups Bisquick

2 Tbsp. sugar plus ¼ cup sugar

¼ cup chopped pecans

3–5 cups cooked sweet potatoes

2 eggs

3 Tbsp. molasses

1 tsp. allspice

½ tsp. nutmeg

1 tsp. vanilla extract

2 cups brown sugar

½ cup pecans

2 egg whites

1 Tbsp. lemon juice (optional)

crushed pecans (optional)

½ tsp. cinnamon

Preheat the oven to 350 degrees F.

For the bottom crust, mix 4 Tbsp. margarine, 1½ cups Bisquick, 2 Tbsp. sugar, and chopped pecans until crumbly. Press into 3-quart casserole dish and bake for 10 minutes. (This can also be done in a shallower pan.)

Next mash the cooked sweet potatoes and mix with 2 Tbsp. margarine, 2 eggs, ¼ cup sugar, molasses, allspice, nutmeg, and vanilla. Pour over baked crust.

Mix 4 Tbsp. margarine, 1 cup brown sugar, ¾ cup Bisquick, and pecans until crumbly. Sprinkle over potato mixture. Bake for 45–50 minutes.

For the top layer, beat 2 egg whites until frothy. Add 1 cup brown sugar and lemon juice. Pour on top of dish and sprinkle with crushed pecans and cinnamon. Put in oven long enough to toast nuts.

Variation: In lieu of the top layer, you may choose to beat 1 egg white and add 1 Tbsp. sugar and ½ tsp. cinnamon. Brush on top of warm casserole and return to oven for 10–15 minutes.

∽ *Submitted by Charlaine Harris*

GRAN'S EASY BAKED APPLES

TIME: 60 MINUTES · SERVES 6

INGREDIENTS:

6 large baking apples

¾ cup raisins, cranberries, or chopped dates

1 cup brown sugar

1 cup water

2 Tbsp. butter

½ tsp. cinnamon

½ tsp. nutmeg

Preheat the oven to 350 degrees F.

Core the apples, paring a strip of peel from the top of each one. Place apples in a 10 × 6" baking dish that is at least 1½" deep. Fill the apples with raisins, cranberries, or dates. Combine the brown sugar, water, butter, cinnamon, and nutmeg in a saucepan. Bring to a boil. Pour the hot syrup around the apples, and be sure to add at least 1 tsp. into each apple cavity. Bake uncovered for about 60 minutes, basting occasionally.

∽ *Submitted by Charlaine Harris*

HOTSHOT HUSH PUPPIES

TIME: PREP TIME 15 MINUTES, FRYING TIME 3–4 MINUTES
PER BATCH · SERVES 6–8

INGREDIENTS:

2 cups white cornmeal (yellow is acceptable)

2 Tbsp. all-purpose flour

1 tsp. baking soda

1 tsp. baking powder

1 tsp. salt

1 Tbsp. sugar

½ cup onion, grated

¼ cup green onion, thinly sliced, or a jalapeño pepper, finely chopped

1 egg yolk

1½–2 cups buttermilk

3 egg whites

Peanut oil for frying

Preheat about 3" oil to 355 degrees F.

Whisk dry ingredients together in a bowl. Add the grated onion, green onion or jalapeño, egg yolk, and 1½ cups of buttermilk. Beat well with fork or whisk until well blended and about the consistency of loose mashed potatoes. Add more buttermilk if it's too stiff. Whip egg whites into soft peaks (not stiff peaks) and fold them into the batter. Drop by tablespoonfuls into preheated oil. They will roll over when done, but you may need to turn them to make sure they brown evenly. Remove with a wire spider and drain on a rack or paper towels. Serve immediately.

～ *Submitted by Treva Jackson*

JANNALYNN'S GOLDEN BISCUITS

TIME: 20 MINUTES • SERVES 8 (16–20 BISCUITS)

INGREDIENTS:

1 medium baked sweet potato

Pinch of apple pie spice or pumpkin pie spice, if desired

2 cups biscuit mix

½ stick butter, room temperature, or a dollop of shortening

½ cup yogurt, buttermilk, or milk (or milk with an egg yolk beaten into it)

Preheat the oven to 450 degrees F.

Comb the sweet potato with a fork to make sure it's done through (nuke if not) and set aside. If using the apple or pumpkin pie spice, stir into the biscuit mix first. Stir the butter and yogurt into the biscuit mix, then stir in the sweet potato until you have lumps of potato but no big lumps of biscuit mix. The dough should look very soft and wet. Drop the dough onto an ungreased biscuit pan or cookie sheet. For tidier biscuits, heavily flour your fingertips and pat down the tops. Bake for about 10 minutes.

Variation: You may also use a handful of sharp shredded cheese in lieu of the sweet potato, leaving out the butter if desired.

ᘉ *Submitted by Terri Pine*

MARDI GRAS CORN SALAD

TIME: 30 MINUTES • SERVES 12

INGREDIENTS:
1 large purple onion, finely chopped
2 large green bell peppers, finely chopped
1 tomato, finely chopped
1 Tbsp. butter
1 package (8 oz.) cream cheese
1 cup mayonnaise or salad dressing
2 cans (15¼ oz. each) whole-kernel yellow corn, drained
2 cans (11 oz. each) white shoepeg corn, drained
2 tsp. lemon juice
Salt and pepper, to taste

Sauté the chopped vegetables in the butter in a large skillet over medium heat for about 5 minutes. Add the cream cheese and mayonnaise and melt. Stir in the corn. Make sure everything is fully coated with the cream cheese–mayonnaise mixture and simmer for an additional 5 minutes. Add the lemon juice, salt, and pepper.

Tip: Serve warm or chilled as a side.

ᘉ *Submitted by Lynda Edwards*

MICHELE'S HOMEMADE BUTTERMILK RANCH DRESSING

TIME: PREP TIME 10 MINUTES, REFRIGERATION
TIME 2 HOURS • SERVES 12

INGREDIENTS:

½ cup sour cream

1 tsp. Worcestershire sauce

1 Tbsp. cider vinegar

½ tsp. salt

1 tsp. dried dill

½ tsp. dried chives

½ tsp. dried parsley

¼ tsp. garlic powder

¼ tsp. onion powder

½ tsp. dried oregano

½ tsp. fresh ground black pepper

⅛ tsp. paprika

¼ tsp. dried mustard

½ tsp. sugar

1 cup buttermilk

Combine all ingredients except buttermilk in a medium mixing bowl. Slowly add the buttermilk and mix well. Refrigerate and let chill at least 2 hours before serving.

Tip: Keeps well for up to a week in a covered container in refrigerator.

∾ *Submitted by Michele Schubert*

MICHELE'S PARMESAN GARLIC CROUTONS

TIME: PREP TIME 15 MINUTES, BAKING TIME 30 MINUTES • SERVES 8

INGREDIENTS:

½ loaf French bread, cut into small cubes

8 tsp. butter, melted

½ tsp. garlic powder

½ cup grated Parmesan cheese

Preheat the oven to 300 degrees F.

Place bread cubes in a large mixing bowl. In a small bowl or measuring cup combine melted butter and garlic powder. Slowly pour butter mixture over bread cubes and toss. Add Parmesan cheese, coating the bread cubes. Place bread on a cookie sheet and bake for 30 minutes or until golden brown, turning occasionally.

Tip: Just about any type of bread can be used for this recipe, so it's a great way to use up bread that would otherwise go to waste.

ᴄᴏ *Submitted by Michele Schubert*

Pinkie's Fried Green Tomatoes

TIME: PREP TIME 20 MINUTES • SERVES 3–4

INGREDIENTS:

Cooking oil

1 cup all-purpose flour

1 cup yellow cornmeal

1½ tsp. salt

1 tsp. black pepper

2 Tbsp. sugar

3 medium green tomatoes, unpeeled

1 cup buttermilk

Heat the oil in a heavy skillet. Mix all the dry ingredients in a shallow pan. Slice the tomatoes about ¼" thick. Place a few slices at a time in the buttermilk. Roll the soaked slices in the dry mixture and fry (one layer at a time) in the hot oil until the slices are brown on both sides. Drain on paper towels.

ᴄᴏ *Submitted by Charlaine Harris*

Sister's Mashed Potato Casserole

TIME: PREP TIME 30 MINUTES, BAKING TIME 30 MINUTES · SERVES 12

INGREDIENTS:

3 lb. small red potatoes, skins on, washed and quartered

Water

½ cup sour cream

½ cup half-and-half

4 Tbsp. butter

2 cups cheddar cheese, shredded (reserve 1 cup for topping)

3 strips of bacon, cooked and crumbled

1 shallot, minced and sautéed

¼ tsp. salt

½ tsp. fresh ground black pepper

Cover potatoes with 1 or 2 inches of water in a large saucepan. Bring to a boil, then reduce heat and cover. Simmer for 15 to 20 minutes, or until tender but not mushy. Remove from heat and drain.

Preheat the oven to 350 degrees F.

Mash potatoes and add sour cream, half-and-half, butter, 1 cup of the cheddar cheese, bacon, shallot, salt, and pepper. Place mashed potatoes in a greased or sprayed 9 × 13" or 3-quart casserole dish and sprinkle with the remaining cup of cheddar cheese. Bake for 30 minutes, or until thoroughly heated and cheese topping is melted.

Tip: The casserole could be made in advance and refrigerated for up to 2 days prior to baking. Allow extra baking time if dish has been prepared in advance and refrigerated.

ᔕ *Submitted by Michele Schubert*

Desserts

ADELE HALE STACKHOUSE'S BLUE-RIBBON CHOCOLATE CAKE

TIME: 65 MINUTES; PREPARE THE ICING BEFORE MAKING
THE CAKE • SERVES 12

INGREDIENTS:

Chocolate Icing:

1⅛ cups whipping cream

1 stick unsalted butter (use a premium brand)

4 Tbsp. unsweetened cocoa powder (use a premium brand)

3 Tbsp. light corn syrup

9 oz. bittersweet or semisweet chocolate (half of each is best; use
    Ghirardelli or another premium brand)

1 tsp. pure vanilla extract

Chocolate Cake:

2 cups flour (sifted, then measured)

2 cups sugar (I prefer ultrafine baker's sugar)

½ cup unsweetened cocoa powder (use a premium brand)

½ tsp. baking soda

¼ tsp. salt

1 cup whole milk

½ cup cold black coffee

½ cup shortening

1 tsp. pure vanilla extract

2 large eggs

⅔ cup chopped pecans, plus pecan halves for garnish

To prepare the icing, whisk the whipping cream, butter, cocoa powder, and corn syrup in a medium saucepan over medium heat until the butter melts and the mixture comes to a simmer. Remove the pan from the heat. Add the chocolate and vanilla, and whisk until the chocolate is melted and smooth. Refrigerate the frosting until slightly thickened but still spreadable, stirring occasionally, about 45 minutes.

Preheat the oven to 350 degrees F. Grease and flour two round 9" cake pans, 2" deep.

To prepare the cake, mix the flour, sugar, cocoa powder, baking soda, and salt in a medium bowl. Beat in the milk, coffee, shortening, and vanilla with an electric mixer at a low speed until combined. Then beat at high speed for 2 minutes. Add the eggs and beat for 2 more minutes. Pour the batter into the prepared pans and smooth with a spatula.

Place in the middle of the oven and bake for 30–35 minutes, or until a toothpick inserted in the center comes out clean. Let the cake layers cool in the pans for 5 minutes. Remove from the pans and place on racks to cool completely.

Place one layer top side down on a plate. Spread with half of the prepared icing; sprinkle with chopped pecans. Top with the other layer, top side up. Frost the top and sides with the remaining icing. Garnish the cake with pecan halves with a star design.

Tip: When frosting the cake, run the knife or spatula under hot water every few minutes to ensure a glossy finish. Also, a tablespoon of mayonnaise can be added to the cake batter for moistness in cold, dry weather.

∾ *Submitted by Michele Schubert*

Aunt Patty's Sour Cream Cake with Praline Frosting

TIME: 2 HOURS 15 MINUTES, PLUS COOLING TIME · SERVES 12

INGREDIENTS:

Cake:

1 cup sour cream

¼ tsp. baking soda

4 cups sugar

2 cups butter, softened

7 egg yolks

7 egg whites, stiffly beaten

3 cups all-purpose flour

½ tsp. salt

2 tsp. vanilla extract

2 Tbsp. almond extract

Praline Frosting (makes 1½ cups):

1 cup chopped pecans

6 Tbsp. butter

1 cup firmly packed light brown sugar

5 Tbsp. heavy cream

1 cup powdered sugar

1 tsp. vanilla extract

Preheat the oven to 325 degrees F. Grease and flour a 10" tube pan.

Stir together the sour cream and baking soda in a bowl; set the mixture aside. Beat the sugar and butter with an electric mixer on medium speed until fluffy. Add the egg yolks, one at a time, beating well after each addition. Fold in the egg whites. Stir the flour and salt together in a separate bowl, and then set the mixture aside.

Alternately add the flour mixture and the sour cream mixture to the egg mixture, beginning and ending with the flour mixture. Beat at low speed just until blended after each addition. Stir in the vanilla and almond extract. Pour the batter into the prepared pan. Bake for 90 minutes, or until a long wooden pick inserted in the center comes out clean. Cool in the pan on a wire rack for 20 minutes. Remove from the pan and cool completely on the wire rack. Increase the oven temperature to 350 degrees F.

To prepare the frosting, place the pecans on a baking sheet and bake for 8 minutes at 350 degrees F. Flip the pecans over and bake for another 8 minutes, or until golden brown.

Place the butter, brown sugar, and cream in a 2-quart saucepan over medium heat and bring to a boil, stirring often. Continue to boil and stir for 2 minutes. Remove from the heat and whisk in the powdered sugar and vanilla until smooth and creamy. Add the toasted pecans; stir gently for 5 minutes, or until the frosting begins to cool and thicken slightly. Spread immediately over the cooled cake.

∽ *Submitted by Lara Nocerino*

Caroline Holliday Bellefleur's Chocolate Cake

TIME: 2 HOURS • SERVES 12

INGREDIENTS:

1 package Swansdown Chocolate Fudge Cake Mix (or Duncan Hines, if you can't find Swansdown anymore)

1 package (8 oz.) seedless dates

1 cup water

¾ cup sugar

2 cups confectioners' sugar

⅛ tsp. salt

3 Tbsp. shortening

½ tsp. vanilla extract

3 Tbsp. brewed coffee

1 cup chopped pecans

I know you'll be surprised, people of Bon Temps, that my recipe contains a mix! This has been my dark secret for many years. I've always driven to Cla-

rice to make the purchase, so no one would see me. So now you know! If you're a purist, please use your favorite chocolate cake recipe, providing it's very moist.

Mix the cake mix and bake in a greased 9 × 13" glass pan, following the box directions.

Cook the dates, water, and sugar in a double boiler for 30–40 minutes. Spread on top of the cooled cake.

While the date mixture is cooling on the cake, mix together the confectioners' sugar, salt, shortening, vanilla, coffee, and pecans. Spread on top of the cake. Sometimes I use pecan halves to create a pattern to make it look prettier.

ᔆ *From Caroline Bellefleur, as told to Charlaine Harris*

DINER KEY LIME PIE

TIME: PREP TIME 30–40 MINUTES, REFRIGERATION TIME
4 HOURS • SERVES 8

INGREDIENTS:
3 Tbsp. butter
25–30 chocolate wafers
1 package lime Jell-O
½ cup hot water
¼ cup lemon juice
¼ cup sugar
1 can (12 oz.) evaporated milk, refrigerated until very cold
Green food coloring
1 tsp. lemon zest

Melt the butter. Crush the wafers and mix with the melted butter. Press the crumb mixture into a 9" pie pan to form a crust. Save crumbs not used for crust to sprinkle on top. Dissolve the Jell-O in hot water, then add the lemon juice and sugar. Whip the evaporated milk until it thickens.

Add the Jell-O mixture to the milk and whip until stiff. Add four drops of green food coloring and lemon zest. Spoon the mixture into the crust. Sprinkle remaining chocolate crumbs on top and refrigerate for at least 4 hours but preferably overnight.

  ∾ *Submitted by Treva Jackson*

Louisiana Pralines

TIME: 30–45 MINUTES · SERVES 5–10

INGREDIENTS:
Butter for greasing the saucepan
1 cup granulated sugar
1 cup firmly packed brown sugar
¾ cup half-and-half
½ tsp. salt
2 Tbsp. butter
1 tsp. vanilla extract
1 cup chopped pecans
24 whole pecans (optional)

Note: Like any candy, this recipe needs a dry day (below 50 percent humidity) to set up perfectly. Higher humidity results in sticky candy. If it's pouring rain, you may end up eating it spooned over ice cream—which is fabulous, too.

You'll need a large, heavy saucepan (at least 2 quarts) with a lid and a very sturdy handle. The boiling syrup must be vigorously beaten, so deep sides and a firmly attached handle are a must. When making candy, the goal is to have it crystallize when you want it to, and not a minute before. That means that if even a grain of sugar or salt falls into the heated syrup before you're ready to spoon it out, the contents of the saucepan will set up like concrete, and you'll get no candy, plus you'll have a nasty mess to clean up. So the following instructions are set up to make certain no untoward grains of sugar destroy your candy before its time.

Butter the sides of your saucepan. As the pan warms, the butter will melt, and any sugar grains sticking to the side will slide into the pan before they cause trouble. Place the sugars, half-and-half, and salt into your prepared pan. Stir constantly over low heat until the mixture blends and the sugars melt into the half-and-half. Raise the heat to medium. Place the lid on the pan and allow it to heat for a few minutes. This will let the steam from the mixture wash any remaining sugar crystals down the side of the pan.

While the candy is cooking, prepare an area to spoon the candy by greasing a cookie sheet or placing a sheet of greased waxed paper on a butcher block or marble slab.

Remove the lid. Once the sugar syrup boils, turn the heat down to a simmer. If any crystals remain on the sides of the pan, carefully remove them with a wet paper towel wrapped around a fork. Never put your fingers into the pot. Bring the syrup to 234 degrees F. If you don't have a candy thermometer, bring it to the soft-ball stage. Remove from the heat.

Add the butter and vanilla, but don't stir—you're just letting the butter melt and the alcohol boil out of the vanilla right now. Wait 5 minutes. Add the chopped pecans. Stir vigorously with a clean wooden (nonconductive) spoon until the candy loses its gloss and thickens. Warning: The syrup is hot enough to inflict serious burns. You're incorporating air into the sugar syrup, which makes the candy soft and easy to eat, like fudge or taffy, instead of hard like a lollipop. Once it thickens, you need to move fast. Quickly spoon the candy into small mounds onto the prepared surface. If it starts to set up or gets too hard to work, beat in a teaspoon of hot water to loosen it up.

When the candy is all spooned out, press a whole pecan into the top of each praline, if desired. Allow the pralines to cool before serving.

Tip: Store the pralines in a tin lined with waxed paper to seal out humidity.

Cleanup note: Place the pan in the sink and fill it with hot water; let it sit for a little, and it'll be a lot easier to clean. If it's still a mess, fill it with water and place it on low heat on a burner. The sugars on the sides of the pan should soon melt away.

     ∾ *Submitted by Denise Little*

PERDITA'S BREAD PUDDING WITH BOURBON SAUCE

TIME: PREP TIME 35 MINUTES, BAKING TIME 60 MINUTES · SERVES 8

INGREDIENTS:

Bread Pudding:

½ cup seedless golden raisins (or dark raisins)

Enough bourbon to soak raisins

10 day-old slices of white bread, torn into pieces

4 cups milk, scalded

1 cup heavy cream

4 large eggs, beaten

1 cup granulated sugar

1 tsp. pure vanilla extract

1 tsp. ground cinnamon

½ tsp. ground nutmeg

½ cup (1 stick) butter, melted

½ cup pecans, roughly chopped

½ cup apple, peeled and chopped

Warm water

Bourbon Sauce:

2 sticks butter

2 cups powdered sugar

2 eggs

3 Tbsp. bourbon (or more to taste)

Preheat the oven to 350 degrees F.

In a bowl, cover raisins in bourbon to soak. Combine the bread, milk, and cream in a large mixing bowl and stir until blended. In a separate bowl, mix the eggs and sugar together till well blended. Pour egg mixture into bread mixture and stir. Add the vanilla, cinnamon, and nutmeg, and stir well. Drain soaked raisins. Stir in the melted butter, raisins, pecans, and apple. Pour the mix into a greased 9 × 13" 2-quart baking dish, set the dish in a larger baking pan filled with warm water about 1" deep, and bake for 1 hour. Remove the dish from the pan of water and let the pudding cool.

To prepare the bourbon sauce, melt butter in a double boiler. Combine sugar and eggs in a mixing bowl and stir until sugar dissolves. Add sugar and egg mixture to butter. Whisk sauce in double boiler over hot water until sauce thickens slightly. Remove from heat and add bourbon to taste.

Portion out the pudding and spoon bourbon sauce over each serving.

∽ *Bread pudding submitted by Belle Franklin; bourbon sauce submitted by Treva Jackson*

PORTIA'S SWEET POTATO PIE

TIME: PREP TIME 15 MINUTES, BAKING TIME 60 MINUTES · SERVES 8

INGREDIENTS:

2 cups canned mashed sweet potatoes

2 eggs

1¼ cups evaporated milk

½ cup sugar

½ tsp. salt

½ tsp. ground cinnamon

½ tsp. ground nutmeg

2 Tbsp. rum

4 Tbsp. melted butter

1 unbaked pie crust (9")

Preheat the oven to 425 degrees F.

Mix the sweet potatoes, eggs, evaporated milk, sugar, salt, cinnamon, nutmeg, rum, and butter with an electric mixer on medium speed until smooth. Pour into the pie crust. Bake for 10 minutes. Reduce the oven temperature to 300 degrees F and bake for an additional 50 minutes, or until the filling is firm.

∽ *Submitted by Ali Katz*

WICKED PEACH CAKE

TIME: BAKING TIME 35–40 MINUTES · SERVES 8–10

INGREDIENTS:

1 box yellow cake mix

1 package peach Jell-O

½ cup peach schnapps, divided

3–4 good-sized peaches, chopped to make 1½ cups

½ box powdered sugar

Preheat the oven to 350 degrees F. Grease and flour a Bundt cake pan.

Prepare cake mix according to box directions. Add Jell-O and ¼ cup schnapps. Fold in peaches. Pour mixture into pan and bake for 35–40 minutes, or until an inserted toothpick comes out clean.

Let cake cool for a few minutes, then turn it onto a cake plate and let cool until just warm. Mix together ¼ cup schnapps and powdered sugar to make a glaze. Poke several holes into the top of the cake with an ice pick or similar-sized utensil before drizzling the glaze over the cake. Add more schnapps if glaze is too thick.

∽ *Submitted in memory of Sharon Hicks*

Drinks

CLASSIC SOUTHERN SWEET TEA

TIME: 15 MINUTES FOR HEATING AND STEEPING · SERVES 8

INGREDIENTS:

1 quart water, preferably filtered

1 cup sugar

6 tea bags (flavor of your choice, but plain old Lipton is traditional)

Ice

Place a heavy 2-quart stainless steel saucepan on the stove. Fill just over halfway with water.

Add the sugar. Heat the water until the sugar melts, stirring frequently. Remove from the heat.

Drop in the tea bags. Allow to steep for roughly 5 minutes, or to taste. The longer the bags steep, the stronger the tea will be. Remove the tea bags and discard. Add ice to the mixture and stir. Pour the tea into a pitcher. Serve by pouring into ice-filled glasses.

Tip: Garnish with mint or lemon balm, if desired.

∾ *Submitted by Denise Little*

COUNTRY PORCH LEMONADE

TIME: 15 MINUTES • SERVES 6

INGREDIENTS:
1 quart water, preferably filtered
1 cup sugar
3 lemons
Ice

Place a heavy 2-quart stainless steel saucepan on the stove. Fill just over halfway with water.

Add the sugar. Heat the water until the sugar melts, stirring frequently. Remove from the heat.

While the water is heating, slice the lemons in half. Cut six perfect round slices to garnish with, one from each cut lemon half. Set aside the garnish slices. Juice the six remaining lemon halves. Strain out the seeds and pulp. Add the lemon juice and ice to the warm sugar water. Stir. Pour the lemonade into a pitcher. Serve by pouring into ice-filled glasses. Garnish each glass with a slice of lemon.

∾ *Submitted by Denise Little*

Inside *True Blood*

Alan Ball Answers Questions from the Fans

Although *True Blood* certainly wouldn't exist without Charlaine's cele-brated bestselling novel series, there's no doubt that the driving force behind the sexy, sassy television show is its creator, producer, and writer, Alan Ball, who was captivated with Charlaine's wonderful characters at first sight and has reimagined them for television while staying true to their original versions at the same time.

When I approached him for an interview about the series and his work, Mr. Ball said yes quickly and graciously. Rather than ask him questions that have no doubt been covered in other venues, I decided to allow the fans a rare chance to ask Mr. Ball questions about his work on *True Blood* and just about anything else Sookie-related that they desired. The response was overwhelming, and I selected the best questions to pass along to him. I'm pleased to reveal his answers here.

How did you first discover the Sookie Stackhouse series?

—RACHEL KLIKA

I was early for a dentist appointment and stumbled upon the books at a nearby Barnes & Noble. I picked up the first book and couldn't put it down. Once I got into the series, I knew it had to be a TV show.

In Season 2 of *True Blood*, the maenad character Maryann Forrester (played brilliantly by Michelle Forbes) was developed to a fuller extent when compared to her role in the book by Ms. Harris. Why did you decide to develop this character further? —DEIRDRE BRENNAN

Part of the challenge in adapting Charlaine's novels is to create strong stories for the characters other than Sookie and still remain very faithful to the spirit of the books. We loved the maenad attacking Sookie and poisoning her with her claws, and then we looked for ways for her to interact with the other characters as well as being dangerous to Sookie. Ultimately, she gave us something for the entire cast to go up against.

What was your motivation for having Bill ask Sookie to marry him in the end of the second season when it was so far from the books? Was it that it was a good way to have Bill kidnapped/disappear? —ADDIE BROWN

I think the motivation was to give them a moment of happiness, a hope that something they thought was off-limits to both of them was actually within their grasp. They've been through so much together during their relatively short relationship, it felt nice to give them a moment of "normalcy" and the hope that they could have a happy ending. Of course, this being *True Blood*, there isn't much chance of that.

What inspired you to make the Sookie books into an HBO series? —KIM MCCOLLOM

I was so deeply entertained by the experience of reading the books, I just thought it would make a great TV show. The world and the characters seemed too large for just a movie—to me, it begged for the larger canvas of a TV series.

Your show has resonated with such a wide demographic group of people—many not typical fans of vampires and the paranormal. What [do you think] sets *True Blood* apart from all the other vampire movies/shows to attract such a following? —KIM MCCOLLOM

I think it's because of several different elements: the characters and the world that Charlaine created; the performances by the amazingly talented cast; the humor, the romance, the scares; the focus we try to keep on making everything, no matter how outlandish, grounded in the emotional lives of the characters. It's just a really fun show to make and hopefully a fun show to watch.

What were your first impressions of the people in Bon Temps?
—NADEEN CUMMINGS

They felt really authentic to me. I grew up in a semismall town in the South (Marietta, Georgia), and the descriptions of the characters, the way they behaved and spoke, it all felt like something I recognized.

I love the character of Lafayette and am so glad that he survived Season 1 of *True Blood*, unlike his less-fortunate counterpart in the books. Did you decide that his character would go beyond Season 1 from the beginning, or was that decision made after seeing how well he came to life on screen? —LAURA CHEQUER

The first scene I shot with Nelsan Ellis in the pilot made it abundantly clear to me that this was a character we could never lose. I am usually not a fan of actors who improvise, but Nelsan doesn't just improvise, he channels from planet Lafayette. In a lesser actor's hands, Lafayette could come across as extreme or one-dimensional; Nelsan makes him strong, fierce, and deeply lovable.

Will you consider casting yourself in a cameo role each season (à la Alfred Hitchcock)? —TEDDI SMITH

Never! I allowed myself to be talked into doing that in an episode of *Six Feet Under* and have always regretted it. I think it would just take viewers out of the story.

Many changes have been made from Charlaine Harris's books to the show, and I'm wondering why you chose to paint Bill and Sophie-Anne in the light you did, as opposed to the way Ms. Harris wrote the characters? While there are a lot of similarities in Bill, it seems your Sophie-Anne is very modern and not the regal, aristocratic French queen portrayed in the series. Any insight to your decisions would be appreciated. —SUSAN MOSS

In *True Blood*, Sophie-Anne appears in the same season Godric appears. We chose not to have two ancient vampires who seem barely older than children in the same season. And ultimately, every nonregular character on our show exists to create conflicts and challenges for our regular characters. Having read all the books at this point, and knowing why Bill appeared in Bon Temps in the first place, we chose to play Sophie-Anne a little differently. We also were setting up a major story line in Season 3.

In the show, it consistently seems as if you are trying to villainize Eric and sanctify Bill, even referring to Eric as the "bad boy" more than once in interviews. This certainly does *not* stay true to the spirit of the books, as Eric is absolutely not a villain or even a bad boy in the books, and likewise Bill is definitely not a saint, nor is he even a "good guy" half the time. Is there a reason that you try to portray these characters in this manner, and if so, what is it? —LISA ROWELL

Hmm...I am not sure I agree with your assessment. We have purposely shown many darker aspects of Bill, such as his penchant for sport-killing during his years with Lorena, his keeping things from Sookie, his interaction with the state patrolman he glamoured in Season 1, taking his gun and pointing it at him, and his murder of Uncle Bartlett. Likewise, we have shown many of the deeper, more tender aspects of Eric—his love for Godric, his grief at Godric's true death. We continue with both of these directions in Season 3. And it seems to me more dramatic to establish certain expectations about a character and then upend them than to just depict everyone as equal parts light and darkness. And when I use the term "bad boy," I am referring to the kind of bad boy that women are consistently attracted to—a man who doesn't play by the rules, a man who is a little dangerous, who is going to create more drama and fun than the good guy who does everything right.

Sex, death, food, and violence play a large role in *True Blood*. Americans have a possibly unhealthy relationship with all four, and yet we are fascinated by them. Is this the secret to the success of the books and series?

—SARA FOSTER

Honestly, I have no idea. I think the success of the series is because these stories and characters are so much fun.

It is not a common thing for the vampires in *True Blood* to be young and beautiful, as it normally is in other vampire television shows and movies. Why did you choose to go in this direction? —ANNE FELDBAK

Well, I think while we have plenty of vampires who are young and beautiful, I like the idea that one can become a vampire at any point in his or her life. This is exactly as it is in Charlaine's books—and I thought that was clever and unexpected. Also, I generally chafe at doing something the same way everyone else does it.

What plot point (so far) has been the most difficult to write, act, and film?   —MISTY PADGETT

Hmm—the storming of Merlotte's by the black-eyed zombies . . . the final Maryann sacrifice/marriage . . . the storming of Steve Newlin's church by the Dallas vampires.

What is your gauge to keep elements in the series that are in the books?
—KERI MCCOY

Instinct. And input by the other writers on staff.

Since art imitates life, explain what _True Blood_ has to say about the American viewing public. What does our "bloodlust" say about the current cultural climate? The archetype has been used throughout history in many cultures, but what do _you_ see this archetype revealing about us?
—JESSICA OHMAN

I leave that to the academics. Anything I say about why vampires are such potent symbols is just going to be me trying to pretend like I know why when I don't. I'm just glad people are intrigued by vampires and other supernatural creatures because working on this show is the most fun I have ever had.

Did the real-life relationship of Anna Paquin and Stephen Moyer have an impact on the decision to diminish the role of Eric in favor of Bill in the _True Blood_ series?   —LINDA J. KERLEY

I don't really buy that the role of Eric has been diminished in favor of Bill. Eric has his own very strong story line in Seasons 2 and 3. Maybe you mean in terms of his relationship to Sookie . . . ? You have to remember we're in the middle of _True Blood_. It is an ongoing story.

I noticed the episodes have different writers. How do multiple writers come to write something continuative? Is there a sit-down session for each episode that you drive? Do you say, "I would like so-and-so to write this particular scene"? —CYNTHIA MEIER

I work with six other writers. We break stories and outline episodes as a group, then a single writer writes the script. We give notes as a group, then that same writer writes a second draft of the script. Sometimes I do a polish if I believe it is necessary. Writers generally volunteer for the episodes they want to write.

What is it about the show *True Blood* that represents you in some way? —AARON HARRIS

I guess I would say the irreverence, the humor, the fascination with the bizarre, the romance, the fun.

What do you find to be most challenging when depicting a fictional world from book to screen (besides the fans wanting certain story lines)? —EMILY MELONAS

Hmm . . . keeping everyone's actions motivated and based in their emotional needs and desires. In the case of Charlaine's books, keeping the characters who are not Sookie active in their own stories.

What inspired you to bring in characters on the show that were not in the books, such as Jessica and Daphne, as well as to keep Lafayette? (We are grateful for these characters, as they are awesome; just curious.) —KIMBERLEE TUCKER

Again, it all comes down to creating stories for characters who are not Sookie, and in Lafayette's case, loving what Nelsan Ellis was doing so much that I wanted to keep him in the show.

My question is regarding the character Bill Compton. I really liked the character in the books and hated to see him pushed to the side so often, so I must say I really enjoy him being a front-burner character in the show. What was it about the character on the page that made you connect with him? What were you looking for in the actors who auditioned for the part, and how did you feel when you finally found the talented and gorgeous Stephen Moyer to fill the role? **—BARBI BARRIER**

Well, just like you, I loved the idea of a man who had basically lost everything; who, because of his and Sookie's circumstances (him being vampire, her being telepathic), is suddenly given a second chance at love and meaning in his life. When casting, I kept looking for a man who seemed like he was from another time, who knew how to play that undercurrent of sadness, and also was dashing and handsome, like a true romantic hero. When we found Stephen, I was thrilled, because we had been looking for a long time prior.

I really enjoy watching the show, but never watch the opening credits, as I find them unnerving. How and why did you come to decide on such a thought-provoking opening sequence? **—OLIVIA PAVEY**

I wanted something primal, something that really communicated Southern gothic, something that alluded to the twin polarities of sex and religion as a means for transcendence, something that was really rooted deeply in nature.

I'd like to thank Alan for taking time out of his very hectic schedule to answer these wonderful questions, and thanks also to all of the fans who submitted them!

From Mystery to Mayhem

The Works of Charlaine Harris

BY BEVERLY BATTILLO

L ong before a telepathic waitress served the first beverage to a handsome vampire at Merlotte's Bar, Charlaine Harris was creating compelling characters and plots that have excited her fans' imaginations and
fueled their fantasies.

Ever since the fourth grade, when she began composing poems about
ghosts, Charlaine wanted to write. Her formal writing career began, however, after her marriage in 1978 to her second husband, Hal. As a wedding
present, the understanding groom presented his bride with an electric
typewriter and encouraged her to follow her longtime dream of becoming
an author. Charlaine's first novel, the mystery *Sweet and Deadly*, was published in 1981 and marked the beginning of a distinguished career that has
now spanned thirty years.

FIRST STEPS

With the publication of her first novel, Charlaine was described as "a
strong new talent whose writing has verve and originality" and as "an
author of rare talent," but it was the release of her second stand-alone

mystery, *A Secret Rage*, in 1984 that led to more critical acclaim and a "cultlike" fan following. The story of a small Southern university town terrorized by a serial rapist "makes brilliant use of the rapidly changing Southern background and handles a difficult theme with sensitivity and insight," according to critics. Fans in the mystery community embraced this new talent and eagerly looked forward to more from her.

Motherhood took up much of Charlaine's attention during these early years, and she quit writing for a while to focus on beginning a family. After the birth of her second child, "she ached to get back to writing, she missed it so." It was at this time that she signed with Joshua Bilmes, who would become her longtime agent and friend. After the five-year hiatus, it was difficult to get back into the publishing world, but, with renewed energy, Charlaine burst back upon the scene with the first of her new mystery series.

THE AURORA TEAGARDEN AND LILY BARD SERIES

Real Murders, the first book in Charlaine's Aurora Teagarden series, was published in 1990. About a small-town Georgia librarian and amateur sleuth whose life doesn't turn out the way she expected, the books have been described as "cozies with teeth." *Real Murders* garnered Charlaine her first Agatha Award nomination for Best Novel of 1990. Fans who gathered at Malice Domestic to meet their new favorite author had a great time, and Charlaine began establishing the warm relationship with readers that she would continue and cherish over the coming years.

The greatest fan reaction to the series came after the publication of *A Fool and His Honey* in 1999. Charlaine outraged many readers with the death of the heroine's husband. This was the first of many indications that Charlaine would write her books according to her vision and her vision alone. The Teagarden series sold steadily over many years, but it was hard to build an audience because of the limited availability of the Worldwide paperback editions. The final book of the series, *Poppy Done to Death*, was released in 2003.

In 1996, Charlaine began her second series, the Lily Bard "Shakespeare" books, set in the fictional town of Shakespeare, Arkansas. Lily is the survivor of a terrible assault that has left her an emotional cripple, and the first book, *Shakespeare's Landlord*, begins her first steps back to a normal life and normal relationships. Drawing on her own experiences, Charlaine has said that writing Lily helped her clean out many of her own dark places. More somber in tone than the Teagarden books, the Lily Bard novels didn't necessarily appeal to the same fans. The books did receive excellent critical response, however, and picked up a good paperback deal. Despite receiving a lot of good press, the series ended in 2001 with the release of *Shakespeare's Counselor*. Lily Bard was a fresh and distinct new character and provided a bridge to the next stage of Charlaine's career.

THE SOOKIE STACKHOUSE SERIES

Hoping to reach a broader audience with her next series, Charlaine began developing a character that was quite unlike any she had ever written before. She hoped to draw on the same reader base she'd created, and the new series' success was helped in many ways by the foundation she had created with the Aurora Teagarden and Lily Bard books. Full of a unique blend of dark humor, unforgettable characters, and a well-developed mystery with a twist of romance, *Dead Until Dark*, the first of the Sookie Stackhouse series, was released in 2001. The book was so different that it had taken her agent nearly two years to find a publisher, but Charlaine had faith in Sookie and her story. Now recognized as the first in a series that helped introduce the new genre called urban fantasy, the Sookie Stackhouse novels have been embraced by an ever-widening audience of fans and have received much critical acclaim. Charlaine established herself as an important and versatile author in this new genre. *Dead Until Dark* won the Anthony Award for Best Paperback Mystery in 2002. Now published in thirty languages, the series, which spans eleven novels, continues to reach new fans all over the world.

Sookie novels and stories in the order they should be read:
Dead Until Dark
Living Dead in Dallas
Club Dead
Dead to the World

"Fairy Dust"
"Dracula Night"
Dead as a Doornail
"One Word Answer"
Definitely Dead
All Together Dead
"Lucky"
From Dead to Worse
"Gift Wrap"
Dead and Gone
"Two Blondes"
Dead in the Family
"Small-Town Wedding"
Dead Reckoning
"If I Had a Hammer"

TRUE BLOOD

The end of 2006 brought a new dimension to the popularity of Sookie Stackhouse when it was announced that Alan Ball and HBO had contracted to turn the popular books into the television series *True Blood*. Fans on the website spent the next year closely following the casting and filming information as they eagerly anticipated their first view of the Sookieverse brought to life.

First scheduled to premiere in March 2008, the pilot was delayed by a screenwriters' strike until September of that year. Almost immediately, the series caught the fancy not only of established book fans but of viewers new to the story of the Louisiana bar waitress and her undead boyfriend. Hits on the Charlaine Harris website exploded within a day of the September 7, 2008, debut, as *True Blood* viewers flocked there to discuss the characters and the story in such numbers that the site was overwhelmed. New fans sought out the books upon which the series was based, and soon all of the published books in the Sookie Stackhouse series were simultaneously in the top twenty-five paperbacks on the *New York Times* bestseller lists.

THE HARPER CONNELLY SERIES

With the release of *Grave Site* in 2005, Charlaine introduced us to a new heroine, Harper Connelly, and her stepbrother, Tolliver Lang. The series was quickly embraced by fans for its quirky characters and darker, noir-like feel. Although the books and characters were popular with readers, Charlaine felt that the story was told, and the series ended with the publication of the fourth book in the series, *Grave Secret*, in 2009.

CHARLAINE AND HER FANS

Charlaine has commented that she has "the greatest readers in the world." Her close relationship with fans led her to establish a website in 2001. Increasing fan usage soon made it obvious that a more flexible site would be needed, and in March 2004, charlaineharris.com became the place where fans could meet to discuss her books and characters, read her weekly blog and book review column, learn of her touring schedule, and share everything from recipes to prayer requests. Charlaine's willingness to visit the website daily and interact with her fans, and her obvious enjoyment of her readers in personal appearances, led to the establishment by fans of her official fan club, Charlaine's Charlatans, in 2006. The fan club voted that its first goal was to help Charlaine reach the number one spot on the *New York Times* hardback bestseller list. In May 2009, *Dead and Gone*, the ninth book in the series, debuted in the number one spot on the *New York Times* hardcover bestseller list. Charlaine's fan club was thrilled!

As *True Blood* enters its fourth hit season and the Sookie Stackhouse series continues, Charlaine's earlier series are experiencing a rebirth. Fans who have been enchanted with Sookie are now turning to Aurora, Lily, and Harper, and finding that these other stories are just as compelling and the characters as fresh as they were when first introduced. Charlaine continues to develop new characters and offer new pleasures for readers all over the world.

Recollections Around the Duckpond

The Fans of Charlaine Harris

BY BEVERLY BATTILLO

F an clubs are very dangerous things. I should know; I started one, and my life will never be the same.

My story began fifty years ago with my best friend Ellen and I playing our favorite game—school. Since Ellen was four years older, she got to be the teacher, and a terror she was! As the hapless student, if I didn't learn my spelling words, Ellen would energetically apply her ruler to my backside. I was soon a most exemplary student and kept my excellent study habits for the remainder of my life. The greatest tribute to Ellen's tenacious teaching style was that by the time I was five years old I could read at first-grade level. Doors began opening in my mind, and reading became my greatest pleasure and one I pursued voraciously. Ironically, Ellen now works for the IRS and continues, at least metaphorically, to apply her ruler.

Reading became my addiction. I took another quantum leap in junior high when I registered for a speed-reading course. Now I not only read a lot, but I read a lot really *fast*. In addition, my ability to completely block out all activity when reading was a talent that drove my parents totally crazy. If we ever have a nuclear war, I doubt I'll know it until the universe is completely annihilated and I complete whatever I happen to be reading and find angels playing harps all around me.

My taste in literature has always been rather eclectic. If it's in print, I'll read it, whether biography, romance, mystery, cereal boxes—I'm sure you get the idea. I can't say my reading has led me to any great revelations or astounding insights. My life in general has remained boringly normal. I have discovered many friends in books—ones that I revisit again and again with great pleasure—and I marvel at the talent and imagination of those who can create worlds within worlds for us to enjoy. It wasn't until late in life that I discovered something that led me to stray from my steadfast and steady existence.

My first breach into a different world came in 1964 when a favorite teacher introduced me to the works of J. R. R. Tolkien. *The Hobbit* and *The Lord of the Rings* were literature the likes of which I had never experienced—a realm filled with astounding characters and a new language of its own. Dipping into fantasy a bit in later years, I happened upon a book by a new writer named Laurell K. Hamilton. Hamilton's first book, *Nightseer*, caught my fancy, and I still believe it to be one of her best works. I discovered Hamilton's Web board and began to explore her Anita Blake series. These books were part of what was being described as an emerging new fictional genre. Booksellers didn't quite know where to put them—some placed them in horror, some in fantasy, and even a few in the romance section. Identifying their place in literature became something of a conundrum. Although I enjoyed the early books in the series, I found the later ones not to my taste and began to look for something new. While I was perusing the horror section in a nearby Barnes & Noble bookstore, my eye was caught by a book with a charming, almost folk art, cover. The book was *Dead Until Dark* by Charlaine Harris. The rest is, as they say, history.

Dead Until Dark was unlike anything I had read in my long history of reading. Since it was written in the first person from the perspective of the heroine, I felt that I actually became Sookie and experienced events through her eyes. I had read first-person perspective in the past, but these books seemed completely fresh, and the world was new and absolutely believable. Following my usual pattern, I visited the author's website, searching to find other readers with whom to discuss the wonders of this new universe. I did not expect to meet the author there!

Charlaine established her website in 2001 and updated it in March 2004 to handle the ever-increasing usage. Charlaine was an active participant, who encouraged discussion and became involved on a personal level with the readers who visited her site. I first visited her board early in 2004 and was able to share in the development of the new site. Imagine my thrill and astonishment the first time Charlaine commented directly to me on the board.

A fan board is an interesting organism. It constantly changes as members come and go and as friendships are forged and cemented. In the early days of the new board, an active core of members was established, and these new friends became closer to me than many of the people whom I had known for decades. As we became more engaged with one another, a sense of community grew among members who were geographically far apart but close in interest and viewpoint. Charlaine was the glue that held us together, but in a very real way we were all a part of something that was much larger than any individual. It is not hard to imagine that many of us were curious to discover whether the friendships we had forged with one another as strangers would carry over into the reality of actually meeting.

As more information became available regarding Charlaine's touring schedule, board members began to plan to meet at these events. My first opportunity came in May 2006 at the Romantic Times Convention in Daytona Beach, Florida. I attended the Saturday author book-signing session and will never forget the first time I met my favorite author.

I approached Charlaine's table shyly, not at all sure how to greet her. Charlaine took matters into her own hands by leaping to her feet, hugging me with apparent delight, and inviting me to sit beside her and talk as she signed books for fans. As we sat together that afternoon, I felt a true friendship form and realized there were ways that fans like me could help bring her terrific books to the attention of new readers. Ideas from that first convention were spinning in my head as I returned home and shared with my family the wonderful experience of meeting Charlaine and several of my online friends.

Returning to the board after my experience at RT, I approached the members with the idea of developing an official fan club whose stated purpose would be to help Charlaine become a number one bestselling author. Members of the board were interested, so I approached Charlaine for permission to pursue the fan club idea, and with some bemusement she agreed. Officers were nominated and elected, and a contest was instituted to choose a name and a logo for the club. During this time, it was announced that the rights to the Sookie Stackhouse books had been sold to producer Alan Ball, who was to develop them into an HBO television series tentatively titled *True Blood*. Excitement was high on many levels, and on June 1, 2006, Charlaine's Charlatans became the official fan club of author Charlaine Harris.

The sale of the merchandising rights to the Sookie series prevented the fan club from using any of the images associated with the Sookie books as we began to discuss what to use as a logo for the club. Charlaine's Web moniker was Duckpond, and we decided to develop identification around that name. Fortunately, a talented artist member and her equally talented husband created the two-ducks-on-the-pond logo that is now recognized wherever we go. Incorporating the motto "Follow me to the Duckpond," our specially designed logo T-shirts soon became familiar to fans and authors alike. Charlaine told us she loved the shirts because wherever she saw them as she traveled she knew she was among friends.

Toward the end of 2006 another idea was gaining ground on the Web board. The Romantic Times Convention was to be held in Houston, Texas, in April 2007, and the club leadership decided that this would be the perfect venue for our first official fan club gathering. Sixteen Charlatans from around the world traveled to Houston to join Charlaine there. I can't express the excitement we felt as the time drew near. I'd never traveled alone so far from my home, so it was a special time for me; as president of the fan club, I felt a real responsibility to make this a memorable event for all of us. I can only say that Houston had never seen anything like the Charlatans! The event was literally one of the high points of my life. The camaraderie we felt was instantaneous; the friendships we had forged as strangers on the board became a face-to-face reality. I can now go almost anywhere in the world and be near a friend who I can call on in need and be absolutely sure will answer. It is an empowering and comforting idea. I won't recount here all the pranks and laughs we shared. Never had so much fun been had with a set of waxed fangs! Before we left, several authors asked Charlaine if they could buy the club from her. High praise indeed!

Our leadership took seriously the pledge to help Charlaine reach new readers. The year 2007 was busy as we continued to design items such as bookmarks and bookplates to distribute to fans at conventions and signings. Charlatans acted as "commandoes" in bookstores, moving Charlaine's books to more advantageous locations. Membership in the fan club steadily increased as new readers came to participate on the board and as Charlaine began to make more personal appearances. The board was buzzing with speculation as reports began to come of progress in the development of *True Blood*. We were especially pleased to learn late in the year that Charlaine was selected to be the guest of honor at the Malice Domestic Convention in April 2008. This was a great honor for her, and the fan club leadership decided to support Charlaine by having our next official gathering at Malice Domestic. The Charlatans were ready to take on Washington, D.C.

Another event that took place in 2007 would institute a new tradition for the fan club. Charlaine shared with the board that one of her most popular characters, Eric Northman, was inspired by a character she had seen in the movie *The Thirteenth Warrior*. She was surprised and delighted when actor Vladimir Kulich contacted her to let her know how pleased he was to have been her inspiration and that he was a great fan of her books. A germ of an idea formed, and I contacted Charlaine to ask if we could invite Mr. Kulich to become an honorary member of Charlaine's Charlatans. On July 25, 2007, Vladimir Kulich was pleased to become our first Honorary Charlatan. Since that time we have recognized many others who have contributed in some significant way to Charlaine's writing.

Excitement was somewhat dimmed by the writers' strike in late 2007, which set back the expected premiere of *True Blood* from March to September 2008. There was a great deal of buzz already about the show, however, when the Charlatans came to Malice, where Charlaine was guest of honor. A very different venue from Romantic Times, Malice Domestic is a mystery writers' convention and was a new experience for the Charlatans. The Charlatans were definitely a new experience for Malice! Few mystery writers have organized fan clubs, and we were a curiosity for the authors who attended. The Charlatans enjoyed meeting them and sharing our experiences as a group and our support for Charlaine. We were very proud of our author as she received this important recognition from her peers. I was particularly proud of our club during the recognition banquet at which Charlaine spoke. We were all dressed to the nines, and as Charlaine came to the podium, we held up small lighted ducks so that she could see our support in the dim light of the banquet hall. Charlaine later told us how much it meant to have us in attendance.

Few members expected the events of September 2008. Familiar with what transpired on Jim Butcher's board when the *Dresden Files* television show premiered, I had spoken online with our webmistress about what might happen on Charlaine's board after the premiere of *True Blood*. None of us, Charlaine included, were prepared, however, for the explosion that actually took place. Within a day of the September 7, 2008, debut, the board was overwhelmed. *True Blood* fans flocked to the board to discuss the characters and the story, and many came to join the fan club. New readers sought out the books on which the series was based, and soon all eight of the published books in the Sookie Stackhouse series were simultaneously in the top twenty-five paperbacks on the *New York Times* bestseller list.

This tremendous influx of new fans soon made it evident that the fan club could not continue in its original form. By the end of 2008, Charlaine's Charlatans became a completely online club and ceased to operate as a conventional fan club. Our support for Charlaine continued, though, and the Charlatans were thrilled in May 2009 when the ninth book in the Sookie series, *Dead and Gone*, premiered at number one on the *New York Times* hardcover bestseller list. Charlaine's Charlatans initial stated goal had been achieved.

Several of us met again at the 2009 Dragon Con in Atlanta, Georgia. Charlaine was appearing, and we planned a gathering in which many new fans would be in attendance. The night before the event, a group of old friends were sitting around a table on the sidewalk outside a busy restaurant long after dinner was eaten, sharing memories and laughing. We were compiling a trivia contest for the meeting the next day and having a few beers and a lot of fun. It was warm and comfortable and absolutely *right*. Soon I would leave to return to Florida; another member would return to Texas; two each to Maryland, Pennsylvania, and California; and one would remain in Georgia—so many friends brought together by admiration of one special person. Charlaine Harris is the catalyst that brought us together and the inspiration that forged us into a formidable unit. As the Charlatans move forward into the future, we will continue to support Charlaine and enjoy the opportunities that arise to strengthen the bonds of friendship that have come to mean so much to us all.

Charlaine Harris Answers Questions from Her Fans

Thanks to all of you for your enthusiastic response to the opportunity to ask me questions. If I didn't get to answer your specific question, I apologize in advance for your disappointment. Here's the selection process we followed: BFF Paula, my invaluable best friend and assistant, sorted the questions into categories. She discarded some of the duplicates, since obviously there was no point in my reading the same thing over and over. I read all her choices, and I narrowed the field down to about fifty questions. Then I eliminated a few more after a second winnowing. This wasn't an easy process, so let me explain why I chose to answer some and not others.

First, if I thought the answer was already in the books, I felt it would be a waste of my time to reply to the question. Second, if I knew the answer would be included in future books . . . I put those aside, too, for the most part. Third, if the question was based on the television show mythology rather than the book mythology, of course I wasn't going to venture my opinion.

Some questions I bypassed simply because I didn't know the answer, or because I hadn't made up my mind yet. In some cases, the development of the books' mythology hadn't led me to a conclusion on the correct response, and in other cases, I simply don't know yet if (for example) Eric's other child will be a factor in Sookie's story.

I've corrected some of the spelling and a bit of the punctuation in some of these questions. I'm compelled to do that.

So, here goes.

Since the *True Blood* TV series began, do you picture your characters as the actors? I mean, when you're writing about Sookie, do you picture Anna Paquin? Or in your head do they just look the way you've always thought of them? —KIM HAMBLETON

They look the way I've always thought of them. I've been writing the books much longer than the show has been on the air.

Here is my big general question for Charlaine. I'm curious about her plotting. How much of it does she do in advance and how much of it is spontaneous? It just amazes me how some seemingly minor details in one book turn out to be huge later on. For example, Sookie mentions her cousin Hadley, but Sookie has no idea what happened to her. Now, many books later, we find out that Hadley mentioned Sookie to Queen Sophie-Anne, which started her whole relationship with vampires. Not to mention that Hadley had a child and that boy is now in the books—yet to be determined whether he becomes a major character.

—DENISE DUNNELL WELLS

I don't plot much in advance. Many of the big turning points in the books have been the result of spur-of-the-moment revelations. I'm always scattering seed in the field, though I'm never sure which will spring up and which will die in the ground. To me, that's the fun of writing. Of course, sometimes instead of scattering seed, I'm planting land mines to blow up in my face in the future.

How much of Sookie's personality is a reflection of yours, or is she more like an alter ego? —JESSICA SMITH

There are definitely elements of Sookie in me—or, more correctly, there are elements of me in her. I think there's a sliver of me in all my characters. I wish I were as brave as she is!

Is there any limit to the animals Sam can shift into? Can he shift into creatures that are more than one animal (like a hippogriff, perhaps)?
—PATRICIA RUOCCO

Sam can't shift into mythical animals, and he refuses to shift into the form of another human being. To a true shifter, that's a disgusting perversion. True shifters almost invariably stick to mammals when they choose their animal form, and most of them have a favorite.

Are some of the minor characters based on people you know/knew?
—SANDRA RUSSELL

The correct answer is, not entirely. I pick up on bits and pieces of people as I go through life: a physical trait, a speech habit, a character flaw or strength. I build my minor characters (though no character is really minor) based on an accumulation of observations.

Bubba seems to like keeping to himself, but I imagine he can get lonely at times. Would he ever consider creating a companion by turning one of those cats he's so fond of?
—LINDSEY NEELY

I got a lot of questions about Bubba, so let me just condense this answer. (Animals can't become vampires in my mythology, by the way.) Bubba does like to keep to himself. He still loves to perform, when he's in the mood, but he hates to be reminded of his former status, so characters don't mention his life name. Most vampires have gone through several names since they died, since they're constantly reinventing themselves, by the way. They had to, before they were able to come out of the coffin. But Bubba will stick to Bubba.

How long did Eric know about Bill's "mission" to seduce Sookie for Sophie-Anne? And why didn't he arrange for her to find out about it earlier?

—LADA KYST

Bill's mission was not to seduce Sookie; it was to investigate Sookie and verify her power. Seduction was just one option in his investigation. Bill was the obvious guy for the job since he already had a home in Bon Temps. Though Bill came to Bon Temps on this assignment for the queen, Eric did not know what Bill's specific mission was until he arrived in New Orleans in *Definitely Dead*. For several different reasons, Eric forced Bill to tell Sookie that he'd had a hidden agenda.

This has been bugging me lately. Did Bill set the Rattrays up? It seems that a vampire would know better than to go with strangers, and he should have been able to overpower them or at least put up a struggle. Also, did he offer Sookie the blood that the Rats drained from him so that she would have a connection to him, which he got anyway when he healed her later?

—JANEL SMITH

Bill did not set the Rattrays up. He should have known better than to go with them, but he was sure they were offering blood and sex. He misread the situation and was taken by surprise. He offered Sookie the blood because it would have been a big clue to her character if she'd taken it.

Did you originally intend the Sookie Stackhouse Southern Vampire Mysteries to be more in the mystery vein, like your previous novels, and instead did you find that they snowballed into a much more intricate supernatural creature than you originally planned?

—STACY WHITMORE

Yes. Before the Sookie novels, my experience had been exclusively in mystery. I did intend each book to contain a separate murder mystery, but as the series grew, that became impractical.

I am interested in the editing process Ms. Harris goes through with her Sookie books. Does she overwrite and then pare down, or sketch and fill in? Does she go back after writing and say, no, Sookie would not do that/ say it that way? Would her editor ever question why Sookie is doing or saying things, or is that the author's determination? —DOROTHY BAKER

Editing is a critical part of the writing process; in fact, it may be the most important part. I wish I overwrote and had to pare down. My problem is the opposite. I tend to write very close to the bone as far as my word count goes. Certainly, I backtrack, delete sections, and steer Sookie in different directions, but after being with her for so many books, it's second nature to me to step into Sookie's skin. My editor certainly does ask questions about the various characters' motivations, and if I can't answer them, I've taken a misstep that I have to correct.

Will Sookie have a happy-ever-after? And if not, why not? I have heard that you said she will not have an HEA, but that seems so harsh for the heroine we all love. —SHARON KNAUER

I think this rumor arises from comments I made while on a panel at Romantic Times. The point I was trying to make is this: Many romance novels have a black-and-white conclusion. Love conquers all, and the good people are all happy. The bad people get what's coming to them. And it's clear what category the characters fall into. There's nothing wrong with this scenario. It can be wonderfully satisfying reading. But the conclusion of Sookie's story may not be like this. Some characters will be happy, but some won't, and all my characters have both good and bad in their natures. There's no way to write an ending to this series that will satisfy all my readers. I can only be true to my own vision of the books.

Your fantasy world of the Sookie Stackhouse series includes many mythical beings: vampires, werewolves, shapeshifters, fairies. Was this because of any outright decision to make sure nothing would be related to actual life (i.e., no political commentary, etc.)? —BRET STEARNS

On the contrary, I think the books are full of commentary, though I see it as social rather than political. I'm writing about mythical creatures, but that doesn't mean they can't represent something else. I definitely have an agenda. But I am also happy for the books to be read as the adventure novels they are. I don't answer questions about my own politics. If the reader "gets" it, great. If not, I think the books are a lot of fun anyway.

Is there a possibility of the fae extending Sookie's life so she will age less quickly? I know you said that Sookie will not become a vampire; do you still feel that way now that *True Blood* and the Sookie novels have a cult-like following? —SOMMER STRACHAN

These questions both relate to things I've said often and publicly. Sookie's little dash of fae blood will not extend her life, nor will she become a vampire. No matter what happens on *True Blood*, and no matter how popular the books get, my vision for Sookie has not changed.

In previous books Sookie has had brushes with evil and has lost loved ones to supernatural as well as garden-variety evil. These losses toughen her little by little. In *Dead and Gone*, Sookie herself experiences radical evil as she is tortured nearly to death by her sadistic captors. Large pieces are torn from her in both the literal and the abstract. I think this was shocking to many readers. Why did you decide to take Sookie's narrative to such a dark place? Her horrible experience has definitely stiffened her resolve to protect those she loves by being more proactive (if a little ruthless) instead of defensive. —BRIDGET PAGE

I'm not always sure why I make the decisions I do, but in this case I knew that eventually Sookie's involvement with the supernatural world would lead to something irrevocable happening to her. And when something terrible has happened, she must change as a result. It would be amazing if she didn't. To me, that's one of the most interesting parts of writing: following the character through growth and change.

Through all the books, anything seems possible to the imagination. Did you ever think of a story line that made you think again and not include it because it was too far-fetched? —ESTHER SCHMIDT

Yes, I did. I had worked out a fantastic story line in which Niall was actually Sookie's father instead of her great-grandfather, but I'd already said too much that contradicted that for it to be a viable part of the mythology. I had a happy two hours thinking it through, though, before "reality" set in. I've also written some passages that my editor deemed too gross to include. No, don't ask!

If Sookie inherited her telepathy as a fairy power from her grandmother's foray into fairy blood, how is it that her cousin Hunter has it, too, unless Gran had another child of fairy descent? Who are Hadley's parents? There's virtually no reference to them in the books, yet Hunter must have fairy blood. —EILEEN PRESCOTT

Though Sookie didn't *exactly* inherit the telepathy from her grandmother's lover (there is more about this in *Dead Reckoning* and possibly in the books to come after), Hunter has a dash of fairy blood through his mom, Hadley, Sookie's first cousin. Hunter's parents are Remy Savoy and Hadley Delahoussaye. Hadley is the daughter of Adele Stackhouse's daughter, Linda (who died of uterine cancer), and Linda's husband, Carey Delahoussaye. Hunter is Adele's great-grandson. This has been asked so frequently I felt I had to address it.

You adapted the catastrophe of Hurricane Katrina into Sookie's story. Do you feel that this event drastically changed your vision of the story? How much of a challenge was it to adapt if necessary?

—JENNIFER MORGAN

The main effect of the inclusion of Hurricane Katrina has been the changes in the timeline of the books. Now they're taking place in the past instead of in an indeterminate present, since Sookie's life is anchored to a real-time event. You'll see timelines in the "Life in Bon Temps" section of this book. When Katrina occurred, I decided it would be disrespectful to the many people affected by it if I left such a disaster out of the narrative of the books. I stick by that decision.

As a pagan and practicing witch, I was very happy to see Wiccans portrayed in a positive light in your books, and not as Satan-worshipping crazy people, which has been my experience. What kind of research did you do to develop your Wiccan characters in the book, and did it change your view of non-Christians, being a Christian yourself?

—WENDY CARROLL

I did a lot of research into both witchcraft and Wicca so I could write about them with some authenticity. There are differences in the two, and I wanted to be accurate. Since I'm a Christian, I feel obliged to try hard to be fair, open-minded, and nonjudgmental; that's my interpretation of our creed. I'm convinced that there are people who are both good and evil in *every* classification, whether it be racial, political, or spiritual—and quite often these contradictory traits are combined in one person.

There seems to be so many vampire mythologies. Some can walk in the sun, some can't; some don't have a problem with garlic, some do; etc. How did you choose which mythologies to take inspiration from? Why are the vampires in your series the way they are? —LUCIA MATEO

The glib answer is, "Because that's the way I needed them to be." It's true that there are a lot of vampire mythologies, and in general I followed the classical *Dracula* pattern, with a dash of Anne Rice's and Laurell K. Hamilton's. However, I had to pick and choose among these other mythologies for what would work for my own storytelling purposes. I hope I've come up with my very own version. My vampires are the way they are because that's what moves Sookie's story forward.

When you started writing this series—which started off as one book— did you have in mind a story arc for Sookie to go on?

—BARBARA CRAMER

When I wrote the first Sookie book, I had no idea I'd ever get to write another one. I did have ideas about things I'd like to do with the characters, and most of those ideas I've been able to incorporate into her story. I have a few surprises left, I hope. From early in the series, I have known how I'll end it.

Eric's character seems to resonate so very well with the female population, myself included. Where did his character come from? Is he your dream man or a product of the plot? Is Alexander Skarsgard what you imagined Eric to be like?

—MARIANNE MCCLEARY

Eric has surprised me over and over. When I began establishing him, I thought it would be fun to include a Viking as a counterpoint to Bill, my Civil War veteran. In many ways, Eric is Bill's opposite, absolutely on purpose. Around that time, I happened to see a movie called *The Thirteenth Warrior*, based on a Michael Crichton book. I thought the actor Vladimir Kulich (a Czechoslovakian who plays Viking leader Buliwyf) was a great presence—commanding, regal, determined (and handsome). Although Eric is not completely based on Kulich's portrayal of Buliwyf, the film character was certainly a factor in fine-tuning Eric. The process of character building is a mysterious one, not least to the writer. So, no; Alexander is not *exactly* what I imagined Eric to be like, but then, no one is.

Would you ever consider bringing someone from the Sookieverse into a different author's books? Maybe Dresden Files ... Amelia could be in the Witch Network for New Orleans. ...

—KRISTINA MINCEY

Jim Butcher would have a few things to say about that, and so would his lawyer. As much fun as such a crossover sounds, not only would I have to agree with the other writer on how such a "visit" would be accomplished, but we'd have to figure out how to blend two different worlds in a seamless way and reconcile two separate publishers (in some cases, though Jim and I have the same publishing house), two separate agents, and two separate contracts. There's a lot more to consider than the fun of it—which would be considerable.

Would you ever do a spin-off series based on any of the characters in your books? —JOHN BONFIGLIO

I don't have any plans for that right now, but I certainly don't rule it out. I will not write the same story from another point of view, which is a related question I get frequently.

As a writer, is it hard to "not bring the work home"? Do you plot literary murders over breakfast? Take a pause to write down an idea while watching a movie? Miss sleep while wondering how to tie up a loose end? —SILJE ARSETH

I do plot murders over breakfast, and while I'm in the car, and while I'm on planes. I have ideas all the time—when I'm showering, when I'm doing the dishes, when I'm having phone conversations . . . and I apologize to the person on the other end of the conversation, here and now. I don't miss a lot of sleep, but sometimes I think over what I've written during the day as I'm drifting off to sleep or just waking up, and I've gotten some resolutions to problems at those times. The trick is remembering them long enough to get them into the book.

I've just finished reading *Dead in the Family*, and I was somewhat confused that Sookie can feel Eric, Alexei, and Appius Livius Ocella in the bond—but not Pam. If they are all from the same blood, surely Pam should be present in the bond between Eric and Sookie. —PATRICIA DE VRIES

The bond works "up." Sookie can feel the one she's bonded with (Eric) and his maker, and therefore the maker's other child (Alexei) . . . but she can't feel "down," which would be Eric's children or Alexei's child, if he'd ever sired one.

In Sookie's world, can vampires be brought back to human life once they are made vampire? —SALLY JOHNS

No. They've already died, so life is not an option for them.

If a vampire has been publicly found guilty of killing a human, will he or she be tried in human court? —BRIAN COTTRELL

Yes, unless the vampires catch him or her first. They don't want bad publicity, and such a trial would definitely be detrimental to the image they're trying to project—if the guilty vampire simply killed from overfeeding or for the pleasure of it. However, if the vampire was being attacked by a group of Drainers, the vampire hierarchy would be glad to see the trial, since it would send a message to those who were thinking of doing the same thing.

It is well-known that when vamps cry, it is blood. So my question is, Do vamps go to the bathroom? We also know that vamps are very sexually active, so if they cry blood, what is in place of their "other" bodily fluids? Is this why Sookie couldn't get pregnant? —JENNIFER VAN HORN

I got lots of questions about vampire bodily fluids, so I guess I have to respond. Vampires do cry blood. Their sexual emissions are tinged with blood, too. Males and females are sterile because birth (and engendering birth) are processes of living, as is using the bathroom. Vampires only ingest blood (though they may occasionally sip a nonblood drink), and they use every bit of the blood as fuel.

During the ride to look for Bill, Alcide tells Sookie that bitten Weres, or the half-man, half-wolf Weres, "don't live long, poor things." Does this apply to the werepanthers as well? What does it mean for Jason?

—SANDY SMITH

In some packs, the halfies are killed as soon as they're discovered. Other packs allow them to live, but running with the pack engenders a lot of wear and tear on bodies that don't heal as quickly as pureblood bodies. (By the way, this is where the legend of the Yeti and of Bigfoot came from: sightings of halfies.) Though Jason has a good chance of remaining a very healthy and vigorous man when his friends are starting to slow down, his life span will not be as long as if he had not been bitten.

A Guide to the World of Sookie Stackhouse

BY VICTORIA KOSKI

Codes for Sookie Stackhouse novels:

DUD: *Dead Until Dark*

LDID: *Living Dead in Dallas*

CD: *Club Dead*

DTTW: *Dead to the World*

DAAD: *Dead as a Doornail*

DD: *Definitely Dead*

ATD: *All Together Dead*

FDTW: *From Dead to Worse*

DAG: *Dead and Gone*

DITF: *Dead in the Family*

DR: *Dead Reckoning*

Codes for Sookie Stackhouse stories:

FD: "Fairy Dust"

DN: "Dracula Night"

OWA: "One Word Answer"

L: "Lucky"

GW: "Gift Wrap"

TB: "Two Blondes"

STW: "Small-Town Wedding"

IIHAH: "If I Had a Hammer"

If a character was deceased before the series started, the word "deceased" immediately follows the entry. The novels and stories in which a character appears are listed in the preceding codes. If a character is only mentioned in a work and does not appear, the word "mentioned" precedes the code. If a character dies in a work, the word "dies" precedes the code.

Unless otherwise indicated, characters are human . . . as far as Sookie knows. But she doesn't always read everyone she meets, so you just never know.

A:

Akiro (vampire): No other name given. Akiro takes Bruno's place as Victor's second-in-command just in time for the assassination party at Fangtasia. He reacts quickly when Eric attempts to stake Victor, bringing his sword down on Eric's arm and hewing through Mindy Simpson's shoulder on the way, killing her almost instantly. He is attacked by Thalia, who manages to do some damage before he cuts off her arm, and is finally killed by Eric after refusing to surrender. (Dies DR)

Alain (vampire): No last name given. A former priest turned into a vampire, Alain discovers Sophie-Anne and Clovis in the woods and, after feeding on Clovis, promises to bring Sophie-Anne over but decides instead to use her in the same way that Clovis had, selling her "services" when he needs money. When Alain is captured in a village that he had visited before and now recognizes him for what he is, Sophie-Anne seeks to rescue him but first has him fulfill his promise and turn her. The village priest returns before she can rise to free Alain, and he meets the dawn at the hands of the villagers. (Deceased; mentioned DD)

Albanese, Marcia: As a member of the Bon Temps school board, Marcia is familiar with the teaching staff and offers to host Halleigh's bridal shower at her home. She is one of the few residents to see Bob after he is returned to his human form, witnessing his awkward behavior when Sookie takes him to Wal-Mart. (ATD, FDTW; mentioned DR)

All-vampire cast of *Hello Dolly!*, the: Enough said. (Mentioned ATD)

al Saud, Basim (wolf): Basim moves to Shreveport from the Houston pack after accidentally killing a human friend of the pack who attacked him with a hoe. Trying to earn the money to pay the blood debt he owes for the killing, he is pulled into fairy Colman's plan to implicate Sookie in a crime so that she will be sent to jail. Basim decides he will not murder again and will instead find a body to fulfill the bargain, but he is murdered by Ham and Patricia. In a twist of irony, it is his body that is buried on Sookie's land. Fortunately, it is found and moved before local law enforcement arrives for a search based on an "anonymous tip." (Dies DITF)

Ancient Pythoness (vampire): The original Oracle consulted by Alexander the Great, the Ancient Pythoness was so revered that she was brought over even in her old age and is now cared for by her handmaidens. She sits in judgment at the trial of Sophie-Anne at the summit in Rhodes, ruling in Sophie-Anne's favor after hearing Sookie's testimony. (ATD)

Antonio (vampire): No last name given. Leather-clad Antonio and Luis are mentally nicknamed the bondage Bobbsey Twins by Sookie as they take her, Eric, and Pam to Victor's table at Vampire's Kiss. After the meeting, he and Luis usher the trio out to the parking lot and make a claim of dissatisfaction with Victor to tempt Eric into betraying their regent, but an astute Eric denies them, believing it is a trap.

Luis and Antonio attend Bubba's performance, entering Fangtasia first to secure the bar for Victor's arrival. Both are entranced as they watch the concert from their positions guarding the front door. When the attack begins, Antonio struggles with Palomino and is staked in the back by Maxwell Lee. (Dies DR)

Anubis Airlines: Established to fly vampires safely both day and night, Anubis Airlines planes are designed and outfitted for sleeping vampires, who are transported in their coffins in large bays that line the walls. Some planes have a few rows of seats for the occasional human passengers and provide flight attendants to check on their comfort.

After several "incidents" on board commercial flights, most vampires are willing to pay extra for the additional security Anubis offers, which often includes safe transportation of the coffin to its final destination once on the ground. However, although security is tight, it is not infallible, as Sookie discovers when she is accosted while waiting for Bill's coffin to be unloaded in Dallas, and again when his coffin is stolen in Mississippi. (LDID, ATD; mentioned CD)

Arlene Fowler's aunt: No name given. Arlene's elderly aunt lives in nearby Clarice. (Mentioned DAG)

Arnett, Pinkie: Pinkie bought the Crawdad Diner and the original recipes from Ralph Tooten with the provision that the name remain the same. (DITF)

Arrowsmith, Bart: Brother Arrowsmith is the pastor at the Gethsemane Baptist Church in Wright, Texas, and presides over Craig and Deidra's wedding. He is a good man but is still questioning the revelation of the shifters and their place in his theology. Whatever his own personal feelings, he is horrified when his son joins the protesters and tries to throw a stink bomb into Bernie's house. During the ceremony, he leads the wedding party in prayer, knowing the crowd outside can hear him over the speaker and hoping the words will sink in. (STW)

Arrowsmith, Mrs.: No first name given. Mrs. Arrowsmith forces her humiliated and ashamed son to attend the Lisle-Merlotte wedding in a show of solidarity with her husband. (STW)

Arrowsmith, Nathan: The only child of Pastor and Mrs. Arrowsmith, Nathan attempts to throw a stink bomb into Bernie Merlotte's house through the back door while other protesters distract the family at the front of the house. The police are called after his arm is broken by a baseball bat–wielding Sookie, and Nathan admits his guilt. (STW)

Art: No last name given. A waiter at the Pyramid in Rhodes, Art dies in the ruins of the hotel even as the rescuers are digging him out. (Dies ATD)

Arturo: No last name given. A room-service waiter at the Silent Shore Hotel, Arturo is well trained to deal with the vampire clientele. (LDID)

Auberjunois, Bill: Arlene wonders if Sookie is dating Bill Auberjunois when Sookie says she has been with Bill, but then Sam announces it is Bill Compton, pulling down Sookie's collar to show the bite marks. (Mentioned DUD)

Aubert, Christy: Christy works part-time for her husband, Greg. (L)

Aubert, Greg (witch): Greg, the local Pelican State Insurance agent, has a thriving client list with very few claims. People say he's a lucky man and that it rubs off on his clients. Actually, Greg is a witch, a talent he inherited from his mother, who educated him in spellcasting. He uses these spells to keep his clients and their properties safer. Unfortunately, by doing so he uses up the luck of the other agents in town, who all suffer more than their fair share of losses—literally. When he realizes his mistake, Greg takes on his share of bad luck, freeing up some of the good fortune for the other agents and their clients. (DAAD, L, DITF)

Aubert, Greg Jr.: Greg Jr. considers his father's job boring and definitely doesn't want to follow in his footsteps. (L)

Aubert, Lindsay: Greg's teenage daughter, Lindsay, never realizes that her "Forbidden Boyfriend" is actually a vampire using her for a light snack. (L)

Aude: No last name given. First the wife of Eric's older brother, Aude married Eric when her husband fell in battle, and they had six children together before she died. (Deceased; mentioned DAG)

Audrey: No last name given. EMT Audrey responds with her partner to the shoot-out at Arlene's trailer. (DAG)

Audrey (vampire): No last name given. The child of Booth Crimmons, Gervaise's lieutenant, Audrey is left in charge of the recovering Sophie-Anne the night of the takeover. It is presumed she perished. (Mentioned FDTW)

Ayres, Hugo: Lawyer Hugo Ayres represents Texas vampire Stan Davis in a court case. Hugo becomes enamored with Isabel Beaumont, one of Stan's nest mates. He is addicted to Isabel and vampire sex but hates himself for it and spies on the Dallas vampires for the Fellowship of the Sun. He delivers Sookie into their clutches as she searches for Farrell. Hugo soon realizes that he is also considered expendable when the Fellowship stashes him in a cell with a hungry Farrell. He is rescued, but his punishment is to remain naked in a room with a naked Isabel for several months, each chained to a wall. Hugo is fed and taken care of but unable to reach the object of his addiction; Isabel is not fed and unable to reach the answer to her thirst. Hugo is unchained first and given a day's head start. (LDID)

B:

Babbitt, Cleo (vampire): The sheriff of Area Three, Cleo survives the bombing at Rhodes only to be killed along with her vampires during the takeover by Nevada when they refuse an offer of surrender. (ATD; mentioned, dies FDTW)

Babcock, Connie: The receptionist at Herveaux and Son, Connie is sleeping with Jackson Herveaux. She resents Jackson's escorting Christine Larrabee to Colonel Flood's funeral. She's unaware that her boss/lover is a werewolf and thus doesn't know that Jackson needs Christine's political support. She retaliates by accepting a bribe to steal personal papers from Jackson, most likely for Patrick Furnan. (DTTW; mentioned DAAD)

Baldwin, Liz: Liz worries about her family, especially her oldest grand-daughter, while trying to relax at Merlotte's. (DAAD)

Ball, Lorena (vampire): Lorena Ball is working as a prostitute in New Orleans when she meets Solomon Brunswick in 1788. Fascinated when Solomon drains a customer whose throat she slit for not paying, she has Solomon turn her and travels with him for a time. She eventually betrays her sire, pretending to be human when she is caught with a dead child she is draining and blaming the death on Solomon, and they go their separate ways.

Lorena sees Bill after he returns home from the Civil War and falls in love as she spies on him and his family. She takes him by surprise one night and fakes his death so that she can have him as a companion and lover. She compels him to stay with her, even going so far as to create a companion for him by turning a woman who resembles his lost wife. Though she finally allows her children to leave her, she calls Bill back again after eighty-odd years when she learns of his profitable vampire database. When she cannot seduce its location from him, she resorts to torture to get not only the database but also the name of the woman Bill is involved with. Lorena attacks Sookie while she is rescuing Bill and meets her final death at Sookie's hands. (Dies CD; mentioned DTTW, DAAD, ATD, DITF, DR)

Ballinger, Bonnie: The daughter of Doke and Mindy, three-year-old Bonnie doesn't understand the protesters' screaming and violence on the day of her uncle's wedding. (STW; mentioned FDTW, DAG, DITF)

Ballinger, Doke: Doke and Mindy Merlotte attended high school together in Wright and married young. They soon moved to nearby Mooney, where Doke has a job with a wind turbine manufacturing plant. Doke's children are his main worry on the day of Craig and Deidra's wedding, but he decides the whole family should stick together and attend the ceremony. (STW; mentioned FDTW)

Ballinger, Mason: Doke and Mindy's five-year-old son, Mason, can't comprehend the animosity directed toward his beloved grandmother Merlotte. (STW; mentioned FDTW, DAG, DITF)

Ballinger, Mindy Merlotte: Sam's sister, Mindy, and her family live in

Mooney, about thirty miles from Wright. She adjusts surprisingly well to the revelation that her mother and brother are shifters. Friendly, plump, and chatty, Mindy is a stay-at-home mom of two young children. The safety of her children concerns her most during the protests at Craig and Deidra's wedding. (STW; mentioned FDTW, DAG, DITF)

Bannister, Annabelle (wolf): As a member of the Air Force, Annabelle is reassigned from South Dakota to the Barksdale Air Force Base near Shreveport. As a werewolf, Annabelle transfers from the Elk Killer pack to the Long Tooth pack. She starts dating Alcide Herveaux. When Basim al Saud's body is found on Sookie's property, she confesses that she was also secretly seeing Basim. She had nothing to do with Basim's death and so ultimately is not convicted of betraying the pack, though she is punished for her unfaithfulness. (DITF)

Barker, Marge: Marge works full-time as Greg Aubert's clerk and is known as much for her unpleasant demeanor as for her efficiency. (L)

Barlowe, Mr.: No first name given. Fellowship of the Sun member Mr. Barlowe demonstrates against shifters in front of Merlotte's. Though he insists that they are all willing to be arrested for their beliefs, his fellow protesters are not so certain, and they all eventually back down and disperse. (DITF)

Barrett, Liz: Liz becomes Jason's regular date and even hopes he will ask her to marry him, especially when she has a pregnancy scare. She's not pregnant, and the relationship just doesn't last. (DUD, LDID; mentioned CD)

Baruch, Christian (vampire): As a human, Christian Baruch designed and managed hotels in western Europe. As a vampire, he does much the same thing, delivering success to a vampire hotelier in exchange for being turned and brought to America. He has his sights set higher, however, and plants the Dr Pepper bomb in the hallway outside Sophie-Anne's room in a misguided attempt for her attention and affections. Christian survives the bombing of his hotel. (ATD)

Batanya (Britlingen): No other name given. A member of the Britlingen Collective. Batanya is five foot eight and very intimidating, with inky black curls and a lithe, muscular body. With her partner, Clovache, Batanya is hired by Isaiah, the King of Kentucky, to guard him during the vampire summit in Rhodes. Batanya kills Kyle Perkins, a vampire assassin who gets too close to Isaiah, decapitating him with a throwing star. Batanya and Clovache are able to carry Isaiah out of the Pyramid of Gizeh before it collapses. (ATD)

Bat's Wing, the: A Dallas vampire club owned by the area vampires, the Bat's Wing is operated as much as a tourist draw, complete with gift shop, as for the vampires themselves. The bar employs both humans and vampires, though a vampire club is not considered the safest place for a human to work. The vampire Farrell is kidnapped by the Fellowship of the Sun at the Bat's Wing. (Mentioned LDID)

Bear shifter: No name given. A young male shifter photographed in midchange, presumably for the first time; his photo appears in Alfred Cumberland's eyes-only supernatural photo album. (Mentioned DD)

Beaumont, Isabel (vampire): One of Stan's Dallas vamps, Isabel has a human lover, a lawyer who successfully defended Stan in court. When it is revealed that her lover, Hugo, has betrayed the Dallas vamps to the Fellowship of the Sun, Isabel is punished by being chained in a room with Hugo for a few months without being allowed to feed. At the end of their sentence, Hugo is given a head start of twenty-four hours before Isabel is unchained to go after him. (LDID)

Beck, Alcee: The only African American detective on the Renard Parish force, Alcee often takes the opportunity to line his own pockets at the expense of his fellow African Americans. However, he's a good detective and fiercely loyal to his wife and family. (LDID, DTTW, DAAD, DD, FDTW, DAG, DITF)

Beck, Dove: Alcee's married cousin Dove has an affair with Crystal and is caught in the act by Sookie and Calvin. (FDTW; mentioned DAG)

Beech, Mrs.: No first name given. Mrs. Beech is Copley Carmichael's housekeeper. (Mentioned FDTW)

Beecham, Chuck: Chuck attends the New Year's Eve party at Merlotte's and can't resist taunting Sookie about Bill being out of the country. (DTTW)

Beeson, Ms.: No first name given. The accounts clerk at the Grainger hospital, Ms. Beeson tells a mystified Sookie that the hospital bill from her shooting has been paid in full by an anonymous donor. (DAAD)

Belinda: No last name given. Belinda works as a waitress at Fangtasia and is tortured by Hallow when she seeks the missing Eric. (DUD, DTTW)

Bellefleur, Andy: Bon Temps police detective Andy Bellefleur is competent and thorough, although slightly hardened by his exposure to crime and criminals. He investigates the murders of several young women associated with both vampires and Jason Stackhouse. Andy arrests Jason. Sookie is attacked by the real murderer, and though he is arrested and Jason released, Andy remains suspicious of the siblings on general principle. Saddened by a child abuse case, Andy becomes drunk in Merlotte's and is taken home by Portia. When the body of Lafayette Reynold is found in his car in the Merlotte's parking lot the next morning, Andy himself becomes a suspect. He eventually follows his leads to Jan Fowler's cabin in the woods, where he encounters not only the orgy participants and Bill, Eric, and Sookie, but Callisto as well. Though the true murderers die, enough evidence is left to exonerate Andy.

Andy and Alcee Beck put in hours on the case when Jason goes missing. After Sookie brings Jason home, Andy doesn't quite buy their story. He also responds to the arson at Sookie's house and encounters Sookie yet again when she is confronted by Sweetie Des Arts. Andy shoots Sweetie when she is distracted by Dawson. Andy believes in Sookie's ability and is even willing to use her when a child goes missing at the local elementary school. He briefly dreams of using her talent to solve every case but is brought back to reality by police officer Kevin Pryor, who reminds him that knowledge of the crime and criminal is not enough and that good old police work will always be necessary. Enlisting Sookie's help when he proposes to Halleigh Robinson in Merlotte's, an anxious Andy asks Sookie if Halleigh really loves him.

The detective works with Agents Lattesta and Weiss when Crystal is found on the cross at Merlotte's. Sookie calls him when she realizes that Arlene's buddies have planned the same crucifixion for her, and he comes to Arlene's trailer along with the two agents and is involved in the shootout, wounding Whit Spradlin.

Andy reacts badly at first to the news that Bill is his great-great-great-grandfather, but Bill puts him in his place by reminding him of his manners, and Andy begins to accept the connection, ultimately deciding with Halleigh to name their daughter Caroline Compton Bellefleur when they find out they are having a girl. Andy is off duty in Merlotte's playing darts with Danny Prideaux when the four toughs hired by Sandra Pelt come in, and he helps subdue the assailants. (DUD, LDID, DTTW, DAAD, DD, ATD, FDTW, DAG, DITF, DR; mentioned CD, IIHAH)

Bellefleur, Caroline Holliday: After the death of her son and his wife, Caroline Holliday Bellefleur raises her two grandchildren, Andrew and Portia. Beset by shrinking finances, the Bellefleur family home, Belle Rive, has fallen into disrepair, and Caroline is extremely pleased by a legacy from an unknown relative that allows her to restore Belle Rive to its former glory. When she finally discovers, on her deathbed, that Bill Compton is her great-grandfather and arranged the bequest, she reacts with humor, grace, and gratitude.

Her last bequest is to leave the recipe of her famous chocolate cake to the town so the legacy of Caroline Holliday Bellefleur, once one of Renard Parish's finest cooks, lives on in the kitchens and dining rooms of Bon Temps. (FDTW; dies DITF; mentioned LDID, CD, DTTW, DD, ATD, DR)

Bellefleur, Halleigh Robinson: When Andy asks Halleigh, a teacher at Betty Ford Elementary, to marry him, her one condition is that they not live at Belle Rive but instead find their own home. They do buy a small house, the old Wechsler place, but a pregnant Halleigh still helps care for her grandmother-in-law at Belle Rive in Caroline's final days. Halleigh and Andy find that they are expecting a daughter and decide to name her Caroline Compton Bellefleur. (DAAD, DD, ATD, FDTW, DAG, DITF; mentioned DR, IIHAH)

Bellefleur, Terry: Terry Bellefleur, cousin of Andy and Portia, is a Vietnam veteran who paid dearly for doing his duty for his country. Held as a POW for two years, he is scarred both mentally and physically. Terry functions best in simple situations but doesn't mind hard work, doing odd jobs around town such as tearing down Sookie's kitchen when it burns, as well as standing in for Sam as bartender at Merlotte's and cleaning the bar after hours to supplement his government pension.

Terry loves training and breeding his Catahoula hunting dogs, and when Sam turns into a collie during the Great Reveal, he takes it all in stride, certain that it is one of the reasons he has always gotten along so well with his bartending boss.

Terry is playing darts in Merlotte's when Sandra Pelt enters to kill Sookie. Sam passes Terry the baseball bat from behind the bar. Terry knocks Sandra out but reacts horribly to the sight of blood. As Sookie comforts him, he tells her that "the shining one" and "that big blond one" told him to watch over her in exchange for ridding him of his nightmares and protecting his beloved dog. (DUD, LDID, DTTW, DAAD, L, FDTW, DAG, DITF, DR; mentioned CD, ATD, IIHAH)

Bellenos (elf): No other name given. The night watchman at Hooligans has the sharp pointy teeth of his species, cannot pass as human, and doesn't even try. When Dermot is attacked and injured by Kelvin and Hod, Sookie calls Claude, but Bellenos answers and comes in his place. He treats Dermot by breathing into him, sharing his breath to heal him. Once Dermot has recovered enough, Bellenos joins him in the hunt for the two men who attacked him, and the two soon return to Sookie's house with Kelvin's and Hod's heads. They then take the heads to Monroe to show the other fae, having already destroyed the bodies. (DR)

Bernard (vampire): No last name given. Also known as Curly, he is one of Russell's many male guests. "Cute as a bunny" Bernard asks Sookie to dance at Josephine's, but his real attention is reserved for Eric, with whom he spends part of the night locating a car for Sookie to use to rescue Bill (unbeknownst to Bernard, of course). When Eric returns to give Sookie the keys to the car, he is sporting a hickey on his neck, courtesy of Bernard. (CD)

Bettina (unspecified shifter): No last name given. Head of the shifter paramedics working at the Pyramid of Gizeh during the Rhodes summit, Bettina looks like a honey bear (Sookie thinks she could indeed be one). She feels it's a privilege to take care of Quinn after he takes the arrow thrown at Sookie by Kyle Perkins. (ATD)

Beverly: No last name given. Clarice Hospital nurse Beverly is in Merlotte's the night that Claude and Claudine come by to see Sookie, and she makes plans to go watch Claude strip at Hooligans. (FDTW)

Biker Babes (unspecified shifters): A Texas motorcycle group with customized jackets. Three of its members, including Brenda Sue, arrive to provide protection at the Lisle-Merlotte rehearsal and wedding. One of the Babes works with Luna to remove the memory chip from Sarah Newlin's camera. (STW)

Bill Compton's house: The Compton family home in Bon Temps reverts to Bill when his descendant, Jessie Compton, dies. Set back from the road on a knoll with a view of the cemetery and surrounded by azalea bushes, the two-story house has undergone renovations since Bill moved in, including new wiring; new wallpaper; refinished hardwood floors; a remodeled, albeit downsized, kitchen; and a luxurious first-floor bathroom with both a stand-alone shower and a hot tub surrounded by a cedar deck. Lacking a basement because of the high water table, the house does boast a light-tight crawl space that can be used as a daytime resting place. The bedrooms, which are rarely used, are all on the second floor. Although modernized, the house retains many old furnishings, including items from Bill's human life, such as his aunt Edwina's Spanish shawl. (DUD, CD, DTTW, DAAD, DITF, DR; mentioned LDID, DD, FDTW, DAG)

Bill Compton's strip mall: Shortly after his arrival in Bon Temps, Bill purchases a strip mall near the highway. It houses a number of businesses, including a restaurant, Lalaurie's, cited as the only fancy restaurant in the town besides the country club dining room; a hair salon called Clip and Curl; and Tara's Togs, a clothing shop owned by Sookie's best friend, Tara Thornton. It becomes a source of tension between Sookie and Bill when he tells her he's set up an unlimited line of credit at the shops for her, which makes her feel like she's being kept. (LDID)

Bison shifter: No name given. A patron at Josephine's on the night Sookie is staked, the bison lumbers past Russell's limo as they are stopped at an intersection. (CD)

Black Moon Productions: Affiliated with Blue Moon Entertainment, Black Moon Productions is the side of the company that handles more adult entertainment, involving both humans and vampires and a willingness to have sex in public. (Mentioned ATD)

Blanchard, Ben: Ben, Sookie's maternal grandfather, dies of a stroke while Sookie is in her teens. (Deceased; mentioned CD)

Blanchard, Olivia: Sookie's maternal grandmother, Olivia, dies of an overdose of sleeping pills about a year after her husband's death. It's suspected her overdose was not an accident. (Deceased; mentioned CD)

Blood in the Quarter, the: After the vampires revealed their existence to the world, this was the first hotel in the world that catered exclusively to vampires. Located in the middle of the French Quarter, it features light-tight rooms and anything else that a traveling vampire might need. Bill stays there while in New Orleans on business. (DUD)

Blue Moon Entertainment: Affiliated with Black Moon Productions,

Blue Moon Entertainment is a dance company that specializes in human/vampire dance teams. Sean O'Rourke and Layla Larue Lemay, professional dancers employed by Blue Moon, perform at the Pyramid of Gizeh during the vampire conference in Rhodes. (Mentioned ATD)

Blythe, Polly: Ceremonies officer of the Fellowship of the Sun in Dallas, Polly helps arrange the planned self-immolation of Godfrey and the forced immolation of Farrell in a dawn ritual. When Luna and Sookie escape in Luna's Outback, Polly and Sarah Newlin pursue them, ramming them with their car and forcing them into an accident. With the help of concerned witnesses, Luna and Sookie are sent to the hospital while Polly and Sarah are questioned by the police. (LDID)

Bodehouse, Jane: One of Merlotte's resident alcoholics, Jane tries repeatedly to stay sober and fails. Despite the effects of alcohol on her brain, she is an expert on old-movie trivia and joins in with the other bar patrons and the employees in guessing the answers to *Jeopardy!* every day. (CD, DAAD, DD, FDTW, DAG, DITF, DR)

Bodehouse, Marvin: Jane's son is sadly accustomed to the calls to pick up his mother. Having seen the effects of alcoholism, Marvin doesn't drink. (CD, DD)

Boling: No first name given. Shreveport patrolman Boling arrives at the scene of the bitten Were attack on Sookie and Quinn outside the Strand Theatre and insists they go down to the police station to make statements and fill out a report. (DD)

Boling, Donny: A member of the Fellowship of the Sun along with his buddy Whit Spradlin, Donny is disgusted and angered the night of the Great Reveal. As a warning to those who fraternize with shifters, he and Whit make plans to crucify Sookie, imitating Crystal's death although they did not commit that murder. Donny is killed in the shoot-out at Arlene's trailer. (Dies DAG)

Bolivar, Anthony (vampire): Anthony worked in a diner during the Depression and still remembers his way around a kitchen, occasionally subbing as a short-order cook at Merlotte's. (DAAD; mentioned LDID)

Bond, Hamilton (wolf): Alcide's childhood friend and neighbor, Hamilton wants to become Alcide's second. He becomes jealous when Alcide chooses Basim instead. Overhearing Colman offering Basim money to plant a body on Sookie's property to frame her, Hamilton decides to take advantage of the situation and kills Basim, burying his body on Sookie's land. He admits his guilt when Sookie confronts him and accepts the judgment of the pack. Assumed deceased. (DITF)

Book, Katherine (vampire): Appointed by the state of Kansas to supervise the welfare of a preadolescent vampire, lawyer Kate Book fights for the parental rights of his human mother and father, who allowed him to be turned because he suffered from a fatal blood disorder. Although the judges at the summit rule that the legal contract between the sire and the parents be honored, leaving the boy with his maker, Book succeeds in securing enforcement of visitation rights for the parents. (ATD)

Boom (vampire): No other name given. Boom works for the Rhodes bomb squad and cheerfully carries the Dr Pepper bomb down the stairs of the Pyramid. (ATD)

Boyle, Mrs.: No first name given. Red Ditch kindergarten teacher Mrs. Boyle is slightly burned out, brisk, and a touch impatient, but not dangerous or malicious. (DR)

Brazell, Bruno (vampire): Victor's second-in-command is by his side during the takeover, standing in Sookie's front yard while Victor negotiates the surrender of Eric and Bill. After the takeover, he continues doing Victor's biding, lying in wait for Sookie and Pam by the side of the interstate to intercept them as Pam takes Sookie home from Shreveport. Pam dispatches Bruno's partner-in-crime Corinna while Sookie grapples with Bruno, driving a silver dagger up into his heart. (FDTW; dies DITF; mentioned DR)

Brenda Sue (unspecified shifter): No last name given. Brenda Sue, a trauma nurse and member of the Biker Babes, arrives with two of her fellow shifter Babes to watch over at the Lisle-Merlotte rehearsal and wedding. (STW)

Brewer, Dan: Dan Brewer is the head of the Michigan state terrorist task force, investigating the bombing of the hotel in Rhodes. (ATD)

Brigant, Binne (fairy): Binne is the wife of Dillon and the mother of Claudine, Claude, and Claudette. (Mentioned DAG)

Brigant, Branna (fairy): Branna is Niall's first wife and the mother of Dillon. (Mentioned DAG)

Brigant, Breandan (fairy): Breandan is Niall's nephew, the son of his departed older brother, Rogan. Since his father's death, Breandan has been on a mission to eradicate those of mixed fae blood, believing that they dilute the magic of the fae, weakening the race. He is pleased to be able to target Niall's own descendents. Breandan sends Lochlan and Neave to scout out Bon Temps, where they discover an injured Crystal at Jason's, take her to Merlotte's, and crucify her. He has them kidnap Sookie to use as a bargaining chip with Niall, counting on Niall's love for his great-granddaughter to force him to accede to Breandan's determination to close off Faery from the human world. Breandan joins the attack on the hospital where Sookie, Bill, and Tray are recuperating after Sookie's rescue. He evades Eric and beheads Clancy as he goes for Bill. Gathering his strength, Tray grabs at Breandan and is killed by the fairy, who in turn meets his own death from Bill by means of Sookie's iron gardening trowel. One of Claudine's knitting needles protrudes from Breandan's shoulder, a sign that he claimed Claudine and her unborn child as victims on his way into the hospital. (Dies DAG; mentioned DITF, DR)

Brigant, Dermot (fairy): Niall Brigant's younger twin son by the human Einin, Dermot defies his father and allies himself with his cousin Breandan, believing Breandan's philosophy that humans and fairies shouldn't mingle. He is also implicated in the death of Sookie's parents. Dermot and his great-nephew, Jason, look very much alike. Dermot is left on the human side when Niall closes Faery. When he finally approaches Sookie, she realizes he is bespelled. He is unable to tell her who put the spell on him as he slips in and out of the confusion caused by the magic. He does tell her he watches over her when he can and that there is another fae on this side who means her harm. He also denies helping to kill her parents and tells her he has come to terms with his half-blood status. Dermot is watching from Sookie's woods when Alexei attacks Claude and the other fae, Colman. After Alexei is killed, Colman attacks Sookie, only to accidentally kill Ocella instead. Dermot throws a dagger that lodges in Colman's back, allowing Eric to catch and drain him. Dermot struggles to speak to Claude and Sookie, and they discover that Niall is the one who bespelled his own son. Together they break the spell the old-fashioned way, with a kiss from each, and Dermot's mind clears. He remains with Sookie and Claude at Sookie's house, trying to adjust to life on this side. When Claude offends Sookie and is told to move out, Dermot admits that he feels he has no purpose in life and tells her he wishes only to stay with her and finish fixing up her attic, a project he has been tackling with great enthusiasm. He is injured by kidnappers searching for Sookie but recovers after Sookie finds him and sends for the elf Bellenos, who breathes into Dermot to heal him. The two fae then go on the hunt, returning with the heads of Dermot's assailants. (DAG, DITF, DR; mentioned FDTW)

Brigant, Dillon (fairy): Niall's full-fairy son, Dillon is the product of Niall's unhappy marriage to his first wife. Dillon is married to Binne and is the father of Claudine, Claude, and Claudette. He has eyes and hair the color of butterscotch. (DAG; mentioned DITF)

Brigant, Fintan (fairy): The elder of Niall Brigant's twin sons by the human Einin, half-fairy Fintan meets Adele Stackhouse while she is out in her yard one day and becomes smitten. Adele desperately wants children, but her husband is infertile. Fintan promises her he can and will give her children, and both Corbett and Linda are the results of Adele's liaisons with the fairy. Fintan visits Adele more than she knows, often appearing as her husband, Mitchell, in order to spend time with her. As a token of his love, he arranges for Mr. Cataliades to deliver a cluviel dor to her after his death.

Fintan stops seeing his human family soon after the birth of Linda and forbids Niall to visit, fearing they will come to harm. He is killed by Lochlan and Neave, setting in motion Niall's contact with Sookie. (Deceased; mentioned FDTW, DAG, DITF, DR)

Brigant, Niall (fairy): Niall is a fairy prince and great-grandfather to Sookie and Jason. His glamour is that of an elegant, handsome older man with green eyes and long, pale gold hair. Like other supernaturals, fairies have interests in a variety of human businesses, including a drug company whose products have uses for the fairies. Niall's son Fintan tries to keep his human descendants hidden from the fae by ceasing all contact with them, but Niall disregards his son's decree to stay away and visits Jason as a child, losing interest when he realizes Jason's complete humanity. When Niall discovers that Sookie has the essential spark, he begins to surreptitiously keep an eye on her, using both Terry Bellefleur and Eric as sources of information. Niall has dinner with her following Fintan's death.

Niall expresses distaste for Jason, associating him with another son, Dermot, to whom Jason bears a remarkable resemblance. Although he wants only to know and love his great-granddaughter, Niall brings tragedy and pain to Sookie's life when her existence becomes known to a faction of fairies led by Breandan, Niall's nephew, who oppose Niall and the idea of mingling in any way with humans. Niall joins Bill in rescuing Sookie when she is kidnapped and tortured as a means to bring about his surrender. Niall ultimately defeats Breandan. Niall is left as the only remaining fairy prince, but the experience causes him to question the wisdom of associating with humans, since they end up the worse for the encounter. He decides to close the portals to Faery, more to save humanity from the fae than to save the fae from humanity. Niall was also behind the events at Sookie's house one Christmas Eve, arranging for a visitor so Sookie wouldn't be alone. (FDTW, DAG, GW; mentioned DITF, DR)

Brigant, Rogan (fairy): Niall's oldest brother. Rogan's followers claim kinship to the sea, with an affinity to and influence over water. After he goes to the Summerland, his son Breandan tries to kill Sookie because of her fairy blood. (Deceased; mentioned DAG)

Briscoe, John Robert: Bon Temps insurance agent John Robert's streak of bad luck with claims has affected him mentally and physically. (L)

Britlingen Collective, the:

> *What is the law?*
> *The client's word.*
> MOTTO OF THE BRITLINGEN COLLECTIVE

Bodyguards from another dimension, Britlingens are reputed to be the best. They must be summoned by a witch, who negotiates a contract with their guild and returns them to their dimension when the contract is fulfilled—and Britlingens always fulfill their contracts.

Batanya and Clovache are hired by Isaiah, the King of Kentucky, to guard him during the vampire summit in Rhodes. The two Britlingens also have their own novella. (ATD)

Broadway, Amelia (witch): With her short brown hair and bright blue eyes, Amelia looks like a suburban mom but is actually a practicing witch who owns the apartment building in New Orleans where Hadley lived. When Hadley is killed, Amelia dutifully seals up the apartment with a stasis spell until Hadley's heir can come to claim her possessions; unfortunately, she inadvertently seals in an unrisen vampire. When he rises and attacks Amelia and Sookie, they manage to escape, although both are injured. Amelia offers to perform an ectoplasmic reconstruction of Hadley's last moments to find out how and why the new vampire, a Were, was turned. It's more successful than anyone had anticipated.

After the melee at the queen's reception, Sookie and Quinn arrive back at Amelia's to find that during a tryst with one of her fellow witches, Bob, she has turned him into a cat and cannot reverse the spell. Amelia and Bob move to Bon Temps with Sookie to get a little distance from her coven while she works on transforming Bob back. Amelia remains with Sookie through the summer and so misses the disaster of Hurricane Katrina. She fills her time with part-time jobs, including filling in at Merlotte's when needed, shopping, and trying to transform Bob. She doesn't seem to lack for income, a condition explained when she tells Quinn and Sookie that her father is Copley Carmichael, a well-known wheeler-dealer. Broadway is her mother's maiden name. She is tracked down by her mentor, coven leader Octavia Fant, who is now living close by in Monroe with a niece after her own home was destroyed by Katrina. After the two perform another ectoplasmic reconstruction to solve the murder of Maria-Star Cooper and then cast a spell on Tanya Grissom to rid her of the influence of Sandra Pelt, Octavia moves in with Sookie and Amelia and changes Bob back to human. Amelia briefly dates Pam and then begins a solid relationship with Were Tray Dawson, a lone-wolf mechanic who also works as a bodyguard. She stands proudly by as Tray shifts in Merlotte's with Sam during the Great Reveal and looks forward to a future with him. But when Tray is poisoned and attacked by fairies and then dies defending Sookie at Dr. Ludwig's hospital, Amelia is heartbroken and decides to return to New Orleans to pick up the pieces of her life there.

Back in New Orleans and working at the Genuine Magic Shop, which is owned by her coven, Amelia gets back together with Bob. They travel to Bon Temps to renew the wards on Sookie's house. Amelia reveals that she has found a way to break Sookie's blood bond with Eric. The two witches successfully perform the ceremony. Amelia shares this news with Alcide Herveaux and encourages him to pursue Sookie, a bad decision that results in Amelia being banished from Sookie's house. She apologizes and continues with Sookie's request for information about the cluviel dor when she gets home. (DD, ATD, FDTW, DAG, DITF, DR; mentioned L, GW, IIHAH)

Bruce: No last name given. Accountant Bruce is understandably nervous as Sookie reads his mind when he is one of the humans questioned about money embezzled from Fangtasia, even though he is innocent. His main concern is what will become of his wife, Lillian, and children, Bobby and Heather, if he is killed by Eric. (DUD)

Brunswick, Solomon (vampire): Solomon is traveling around New England in 1768, making a living as a tinker and trader, when he encounters a vampire in the woods one night. The vampire follows him and drinks from him a second time, accidentally turning him and leaving him to fend for himself. Solomon makes his way to New Orleans, and while leaving a brothel, he sees a prostitute cutting the throat of a customer who has tried to skip paying for her services. He reveals his nature by partaking of the victim's blood and finds a kindred spirit of sorts in prostitute Lorena Ball, turning the willing woman to become his companion.

Solomon is ultimately betrayed by Lorena, and the two part ways. He currently resides in Europe. (Mentioned DITF, DR)

Bubba (vampire): No real first or last name given. Also known as the Man from Memphis, Bubba has a famous face and an even more famous voice. When he was taken down to the morgue on that August evening in 1977, one of the morgue attendants was not only a vampire but also a huge fan. Detecting a faint spark of life, the attendant hastily brought him over. Unfortunately, the drugs that had plagued him in life made his transition less than perfect. He is a loyal soldier who will follow orders to the letter, but he is not capable of much independent thought. His fans in the vampire world try to keep him hidden and protected. He doesn't always remember to stay out of sight when left on his own, so the public does get an occasional glimpse of the real thing. Bubba gets upset when called by his birth name, answering only to his nickname. He prefers not to feed on human beings and survives on a diet of animal blood, mainly cats—an aberration in the vampire world—and synthetic blood.

Bill introduces Bubba to Sookie, and Bubba often looks after her, sometimes successfully, sometimes not. Bubba is fond of Bill.

He is drawn into the plot to assassinate Victor by being the bait used to lure the Elvis fan to Fangtasia. Although reluctant at first, he agrees when Bill is called to convince him that it is necessary. He does his job the following night, captivating his audience (for the most part) and distracting Victor before the attack. Upset by the carnage happening around him,

Bubba is taken to safety by Bill. (DUD, CD, DTTW, DAAD, OWA, DD, DAG, DR; mentioned ATD, FDTW, DITF)

Bureau of Vampire Affairs (BVA): The BVA is in charge of overseeing federal legislation regarding vampire issues, setting the guidelines for vampire behavior, and investigating any claims involving vampires. Following the announcement of the existence of shifters, Congress is considering expanding the BVA's authority to include the weres and changing the name to the Bureau of Vampire and Supernatural Affairs, which would conveniently cover the revelation of any other type of supernatural being. (Mentioned FDTW, DITF, STW)

Burgess, Randy: Randy Burgess of Burgess and Son gravels Sookie's driveway on Eric's orders. (Mentioned CD)

Burley, Amy: Barmaid Amy puts in an application at Merlotte's while subbing at the Good Times Bar but is murdered before Sam can speak to her about a job. (Mentioned, dies DUD)

Burnham, Bobby: Bobby works as Eric's daytime employee, accomplishing tasks the vampire cannot do while the sun is out, including delivering the package containing the knife to Sookie at Merlotte's. He openly dislikes Sookie, not understanding why Eric and Pam hold her in such regard. Bobby is fiercely loyal to Eric and stays at Eric's home to try to help him deal with Alexei the night he goes insane. Bobby and Felicia, whom he is dating, both die at Alexei's hands. (ATD, DAG; dies DITF; mentioned DR)

C:

Cait (fairy): No last name given. Cait is captured and her blood rubbed onto glasses offered by Victor to Eric and Pam at Vampire's Kiss in an attempt to intoxicate them. There is little hope for her survival because she was taken by vampires, and the fae are called together to find out if she has family and if they have had a death vision. (Mentioned, dies DR)

Callaway, Donald: Donald, along with partner Brenda Hesterman, buys, sells, and appraises antiques at their shop, Splendide, in Shreveport. He accompanies Brenda to Sookie's house to appraise the items from her attic and finds a secret compartment in Mitchell's old desk that contains a letter from Gran and the cluviel dor. (DR)

Callisto (maenad): No last name given. Callisto arrives in Bon Temps seeking those who provide and enjoy drink and pleasures of the flesh. She uses Sookie as a messenger to Eric to demand tribute, viciously scratching and poisoning her back. Although Eric sacrifices a bull to her, she is not satisfied and wanders the woods with Sam in collie form as her companion. When the orgy is held at Jan Fowler's lake house, Callisto is attracted to the lust and drunkenness and arrives to take her own tribute, sending her madness into the partygoers, destroying them. Sated, she bids a fond farewell to Sam and continues on her way. (LDID)

Cannon, Velda: As a member of the Descendants of the Glorious Dead, Velda is part of the group that heads to Vicksburg to see the battlefields. Despite a little incident with inadequate Depends, Velda, her comrades, and Sookie all have a wonderful time. (Mentioned CD)

Carmichael, Copley: Copley Carmichael, Amelia's father, has his dirty fingers in many financial and political pies. A builder by trade, he owns large lumberyards and is eager to establish a business relationship with the Nevada vampires after the takeover to continue his rebuilding efforts in New Orleans. To that end, he meets with Sandy Sechrest, Felipe de Castro's area rep for Louisiana. (FDTW; mentioned ATD, DAG, DITF)

Carpenter, Porter: Officer Carpenter, of Wright, Texas, is uneasy about the shifter revelation but promises police assistance for the wedding of Craig Merlotte and Deidra Lisle. He and another deputy are at the church for the service but are struggling to keep protesters out, so they cannot help the Merlottes as they are trying to get there.

Porter responds to the 911 call made by Luna at Jim Collins's house and arrests Sarah Newlin before taking her for medical treatment. (STW)

Carson: No other name given. Ex-army man Carson works for a short time as a cook at Merlotte's. (FDTW)

Carson, Brother: No first name given. Brother Carson is the new Calgary Baptist preacher. (DR)

Casey: No last name given. Casey already had a history of abusing women when Kennedy Keyes killed him in self-defense. (Deceased; mentioned DR, IIHAH)

Cassidy, Mrs.: No first name given. Mrs. Cassidy is laid out for visitation back at Spencer and Sons Funeral Home as Mike Spencer stops by Merlotte's to invite Sookie to an orgy. (Deceased; mentioned LDID)

Cataliades, Desmond (mostly demon): A demon with a law degree is a lethal combination. Well-known as a specialist in vampire law, Mr. Cataliades serves as Sophie-Anne's attorney and, as such, notifies Sookie of her cousin Hadley's final death while delivering Waldo to her doorstep so that she can avenge her cousin. When his niece Gladiola is later murdered while trying to deliver a letter to Sookie regarding Hadley's estate, Mr. Cataliades seeks out a bit of vengeance of his own when Sookie gives him the identity of Glad's assailant. He has no visible weapons as he confronts Jade Flower, so exactly how she loses her leg remains a mystery. Mr. Cataliades personally rescues Sophie-Anne Leclerq from the Pyramid of Gizeh in Rhodes and continues to manage her affairs as she recovers. After her death during the takeover of Louisiana by the Nevada vamps, the esteemed lawyer is hired to represent Felipe de Castro's interests in Louisiana. Even though he must appear to remain neutral in his dealings in the supe world, he is grateful for Sookie's aid during the Rhodes bombing and its aftermath, so he sends his niece Diantha to warn her about the fairies moving about in the human world. He also ensures that she receives payment for her services at the summit from the late queen's estate, and sends Sookie her inheritance after handling Claudine Crane's will.

A letter from Adele reveals just how much influence Mr. Cataliades has had in Sookie's life and why he feels a responsibility toward her. As a friend of her grandfather, Fintan, Mr. Cataliades bestowed the gift of telepathy on all of Fintan and Adele's descendants who possessed the essential spark. After Fintan's death, he gave Adele the cluviel dor on Fintan's behalf. (OWA, DD, ATD, DR; mentioned FDTW, DAG, DITF)

Cater, Jennifer (vampire): Peter Threadgill's lieutenant-in-training, Jennifer presses the case against Sophie-Anne after his death. She and two of her retinue are murdered in their suite at the Pyramid of Gizeh by Sigebert. (Dies ATD)

Cecile: No last name given. The King of Texas's executive assistant, Cecile attends the summit at Rhodes, sharing a room with Barry. When the impending bombing is uncovered, she smartly pulls the fire alarm to alert the human guests, only to become a victim herself and perish in the explosion. (Dies ATD)

Charity (vampire): No last name given. After Waldo reports that he and Hadley had been attacked by Fellowship of the Sun members at

St. Louis Cemetery #1 while trying to raise Marie Laveau, Charity and Valentine are sent by Sophie-Anne to investigate the incident. They find no sign or scent of humans at the site. (Mentioned OWA)

Charlie: No last name given. Vampire Heidi's son, Charlie languishes as a drug addict in Reno. Heidi has accepted Eric's offer to allow her to relocate her son to Shreveport. (Mentioned DITF, DR)

Chenier, Willie: Along with Jane Bodehouse, Willie is a regular heavy drinker at Merlotte's until his death. (Deceased; mentioned DAG)

Chester (vampire): No last name given. One of Sophie-Anne's guards, Chester was once a backwoods kid with sandy hair and a pleasant demeanor. He and fellow guard Melanie are among the vampires who perish during the Katrina disaster. (DD; dies; mentioned ATD)

Chico (vampire): No last name given. Heidi tells Eric the story of Chico, a new vampire who was disrespectful to Victor. To punish him, Victor had his mother kidnapped, cut out her tongue, and fed it to her son. Chico was unable to save his mother as she bled to death. Chico's half brother, Colton, refers to the same incident when asked why he wants to kill Victor. (Mentioned DR)

Child, Rita: While owner of the strip club Hooligans, Rita makes the potentially deadly mistake of killing a fairy with two vengeful siblings. Claudette Crane and her brother, Claude, both work for her as strippers. Claudette makes plans to leave for another club and take Claude with her, so Rita (who lusts after Claude as well as values him as a moneymaker) rubs the inside of the money pouch Claudette is using with lemon juice. After Sookie uncovers her guilt, Claude and his remaining sister, Claudine, have Rita sign over Hooligans to them for a dollar. They then release her, informing her that she also owes them the hunt for murdering their sister and that if she can dodge them for a year, she can live. The year is up. Her status is unknown. (FD)

Chow (vampire): No last name given. With his tattoo-covered body, Chow, bartender and part owner of Fangtasia, is quite a draw for the tourists who frequent the bar. When given Hallow's terms by the young witch acting as messenger, he angrily attacks, causing the spell attached to the witch to activate and poofing Eric from the office. Chow pays the ultimate price during the Witch War, succumbing to his final death at the hands of a witch with a wooden knife. (LDID, CD; dies DTTW; mentioned DAAD)

Chuck: No last name given. Chuck is hired as the bartender at the welcome-home party for Farrell at Stan's house. He is wounded when the Fellowship of the Sun opens fire on the mixed crowd of vampires and humans. (LDID)

Clancy (vampire): No other name given. One of Pam's nest mates, Fangtasia bar manager Clancy is kidnapped and drained almost to the point of second death by Hallow and her coven. He survives but is embittered by the experience. Though he obeys Eric's summons to defend Sookie against the fae in the supe hospital, he requests to be released from his vow to Eric if he survives. He is taken down by a mace swung by one of Breandan's followers, and Breandan decapitates him as he leaps over his body to get to Bill. (DN, ATD, FDTW; dies DAG; mentioned CD, DTTW, DAAD, DITF)

Clausen, Charles (owl): Charles gets engaged to Debbie Pelt during one of her breakups with Alcide, but Debbie can't get over her former boyfriend so the engagement is called off. (CD; mentioned DAAD, DD)

Clayton, Errol: Errol manages the *Bon Temps Bugle*, the local newspaper, on a tight budget, writing about half of the stories himself. (DITF)

Clearwater, Hank: When the water heater stops working, Sookie suggests that Claude call Hank to see about repairing it, but Terry offers to take a look and easily replaces the element. (Mentioned DITF)

Cleary, Allie: Allie is the new wife of Holly's ex-husband, David. She has two children from a previous marriage. (Mentioned DTTW)

Cleary, Cody: Holly's son, Cody, almost dies when he is involved in an altercation at school with the school custodian and ends up stuffed into a large garbage can. He is rescued by Kenya Jones, who is told by Sookie where to look. (DD; mentioned LDID, DTTW, FDTW, DAG, DITF, DR)

Cleary, David: Holly's ex-husband, David, lives in Springfield with his new wife, Allie, and her two children. (Mentioned DTTW, DD)

Cleary, Holly (witch): Holly works with Sookie at Merlotte's bar along with her good friend Danielle Gray. Divorced with one son, six-year-old Cody, Holly practices the Wiccan faith. She is pulled into Hallow's attempt to ensnare Eric Northman through threats to her son. Blackmailed into acting as a lookout for Hallow, Holly accosts Sookie as the vampires and Weres are beginning their attack but winds up giving Sookie information instead, hoping that Hallow's coven will be destroyed. When Holly's son later goes missing at his school, Sookie is able to locate him in time to save him from an accident gone terribly wrong. Holly is one of the few humans who knows about the existence of the shifters, and she speaks out on behalf of Sam and Tray during their reveal at Merlotte's. She has grown into a confident woman who stands up for her friends and is engaged to Hoyt Fortenberry, Jason's best friend. That change is reflected in Holly's appearance, as she has gone from a bleached blonde to a black-haired Goth and is now back to her natural brown hair. When she and Hoyt set the date for their wedding, she asks Sookie to serve the punch, an honor reserved for good friends. (LDID, DTTW, DAAD, DD, ATD, FDTW, DAG, DITF, DR)

Clete (wolf): No last name given. Clete and several other Weres are hired by the Pelts to grab Sookie in New Orleans and bring her to an isolated house in the swamp for interrogation about Debbie's death. During the drive there, Sookie stabs Clete in the face with a screwdriver to force the driver, George, to panic and pull over so that she and Quinn can make their escape into the swamp. Quinn is outraged at Clete's handling of Sookie and makes certain Clete pays when, in tiger form, he tracks the Weres to the isolated house where the Pelts are waiting and surprises the abductors sitting outside having a smoke. (DD)

Clovache (Britlingen): No other name given. A member of the Britlingen Collective, she is a slightly smaller version of her partner, Batanya, with feathery brown hair that needs styling and big green eyes below high, arched brows. The Britlingens are hired by Isaiah, the King of Kentucky, to guard him during the vampire summit in Rhodes. It is Clovache who fills Sookie in on Isaiah's discovery of a spy in his organization. She and Batanya fulfill their duties by carrying their sleeping client to safety before the Pyramid of Gizeh explodes, then return to their own dimension. (ATD)

Clovis: No last name given. Clovis and Sophie-Anne are the sole survivors when a sickness wipes out their village. He rapes Sophie-Anne and forces her into prostitution, traveling from town to town until they are caught by Alain in the woods and he is drained. (Deceased; mentioned DD)

Cluviel dor: A fairy love token. The cluviel dor grants just one wish to the one to whom it is given, but its potential is enormous as long as the wish is based in love. (DR)

Coburn, Parker (vampire): Parker, Palomino, and Rubio wind up staying in Eric's Area Five after Katrina, nesting together in Minden. The trio is called upon to help with Victor's assassination. Though not much of a brawler, Parker does his best to help Palomino as she takes down Unknown Enemy Vamp #2. (DR)

Collins, Reverend: No first name given. Reverend Collins preaches at Sookie's Methodist church. (FDTW)

Collins, Callie: Heavyset Callie is just one of many cooks who briefly works at Merlotte's. (DD)

Collins, Jim: Jim's wife, Della, dies around the time of the vampires' Great Revelation, and the Texan's loneliness morphs into hatred toward first the vampires and then the shifters; he blogs about them on his website, set up to espouse his views. He is a good friend of Don, Bernie Merlotte's second husband. Jim considers Don's shooting of Bernie justified. His extremism eliminates his compassion toward all animals, and he shoots all of the dogs at the local animal shelter to drive his point home after posting a sign on Bernie's lawn about dogs belonging at the pound.

Jim and Sarah Newlin connect online, and she sneaks into the area to encourage like-minded people to disrupt Craig and Deidra's wedding. Jim suggests and then demands that he and Sarah go next door and start shooting people in Bernie's backyard at the after-party. When she refuses, he calls her a hypocrite and shoots her. Sarah is wounded but shoots back, and Jim collapses and dies. Jim's body and the injured Sarah are found in his house by Sookie and Luna, whose sensitive shifter nose picks up the scent of something dead. (Dies STW)

Colman (fairy): No other name given. Colman is the father of Claudine's child and seeks revenge on Sookie for their deaths. At first he cannot bring himself to kill her outright, so he considers and dismisses a plan to kidnap Hunter, then concocts a scheme involving Basim al Saud, a dead body on Sookie's land, and an anonymous tip to the police to have her arrested and incarcerated. When that fails, he watches her, waiting for an opportunity to do harm. He stands with Claude when they are attacked by Alexei and attempts to stab Sookie after Alexei is staked, but skewers Ocella instead, killing him. Disabled by a knife thrown by Dermot, Colman cannot defend himself when Eric seizes him and drains him for killing his maker. (Dies DITF; mentioned DAG)

Colton: No last name given. At the urging of his girlfriend, Audrina, Colton moved from Reno, where he worked in a club for Felipe, and he's now a server at Vampire's Kiss. He is more aware of the goings-on of the supernatural world than most humans, courtesy of his half brother, Chico, a vampire. Having heard about Sookie, Colton is able to send her a mental message to keep Eric and Pam from using fairy blood–tainted glasses at the bar. Furious at Victor for punishing Chico's insubordination by killing their mother, he and Audrina participate in the massacre at Fangtasia. Colton survives the night but loses Audrina in the battle. (DR)

Colton and Chico's mother: No name given. Mother to both Colton and vampire Chico, she becomes a victim of Chico's insolence to Victor. Victor has her kidnapped, cuts out her tongue, and force-feeds it to Chico. Violently ill from ingesting the bloodied flesh, Chico is unable to save his mother as she bleeds to death. (Deceased; mentioned DR)

Compton, Caroline: Bill's wife, Caroline, celebrates his safe return home from the war only to find herself a widow after Bill is attacked and taken by Lorena, leaving her to raise their two children alone. (Deceased; mentioned DUD, LDID, DITF, DR)

Compton, Fuller: Fuller, one of Bill's descendants, was the sole policeman in Bon Temps back in the 1930s and investigated the Isaiah Wechsler murder. (Deceased; mentioned IIHAH)

Compton, Jessie: Jessie is descended from Bill's son Tom and is the last "living" Compton of that family. When he dies, the family home reverts back to Bill. (Deceased; mentioned DUD, LDID, DD)

Compton, Mr.: No first name given. Bill's father died while he was away soldiering in the Civil War. (Deceased; mentioned DUD)

Compton, Mrs.: No first name given. Bill's mother's maiden name was Loudermilk. (Deceased; mentioned DUD)

Compton, Robert: Bill's older brother Robert dies at age twelve of an infection. (Deceased; mentioned DUD, LDID)

Compton, Sarah: Bill's sister Sarah's young man dies in the Civil War, and she remains unmarried. (Deceased; mentioned DUD, LDID)

Compton, Sarah Isabelle: Bill's daughter, named for her aunt, has a daughter named Caroline, who marries her cousin and has her own daughter Caroline, who marries a Bellefleur. (Deceased; mentioned DUD, LDID, DITF)

Compton, William "Bill" (vampire): Under the orders of his queen, Bill Compton, Confederate soldier, returns to claim his family home in Bon Temps upon the death of his last direct descendant. Told to seek out

Sookie Stackhouse, he finds her at her job at Merlotte's, but when he foolishly goes out to the parking lot with a couple who offer him blood and sex, he is bound with silver chains as they try to drain him to sell his blood, and he is rescued by the very woman he has been sent to evaluate. A few nights later he returns the favor when she is attacked by the couple who attempted to drain him; he kills them both and gives a gravely injured Sookie his blood to heal. Sookie soon becomes far more than an assignment.

After taking Sookie to Fangtasia, looking for information about several women murdered in the area, Bill is dismayed that she catches the attention of Eric Northman, vampire sheriff of Area Five. Bill seeks a position in the vampire hierarchy himself to protect Sookie. He successfully campaigns for and becomes the Area Five investigator. Under Eric's orders, they travel together to Dallas to find Farrell, the nest mate of sheriff Stan Davis. Sookie is sent to infiltrate the Fellowship of the Sun during the day, and upon waking, Bill is alerted to the fact that she is in trouble by a young telepath whom Sookie was able to contact at the hotel. Bill is searching for her when she is brought back to the hotel, and he rushes back to her side. During the celebration of Farrell's safe rescue, the Fellowship of the Sun fires on Stan's house, and Bill is among the vampires who give chase to their assailants, leaving Sookie in the company of Eric. Disappointed in Bill, Sookie returns home, and they remain estranged for several weeks. After their reconciliation, Bill must leave town, and he returns to find that Sookie has asked Eric to protect her during an orgy she is attending to gather information about the death of Lafayette Reynold. Bill arrives in time to witness maenad Callisto's madness infect the orgy participants, and he takes Sookie home after he and Eric clean up the mess.

Looking through his family Bible, Bill realizes that he still has descendants in the area, the Bellefleur family, and sets up an anonymous legacy. When he's summoned by his maker, Lorena, he stashes his computer in Sookie's hidden vampire retreat. He briefly surrenders to the will of his maker, becoming her lover once again, but she soon reveals that her true intent is to acquire the database. When seduction doesn't bring the results she wants, she turns to torture. Sookie kills Lorena during Bill's rescue, and she angrily questions his feelings for her. Bill continues to profess his love and explain the situation with his maker, but he soon leaves on a research trip for the database. Upon his return, he discovers that Sookie and an amnesic Eric have become intimate. Still trying to win her back, Bill takes Sookie back to his house after her kitchen is set on fire, ready to care for her. He reacts badly when he walks in on Sookie and Sam kissing at Merlotte's, and he soon brings in a date to retaliate. After helping Sookie by staking her cousin's killer, Bill offers his services should she need help settling her cousin's estate. Although she declines, he joins her on her trip to New Orleans. After she is attacked by Jake Purifoy, Eric forces Bill to admit to Sookie that she was an assignment from the queen. Devastated, Sookie sends him away. He saves her from Jade Flower at the queen's spring party and shows up at her door to wearily tell her that he genuinely loves her, but Sookie is unable to forgive him.

Bill continues seeing Selah Pumphrey while Sookie moves on, but he remains adamant in his love for her and watches over her. He arrives at her house the night of the takeover, worried that several vampires have suddenly lost touch. After the arrival of Victor Madden, Bill agrees to the terms of surrender, but not before telling Victor that he would willingly die for Sookie. He proves his words when Sookie is kidnapped by fairies Lochlan and Neave. Bill and Niall track her, and Bill kills Neave, who manages to bite him with her silver-capped teeth. Sickened with silver poisoning, Bill still manages to stand in front of Sookie when Breandan's forces arrive, killing Breandan himself with Sookie's trowel.

Although deathly ill, Bill takes his family Bible to Caroline Bellefleur and tells her of their family connection—she is his great-granddaughter. Caroline is amused and delighted by the news, but passes away the next day. At Bill's request, Portia arranges a nighttime funeral so that he can attend. While he is with his newfound family after the funeral, Sookie sneaks into his home to find out how to contact his one vampire sibling, whose blood can help him heal. Judith Vardamon arrives, pleased to be able to see Bill again, but he soon realizes that Judith continues to have feelings for him, which he still does not return. That is the reason they parted before. She overhears him speaking to Sookie about it and tells them that she will leave because she deserves better. When Bud Dearborn calls with word that Sandra Pelt, who was arrested earlier in the evening for her attempts on Sookie's life, has escaped custody, Bill offers to watch over Sookie's house to keep her safe.

Bill is in his daytime sleep when Sookie runs to his house to escape two men who have come to kidnap her, but she is able to locate him in the crawl space under his kitchen. As Sookie crouches over him, he surfaces several times, only to fall back asleep. He finally rouses and comes to her aid, making certain the kidnappers have left before escorting her home. Finding Dermot bleeding in the attic, Bill must leave as he fights off the intoxicating scent of the fairy blood. Bill returns to his own home, but he is called back to Sookie's later that night to convince Bubba to play his part in the plot to assassinate Victor. Bill is responsible for getting Bubba to and from Fangtasia when the time comes, and he leads the frazzled singer to safety when the mayhem begins, pausing briefly to kill one of Victor's vamps. After Bubba leaves to find his own place to sleep, Bill returns and speaks to Eric, who has not bothered to soothe Sookie's pain while taking her blood. Bill drives Sookie home, allowing her the silence for her own thoughts, but they begin to talk once they're at her house, and she describes her feelings about the deaths at Fangtasia and then tells him the whole story of Eric's contract with Freyda, admitting that she had broken the blood bond even before finding out. Although he dislikes and distrusts Eric, Bill offers advice as a friend, telling her to let Eric make up his own mind about what to do. (DUD, LDID, CD, DTTW, DN, DAAD, OWA, DD, ATD, L, FDTW, DAG, DITF, DR; mentioned FD, GW, STW, IIHAH)

Connie the Corpse (vampire): No other name given. Connie, with her smooth voice, is the early night DJ on KDED, the Baton Rouge–based all-vampire radio station. (DAAD)

Cooper, Maria-Star (wolf): Gentle Maria-Star joins her pack to attack Hallow and Mark Stonebrook at Bill Compton's house and is gravely injured when she is hit by their car as the witches flee the scene. Taken to the hospital by Sookie, she manages to comprehend the story Sookie has concocted about her injuries and play along for the police investigating her hit-and-run. She has recovered in time for the packmaster contest, where she comforts a distraught Alcide Herveaux after his father's defeat and death, and they begin dating soon after.

Maria-Star is content in her professional life, working for photographer Al Cumberland as his assistant and makeup artist, and in her personal life, as she and Alcide become serious. They have just started discussing her moving in with him when she is brutally murdered in her apartment.

Alcide is devastated and vows vengeance on Patrick Furnan, who he believes is behind her murder, only to find that Patrick's wife, Libby, is also a victim of a female Were packleader named Priscilla Hebert. Alcide and Patrick work together to kill Cal Myers, the actual killer of Maria-Star, Libby, and Christine Larrabee. Patrick Furnan is killed during the ensuing battle with Priscilla's pack, and Alcide ascends to packmaster without Maria-Star by his side. She is survived by her parents and three younger brothers. (DTTW, DAAD, DD; dies FDTW; mentioned DITF)

Cooper, Matthew and Stella (wolves): The parents of Maria-Star; they mourn her death along with her three nonshifter brothers. (Mentioned FDTW)

Copper: No other name given. Copper's willingness to show Sookie and Barry the security tapes at the Monteagle Archery Company in Rhodes is her undoing. She is murdered before they return to view the tapes. (Dies ATD)

Corinna (vampire): No last name given. Victor's vamp Corinna joins Bruno in an attempt to kill Sookie and Pam, waiting on the side of the road and flagging them down as they drive back to Bon Temps late one night. Pam easily defeats her with her bare hands, leaving Sookie with a knife to tackle Bruno. (FDTW; dies DITF; mentioned DR)

Corinne: No last name given. Corinne, the manicurist and pedicurist at Janice Herveaux Phillips's salon, cheerfully pampers Sookie during her stay in Jackson. (CD)

Coughlin, Mike: Shreveport detective Coughlin investigates the killings at Verena Rose's Bridal and Formal Shop, unaware that the bodies he is looking at are supernatural in nature. He inadvertently remains connected to the supe world when he is partnered with Were Cal Myers but does suspect something odd about his new co-worker. (DTTW, DD; mentioned FDTW)

Coyote shifter: No name given. A beautician who comes out around the Great Reveal, much to the dismay of one of her longtime clients, who also discovers that she is the granddaughter of a werelynx. (Mentioned DAG)

Crane, Claude (fairy): Claudine's brother, Claude, is six feet tall, with brown eyes, long dark hair, and ears surgically altered to appear more human. He is an exotic dancer who prefers men to women but who has "visited the other side of the fence." Narcissistic in the extreme, Claude generally does what is best for Claude. After losing both of his sisters, however, Claude moves in with Sookie, ostensibly for companionship but in reality to protect her from Colman, the father of his late sister Claudine's child, both lost in the Fae War. Claude proves to be a surprisingly pleasant roommate for Sookie and actually seems to enjoy playing with Hunter Savoy when Sookie babysits him for the night. Together, Claude and Sookie are able to break the spell on Sookie's great-uncle (and Claude's half-uncle) Dermot. As fairies draw comfort from other fae, Claude and Dermot remain living with Sookie until Claude is told to move out after allowing Alcide Herveaux into Sookie's bed to wait for her, despite the fact that she is involved with Eric. (FD, DAAD, DD, FDTW, DAG, DITF, DR)

Crane, Claudette (fairy): Triplet to Claudine and Claude, Claudette apparently does not share the caring nature of Claudine and often doesn't even bother to put on the charm Claude can assume when he pleases. When Claudette is murdered with pure lemon juice, Claudine asks Sookie for her help identifying the murderer by reading three potential human suspects. When the culprit turns out to be the owner of the strip club where both Claude and Claudette worked as exotic dancers, instead of human justice, the payment for the murder is the deed to the club—and the hunt. As Claudine says, "Fair is only part of fairy as letters of the alphabet." (Deceased; mentioned FD, DAG, DITF, DR)

Crane, Claudine (fairy): Tall, dark-haired, dark-eyed, well-endowed Claudine first strolls into Merlotte's on New Year's Eve. She eventually reveals that she is Sookie's fairy godmother, and her mission is to try to prevent disasters in Sookie's life and help her recover from those she can't prevent. Sometimes it is with advice—ranging from fashion tips to telling Sookie not to attend the summit in Rhodes and warning her about Dermot and Breandan. Other times Claudine's help is more action-packed. She pops into Sookie's car when Sookie almost falls asleep and also pops into the middle of the Were war to stand over Sookie and guard her from the battling Weres. Her last act is protecting Sookie when Breandan attacks Dr. Ludwig's clinic. A pregnant Claudine attempts to stop Breandan from killing Sookie, but she dies in the process. Claudine once told Sookie that she was working on becoming an angel, but she appears to her father, Dillon, as part of her death ritual, so she currently resides in the Summerland. (DTTW, FD, DAAD, DD, ATD, FDTW; dies DAG; mentioned DITF, DR)

Crawdad Diner: Perdita and Crawdad Jones opened their diner in the 1940s. After Perdita's retirement, she gave her recipes to subsequent owner Ralph Tooten with the caveat that the business remain named for her late husband. Ralph's arthritis didn't allow him to keep the diner for long, but he maintained Crawdad's name by selling to Pinkie Arnett with the same condition. Located in the oldest part of Bon Temps and once somewhat of a dive, the restaurant is well-known by locals who go there to enjoy traditional Southern foods, including fried green tomatoes, country-fried steak, and Perdita's bread pudding. (DUD, DITF; mentioned DR)

Crimmins, Patricia (wolf): Patricia is one of the three St. Catherine Parish wolves who surrender to Alcide after Priscilla Hebert's failed attempt to take over the Shreveport pack. Alcide chooses her to reveal herself on camera when the shifters come out because she is pretty, shapely, and, quite frankly, the new girl. When Alcide begins seeing Annabelle, Patricia is jealous, even though she is seeing Hamilton Bond, and she aids and abets Ham when he kills Basim and buries him on Sookie's property. When Sookie "sees" her guilt, Patricia throws herself on the mercy of the pack, but Jannalynn convinces Alcide that Patricia is a traitor and should die with Hamilton. Assumed deceased. (FDTW, DAG, DITF)

Crimmons, Booth (vampire): Gervaise's second-in-command. Booth and his vamps, along with Sigebert, are guarding Sophie-Anne during her recovery. He is out during the actual takeover, having left his child Audrey in charge. His status remains unknown. (Mentioned FDTW)

Cromwell, Willie: Detective Cromwell is part of the investigation into the people missing after Priscilla Hebert's attack on the Shreveport Weres. He'll never find out what really happened. (Mentioned FDTW)

Crowe, Bartlett (vampire): The King of Indiana, Bart marries Russell Edgington at the summit in Rhodes. He and his husband both survive the explosion with minimal injury. (ATD; mentioned DAG)

Culpepper (wolf): No first name given. When Hallow and her coven target the Shreveport Weres and vampires, Culpepper pairs with fellow Were Portugal to ensure that the local Wiccans either help or stay clear of the upcoming Witch War. When Portugal is among those killed in the war, Culpepper sits beside his body, mourning his death. (DTTW)

Cumberland, Alfred (wolf): From the nuptials of a vampire king and queen to the double wedding of small-town royalty, Al, photographer of the supernatural and the mundane, is privy to the rituals of both worlds as he records them for posterity. (DD, FDTW)

Cummins, Jesse Wayne: Jesse Wayne frequents Merlotte's. (DITF)

Cunningham, Riki: Riki has a prom dress for her daughter on layaway at Tara's Togs. (DAG)

Curlew: No first name given. Officer Curlew interviews Sookie along with his partner, Jay Stans, when she brings Maria-Star to the hospital, claiming she found her on the side of the road after she was hit by a car. (DTTW)

Curt (wolf): No last name given. Curt, who works for Niall as a courier and does community theater, plays the part of Other Brute, the unseen Were at Sookie's door on Christmas Eve. (GW)

Cyndee (vampire): No last name given. One of Fangtasia's human barmaids, Cyndee brings the Bureau of Vampire Affairs down on the bar when she promises to bribe a vampire to bite a female customer. Eric is certain they will be exonerated, as he doesn't allow such things in his bar and has no history of doing so, but is annoyed that he must deal with an investigation. Cyndee is fired, of course, which is Eric's only legal recourse. (Mentioned STW)

D:

Dallas Midnight Massacre, the: The name various newsmagazines give to the attack on Stan Davis's house by members of the Fellowship of the Sun, citing it as the perfect example of a hate crime. (LDID)

Dan: No last name given. Dan is one of the gate guards for Eric's community. (DITF)

Dana: No last name given. Bridesmaid Dana coaches Sookie on the procedures when she takes Tiffany's place in Halleigh's wedding. Her husband and baby attend the wedding as well. (FDTW)

Danvers, Carla: Gervaise's girlfriend is a mix of wholesome prom queen and pierced free spirit, blithely parading naked around the hotel room she shares with Sookie at the summit. Carla enjoys being with "Gerry," the sheriff of Area Four—and all the perks that come with it. She is one of the victims of the bombing of the hotel. (Dies ATD)

Dave: No last name given. Dave, a serviceman from Barksdale Air

Force Base, drunkenly approaches Sookie as she sits with Eric in Fang-tasia, telling her she shouldn't associate with vampires. He is surprised when she knows his name, and he calms down enough to offer an apology of sorts. (DAAD)

David and Van Such Printing Company: David and Van Such is a defunct printing company located in an industrial park at 2005 Claire-mont in Shreveport. The site consists of several vacant buildings and load-ing docks, making it a perfect place to hold supernatural events. Quinn's Special Events team sets up the various tests for the Long Tooth packmas-ter contest in a large empty area in the main building, and the two result-ing factions of the Shreveport Weres, along with Sookie and Sam, later face each other outside in one of the large loading bays to find the truth behind the murders and abductions of several Were females from their pack before joining forces to defeat interloper Priscilla Hebert and her St. Catherine Parish Weres. (DAAD, FDTW)

Davis, Stan (vampire): The former Stanislaus Davidowitz has been working his way through the vampire hierarchy, first controlling Area Six in Texas as sheriff and then taking the entire state as king. While still sher-iff, he wins a lawsuit in human court against his neighbors, who are suing to have vampires barred from their community, and then becomes a sym-pathetic figure as he, his vampires, and the humans at his home suffer sev-eral casualties when they are attacked by members of the Fellowship of the Sun during what becomes known as the Dallas Midnight Massacre.

King Stan attends the summit in Rhodes even though Texas is not part of the clan holding the event, as he is proposing a business arrangement with Mississippi's Russell for a resort development. Unfortunately for Stan, he is badly injured in the bombing, losing his child Rachel as well. His second, Joseph Velasquez, struggles to hold Texas for his king as he recovers. (LDID, ATD; mentioned DD, DAG, DITF)

Dawn, Devon (vampire): A fashion "victim" on the TV show *The Best Dressed Vamp*, Devon at first stubbornly resists the help offered by hosts Bev and Todd, ripping Todd's throat out and getting a broken arm in return. (DAG)

Dawson, Tray (wolf): Ex-cop Tray Dawson is literally a lone wolf. Divorced with one son, he doesn't belong to a pack. He chooses to stay neutral in most two-natured affairs. Tray owns a small engine repair shop and supplements his income by working as a bodyguard. Hired to guard Calvin Norris while he is in the hospital, Tray spends the last day of his contract guarding Sookie at Calvin's request. He is shot by Sweetie Des Arts as she is confronting Sookie and Andy Bellefleur. Tray is a friend of Sam's and occasionally fills in for him behind the bar. After witnessing Maria-Star Cooper's death via the ectoplasmic reconstruction, Tray chooses to stand on Alcide Herveaux's side against Patrick Furnan, who is believed to be behind Maria-Star's death. When the true perpetrator is revealed, Tray fights with the pack but does not join it. He begins dating Amelia and accepts a job from Alcide to provide protection for Sookie when she is being threatened by the fae, partly because his presence will also protect Amelia. Tray is compelled to drink poisoned vampire blood by a fairy in Sookie's woods. He becomes too ill to guard her. Taken from his home by Lochlan and Neave so that he cannot come to Sookie's aid, Tray is tortured to the point of death. He is rescued and taken to Dr. Ludwig's hospital, but he knows he is dying. When Breandan and his followers attack, Tray summons all his remaining strength to distract Breandan, and he dies under his sword, giving Bill the few seconds he needs to kill the fairy. (DAAD, ATD, FDTW; dies DAG; mentioned DITF)

Dead Man Dance Band, the (vampires): The "live" band performs at the summit in Rhodes. (ATD)

Dean, Alma: Meek Alma is Diane Porchia's clerk. (L)

Dearborn, Bud: Sheriff Bud Dearborn was a friend of Corbett Stackhouse, but that doesn't alleviate his misgivings about both Sookie and Jason. The sheriff is a good man who honestly seeks justice. Just how well he knows his parish is revealed when he seeks to comfort a partially shifted Calvin Norris after the discovery of Crystal's body. Sookie is not the only one who already knew about the existence of the panthers.

Bud is in Merlotte's when Sandra Pelt makes another attempt to kill Sookie. After Sandra escapes from custody, he calls Sookie to let her know that her enemy is loose. (DUD, LDID, DTTW, DAAD, DD, FDTW, DAG, DITF, DR; mentioned ATD)

Dearborn, Greta: Greta's happy and unsuspicious nature, the flip side of her sheriff husband, is a perfect fit for her job with Bon Temps Florist. (DAAD)

Dearborn, Jean-Anne: The daughter of Bud and Greta Dearborn,

Jean-Anne was caught making out with Jason in the bed of his truck by her father. (Mentioned DUD)

Death by Fashion: At Death by Fashion, a high-end hair salon, stylist Immanuel Earnest is able to charge the highest prices in Shreveport. (Mentioned DR)

Deb (wolf): No last name given. Deb is the driver arranged by Dr. Josephus to take Sookie from the Dallas hospital to the Silent Shore Hotel after the car wreck. Blindfolded, Sookie listens to the talk among Deb, her fellow Were passenger riding shotgun, and Luna, including Deb's comments when she sees Eric standing outside the hotel. Deb thinks he's attractive but is told by Luna that she "can't date a deader." (LDID, STW)

de Castro, Felipe (vampire): The current King of Nevada, Louisiana, and Arkansas owns a number of businesses throughout Nevada, including a casino, several restaurants, and a talent management company that handles vampire entertainers. He is also reputed to have a publishing empire, although no specifics are given. With his experience dealing with tourists and, therefore, making money, he seems to be the right person to rebuild the vampire holdings in New Orleans.

Striking when Sophie-Anne is financially drained and physically disabled, Felipe orchestrates the takeover of Louisiana and Arkansas, sending his vampires to either assimilate or assassinate the vamps in both states. Felipe is captured along with Eric and Sam in Merlotte's parking lot by a vengeful Sigebert. Rescued by Sookie, he shows his gratitude by offering formal vampire protection to her.

Felipe's control over Louisiana is tenuous as his regent, Victor, seeks to gain more and more power. But Felipe is aware of that and, as it turns out, had his own plans for Victor. (FDTW; mentioned DAG, TB, DITF, DR)

DeeAnne: No last name given. DeeAnne starts her night in Merlotte's with a trucker from Hammond but ends it by going home with Jason. (DUD)

Delagardie: No first name given. After Jake Purifoy's attack, paramedic Delagardie patches Sookie up at Hadley's apartment before sending her to the hospital. He gives Sookie some free advice. (DD)

Delahoussaye, Carey: The husband of Sookie's aunt Linda, he returns to his family in New Orleans when they divorce. Sookie has only faint childhood memories of him. (Mentioned OWA, DAG)

Delahoussaye, Linda Stackhouse (quarter fairy): Linda, the daughter of Adele and Fintan, apparently never benefits from her fairy heritage. As a child, she's molested by her uncle Bartlett. Linda's husband, Carey, leaves her to return to New Orleans. Her daughter, Hadley, also leaves home, disappearing from her life. Linda dies of uterine cancer shortly thereafter. (Deceased; mentioned DUD, OWA, DD, ATD, FDTW, DAG, DITF, DR)

Denissa: No last name given. Denissa is planning on singing at the Lisle-Merlotte wedding with Mary. She makes it to the rehearsal in the morning but is either unable or unwilling to brave the protesters for the service. (STW)

D'Eriq: No last name given. D'Eriq works as cook Antoine's helper while also busing tables at Merlotte's, so he is there the night Sam and Tray shift as the two-natured announce themselves on TV. He takes the reveal in stride, discovering not only that he works for a shifter but also that his cousin is married to a werewolf. (DAG, DITF)

D'Eriq's cousin: No name given. D'Eriq's cousin in Monroe calls him after the Great Reveal to let him know that he (the cousin) is married to a werewolf. (Mentioned DAG)

Derrick: No last name given. Derrick, Arlene's cousin, is brave enough to work the night shift at a gas station in Bon Temps. (LDID)

Derrick (panther): No last name given. As far as Amelia Broadway is concerned, her night spent with Calvin's cousin Derrick after Jason and Crystal's wedding is a onetime thing. In Derrick's mind, that one night makes them a couple, and he continues to call for a time, hoping for more. Unfortunately, his dirty sheets mean he doesn't stand a chance of a future with clean-freak Amelia, even if the sex had been good (which, according to her, it hadn't). (ATD; mentioned FDTW)

Des Arts, Sweetie (wolf): Bitten by a Were while lying injured in a car wreck, former stripper Sweetie partially shifts at the next full moon. She resents what she has become and hates all shifters with a passion, taking her revenge with a gun. She moves from place to place, working in bars, identifying local shifters not only through her customers but also through churches, restaurants, and day care centers. While working as a cook at Merlotte's, Sweetie kills teenager Heather Kinman, a werefox. She also shoots Calvin Norris, a werepanther, who barely survives, and wings Sookie, mistaking her for a shifter because of the scent of shifter on her. Sweetie meets her end in an alley, shot by Andy Bellefleur. In the three years after she was bitten, Sweetie randomly killed twenty-two shifters and wounded forty-one. (Dies DAAD)

Desiree: No last name given. Desiree is sent by Eric as a reward for Bill. Bill returns his present unopened, relieved when Jason offers to give her a ride home. (DUD)

DeWitt, Mr.: No first name given. Mr. DeWitt, Caroline Bellefleur's neighbor, hires her nurse, Doreen, after Caroline's passing. (Mentioned DITF)

Diane (vampire): No last name given. Monroe vampire Diane doesn't care about mainstreaming and takes pains to offend humans while visiting old acquaintance Bill in Bon Temps. Because of their arrogance, she and nest mates Liam and Malcolm are targeted by unhappy locals who burn down their house just after sunrise, trapping them in their coffins. (Dies DUD)

Diantha (half demon): No last name given. Diminutive half-demon Diantha is the niece of Mr. Cataliades and, along with her now-deceased sister, Gladiola, worked as a messenger for the late Sophie-Anne Leclerq as well as for her own uncle. She tends to dress very colorfully and quite often speaks without taking a breath, running her words together. She survives the bombing of the Pyramid of Gizeh in Rhodes after being trapped in the rubble for twelve hours. She conveys her uncle's personal message to warn Sookie about the fairies as well as delivers Sookie's inheritance from Claudine. Diantha can conjure small flames in the palm of her hand, loves to hunt, and has been known to bring down not just deer but also people (in her own defense) and even the occasional rogue vampire. (DD, ATD, DAG, DITF; mentioned DR)

Dinwiddie, Dr.: No first name given. Tara chooses Clarice obstetrician Dr. Dinwiddie as her doctor during her pregnancy. (Mentioned DITF)

Dominica, Don: The owner of Don's RV Park reports that the owners of three RVs registered to Priscilla Hebert haven't been seen in several days. (Mentioned FDTW)

Don: No last name given. Bernie Merlotte's second husband shoots her when she shifts in front of him the night of the Great Reveal. Arrested, he remains in jail waiting for trial, unable to make bail. (Mentioned FDTW, DAG, DITF, STW)

Donati, Todd: Chief of security at the Pyramid of Gizeh, terminally ill Todd wants nothing more than to put in his time so that his family will be taken care of after his death. He is frustrated by the machinations of the vampires at the summit. He survives the bombing and is able to tell Sookie that hotelier Christian Baruch set the Dr Pepper bomb in the hallway outside Sophie-Anne's room. (ATD)

Doreen: No last name given. Calm and competent Doreen takes care of Caroline Bellefleur in her final days and is with Caroline when Bill reveals their family connection. After Caroline passes, she moves next door to take care of neighbor Mr. DeWitt. (DITF)

Doug (wolf): No last name given. When Sookie drives off Russell's property at dawn with Bill stashed in the trunk, gate guard Doug casually asks her if she's returning for the "crucifixion." If he hadn't mentioned it, Bubba might have met his second end in his home state at the hands of vampires and werewolves who didn't recognize him as the real thing. (CD)

Dowdy, John: Former Renard Parish sheriff John Dowdy heads out to Hotshot to arrest Carlton Norris for statutory rape and is never heard from again. (DTTW)

Downey, Jim: Mechanic Jim occasionally works on Sookie's car. He is married with three children. (CD)

Duchesne, Kristen: Kristen loves Remy Savoy but ultimately cannot deal with Hunter's special abilities. (FDTW; mentioned DAG, DITF, DR)

Duff: No other name given. Duff regularly delivers the beer to Merlotte's. (DAG)

Duffy, Mark: A student at Louisiana Tech, Mark gets into a class war with Jeff LaBeff in Merlotte's, eventually leading to violence. (DAAD)

Duke of Death, the (vampire): "Live" DJ Duke of Death provides the music for Fangtasia's birthday party for Dracula, taking guests on a musical journey in honor of Vlad Tepes. (DN)

Dumas, Desiree: Desiree Dumas works in the gift shop of the Bat's Wing bar in Dallas and shares a small apartment with fellow employee Bethany Rogers. (Mentioned LDID)

du Rone, JB: Lovely JB du Rone sees life in the simplest terms. He has been friends with Sookie since high school because his thoughts are easy and direct, causing no stress to Sookie's telepathic mind. They reconnect after Dawn's murder, and JB values Sookie's continued friendship, eventually working with her to recover from what the town believes is a hit-and-run accident but is actually the result of a fairy attack. He also reconnects with fellow high school friend Tara, who is seeking a man who is not controlling or abusive after her encounters with vampires. Sweet JB fits the bill nicely, and they marry, soon welcoming twins Robert Thornton du Rone and Sara Sookie du Rone.

While tearing down a wall in the du Rones' bungalow, JB and Sam discover a hammer hidden inside and identify it as the weapon used in the murder of Isaiah Wechsler, who lived in the house next door in the 1930s. The murderer's spirit is disturbed, casting a pall over the house until his bones are uncovered and identified with the help of Sookie and the du Rones' nanny, Quiana Wong, who is a psychic. The spirit rests when the bones are reinterred in Sookie's family plot. JB returns the group to normalcy by confirming plans to finish the work in the house. (DUD, LDID, DD, ATD, DITF, IIHAH; mentioned FDTW, DAG, DR)

du Rone, Mrs.: No first name given. JB's mother attends Tara's baby shower for her soon-to-be grandchildren held at Sookie's house. (Mentioned DR)

du Rone, Robert Thornton: JB and Tara's son is given his mother's maiden name as his middle name. (IIHAH)

du Rone, Sara Sookie: Tara and JB's daughter's middle name is in honor of her "aunt" Sookie. (IIHAH)

du Rone, Tara Thornton: Sookie's longtime friend Tara overcomes a tough childhood to own her own business, a clothing store called Tara's Togs. Tara doesn't always exercise the best judgment in men and is briefly engaged to Eggs Benedict. She attends the local orgies at his urging, and it is only dumb luck that keeps her alive when Callisto arrives. Her next lover, vampire Franklin Mott, soon passes her to another vampire as payment for a debt. Sookie extricates her from that situation, and Tara eventually recognizes a good man right in front of her in her old high school friend JB du Rone. JB's simplistic approach to life appeals to Tara, and they marry. When she finds out she is pregnant, Tara vows to give her baby all the love and support that she lacked as a child. To the surprise of Tara, JB, and their doctor, Tara discovers she is pregnant with twins, and soon safely delivers Robert Thornton du Rone and Sara Sookie du Rone.

Living in the old Summerlin bungalow that she purchased a few years ago, Tara and JB decide to renovate to make room for the babies, and they enlist Sookie and Sam to help. When an old hammer is found concealed in a wall, they realize that it was used in the 1930s murder of neighbor Isaiah

Wechsler. By unearthing the hammer, they inadvertently unleash the spirit of the murderer. The babies' nanny, Quiana Wong, reveals that she is a psychic, and with Sookie's help they are able to identify the murderer as the youngest son of the family that built the house, the Summerlins. He committed suicide after the murder and was secretly buried in the yard by his parents. His bones are taken to Sookie's family plot and buried, putting the spirit to rest. (LDID, CD, DTTW, DAAD, DD, ATD, FDTW, DAG, DITF, DR, IIHAH)

Dustin (vampire): No last name given. Unschooled in being a vampire because his maker met his final death shortly after he was made, Dustin makes his way to Bon Temps, where he seduces and glamours Greg Aubert's daughter, Lindsay, in order to get fresh blood. When he is discovered by Sookie and Amelia, they call on Bill to take him to Fangtasia to meet Eric and, hopefully, learn the ropes. (L)

E:

Earnest, Immanuel: A hairstylist at Death by Fashion salon in Shreveport, brightly tattooed Immanuel is brought by Pam, who is his sister's lover, to Sookie's house to cut her hair after the firebombing at Merlotte's. Immanuel remains calm when Eric and Pam fight. He tells Sookie that his sister, Miriam, is critically ill and that Pam wants to bring her over. When his sister dies, Immanuel is only too happy to join the attack on Victor and his people at Fangtasia. He survives and leaves with Colton, united in grief after the loss of Miriam and Colton's girlfriend, Audrina. (DR)

Earnest, Miriam: Miriam is suffering with leukemia, so her lover, Pam, wants to turn her into a vampire before she sickens further, but Victor denies Pam's request to make a child. Having summoned Eric and Sookie to Vampire's Kiss and knowing that Pam will accompany them as Eric's second-in-command, Victor callously forces Miriam to attend as well. The desperately ill woman struggles to maintain control until Pam is able to get her out of the club and take her home.

Miriam succumbs to her illness, and Pam takes vengeance on Victor. (Dies DR)

Ectoplasmic reconstruction: A magical method of viewing past events involving people or other living creatures, it is rarely attempted because of the amount of time, energy, and skill required by the witches involved. Amelia Broadway successfully performs the ritual twice, once with three other witches after Hadley's death and once with Octavia after Maria-Star's death. The number of witches needed depends on the amount of area covered by the reconstruction, and the witches must recite the chants in unison, building the power and concentrating to keep the visual going. During the reconstruction, the subject appears translucent, with surrounding objects appearing only when touched by the subject. (DD, FDTW)

Edgington, Russell (vampire): Russell Edgington, the vampire King of Mississippi, does not intervene when Lorena Ball takes up residence on his property to torture information about the database out of Bill, but he is able to reach a tentative peace with Bill after his escape.

While at the Rhodes summit, Russell completes marriage negotiations with the King of Indiana, Bartlett Crowe, and they are married in full regalia by Eric. The happy couple survives the bombing with only minor injuries. (CD, ATD; mentioned DAAD, DAG, TB)

Einin: No last name given. Lovely Einin catches Niall's eye in the woods one day and ultimately bears him twin sons, Fintan and Dermot, but she lives the rest of her life in misery when Niall stops visiting her. (Deceased; mentioned FDTW, DAG, DITF)

Ellis, Helen: While Arlene sets the trap for Sookie, Helen takes Coby and Lisa away for the day. After the shoot-out, she claims she didn't know the plans and only took the children for a treat because they'd done well at school. (DAG)

Elvira: No last name given. Fangbanger Elvira works at Fangtasia. (FDTW)

Elvis Undead Review, the (vampires): This troupe, represented by Felipe de Castro's management company, doesn't include the real thing as it performs in Vegas. The company also manages several all-vampire dance groups. (Mentioned FDTW)

Emilio (wolf): No last name given. Shreveport Weres Emilio and Sid track Hallow and her coven to the empty business in Shreveport where the Witch War takes place. (DTTW)

Enda (fairy): No last name given. Enda, a shy fairy female, is caught and killed by Breandan in retaliation for Murry's death. (Dies DAG)

Engelbright, Dennis: Dennis is a former classmate of Sookie's who hooks up with her friend Marianne on a senior class trip to Six Flags in Dallas. (Mentioned LDID)

Eric Northman's children: Eric had six children with his wife, Aude. Two boys and a girl lived to adulthood. (Deceased; mentioned DAG)

Eric Northman's family: Eric's older brother died in battle, but his parents and other siblings were left to take care of his children when widower Eric vanished from their lives. (Deceased; mentioned DAG)

Eric Northman's house: Eric's fieldstone house is located in a gated community in Shreveport with a twenty-four-hour guard and a lawn service. Built on a slope, it has a lower-level game room that originally had a walk-out but has been sealed up to be a light-tight master bedroom with a heavy door barring the stairs to the main floor. The garage, empty save for Eric's Corvette, opens into a sparsely decorated and relatively unused kitchen. The living room, sporting new carpeting and new paint, is full of deep, rich colors and furnished with heavy furniture suitable for a man Eric's size. The bedrooms on the upper floor have all been fitted with shutters and heavy curtains, and the guest bedrooms have sleek coffins stowed under the beds. (DITF, DR; mentioned DTTW, FDTW, DAG)

Erin: No last name given. Erin begins dating Remy Savoy after his breakup with Kristen. When she runs into Sookie, Remy, and Hunter after Hunter's kindergarten orientation, she takes the opportunity to question Sookie about Kristen's comments that there is something strange about the child. Erin's feelings for the father are growing, and she already loves the little boy, so she accepts Sookie's assurance that although Hunter is different, there is nothing wrong with him. (DR)

Extreme(ly Elegant) Events: A nationwide event-planning company well known by its triple E logo. The company's secret division, Special Events, does the same sort of thing but for the supernatural community. (FDTW; mentioned DD, ATD)

F:

Fae creature (part fairy): No name given. A short, blond, unidentifiable creature of undeterminable gender acknowledges Sookie as having fairy blood and asks if she is joining the fae gathering at Hooligans. (DR)

Fae female (part elf): No name given. Beautiful with red hair, the female part elf has her teeth filed down so that she can pass as human but still desires the company of her fellow fae at Hooligans. (DR)

Fae male (part fairy): No name given. A long, slim, male creature of unknown origin sits in with the other fae at Hooligans. (DR)

Fairy child: No name given. He is the child of the fairy Breandan and an unnamed mother; the mother's life is spared, but the child is killed. (Mentioned, dies DAG)

Fairy warrior, female: No name given. A very tall female warrior wielding a mace follows Breandan through the door of Bill and Tray's room at Dr. Ludwig's clinic. She misses Eric, but her blow catches Clancy in the side of the head, enabling Breandan to behead him. She abandons her attack on Eric when Bill kills Breandan and aims her sword at Sookie, who squirts her with lemon juice. Distracted by the pain, she is killed by Eric. (Dies DAG)

Fairy warrior, male: No name given. A tall, thin male with gossamer hair is the first through the door during the final confrontation at the hospital and is the first to die, beheaded by Clancy. (Dies DAG)

Fairy warrior, male: No name given. The second through the door suffers a knife in the throat, thrown by Bill. (Dies DAG)

Fairy women: No names given. Two of Breandan's followers, including the mother of his child, are spared by Niall at the end of the Fae War because females are needed in the fairy world. (Mentioned DAG)

Falcon, Jerry (wolf): Hounds of Hell gang member Jerry Falcon accosts Sookie at Josephine's, drawing the wrath of Mr. Hob and the disapproval of his employer, Russell Edgington, the vampire King of Mississippi. After complaining to the Jackson packmaster about Alcide, Jerry attempts to break into Alcide's condo, only to be seen and killed by Bubba, who stuffs his body in the closet for Eric to dispose of. Unfortunately, Bubba doesn't tell Eric, Sookie, or Alcide, so when Sookie finds his body, neither she nor Alcide knows how it got there, but they do know they need to get rid of it. Jerry's body is wrapped in a shower curtain, driven to the Kiley-Odum Hunt Club, unwrapped, and left in an isolated area of the property. (Dies CD; mentioned DD)

Fangtasia: "Shreveport's Premier Vampire Bar" is located in a suburban shopping area of Shreveport, Louisiana, set in a strip mall not far from a Sam's Discount Center and a Toys "R" Us. The club is currently owned by vampires Eric Northman and Pam Ravenscroft. Its façade is painted steel gray, with a red main door, and a red neon sign proclaims the business's name. That color scheme continues in the interior, which is done in gray, red, and black with dim lighting. The atmosphere is enhanced by female employees in long black dresses and framed pictures of movie vampires on the walls. The clientele mainly consists of fangbangers and tourists visiting for the thrill of seeing a real vampire up close. Other supes unrevealed to the public frequent the bar as well. As part of the fealty owed to Eric as sheriff of Area Five, many of his vampires are required to put in hours on display at the bar, and he often sits at a table or booth himself.

Patrons are greeted at the entrance by a vampire at a lectern who takes the cover charge and shows them to their seats, and there are also stools at the bar. Spread around the main area are a number of placards with rules and warnings, such as NO BITING ON PREMISES, CONDUCT YOUR PERSONAL BUSINESS ELSEWHERE, and YOUR PATRONAGE IS APPRECIATED. PROCEED AT YOUR OWN RISK. There is an area for a band and a gift shop for souvenirs, including T-shirts and the Fangtasia calendars. The bar is open six nights a week, Tuesday through Sunday, from six p.m. on, although the vampires do not appear until after full dark. Along with the area vampires, Fangtasia has a number of human employees who are covered by a group health insurance policy.

The club hosts a rare concert by Bubba, given to lure Victor Madden and his crew to their deaths. (DUD, LDID, DTTW, DN, DAAD, ATD, DAG, DITF, DR; mentioned CD, DD, L, FDTW, TB)

Fant, Octavia (witch): Amelia's witch mentor and head of her coven, Octavia can look and behave like a sweet, elderly African American grandmother when she chooses. She lost everything in Hurricane Katrina and is staying with her niece in nearby Monroe when she finally finds her student at Sookie's house. Amelia's coven is upset because Amelia used transformational magic when she accidentally turned Bob Jessup into a cat and has been unable to turn him back. Octavia herself apparently fails in her attempts to return Bob to human form. Although disapproving, Octavia helps Amelia perform an ectoplasmic reconstruction to find the murderer of Maria-Star Cooper. The two witches work together again to rid Tanya Grissom of Sandra Pelt's influence so that she will stop causing trouble for Sookie and for Jason and Crystal, and Sookie invites Octavia to move in as a favor to Amelia. Octavia finally changes Bob back, admitting that her first attempts failed on purpose and that she left him that way so Amelia and Sookie would need her and allow her to stay. Octavia is eventually found by her boyfriend, Louis Chambers, a powerful man in his own right, who has been looking for her since Katrina. He comes to Bon Temps to take Octavia home with him to New Orleans. (FDTW, DAG; mentioned ATD, DITF, DR)

Farrell (vampire): No other name given. Farrell dresses like a cowboy and drinks like a vampire. Lured into the bathroom of the Bat's Wing bar by Godfrey, Farrell is taken prisoner by the Fellowship of the Sun, who plan to force him to be an unwilling partner to Godfrey's decision to meet the dawn. Farrell is rescued by Bill and the Dallas vamps as they search for Sookie. (LDID)

Fay: No last name given. Halleigh's sister Fay is one of her bridesmaids. (FDTW)

Fedor (vampire): No last name given. Along with Velislava, one of many vampires known by both Eric and Ocella and killed by the Bolsheviks. (Deceased; mentioned DITF)

Feith, Henrik (vampire): Henrik Feith is down in the lobby complaining about towels when Jennifer Cater and the other two Arkansas vamps at the summit are murdered in their hotel room. Sophie-Anne offers him a place in her entourage, but he is misled about her intentions and continues the suit against her for his king's death. After Sophie-Anne is declared innocent, Henrik is dispatched with an arrow thrown by a vampire onlooker before he can announce who has been lying to him. (Dies ATD)

Felicia (vampire): No last name given. The lovely Felicia is still too new to understand Pam's humor when she is sent by Pam to introduce herself to Sookie. Though she prefers the company of women, Felicia becomes involved with Bobby Burnham, Eric's daytime guy. Whether the romance is rooted in attraction or politics is unknown. Eric surmises that Felicia has been planted in Louisiana as a spy.

Whatever her true allegiance, Felicia dutifully follows Eric's orders, helping Bill with the database and even giving him blood. Both her romance and her career as a spy are ended when she and Bobby become victims of Alexei's madness. (DD, ATD, DAG; dies DITF; mentioned DR)

Fellowship of the Sun (FotS): A militant anti-vampire organization, the FotS is the fastest-growing cult in America and is dedicated to the elimination of vampires from society. Founded by G. Steve Newlin and his wife, Sarah, the movement has several branches and holds services preaching intolerance of the undead and condemning the humans who have any type of contact with vampires. Their most lucrative location, in Dallas, is raided by the FBI and shut down when the raid uncovers a basement dungeon complete with silver chains, weapons adapted to shoot wooden stakes, and the dead body of a Fellowship enforcer. Members of the FotS attack a vampire celebration in retaliation, killing several vampires and human participants. The assault prompts calls for legislation beneficial to vampires, and forces Steve and Sarah to go underground to continue spreading their message against the undead and promoting their program of eradication. The main organization publicly claims not to be involved in any violent incidents and is quick to deny responsibility for the bombing of the vampire summit in Rhodes that killed not just vampires but humans, including many employees of the Pyramid of Gizeh. The Fellowship blames a splinter group that has its own agenda.

The FotS targets shifters after their reveal as well, encouraging protests and surreptitiously inciting violence against them and those associating with them. (LDID; mentioned CD, DAAD, DD, OWA, ATD, FDTW, DAG, STW)

Flood, James (wolf): Retired Air Force colonel James Flood serves as the Shreveport packmaster, leading the Long Tooth pack in the Witch War against Hallow and her coven of Were witches. It is he who names Sookie a "friend of the pack" after she brings news of the coven to Alcide. His death in a car accident sparks the contest between Jackson Herveaux and Patrick Furnan. (DTTW, DN; dies; mentioned DAAD, DD)

Foley, Buck: Buck is briefly one of Arlene's beaus. (CD)

Fortenberry, Ed: Shy and quiet Ed lets his wife do most of the talking. (FDTW)

Fortenberry, Hoyt: Jason's best friend, Hoyt is loyal to a fault and feels lost when Jason marries Crystal. He soon recovers and becomes involved with Holly Cleary, happily including both Holly and her son in his life as he asks her to marry him. (DUD, LDID, DTTW, DAAD, DD, ATD, FDTW, DITF; mentioned DAG, DR)

Fortenberry, Maxine: Large and formidable, Maxine has a heart of gold and genuine affection for Sookie and Jason. She does what she can to help out in her community, be it taking Sookie's laundry for a washing to rid it of the smell of smoke after her house fire, organizing refreshments during the search party for Jason, or arranging meals for displaced Katrina evacuees. She is thrilled when her son Hoyt begins dating Holly Cleary, welcoming Holly and her son into her life. (DUD, DTTW, DAAD, ATD, FDTW, DITF, DR; mentioned CD)

Fowler, Arlene: Fellow Merlotte's waitress Arlene is the closest thing to a friend Sookie has for a long time. She acknowledges Sookie's ability and expects Sookie to respect her enough to keep out of her head. Married four times, Arlene is constantly on the lookout for number five but doesn't have good judgment when it comes to men. She is dating Rene Lenier, one of her previous husbands, while he is on his murderous spree. Always a follower, Arlene adapts to the man she is interested in, and soon finds herself involved with the Fellowship of the Sun simply because her onetime beau Rafe Prudhomme is involved. She switches her affections to Whit Spradlin, becoming more and more militant about her dislike of vampires. When the shifters reveal themselves, she quits work and leaves Merlotte's.

She pretends to extend an olive branch to Sookie and invites her over to her trailer, but it is all part of a plot to enable Whit and his friend Donny Boling to crucify Sookie in the same manner as Crystal as an example of what happens to those that fraternize with supes. Sookie is able to zero in on the plot while suspiciously scoping out the trailer, and calls the police. Arlene is wounded in the shoot-out with law enforcement and arrested. (DUD, LDID, CD, DTTW, DAAD, DD, ATD, FDTW, DAG; mentioned DITF)

Fowler, Coby: Arlene's son is very fond of his "aunt" Sookie, who often babysits him and his sister, Lisa. When he finds out that Sookie has a boyfriend, protective Coby tells her that Bill better be nice to her, but relaxes after meeting the vampire. As Sookie's world expands and Arlene's narrows, Sookie loses touch with Coby and Lisa, who are taken away by Helen Ellis as Whit and Donny wait to carry out their plan. (DUD, DAG; mentioned CD, DAAD, DITF)

Fowler, Jan: Multiple divorcée Jan Fowler uses her private cabin at Mimosa Lake to hold orgies with a select group of Bon Temps residents.

She and her fellow participants are killed when maenad Callisto, drawn by the lust and drunkenness, infects them with her madness. (Dies LDID)

Fowler, Lisa: Arlene's daughter loves her "aunt" Sookie, a frequent babysitter. She is intrigued when she meets Bill, questioning his paleness, but gives tacit approval to his courtship of Sookie. As Sookie and Arlene go their increasingly separate ways, Arlene cuts off the children's contact with Sookie. She sends Lisa and Coby away with Helen Ellis as Whit and Donny prepare for their planned crucifixion of Sookie. (DUD, DAG; mentioned CD, DAAD, DITF)

Freyda (vampire): No last name given. Freyda is the Queen of Oklahoma; it's possible that she sent Felicia to spy on Eric prior to the Nevada takeover and kept her there to continue to report on both Eric and the new king. Ocella arranges a marriage between Eric and Freyda, and she intends to hold Eric to the bargain despite his maker's death. (Mentioned DITF, DR)

Fullenwilder, Jimmy: Baptist minister Fullenwilder joins the search for the missing Jason and is put in a group with Sookie, Calvin Norris, Crystal Norris, and Felton Norris, as the rifleman. He is able to shoot and kill the feral pig that attacks Crystal. (DTTW)

Furnan, Libby (wolf): Patrick's wife, Libby, fully supports her husband in his bid to become packmaster, even accepting his ceremonial mating with a willing female pack member after he wins the title, knowing he will return to being a faithful husband after the ritual. When she goes missing, Furnan suspects Alcide. The men discover that Priscilla Hebert, widow of the St. Catherine Parish packmaster, has killed Libby, Maria-Star Cooper, and Christine Larrabee in an effort to start a war between them. (DAAD; mentioned, dies FDTW)

Furnan, Patrick (wolf): After the death of Shreveport packmaster Colonel Flood, Harley-Davidson dealership owner Patrick vies with Jackson Herveaux for the job. Both men begin their campaigns in their eulogies for Colonel Flood. Patrick emphasizes Jackson's weakness for gambling to cast doubt on his rival's suitability for the position. The packmaster contest consists of three tests taken in wolf form; although Patrick cheats, forfeiting the first and second tests, the pack votes to allow him to continue. He wins the third test, a test of battle, decisively and opts to kill his rival. His methods are not appreciated by the entire pack, and they remain split even after he takes his place as packmaster.

When Maria-Star Cooper is killed, Alcide immediately suspects Patrick. Patrick's wife, Libby, is missing, and he immediately suspects Alcide. They call upon Sookie to help them find the truth. Priscilla Hebert reveals herself and her pack, announcing that she is behind the loss of Maria-Star and Libby, as well as Christine Larrabee. The pack unites to fight Priscilla and her Weres. Patrick dies bravely, surrounded by the dead bodies of his enemies, and the pack howls the loss of their packmaster before celebrating their victory. (DAAD; mentioned DD; dies FDTW)

Furnan children (wolf and human): No names given. Patrick and Libby Furnan have two children, a boy who will be a Were and a girl who will remain human. After the deaths of their parents, the children go to live with Libby's sister, who is told that Patrick was a member of a secret society to explain why members of the pack will continue to be in the son's life. (DAAD; mentioned FDTW)

G:

Gabe: No last name given. A member of the Dallas Fellowship of the Sun, Gabe keeps Farrell imprisoned in the cellar of the church. He happily locks Hugo and Sookie up as well. Having already badly injured Sookie when she tried to escape, Gabe is willing to continue the abuse. After shutting Hugo in with Farrell, Gabe attempts to molest Sookie. He is stopped by Godfrey, who unintentionally kills him. (Dies LDID)

Garfield, Mrs.: No first name given. Mrs. Garfield, the wife of a Methodist-Episcopal minister, is the principal of Betty Ford Elementary School when Cody Cleary goes missing. She happily attends the wedding shower of Halleigh, one of her teachers. (DAAD, ATD)

Garza, Luna (bat): Petite werebat Luna successfully infiltrates the Fellowship of the Sun in Dallas to gather information for the local shifter groups. When she realizes that Sookie knows she is a shifter and sees that she is in trouble, Luna blows her cover helping Sookie escape the church, which is locked down for the night. After getting rear-ended by Sarah Newlin and Polly Blythe, Luna contacts a shifter doctor at the hospital Sookie is taken to, has all traces of her treatment erased, and arranges a ride back to the hotel.

Divorced with no children, Luna gets out of the spy business and takes a job with a PR firm in Dallas. She hears about Sam's brother's wedding and travels with other two-natured to Wright to help stave off any violence. Afterward, she joins the impromptu party at Bernie's and, while spending some quality time with a cute Chinese Were cop from Fort Worth, scents a dead body in the house next door. She and Sookie cautiously enter the house to find Sarah Newlin of the Fellowship of the Sun injured on the floor, shot by house owner Jim Collins, whom she shot and killed in return. After calling the police, explaining the situation, and seeing Sarah taken into custody, Luna and Sookie return to the party. At the end of the night, Luna hugs Sookie good-bye and leaves with her newly found Were friend. (LDID, STW)

Genuine Magic Shop, the: Run by members of Amelia Broadway's coven, the Genuine Magic Shop is in the French Quarter. Amelia works at the shop when she goes back to New Orleans. (Mentioned DR)

George (wolf): No last name given. A member of the gang that kidnaps Sookie and Quinn from Hadley's apartment, George drives the van taking them to the Pelts. He and Clete continue to the cabin the Pelts are using after the prisoners escape. As they smoke outside, Quinn (in his tiger form) pounces. (DD)

Gerald (vampire): No last name given. Gerald, one of Pam's nest mates, fights in and survives the Witch War. Gerald generally keeps to himself, though he puts in his time at Fangtasia. (DTTW)

German shepherd shifter: No name given. A German shepherd stares at Sookie with luminous yellow eyes as she lies staked on the floor of Josephine's. (CD)

Gervaise (vampire): No other name given. After the devastation of New Orleans and Area One by Hurricane Katrina, Sheriff Gervaise hosts Sophie-Anne in his nearby Area Four. He attends the summit along with his human lover, Carla, and both perish in the hotel bombing. (Dies ATD; mentioned FDTW)

Ginger: No last name given. Fangtasia fangbanger Ginger is accidentally killed when Hallow, in her search for Eric, casts a spell on the human Fangtasia employees that causes their leg muscles to cramp up. Ginger falls, hitting her head on a bathroom sink. (DUD; dies DTTW)

Gladiola (half demon): No last name given. Gladiola is Diantha's sister and Mr. Cataliades's niece. Mr. Cataliades dispatches Gladiola with a message to Sookie, but she is intercepted and is killed by Jade Flower. Glad's body is burned by Diantha and Mr. Cataliades on Sookie's driveway. (Dies DD; mentioned ATD, DAG)

Glassport, Johan: Attorney Johan is hired by Sophie-Anne to defend her against the charges brought by the Arkansas vampires for Peter Threadgill's death. Although he preps for the case, his services prove unnecessary when the Ancient Pythoness rules in Sophie-Anne's favor. Nonetheless, Johan manages to collect his fee from Sophie-Anne's estate and return to Mexico, where he had previously served time for striking a prostitute. He is guilty of many worse things. (ATD; mentioned DAG)

Godric/Godfrey (vampire): No last name given. Just a teenager when he was turned centuries ago, tattooed Godric—or Godfrey, as he has been known for the past century—has decided that vampires are an abomination. He himself is far too fond of children, in a very unhealthy way. Believing that only his death will stop him from continuing to sin, he has allied himself with the Fellowship of the Sun. He plans to meet the sun in a ritual. He lures Farrell into the hands of the Fellowship so Farrell will die with him. Godfrey reluctantly saves Sookie from Gabe and helps her escape. Although the Fellowship of the Sun is thrown into a panic and cancels their morning ceremony, Godfrey carries through with his own plans. He meets the dawn while Sookie bears witness, believing that in his repentance he will see the face of God. (Dies LDID)

Golden, Phoebe (vampire): The Queen of Iowa, Phoebe is married to the King of Ohio, and both attend the summit at Rhodes. (ATD)

Graham, Parfit: Shreveport police chief Graham investigates the missing people after the Were war, unaware that there are motives and actions that he will never understand and bodies that he will never find. (FDTW)

Gray, Ashley: Ashley is the daughter of Merlotte's waitress Danielle. (Mentioned LDID, DAAD, DD, ATD, FDTW, DAG)

Gray, Danielle: Danielle has been Holly Cleary's best friend all through high school. She and Holly support each other through their respective divorces and raising their children. The two begin to part ways as Holly delves deeper into the Wiccan religion and each gains a steady boyfriend. (LDID, DAAD, DD, FDTW, DR; mentioned DTTW, ATD, DAG)

Gray, Mark Robert: Mark Robert is the son of Merlotte's waitress Danielle. (Mentioned LDID, DD, ATD, FDTW, DAG)

Green, Dawn: Dawn works as a barmaid at Merlotte's and is fairly easy with all males, both human and vampire. She does not object to being filmed during sex, and she enjoys it rough. Her body is found when Sam asks Sookie to stop by Dawn's apartment to check on her. (Dies DUD)

Gregory (vampire): No last name given. Gregory, known by Eric and Ocella, had to be staked after being infected by maenad Phryne's madness at the Halloween Massacre of 1876 in St. Petersburg. (Deceased; mentioned LDID, DITF)

Griesniki, Milos (vampire): A recent immigrant from the old country, Milos Griesniki gets a job bartending at Fangtasia and immediately begins to pry into the financial matters of Eric and the bar. When Eric calls for the Lord of Darkness to reveal himself at Fangtasia's Dracula Night party, Milos claims to be Vlad Tepes III, aka Dracula, and announces that he plans to stay on at Fangtasia for a year, expecting not only tribute, tithe, and vampire servants but also fresh blood from the source, with Sookie being his first meal. He attempts to glamour Sookie to obey him but is tricked by her into revealing his lack of knowledge of the burial place of the real Dracula. Staked by Sookie, Milos flakes away even as Eric and Pam defend her actions to the other attending vampires, stating that, as Milos was not really Dracula, it was he who committed a crime by pretending to be their founder, not Sookie. (Dies DN)

Gristede, Mrs.: No first name given. Mrs. Gristede's class meets in the Pony Room at the Red Ditch kindergarten. (DR)

Guglielmi, Antonio "Dago": Dago works on the road crew with Catfish and Jason and frequents Merlotte's with his friends. (DTTW, DAAD, DD)

H:

Hair of the Dog: Owned by Were Amanda Whatley and catering to shifters of all kinds, the Hair of the Dog is located in an old brick storefront near Centenary College, just off Kings Highway in Shreveport. The door is warded by a top-of-the-line go-away spell that causes any humans who approach to have an uncontrollable urge to turn around and leave, and only the aura of a shifter can negate the spell for a human until he or she is inside. After Quinn and Sookie are attacked by bitten Weres on their first date, Quinn takes her to the Hair of the Dog to inform the Shreveport pack. One of the employees at the club that night is Jannalynn Hopper, whom Sam eventually starts dating. When Amanda is killed in the Were war, the bar passes to Alcide, who retains Jannalynn as manager. (DD; mentioned FDTW, DITF, DR)

Hale, Bartlett: Adele's brother, Bartlett, takes advantage of his family connections to molest Adele's daughter, Linda; Linda's daughter, Hadley; and Sookie. He is forbidden to come to the house after Sookie manages to tell Adele what has happened. Bartlett is killed by persons unknown shortly after Sookie tells Bill of her abuse at her great-uncle's hands. He leaves Sookie money. (Dies DUD; mentioned DD, FDTW, DITF)

Hallow's coven members (shifters): Hallow's coven is made up of shifters, all of whom also drink vampire blood. They follow her lead as she makes her play for the assets of both Eric and Area Five, and seeks to destroy the Long Tooth pack. (DTTW)

Hanson, Mrs.: No first name given. Mrs. Hanson has had two car accidents since signing with John Robert Briscoe's insurance agency. (L)

Happy Cutter, the: Three blocks from the Genuine Magic Shop in the French Quarter is the Happy Cutter, a unisex hair salon where Bob Jessup gets a job when he returns to New Orleans. (Mentioned DR)

Hardaway, Cleo: Cleo runs the high school cafeteria during the day and attends orgies with her husband at night. They are infected with maenad Callisto's madness and die together at the lake house with Jan Fowler and Mike Spencer. (Dies LDID)

Hardaway, Tom: Tom and his wife, Cleo, attend the orgy at the lake house, where Sookie is able to read in Tom's mind their involvement in the death of Lafayette Reynold. Both Tom and Cleo fall victim to maenad Callisto's madness, dying on the porch with Jan Fowler and Mike Spencer. (Dies LDID)

Harley-Davidson dealership: No name given. A motorcycle dealership owned by Patrick Furnan. It not only sells Harley-Davidsons but also does repairs and sells parts and accessories that bike riders need, such as saddlebags, riding leathers, helmets, and goggles, along with a stock of

T-shirts and other authorized items with the H-D insignia. (Mentioned DAAD, FDTW)

Harrow, Matthew: Newscaster Matthew watches nervously as Patricia Crimmins announces the existence of shifters and changes into her werewolf form on camera. (DAG)

Hart, Ginjer (panther): Mel Hart's ex-wife, Ginjer, occasionally stops by Merlotte's for a margarita. According to Mel, their marriage didn't work out because they both had unconventional sexual interests. (DAG)

Hart, Mel (panther): One of the rare local panthers who chooses to live outside Hotshot, Mel Hart rents a duplex from Sam and works at Bon Temps Auto Parts. When Jason's best friend, Hoyt, becomes engaged to Holly Cleary, Mel takes his place in Jason's life. They go to bars, work on their cars—all the things guys do when they're hanging out. But Mel has a secret. He left Hotshot when he was unable to fulfill his duty to the pack by producing a full panther child with his now ex-wife, Ginjer. Mel is gay, and he has fallen in love with Jason. He stops by to see Jason one day, but he's not home. Crystal arrives and taunts him sexually. He slaps her in a fit of anger. Thinking she's dead, he tosses her into his truck and goes into Jason's house for a drink to calm his nerves. When he returns, Crystal is gone. He is as surprised as everyone else when her body is found on the cross in Merlotte's parking lot. Dermot knows what really happened and goes to Jason's house later to confront Mel, but he is unable to clearly communicate what went on and throws Mel across the room, calling him a killer. Sookie realizes the implication of Dermot's visit to Jason and his attack on Mel and confronts Mel at Jason's house after notifying Calvin. Mel admits his guilt and accepts his fate at the hands of his packmaster, Jason, Crystal's sister Dawn, and their first cousin Jacky. (Dies DAG)

Harvey (unknown): No last name given. Harvey searches Bill's house for the database but comes up empty-handed. (Mentioned CD)

Hawk shifter: No name given. A hawk narrowly misses the ceiling fan at Josephine's while flying away after shifting when Sookie is staked. (CD)

Hebert, Arthur (wolf): Arthur was the packleader of the St. Catherine Parish Weres. After his death, his wife, Priscilla, looks for a new place for her pack. (Deceased; mentioned FDTW)

Hebert, Priscilla (wolf): Widow of the St. Catherine Parish Were packmaster, Priscilla seeks a new home for her remaining pack after the destruction of Hurricane Katrina. Her attempt to instigate a war between Patrick Furnan and Alcide by killing females of the Long Tooth pack almost succeeds but is derailed when Sookie arranges a meeting between the two Weres. Even though Cal Myers, supposedly loyal to Furnan, is identified as Maria-Star Cooper's killer, both men accept that neither ordered the deaths of Maria-Star, Libby Furnan, and Christine Larrabee. Cal is revealed as Priscilla's half brother. As the Weres battle it out in wolf form, Priscilla kills Amanda and then is killed by Sam, who has wisely changed into a lion instead of a collie. (Dies FDTW)

Heffernan, Mr.: No first name given. Mr. Heffernan is the principal at Betty Ford Elementary School during Sookie's term there. (Mentioned DD)

Heidi (vampire): No last name given. Heidi, a superior tracker, is sent to Shreveport by Victor to spy on Eric. When fairies and a body are scented by the Weres in Sookie's woods, Heidi arrives to try to sort it all out. She informs Sookie that two fairies, many werewolves, and one vampire have been traipsing around, and that two bodies, one killed very recently, are buried on the land.

Heidi talks of her son, now grown and drug addicted, living in Reno, and is surprisingly gentle and careful with Hunter, kneeling to speak to him on his level and spelling out words she doesn't want him to understand. When Eric offers to allow her to move her son to Shreveport, she readily accepts and gives her loyalty to her new sheriff, taking his side against Victor in the assassination. (DITF, DR)

Hennessy, Shirley "Catfish": Jason's boss, Catfish, is never called Shirley by his men. A loyal friend, Catfish protests Andy Bellefleur's and Alcee Beck's treatment of Sookie when Jason goes missing. He also organizes the search party for the woods around Jason's house. Catfish occasionally takes his wife to Merlotte's. (DTTW, DAAD, DD, ATD, FDTW, DAG, DITF)

Hermosa, Rubio (vampire): Rubio finds a new home in Area Five after fleeing Katrina, living together in a nest in Minden with Parker and Palomino. The threesome are summoned to participate in the assassination of Victor, and Rubio does his part by staking Luis. (DR)

Herve: No last name given. Cleo Babbitt's human squeeze attends the summit with her. (ATD)

Herveaux, Alcide (wolf): A partner with his father in Herveaux and Son, AAA Accurate Surveys, Alcide, like most shifters, doesn't want to become involved in vampire affairs; but when the Shreveport vamps call in a marker on his father's gambling debts that would destroy their company, he must agree to escort Sookie to Jackson in her search for a missing Bill. He is attracted to Sookie and she to him, but just as she is sorting through her feelings of betrayal with Bill, he is sorting through his own feelings about his ex-girlfriend, Debbie Pelt. Although Alcide claims he is determined to rid himself of Debbie, he is willfully blind when it comes to her faults, even Debbie's vicious act of pushing Sookie into the trunk of a car with a starving Bill. And when Debbie lies and tells him later that Sookie and Bill have reconciled, he believes her and resumes their relationship.

He is finally forced to face reality when Bill confirms that not only did Debbie lock Sookie and him together in the trunk, but she also participated in his torture at Russell's mansion. Alcide abjures Debbie in an irrevocable ritual.

Alcide contacts Sookie again after the death of packmaster Colonel Flood, asking her to attend the funeral as a friend of the pack. He uses her presence to imply her unspoken support for his father as Colonel Flood's successor. He also wants her to read the other candidate's mind. He rationalizes that Sookie might think she owes him, as he has realized that she killed Debbie. Although he claims he doesn't care, Sookie is hurt and angered by his actions and asks him to stay away.

Alcide rushes to Sookie when her kitchen burns. He asks her to move in with him to explore their relationship, but Sookie questions whether he is fully recovered from Debbie and whether he can forgive her for Debbie's death. Alcide turns from Sookie into the arms of Were Maria-Star Cooper after his father dies during the packmaster contest with Patrick Furnan. The Were pack remains splintered by the cheating during the contest and the outcome, with Alcide heading the anti-Furnan faction.

When Maria-Star is murdered, Alcide first suspects Furnan but soon discovers that Patrick's wife is missing as well. At an arranged parley, the two are attacked by a band of Weres led by Priscilla Hebert, who wants the Long Tooth pack's territory. The Long Tooth pack unites to take down the interlopers, and when Patrick is killed, Alcide ascends to packmaster. As such, he continues viewing Sookie as a friend of the pack, and they tentatively establish a friendship. He sends Tray Dawson to guard her when she is threatened by the fae.

Alcide contacts Sookie and Bill to ask if the Long Tooth pack can run on their land at the full moon, as there is a party of human campers on the Herveaux land. Unbeknownst to him, his childhood friend, Hamilton Bond, has conspired to kill his newly appointed second, Basim al Saud, out of jealousy for not being named to the position, foolishly becoming involved with fairy Colman's plan to get Sookie in trouble with the law. Ham buries Basim's body on Sookie's land, but the body is scented by a vampire tracker sent by Eric to check the woods for intruders. Alcide; his new girlfriend, Annabelle; and pack member Jannalynn Hopper arrive to investigate. Along with Ocella, Alexei, Eric, Sookie, and Jason, they dig up the body, and Annabelle is forced to admit that she was having an affair with Basim, but she denies any involvement in his death.

The pack holds a meeting at Alcide's house, with Sookie and Jason sitting in. When they arrive, Alcide asks Sookie to act as a shaman, giving her a potion that will help her see the truth among the Weres. She identifies Ham as the culprit and new pack member Patricia Crimmins, one of the few survivors of Hebert's pack, as his partner-in-crime. Alcide spares Annabelle, but Sookie leaves the meeting knowing that Jannalynn, his newly appointed second, will successfully campaign for the deaths of Ham and Patricia.

When Alcide hears from Amelia that Sookie has broken the blood bond with Eric, he goes to Sookie's house to wait for her in her bed. He winds up falling asleep because Sookie spends the night with Eric, but Alcide expresses his desire to have a chance with her when she wakes him in the morning. He reassures her of his genuine interest when she implies that he wants her because the pack needs a shaman, but he becomes upset and leaves when she tells him she doesn't like the way he has changed since becoming packmaster. (CD, DTTW, DAAD, FDTW, DITF, DR; mentioned DD, ATD)

Herveaux, Jackson (wolf): Alcide's father, a self-made man who owns a successful surveying business, begins to gamble too much after his wife's death, paving the way for the vampires who hold his markers to exact a favor from Alcide. When Colonel Flood is killed in an accident, Jackson decides to run for packmaster, but his opponent, Patrick Furnan, uses Jackson's gambling problems to suggest that he would be unsuitable as a leader. Jackson is having an affair with Connie Babcock, his secretary.

When he escorts Christine Larrabee to Colonel Flood's funeral instead of her, Furnan persuades a scorned Connie to steal personal papers from Jackson's office in an attempt to get more dirt. Connie is caught and arrested, but the damage is done. Furnan continues to spread the word that Jackson cannot handle his own life, let alone the pack. During the packmaster contest, Jackson is declared the winner of the first two tests when Furnan is caught cheating, but the pack, torn by concerns over Jackson's personal life, votes to allow the third challenge, calling for a decisive win in battle. Furnan defeats Jackson, killing him. Jackson's body is taken to the Herveaux farm, and an accident is staged to account for his death. (Dies DAAD; mentioned CD, DD, ATD, FDTW, DITF)

Herveaux and Son, AAA Accurate Surveys: A bi-state survey company owned and operated by Jackson and Alcide Herveaux, the business has offices in Jackson, Mississippi, and in Monroe, Shreveport, and Baton Rouge, Louisiana. Their main office is in Shreveport, where they own the building housing the company headquarters, and they also keep an apartment in Jackson. After his father's death in the packmaster contest, Alcide assumes control of the company. (DTTW; mentioned CD, DAAD)

Hesterman, Brenda: Brenda and her business partner, Donald Callaway, own Splendide in Shreveport. They buy, sell, and appraise antiques. She and Donald travel to Sookie's house to appraise the items brought down from the attic, purchasing several pieces for resale in their shop. (DR)

Hob, Mr. (goblin): No first name given. The doorman and bouncer at Josephine's, short and cranky Mr. Hob guards the entry to the club and maintains strict order inside. Although his full ability is not known, he easily lifts a biker who violates the rules off the floor and causes the man's flesh to start burning as he carries him out. (CD)

Hondo (unspecified shifter): No last name given. One of the paramedics working the summit in Rhodes to care for any injuries to the attending supes. He takes care of Quinn after the weretiger is hit by the arrow thrown by Kyle Perkins. (ATD)

Hooligans: Hooligans is a strip club co-owned by fairy twins Claude and Claudine. The twins took possession of the club as partial payment when their triplet, Claudette, also a stripper, was murdered by the previous owner. A small club with a fair-sized parking lot, it boasts electric-blue siding and a shocking-pink neon sign. Claude manages the club and also strips on ladies' night. After Niall closes the door to Faery, Hooligans becomes a meeting place for exiled fae. (DR; mentioned FD, DAAD, DD, FDTW, DAG, DITF)

Hopper, Ellie: Like many teenagers, Ellie and seventeen-year-old Quinn make out in the backseat of his father's car. (Mentioned DD)

Hopper, Jannalynn (wolf): Young Jannalynn is loyal, ruthless, and a flashy dresser. Given the task of executing the fallen enemies after the Were war, she does so with a savage efficiency. Upon the death of Amanda Whatley in that war, ownership of her bar passes to Alcide, who appoints Jannalynn manager despite her youth. He further demonstrates his faith in her by naming her his second after the death of Basim al Saud. Alcide's faith in her is repaid by her absolute devotion to him. When Hamilton Bond and Patricia Crimmins admit to the murder of Basim, Jannalynn convinces Alcide that the punishment for their betrayal should be death. Even though she is a full Were, Jannalynn is "into lions" and calls Sam for a date after the battle. Although Sam seems to be enjoying their blossoming relationship, he feels that Jannalynn is not exactly a girl one takes home to meet Mom, so having already asked Sookie to accompany him to his brother's wedding, he takes her as his date instead of his new girlfriend. Jannalynn is hurt and resentful, and shows up anyway. They plan a date to discuss their relationship and decide to keep seeing each other. Jannalynn is at Merlotte's to see Sam when the four thugs hired by Sandra Pelt attack, and she throws herself into the fight, easily breaking bones to disable her target. Still brooding over Sookie's presence in Sam's life, Jannalynn encourages Alcide Herveaux, her packmaster, to steal into Sookie's bed and perhaps steal her heart after Sookie breaks the blood bond with Eric.

When Jannalynn and Sam are forced at gunpoint to take Sandra Pelt to Sookie's house, an infuriated Jannalynn sees her chance to attack Sandra when Sookie fires at her from the woods. Jannalynn finally manages to break Sandra's neck, then crushes her skull to finish the job. She is impressed that Sookie has a fairy portal in her woods, and watches curiously as Sam and Sookie force Sandra's body through the portal. (DD, FDTW, DITF, STW, DR)

Horowitz, Barry (telepath): Barry is an undisciplined telepath working as a bellboy at the Silent Shore vampire hotel in Dallas when he meets a fellow telepath for the first time. Sookie is able to send Barry a message when she is captured by the Fellowship of the Sun, giving him her location so he can notify Bill and Eric. His actions bring him to the attention of Stan Davis, who shortly becomes the King of Texas and hires Barry as a permanent part of his entourage. He is much more in control of his abilities when he sees Sookie again at the summit in Rhodes, and after the explosion, they work together to locate survivors in the wreckage. (LDID, ATD; mentioned DAG)

Hot Rain (vampire): Long Shadow's sire and grand-sire to Charles Twining, he is unhappy with the penalty levied at Eric for Long Shadow's death and seeks revenge by having Charles kill Sookie. (Mentioned DAAD)

Hotshot: Located on a crossroads about ten miles southeast of Bon Temps, Hotshot is an isolated little community, the home of a werepanther pack consisting mainly of the multigenerational Norris and Hart families. Therefore, its residents tend to have one of two basic heritages: stocky and fair with green-gold eyes, or small and dark with dark eyes. They keep to themselves and do for themselves, taking care of one another and seeing to their own justice. The roads leading into the community are not well maintained, there are no streetlights, and the people are secretive. Outsiders rarely venture into Hotshot.

Within the pack, they are all family. They take responsibility for one another. They work as a community to ensure that needs are met. They share the raising of children, considered precious in this small pack. Each member is expected to add to the pack, often more than once, which requires multiple partners, as only the first child of any full-blooded shifter pair is a full-blooded shifter. Though the panthers are not incestuous, they are inbred.

Calvin Norris, a man well respected both inside and outside the pack, is the leader of Hotshot. He does not hold this position lightly and can be ruthless when enforcing pack laws or meting out justice. When Felton Norris kidnaps Jason Stackhouse, holding him in a metal shed and repeatedly biting him to turn him into a panther, Calvin makes certain Felton pays the ultimate price in exchange for Jason and Sookie not going to the police. Needless to say, death certificates are not always filed when pack members pass away and are quietly buried behind the Tabernacle Holiness Church, where Calvin's uncle Marvin Norris is the pastor. And, in the past, the need for secrecy has sometimes overwhelmed all else: Sheriff

John Dowdy disappeared while serving a warrant in Hotshot, never to be seen again.

Calvin does not bring the pack out publicly when the shifters announce their presence during the Great Reveal, preferring to allow his panthers to choose when and to whom to disclose their second nature. But Sheriff Bud Dearborn's careful and caring handling of a grief-stricken Calvin after the death of Crystal Norris Stackhouse indicates that the secrets of Hotshot have been known for some time to at least a few. (DTTW, DAAD, ATD, FDTW; mentioned DAG, DITF)

Humphries, Tolliver: The death of Bill's friend and fellow Civil War soldier Tolliver—who was killed while trying to rescue a wounded Jebediah Bellefleur—causes Bill to loathe the Bellefleurs for the next hundred and forty-odd years. (Deceased; mentioned DUD, LDID)

I:

India: No last name given. Merlotte's new waitress, India, has cornrows and a nose piercing and is naturally cheerful. She's currently dating Lola Rushton. (DR)

Indira (vampire): No last name given. Tiny Indira puts in her time at Fangtasia, content that servitude with Eric does not require sexual favors unless she is so inclined. She is among the select vamps Eric calls to Fangtasia for the attack on Victor, and she does her part by first emasculating and then staking the new bartender, Jock, a former employee of Victor who's still loyal to his old boss. (DAAD, ATD, DR; mentioned DD)

Isaiah (vampire): No last name given. King of Kentucky Isaiah finds a Fellowship of the Sun spy in his retinue. Based on information tortured out of her, he is convinced the Fellowship of the Sun will attack the summit. He hires Britlingens as bodyguards. While at the summit, he attempts to court Sophie-Anne and is chosen to preside over her trial for the death of Peter Threadgill. He survives the disaster thanks to the Britlingens. (ATD)

Ives, Harlen (vampire): Harlen is traveling from Minnesota to New Orleans when he stops in Bon Temps for a visit with Bill and then heads to Monroe to spend some time with Diane, Liam, and Malcolm. He perishes with them when their house is set on fire by an angry mob. (Dies DUD)

J:

Jacky (panther): No last name given. Crystal's oldest first cousin, teenager Jacky participates in the Hotshot justice meted out to Mel Hart for his part in Crystal's death. (DAG)

Jada: No last name given. Jada is a new girl working at Merlotte's who, in Arlene's opinion, is better than Danielle. (DAAD)

Jade Flower (vampire): No last name given. As Peter Threadgill's loyal second, Jade Flower does everything within her power to ensure his triumph in his plan to dethrone his queen, including draining E(E)E employee Jake Purifoy in Hadley's courtyard in an attempt to discredit the queen's former lover, and tracking Mr. Cataliades's niece Gladiola to Bon Temps to kill her before she can deliver a message to Sookie.

During the melee at the queen's spring ball, Jade Flower must defend herself against Mr. Cataliades, who has discovered that she murdered his niece. By the time she is able to attack Sookie, whom she holds responsible for Peter's downfall, she is mysteriously missing one leg. She is beheaded by Bill as he comes to Sookie's aid. (Dies DD)

Jan: No last name given. Firefighter and nurse Jan responds to the fire at Sookie's house. (DAAD)

Janesha: No last name given. Octavia Fant first stays with her niece Janesha, her boyfriend, and her three children after Hurricane Katrina destroys her home. (Mentioned FDTW, DAG)

Jarvis: No last name given. The hairstylist at Janice Herveaux Phillips's beauty salon, Jarvis does Sookie's hair for her first night at Josephine's. (CD)

Jarvis, Mrs.: No first name given. Jarvis is on the phone with his mom when Sookie leaves after being styled. (Mentioned CD)

Jason Stackhouse's house: Corbett and Michelle Stackhouse built their home in Bon Temps when they were first married and expecting Jason. Left to both children after their deaths, it sat vacant until Jason moved in alone, eventually gaining sole ownership after Gran's death, when Sookie inherited her house. Jason's house is well maintained and currently painted a buff color with bright white trim. Although the house is visible from the road, the property extends several acres behind it.

A branch off of the circular driveway in the front leads to a porte cochere in the rear, and the ground slopes down from the back deck to a pond with a small pier. A makeshift shooting range in the yard is oriented so that shooters aim into the woods. Inside, the one bathroom has been fully renovated, and there is a kitchen, a small dining room, a living room, a family room, one master bedroom, and two smaller ones. (DUD, DTTW, DAAD, FDTW, DAG)

Jasper, Mary Jane: Danielle's mother, Mary Jane, and father are there to support their daughter, including picking up Ashley from school and watching both grandchildren when necessary. (Mentioned LDID, DTTW, DD, FDTW)

JB du Rone's boss: No name given. JB's boss at the gym allows JB to use the facilities to work with Sookie to keep JB happy. (Mentioned DITF)

JB du Rone's grandmother: No name given. At Tara's baby shower, JB's grandmother tells Sookie a lovely story about Gran. (Mentioned DR)

Jennings, Melba: Melba Jennings is the only African American female lawyer in Bon Temps and takes Arlene's case when she is arrested for the plot to kill Sookie and the ensuing shoot-out at the trailer. (Mentioned DAG)

Jerry: No last name given. Infected with Sino-AIDS by a lover who ultimately leaves him for a vampire, Jerry seeks to infect vampires as revenge. He attacks Sookie when she reveals his duplicity, and Bill breaks Jerry's wrist to free her. Jerry's current vampire lover, Malcolm, takes him from Bill's home to deal with him privately. Assumed deceased. (DUD)

Jerry: No last name given. Sookie is able to pick memories of hairdresser Jerry from Bethany Rogers's mind, and uses the memories to soothe the frightened girl as she attempts to read her. (Mentioned LDID)

Jessup, Bob (witch): Bob is one of the three witches Amelia hires to do the ectoplasmic reconstruction at Hadley's apartment with her. Although he looks somewhat like a Mormon missionary, Bob is actually a hairdresser with a sardonic, intellectual sexiness that catches Amelia's attention. They indulge in a night of sex afterward, rousing the next afternoon in time to alert the queen's headquarters that Sookie and Quinn have been kidnapped. Bob stays with Amelia again the night of the queen's reception, and their play takes an unexpected downturn when Amelia mistakenly transforms him into a cat. When Amelia moves to Bon Temps, Bob lives as a cat with Sookie and Amelia until Amelia's mentor, Octavia Fant, is able to transform him back to human. While in feline form, he misses the catastrophe of Hurricane Katrina, and upon his return to human form, he leaves almost immediately to reestablish contact with his family and friends.

After finding that the aunt and uncle who raised him are safe in Natchez, Bob eventually wends his way back to New Orleans, taking a job at the Happy Cutter and going to the Genuine Magic Shop just three blocks away to ask about Amelia. They reestablish their relationship. He joins his girlfriend when she travels to Bon Temps to renew the wards around Sookie's house, and he participates in the ceremony to break Sookie's blood bond with Eric. (DD, ATD, L, FDTW, DR; mentioned DAG, DITF)

Jock (vampire): No last name given. New Fangtasia employee Jock worked for Victor in Reno before moving to Shreveport to tend bar after Felicia's death. He is there to take up her role as a spy. He is on the job when Bubba sings for Victor and naturally fights on Victor's side. Although he is emasculated by Indira during the melee, he still manages to stun her with a blow to the head. He is distracted by Sookie before he can continue his attack, giving Indira time to recover and stake him. (Dies DR)

Jodi (vampire): No last name given. Vampire Jodi breaks off one of fellow vampire Michael's canines with pliers while he sleeps after he abducts and tortures the sister of one of her human employees. Sued by Michael and brought before vampire judges, including Bill and Dahlia, at the summit, Jodi pleads her case, wins, and is allowed to stake an unrepentant Michael. (ATD)

Joe: No last name given. Joe works at the Pyramid and calls the rooms to notify them of misplaced luggage that needs to be personally collected. When Sookie tries to read him while she locates a suitcase supposedly belonging to the Louisiana vampire party, she finds that Joe essentially has a metaphysical helmet around his mind, blocking his thoughts. (ATD)

Johnson, Brock and Chessie: Brock and his wife, Chessie, own the house and upholstery shop next to Tray Dawson's house and shop. (Mentioned DAG)

Jonathan (vampire): No last name given. Nevada vampire Jonathan introduces himself to Sookie at the Bellefleur-Vick wedding as a guest of Hamilton Tharp and claims to have dutifully checked in with Area Five sheriff Eric Northman, as protocol demands.

He lied. (FDTW)

Jones, Crawdad: Crawdad is the original owner of the Crawdad Diner with Perdita Jones. After his death, his wife sells their recipes along with the diner to Ralph Tooten in order to keep the name Crawdad on the sign. (Deceased; mentioned DITF)

Jones, Kenya: Built like an Amazon, Kenya is the opposite of her patrolman partner, Kevin, in almost every way, but they work well together, eventually beginning a romantic relationship that culminates with them moving in together. (DUD, DTTW, DAAD, DD, DAG, DITF; mentioned LDID, CD, DR)

Jones, Perdita: Perdita is the former co-owner of the Crawdad Diner with her husband, Crawdad. When she sells the diner to Ralph Tooten, she sells him the recipes as well with the stipulation that the diner keep Crawdad's name. (Mentioned DITF)

Josephine's: Known as Club Dead among the Weres, vampire-owned Josephine's is located on the outskirts of downtown Jackson, Mississippi, on or near Amite Street. The supes leave their keys in their cars, which then drive away on their own so that the streets in front of the bar are kept deserted. The club is surrounded by an ominous, watchful air; most humans experience a feeling of dread when they approach the door, and if they do get in, they are treated to a costly cover charge, terrible drinks, and poor service. Those who manage to stay soon find themselves on the sidewalk with no memories of leaving the bar.

The doorman and bouncer is Mr. Hob, a goblin, who treats all strangers with suspicion. The interior of Josephine's looks a lot like any other bar: dim lighting, low music, glasses suspended on racks over a large square bar surrounded by polished bar stools, a small dance floor and stage just to the left of the bar. The club is run as a neutral ground, with specific rules on how both vampires and shifters are to behave: "No Changing on the Premises," "No Biting of Any Kind," "No Live Snacks." Alcide Herveaux escorts Sookie to Club Dead to gather information on Bill's whereabouts after his kidnapping. During their second visit, Sookie picks up the thoughts of a Fellowship of the Sun member determined to become a martyr and is staked when she confronts the assassin. (CD; mentioned DTTW, DAAD, ATD)

Josephus, Dr. (unspecified shifter): No first name given. Luna Garza asks for fellow shifter Dr. Josephus when she and Sookie are taken to the hospital in Dallas after the car accident caused by Sarah Newlin and Polly Blythe. Dr. Josephus treats Sookie and releases her in short order, arranging transportation with two Weres to get her safely back to the Silent Shore Hotel. (LDID)

Julia: No last name given. Sookie's great-aunt Julia embroidered the pattern on the edge of the bedspread Sookie still uses. (Deceased; mentioned DAAD)

K:

Kelly: No last name given. Halleigh's cousin Kelly is a member of her bridal party. (FDTW)

Kelner, Tawny: Dallas police detective Tawny Kelner grimly investigates the murder of Bethany Rogers, aware that she worked at a vampire bar but convinced that the murder was actually a message to vampires, not committed by them. (LDID)

Kent, Kendell (wolf): Kendell works as a waiter at Les Deux Poissons and is almost certainly the person who notifies Lucky Owens that Sookie has left the restaurant after her dinner with Niall, setting the scene for Lucky to make an attempt on her life. Alcide is saddened by the news, thinking Kendell has sided with Patrick Furnan. In reality, both Kendell and Lucky are working for Priscilla Hebert. (FDTW)

Kenya Jones's brother: No name given. Kenya's brother is not happy when she moves in with Kevin. (Mentioned DAG)

Kershaw, Angela Beck: Alcee's cousin and Dove's sister, Angela went to school with Sookie and is now married with a son. (Mentioned FDTW)

Kershaw, Maurice: Maurice is married to Dove Beck's sister Angela. (Mentioned FDTW)

Keyes, Kennedy: Kennedy finds her way into Merlotte's after serving time for manslaughter, having killed a man who brutally abused her. She eagerly accepts Sam's job offer, studying to learn bartending and quickly adjusting to her new position. Worried that Kennedy will be hassled, not just because of her past but because she is a woman, Sam arranges for Danny Prideaux to come in as a bouncer when Kennedy works nights. She and Danny begin spending time together outside of work, and they are off duty in the bar when a firebomb is thrown through the window. Neither is injured, but Kennedy wonders if the attack was aimed at her, possibly carried out by a member of her abuser's family in retaliation for her past crime. (DITF, DR)

Khan: No other name given. After Lafayette's death, his friend Khan takes over as cook at Merlotte's. (Mentioned LDID)

Khan, Mustapha (wolf): The former KeShawn Johnson has obviously faced hard times but has come out on top as Mustapha Khan, proud to be his own man. Bubba recommends the lone wolf to Eric after learning of the death of Bobby Burnham, and Eric hires him as his assistant because Mustapha knows how to keep his mouth shut and hates Victor Madden, although Eric does not know why. Mustapha gladly participates in Victor's demise, arming himself with a long knife and having his human friend Warren as a shooter on the outside in case anyone escapes. When vampire Luis does run from the club, a bullet from Warren sends him back to Mustapha's blade. Luis puts up a fight but is finally staked by Rubio, and Mustapha then goes to the aid of Palomino and Parker, who are fighting Unknown Vampire #2. Mustapha beheads the vampire in one swing. After the battle, an injured Pam asks to drink from him, and he agrees, knowing that it comes with the job. (DR)

Kinman, Heather (fox): One of Sweetie Des Arts's victims, nineteen-year-old Heather Kinman is shot and killed on the sidewalk outside the local Sonic while drinking a chocolate milkshake. She had just graduated from high school and was working at her first job at Bon Temps Office Supplies. (Mentioned, dies DAAD)

Kiss of Pain, the: An S&M club in Rhodes, the Kiss of Pain specializes in supplying its clientele with services dedicated to "the particular enjoyment of those who enjoy their pleasures on the darker side." Gervaise takes Carla there during the conference. (Mentioned ATD)

Kolinchek, Dusty: Dusty is continuing the family yard-work business, and his customers include Victor Madden. (Mentioned DR)

Krause, Lindsey: Lindsey works at Merlotte's but quits to move to Little Rock. (Mentioned DUD)

L:

Labeff, Jeff: Jeff gets into a shouting match in Merlotte's with Louisiana Tech student Mark Duffy that soon gets out of hand. He returns the next night to apologize and is warned by Sam to behave in his bar. (DAAD)

Lancaster, Elva Deene: Sid Matt's wife, Elva Deene, passes away before the shifters' Great Reveal. Her husband believes she would have enjoyed finding out about even more supes among them. (Mentioned DUD, LDID; dies; mentioned DAG)

Lancaster, Sid Matt: When Jason is suspected of the murders of several local women, he and Sookie hire Sid Matt, who is said to be the most aggressive trial lawyer in Renard Parish. His experience isn't necessary once Rene confesses to the crimes. Sid Matt takes the Great Reveal of the shifters in stride, even taking on werewolves as clients, and wishes that his wife, Elva Deene, had lived to see it. Suffering from cancer, he knows he'll be joining her soon. (DUD, LDID, DTTW, DD, DAG; mentioned FDTW)

Landry: No first name given. Pyramid security officer Landry overreacts when Sookie questions procedure during the investigation into the deaths of the Arkansas vampires, roughing up Sookie and handcuffing her. Landry's boss, Todd Donati, instructs her to release Sookie and apologize in writing. (ATD)

Larrabee, Christine (wolf): The widow of the packmaster preceding Colonel Flood, Christine would prefer to stay neutral in the contest for Flood's successor, but Jackson Herveaux calls on their friendship for her support. When it comes time for the actual contest, Christine agrees with Alcide that Sookie should be invited to serve as a witness and subtly encourages Sookie to use her talents to ensure an honest competition. Christine is among the females of the pack killed by Priscilla's wolves in their attempt to take over Shreveport. (DAAD; mentioned, dies FDTW)

La Salle, Truman: The fire chief of the city of Bon Temps, Truman and his crew respond to the firebombing at Merlotte's even though the bar is outside the city limits. (DR)

Lattesta, Tom: FBI Special Agent Lattesta travels from Rhodes to question Sookie about her involvement in the rescues at the Pyramid of Gizeh hotel. He and Agent Weiss are at her house when she gets the call about Crystal. They consider investigating the murder as a possible hate crime.

Lattesta doesn't trust Sookie but does believe that there is something different about her. He also knows about shifters even before the Great Reveal and has sent Antoine Lebrun in as an unwilling informant. When his interest in Sookie is stymied by powerful higher-ups (influenced by Niall and his money), Lattesta is resentful and vows to renew his pursuit if he is able to tie her to any new investigations. (DAG, DITF)

Laveau, Marie (voodoo queen): Among the vampires of New Orleans, legend has it that Marie Laveau can be called on for favors by marking her tomb in St. Louis Cemetery #1 with three Xs, the blood of the dead, and words of magic. Hadley is attempting this ritual when she is killed by Waldo. (Deceased; mentioned OWA, DD)

Lebrun, Antoine: Left homeless by Katrina, Antoine is arrested after stealing a car and unwillingly makes a deal with FBI Agent Lattesta to avoid jail. Agent Lattesta, aware of the existence of shifters and certain that they will come out, orders Antoine to spy on Sam—and Sookie. He takes a job as a short-order cook at Merlotte's but determines to rid himself of Lattesta's presence in his life and is relieved when Sookie accidentally reads his dilemma from his own mind. He confesses all to Sam and Sookie, promising not to give Lattesta any more information, happy to keep his job and new life in Bon Temps. Antoine is working the night of the firebombing and reacts quickly to shut down the appliances and protect the kitchen. (DAG, DITF, DR)

Leclerq, Sophie-Anne (vampire): Sophie-Anne begins her life as Judith in a small village in northwest Europe approximately eleven hundred years ago. When she is around twelve years old, an illness decimates her village and she is forced into prostitution by the only other survivor, a slightly older boy named Clovis. They are camped in the woods when they are found by Alain, a vampire, who immediately drains Clovis but decides to spare Judith to use as a companion, continuing to prostitute her to pay for her upkeep, all the while promising to turn her. Alain is taken captive in a village that he had visited before, where he is recognized for what he is. Judith is left unbound as she is clearly human and a victim of Alain's abuse, so she sneaks into the hut he is being held in and bargains with him to be turned in exchange for setting him free when she rises. Alain begins the process, but the village priest returns from a trip while she remains buried in the earth. Alain is killed before she awakens. She wanders alone for a few years until she finds a young boy being abused and turns him for companionship. Andre becomes her devoted servant and lover for centuries. By the time she works her way through the vampire hierarchy to be named the Queen of Louisiana, she has become Sophie-Anne Leclerq and keeps her background private. She meets Hadley Delahoussaye Savoy and begins an affair with her, eventually turning her. Hadley tells Sophie-Anne of her past, including tales of the unusual abilities of her cousin Sookie, setting in motion the chain of events that sends Bill to Bon Temps in the service of his queen.

Sophie-Anne arranges a political marriage with Peter Threadgill, the King of Arkansas, but Peter has plans to take over her holdings by proving that she has given another lover one of his wedding gifts—a diamond bracelet actually stolen by Hadley in a fit of jealousy. When Sookie finds the bracelet and returns it to Sophie-Anne in time for her spring party, Peter starts a war anyway, leading to the defeat of the Arkansas vampires and his own death at Andre's hands. Sophie-Anne faces a trial for the death of her husband at the summit in Rhodes. She is found innocent and granted the kingdom of Arkansas. Her relief is short-lived, as she is badly injured in the bombing, losing both her legs. She is still trying to recover when Felipe de Castro wages his campaign to take over Louisiana and Arkansas, killing her and her remaining sheriffs save for Eric. (OWA, DD, ATD; mentioned CD, DAG, DITF, DR; mentioned, dies FDTW)

Lee (fairy): No other name given. One of Breandan's followers. He and a few brownies try to ambush Claudine, who ably defends herself and leaves them all dead. (Dies DAG)

Lee, Maxwell (vampire): One of the vampires owing loyalty to Eric, Maxwell, an investment banker, dutifully puts in his time at Fangtasia. In his free time, he enjoys a close shave from Barry Barber at Hooligans. He helps Pam evacuate Sookie and Bill after the battle with Breandan and his followers at the hospital, and Maxwell does his part in the assassination of Victor by staking Victor's bodyguard Antonio. (DAAD, ATD, DAG, DITF, DR; mentioned FD)

Leeds, Jack: Private investigator Jack Leeds and his wife, Lily, are hired by the Pelts to find out what happened to their daughter Debbie. After interviewing many people, including Sookie, they inform the family that, as there are no leads, they cannot continue with the case. They are later hired by Mr. Cataliades, who is handling Gordon and Barbara Pelt's estate after their deaths, and are told to be in Merlotte's at an exact time to inform Sookie that Sandra Pelt is gunning for her. While they are there, four toughs, hired by Sandra, come into the bar and start trouble. When one of the thugs pulls a knife and another charges, Jack draws his gun but is shot in the arm by a third. After the assailants are subdued and the authorities arrive, Jack and Lily leave for the hospital so that Jack can be treated. (DAAD, DR; mentioned DD)

Leeds, Lily Bard: Lily and her husband, Jack, are investigating the disappearance of Debbie Pelt, but when there are no leads, they inform the family that the case is cold. Sookie is able to read from Lily's mind that she knows people are capable of horrible things, a knowledge Sookie sadly shares. The couple returns to Bon Temps when they are hired by Mr. Cataliades to warn Sookie that Sandra Pelt, who has been in jail for assault and battery, has been released and is after Sookie. Given a precise time to be at Merlotte's, the Leedses are present when the four men hired by Sandra enter the bar. Jack is shot in the resulting mayhem, and Lily coldly disarms and disables his attacker, furious at her spouse's injury, however minor. She takes Jack to the hospital herself after the authorities arrive. (DAAD, DR; mentioned DD)

Lemay, Layla Larue (vampire): Partners in dance and partners in undeath, Layla and Sean O'Rourke work for Blue Moon Productions, putting on dance shows with both vampires and humans, including dancing at the Rhodes summit. Although most vampire couples, even makers and children, don't remain together very long, Layla and Sean seem to be beating the odds. Layla and Sean have their own novella. (ATD)

Lena: No last name given. Lena works as a bathroom attendant at the Pyramid of Gizeh yet despises the vampires who are the hotel's main clientele as well as the humans who associate with them. (ATD)

Lenier, Cindy: Rene's sister, Cindy, is working in a hospital cafeteria in Baton Rouge and dating a vampire when she is killed by her brother. (Deceased; mentioned DUD)

Lenier, Rene: Rene, one of Arlene's ex-husbands, works on the road crew with Jason. He kills his sister, Cindy, because she is dating a vampire. In his madness, he begins to target other women with vampire lovers. After several other murders he goes after Sookie, but when she is not home he murders Gran instead. He does not waver in his intent, however, waiting for his chance, finally cutting her phone line one night when she is alone and catching her as she runs through the cemetery toward the safety of Bill's house. Although he beats her savagely, Sookie is able to grab his knife from his belt and stab him. Rene survives to be tried for his crimes. (DUD; mentioned ATD)

Lennox, Janella: Janella accompanies Liam, Malcolm, and Diane to Bill's house, casually performing a sexual act with Liam on the couch. (DUD)

Leonard: No last name given. Sam's friend Leonard joins other supporters to watch over the Merlottes as they are leaving for the Lisle-Merlotte wedding ceremony. (STW)

Leopard shifter: No name given. A British tennis player's mother comes out as a leopard during the Great Reveal. (DAG)

Leveto, Bev (vampire): Co-host of *The Best Dressed Vamp* with Todd Seabrook, Bev is relentlessly enthusiastic as she carries on with Devon Dawn's fashion makeover while Todd, suffering from a torn throat courtesy of Devon, heals on the floor. (DAG)

Liam (vampire): No last name given. Vampire Liam finds plenty of willing human females as he and nest mates Malcolm and Diane party their way through towns around Bon Temps. The trio's total disregard of propriety makes them the focus of increasing rage by locals who suspect that vampires are responsible for the recent deaths in the area. He dies with his nest mates, vampire visitor Harlen Ives, and an unidentified human female when their house in Monroe is burned down. (Dies DUD)

Lisle, Angie: The younger sister of Craig Merlotte's fiancée, Deidra, Angie rings the church bell with Sookie's help to announce the wedding, and turns on the outside speaker before rejoining her sister to stand as one of Deidra's bridesmaids. The other two bridesmaids, Deidra's friends, backed out after Bernie's shooting and the revelation that Deidra's future mother-in-law and brother-in-law are shifters. (STW)

Lisle, Jared: Jared, whose army unit is shipping out to Afghanistan in a month, keeps watch over the church and the wedding party on his sister's wedding day, alert for the first signs of trouble. (STW)

Lisle, Mr.: No first name given. Mr. and Mrs. Lisle are shocked when they discover that Craig's mother and brother are shifters, and they insist on postponing the wedding while the young lovers get both marital and genetic counseling. Although they genuinely like Craig, they will probably always view his family with trepidation. When Mr. Lisle arrives at the altar after walking his daughter down the aisle, he quietly suggests to Brother Arrowsmith that he lead the attendants in prayer, knowing it will be heard outside as well. (STW; mentioned DAG, DITF)

Lisle, Mrs.: No first name given. Deidra's mother and father are taken aback when Craig's mother and brother are revealed as shifters, and demand that the engaged couple delay their wedding until they receive marital and genetic counseling. They like Craig and the Merlotte family, but will always be a bit leery around them. (STW; mentioned DAG, DITF)

Littrell, Kempton: Father Littrell holds Holy Eucharist in the small Episcopal church in Clarice every two weeks and visits Bon Temps on those weekends to have dinner with Catholic priest Father Riordan, who comes to town on Saturdays to celebrate mass. He officiates at the Bellefleur weddings. (DD, FDTW)

Lizbet (vampire): No last name given. Voluptuous Lizbet works at Fangtasia. (FDTW)

Lochlan (fairy): No last name given. Lochlan is Neave's brother and lover, and they are both followers of Breandan and enemies of Niall, Sookie's great-grandfather. Lochlan and Neave kidnap Sookie on Breandan's orders to force Niall to step down as Prince of Faery. The siblings murdered Sookie's grandfather, Fintan Brigant, and also killed Crystal, Jason Stackhouse's wife, and her unborn child. Lochlan and Neave joyously torture Sookie for an hour before she is rescued by Bill and Niall, with Niall beheading Lochlan during the fight. (Dies DAG; mentioned DITF)

Long Shadow (vampire): Fangtasia bartender Long Shadow foolishly embezzles money from the bar instead of approaching Eric for a loan. His duplicity is discovered when Eric has Sookie brought to the bar to read his human employees. She is able to discern the truth by penetrating the glamour Long Shadow has used on a waitress. Attacking Sookie in a fury, he is staked by Eric.

His maker, Hot Rain, mourns his loss and is not satisfied by the monetary penalty paid by Eric, so he sends his "grandchild" to seek vengeance.

The attempt is not successful and ends in yet another loss to Hot Rain. (Dies DUD; mentioned DAAD)

Loomis, Audrina: A Louisiana native, Audrina takes a job as a book-keeper at Vic's Redneck Roadhouse when she returns to the Shreveport area with her boyfriend, Colton, to be closer to her grandmother. Loyal to her lover, whose mother was murdered by Victor, she joins Colton, Sookie, Eric, and Eric's vampires in planning and carrying out the assassinations of Victor and his crew. Audrina is killed in the melee at Fangtasia. (Dies DR)

Ludwig, Dr. Amy (unknown): A very short, hunchbacked woman, Dr. Amy Ludwig is knowledgeable in both human and supernatural medicine and specializes in treating supernaturals—and those attacked by the supernatural. She is also notoriously ill-tempered and has been known to employ a Were as her chauffeur and (presumably) bodyguard.

Dr. Ludwig first encounters Sookie when summoned to treat her after Callisto's attack. Sookie is appalled when Dr. Ludwig licks the maenad's poison from her back, but the good doctor knows best. After a massive blood transfusion, Sookie is healed with a minimum of scarring. They meet again during the packmaster contest, and when Crystal later suffers a miscarriage, Sookie calls on Dr. Ludwig for help.

It is to her hospital for supernatural patients that Sookie is taken after her rescue from Lochlan and Neave, along with a gravely ill Bill and a mortally wounded Tray Dawson, and it is there that the final confrontation between Niall and Breandan takes place. (LDID, DAAD, DD, DAG; mentioned DITF)

Luis (vampire): No last name given. The taller of the two vampires Sookie mentally dubs the bondage Bobbsey Twins for their brief leather working attire, Luis closely guards Victor at Vampire's Kiss. He and his partner, Antonio, escort Eric, Pam, and Sookie into the parking lot as they leave the bar. The guards voice dissatisfaction with Victor's rule, attempting to lure Eric into betraying him, but they are spurned by a shrewd Eric.

Luis and Antonio enter Fangtasia first on the night of Bubba's performance, carefully checking out the club. As drinks are served, Luis samples a random glass before any of the others drink and then takes up position at the front door. He and Antonio are captivated by Bubba's show, but he reacts quickly when Eric attempts to stake Victor, rushing to his master's defense. He does try to leave Fangtasia but is driven back in by Warren, who shoots him in the shoulder. Although wounded, he puts up a fight and is finally dispatched by Rubio. (Dies DR)

Lundy, Sally: Vigilant Sally is John Robert Briscoe's loyal clerk and is the only person who figures out that Greg Aubert is hogging the luck of the insurance agents in Bon Temps. Amelia is able to cast a spell to make both Sally and John Robert forget Sally's assertions. (L)

Lyle (vampire): No last name given. Lyle attends the Fangtasia birthday party for Dracula while visiting from Alexandria to learn about running a vampire club. (DN)

Lynley-Chivers, Dahlia (vampire): Dahlia is a good choice to be a judge at the vampire trials at the Rhodes summit, listening to the testimony of Jodi and Michael and asking the questions that enable her to come to a unanimous decision with her fellow judges, including Bill. She survives the explosion at the hotel. The petite vampire stars in her own set of short stories. (ATD)

Lynx shifter: No name given. Sookie is eyed by a lynx after she is staked at Josephine's. (CD)

Lynx shifter: No name given. When a grandfather comes out during the Great Reveal, his granddaughter feels betrayed. She's also not pleased that her beautician is a coyote. (DAG)

Lyudmila, Ana (vampire): Although not one of the vamps who attack Pam at Vampire's Kiss, Ana Lyudmila openly ignores both Eric's second-in-command and Sookie as they enter with Eric until Sookie reminds her of her manners. She attends Bubba's performance as part of Victor's retinue but sits off alone, bored, and is the first to fall during the assassination, courtesy of a drink delivered by Thalia. (Dies DR)

M:

Madden, Victor (vampire): Victor Madden cheerfully announces himself when he arrives at Sookie's house the night of the takeover by Nevada king Felipe de Castro, secure in the knowledge that his side has prevailed thus far. He is willing to burn down both Fangtasia and Sookie's house if Eric and Bill don't capitulate. For a time, Victor remains in New Orleans to oversee Area One personally, but eventually he sends Felipe de Castro's representative back to Nevada and attempts to watch over the entire state himself as he begins to consolidate his power.

Victor witnesses Sookie's presentation of the knife to Eric, as Eric planned. Victor knows that she is Eric's wife and that Felipe has extended his protection to Sookie. But when Sookie asks for help while she is being hunted by Breandan's people, Victor ignores Eric's petition for her protection. When Bill calls Eric with the news that Sookie has been kidnapped, Victor chains Eric and restrains Pam to keep them from going to her aid, unwilling to let the vampires get involved in the Fae War. At first he pretends to disbelieve that Felipe has made any promises to Sookie. And when Pam is finally able to contact the king, Victor tells Felipe he had forgotten that Eric and Sookie are married. Felipe forces Victor to let Eric go to her aid.

The ambitious vampire continues to amass more power and begins plotting to discredit Eric, the only sheriff left from Sophie-Anne's regime. Unwilling to allow Eric to have use of Sookie's telepathic ability and worried about her powerful grandfather, he secretly sends his second, Bruno Brazell, and a female vampire named Corinna to waylay Sookie and Pam. Sookie and Pam prevail and cover their tracks. When his two vampires don't show up for work, Victor can make no accusations against the Area Five vamps or Sookie, as Bruno and Corinna were never officially there. Although Victor is named regent of the state, he soon moves his power base to Area Five, opening Vampire's Kiss and Vic's Redneck Roadhouse while living in a mansion between Musgrave and Toniton. He continues to bait Eric, summoning him for a meeting at Vampire's Kiss and then preventing Pam from checking security, bringing Pam's sickly human lover to the bar in an effort to goad her to react, rubbing fairy blood on glasses in the hope that Eric and Pam will drink from them and cause problems. Victor's actions cement the decision that he must die, and he is lured to Fangtasia by the promise of a performance by Bubba. An ardent fan, Victor does indeed get to hear his idol sing. But the performance is cut short when Eric and his supporters make their move. In the ensuing fight, Victor meets his final death at Pam's hands. (FDTW, DAG; dies DR; mentioned TB, DITF)

Maimonides, Simon (demon): Brother-in-law to Mr. Cataliades, Simon, also a lawyer, represents the state of Arkansas in the murder trial of Sophie-Anne, accused of killing her signed-and-sealed spouse, Peter Threadgill, King of Arkansas. (ATD)

Malcolm (vampire): No last name given. Vampire Malcolm brings his human Jerry with him to Bill's when he, Liam, and Diane visit, offering Bill a taste of the real thing. When it is revealed that Jerry knows that he has Sino-AIDS, one of the few diseases that can infect vampires, Malcolm takes his human lover away to deal with him privately. Jerry has been disposed of by the time Malcolm, Diane, and Liam are incinerated along with Harlen Ives—a vampire visiting on his way to New Orleans—and an unidentified human female when their house is set on fire. (Dies DUD)

Marianne: No last name given. Sookie's high school friend deserts her on a senior trip to Six Flags in Dallas to pair up with fellow classmate Dennis Engelbright. (Mentioned LDID)

Marley, Tyrese: Tyrese is Copley Carmichael's bodyguard and chauffeur. (FDTW)

Marriot, Jay: Jeff's twin brother, Jay, and their mother, Justine, search desperately for answers about Jeff's death but accept his guilt when his car is found on a side road across from Sookie's driveway. (DAAD)

Marriot, Jeff: Jeff Marriot is killed by Charles Twining and set up to take the blame for the fire at Sookie's house. (Dies DAAD)

Marriot, Justine: Jeff Marriot's mother, Justine, is devastated by his death and the report of his arson of Sookie's house. (DAAD)

Martinez, Julio (wolf): An airman from Barksdale Air Force Base, Shreveport pack member Julio is one of the local victims of the Were war. (Dies FDTW)

Mary: No last name given. Mary and Denissa are planning on singing at the Lisle-Merlotte wedding. Although Mary attends the rehearsal in the morning, she doesn't show up for the service, either unwilling or unable to make her way through the protesters. (STW)

Mason, Everlee: Gran's friend Everlee likes to call with all the local gossip. (Mentioned DUD)

Maude (vampire): No last name given. The Queen of Minnesota, Maude and her husband, the King of Wisconsin, attend the summit at Rhodes. (ATD)

Mayfield, Hod: Hod and Kelvin are hired to kidnap Sookie but fail in their assignment when she hides at Bill's house. They injure Dermot while looking for her, so he and Bellenos hunt them down and take their heads. Hod leaves behind his wife, Marge. (Dies DR)

Mayfield, Kelvin: Having been hired to kidnap Sookie, Kelvin and Hod knock Dermot out while searching for her, but she successfully hides at Bill's house. The two men are hunted down and beheaded by Dermot and Bellenos. Kelvin leaves three children. (Dies DR)

Mayhew, Darryl: Prior to the murders by Rene Lenier, the most recent murder in Bon Temps was the shooting of Sue Mayhew by her husband, Darryl. (Mentioned DUD)

Mayhew, Dixie (panther): Dixie Mayhew, Dixon's fraternal twin sister, has the dark, almost black, eyes of many of the Hotshot panthers. She and Dixon stand guard in the Grainger hospital lobby as Calvin recovers, and they continue watching over him after he is released. When Victor Madden moves to a mansion located between Musgrave and Toniton, he hires the twins as his daytime guards. (DAAD; mentioned DR)

Mayhew, Dixon (panther): Dixon takes after the other side of the Hotshot panthers, with lighter hair and a stocky build. He and his fraternal twin, Dixie, are stationed in the Grainger hospital lobby after Calvin is shot, and they guard him while he recovers at his home in Hotshot. The siblings are hired by Victor Madden to watch over him during the day at his mansion situated between Musgrave and Toniton. (DAAD; mentioned DR)

Mayhew, Sue: Prior to Rene Lenier's murders, Sue's death was the most recent murder in Bon Temps. She was shot by her husband. (Deceased; mentioned DUD)

McKenna: No last name given. McKenna works part-time as Tara's assistant at Tara's Togs. (DTTW, ATD, DR; mentioned DAG, DITF, IIHAH)

Melanie (vampire): No last name given. Petite Melanie is one of Sophie-Anne's trusted guards, along with Chester and Rasul. Both she and Chester are casualties of Hurricane Katrina. (DD; dies; mentioned ATD)

Mendoza, Sister: Deputy Mendoza has been friends with Sam for a long time, and her affection hasn't wavered. Even though they are off duty, Sister (yes, that's her name) and her partner, Tony, stand guard at Bernie's house while the family goes to the rehearsal. (STW)

Merlotte, Bernadette "Bernie" (pure shifter): The mother of Mindy, Craig, and Sam, Bernie remarries about two years after the death of Sam's father and keeps her shifter status a secret, making excuses to explain her absence on full-moon nights. As they watch the Great Reveal on television, Bernie finally tells her husband, Don, her secret and shifts in front of him, but Don does not react as she hopes: He shoots her. He is charged and taken into custody, and they divorce while he remains incarcerated awaiting his trial, unable to make bail.

Bernie is working as a receptionist/secretary at an elementary school when she is shot. They hire a replacement for her while she heals, but she's not at all certain she'll still have a job when the new school year starts. Longtime friends become strangers, but she remains determined to see her son Craig safely married even as her town struggles with the presence of shifters in their midst. (STW; mentioned FDTW, DAG, DITF)

Merlotte, Craig: Craig, Sam's brother, has plans to get married when the shifters reveal themselves, but his engagement is put on hold while his fiancée's family adjusts to the fact that his brother and mother are shifters. Like his older brother, Craig proudly served his time in the military and now does tech support for a large accounting firm in Houston after graduating from UT Dallas. (STW; mentioned FDTW, DAG, DITF)

Merlotte, Deidra Lisle: Pretty Deidra is married to Craig, Sam's brother. Although her parents are uncertain about the shifters in their new son-in-law's family, Deidra is not worried about the effects on her future children. She's currently training to become an EMT but may have to put her career on hold for a bit as she and Craig start their new life together by preparing for the baby that's already on the way. (STW; mentioned FDTW, DAG, DITF)

Merlotte, Sam (pure shifter): Sam Merlotte did his duty for his country, serving in the army for four years before buying his bar with money left after the death of his father, a former military man and pure shifter himself, and settling in Bon Temps. A rare pure shifter, Sam can become anything he wants but prefers the form of a collie, and it is in this form that Sookie takes him home from the bar, thinking he is really a dog. Sam fully intends to wake first and leave, but he oversleeps and surprises Sookie in her bed. Sam tells her about himself and also informs her that vampires are really dead.

When Callisto arrives, he spends time with the maenad, offering his companionship as tribute, and they enjoy their romps in the woods around Bon Temps together.

Sam watches over Sookie as she goes deeper and deeper into the supernatural world. He's especially worried about her involvement with vampires. Although he normally remains neutral in supernatural goings-on, he accompanies Sookie to the parley between Alcide and Furnan and changes into a lion to protect her when they are attacked by Priscilla Hebert and her Weres. He is then drawn into vampire affairs when he is captured by Sigebert, who, seeking revenge on Eric and Felipe, finds them in Merlotte's parking lot. Freed by Sookie, Sam is saddened by the fact that he was attacked walking the short distance from his bar to his trailer and worries what more will come.

When the shifters announce the Great Reveal on TV, Sam and Tray Dawson shift at the same time in Merlotte's. Across the world shifters are revealing themselves, including Sam's mother, who is shot by her second husband when she shifts in front of him. Sam rushes to her side, leaving Sookie to manage the bar in his absence. While he is gone, Crystal is found crucified in the parking lot. Like many people, Sam wonders whether she was killed because she was a shifter or because of her actions. He returns as quickly as possible to take over from Sookie and finds out that she has unwittingly married Eric. He reacts badly. His overall concern for her grows as her new involvement with the fae leads to her kidnapping and torture.

The wedding of Sam's brother, Craig, has been postponed as Craig's fiancée's family struggles with the shifter aspect of their future son-in-law's family, and Sam continues to hope for a new date to be set. Having asked Sookie if she would accompany him months before, he confirms that she will attend with him even after he begins dating Jannalynn Hopper. Sam fears that Were Jannalynn is too intense for his family. When the wedding finally takes place, the families are faced with protests but wind up surrounded by shifters who have come from all around to offer support and protection. Jannalynn shows up unannounced, hurt and angry that Sam didn't think she was appropriate to bring to a family function, and the two agree to discuss their relationship when they both get home. They do and decide to continue dating.

Sam is already worried about the future of his bar when a firebomb is thrown through the front window. Damages and injuries are minimal, and he is quickly able to reopen, but business continues to slide as customers are drawn to Vic's Redneck Roadhouse, a new bar that Victor Madden has opened nearby. Sam's problems increase when four thugs high on vampire blood enter Merlotte's, intent on causing trouble and taking Sookie. Sam, Jannalynn, an off-duty Andy Bellefleur, and the suspiciously well-placed and well-timed private detectives Jack and Lily Leeds subdue the men. The motive behind both attacks is eventually revealed when a wild-eyed Sandra Pelt shows up at Merlotte's, publicly admitting that she has been attempting to kill Sookie. With Sam's help, Terry Bellefleur manages to disable Sandra, and she is taken first to the hospital and then to jail, but she manages to escape. Struggling with the bar's mounting costs and lack of business, Sam reluctantly accepts a sizable loan from Sookie to tide the bar over. He and Jannalynn are spending the afternoon together at his trailer when they are accosted by Sandra and held at gunpoint. She forces Sam to call Sookie to lure her to his trailer, but sensing something is wrong, Sookie has Sam drive out to her house instead. When the trio arrives, Jannalynn takes advantage of a distraction and viciously attacks Sandra while Sam and Sookie stay on the fringes, trying to help. Sam's nose is broken when he grabs Sandra's hair and she punches him, but Jannalynn ultimately gets the upper hand and breaks Sandra's neck, then crushes her skull to finish the job. Worried about the ramifications of reporting the death, Sam and Sookie decide to dispose of the body instead and, followed by a wounded Jannalynn, carry Sandra into the woods to the fairy portal and shove her through. After returning to the house, Jannalynn sets Sam's broken nose before the pair leave for his trailer, disposing of Sandra's rifle along the way.

When Tara and JB du Rone decide to renovate their bungalow to make a room for their new twins, Sam agrees to help and then gets some tips from Terry Bellefleur. As he is tearing down a wall, Sam finds the hammer used to murder Isaiah Wechsler in the 1930s. The handling of the hammer disturbs the murderer's spirit, and both the adults and the babies react to the negative energy in the house. JB and Tara's nanny, Quiana Wong, is a psychic who is able to channel the spirit and realizes that his bones must be buried nearby. Sam shifts to a bloodhound to scent the area and is able to locate the remains in the yard. Sookie and Quiana work together to identify the killer as the youngest son of the Summerlins, the family that lived in the house at the time. He was secretly buried in the yard by his parents after committing suicide. After the bones are uncovered and reinterred in

Sookie's family plot, the spirit finally rests, and Sam and JB make plans to continue the renovations. (DUD, LDID, CD, DTTW, FD, DN, DAAD, DD, ATD, FDTW, DAG, DITF, STW, DR, IIHAH; mentioned L, GW)

Merlotte's Bar and Grill: Shifter Sam Merlotte bought a failing bar with an inheritance from his father, renamed it, renovated it, and turned it around. Carved out of the woods that still surround the parking lot, Merlotte's attracts a wide range of clientele of both the human and supernatural kind. The bar is open till midnight on weekdays and one a.m. on Fridays and Saturdays, serving light meals as well as drinks, including synthetic blood. Sam is still undecided about being open on Sundays and periodically gives it a try. He lives in a double-wide trailer placed at a right angle behind his bar.

Customers park on the black-topped front lot while employees park behind the building on the gravel, using the rear door to enter the bar, passing by Sam's office and the kitchen on their way through to the main room. Merlotte's has been through many cooks, including a vampire and a shifter, and many waitresses. Several come to tragic ends: waitress Dawn Green is killed by Rene Lenier, cook Lafayette Reynold is murdered by Mike Spencer and the Hardaways, and cook Sweetie Des Arts is a sniper who is killed by Detective Andy Bellefleur. Sam normally handles most of the bartending himself, but when he borrows bartender Charles Twining from Fangtasia after being shot in the leg (by Charles, as it turns out), the vampire attacks Sookie in retaliation for her involvement in another vampire's death. Charles asks to be staked rather than turned over to the police, and the patrons oblige. Sam has recently hired Kennedy Keyes, a former beauty queen who has done time for manslaughter, as a regular bartender, with Terry Bellefleur still taking a shift here and there as necessary. Overall, work hours for all employees are flexible and balanced.

The bar takes a double hit when first Vic's Redneck Roadhouse, a bar full of gimmicks and contests, opens nearby, and then Merlotte's is firebombed by Sandra Pelt in an attempt to kill Sookie. Suffering financially, Sam struggles to keep his bar going and is both grudging and grateful when Sookie offers part of her inheritance to keep it afloat.

The moment Bill Compton walks in the door, Merlotte's seemingly becomes the eye of the storm for supernatural events in Bon Temps.

Whether it's vampires as fellow customers, Sam and Tray Dawson shifting in the bar as the shifters announce themselves on TV, or even the crucifixion of Crystal in the parking lot, the regulars at Merlotte's watch, wonder, and then order another round, apparently taking it all in stride. (DUD, LDID, CD, DTTW, FD, DN, DAAD, DD, ATD, L, FDTW, DAG, DITF, DR; mentioned OWA, GW, TB, STW)

Michael (vampire): No last name given. Michael, an Illinois vampire, abducts and tortures the sister of Wisconsin vamp Jodi's employee despite repeated warnings to stay away from the girl. In retaliation, Jodi breaks off one of his canines with a pair of pliers while he sleeps, so Michael brings suit against her. His behavior is deemed detrimental to vampires in general, and Jodi is allowed to stake him. (Dies ATD)

Michael (vampire): No last name given. Owner of the gentlemen's club Blonde in Mississippi, devious Michael pretends to want to ally himself with the Nevada vamps as they attempt to take pieces of Mississippi from Russell, but he is actually playing his own game for financial gain. Unfortunately for him, so is his employee Mohawk, who takes advantage of the situation when Pam literally takes pieces of Michael, leaving him vulnerable and in agony. (Dies TB)

Mickey (vampire): No last name given. Mickey begins a relationship with an unwilling Tara, who has been passed to him as payment of a debt owed by her previous lover, Franklin Mott. Sookie calls in a favor from Eric for help for her friend, and he contacts Mickey's maker, Salome. She orders Mickey to her side. Angered by Sookie's interference, Mickey savagely abuses Tara and drags her with him to the duplex Sookie has made her temporary home. He first disables Eric with a rock to the head and then forces Sookie to invite him in. He attempts to attack her, but she is able to rescind his invitation in time and he is forced to retreat, unwillingly leaving Tara behind. Mickey clearly hears his maker's call but tries to resist, fleeing into the night. Eric is confident that Salome will find and punish her child. (DAAD)

Minas: Minas was the yard slave of Jonas Stackhouse, Mitchell's great-great-great-great-grandfather. (Deceased; mentioned DUD)

Mitchell, Susanne: Susanne is one of the few longtime barmaids at Merlotte's. (Mentioned DUD)

Mohawk (vampire): No last name given. An employee at Blonde, a gentlemen's club run by Michael in Mississippi, Mohawk—as Sookie refers to him—has his own agenda and happily seizes the opportunity to take over the club by finishing off Michael and his half-elf companion Rudy when they are incapacitated. (TB)

Mott, Franklin (vampire): Born in Sicily in 1756, urbane Franklin dates Tara, treating her as his mistress with Tara's tacit consent. Owing a debt to fellow vampire Mickey, Franklin pays by passing Tara along to Mickey to be used both sexually and for blood. (CD; mentioned DTTW, DAAD)

Murray, Debi: Clarice nurse Debi has seen Claude strip at Hooligans. (FDTW)

Murry (fairy): No last name given. A close friend of Breandan, Murry sneaks up on Sookie while she is weeding her flower beds. He arrogantly announces that he'll enjoy killing Sookie, which proves to be a fatal mistake. Sookie lunges up at him, metal garden trowel in hand, and stabs him in the stomach. The cold steel does its job and Murry dies, pale blue eyes wide with surprise. (Dies DAG)

Myers, Cal (wolf): Shreveport detective Cal Myers stands as Patrick Furnan's second during the packmaster challenge between Furnan and Jackson Herveaux, cheating by using gloves laced with a desensitizing drug to handle a silver bar during the second part of the contest so that Furnan can hold the bar longer. Cal's own thoughts betray him, and Sookie reveals their treachery. Although Furnan remains in the contest and does triumph, Cal is eventually punished by having his head shaved. Cal appears in the ectoplasmic reconstruction performed by Amelia and Octavia to determine who murdered Maria-Star Cooper. He is seen repeatedly stabbing the defenseless woman as another Were holds her down after breaking into her apartment. He is exposed as working with Priscilla Hebert, his half sister, against the Shreveport pack and is no doubt at least partially responsible for the deaths of Libby Furnan and Christine Larrabee as well. He is the first victim in the Were war, eviscerated by Furnan while simultaneously being partially beheaded by Alcide. (DAAD, DD; dies FDTW)

N:

Neave (fairy): No last name given. Lochlan's sister and lover, Neave helps kidnap Sookie on Breandan's orders in an attempt to force Niall to step down as Prince of Faery. Neave and Lochlan also gleefully murdered Sookie's grandfather, Fintan Brigant, as well as her pregnant sister-in-law, Crystal Stackhouse. The siblings are true sadists and take joy in torturing Sookie. When Bill and Niall come to Sookie's rescue, Bill dispatches Neave, but not before she seriously wounds him with her silver knife and silver-capped teeth. (Dies DAG; mentioned DITF)

Nella Jean: No last name given. Claude's secretary Nella Jean does her job for Hooligans but stays out of supernatural business. (DR)

Nergal (demon): No last name given. A demon, Nergal is Mr. Cataliades's half brother and the father of Diantha and Gladiola (by different mothers, of course). (Mentioned DD)

Newlin, G. Steve: G. Steve Newlin and his wife, Sarah, head the Fellowship of the Sun church in Dallas. After the revelation that they were planning to immolate a vampire and a human victim, and their involvement in the ensuing Dallas Midnight Massacre, they go underground. Steve surfaces briefly to encourage a devout follower on a suicide mission in Josephine's as he plans to stake Betty Joe Pickard—Mississippi vampire King Russell Edgington's second-in-command—but he flees when the attack is thwarted by Sookie and disappears once again. (LDID, CD; mentioned DAAD, DD, STW)

Newlin, Sarah: Sarah and her husband, Steve, go underground when their Fellowship of the Sun ministry in Dallas is raided, but they remain active in their hate campaign toward supes. After making contact with Jim Collins online, Sarah comes to Wright, Texas, incognito to protest Craig Merlotte's wedding but is recognized by Luna and Sookie.

After the reception at the church, the shifters gather at Bernie's, and Sarah visits Jim Collins next door to find out why he didn't attend the protest. Jim suggests that he and Sarah go next door and start shooting, but she rejects being a martyr, believing that she has more work to do against the shifters. Jim gets angry and shoots her, and Sarah, wounded, shoots back, killing him. Injured enough that she cannot flee the scene, Sarah is discovered by Luna and Sookie, who gleefully call the police. She is arrested for murder before being taken for treatment. (LDID, STW; mentioned DAAD, DD)

Norris, Calvin (panther): Calvin Norris is a steady man. He works hard as a crew leader at Norcross, the lumber-processing plant, and at leading his extended family of werepanthers in the strange little community of Hotshot. He briefly courts Sookie, helping her look for her missing brother, Jason, and then helps Jason adjust to his new life as a bitten werepanther. Shot by a sniper targeting shifters, a badly wounded Calvin promises Sookie that Jason, who is a suspect because of his forced transformation to panther, will not be punished until all of the facts are known and his guilt is certain. His concern for Sookie when she is shot leads him to send Tray Dawson to watch over her, and during the confrontation with sniper Sweetie Des Arts, Tray's presence distracts her, allowing Andy Bellefleur to shoot first.

Realizing that Sookie cannot adjust to his life and duties as packmaster, including his four children by different mothers, Calvin settles for being her friend and stands for his niece Crystal while Sookie stands for Jason at their wedding, even though they both have their doubts about the union. After a time he begins dating Tanya Grissom, and when Sookie tells him that Tanya has been bespelled by Sandra Pelt, he asks Amelia and Octavia to rid her of Sandra's influence rather than having them cast a simpler spell that would force Tanya to leave.

A pregnant Crystal breaks her wedding vows, and as her punishment will be taken by Calvin, Jason selfishly decides that Sookie will take his place in administering the penalty. Calvin comforts Sookie even as she is forced to break his fingers, symbolic of his panther claws. Calvin is shattered when Crystal's crucified body is found in Merlotte's parking lot and is comforted by his now live-in companion Tanya. In keeping with the traditions of Hotshot, he, Jason, Crystal's sister Dawn, and her cousin Jacky deal with Crystal's killer themselves.

Calvin and Tanya decide to go to Arkansas to get married without fanfare but enjoy a Hotshot celebration when they get home. No word on who stands for Calvin or Tanya. (DTTW, DAAD, DD, ATD, FDTW, DAG; mentioned DITF, DR)

Norris, Carlton (panther): Carlton is Calvin Norris's oldest brother.

When Carlton is accused of statutory rape by the stepfather of a willing and experienced, albeit underage, girl, Bon Temps sheriff John Dowdy rides out to Hotshot to arrest him. Sheriff Dowdy's car is found halfway between Bon Temps and Hotshot without a trace of either man in it, and neither is ever seen again. Carlton's current whereabouts are unknown, although he is presumed dead. (DTTW)

Norris, Dawn (panther): Crystal's younger sister, Dawn, has a son named Matthew. When first seen by Sookie, she is obviously pregnant, apparently doing her part to maintain the Hotshot panther pack. When Crystal is murdered and Mel Hart is suspected, Dawn joins her uncle Calvin, brother-in-law Jason, and young cousin Jacky to dispense the Hotshot version of justice. (DTTW, DAG)

Norris, Felton (panther): Obsessed with Crystal, Felton kidnaps Jason and repeatedly bites him to turn him into a panther in a twisted attempt to decrease Crystal's interest in him. After Jason's rescue from Felton's shed, Calvin and the panthers of Hotshot kill Felton so that Sookie and Jason will not go to the police. (Dies DTTW)

Norris, Marvin (panther): Calvin's uncle Marvin is the pastor of the Tabernacle Holiness Church, where the funerals of Hotshot residents are held. (Mentioned DAG)

Norris, Maryelizabeth (panther): The mother of Calvin's daughter Terry, Maryelizabeth warmly welcomes Sookie into Calvin's home and introduces her around when Sookie visits while he is recovering after being shot. As Calvin stands in to take pregnant Crystal's punishment after her infidelity is revealed, Maryelizabeth leads the ceremony and tells Sookie, standing in for Jason, what she must do as punishment, even handing her the brick with which to do it. (DAAD, FDTW; mentioned DD, ATD)

Norris, Matthew (panther): Dawn Norris's son is just a toddler when his aunt Crystal becomes involved with Jason. (DTTW)

Norris, Mitch (panther): As a member of the Bon Temps police department, Mitch helps remove Crystal's body from the cross in Merlotte's parking lot. (DAG)

Norris, Sterling: Mayor of Bon Temps, Sterling Norris is not one of the Hotshot Norrises. (DUD)

Norris, Tanya Grissom (fox): Cousin by birth to Debbie Pelt, werefox Tanya is sent to Bon Temps to spy on Sookie by the Pelts, desperate for information about their missing daughter. She gets a job subbing at Merlotte's and attempts to befriend Sookie but is rebuffed by the suspicious telepath. After the Pelts find out the truth of Debbie's death, Tanya decides to stay on in Bon Temps and pursue her interest in Sam. When that interest doesn't pan out, she eventually connects with the panthers in Hotshot, attending the Bellefleur-Vick wedding with Calvin Norris. Tanya begins spending an inordinate amount of time with Crystal Stackhouse, encouraging her to spend liberally during frequent trips to the mall in Monroe. Sookie realizes that Tanya is deliberately causing friction between Jason and Crystal as a result of a spell by Sandra Pelt. At Calvin's request, Amelia and Octavia break Sandra's hold on Tanya. She proves her steadfast affection for Calvin as she supports him when Crystal is murdered. She and Calvin drive over the state line to Arkansas and get married in a simple courthouse ceremony. When they get home, they enjoy a fun reception out at Hotshot. (DD, FDTW, DAG, DITF; mentioned DR)

Norris, Terry (panther): Calvin's daughter by Maryelizabeth Norris, Terry is a forthright teenager who views Sookie with a strange mixture of hostility and respect. She is among the witnesses at the ceremony of the punishment for Crystal's infidelity, watching as Sookie, standing in for Jason, breaks Calvin's fingers as he stands in for his pregnant niece. (DAAD, DD, FDTW)

Northman, Eric (vampire): More than a thousand years ago, a tipsy Viking warrior stopped to offer aid to a fallen stranger and died for his effort, rising as vampire Eric Northman. Fatally cured of his good Samaritanism, Eric uses his innate intelligence and cunning to grow into a powerful and prosperous vampire. He eventually settles in Louisiana and becomes the sheriff of Area Five, a position that puts all the vampires in his area under his protection and his control. He uses his position to his advantage by requiring his vamps to spend time in Fangtasia, a vampire bar he opens in Shreveport with Pam after the Great Revelation.

Eric is intrigued when Bill Compton brings Sookie to Fangtasia in her search for clues about murders happening in her hometown of Bon Temps, and his interest is further piqued when Sookie reads the mind of an undercover cop in the bar and is able to alert Bill to an imminent police raid. The two signal Eric and bartender Long Shadow on their way out, and Sookie must admit that she is a telepath when Eric questions how she knew. When he discovers that someone is embezzling from the bar, he orders Bill to bring her back to Fangtasia to read his employees' minds. When she worries that she could be sentencing a human to death by identifying him, Eric agrees to turn the thief over to the police if she will make herself available for further use. Although she cannot read vampire minds, Sookie does get the image of the embezzler from one of the waitresses and names Long Shadow. Eric is forced to stake his bartender when Long Shadow attacks Sookie. Even though the circumstances made it impossible to turn Long Shadow over to the police as promised, Eric holds Sookie to her end of the bargain.

A maenad passing through the area uses Sookie's back as a billboard to tell Eric that she expects tribute. Eric arranges for a supernatural doctor to attend to Sookie's wounds and provide a transfusion, joining Pam, Bill, and new bartender Chow in draining Sookie of most of her poisoned blood. After her recovery, he sends her to Dallas to help locate the missing nest mate of vampire sheriff Stan Davis. Although the deal calls for only Sookie and Bill, Eric decides to go in undercover as a visiting California vampire named Leif. When the Fellowship of the Sun attacks Stan's house as the vampires are celebrating Farrell's safe return, Eric takes a bullet while covering Sookie. He uses the situation to his advantage by telling Sookie she must suck out the bullet, even though he knows it will pop out on its own. By getting his blood in her, even a drop, he will have insight into her feelings.

Eric accepts Sookie's invitation to an orgy but is taken aback when she requests that he pretend to be gay. Their attendance is, of course, a ploy to gain information on the murder of Lafayette Reynold, Sookie's friend and co-worker at Merlotte's. Eric shows up at Sookie's house on time, resplendent in pink and aqua Lycra, and promises to keep her safe. Sookie does discover the killers through their thoughts and Eric gets her out of the immediate situation, but unfortunately for everyone involved, the maenad, Callisto, attends the orgy as well, attracted by the alcohol and debauchery. She sends her madness into the participants, sparing only Sookie, Tara, Eggs, Eric, and a newly arrived Bill, and the vampires clean up the mess afterward.

Eric relies on Sookie's affection for Bill when Bill goes missing along with a valuable project he was working on for their queen, and he sends werewolf Alcide Herveaux to escort her to Jackson in search of her missing lover. Once again, he shows up on the scene loosely disguised as Leif, coming to Sookie's aid when she is staked at Club Dead. They are taken to the King of Mississippi's mansion so she can be healed, and after she confirms that Bill is there, Eric finds her transportation so that she can rescue Bill during the day and escape. In the meantime, Eric spends his time with an adorable vampire named Bernard who has taken a shine to the big Viking. Eric plays along to help facilitate their plan. While Eric drives Sookie back to Bon Temps, the two are attacked first at a gas station by thugs (hired by a biker gang involved with Bill's captivity) and then by the gang members themselves at Sookie's home. As payment for Sookie's services, Eric has her entire driveway repaved.

A witch coven composed mainly of shifters who drink vampire blood comes to Shreveport to try to take over Eric's business network. He refuses the coven leader's offer of a better deal if he pleases her sexually and is cursed with amnesia when Chow attacks the witch who delivers the offer. Frightened, confused, and alone, he finds himself running down the road toward Sookie's house early New Year's morning and is taken in by a sympathetic Sookie. Jason makes a deal with Pam and Chow for Eric to remain at Sookie's house as a paying guest while the witches are dealt with, and Eric and Sookie begin a brief, passionate affair. The witches are defeated in a joint effort by the local vampires and local Weres, and Eric and Sookie return to her house because his memory hasn't yet returned. Upon entering the back door, they are surprised to find Debbie Pelt waiting for them with a gun. Eric steps in front of Sookie to take the bullet, giving Sookie time to grab a shotgun and blow most of Debbie's head off. Eric disposes of the body and Debbie's car while Sookie cleans up the mess. He returns in time to kiss her good night and climb into the hidey-hole in her guest room closet. By the time he awakens the next night, his memory is restored, but he has no recollection of what happened while he had amnesia, although he suspects it was more than a simple stay-over at Sookie's.

When Sam is shot and it's discovered that shifters are being targeted, he asks Sookie to ask Eric if he can borrow a bartender. Eric readily agrees, always happy to be owed a favor, and sends Charles Twining, a newly hired bartender from Mississippi. Eric is unhappy to learn that Mickey, vampire child of Salome, is in the area and tells Sookie to stay away from him. Tara becomes involved with Mickey, passed to him by another vampire she was dating, and Sookie asks for Eric's aid again, this time for her friend. Eric uses the favor to call in one from Sookie: He wants to know everything that happened while he had amnesia, and she tells him. In return, he calls Salome to call off her child, who is violating the new rules the vampires are trying to live by. Eric becomes suspicious of Charles Twining and decides to further check his references. To his horror, he discovers that Charles is pledged to Hot Rain, the sire of Long Shadow, and is there to take vengeance on Eric by harming Sookie. By the time he reaches Merlotte's, the human patrons have taken care of the problem.

Eric is unhappy when he has Pam call Sookie to a meeting and Sookie will not attend as she has a date with weretiger Quinn. Eric goes to her house instead and becomes enraged that not only is Sookie going on a date with the weretiger, but Quinn has delivered the news that vampire Queen Sophie-Anne Leclerq is claiming Sookie's services for the upcoming vampire summit, usurping Eric. Eric travels separately to New Orleans as Sookie is heading down with Mr. Cataliades to take care of her late cousin Hadley's apartment and legal affairs, with Bill as a passenger. Eric finds her in the hospital after she is attacked by Jake Purifoy and, when Bill enters as well, forces him to tell Sookie that he was sent by Sophie-Anne to gain her confidence. Because Sookie and he have had each other's blood, Eric is called upon to track her after she and Quinn are kidnapped. When the melee breaks out at Sophie-Anne's spring party, Eric slays the Arkansas vampire who decapitated Wybert.

As planned, Eric, Bill, and Sookie all travel to the summit as part of the queen's entourage. The King of Mississippi and the King of Indiana conclude their marriage contracts and decide to marry at the summit, but the priest doesn't show up for the wedding. Ordained online by the Church of the Loving Spirit, Eric steps in as priest and performs the ceremony, keeping the ceremonial knife and cloak afterward. When Andre decides to force Sookie into a blood bond to tie her closer to the Louisiana vamps, Eric steps in again and offers himself in Andre's stead, using the ceremonial knife to cut himself for Sookie. Eric and Pam are saved by Sookie during the bombing of the hotel and return to Shreveport to recover.

After calling in all his vampires, Eric himself is cut off from Fangtasia when the Nevada vamps arrive to take over Louisiana. He makes his way to Sookie's house but has been tracked by Victor Madden and his crew. Victor makes an offer of surrender to Eric and Bill, informing them that he has Fangtasia surrounded and ready to burn. The vampires accept his terms, and Eric becomes the only sheriff from the old regime to survive the takeover. Fearful that King Felipe de Castro will force Sookie to work for him, taking her from her home, Eric sends her a wrapped bundle containing the ceremonial knife from the summit with instructions to present it to him in front of Victor. The formal presentation and acceptance signify a vampire marriage, making Sookie off-limits to other vamps. They eventually begin a romantic relationship, and though Sookie does not truly acknowledge the marriage, as it is not legal in human terms, Eric considers her his wife in every way that matters to him.

When Eric's maker, Appius Livius Ocella, arrives with another child in tow, Eric takes them in. Ocella hopes that Eric's presence will calm the child, Alexei Romanov, whom he saved from execution by Bolsheviks, but Alexei is a drain on Ocella and Eric and, through their blood bond, on Sookie as well. Alexei becomes uncontrollable, killing Bobby and Felicia at Eric's house and badly injuring both Eric and Pam. He is finally stopped by silver chains in Sookie's front yard, and Eric stakes his brother with a tree branch. Ocella is killed by a crazed fae intent on killing Sookie, and Eric mourns his maker even as he rejoices in his freedom.

His freedom is short-lived, as he soon receives word that Ocella arranged a marriage for him to Freyda, the vampire Queen of Oklahoma. He tries to extricate himself from the contract, even as he struggles under Victor Madden's rule as Regent of Louisiana. Fangtasia is facing stiff competition from Victor's new club, Vampire's Kiss, and Victor himself is causing pain for Eric's child Pam, denying her permission to turn her seriously ill lover. Eric includes Sookie in planning Victor's demise but tries to hide his seemingly unavoidable nuptials to Freyda, finally admitting to the contract after pointed prodding from Pam. He tells Sookie that he will have to dissolve their vampire marriage. Unable to convince her of the need to honor his maker's wishes, Eric concentrates his efforts on the assassination of Victor, persuading Bubba to sing at Fangtasia after hours to lure Victor to the club. The event goes fairly smoothly and culminates in the death of Victor at the hands of a vengeful Pam, while Eric kills Victor's powerful second, Akiro. Eric becomes angry and frustrated with Sookie for what he perceives as her hypocrisy in not rejoicing over the death of Victor (when she knew it was necessary and even participated in both the planning and the deed), and without regard for her comfort, he takes the blood she offers to help him heal from his battle wounds. He lets Bill take Sookie home as he and his vampires begin to clean up the club. (DUD, LDID, CD, DTTW, DN, DAAD, DD, ATD, FDTW, DAG, DITF, DR; mentioned L, GW, TB, STW)

O:

Ocella, Appius Livius (vampire): Appius Livius Ocella was turned around the time of Jesus, so he is already centuries old when he turns Eric, his first success at siring a child. He teaches Eric how to be a vampire, educates Eric in Ocella's own sexual proclivities, and finally sets Eric free after several centuries. Ocella is also successful in saving Alexei Romanov, the tsarevitch of Russia, from execution shortly after the Russian Revolution. Able to track the royal family because Rasputin has been giving hemophiliac Alexei his blood, the ancient vampire finds the royal family and watches as their bullet-ridden bodies are first thrown down a well and then dug up and reburied. Sensing a spark of life in Alexei, he can't resist trying to save him. He arrives at Sookie's house with Alexei in tow, hoping the presence of Eric will calm his troubled child. Spoiled in life, Alexei has descended into madness in death, haunted by the memories of the slaughter of his entire family. Even with Eric's assistance, Ocella is unable to control Alexei, who sneaks out twice, resulting in a human death both times. Alexei finally completely snaps, killing Bobby Burnham and Felicia and badly wounding Eric and Pam. Ocella goes after his child, but Alexei severs his spinal column. Ocella lies in Sookie's front yard, incapable of stopping Alexei, who is gleefully battling fairies Claude and Colman. After Alexei is finally killed by Eric, Ocella knows that Sookie is tempted to kill him as he lies helpless. She approaches him while Eric pleads for her not to do it, and she decides against it. Ocella realizes that Sookie is about to be impaled by Colman and mentally tells her to move, taking the fairy's sword to the chest and dying almost instantly. For all his sins, Ocella is mourned by Eric, who soon learns that his maker has arranged a marriage between him and Freyda, the Queen of Oklahoma. Eric feels he must honor Ocella's contract. (Dies DITF; mentioned DAG, DR)

O'Fallon, Miss: No first name given. Pretty Miss O'Fallon teaches in the Puppy Room of the kindergarten in Red Ditch. Her outward appearance belies a sick mind, as she fights the temptation to hurt the children in her care. Her thoughts frighten Hunter and cause Sookie to tell Remy to exclude Miss O'Fallon from consideration as Hunter's teacher. Miss O'Fallon is surprised when Sookie approaches her and urges her to get help before she actually does damage. Stunned and scared by Sookie's perception, the woman promises to do so. (DR)

Older Lisle brother: No name given. Deidra's oldest brother is one of Craig Merlotte's groomsmen, along with Sam Merlotte. (STW)

Olympio, Togo (unspecified shifter): Togo is in Wright to visit his lover, Trish, when he finds himself in the midst of the controversy over Craig Merlotte and Deidra Lisle's wedding. Angered by the deaths of the shelter dogs, Togo joins in with Quinn, Trish, and other shifters to protect the Merlotte family and ensure that the ceremony does take place. Walking alongside the car as they head out for the actual ceremony, both Togo and Trish become battered and bloody by the time they reach the church. (STW)

O'Malley, Jake: Competing businessman Jake O'Malley plans to screw over Herveaux and Son by bribing one of their office staff for information on bids. His much younger wife has plans of her own for Alcide. (CD)

O'Malley, Mrs.: No first name given. Some twenty years younger than her sixtyish husband, Mrs. O'Malley thinks of jumping Alcide's bones while her husband thinks about screwing him over another way. (CD)

O'Rourke, Sean (vampire): Lovers and dance partners, Sean and Layla Larue Lemay work for Blue Moon Productions, dancing in front of both human and vampire audiences. Sean turned Layla when she was mortally wounded by a former boyfriend. They seem to be beating the odds, because most vampire couples, even makers and children, don't have long-term relationships. They dance at the summit in Rhodes and help defuse the tension between Sookie and Eric on the dance floor. Sean and Layla have their own novella. (ATD)

Osburgh, Mrs. Charles III: Elderly Mrs. Osburgh is one of Alcide's neighbors at the condo building in Jackson, living in #502 with her nurse. (Mentioned CD)

Owens, Lucky (wolf): After receiving word from waiter Kendell Kent that Sookie and Eric are headed back to Bon Temps, Lucky, pretending to be a policeman, pulls them over and takes a shot at Sookie. Eric protects her, taking the bullet in the neck before he grabs Lucky and begins pulling him into the car. Lucky begs Sookie not to let Eric turn him into a vampire, but that is not Eric's intent. The vampire has a fresh meal to help him heal from the bullet before disposing of Lucky's body somewhere off the interstate. (Dies FDTW)

P:

Palomino (vampire): No last name given. After surviving Katrina, vampires Palomino, Parker, and Rubio get permission to settle in Area Five in Minden. As Eric's vamps, they are called to take part in Victor's assassination. Palomino struggles with Antonio until Maxwell Lee is able to stake him, then goes after Unknown Enemy Vamp #2 with Parker. (DR)

Pardloe, Preston (fairy): To repay a debt to Niall, fairy Preston pretends to be a Were and lies naked in Sookie's woods on Christmas Eve, waiting for her to find him and counting on her innate kindness to get him into her home. Once safely inside, he uses just a touch of magic to spark the attraction between them, and they spend a satisfying night together. As the fairy magic fades, so do Sookie's detailed memories of the encounter, but she retains the feelings of guilt-free pleasure and happiness. Preston retains all his memories but knows he must follow Niall's instructions and have no further contact with Sookie, no matter how much he would like to. (GW)

Parnell (wolf): No last name given. Amanda's partner at the meeting of the Weres and the vampires at Merlotte's, Parnell almost overreacts when Eric leaps to Sookie's defense after Amanda calls her a "vamp humper." (DTTW)

Patty: No last name given. Michelle Stackhouse's best friend, Patty does her best to be an honorary aunt to Sookie after Michelle's death. (Mentioned LDID)

Paul, Andre (vampire): Andre is Queen Sophie-Anne Leclerq's faithful second-in-command. Orphaned as a teenager, he was found in the .

woods and turned by Sophie-Anne a few years after her own turning and has been her most loyal bodyguard, companion, and lover ever since. During the ectoplasmic reconstruction of Jake Purifoy's turning at Hadley's apartment, Andre is able to read lips and let the other watchers know what is being said. Afterward it is Andre who tells Sookie that she has fairy blood when they pretend to have sex as an excuse for time alone with Sophie-Anne to tell their story. Andre's only concern is the well-being of Sophie-Anne; he kills her husband, Peter Threadgill, after Peter's vampires attack at the reception for the couple at Sophie-Anne's monastery and escorts his queen safely away. After the disaster of Hurricane Katrina, Andre arranges a meeting with Sookie, Eric, and his vampires to make plans for the upcoming vampire summit, where Sophie-Anne will face charges for the death of Peter. Once at the summit, Andre demonstrates his willingness to do anything he feels necessary to benefit his queen by trying to force Sookie into a blood bond to strengthen her connection to him. He is interrupted by Eric, who bonds with Sookie instead. Quinn comes upon the scene and is furious that the vampires are attempting to control Sookie. After the hotel explodes, an injured Andre is found by Sookie at the same time she finds Quinn, and she walks away knowing that Quinn is moving toward Andre to eliminate the threat to Sookie's free will. Andre meets his final death in the ruins of the Pyramid of Gizeh. (DD; dies ATD; mentioned FDTW, DAG)

Pearl (vampire): No last name given. Victor's vamp Pearl and two of her cohorts forcibly stop Pam as she tries to enter Vampire's Kiss to check out the club before Eric and Sookie arrive. Pearl suffers an injured arm for her trouble, and all three require blood to heal. (Mentioned DR)

Pelt, Barbara (wolf): The adoptive mother of Debbie and Sandra Pelt. Barbara and her husband, Gordon, indulge their Were daughter Sandra's determination to find the truth of her werefox sister's disappearance, hiring first private detectives to search for clues and then a private hit man to clean up when Sandra, breaking the rules of their Mississippi pack, bites and turns two young men, sending them after Sookie. They also send Debbie's birth cousin, werefox Tanya Grissom, to spy on Sookie by getting hired as a waitress at Merlotte's. When their plan to kidnap Sookie in New Orleans to force her to tell the truth fails and they are taken captive by Sookie, Quinn, Eric, and Rasul instead, they listen and accept Sookie's recounting of the night Debbie was killed and give their word that there will be no further attempts on Sookie. Barbara and Gordon are killed in a traffic accident, leaving Sandra free to seek vengeance against Sookie. (DD; dies; mentioned DAAD, FDTW, DR)

Pelt, Debbie (fox): Debbie Pelt won't let go of Alcide Herveaux. Even during her engagement celebration to another man, werefox Debbie can't resist a few pointed comments to Alcide and Sookie, his date. After being bested verbally by Sookie, Debbie retaliates by burning a hole in Sookie's shawl. That altercation is indicative of Debbie: She always retaliates. After breaking off her engagement and convincing Alcide that Sookie has reunited with Bill, Debbie renews her relationship with Alcide, who is dismayed when he realizes that she lied about Sookie and Bill being together. When Debbie joins the Weres for the Witch War, everyone is appalled when Bill identifies Debbie as one of the shifters who tortured him at Russell's compound, and Alcide finally abjures her, essentially banishing her existence from his life. Debbie is not allowed to leave after being abjured for fear she will betray them all to Hallow, and she enters the building when the skirmish begins, trying to take advantage of the chaos to kill Sookie. She is stopped by Eric but gets away, only to break into Sookie's house and lie in wait with a gun. Eric takes the bullet meant for Sookie, and Debbie is cut down by a blast fired by Sookie from Jason's Benelli shotgun. Eric disposes of Debbie's body and her car and promptly forgets how and where as the amnesia spelled on him by Hallow is lifted and he regains his full memory but loses his recent memory of events during the time he was cursed. Debbie's sister and parents search for clues to her disappearance, hiring private detectives to trace her, but the only person who truly knows what happened is Sookie, who lives in fear that Eric will remember and realize the hold he has over her. The Pelt family finally learns what happened to Debbie after attempting to kidnap Sookie, and almost a year after that night, Eric finally remembers where he hid her body and her car. (CD; dies DTTW; mentioned DAAD, DD, FDTW, DITF, DR)

Pelt, Gordon (wolf): Debbie and Sandra Pelt's adoptive father, Gordon, and his wife, Barbara, use private detectives to search for clues into Debbie's disappearance, at daughter Sandra's insistence, and arrange for Tanya Grissom, Debbie's cousin by birth, to spy on Sookie in Bon Temps. The Pelts also hire a Were to take care of the problem when Sandra violates the rules of the Mississippi pack, biting and turning two young men to send after Sookie. The Pelts all work together to have Sookie kidnapped in New Orleans, but the plan backfires when Sookie and Quinn escape, and the family is captured by Sookie, Quinn, Rasul, and Eric instead. Sookie tells them the truth about what happened to Debbie and, knowing their daughter, they accept Sookie's story and promise that they will no longer interfere in her life. Gordon informs Sandra that they have given their word and that he will take her down himself if she breaks it. She abides by the vow until Gordon and Barbara are killed in a traffic accident and then begins to plot revenge against Sookie once more. (DD; dies; mentioned DAAD, FDTW, DR)

Pelt, Sandra (wolf): Sandra adores her adopted older sister, Debbie, and is determined to investigate her disappearance. Unsatisfied by the report from the private detectives hired by her parents, Sandra decides to take matters into her own hands to find the truth. Violating the rules of her Mississippi pack, she turns two young men, and sends them to attack Sookie. When Sookie is defended by Quinn and the young men are arrested, Sandra's parents arrange for their elimination to protect their daughter. Sandra then makes arrangements with her parents to kidnap Sookie, take her to an isolated house, and force her to talk. That plan fails when Quinn is captured as well, and he and Sookie are able to escape, tracking their captors to the house and taking the Pelts prisoner with the help of Eric and Rasul. Sandra is forced by her parents to accept the fact that Debbie attacked Sookie and was killed in self-defense, and reluctantly promises that no further harm will come to Sookie, a promise she keeps until her parents are killed in a car accident. Sandra then reestablishes contact with Debbie's birth cousin, werefox Tanya Grissom, who had originally been sent to spy on Sookie but stayed in Bon Temps of her own accord. She bespells Tanya, persuading her to cause problems in Jason and Crystal's marriage, but Amelia and Octavia are able to remove Sandra's influence.

Sandra's instability increases, and she spends time in jail for assault and battery on a cousin who benefited from the Pelts' estate. After her release, she again focuses on Sookie, first firebombing Merlotte's in an attempt to kill her and then hiring four thugs to grab her from the bar. She even attempts to enter Sookie's house, but Amelia's wards keep her out. Sandra finally goes to Merlotte's, screams out her frustration at Sookie's failure to die, and pulls a gun, only to be thwarted once again, this time by a baseball bat–swinging Terry Bellefleur. Sandra manages to escape from custody while at the hospital being treated for her injuries and lies low until she is able to take Sam and Jannalynn hostage at his trailer in an attempt to lure Sookie from her house. When Sookie balks at going to Sam's, sensing something is wrong, Sandra forces Sam and Jannalynn to take her to Sookie's, not knowing that Sookie's suspicions have her lying in wait in the woods with her shotgun. The blast from the shotgun barely slows Sandra down, but a furious Jannalynn takes advantage and attacks, ultimately breaking Sandra's neck and then crushing her skull. The body is disposed of through the fairy portal in the woods, much to the savage delight of whatever is just on the other side. (DD; mentioned DAAD, FDTW; dies DR)

Pepper, Madelyn: Betty Ford Elementary School custodian Madelyn panics when she yells at Cody Cleary, startling him into losing his balance and hitting his head. Mistakenly believing he is dead, she impulsively hides his body in her large garbage bin. She is miserable, and her thoughts betray her to Sookie, who instructs Kenya where to find the child in time to save him. (DD)

Perkins, Kyle (vampire): Illinois vampire Kyle Perkins is hired to make certain that Henrik Feith does not reveal the identity of the person who encouraged him to pursue the Arkansas case against Sophie-Anne. He hurls wooden arrows at Henrik as he stands on the stage before the court, killing him and wounding Quinn. He loses his own head to the blade of Britlingen Batanya's throwing star. (Dies ATD)

Petacki, Alphonse "Tack": One of Merlotte's many temporary short-order cooks, Tack briefly dates Arlene before running off with her plates, forks, and CD player. (DTTW; mentioned DAAD)

Pettibone, Dennis: Dennis is the arson investigator who looks into the fire at Sookie's house. Divorced with a daughter, Katy, he briefly dates Arlene. (DAAD)

Pettibone, Katy: Katy is the daughter of Dennis Pettibone. (DAAD)

Pfeiffer, Trudi: College student Trudi is dating Joseph Velasquez when they are caught in the Midnight Massacre at Stan's house. She is mortally wounded, and Eric offers to bring her over, but she dies before Sookie can even consider making that decision for her. (Dies LDID)

Pharr: No other name given. Pharr is the cousin of Holly's ex-husband, David Cleary. (Mentioned DTTW)

Phillips, Dell: Dell is as judgmental as his wife is not. He disapproves of Sookie staying with Alcide in Jackson even though they are adults and in separate bedrooms. (CD; mentioned DAAD)

Phillips, Janice Herveaux: Alcide Herveaux's younger sister owns a beauty salon in Jackson. Married with one child, Janice hopes Alcide will settle down with Sookie and be able to cut Debbie Pelt from his life. She knows about her brother's second nature and loves him unconditionally. (CD, DAAD, DD)

Phillips, Tommy: Tommy is Janice and Dell's son. (Mentioned CD, DAAD)

Phryne (maenad): No last name given. The maenad Phryne sent her madness into the vampire Gregory in St. Petersburg, causing the Halloween Massacre of 1876. Gregory had to be staked, and it took twenty vampires to clean up the results of his insanity. (Mentioned LDID)

Pickard, Betty Joe (vampire): King Russell Edgington's second-in-command, Betty Joe dresses like Mamie Eisenhower and hits like Muhammad Ali. When a Fellowship of the Sun member attempts to stake her in Josephine's, Betty Joe takes him out with two quick punches, snapping his neck and shattering his skull. Fortunately for Bubba, who is captured at Russell's mansion after Sookie leaves, Betty Joe accepts a phone call from Sookie and believes her when she tells her Bubba's true identity. She is able to stop the planned crucifixion of the "Elvis impersonator." (CD)

Pickens, Maudette: Maudette is the first Bon Temps woman murdered, and the marks on her thighs attest to the rumor that she liked being bitten, leading the investigators to consider a vampire as the killer; but she died of strangulation, not exsanguination. After tapes are discovered of Jason having sex with Maudette, he falls under suspicion for her death and the deaths that follow until the real killer is revealed as Rene Lenier. (Dies DUD)

Polk, Francie: Francie, her husband, and her three children bed down in the Fellowship of the Sun building for the lock-in so that they can be there to watch the self-immolation of Godfrey and the unwilling immolation of Farrell come the dawn. (LDID)

Popken, Lindsay: Popular Lindsay is voted Miss Bon Temps the year Sookie graduates from high school. (Mentioned DD)

Porchia, Diane: Insurance agent Diane is seriously considering selling her business in Bon Temps after processing numerous claims. (L)

Portugal (wolf): No first name given. On the order of Colonel Flood, Portugal works to ensure that the local Wiccans either assist the Weres and vampires or stay clear of the upcoming Witch War. He is among the victims and is mourned by Culpepper, who sits beside his body and keens her sorrow. (Dies DTTW)

Prescott, Lorinda: Lorinda artfully decorates her family's home, located between Sookie's and Merlotte's, for Halloween. (Mentioned FDTW)

Prideaux, Danny: Recently honorably discharged from the army, Danny is working part-time at the home builders' supply store and several nights a week as a bouncer at Merlotte's, keeping an eye on new bartender Kennedy Keyes. His interest is more than professional, and his attentions pay off when they begin seeing each other outside of work. They are at Merlotte's for a drink when the bar is firebombed, and Danny reacts quickly to get Kennedy out of danger. He, Sam, Terry, and Antoine work to get the bar back in order so it can reopen. Danny also spends time in Merlotte's without Kennedy and is there playing darts with Andy Bellefleur the night four thugs come in and start trouble. He stands his ground, along with Andy, and throws a dart at one of the assailants to distract him before the thug can deliver a blow. (DITF, DR)

Prudhomme, Rafe: Rafe, a Pelican State Title Company employee, briefly dates Arlene, getting her involved in his church, the Fellowship of the Sun. (Mentioned DD)

Pryor, Jeneen: Kevin's mother is controlling of her son, keeping him close. (Mentioned DUD, CD, DTTW, DD, DAG)

Pryor, Kevin: Quiet and lean patrolman Kevin is usually partnered with Kenya, working the same shifts whenever possible. Notoriously mother-ridden, he shocks Andy Bellefleur when he speaks up to tell him that he cannot use Sookie's abilities to solve cases after she finds Cody Cleary. He's convinced that the answers must be found through evidence, not telepathy.

Kevin stands up for himself again when he and Kenya decide to move in together, despite the dismay of both families. (DUD, LDID, CD, DTTW, DAAD, DD, DAG, DITF; mentioned DR)

Puckett, Jeff: Jeff works as a bouncer at Hooligans, where his former lover Claude Crane strips. He is angry with Claude's sister Claudette because she interfered in his relationship with Claude, so he becomes a suspect in Claudette's death, but he cares too much for Claude to have hurt his sister. Claudine erases his memories of the evening when he is cleared, and Jeff leaves relaxed and happy, having gotten a good-night kiss from Claude. (FD)

Pulaski, Trish Graham (unspecified shifter): Wright ranch owner Trish monitors the anti-supe websites and is not surprised when told that Jim Collins is involved in the deaths of the dogs at the Los Colmillos County Animal Shelter, a shelter she personally raised the money to build. She joins her lover, Togo, and the other shifters to guard the Merlottes, escorting their cars to the church for Craig and Deidra's wedding and taking blows herself while protecting them when the crowd gets violent. Trish is dazed and bleeding by the time they reach the church. (STW)

Pumphrey, Selah: Real estate agent Selah begins dating Bill after he and Sookie break up. She resents Bill's obvious continued feelings for Sookie and finally moves to Little Rock to work for a large firm that deals with vampire properties. (DAAD, DD, ATD, FDTW; mentioned DITF)

Purifoy, Jake (former wolf, current vampire): Jake is working on Sophie-Anne's wedding with Special Events, the supernatural offshoot of the highly regarded Extreme(ly Elegant) Events, when he suddenly disappears. He is found by Sookie in the closet of her cousin Hadley's apartment in New Orleans, turned into a vampire by Hadley after she finds him drained by Jade Flower outside her gates. He has been kept from rising by the stasis spell cast on the apartment by Amelia under Sophie-Anne's orders. Jake rises, attacks Sookie and Amelia, and is taken into custody to the queen's headquarters to adjust to being a vampire. A rarity, former Were, current vampire Jake is a stranger in a strange land. He is unable to shift with the moon, so he is no longer part of the pack, but as a Were he is isolated among the vampires. His frustration and loneliness culminate in his alliance with the Fellowship of the Sun in planning the bombing of the Pyramid of Gizeh at the summit in Rhodes. He does suggest that Quinn take Sookie out for the day, in an attempt to spare them, and is last seen lying in his daytime sleep in the hallway of the hotel, apparently headed for Sookie's room in another last-ditch effort to save her. (DD, ATD)

Pyramid of Gizeh Hotel: Located in Rhodes outside Chicago, the hotel has a view of the Great Lakes. Built roughly in the shape of a pyramid, all the walls are made of opaque, bronze-colored reflective glass, except for the floor designated for use by guests' human companions. The main doors are manned by uniformed men to check the guests' IDs, and there are reproductions of sarcophagi standing in an upright position on each side of the lobby doors.

The lobby is brightly lit and decorated with murals depicting Egyptian tomb art in an attempt to look like a human hotel. The floors are numbered in reverse order, with number one being the penthouse and number fifteen, the largest and the one used by humans, being the bottom, and a mezzanine area between the human floor and the lobby. The big selling point for any vampire hotel is the security and privacy of its guests, and the Pyramid is no exception: there are armed guards and a metal detector, as well as security cameras spread throughout the building. The staff is specially trained to cater to the needs of their vampire guests, and there is a small restaurant for the human guests.

The vampire summit is held at the Pyramid, with vampire kings and queens from at least sixteen states attending with their entourages. Sookie works for Louisiana queen Sophie-Anne Leclerq, reading the human companions of the vampire attendees, and testifies when the queen is put on trial for murdering her husband, Peter Threadgill, the former King of Arkansas. The hotel is blown up during the summit by a splinter group of the Fellowship of the Sun. (ATD; mentioned FDTW, DAG)

Q:

Queen's monastery: An abandoned monastery deep in the Garden District of New Orleans, the property is owned by Sophie-Anne Leclerq, the vampire Queen of Louisiana, who uses it as a place to entertain. Located among the expensive houses of the area, it is a two-story building surrounded by a high wall. A large featureless structure with only a single small door in the middle of the façade, it is easily defensible with small windows regularly placed. Inside, one of the walls has murals depicting scenes from around the state: a swamp scene, a Bourbon Street montage, a field being plowed and lumber being cut, and a fisherman hoisting up a net in the Gulf Coast. These all seem to be scenes featuring humans. The wall surrounding the doorway shows the vampire side of Louisiana life: a group of happy vampires playing fiddles, a vampire police officer patrolling the French Quarter, and a vampire guide leading tourists through one of the Cities of the Dead. It is the site of Peter Threadgill's assassination attempt against Sophie-Anne and the fierce battle between the Arkansas and Louisiana vampires. (DD)

Quiana Wong's mother: No name given. Half-Chinese, half–African American, Quiana's mother is killed along with Quiana's father, Coop, when their car stalls on the railroad tracks. They leave behind their sixteen-year-old daughter and rumors that it wasn't an accident. (Deceased; mentioned IIHAH)

Quinn, Francine: Frannie is the result of the brutal rape of her mother at the hands of hunters who captured her while she was in tiger form, causing her to revert to human. Frannie tries to take care of her now mentally unstable mother, while her mother tries to deal with her emotionally troubled child. She joins her brother, Quinn, at the summit, surviving the explosion thanks to Sookie's call, and makes a tentative peace with her brother's new girlfriend.

When their mother escapes from the home Quinn has had her committed to and the resultant mess is taken care of by the Nevada vampires, the siblings are first given the choice of Frannie becoming a blood whore or Quinn fighting in the pits. The vampires settle for blackmailing Quinn into providing them with information to help with the takeover of Louisiana and Arkansas. (ATD, FDTW; mentioned DAG, STW)

Quinn, John (tiger): Widely recognized and respected in the supernatural world, weretiger Quinn is known not only for being a partner in Special Events, the supernatural offshoot of a national event-planning company, but also for his past. After attacking the humans that captured his mother in tiger form and raped her after she shifted back to human, a teenage Quinn was forced to ask the local vampire nest for help cleaning up the scene and so became indebted to them. He worked off his debt by fighting in the pits for three years. The fact that he is one of the few to survive this brutal sport makes him something of a star among the supes.

Quinn attends Colonel Flood's funeral in preparation for his upcoming job refereeing the Long Tooth packmaster contest between Jackson

Herveaux and Patrick Furnan. He notices Sookie, first with Alcide at the funeral and then with Claudine and Claude at the contest. When she steps forward to accuse Furnan of cheating, Quinn listens to her claims and concurs, sending the pack into a vote on whether to disqualify Furnan. He asks Sookie to try to read the two Weres again just before the final test, and when she is scratched by an apparatus, he licks the blood from her leg and promises that she will see him again. Indeed, he walks into Merlotte's one night and asks Sookie for a private conversation about both business and pleasure. She agrees, and he follows her to her house, where he first asks her out and then informs her that Queen Sophie-Anne Leclerq is requesting her services at the vampire summit, trumping Eric's prior request.

Quinn takes Sookie to the Strand Theatre to see *The Producers*, and they are attacked by bitten Weres in the parking lot after the show. After filing police reports, he takes Sookie to Hair of the Dog, a shifter bar in the area, where he informs Alcide Herveaux and owner Amanda Whatley that they were attacked and that he expects the local pack to investigate. He next sees Sookie in New Orleans after she has to break their second date to accompany Mr. Cataliades to settle Hadley's estate. While Quinn is helping her pack up Hadley's apartment, they are kidnapped by Weres hired by the Pelts, who are convinced that Sookie knows what happened to Debbie. They escape their captors and turn the tables on the Pelts with the help of Eric and Rasul.

Quinn tries to see Sookie as much as possible but has a hectic schedule. He arranges to take a month off after the vampire summit, where he is also working, to spend time with her, and they consummate their relationship with great hope for the future. They are only able to grab a few moments at the summit. When Quinn comes across Andre forcing Eric to forge a blood bond with Sookie, he becomes enraged with the vampires. Quinn later gets word that Sookie has found a bomb in the hallway outside Sophie-Anne's room, so he rushes upstairs and tries to persuade her to hand him the bomb, telling her that he will heal faster than she will and that he doesn't want anything to happen to her. A vampire bomb-disposal expert finally comes and carries the bomb away. After answering all manner of questions, Sookie finally gets to her room, where she finds Quinn waiting outside her door, and they spend the night just holding each other. During the trial of Sophie-Anne the next evening, a vampire in the audience hurls arrows at the stage to kill the last remaining Arkansas vamp at the summit, and Quinn jumps in front of Sookie, taking an arrow to protect her. When Sookie realizes that the hotel is going to blow up, her first action is to warn Quinn and his sister Frannie. Quinn suffers two broken legs but manages to kill Andre, who is lying injured nearby in the rubble, in an attempt to free Sookie from the vampires' control.

When Quinn doesn't contact Sookie after the summit, she assumes the worst—that he has lost interest. In truth, Quinn is dealing with his mentally ill mother, who has escaped from the home in Nevada where he had her committed and killed several tourists. She is found first by the Nevada vamps, who clean up after her and then hold Quinn accountable, telling him they will make his little sister, Frannie, a blood whore, he can fight in the pits, or he can pony up information about the Louisiana vamps. He tries to resist and refrains from contacting Sookie at all, fearing she will become another hostage to be used against him. He is waiting for Sookie in her room when she wakes after the takeover and is devastated when she breaks off their relationship. He tries to see her but is banned from Area Five by Eric. When he sneaks in anyway, Eric sends Bill to divert him, and they get into a fight that ends up injuring Sookie.

Quinn finally sees Sookie again at the wedding of Sam's brother. He accepts her relationship with Eric but tells her that if she ever needs him, he will be there for her. (DAAD, DD, ATD, FDTW, DAG, STW; mentioned GW)

R:

Rachel (vampire): No last name given. Stan's child, Rachel is also his nest mate. She is killed at the summit when the Pyramid explodes. (LDID; dies ATD)

Ralph (wolf): No last name given. Ralph works for one of Niall's businesses as a courier. The huge Were does community theater, so he is the natural choice to play the part of Big Threatening Brute for Niall in his presentation of his Christmas gift to his great-granddaughter Sookie. (GW)

Rasputin: Grigori Rasputin, a Russian monk, claims to have powers of healing and prediction, taking on the care of the tsarevitch Alexei, who suffers from hemophilia. He uses Ocella's blood to heal the boy during his episodes with the disease, creating a tie between Ocella and Alexei that Ocella uses to find the boy during the execution of the Russian royal family. (Deceased; mentioned DITF)

Rasul (vampire): No other name given. After his comrades Melanie and Chester die during Katrina, Rasul is paired with were-vampire Jake Purifoy for guard duty at the summit. Rasul survives both the bombing at the Pyramid and the Nevada takeover of Louisiana and is sent to Michigan as a spy by Victor and Felipe. (DD, ATD; mentioned FDTW, DITF)

Rattray, Denise: Denise and her husband, Mack, have already spent time in jail for draining vampires, but that doesn't stop them from luring Bill to the Merlotte's parking lot, wrapping him in silver chains, and slapping a tourniquet on his arm. Enraged when Sookie rescues Bill, the couple lie in wait for her in the parking lot a few nights later, viciously beating and kicking her until Bill comes to her aid and puts a permanent end to their criminal ways. Bill later destroys their trailer and the surrounding area, making it look as if the two were victims of a tornado. (Dies DUD)

Rattray, Mack: Mack and his wife, Denise, don't learn their lesson even after doing time in jail for draining vampires and immediately target Bill when he comes into Merlotte's, luring him to the parking lot and trapping him with silver chains. They are both furious when Sookie rescues Bill and return to the bar a few nights later to take their revenge, savagely beating her until they are stopped—permanently—by Bill. Bill disguises their deaths as the result of a tornado touching down at their trailer at Four Tracks Corner. (Dies DUD)

Ravenscroft, Pam (vampire): Turned by Eric at age nineteen in Victorian London, Pam immediately adjusts to the life of a vampire. After spending many years with her maker, first as lover and then as companion, they travel to North America together, where he releases her to go her own way. She remains his loyal child and returns from Minnesota when he calls her to Louisiana to open Fangtasia with him. Like all children, Pam obeys her maker, but unlike some, she does so willingly.

With a better sense of humor than most vampires and a stunning sense of style, Pam becomes something of a friend to Sookie, and she insists on Sookie being told of Bill's betrayal so that she knows the truth. Yet she is still a vampire who believes that vampires come first and momentarily considers killing both Sookie and Jason when Eric has amnesia and is hiding at

Sookie's house. As Eric's second-in-command, she leads the vampires into the Witch War, capturing Hallow herself and forcing her to undo the spell on Eric. Pam is among those who attend the summit at Rhodes and is saved during the bombing by Sookie with Eric's help.

Pam briefly dates Amelia Broadway while she is staying in Bon Temps, using her interest to disguise the fact that she is keeping an eye on Sookie. During the actual takeover by the Nevada vamps, Pam escapes Fangtasia and systematically picks off any enemy vampire who strays too far from the group.

While driving Sookie back home one night after a visit with Eric, Pam and Sookie are waylaid by Victor Madden's second, Bruno Brazell, and a female vampire named Corinna. Pam hands Sookie a knife to fight with Bruno while she takes on Corinna, and soon both of Victor's vampires are disintegrating in the rain. Surprised and not at all pleased when Ocella shows up, Pam does her best to help Eric through the difficult times with his brother. Although she suffers a broken arm and leg, broken ribs, and various cuts and bruises when attacked by an insane Alexei, she still protests as she is left behind at Eric's when Sookie and Eric race to confront him.

Pam quietly takes a human female as a lover, asking permission to turn Miriam, since she suffers from leukemia and is growing increasingly weaker. When Victor refuses to allow it and actually uses Miriam to taunt Pam instead, Pam becomes even more enthusiastic about eliminating him from their lives. She makes plans to turn Miriam in secret, but her lover takes a sudden turn for the worse and dies before she can do so. Pam teams up with Eric at Fangtasia to take Victor down, and she ends up beneath him, his teeth at her throat. Seeing Sookie standing above her with Akiro's sword in her hands, Pam urges her to bring it down on Victor's neck. Sookie checks her swing in an effort not to hurt Pam, who jumps up and grabs the sword, finishing the job herself. (DUD, LDID, CD, DTTW, DN, DAAD, DD, ATD, FDTW, DAG, TB, DITF, DR; mentioned L)

Ray Don (vampire): No last name given. Ray Don's talent is an overabundance of the chemicals in his saliva that promote healing, and he cleans Sookie's wound after she is staked at Josephine's. (CD)

Re-Bar: No other name given. Re-Bar is the bouncer at the Bat's Wing in Dallas; his mind is permanently damaged when a vampire, probably Godfrey, removes his memories. Stan promises to take care of the now mentally impaired human because he was injured while working for vampires. (LDID)

Red Rita (vampire): No other name given. King Felipe de Castro appoints the formidable Red Rita as Regent of Arkansas. (Mentioned DR)

Remy Savoy's aunt: No name given. When Remy's father's sister passes away, Remy asks Sookie to babysit Hunter overnight so that he can attend the funeral and a family lunch over in Homer. (Deceased; mentioned DITF)

Renfield: No other name given. Dracula's human servant, Renfield is totally controlled by his master and eagerly does his bidding. Eric refers to any human who is controlled in such a way as a Renfield. (Mentioned DAG)

Renfield's Masters (vampires): This "live" band played at Fangtasia on their way to New Orleans. (Mentioned DAAD)

Reynold, Lafayette: Merlotte's cook Lafayette is cheerful, entertaining, clever, a good cook, and openly gay. His willingness to experiment brings a fatal result when he is killed at an orgy, and his body is dumped in Andy Bellefleur's car in Merlotte's parking lot. His killers are uncovered by Sookie, who has no real proof until his belongings are found in Mike Spencer's car after the orgy regulars fall victim to maenad Callisto's madness. (DUD; dies LDID; mentioned DITF)

Riordan, Dan: Father Riordan comes to Bon Temps every Saturday to celebrate mass with his Catholic parishioners. He freely expresses his prejudice against vampires, even attending Fellowship of the Sun meetings in nearby Minden, and tells Sookie that consorting with vampires is a type of death wish.

Approached by the Pelts in their search for their daughter, Father Riordan asks Sookie to meet with them and is disappointed in her when she refuses. He reluctantly ambushes her, bringing the insistent Pelts to Merlotte's to speak with her anyway. (DD)

Robinson, Fay: Halleigh's sister Fay is one of her bridesmaids. (FDTW)

Robinson, Linette: Despite Halleigh's mother Linette's discomfort around crowds, she manages to get through her daughter's wedding shower and then celebrate her wedding. (ATD, FDTW)

Robinson, Mr.: No first name given. Mr. Robinson doesn't walk his daughter down the aisle in deference to Portia's solo walk but does meet his daughter at the altar to ceremoniously give her away. (FDTW)

Rodriguez, Carla: Carla, one of Jason's ex-girlfriends, is in town the night he disappears but is being truthful when she tells Sookie that she did not see Jason and would have turned her back on him if she had. (DTTW)

Rodriguez, Dovie: Sookie calls on Dovie in Shreveport to question her visiting cousin Carla about Jason after he disappears shortly after New Year's. (DTTW)

Rodriguez, Terencia "Terry": Along with Amelia Broadway, Bob Jessup, and Patsy Sellers, Terry helps perform the ectoplasmic reconstruction for the Queen of Louisiana after a Were turned by a vampire rises in Hadley's apartment and attacks Amelia and Sookie. Terry is Hispanic, in her mid- to late twenties, with full cheeks, bright red lips, and rippling black hair. She is short and, in Sookie's words, "has more curves than an S-turn." (DD)

Rogers, Bethany: A waitress at the Bat's Wing, Bethany is working the night that Farrell is kidnapped and, with Sookie's help, is able to recall what she saw. Stan keeps his word that she will leave unharmed, but the Fellowship of the Sun is not so forgiving of her interaction with vampires and executes her, leaving her body behind the Silent Shore Hotel. (Dies LDID)

Romanov, Alexei (vampire): Alexei is the progeny of Ocella. The tsarevitch of Russia is given the Roman vampire's blood by Rasputin to help with his hemophilia, so when the Bolsheviks execute the royal family, Ocella is able to locate the boy and save him by turning him. In the beginning, Ocella enjoys Alexei's company in every way, but Alexei's spoiled childhood and the trauma of his family's confinement and execution turn him sociopathic, and he begins draining the energy of his maker. Hoping his older child can help his younger one, Ocella brings Alexei to Eric, but Alexei becomes a drain on Eric and Sookie as well. He escapes custody twice, resulting in the death of a human each time. Alexei finally becomes completely insane, badly injuring Eric and Pam and killing Bobby Burnham and Felicia. With Ocella in pursuit, he runs first to Jason's house and then to Sookie's, where he severs Ocella's spinal column before gleefully engaging Claude and Colman, the father of Claudine's child, in battle. Sookie is able to ensnare him with a silver chain, and Eric uses a tree branch to send his brother to his final death. (Dies DITF; mentioned DR)

Romanov, Maria: During the assassination of the Russian royal family by Bolsheviks, the bodies of Maria and Alexei are buried separately and not found until sixteen years after the discovery of the burial place of the rest of their family. (Deceased; mentioned DITF)

Rose-Anne (vampire): No last name given. Rose-Anne works for Salome at the Seven Veils Casino. (DAAD)

Rudy (half elf): No last name given. Half-elf, half-human Rudy is Michael's companion—sexually and criminally. His sharp, pointy teeth traumatize Sookie, reminding her of her experiences with the fairies, but not so much so that she cannot react to Rudy's and Michael's threats, shooting Rudy in the face and chest. (Dies TB)

Rushton, Lola: Lola had a crush on Sookie in high school but now dates India, a waitress at Merlotte's. (Mentioned DR)

S:

Sadie: No last name given. Sam's friend Sadie joins other supporters to watch over the Merlottes as they leave for Craig's wedding. (STW)

Salazar: No last name given. Cute paramedic Salazar treats Sookie after Luna's car is deliberately hit by Polly Blythe and Sarah Newlin. (LDID)

Sallie: No last name given. Sallie is the romantic partner of Katherine Boudreaux, the area representative for the BVA. (DITF)

Salome (vampire): No last name given. Mickey's sire, Salome runs the Seven Veils Casino in Baton Rouge. Rumor has it she's one hell of a dancer. (DAAD)

Sam Merlotte's duplexes: Sam owns a block of three duplexes on Berry Street, a block or two behind the oldest part of downtown Bon Temps. They are small but well maintained. After the fire at Sookie's house, he lets her move into one until the repairs are completed. (DUD, DAAD)

Sam Merlotte's trailer: Sam's three-bedroom double-wide is situated behind Merlotte's at a right angle to the bar and facing the employee parking lot, which is illuminated by a security light on the electricity pole in front of his home. The small yard is enclosed by a boxwood hedge with a gate in lieu of a fence, and a covered deck leads to the front door.

Sam manages to keep his private life separate from the bar in spite of the proximity, enjoying his time in his home with friends and girlfriends. (DUD, CD, DTTW, DAAD, DD, ATD, FDTW; mentioned DAG, DR)

Sandra Pelt's thugs: No names given. Sookie nicknames the four men

Bearded Leader, Blond Bristles, Pouty Lips, and Crazy Guy when they enter Merlotte's and threaten the patrons. Hired by Sandra Pelt and paid with sex and vampire blood, the four are aggressive and unstable as they proclaim that they have come for the blonde, meaning Sookie, who is standing next to Lily Bard Leeds (also a blonde) and Lily's husband. Both Jack Leeds and an off-duty Andy Bellefleur pull out their guns when Bearded Leader brandishes a knife. Crazy Guy, who is the most affected by the vampire blood, charges Sam, and bedlam breaks out. Pouty Lips fires his own gun, winging Jack, and is taken down by Lily in a series of moves that breaks his arm. Jannalynn, in the bar to see Sam, attacks Crazy Guy at the same time as Sam, breaking the thug's jaw and femur. Andy is able to easily subdue Bearded Leader by putting his gun in the thug's back, and Blond Bristles takes a dart, thrown by Danny, in the arm before being punched out by Sam. Andy calls for backup, and the four hoodlums are taken into custody. (DR)

Santiago: No first name given. Ms. Santiago is rescued by Sookie and Barry from the wreckage of the Pyramid of Gizeh. (ATD)

Sara (vampire): No last name given. Former stripper Sara hates her present job in Tunica, Mississippi, and makes arrangements to move to Shreveport to work at Fangtasia. (TB)

Sarah: No last name given. One of Halleigh's best friends, Sarah is a bridesmaid at her wedding. (FDTW)

Sarah Jen: No last name given. Sarah Jen picks up the local gossip as she delivers the mail of Bon Temps. (DAG)

Savoy, Hadley Delahoussaye (vampire): Sookie's first cousin, Hadley leaves the family behind and disappears into New Orleans to live by her wits and her body. She eventually comes into contact with Queen Sophie-Anne Leclerq, who turns her as they become lovers. Devastated when Sophie-Anne arranges a marriage with Arkansas king Peter Threadgill, Hadley takes a diamond bracelet given to her lover by the king, a loss that could bring about the downfall of Sophie-Anne.

Finding Jake Purifoy drained in her driveway, Hadley turns the Were in a panic. Seeking answers, she arranges a visit to St. Louis Cemetery #1 with Waldo, the queen's former favorite, to commune with voodoo priestess Marie Laveau. Waldo, jealous at being replaced in the queen's affections, murders an unsuspecting Hadley.

Hadley's estate passes to Sookie, who finds a marriage and divorce cer-
tificate among the papers in Hadley's safe-deposit box. Unbeknownst to
her family, the marriage produced a child, Hunter, who is ultimately found
by Sookie. (Mentioned DUD; dies; mentioned OWA, DD, ATD, FDTW,
DAG, DITF, DR)

Savoy, Hank: Hank, Remy's great-uncle, lives with his wife in Red
Ditch. (Mentioned DR)

Savoy, Hunter (telepath): The child of Sookie's late cousin Hadley,
Hunter is thrilled when he meets Sookie and realizes that she is like him.
Just a child, he struggles with his telepathy, not quite understanding why
he can hear what people think and why he shouldn't speak of it. His father,
Remy, is relieved when Sookie offers to help Hunter, hoping she can train
him to control his mind—and his tongue.

Hunter is fascinated when he realizes that he can't "hear" vampires,
and he already knows that there are other things out there, things he cannot yet identify but is open to because he carries the essential spark. He
discovers that there is plenty to fear in human minds, from a mother's
thoughts of running away from her children, to a kindergarten teacher's
dark fantasies of abuse. (FDTW, DITF, DR; mentioned DAG)

Savoy, Remy: Hadley's ex-husband is raising their son in nearby Red
Ditch, having left New Orleans after Katrina. He is first wary, then grateful,
when Sookie enters their lives and recognizes his son's telepathic ability,
offering to help his child. Remy encourages contact between Sookie and
Hunter, trusting her to babysit while he attends a family funeral, and then
asking her to Hunter's kindergarten orientation, where he also trusts her
advice about the teaching staff. He is dating Kristen Duchesne when he
first meets Sookie, but the relationship turns sour when Kristen becomes
spooked by Hunter's abilities and tells others that something is wrong
with the boy. Remy begins dating Erin, a young woman who already truly
loves his son. When Sookie offers him Hadley's estate, Remy turns her
down, still bitter about Hadley's abandonment of their son, and tells her
that his great-aunt plans to leave her estate to Hunter, as she has no children of her own. (FDTW, DAG, DITF, DR)

Schubert, Michele: Jason may have finally met his match in divorcée
Michele, with her no-nonsense attitude and forthright personality. She
begins seeing him while he is separated from Crystal, and their relation-

ship survives Crystal's death and the ensuing investigation. When approached by Alexei at Jason's house, Michele sends him over to Sookie's, feeling that vamps are Sookie's problem, not Jason's. (DAG, DITF, DR)

Schubert, Pop: Michele Schubert's former father-in-law relies on his son's ex-wife at his Ford dealer's repair shop. (DITF)

Seabrook, Todd (vampire): The co-host of *The Best Dressed Vamp* with Bev Leveto, Todd has his throat ripped open on national TV when Devon Dawn doesn't respond well to their criticism of her wardrobe. The show must go on, and he soon recovers. (DAG)

Seal shifter: No name given. Unsurprisingly, the father of an Olympic swimmer reveals himself as a wereseal. (DAG)

Sechrest, Sandy (vampire): Felipe de Castro's area representative in Louisiana, Sandy is soon sent back to Nevada by Victor as he seeks more power over the state. (FDTW; mentioned DAG, DITF)

Sellers, Patsy (witch): Along with witches Amelia Broadway, Bob Jessup, and Terry Rodriguez, Patsy assists in performing the ectoplasmic reconstruction for the Queen of Louisiana after a Were turned by a vampire rises in Hadley's apartment and attacks Amelia and Sookie. She is in her sixties and has a Bowflex body. (DD)

Seven Veils Casino, the: Located in Baton Rouge, like all casinos it is open 24/7. A female vampire named Salome is one of the powers that be at the casino. Mickey the vampire takes Tara there several times during their relationship. (Mentioned DAAD)

Sharp Teeth (wolf): No other name given. The unidentified St. Catherine's Were attacks Sookie and Barbara Beck at the library. Whacked in the head by a book thrown by Sookie, he dies when he falls on his own knife. (Dies FDTW)

Shawn, Ra (vampire): Dreadlocked Ra Shawn precipitates the war between his home state of Arkansas and Louisiana by decapitating the guard Wybert at Sophie-Anne's spring party. He is killed in the ensuing battle. (Dies DD)

Shelley: No last name given. Shelley is David Cleary's stepdaughter. (Mentioned DTTW)

Shifter library: On each continent, the shifters maintain a library containing their history and their observations of other supes. Now online as well, the sites, both physical and electronic, remain closely guarded and are not made available to anyone other than shifters. The two-natured also maintain private message boards and monitor anti-shifter sites. (Mentioned DR)

Shreveport vampire bar: Though there are a number of "vampire bars," including Fangtasia, located in different cities, they cater to both vampires and humans. There is another bar in the Shreveport area that caters only to vampires. Beyond being in or near Shreveport, its name and exact location have never been stated. (LDID)

Shreveport witches, the: The Shreveport Weres recruit local Wiccans to join the Weres and the Area Five vampires in attacking Hallow's coven. The three witches—an older African American woman, a clean-cut young man, and a young woman—cast spells to make the coven members weak and indecisive and to identify the three innocent Wiccans who are being forced to help Hallow. As Mark Stonebrook begins a spell to cause a mist to permeate the room and confuse the space, the Shreveport witches, kept aware of the events through a scryer, retaliate by making it rain in the building to dissipate the mist. (DTTW)

Shurtliff, Delia: Wife and partner to contractor Randall Shurtliff, Delia runs their business very efficiently, making enough profit to easily provide for Randall's ex-wife, Mary Helen, and his three children from his first marriage. Delia and Randall rebuild Sookie's kitchen after it burns down. (DAAD)

Shurtliff, Mary Helen: Mary Helen is the ex-wife of Randall Shurtliff and mother of his three sons. (Mentioned DAAD)

Shurtliff, Randall: Contractor Randall and his second wife and partner, Delia, take the job of rebuilding Sookie's kitchen after the arson by Charles Twining. (DAAD)

Sid (wolf): No last name given. Shreveport Weres Emilio and Sid track Hallow and her coven to the empty business in Shreveport where the Witch War takes place. Sid files his teeth into points in preparation for the battle with the witches. (DTTW)

Sigebert (vampire): No other name given. Along with his brother Wybert, Saxon warrior Sigebert, whose name means "Bright Victory," is one of the Queen of Louisiana's trusted bodyguards. Turned centuries ago when Sophie-Anne approached them before a battle, the brothers didn't realize at first that the strength she promised meant they would be able to fight only at night from then on. After Wybert's death during the battle at the monastery, Sigebert loyally continues guarding his queen and maker. At Sophie-Anne's command, he slaughters Jennifer Cater and two of her party members at the vampire summit in Rhodes. He survives the hotel explosion and watches over Sophie-Anne in Baton Rouge as she attempts to recover from her injuries. He defends her from the invading Las Vegas vamps but to no avail, and he barely escapes with his own life. Intent on revenge, he targets Eric, whom he considers a traitor because he is the only surviving Louisiana sheriff. He ambushes Eric, King of Nevada Felipe de Castro, and Sam in the Merlotte's parking lot. Sookie runs him over with her car and helps Eric and Sam escape, whereupon Eric decapitates Sigebert. (DD, ATD; dies FDTW; mentioned DAG, DITF)

Silent Shore Hotel, the: The Silent Shore, one of the grand old hotels in Dallas, is the only hotel in the area that has undergone the extensive renovations necessary to accommodate vampire patrons: light-tight rooms, blood supplies (both natural and artificial), and rooms for any human companions that may be traveling with the vampires. Sookie and Bill stay there during their trip to Dallas, and for the first time Sookie meets another telepath in Barry (the Bellboy) Horowitz. (LDID)

Simpson, Ben: Hooligans stripper Ben sometimes performs as a cop, and he uses the stage name Barry Barber because he likes to shave people by private appointment. A suspect in Claudette Crane's death, Ben is cleared by Sookie, and his memories of her questioning are erased by Claudine. (FD)

Simpson, Mark: Fangbangers Mark and Mindy are part of Victor's entourage, accompanying him and his vampires to Fangtasia to hear Bubba's performance. When the battle begins and his wife is killed, Mark tries to join the fight but is hit with a bottle by Colton. He doesn't get up. (Dies DR)

Simpson, Mindy: Mindy and her husband, Mark, are fangbangers in Victor's retinue and join him and his vampires at Fangtasia to listen to Bubba sing. When Eric swings a stake at Victor, Victor's second, Akiro, blocks his arm and cleaves through Mindy's shoulder, killing her almost instantly. (DR dies)

Sino-AIDS: A variant of the blood-borne immune system disease, it is one of the few illnesses that can affect vampires, leaving them very weak for a month after drinking the infected blood. At the Monroe vampires' house, Sookie warns Bill against drinking from Jerry, telling him the man is infected with the disease. (DUD)

Skinner, Dr.: No first name given. Dr. Skinner treats Maria-Star Cooper at the Clarice hospital, unaware that her patient is a werewolf whose injuries were sustained when she was hit while in her wolf form by a car driven by a witch. (DTTW)

Smith, Bailey: A high school classmate of Jason's, Bailey is now a local insurance agent. Like the other agents, Bailey suffers a run of bad luck. (L)

Smith, Everett O'Dell: A student at Tulane Business School, Everett is Mr. Cataliades's gofer and helps Sookie pack up Hadley's apartment. He decides to rent Hadley's place from Amelia, watching over her apartment as well when she heads to Bon Temps with Sookie. He and the building survive Katrina relatively intact. (DD; mentioned FDTW)

Sonntag, Dr.: No first name given. Attractive Dr. Sonntag takes care of Sookie after she is attacked by Rene Lenier and briefly dates JB du Rone. (DUD; mentioned LDID)

Sookie Stackhouse's house: The Stackhouse farmhouse sits on twenty acres of land, well hidden from the road, and the long gravel driveway leads to a parking area in front with an additional area in the back. Built as a single-story home in the 1850s, the original rectangular house consisted of what is now the living room. The kitchen, bathrooms, downstairs bedrooms, and partial second story were added later. The second floor is currently comprised of two small bedrooms and an attic storage area, with room for another bedroom. The front door opens into the living room, with a hallway leading off of the back wall. On the left side of the hallway is a master bedroom with an en suite bath, and on the right is a smaller bedroom, complete with a light-tight vampire hidey-hole in the closet, a separate bathroom, and coat and linen cupboards. The hall continues to the kitchen, which is large enough to serve as the family dining room. After a fire destroys the kitchen and the screened-in back porch, the kitchen is renovated and the back porch, which doubles as a laundry room, is widened and enclosed. Overall, the furniture in the house is old and comfortable, just like the house itself. A tin roof adds to the charm, as does a bench swing on the front porch.

Humans, shifters, vampires, and fairies regularly roam the woods around the house, and the property has been the site of murder, arson, a demon's pyre, buried bodies, staked vampires, and disintegrating fairies. (DUD, LDID, CD, DTTW, DAAD, OWA, DD, ATD, L, FDTW, GW, DAG, DITF, DR; mentioned FD, DN)

Sophie-Anne Leclerq's headquarters: The Queen of Louisiana, Sophie-Anne Leclerq maintains her business headquarters near downtown New Orleans. She owns a block of buildings near the edge of the French Quarter, a not inexpensive area. The three-story office building takes up an entire city block. The windows have all been covered with panels that are decorated in a Mardi Gras theme, with pink, purple, and green designs on a white or black background to offer protection to the vampires who use the place as a retreat or reside there. The iridescent patches on the shutters give them a look like Mardi Gras beads. Because it is publicly known where Sophie-Anne holds "court," the sidewalks teem at all hours with souvenir peddlers, tour guides, and the curious who have just come to gawk at the vampires. (DD; mentioned ATD)

Special Events: Special Events is a secret division of Extreme(ly Elegant) Events, a nationwide event-planning company well known by its E(E)E logo. Special Events does the same sort of thing for the supernatural community, handling events such as packmaster contests, rites of ascension, and vampire hierarchal weddings. Basically, if you want your supe events done right, you go to Special Events. As one of four partners in the company, weretiger John Quinn arranges the staging of the Shreveport packmaster contest, the wedding of Sophie-Anne and Peter Threadgill, and all the official ceremonies at the summit in Rhodes. (Mentioned DD, ATD, FDTW, DAG, STW)

Spencer, Mike: Mike Spencer, owner of Spencer and Sons Funeral Home, is also the Renard Parish coroner. This seemingly upright citizen becomes involved in group sex parties and is directly responsible for the death of Lafayette Reynold, along with fellow partier Tom Hardaway. Mike succumbs to maenad Callisto's madness when she's drawn to their orgy, and Lafayette's belongings are found in his car. (DUD; dies LDID)

Splendide: A real bell rings when the door opens at Brenda Hesterman and Donald Callaway's antiques shop, Splendide, in Shreveport. The two owners appraise and buy antiques of all shapes and sizes, including jewelry, furniture, and clothing. When Sookie cleans out her attic, the partners come to her home to appraise the items, and they purchase several pieces of furniture, including Mitchell's desk, as well as some smaller objects. (DR)

Spradlin, Whit: Arlene's latest boyfriend, Fellowship of the Sun official Whit is both furious and appalled when the shifters are revealed. Although they know Sookie is not a shifter, he decides to make her an example of what happens to shifter sympathizers and crucify her, aping Crystal's death even though he and his cohorts had nothing to do with it. Whit persuades Arlene to go along with the despicable plan and gets her to lure Sookie to her trailer. Sookie is able to discern their intentions from a distance and calls Andy, who soon arrives with Agents Lattesta and Weiss. Whit is badly wounded in the shoot-out, his co-conspirator Donny is killed, and Arlene suffers a minor injury. (DAG)

Stackhouse, Adele Hale: Adele raises her two grandchildren after her son's death and is murdered in her own kitchen by Rene Lenier, a substitute victim of his insane rage against women involved with vampires.

It is eventually revealed that Adele's two children were fathered by half-fairy Fintan. Because her husband, Mitchell, was rendered infertile by mumps, Adele got involved with Fintan when he promised her the children she so desperately wanted. (Dies DUD; mentioned LDID, CD, DTTW, DN, DAAD, OWA, DD, ATD, FDTW, GW, DAG, DITF, DR)

Stackhouse, Corbett Hale (half fairy): Sookie's father, Corbett, never knows that he is the son of half-fairy Fintan, but he dies because of it, killed with his wife by the fairies and water sprites loyal to Breandan, the enemy of his grandfather Niall. (Deceased; mentioned DUD, CD, DAAD, FDTW, DITF)

Stackhouse, Crystal Norris (panther): Thin and intense, with short, curly, dusty-looking black hair, Crystal looks younger than her real mid-twenties age. Looking for a good time, werepanther Crystal accepts a date for New Year's Eve with Jason after meeting him in a Wal-Mart. After suffering a miscarriage, she has been excused from her responsibility to contribute to the pack because she is too inbred and can barely change with the moon. She sees Jason as both an exciting challenge and a chance for a different life. But fellow Hotshot werepanther Felton Norris is so obsessed with Crystal that he kidnaps Jason and bites him until he is turned in a warped attempt to level the playing field, feeling that if Jason is a panther,

Crystal will not find him as desirable. Sookie and Sam go to Calvin Norris and are able to rescue Jason, and Felton pays for his crime at the claws of the pack so that they don't go to the police. After suffering another miscarriage, Crystal becomes pregnant again, so she and Jason marry. Although she makes her vows, she isn't sincere about keeping them and begins an affair with Dove Beck, one of Jason's co-workers. She further jeopardizes her marriage by spending money recklessly, a task she is encouraged in by a bespelled Tanya Grissom on behalf of Sandra Pelt. Suspecting the lovers will meet at his house while he is on errands, Jason arranges for both Calvin and Sookie to witness them together. Because Calvin stood for Crystal at the wedding and she is pregnant, he will take her punishment. Sookie stood for Jason, so Jason chooses to have her deliver the punishment instead of doing it himself. Sookie has no choice but to break Calvin's "claw" just as Crystal broke her vows, and she brings a brick down on his hand. Crystal moves back to Hotshot but continues to be a presence in Jason's life. When she drops by his house and finds Mel Hart waiting for him, she taunts Mel until he slaps her unconscious, and he leaves her in the truck, still out cold, as he goes into Jason's house to settle his nerves. While he's inside, she is found by Lochlan and Neave, who crucify her in Merlotte's parking lot in their depraved version of fun. Jason and Sookie both mourn the loss of Jason's child and are saddened by Crystal's death, believing that, for all her sins, she did not deserve to die afraid and alone at the hands of two twisted and perverted fairies. (DTTW, ATD, FDTW; dies DAG; mentioned DITF, DR)

Stackhouse, Jason (panther): Jason Stackhouse is a ladies' man, romancing his way through Bon Temps and surrounding areas. His carefree ways almost prove to be his undoing when he is suspected of killing several women, including his own grandmother, but he is cleared when his sister, Sookie, is attacked by Jason's co-worker Rene Lenier, the real killer, and is able to defend herself, leading to Rene's arrest. Jason attempts to change his ways but is unable to stick with one woman for long until he meets Crystal Norris, a werepanther from the nearby town of Hotshot. Crystal decides to find a man outside Hotshot and the panther pack, and his involvement with her causes another local werepanther, Felton Norris, to kidnap Jason and change him into a werepanther to level the playing field in the competition for Crystal's affections. Jason is "bitten, not blood," so he only partially changes with the moon, but he runs with the pack and continues dating Crystal. They marry on the spur of the moment when Crystal finds out she is pregnant again after an earlier miscarriage. Jason soon regrets his impulses, both sexual and legal, as Crystal turns out to be a most unsuitable wife. When he discovers that she is being unfaithful, he sets up Sookie and Calvin Norris, Crystal's uncle, to catch her in the act with her lover. Sookie and Calvin stood for Jason and Crystal at their wedding, pledging responsibility for them, and when it comes time for the punishment of Crystal by the panther pack, Calvin stands for her, as she is pregnant, and Jason selfishly has Sookie stand for him. His sister must shatter Calvin's fingers, symbolic of his panther claws, with a brick, and she vows to never speak to Jason again. Jason attempts to mend fences with his sister, but his charm is lost on her and he is finally forced to change his self-centered nature. Separated from Crystal, he begins dating Michele Schubert, a local divorcée with a no-nonsense attitude. When Crystal is found crucified in the parking lot at Merlotte's, Sookie mourns the loss of his wife and baby with him, and they begin to reconnect. Jason suffers another loss when his new friend, fellow werepanther Mel Hart, is revealed to have injured Crystal after she taunted him about his feelings for Jason, leaving her vulnerable to her real killers. Mel admits his love for his friend before Jason, Calvin, and Crystal's sister and cousin exact justice for his actions. Jason finds out about his fairy heritage from Sookie and is angered that his great-grandfather doesn't want to know him because of his selfishness and his close resemblance to his great-uncle Dermot, and he says a bitter good-bye to Niall when he closes the door to Faery. He continues rebuilding his relationship with Sookie, escorting her to the Were trial at Alcide's house, and continues dating Michele, seemingly serious about their relationship.

For all his charm, Jason lacks the essential spark so treasured by his fairy grandfather, Fintan, so the telepathy gifted to his family by Desmond Cataliades passes him by, as it did with his father and aunt. (DUD, LDID, CD, DTTW, DAAD, DD, ATD, FDTW, DAG, DITF, DR; mentioned FD, OWA, L, GW)

Stackhouse, Jonas: Jonas, Mitchell Stackhouse's great-great-great-great-grandfather, knew Bill before he was turned. He lived at the Stackhouse family home with his wife and four children and owned two slaves, although he worked his own fields. (Deceased; mentioned DUD)

Stackhouse, Michelle: Michelle Stackhouse never realizes that it is her husband's fairy heritage that enthralls her, making her jealous even of the attention he pays his own children. That same heritage is responsible for her death alongside her husband when they are drowned by water sprites loyal to the enemy of his birth grandfather Niall. (Deceased; mentioned DUD, CD, FDTW, DAG, DITF, DR)

Stackhouse, Mitchell: Adele's husband, Mitchell, becomes sterile after having the mumps and is not the father of Corbett and Linda. (Deceased; mentioned DUD, FDTW, DAG, DITF, DR)

Stackhouse, Sookie (telepath): Small-town girl Sookie Stackhouse waits tables and reads minds. She is never alone in her own head, constantly barraged by the thoughts of those around her. Vampires have been "out of the coffin" for two years when one comes into the bar and Sookie meets Bill Compton, former Confederate soldier and local landowner. When Bill foolishly leaves the bar with a couple who turn out to be Drainers (people who drain vampires of their blood to sell it), Sookie comes to his rescue. Bill returns the favor a few nights later when the couple return to retaliate against Sookie, beating her badly. Sookie discovers that she cannot "hear" Bill, and she finds in Bill that which she wants and needs most: companionship that gives her a respite from the "blah blah blah" of other people's thoughts that crowd her brain. They begin a relationship that continues even after several local women connected with vampires are murdered. When suspicion falls on her brother, Jason, Sookie seeks information to clear him, going with Bill to a vampire bar in Shreveport to ask questions. She comes to the attention of Fangtasia bar owner Eric Northman, who is doubly interested when he realizes her telepathic abilities.

Believing she was the intended target when her grandmother becomes a victim of the killer, Sookie struggles with her guilt even as her relationship with Bill deepens. Adding to her problems, Eric Northman has decided to use her abilities to uncover an embezzler at Fangtasia. When the culprit is revealed as vampire Long Shadow, the bartender, Eric stakes Long Shadow as he attacks Sookie. Bill leaves town to campaign for a place in the vampire hierarchy as a measure against Eric, and Sookie is assaulted by the murderer, Rene Lenier, stabbing him in self-defense. Bill returns with the news that he has been named Area Five investigator, placing him under Eric's protection.

Bill and Sookie are on the way to Fangtasia to get an assignment from Eric when the car breaks down and they quarrel. Sookie is attacked by a maenad as she walks home. Bill is able to get her to Fangtasia, where blood draining and then transfusions wash the maenad's poison from her system, and after some recovery time, Eric informs them that they are going to Dallas to help find a missing vamp. Once there, Sookie and a human companion attempt to infiltrate the Fellowship of the Sun, an anti-vampire "church," but her companion betrays her. Sookie is injured while escaping, with the help of first Godfrey, a vampire renouncer who seeks to meet the dawn, and then Luna, a shifter who has also infiltrated the organization. After Bill and the local vamps rescue the missing vamp, Sookie returns in the morning to the deserted compound to witness Godfrey's self-immolation. Upon her return to Bon Temps, Sookie becomes involved in finding the murderer of the cook at Merlotte's, Lafayette Reynold, whose body she had found in the bar's parking lot in Andy Bellefleur's car before going to Dallas. Invited to an orgy by those she suspects, Sookie asks Eric to escort her, as Bill has had to make a brief trip back to Dallas. She finds out the identity of the murderers, but before she, Eric, and a just-returned Bill can leave the orgy, a drunken Andy stumbles from the woods. Desperate to find the murderer and clear his name, he calls on Sookie to read the minds of the orgy participants. Callisto, the maenad, arrives, drawn by the atmosphere of lust and drunkenness. She sends her madness into the orgy, and Sookie is almost drawn into the insanity through her telepathy. Satisfied by her tribute, the maenad moves on, leaving Bill and Eric to clean up her mess. Andy is cleared when evidence of the murder is found in one of the automobiles of the deceased partygoers. Bill and Sookie relax at her home, finding a cake from Andy's grandmother on her doorstep the next day as a gesture of thanks. Hearing her full name, Bill realizes that the Bellefleurs are his descendants through his daughter Sarah.

When Bill leaves town under suspicious circumstances, Sookie is hurt and angry but nevertheless becomes determined to find him when told he is now missing and considered kidnapped. Accompanied by werewolf

Alcide Herveaux, she travels to Jackson and goes to Josephine's, a supe bar nicknamed Club Dead, hoping to "hear" something about Bill. After being staked while protecting the King of Mississippi's second-in-command, she locates Bill at the king's mansion and is able to rescue him after killing his maker. Locked in a car trunk by Debbie Pelt, Alcide's jealous ex-girlfriend, Sookie suffers a physical assault from a starved and tortured Bill, who is lost in bloodlust. They are finally able to escape the trunk, and Sookie has Eric, who has tagged along, take her home. Eric is attacked by thugs hired by the biker gang that frequents Club Dead when they stop for gas, and Sookie hurries to save both him and the young clerk. When they finally get to her house, they are attacked again by some of the gang members themselves. Sookie is beaten, but Eric and Bill, who drove home as well, burst in to kill all the bikers.

Sookie and Bill remain estranged, and soon after he goes on a research trip, she finds Eric running down the road to her home early on New Year's morning. Confused and half-naked, Eric has been cursed with amnesia by a witch who wants to take over part of his holdings. Sookie agrees to shelter the befuddled vamp while Pam and Chow plan to restore Eric's memory. Sookie's brother, Jason, goes missing, and even as she worries about him, she heads to Shreveport to warn Alcide about the witches because some of them are Weres, and together they find that the coven has killed the Long Tooth pack's second, Adabelle Yancy. Returning to Bon Temps, Sookie finds comfort with Eric, and the two begin a brief, passionate affair.

Sookie locates Crystal Norris, Jason's date on New Year's Eve, in the tiny town of Hotshot, hoping the young woman can offer some information. Although Crystal is unable to help, her uncle, Calvin Norris, offers Sookie his protection. Admitting that he has seen her in Merlotte's, the Hotshot packleader begins a quiet courtship of Sookie, joining in an organized search of the woods surrounding Jason's house with Bon Temps locals, along with Crystal and Hotshot's best tracker, Felton Norris. Sookie despairs when there is no sign of Jason.

The Weres decide to partner with the vamps to destroy the coven, and Sookie attends the conflict with Eric, using her abilities to identify the innocent local witches who are being forced to participate. The Weres and vampires prevail, and Pam takes Hallow, the coven leader, captive to force her to break the spell on Eric. Attacked by Debbie Pelt on their return home, Sookie is forced to shoot and kill her. Eric disposes of her body and her car while Sookie cleans up the mess. When he awakens the next evening, the spell has been broken, his memories are restored, and he has no recollection of the time they spent together. Pam arrives to take him home and fill him in on the Were war and the damage done to Fangtasia by the coven. When Sam informs Sookie that the Hotshot shifters are panthers, she tells him that a panther track was found at Jason's, and the two race out to Hotshot. With Calvin's help they locate a badly bitten and freezing Jason in Felton's toolshed. Calvin assures them that Hotshot will see that Jason's kidnapper is punished, and Sookie takes her brother home, knowing the chances are good that he will now shift with the moon.

Sookie approaches Eric on Sam's behalf when Sam is shot by a sniper targeting local shifters and needs to borrow a bartender. He complies, sending newly hired Charles Twining back to Bon Temps with her. Shortly thereafter, Alcide Herveaux escorts Sookie to the funeral of the Shreveport packmaster, who has died in a car accident. Sookie doesn't realize at first that Alcide is also hoping she will use her ability for his father's benefit on the Were running against his father for the packmaster position. At the funeral, her attention is caught by a tall, bald man who seems to be watching over the proceedings, including her furious albeit hushed discussion with Alcide on the church steps about his deceit. After work that night she takes Charles home with her to stay in the vampire hidey-hole. She is awakened in the night first by Charles confronting Bill in her yard and then by a fire. Claudine pops in to rescue her, and Charles claims he killed the arsonist in self-defense. Sookie is shaken but soon begins to rebuild her damaged kitchen, staying in a rental house in town. While returning books to the library, Sookie is winged by a sniper.

Sookie asks Eric for assistance for her friend Tara, who is being abused by a vampire named Mickey. Eric is happy to do a favor for Sookie, providing she repay it by telling him the truth about what happened while he had amnesia. She complies, and he is stunned to find that he was willing to give up everything to be with her.

She attends the packmaster contest and finds Quinn, the tall man from the funeral, officiating. Although she catches Alcide's father's opponent, Patrick Furnan, cheating, the pack decides to allow the contest to continue anyway, and Alcide's father is ultimately killed by his opponent. Alcide turns from her, seeking comfort with another Were, and she goes to work that night with a heavy heart. She realizes that the bartender Eric lent to Sam is not who he says he is, and the vampire admits that he is there to kill her in revenge for the staking of Long Shadow. She is able to stuff her silver chain in his mouth and escape, and the vampire is staked by the regular patrons at Merlotte's.

Sookie meets up with weretiger Quinn again a month later, when he walks into Merlotte's with two purposes: to deliver a message from the vampire Queen of Louisiana, whose wedding he has just overseen for his company, and to ask Sookie out. She is delighted to go out on a real date, but their good time is ruined when they are attacked by two bitten Weres while leaving the theater. After filing a police report, Quinn takes Sookie to a shifter bar to inform them of the attack and remind them that she is a friend of the pack. Quinn takes her home, and they set up another date, but Mr. Cataliades arrives to take her to New Orleans to settle her late, twice-deceased vampire cousin Hadley's estate. Bill accompanies them to New Orleans, where Sookie and Amelia, Hadley's landlord, are attacked by a vampire whom no one realizes Hadley has created. A Were who has been missing for several months, Jake has lain hidden in Hadley's closet, held in stasis by a spell Amelia cast. Bill and Eric both come to the hospital where Sookie waits for treatment, and Eric forces Bill to admit that his pursuit of Sookie began as an assignment from the queen. Devastated, she leaves the hospital and wanders back to the apartment. The next night, Sookie, Queen Sophie-Anne Leclerq, and her bodyguards watch an ectoplasmic reconstruction arranged by Amelia to determine why Hadley, the queen's favorite, turned the Were. Quinn arrives to break the tension, having come to New Orleans to look for the missing Were, Jake, one of his employees. Sookie welcomes him the next day to help her pack, but they are attacked again and kidnapped by Weres, who drive them toward the swamps. They escape, track their attackers to a cabin in the woods, and discover that the family of Debbie Pelt is behind their troubles. Sookie decides to tell the family the story of Debbie's death. They believe that it was self-defense, and Debbie's parents promise that they will not seek vengeance. Sookie and Quinn attend the queen's spring ball, where a battle breaks out between the Louisiana vamps and the Arkansas vamps of the queen's new husband.

Sookie escapes with Quinn and is happy to finish her business and leave New Orleans the next day.

Although initially asked by Eric, Sookie attends a summit of vampires in the city of Rhodes as part of the queen's entourage. She and Quinn have become serious, and she hopes to spend time with him at the summit, which he is overseeing for his company. Sookie is the only witness to the death of Peter Threadgill, Sophie-Anne's husband, and expects to be called to testify on the queen's behalf. The queen's second, Andre Paul, believes Sookie can be of more use to the queen if she is connected to him by a blood bond. Eric interrupts as Sookie tries to resist. He suggests that Andre allow him to forge the blood bond with Sookie instead, since they have already had each other's blood. Andre allows this, and Sookie unwillingly gives and receives blood with Eric. Quinn bursts onto the scene, furious that the vampires have forced Sookie into such a situation. Sookie tries to walk away with her head held high but breaks down in a stairwell.

Barry, the telepath she met while in Dallas, is in service to Stan Davis, who is now King of Texas. They both sense that something is wrong at the summit, and Barry awakens Sookie on the final morning in a panic. They discover that there are bombs planted throughout the hotel and frantically try to save both the humans and the vampires with the help of Mr. Cataliades, his niece Diantha, and a human named Cecile, who is also in service to Stan. Sookie alerts Quinn to get out of the hotel, Cecile pulls the fire alarm to evacuate the humans, and they rush to get their vampires to safety. Sookie manages to rouse Eric long enough to stuff Pam into her traveling coffin and get them all out of a window, while Mr. Cataliades is able to save Sophie-Anne. Working to rescue both humans and vampires, Sookie spies an injured Quinn in the rubble, with his sister and Andre lying nearby. Although badly hurt, Quinn insists that Sookie leave to help others, and she walks away knowing that he is going to stake Andre to protect her from his influence. After Sookie and Barry combine their talents to save people from the wreckage, they finally make their way to a motel in exhaustion. Although Mr. Cataliades has arranged a flight the next afternoon, Sookie decides to see Quinn instead and then makes her own way home.

Sookie is back in Bon Temps waiting to hear from Quinn when Eric calls and asks her to dinner on behalf of someone who wishes to meet her. He takes her to a restaurant in Shreveport, where she is surprised to be introduced to a fairy who explains that he is her great-grandfather. His half-human son Fintan had an affair with Gran, fathering both Sookie's father and his sister, Linda. On the way home, Sookie and Eric are stopped by a Were pretending to be a policeman, who takes a shot at Sookie. The next day she discovers that Maria-Star Cooper, Alcide Herveaux's girlfriend, has been murdered, and that Alcide suspects the packmaster is behind it. Sookie arranges a meeting between the two Weres, acting as a go-between and truth barometer, and Patrick's innocence is proven as he tells them his own wife is missing. They are ambushed by a female packmaster seeking to take over their territory. Among the casualties are Patrick, Amanda, and most of the enemy Weres. Sam surprises Sookie by shifting into a lion and fighting to protect her. Once again, Claudine pops in to rescue Sookie and reveals that Sookie's great-grandfather Niall is also Claudine's grandfather.

No sooner has Sookie caught her breath from the Were war than another war literally lands on her doorstep. Knowing that Sophie-Anne Leclerq was injured in the summit bombing, the Nevada vamps launch a takeover and follow Eric to Sookie's house, where he has fled after being cut off from Fangtasia. Quinn sends his sister, Frannie, to warn them. She tells Sookie that Quinn has been forced to work with the Nevada vamps. When the King of Nevada's second shows up in Sookie's front yard with his crew, Quinn accompanies them. He is waiting for Sookie when she wakes in the morning, and she breaks up with him because she feels that his responsibility to his mentally ill mother and younger sister will always stand in the way of a relationship with her.

After finding out that Jason and his new wife, Crystal, are having problems and that Sandra Pelt, Debbie's younger sister, is manipulating Tanya Grissom to cause trouble, Sookie asks Calvin, who has been seeing Tanya, to bring her to Amelia and her mentor, Octavia, to be unspelled. They are able to clear Tanya of Sandra's influence, but even pregnant, Crystal is trouble all on her own. Jason sets up Sookie and Calvin to catch his wife cheating, and Sookie is forced to inflict punishment on Calvin, breaking his fingers with a brick, because she and Calvin stood for Jason and Crystal at their wedding. Sookie is so disgusted with her brother for making her take his place that she vows to never forgive him.

When Eric and King Felipe de Castro are attacked in the Merlotte's parking lot (along with innocent bystander Sam), Sookie runs over Sigebert, Sophie-Anne's child and bodyguard, to save them, a gesture that earns her the promise of protection from the king. Great-grandfather Niall visits, asking Sookie if there is anything he can do for her, and she asks him to find her late cousin Hadley's ex-husband, since she's discovered Hadley left a child. He sends her the address and she visits them in Red Ditch, discovering that the child, Hunter, is a fellow telepath. She offers to help in any way she can.

At work at Merlotte's on the night the shifters come out live on TV, Sookie also sees action in the bar as Sam and Tray Dawson both shift in front of the patrons. Sookie is happy that it seems to go well, but Sam gets the news that his stepfather shot his mother when she shifted in front of him. Sam immediately heads out for Texas, leaving Sookie in charge of the bar. A few days later, Eric's daytime guy, Bobby Burnham, brings her a wrapped package and tells her to present it to Eric in front of Victor Madden, King Felipe de Castro's second-in-command. Doing so, she finds that she has inadvertently married Eric by vampire law, a strategy that Eric swears is for her own protection. She leaves Fangtasia angry at herself and Eric. The next morning she is visited by two FBI agents who want to discover exactly how she and her unidentified companion (Barry) helped save people at the summit. When Sookie is called to Merlotte's by a report of a body in the parking lot, the agents follow, and they find that Crystal Norris Stackhouse has been crucified behind the bar. While the police and the FBI investigate the crime scene, Sookie heads back to Fangtasia at dark to speak with Eric, and he tells her about his past. Merlotte's is allowed to open the next day, and Niall comes to visit, letting Sookie know that there is trouble among the fairies and that she should be careful. Mr. Cataliades also sends Diantha with a warning that fairies are indeed moving about in this world. Sookie calls Claude to get more information. She meets Claude and Claudine for lunch, and they explain Niall's family tree, his position as the fairy prince, and the issues with his nephew Breandan, who despises humans, especially the offspring that have come from human and fairy couplings. Breandan wants to close off Faery so there will be no further contact with humanity. After Sookie returns home, she is attacked by a fairy in her yard but is able to kill him. Quinn arrives to speak with her and is accosted by Bill, sent by Eric, who has banned Quinn from Area Five. Sookie is injured during their brawl and is given blood by Eric when he arrives. They rekindle their relationship, spending the night together.

Arlene—Sookie's co-worker and onetime friend, who quit over the shifters coming out—calls, claiming she wants to make amends. Sookie is suspicious and stealthily approaches Arlene's trailer. She is horrified to learn that Arlene's friends from the Fellowship of the Sun are planning on crucifying her, although she realizes that they were not the ones who killed Crystal. She is able to call Andy Bellefleur, and police and FBI agents soon arrive, but a shoot-out ensues, killing one of the Fellowship of the Sun members and injuring one of the agents. Hearing that there has been trouble, Alcide sends Tray to guard Sookie. She asks for the protection promised by Felipe, but only Bubba comes to her aid. Both he and Tray are sickened by enemy fairies. Sookie is forced to tell Jason about their fairy heritage when he is confronted in his house by their great-uncle Dermot, who is trying to tell him that his friend and fellow werepanther Mel Hart killed Crystal. Mel admits having been goaded by Crystal and striking her but denies crucifying her. Sookie leaves as Jason, Calvin, Crystal's sister, and their cousin exact justice for Crystal. When Sookie is unable to get an answer from either Tray or Amelia, who have been dating, she calls Bill for help. He enters Tray's house to find blood, not all of it the Were's, and follows Sookie back to her house. She loses him at a light. Sookie decides to run from her car into her house, knowing Amelia is waiting, but she is seized by two of Breandan's fairies, Lochlan and Neave. They take her to a deserted house in Arkansas to torture her, hoping her abduction will induce Niall to cede his right to the fairy throne. She is rescued along with Tray by Niall and Bill, who is badly injured by Neave and her silver-tipped teeth. Taken to Dr. Ludwig's hospital, Sookie is given blood by Eric to heal, since they are sure the fairies are going to attack soon. Breandan and his forces arrive, determined to wipe out the opposition. A pregnant Claudine dies, along with Eric's henchman Clancy, and Tray. The severely wounded Bill kills Breandan as he goes for Sookie. Sookie sadly surveys the carnage as Niall arrives, having defeated Breandan's forces on every front. Sookie is home trying to recover when Niall visits and meets Jason for the first time. He tells them that he will seal off Faery because the fairies are too dangerous to humankind, and kisses his great-grandchildren good-bye.

Sookie and Eric continue to strengthen their relationship as Sookie tries to restore her physical and mental health. She reestablishes her connection with Jason as well, happy to see him seemingly settled in a good relationship. She allows the Weres to have their full-moon run on her property. They tell her that fairies have been in her woods and that there is a body buried there. Realizing that the body must be Debbie Pelt's, Sookie tells Eric when she visits him in Shreveport; but she forgets to tell him that Claude has moved in, seeking the company of family and fairy. As Pam is driving Sookie home, they are stopped by Bruno Brazell, Victor's second, and a female vampire named Corinna. Pam tells Sookie that Victor's vampires are going to try to kill them. Sookie and Pam manage to turn the tables.

Feeling safe from any threat for the moment, Sookie agrees to watch Hunter overnight while Remy attends a family funeral. Sookie tries to help Hunter cope with his ability and works with him to control it—and what he says about it. After Remy picks him up the next day, Eric awakens in the hidey-hole and they spend the evening together until Eric's maker, Appius Livius Ocella, and his child Alexei arrive. Since Sookie was told earlier that a second body lies in her woods, Eric is convinced it has been planted there by the Weres. He contacts Alcide, who soon arrives with a small coterie. The whole party troops out to the woods, where the remains of Alcide's second, Basim al Saud, are discovered.

Bill decides to deliver the family Bible to Caroline Bellefleur when he is told she has inquired about it, and he asks Sookie to accompany him as he reveals his family connection to the dying Caroline. Sookie is worried at his inability to recover from the silver poisoning. Upon discovering that his maker's blood would have helped him, she uses his database to seek out his sibling, Judith, hoping her blood will serve the same purpose. When Judith arrives, Sookie tells her of the death of her maker, and the vampire happily heads off to help Bill. The following evening, Sookie and Jason attend the Were meeting, where Sookie acts as shaman and identifies the murderers of Basim. Afterward, she feels that something is wrong with Eric, and they rush to his house to find both Eric and Pam badly injured, and Bobby Burnham and vampire bartender Felicia dead—all at the hands of Alexei, who has descended into madness. Sookie drives Eric to her house, where they find Ocella, his back broken by Alexei, lying helpless as Alexei teasingly attacks Claude and an unknown fairy in her yard. Sookie is able to subdue Alexei with a silver chain so Eric can stake him. As she approaches Ocella, considering killing him, she decides instead to ask him to kill Victor Madden in return for sparing his life. While leaning over him, she is attacked by the second fairy, Colman, the father of the late Claudine's unborn child. Ocella mentally urges her to move out of the way and takes Colman's sword thrust himself. Colman is stunned by his deed and by the knife suddenly lodged in his back, and Eric is able to seize him and drain him. Sookie's great-uncle Dermot emerges from the woods, having thrown the knife to save her, and she realizes that he has been bespelled. She and Claude are able to break the spell. After Eric leaves, the fairies climb into bed with her and she relaxes, surrounded by family.

Sookie is working the evening a Molotov cocktail is thrown through the window at Merlotte's, and she suffers singed hair and skin as she helps put out the flames. Business at the bar has been sparse lately, due to a rival establishment opening nearby, and she, Sam, and the other employees worry that Merlotte's clientele will dwindle even more when word of the firebombing gets around. Eric arrives, having felt her panic through their blood bond, and sends for Pam and a hairdresser. As Sookie showers after getting her hair trimmed, she comes to the conclusion that the thoughts she picked up from outside just before the bomb was thrown did not come from a human. She is stunned when Eric and Pam come to blows in her kitchen, and then angry at the damage they are doing. When the vampires calm down, she sends them both home.

After cleaning out her attic with Dermot and Claude, Sookie rides with Sam to a Shreveport antiques store to arrange an appraisal. They stop by Hooligans on the way back and find the club full of assorted fae. Sookie questions her great-uncle and cousin about her fae heritage but receives only a promise to talk later; however, neither fairy returns home that night. The following night, Eric takes Sookie to Victor's new dance club, Vampire's Kiss, where she finds out that Victor also owns Vic's Redneck Roadhouse, the bar that is drawing customers from Merlotte's. She meets Pam's lover, Miriam, who is dying of leukemia and whom Victor has forbidden Pam to turn. On the ride home, Sookie is shocked again when Eric physically stops Pam from speaking after she brings up a mysterious letter. Sookie spends another night alone. When Dermot and Claude finally show up for their promised talk, Sookie learns more about her great-grandfather Niall and discovers that he had been getting information about her for some time from Eric. She also realizes that her fae blood is accentuated by her contact with Dermot and Claude. The appraisers arrive as scheduled, and Sookie sells them several items, including her grand-father Mitchell's desk. Before taking it away, one of the appraisers searches the desk and finds a hidden compartment, which contains an old dress-pattern envelope and a small velvet bag. Sookie recognizes Gran's hand-writing on a letter in the envelope and puts the letter and bag away until she has some time alone to examine them. Jack and Lily Leeds, the detec-tives who were investigating Debbie Pelt's disappearance, come into the bar that night. The couple tells Sookie that they have been sent by Mr. Cataliades to warn her about Sandra Pelt's continuing vendetta against her. Four thugs, high on vampire blood, come into the bar while the Leedses are there. After making threats and pulling weapons, the toughs are sub-dued and arrested, and no one (except Sookie) realizes she was the target. Sookie calls Amelia the next day to ask if the wards around the house are still strong and if she can find Sandra, and Amelia decides to visit. Sookie reads Gran's letter and learns even more about her fairy grandfather, including the fact that Mr. Cataliades was his trusted friend and was asked to act as the family sponsor, which explains the demon lawyer's interest in Sookie. The item in the bag is a cluviel dor, a powerful fairy love token that can grant one wish, a wish capable of changing lives.

Sandra storms into the bar two days later, pulling a gun on Sookie, but is disabled by Terry Bellefleur wielding a baseball bat. Terry's bad memo-ries come to the fore, and he requires mild sedation from the paramedics who are there to treat Sandra. In his stupor, Terry reveals that he has been visited by Eric and Niall, and given instructions to watch over Sookie. Amelia arrives at Sookie's house with Bob in tow, and Bill stops by later as well. When Bud Dearborn calls to tell Sookie that Sandra escaped, Bill promises her that he will guard her house that night. Sookie spends the next afternoon with Hunter and Remy at Hunter's kindergarten orienta-tion and returns home to find Amelia renewing the wards. Amelia informs Sookie that there is a way to break the blood bond, and Sookie decides to do it without telling Eric, who calls her in a panic when suddenly he can no longer feel her through the bond. He comes over the next night and they reaffirm their love. They decide to drive out to Vampire's Kiss to way-lay one of the waiters, Colton, who mentally warned Sookie that there was fairy blood on the glasses the night she, Eric, and Pam went to the club. Colton has no love for Victor, since Victor murdered his mother, and agrees to a meeting to plan Victor's assassination.

Sookie is attacked by Hod and Kelvin in her driveway as she comes home from work. She seeks refuge at Bill's, waiting with him in one of his daytime sleeping places until he awakes. They return to her house to find Dermot injured and unconscious on the attic floor. Dermot recovers with the help of another fae and leaves for the evening. Eric and Pam arrive, and again there is tension between them. Sending Pam outside, Eric finally reveals that his maker, Ocella, arranged a marriage for him with the Queen of Oklahoma, and that he has been unable to get out of the con-tract. He tells Sookie that he will have to set her aside as his wife to marry the queen, news that does not go over well with Sookie, but she puts away her feelings in order to make plans to kill Victor. Sookie spends the next day preparing for the baby shower she is throwing for Tara, but she takes the time to hand-deliver a sizable check to Sam to help get Merlotte's through the hard times. She tells him it is a loan that he can pay back. The plan works, and Victor and his crew are lured to Fangtasia the next night by the promise of a performance by Bubba. They are set upon and killed.

Sookie is surprised when Mr. Cataliades visits during the baby shower. He stays in the kitchen until the guests depart, at which point he explains a bit more about his involvement with Fintan and Gran but tells Sookie that he is on the run and must leave abruptly. Sam calls and asks her to come to his trailer to pick up a package, but she senses something is amiss and requests that he come to her house instead. She lies in wait in the woods and sees Sam and Jannalynn arrive, held at gunpoint by Sandra. Sookie shoots Sandra, providing an opportunity for Jannalynn to act, and after a pitched battle, the little Were is able to kill Sandra. Sookie and Sam stuff the body through the fairy portal in her woods, and Sam and Janna-lynn take Sandra's gun to dispose of on the way back to Sam's trailer. Sookie relaxes with a glass of ice tea while she watches *Jeopardy!*

Sookie and Sam are enlisted to help out when friends Tara and JB want to renovate their house to accommodate their new twins. While knocking down a wall, Sam uncovers an old hammer hidden inside. Sookie, Tara, and JB tell Sam the tale of the 1930s murder of Isaiah Wechsler, who was beaten to death in his bed next door, in what is now Andy and Halleigh's house. Tara's house belonged to the Summerlins at the time, and their oldest son was suspected of the crime but never charged, and the murder remained unsolved. Unearthing the murder weapon disturbs the spirit of the killer, bringing a powerful negative energy to the little home. Quiana Wong, the twins' nanny, proves to be a psychic and is briefly possessed when she tries to get a read on the house. She tells them that uneasy spirits tend to stay in places where trauma took place. Sam shifts to a bloodhound and begins to search for bones, which he finds buried in the yard. Quiana is again briefly possessed by the spirit, so she and Sookie decide closer contact may allow Sookie to read Quiana's mind to determine what the spirit wants. Sookie is able to see through the murderer's eyes and identifies him as the Summerlins' youngest son, who committed suicide after the murder and was secretly buried by his family to protect what was left of their good name. They take the bones to the cemetery and bury them in Sookie's family plot, putting the spirit to rest. (All)

Stans, Jay: Police officer Jay Stans interviews Sookie along with his partner, Curlew, when she brings Maria-Star to the hospital in Clarice. (DTTW)

Stonebrook, Mark (wolf/witch): Mark and Marnie are sibling Were witches who drink vampire blood for increased power. They bring their coven to Shreveport with plans to take a large cut of Eric's businesses, and send a representative to meet with Eric, Pam, and Chow to give the vampires their terms. Angered by the witches' threats and Eric's unwillingness to personally negotiate, Chow grabs the witch, activating a spell that abruptly takes Eric from his office and deposits him, minus shirt, shoes, and memory, on the road leading to Sookie's house. The coven then sets its sights on the Shreveport Weres, killing their second-in-command. All the while, they continue the search for Eric, plastering Bon Temps with flyers with his face and their contact number. The Weres and the vampires decide to join together, enlisting their own witches to help counteract the coven, and attack the Stonebrooks' headquarters. Despite plans to take Mark alive, he is killed during what becomes known as the Witch War. (Dies DTTW)

Stonebrook, Marnie "Hallow" (wolf/witch): Hallow and her brother,

Mark, are Weres who practice witchcraft and drink vampire blood. They arrive in Shreveport with their coven, planning to take over Eric's businesses. During the negotiations, Chow assaults the witch representative, triggering a spell that poofs Eric out of his office and gives him amnesia, leaving him running down the road near Sookie's house with no shirt or shoes. Hallow's spell doesn't work as she planned, and she has no idea where Eric is. Determined to find him, she induces some local witches and Wiccans to help out. When the Were witches attack and kill the Shreveport pack's second-in-command, the local Weres join the vampires in an unprecedented alliance to rid themselves of the coven. Together they stage an attack on the Stonebrooks' headquarters. Mark and most of the coven members are killed in the battle, leaving only Hallow and one badly injured witch alive. Pam forces Hallow to reveal that her parents (witches who ran confidence games) were abandoned by the supe community when they were incarcerated and that this fueled Hallow's desire for vengeance on both the Shreveport vamps and Weres. Before killing her, Pam also forces Hallow to reverse the spell on Eric, restoring him to his normal state of mind, and he returns to Shreveport to take control of his area once again. (Dies DTTW; mentioned DAG)

Summerlin, Albert: Albert is around sixteen years old in the 1930s when his neighbor Isaiah Wechsler is murdered in his bed. Having recently had a fight with Isaiah, Albert is the prime suspect, but nothing is ever proven, and eventually the speculation dies down. Albert marries, has children, and raises them in the family home. (Deceased; mentioned IIHAH)

Summerlin, Bucky: Bucky, a descendant of Albert, sells the family home to Tara. (Mentioned IIHAH)

Summerlin, Carter: Carter is about thirteen in the 1930s when his older brother gets into a fight with neighbor Isaiah Wechsler over Isaiah's cruel words about Carter. Carter murders Isaiah with a hammer and kills himself the following week. His family secretly buries him in the yard, telling everyone that he has been sent to live with relatives. When the hammer is discovered during renovations to the home—now owned by Tara and JB du Rone—Carter's spirit reawakens until Sookie and the du Rones' nanny are able to discover the truth about the murder. His remains are unearthed, and he is laid to rest in Sookie's family plot. (Deceased; mentioned IIHAH)

Summerlin, Daisy and Hiram: Daisy and Hiram secretly bury their youngest son, Carter, in the yard when he commits suicide after killing neighbor Isaiah Wechsler. In order to protect the family's name, they then announce that Carter has been sent to live with relatives. The couple loses their only daughter to scarlet fever, but their oldest son, Albert, marries and raises his own children in the family home. (Deceased; mentioned IIHAH)

Suskin, Cindy Lou (vampire): Kansas City vamp Cindy Lou wants a child. Since she can't have her own, she is granted permission by the parents of a dying preteen to turn him into a vampire. The legal agreement gives the parents visitation rights with their now eternally undead child, an agreement that Cindy Lou and the boy are not honoring. They are brought before a judicial panel at the summit in Rhodes and told to abide by their legal arrangement with the parents. (ATD)

Synthetic blood: Developed by the Japanese as a medical adjunct for emergency rooms and surgical procedures, this discovery turns out to be the key to the vampire nation revealing its existence to the rest of humanity. It satisfies all the nutritional needs of vampires, thus allowing them to appear to be far less of a threat to humans than they have traditionally been. Synthetic blood needs to be kept refrigerated before use and is usually warmed up in a microwave before being drunk. Marketed under brand names such as Life Flow and TrueBlood, the latter having become an almost generic designation for the product, it is available in various blood types. As with any product, there is a variety of quality and price, ranging from low-end Red Stuff to Royalty, a part-synthetic, part-real blood mixture that includes actual blood from European royalty. (DUD, LDID, CD, DTTW, DN, DAAD, OWA, DD, ATD, L, FDTW, GW, DAG, TB, DITF, DR)

T:

Talbot: No other name given. Talbot is Russell Edgington's steady human companion until Russell's marriage to fellow vampire Bartlett Crowe. (CD; mentioned DAAD)

Tallie, Benedict "Eggs": Tara's fiancé, Eggs, shows an unhealthy interest in Eric when Sookie and the vampire show up at the orgy by the lake. Despite his drunken lust, he survives Callisto's madness, only to die shortly thereafter in a fire. (Dies LDID; mentioned DAAD)

Tepes, Vlad (vampire): The infamous Dracula, Vlad III was a blood-thirsty Wallachian king nicknamed Vlad the Impaler for his practice of impaling his enemies on large wooden stakes. After he was turned and rose on the island of Snagov, he continued to live like a king and is credited with being the first modern vampire. (Mentioned DN, DAG)

Terence (wolf): No last name given. The packmaster of the Jackson pack, Terence is not pleased when one of his Jackson Weres blames Alcide for causing trouble at Josephine's. His displeasure at Alcide is mitigated when he is informed that his Were, Jerry Falcon, drew blood when he grabbed Sookie, but he still wants Alcide out of his territory as soon as possible. (CD)

Terrell: No last name given. Terrell and his friend Chuck taunt Sookie about Bill's absence on New Year's Eve. (DTTW)

Thalia (vampire): No last name given. Thalia is very old and very moody. She was thrown out of Illinois for aggressiveness after the Great Revelation and was allowed by Eric to take up residence in Area Five in exchange for her presence at Fangtasia and her promise of good behavior. Despite (or because of) her obvious disdain for the humans who flock to her, Thalia has a website devoted to her, established and maintained by her avid fans. The ancient vampire is uncharacteristically happy to participate in the planned attack on Victor and his crew at Fangtasia, first discreetly offering a drink to Ana Lyudmila that permanently decommissions her, then launching herself at Victor's second when the fight begins. When Akiro is able to hack off Thalia's arm, she promptly picks it up and hits him with it as Heidi joins in, stabbing Akiro through the neck. Eric finishes the job when Akiro refuses to surrender. Thalia is so old that her ability to regenerate is not limited to the growing of new limbs but also applies to the reattachment of old. Indira holds the severed limb to Thalia's shoulder while Thalia drinks from a willing Immanuel. (DN, DAAD, ATD, DAG, DR)

Thomasina: No last name given. Thomasina works for Herveaux and Son but takes a bribe to reveal bids to a competitor. (Mentioned CD)

Thornton, Myrna: Myrna and her husband were both abusive alcoholics who put their children (including Sookie's friend Tara) through hell. (Deceased; mentioned DTTW, DAAD, DAG)

Thrash, David (wolf): The lieutenant governor of Louisiana, David and his wife are guests at Sophie-Anne's ball at the monastery. When Sookie warns David's wife that there will be trouble, they have one dance, then leave. (DD)

Thrash, Genevieve (wolf): The wife of Lieutenant Governor David Thrash, she accompanies him to Sophie-Anne's ball at the monastery. Sookie warns Genevieve that there will probably be problems, so she feigns a headache. They have one dance and then leave before the melee begins. (DD)

Threadgill, Peter (vampire): The vampire King of Arkansas, Peter Threadgill pursues Sophie-Anne, who finally agrees to marry him. Once the contract is signed, he becomes dissatisfied with their purely political marriage and plots to get Sophie-Anne to break their covenant, thereby forfeiting her state and wealth. When his scheme to discredit her fails, he has one of his vampires instigate a fight with her bodyguard Wybert, decapitating him and beginning the battle between Louisiana and Arkansas that ultimately results in Peter's demise at Andre's hands. (Dies DD; mentioned ATD, FDTW)

Tiffany: No last name given. Halleigh's bridesmaid Tiffany suffers an attack of appendicitis just before the wedding and is rushed to the hospital, leaving Sookie to take her place in the bridal party. Fortunately, Halleigh gets the dress off her before she leaves. (Mentioned FDTW)

Tijgerin (tiger): No other name given. Tijgerin, recently transferred from the European division of Special Events, teams up with Quinn to lead the Merlottes to the church for Craig and Deidra's wedding. She joins the shifters afterward at the Merlottes' impromptu party. She is happy to meet another weretiger (a male!) while she gains the "American experience" her company wants for her, and she informs Sookie that there were demonstrations in the Netherlands that were just as bad as anything being faced in the States. (STW)

Tom: No last name given. Tom is a news anchor for a Dallas station. (LDID)

Tonnesen, Dr. Linda: Dr. Tonnesen pronounces Jeff Marriot officially dead at Sookie's house after the fire. Although not a drinker, she occasionally stops in Merlotte's. (DAAD, DITF; mentioned DR)

Tony: No last name given. Tony played high school football with his friend Sam Merlotte, and their friendship continues to this day. Though off duty, the deputy accompanies his partner, Sister Mendoza, to Bernie's house to keep watch while the family attends the wedding rehearsal. (STW)

Tooten, Charlsie: Good-natured Charlsie subs at Merlotte's until her oldest daughter has a baby, when she leaves to spend time with her grand-child. (DUD, CD, DITF; mentioned LDID, DTTW, DAAD, DD, DAG)

Tooten, Ralph: Charlsie's husband, Ralph, quits his job at the chicken processing plant and buys the Crawdad Diner, but his arthritis soon forces him to sell to Pinkie Arnett. (DUD, LDID, DAAD; mentioned DTTW, DITF)

Travis (wolf): No last name given. A lone wolf unaffiliated with any pack, Travis is a trucker who stops by Merlotte's every two weeks or so. (STW)

Tray Dawson's engine repair shop: No name given. A one-man oper-ation, Dawson's small engine repair shop is located alongside his home out in the country between Hotshot and Grainger. (FDTW, DAG; mentioned DAAD, ATD)

Trout, Julian (witch): When the summit is conveniently postponed until after Hurricane Katrina lays waste to New Orleans, Sookie wonders if one of the other kings or queens has a weather witch who was able to predict the hurricane and therefore delay the summit to force Sophie-Anne and the Louisiana vampires to attend in a weakened position. Her supposition turns out to be true: The culprit is Julian Trout, the Rhodes Channel 7 weatherman. He attends the summit ball with his wife, Olive, and is guided by first Sookie and then Carla and Gervaise to Sophie-Anne's attention. Fortunately, Sophie-Anne believes that Julian was a pawn who didn't understand exactly what his information would be used for, and she promises Sookie she will not harm the Trouts. (ATD)

Trout, Olive: The wife of the Channel 7 weatherman in Rhodes, Olive is unaware of her husband's involvement with the vampires who post-poned the summit based on his prediction of Hurricane Katrina. (ATD)

Twining, Charles (vampire): Pirate vampire Charles is sent to Louisi-ana by his grand-sire Hot Rain to retaliate against Eric for the death of Hot Rain's child Long Shadow. Eric believes that Charles has come to Louisi-ana from Mississippi, where he was employed by King Russell Edgington. After listening to local gossip, Charles decides that killing Eric's beloved

Sookie will be an appropriate revenge. Eric inadvertently plays right into Hot Rain's hands by sending Charles to Bon Temps when Sam needs a temporary bartender. Charles then finagles an invitation from Sookie to stay at her house, and he sets the place on fire. He's already killed a human who has been set up to take the blame. Sookie's fairy godmother rescues the unsuspecting Sookie, and the fire is put out. It isn't until Charles sees Bubba and comments that he's never heard him sing that Sookie realizes Charles could not have been in Russell's employ and thus is not who he has claimed to be, since Bubba did perform for Russell and his vamps. Charles makes a desperate attempt to kill Sookie at Merlotte's, but the attempt is thwarted when she stuffs a silver chain in his mouth, giving the bar regulars time to overpower him. Admitting that he failed in his task and preferring final death to imprisonment, Charles is staked by Catfish Hennessy. (Dies DAAD; mentioned DR)

U:

Unknown Enemy Vamp #1: No name given. One of two young vampires who attend Bubba's concert at Fangtasia, #1 is killed by Bill during the brawl. (Dies DR)

Unknown Enemy Vamp #2: No name given. The second of two young vampires who attend the performance at Fangtasia. A hefty man turned while in his thirties, #2 grapples with a tiring Palomino while Parker stabs him from behind with an ice pick until he is beheaded by Mustapha Khan. (Dies DR)

V:

Valentine (vampire): No last name given. Valentine and Charity are sent by Sophie-Anne to investigate St. Louis Cemetery #1 after Waldo reports that he and Hadley were attacked by Fellowship of the Sun members. They find no trace of humans at the site. (Mentioned OWA)

Vampire database: At the request of Queen of Louisiana Sophie-Anne Leclerq, Bill Compton has developed an extensive database to allow for the identification of as many vampires as possible with as much information on each as he can gather. Bill has traveled as far away as Peru and (it is presumed) to other countries to interview vampires for the project. The value of the information, or perhaps the profit potential, contained in this database is considered so great that Bill is kidnapped and tortured to get it before he can turn it over to the queen. Later, at her behest, he makes copies of it available in the dealer's room at the Rhodes conference, for a steep price. He then sets up a home business to sell the database on the Internet. (CD, DTTW, DAAD, ATD, FDTW, DITF)

Vampire's Kiss: The lights of Vampire's Kiss, which is located off an exit ramp in the middle of nowhere between Bon Temps and Shreveport, shine brightly to attract customers. Victor Madden's vampire club is decorated in a tacky bordello theme with dark wood, flocked wallpaper, red velvet, and leather, with images of Elvis scattered throughout. The vampire employees dress in a caveman–sex slave fashion, while the human employees are clad in skimpy leather outfits. Live music is provided by a vampire band playing a mix of blues and rock. (DR)

Vardamon, Judith (vampire): Lorena's other child is wary when Sookie contacts her on Bill's behalf, but she happily helps him recover from silver poisoning after she learns of their maker's final death. Judith feared Lorena, who turned her to keep Bill's interest when she realized Judith resembled Bill's late wife. Judith and Bill originally parted ways because of her unhealthy obsession with him, and that infatuation leads to another parting when Judith accepts that Bill will never love her as she desires. (DITF, DR; mentioned STW)

Vasco, Jenny: When asked by Sookie if he knows any children with visible problems, Hunter tells her about Jenny, who has a birthmark on her face. (Mentioned DITF)

Vaudry, Elmer Claire: Elmer Claire, a teacher at Betty Ford Elementary, delights in bawdy comments at Halleigh's shower. She has an ancient white Persian cat and innocently suggests that Amelia have Bob the cat neutered when they are both at the vet's one day. (ATD, DR)

Velasquez, Joseph (vampire): Stan's loyal second, Joseph survives the Pyramid explosion that badly injures his king. He continues to hold Texas while Stan recovers, although he will surely face challenges. For now, at least, Texas has been bypassed in Felipe's bid for power. (LDID, ATD)

Velislava (vampire): No last name given. One of many vampires known by both Eric and Ocella who was killed by the Bolsheviks. (Deceased; mentioned DITF)

Verena Rose's Bridal and Formal Shop: Founded by Verena Rose Yancy, Verena Rose's Bridal and Formal Shop is now in the hands of her daughter, Adabelle. It is located in a two-story house with a large bay window in the front, on a block filled with similar older homes. It's set a little back from the street, with parking behind the store. The renovated building has an elegant appearance: white-painted brick, dark green shutters, glossy black ironwork railings on the stairs, and brass details on the door. It is considered *the* place to come to get wedding gear if a family has aspirations of class. (DAAD)

Vick, Glen: Portia's husband, Glen, is an accountant whose clientele includes vampires, several of whom were invited to his wedding, much to his new wife's dismay. Less than a year after their wedding, he and Portia are pleased to learn that they are expecting their first child. (DAAD, FDTW; mentioned DD, ATD, DITF, DR)

Vick, Portia Bellefleur: Lawyer Portia Bellefleur is intelligent, educated, from a good family, and fiercely loyal to her brother. Although completely unnerved by vampires, she bravely pursues Bill while trying to prove her brother Andy's innocence in the murder of Lafayette Reynold. She hopes that her association with a vampire will encourage the orgy participants Lafayette spoke of to invite her to a party so she can learn their identities. Bill, though no fan of the Bellefleurs, finds something noble in her and plays along, but it is Sookie who gets the invitation and clears Andy's name. Portia's bravery comes through again as she scrambles to help Sookie when she is shot in the library parking lot, crouching beside Sookie as she phones for help.

Portia happily plans a double wedding when her boyfriend, Glen Vick, proposes around the same time Andy proposes to Halleigh Robinson. The wedding plans change as her grandmother becomes ill, but Portia is determined to have her wedding while her grandmother is alive to attend. Her plans work out.

When Bill delivers the family Bible to a dying Caroline and his connection to the Bellefleurs is revealed, Portia, though nonplussed, strives to behave with the graciousness of her grandmother and, at his request, arranges to have Caroline's funeral at night so that Bill can attend. Soon after that, she and Glen are excited to find out that Portia is pregnant. (DUD, LDID, DTTW, DAAD, DD, ATD, FDTW, DITF; mentioned CD, DR)

Vic's Redneck Roadhouse: Situated about ten miles from the interstate, Vic's Redneck Roadhouse lives up to its name with wet T-shirt contests, beer pong tournaments, and promotions, such as free-drink cards and "Bring in a Bubba Night." Owned by Victor Madden, the bar is pulling customers from Merlotte's, severely affecting the smaller bar's revenues. (Mentioned DR)

Vlad Tepes's handler (vampire): No name given. Vlad's handler and Eric have a personal discussion about whether Vlad will attend the Fangtasia birthday party held in his honor. (Mentioned DN)

Voss, Jasper: Jasper is a patron at Merlotte's. (FDTW)

W:

Wacker, General Scott (wolf): General Wacker comes out during the Great Reveal and speaks out against proposed shifter registration. His daughter is serving in Iraq. (Mentioned DITF)

Waldo (vampire): No last name given. One of Sophie-Anne's former favorites, albino Waldo's appearance is permanently damaged when he spends a few years in a tank of salt water as punishment for some unknown transgression. He kills Hadley out of jealousy, knowing she has taken his place in the queen's affections, and attempts to blame the Fellowship of the Sun. The queen is not fooled and has him drive Mr. Cataliades to Sookie's house to deliver the news of Hadley's death, masking her own presence in the car. Offered the chance to kill Waldo to avenge her cousin, Sookie declines, but Waldo, heartbroken when he realizes that the queen knows of his duplicity, attacks her and is staked by Bill. (Dies OWA; mentioned DD)

Warren: No last name given. A friend of Mustapha Khan, Were and Eric's new daytime guy, Warren spent fifteen years in the army, service that comes in handy when he is positioned as a sniper to take out any of Victor's crew who make it out of Fangtasia when the battle begins. (DR)

Washington, Detective: No first name given. Detective Washington and his partner (Windbreaker Guy) arrive at Blonde to investigate the murders of owner Michael and his associate Rudy. They question everyone present, including Mohawk, Sookie, and Pam, and release them when all the stories point to a stranger with an appointment with the two men in Michael's office. (TB)

Wechsler, Cathy: Now in her seventies and living near Clarice, Cathy is the widow of the last Wechsler. (Mentioned IIHAH)

Wechsler, Isaiah: In the 1930s, Isaiah is around fifteen years old when he gets into a fight with his next-door neighbor, Albert Summerlin, after Isaiah casts aspersions on Albert's younger brother, Carter. The boys do not reveal the cause of their animosity, but suspicion naturally falls on Albert when Isaiah is found brutally beaten to death in his bed. His murder remains unsolved for more than seventy years, until the murder weapon, a hammer, is found hidden in the Summerlins' home, now owned by the du Rones. Carter's disturbed spirit reveals that he was the culprit. (Deceased; mentioned IIHAH)

Wechsler, Jacob and Sarah Jane: Jacob and his wife, Sarah Jane, accuse neighbor Albert Summerlin when their son, Isaiah, is murdered in his bed in the 1930s. Although no one is ever charged with the crime, the couple remains convinced of Albert's guilt. They are determined to stay in their house as a constant reproach to the Summerlins. (Deceased; mentioned IIHAH)

Weiss, Sara: New Orleans FBI agent Weiss is sent to investigate Sookie's involvement in the rescues from the Pyramid, accompanied by Agent Lattesta. She wants to believe in Sookie's ability and is disappointed when Sookie denies being a psychic. When Crystal is found crucified at Merlotte's, Weiss and Lattesta investigate the case as a potential hate crime. Weiss is badly wounded at the shoot-out at Arlene's trailer.

Home recuperating with her husband, two teenagers, and three dogs, the agent questions her beliefs and begins exploring the paranormal, leading her boss to have doubts about putting her back in the field. (DAG; mentioned DITF)

Were cop: No name given. A Were cop of Chinese descent, he makes out with Luna Garza at Sam's brother's wedding in Wright. (STW)

Whatley, Amanda (wolf): A loyal member of the Long Tooth pack, Amanda participates in the Witch War and gains a grudging respect for Sookie, to whom she had previously referred as a "vamp humper." She attends the packmaster contest where Alcide's father is defeated and executed by Patrick Furnan, and finds her loyalty tested by Furnan's unscrupulous behavior.

Owner of Hair of the Dog, a bar in Shreveport that caters to the shifter crowd, Amanda is first honored, then concerned, when Quinn brings Sookie in one Friday night to complain that they had been attacked by bitten Weres earlier in the evening. Amanda reminds those present that Sookie had been made a "friend of the pack" by the late packmaster Colonel Flood, and she assures Quinn that there will be an investigation.

After Maria-Star Cooper and Christine Larrabee are murdered and Patrick Furnan is suspected, Amanda backs Alcide as they attempt to get to the truth. She attends the gathering of the pack and is consequently involved in the fight with the interloping female Were Priscilla Hebert and her pack. Amanda is killed by Hebert and mourned even as Alcide ascends to packmaster. (DTTW, DAAD, DD; dies FDTW; mentioned DITF)

Whispering Palms: An assisted-living center owned by vampires, Whispering Palms is located outside Las Vegas and specializes in caring for supernaturals, such as John Quinn's mentally ill mother. (Mentioned FDTW)

Williston, Mr.: No first name given. The town of Wright installed a speaker outside the church for the funeral of Mr. Williston, a member of the Texas legislature. (Deceased; mentioned STW)

Wong, Quiana (psychic): Hired by Tara and JB du Rone as a nanny when their twins are born, eighteen-year-old Quiana is something of a misfit. Born of a redneck father and a half-Chinese, half–African American mother, she is orphaned at sixteen. Quiana is left to stay with whichever family member can take her in. She has strange abilities that she conceals until she's at the du Rone house and a hammer is removed from a wall during a home renovation. The hammer, used as a murder weapon, triggers the presence of Carter Summerlin, who gradually possesses Quiana. When Carter is put to rest, Quiana is no longer haunted. (IIHAH)

Woods, Coop: Quiana Wong's father dies with her mother when their car is hit by a train. There are rumors that their car didn't just stall on the railroad tracks, that Coop carried out a murder-suicide. (Deceased; mentioned IIHAH)

Wybert (vampire): No other name given. Saxon warrior Wybert, whose name means "Bright Battle," was turned with his brother, Sigebert, centuries ago by Sophie-Anne, who lured them with the promise of strength. They were unaware that the strength would be limited to the night. Nonetheless, both willingly remain with Sophie-Anne as her loyal bodyguards. At the party at the monastery Wybert is decapitated by Ra Shawn, one of Peter's Arkansas vamps, during the assassination attempt on Sophie-Anne. (Dies DD; mentioned ATD, FDTW)

Y:

Yancy, Adabelle (wolf): Adabelle Yancy is Colonel Flood's second in the Shreveport pack and the pack's best tracker. She lives with her mother in Shreveport and is, according to her mother, gay. She has taken over running Verena Rose's Bridal and Formal Shop, started by her mother, and is killed at the shop by the Stonebrooks' coven. From the remains found at the scene, it's obvious that Adabelle put up a fight and took one of her attackers down with her. (Mentioned, dies DTTW)

Yancy, Verena Rose (wolf): Founder of Verena Rose's Bridal and Formal Shop and mother of Adabelle, Verena worries when her daughter calls from the shop to say she has a meeting right at closing time and then Verena never hears from her again. When Sookie and Alcide find the bloody scene at the shop, Alcide has Colonel Flood deliver the sad news that her daughter has been killed. (DTTW)

Youngest Lisle sister: No name given. Deidra's sisters stand as her bridesmaids at her wedding to Craig Merlotte. The youngest waits nervously with the bride while sister Angie and Sookie ring the church bell at the beginning of the ceremony. Two other bridesmaids, friends of Deidra's, decided against being in the wedding party after discovering that Deidra is marrying into a family with shifters. (STW)

Yvonne, Arla (vampire): The sheriff of Area Two, Arla is killed during the takeover while attempting to make her way to Shreveport with six of her vampires. (Mentioned ATD; mentioned, dies FDTW)

ABOUT THE EDITOR

Charlaine Harris, #1 *New York Times* bestselling author, has been writing for thirty years. Her body of work includes many novels, a few novellas, and a growing body of short stories in such genres as mystery, science fiction, and romance. Married and the mother of three, Charlaine lives in rural Arkansas with her family and three dogs. She pretty much works all the time. The HBO series *True Blood* is based on Charlaine's Sookie Stackhouse novels.